TALES OF THE SEA
JOSEPH CONRAD

LORD JIM · TYPHOON · CHILDREN OF THE SEA ·
AMY FOSTER · YOUTH and OTHERS

CASTLE BOOKS

Table of Contents

INTRODUCTION

Joseph Conrad is recognized as one of the great English writers–yet he was born a Pole. He is recognized as a master of the English language–yet when he arrived in England at the age of 20, he could speak only a few words of the language.

A seaman for 20 years, Conrad is known for his tales of the seas, the adventures that befell Englishmen–often taken from his own personal experiences–in far off exotic lands where the vast and far-flung British merchant sea routes took them. He loved and respected the sea and its effects upon mere men–aship and ashore.

In this volume are reprinted some of his best known works, from the thrilling adventure of storm-tossed seas in *Typhoon*, to the proving of a man in *Lord Jim*. Some, like *Youth*, were taken directly from his own adventures as he sailed throughout the world.

Joseph Conrad was born Jozef Teodor Konrad Nalecz Korzeniowski on December 6, 1857, in Berdichev, Polish Ukraine, a part of Poland which was then under Russian rule. His parents were Polish landowners, well educated and zealous Polish patriots. His father, Apollo Korzeniowski, was a talented poet who translated French and English literature. He was also active in the revolutionary Polish underground which was seeking freedom for a divided and conquered Poland.

When Joseph Conrad was five years old, his father's underground activities were discovered. Apollo, his wife and young son were exiled to Northern Russia, where both parents died of the severe conditions before the boy was 10. Returned and placed under the guardianship of his maternal uncle, Thaddeus Bobrowski, the lonely orphan read a great deal, falling under the spell of the exciting adventure stories of British Naval Captain Frederick Marryat and the novels of Charles Dickens.

At 16, the unhappy boy persuaded his uncle to let him go to sea, and he left for Marseilles, France, where he apprenticed in the French merchant marine and made three voyages to the West Indies and South America between 1875 and 1878.

At 20 he was severely wounded in a duel over a girl. Upon his recovery, his uncle suggested that he leave France for England. When he arrived in that country, he signed on a British freighter and was determined to make a career of the merchant service. From ordinary seaman, he rose through the ranks to master of his own ship in 1886–just 29 years old. At that time he legally adopted his new name and became an English citizen.

He sailed to Australia, Borneo, the Malay States, South America, the islands of the South Pacific and to the teeming ports on the Indian Ocean. Sometime during those voyages he began to while away the time writing.

In 1890 he went to Africa in the Belgian Colonial service and sailed up the Congo River. After nearly four years he was so wasted by fever and dysentery, he was forced home. He based *Heart of Darkness* on some of those experiences in the Congo.

Because of continuing ill health–he suffered the rest of his life from rheumatic gout, resulting from African fevers–he gave up the sea and settled down to build a literary career. Just as he was selling stories successfully, he met and married a young English secretary, Jessie George.

They had two sons, Borys, born in January 1898, and John Alexander, born in August 1905. Added to the pressures of his recurring ill health was Jessie's severe fall on a London street in 1903. Her knees were so badly injured that she became a semi-invalid for the rest of her life. The cost of the medical treatments and operations inspired Conrad to turn out work in spurts of concentrated energy.

Although he always maintained that finishing a novel was "like recovering from a severe illness," his output was as high as 110,000 words of finished manuscript in a year–and he did most of his own redrafting and final copying by hand!

His literary friends, like the young English writer Ford Maddox Ford (with whom he collaborated on two novels) were astonished by his working on several stories and novels at the same time, but he once replied, "All of the stories are in my head; I must just sort through to determine where I left off."

Most of these stories originated in things he had seen, heard or experienced. One of his short stories came directly from the experiences of his wife. Shortly after they were married, they went to live in Southern France. There he became gravely ill, and she–with only a few words of French–had to obtain a doctor and see to his care for several weeks. She was able to cope, but the sense of alienation she felt comes through translated into the story of the castaway in *Amy Foster*.

Conrad's writing, both long and short, can be enjoyed on two levels. They can be read as adventurous tales of the sea, of exotic lands or mysterious seamen. Or they can be seen as explorations of the effects of the might and power of nature upon mortal men. His stories seem to imply that the stolidly unimaginative, practical man of the sea, like Capt. MacWhirr of *Typhoon*, copes far better than sensitive, emotional intellects, like Jim in *Lord Jim* or Kurtz in *Heart of Darkness*.

Conrad lived in the turbulent period when sail was giving way to steam power on the oceans of the world. He died August 3, 1924, leaving behind his stories of excitement and adventures of men on the frontiers of these two contiguous but conflicting ways of life.

Robert O. Patterson

LORD
JIM

CHAPTER I.

He was an inch, perhaps two, under six feet, powerfully built, and he advanced straight at you with a slight stoop of the shoulders, head forward, and a fixed from-under stare which made you think of a charging bull. His voice was deep, loud, and his manner displayed a kind of dogged self-assertion which had nothing aggressive in it. It seemed a necessity, and it was directed apparently as much at himself as at anybody else. He was spotlessly neat, apparelled in immaculate white from shoes to hat, and in the various Eastern ports where he got his living as ship-chandler's water-clerk he was very popular.

A water-clerk need not pass an examination in anything under the sun, but he must have Ability in the abstract and demonstrate it practically. His work consists in racing under sail, steam, or oars against other water-clerks for any ship about to anchor, greeting her captain cheerily, forcing upon him a card—the business card of the ship-chandler—and on his first visit on shore piloting him firmly but without ostentation to a vast, cavern-like shop which is full of things that are eaten and drunk on board ship; where you can get everything to make her seaworthy and beautiful, from a set of chain-hooks for her cable to a book of gold-leaf for the carvings of her stern; and where her commander is received like a brother by a ship-chandler he has never seen before. There is a cool parlour, easy-chairs, bottles, cigars, writing implements, a copy of harbour regulations, and a warmth of welcome that melts the salt of a three months' passage out of a seaman's heart. The connection thus begun is kept up, as long as the ship remains in harbour, by the daily visits of the water-clerk. To the captain he is faithful like a friend and attentive like a son, with the patience of Job, the unselfish devotion of a woman, and the jollity of a boon companion. Later on the bill is sent in. It is a beautiful humane occupation. Therefore good water-clerks are scarce. When a water-clerk who possesses Ability in the abstract has also the advantage of having been brought up to the sea, he is worth to his employer a lot of money and some humouring. Jim had always good wages and as much humouring as would have bought the fidelity of a fiend. Nevertheless, with black ingratitude he would throw up the job suddenly and depart. To his employers the reasons he gave were obviously inadequate. They said "Confounded fool!" as soon as his back was turned. This was their criticism on his exquisite sensibility.

To the white men in the waterside business and to the captains of ships he was just Jim—nothing more. He had, of course, another name, but he was anxious that it should not be pronounced. His incognito, which had as many holes as a sieve, was not meant to hide a personality but a fact. When the fact broke through the

3

incognito he would leave suddenly the seaport where he happened to be at the time and go to another—generally farther east. He kept to seaports because he was a seaman in exile from the sea, and had Ability in the abstract, which is good for no other work but that of a water-clerk. He retreated in good order towards the rising sun, and the fact followed him casually but inevitably. Thus in the course of years he was known successively in Bombay, in Calcutta, in Rangoon, in Penang, in Batavia—and in each of these halting-places was just Jim the water-clerk. Afterwards, when his keen perception of the Intolerable drove him away for good from seaports and white men, even into the virgin forest, the Malays of the jungle village, where he had elected to conceal his deplorable faculty, added a word to the monosyllable of his incognito. They called him Tuan Jim: as one might say—Lord Jim.

Originally he came from a parsonage. Many commanders of fine merchant-ships come from these abodes of piety and peace. Jim's father possessed such certain knowledge of the Unknowable as made for the righteousness of people in cottages without disturbing the ease of mind of those whom an unerring Providence enables to live in mansions. The little church on a hill had the mossy greyness of a rock seen through a ragged screen of leaves. It had stood there for centuries, but the trees around probably remembered the laying of the first stone. Below, the red front of the rectory gleamed with a warm tint in the midst of grass-plots, flower-beds, and fir-trees, with an orchard at the back, a paved stable-yard to the left, and the sloping glass of greenhouses tacked along a wall of bricks. The living had belonged to the family for generations; but Jim was one of five sons, and when after a course of light holiday literature his vocation for the sea had declared itself, he was sent at once to a "training-ship for officers of the mercantile marine."

He learned there a little trigonometry and how to cross top-gallant yards. He was generally liked. He had the third place in navigation and pulled stroke in the first cutter. Having a steady head with an excellent physique, he was very smart aloft. His station was in the fore-top, and often from there he looked down, with the contempt of a man destined to shine in the midst of dangers, at the peaceful multitude of roofs cut in two by the brown tide of the stream, while scattered on the outskirts of the surrounding plain the factory chimneys rose perpendicular against a grimy sky, each slender like a pencil, and belching out smoke like a volcano. He could see the big ships departing, the broad-beamed ferries constantly on the move, the little boats floating far below his feet, with the hazy splendour of the sea in the distance, and the hope of a stirring life in the world of adventure.

On the lower deck in the babel of two hundred voices he would forget himself, and beforehand live in his mind the sea-life of light literature. He saw himself saving people from sinking ships, cutting away masts in a hurricane, swimming through a surf with a line; or as a lonely castaway, barefooted and half naked, walking on uncovered reefs in search of shellfish to stave off starvation. He confronted savages on tropical shores, quelled mutinies on the high seas, and in a small boat upon the ocean kept up the hearts of despairing men—always an example of devotion to duty, and as unflinching as a hero in a book.

"Something's up. Come along."

He leaped to his feet. The boys were streaming up the ladders. Above could be heard a great scurrying about and shouting, and when he got through the hatchway he stood still—as if confounded.

It was the dusk of a winter's day. The gale had freshened since noon, stopping the traffic on the river, and now blew with the strength of a hurricane in fitful bursts that boomed like salvoes of great guns firing over the ocean. The rain slanted in sheets that flicked and subsided, and between whiles Jim had threatening glimpses of the tumbling tide, the small craft jumbled and tossing along the shore, the motionless buildings in the driving mist, the broad ferry-boats pitching ponderously at anchor, the vast landing-stages heaving up and down and smothered in sprays. The next gust seemed to blow all this away. The air was full of flying water. There was a fierce purpose in the gale, a furious earnestness in the screech of the wind, in the brutal tumult of earth and sky, that seemed directed at him, and made him hold his breath in awe. He stood still. It seemed to him he was whirled around.

He was jostled. "Man the cutter!" Boys rushed past him. A coaster running in for shelter had crashed through a schooner at anchor, and one of the ship's instructors had seen the accident. A mob of boys clambered on the rails, clustered round the davits. "Collision. Just ahead of us. Mr Symons saw it." A push made him stagger against the mizzen-mast, and he caught hold of a rope. The old training-ship chained to her moorings quivered all over, bowing gently head to wind, and with her scanty rigging humming in a deep bass the breathless song of her youth at sea. "Lower away!" He saw the boat, manned, drop swiftly below the rail, and rushed after her. He heard a splash. "Let go; clear the falls!" He leaned over. The river alongside seethed in frothy streaks. The cutter could be seen in the falling darkness under the spell of tide and wind, that for a moment held her bound, and tossing abreast of the ship. A yelling voice in her reached him faintly: "Keep stroke, you young whelps, if you want to save anybody! Keep stroke!" And suddenly she lifted high her bow, and, leaping with raised oars over a wave, broke the spell cast upon her by the wind and tide.

Jim felt his shoulder gripped firmly. "Too late, youngster." The captain of the ship laid a restraining hand on that boy, who seemed on the point of leaping overboard, and Jim looked up with the pain of conscious defeat in his eyes. The captain smiled sympathetically. "Better luck next time. This will teach you to be smart."

A shrill cheer greeted the cutter. She came dancing back half full of water, and with two exhausted men washing about on her bottom boards. The tumult and the menace of wind and sea now appeared very contemptible to Jim, increasing the regret of his awe at their inefficient menace. Now he knew what to think of it. It seemed to him he cared nothing for the gale. He could affront greater perils. He would do so—better than anybody. Not a particle of fear was left. Nevertheless he brooded apart that evening while the bowman of the cutter—a boy with a face like a girl's and big grey eyes—was the hero of the lower deck. Eager questioners crowded round him. He narrated: "I just saw his head bobbing, and I dashed my boat-hook in the water. It caught in his breeches and I nearly went overboard, as I thought I would, only old Symons let go the tiller and grabbed my legs—the boat nearly swamped. Old Symons is a fine old chap. I don't mind a bit him being grumpy with us. He swore at me all the time he held my leg, but that was only his way of telling me to stick to the boat-hook. Old Symons is awfully excitable—isn't he? No—not the little fair chap—the other, the big one with a beard. When we pulled him in he groaned, 'Oh, my leg! oh, my leg!' and turned up his eyes. Fancy such a big chap fainting like a girl. Would any of you fellows faint for a jab with a boat-hook?—I wouldn't. It went into his leg so far." He showed the boat-hook, which he had carried below for the purpose, and produced a sensation. "No, silly! It was not his flesh that held him—his breeches did. Lots of blood, of course."

Jim thought it a pitiful display of vanity. The gale had ministered to a heroism as spurious as its own pretence of terror. He felt angry with the brutal tumult of earth and sky for taking him unawares and checking unfairly a generous readiness for narrow escapes. Otherwise he was rather glad he had not gone into the cutter, since a lower achievement had served the turn. He had enlarged his knowledge more than those who had done the work. When all men flinched, then—he felt sure—he alone would know how to deal with the spurious menace of wind and seas. He knew what to think of it. Seen dispassionately, it seemed contemptible. He could detect no trace of emotion in himself, and the final effect of a staggering event was that, unnoticed and apart from the noisy crowd of boys, he exulted with fresh certitude in his avidity for adventure, and in a sense of many-sided courage.

CHAPTER II.

After two years of training he went to sea, and entering the regions so well known to his imagination, found them strangely barren of adventure. He made many voyages. He knew the magic monotony of existence between sky and water: he had to bear the criticism of men, the exactions of the sea, and the prosaic severity of the daily task that gives bread—but whose only reward is in the perfect love of the work. This reward eluded him. Yet he could not go back, because there is nothing more enticing, disenchanting, and enslaving than the life at sea. Besides, his prospects were good. He was gentlemanly, steady, tractable, with a thorough knowledge of his duties; and in time, when yet very young, he became chief mate of a fine ship, without ever having been tested by those events of the sea that show in the light of day the inner worth of a man, the edge of his temper, and the fibre of his stuff; that reveal the quality of his resistance and the secret truth of his pretences, not only to others but also to himself.

Only once in all that time he had again the glimpse of the earnestness in the anger of the sea. That truth is not so often made apparent as people might think. There are many shades in the danger of adventures and gales, and it is only now and then that there appears on the face of facts a sinister violence of intention—that indefinable something which forces it upon the mind and the heart of a man, that this complication of accidents or these elemental furies are coming at him with a purpose of malice, with a strength beyond control, with an unbridled cruelty that means to tear out of him his hope and his fear, the pain of his fatigue and his longing for rest: which means to smash, to destroy, to annihilate all he had seen, known, loved, enjoyed, or hated; all that is priceless and necessary—the sunshine, the memories, the future,—which means to sweep the whole precious world utterly away from his sight by the simple and appalling act of taking his life.

Jim, disabled by a falling spar at the beginning of a week of which his Scottish captain used to say afterwards, "Man! it's a pairfect meeracle to me how she lived through it!" spent many days stretched on his back, dazed, battered, hopeless, and tormented as if at the bottom of an abyss of unrest. He did not care what the end would be, and in his lucid moments overvalued his indifference. The danger, when not seen, has the imperfect vagueness of human thought. The fear grows shadowy; and Imagination, the enemy of men, the father of all terrors, unstimulated, sinks to rest in the dulness of exhausted emotion. Jim saw nothing but the disorder of his tossed cabin. He lay there battened down in the midst of a small devastation, and felt secretly glad he had not to go on deck. But now and again an uncontrollable rush of anguish would grip him bodily, make him gasp and writhe under the blankets, and then the unintelligent brutality of an existence liable to the agony of such sensations filled him with a despairing desire to escape at any cost. Then fine weather returned, and he thought no more about it.

His lameness, however, persisted, and when the ship arrived at an Eastern port he had to go to the hospital. His recovery was slow, and he was left behind.

There were only two other patients in the white men's ward: the purser of a gunboat, who had broken his leg falling down a hatchway; and a kind of railway contractor from a neighbouring province, afflicted by some mysterious tropical disease, who held the doctor for an ass, and indulged in secret debaucheries of patent medicine which his Tamil servant used to smuggle in with unwearied devotion. They told each other the story of their lives, played cards a little, or, yawning and in pyjamas, lounged through the day in easy-chairs without saying a word. The hospital stood on a hill, and a gentle breeze entering through the windows, always flung wide open, brought into the bare room the softness of the sky, the languor of the earth, the bewitching breath of the Eastern waters. There were perfumes in it, suggestions of infinite repose, the gift of endless dreams. Jim looked every day over the thickets of gardens, beyond the roofs of the town, over the fronds of palms growing on the shore, at that roadstead which is a thoroughfare to the East,—at the roadstead dotted by garlanded islets, lighted by festal sunshine, its ships like toys, its brilliant activity resembling a holiday pageant, with the eternal serenity of the Eastern sky overhead and the smiling peace of the Eastern seas possessing the space as far as the horizon.

Directly he could walk without a stick, he descended into the town to look for some opportunity to get home. Nothing offered just then, and, while waiting, he associated naturally with the men of his calling in the port. These were of two kinds. Some, very few and seen there but seldom, led mysterious lives, had preserved an undefaced energy with the temper of buccaneers and the eyes of dreamers. They appeared to live in a crazy maze of plans, hopes, dangers, enterprises, ahead of civilisation, in the dark places of the sea; and their death was the only event of their fantastic existence that seemed to have a reasonable certitude of achievement. The majority were men who, like himself, thrown there by some accident, had remained as officers of country ships. They had now a horror of the home service, with its harder conditions, severer view of duty, and the hazard of stormy oceans. They were attuned to the eternal peace of Eastern sky and sea. They loved short passages, good deck-chairs, large native crews, and the distinction of being white. They shuddered at the thought of hard work, and led precariously easy lives, always on the verge of dismissal, always on the verge of engagement, serving Chinamen, Arabs, half-castes—would have served the devil himself had he made it easy enough. They talked everlastingly of turns of luck: how So-and-so got charge of a boat on the coast of China—a soft thing; how this one had an easy billet in Japan somewhere, and that one was doing well in the Siamese navy; and in all they said—in their actions, in their looks, in their persons—could be detected the soft spot, the place of decay, the determination to lounge safely through existence.

To Jim that gossiping crowd, viewed as seamen, seemed at first more unsubstantial than so many shadows. But at length he found a fascination in the sight of those men, in their appearance of doing so well on such a small allowance of danger and toil. In time, beside the original disdain there grew up slowly another sentiment; and suddenly, giving up the idea of going home, he took a berth as chief mate of the *Patna.*

The *Patna* was a local steamer as old as the hills, lean like a greyhound, and eaten up with rust worse than a condemned water-tank. She was owned by a Chinaman, chartered by an Arab, and commanded by a sort of renegade New South Wales German, very anxious to curse publicly his native country, but who, apparently on the strength of Bismarck's victorious policy, brutalised all those he was not afraid of, and wore a "blood-and-iron" air, combined with a purple nose and a red moustache. After she had been painted outside and whitewashed inside, eight hundred pilgrims (more or less) were driven on board of her as she lay with steam up alongside a wooden jetty.

They streamed aboard over three gangways, they streamed in urged by faith and the hope of paradise, they streamed in with a continuous tramp and shuffle of bare feet, without a word, a murmur, or a look back; and when clear of confining rails spread on all sides over the deck, flowed forward and aft, overflowed down the yawning hatchways, filled the inner recesses of the ship—like water filling a cistern, like water flowing into crevices and crannies, like water rising silently even with the rim. Eight hundred men and women with faith and hopes, with affections and memories, they had collected there, coming from north and south and from the outskirts of the East, after treading the jungle paths, descending the rivers, coasting in praus along the shallows, crossing in small canoes from island to island, passing through suffering, meeting strange sights, beset by strange fears, upheld by one desire. They came from solitary huts in the wilderness, from populous campongs, from villages by the sea. At the call of an idea they had left their forests, their clearings, the protection of their rulers, their prosperity, their poverty, the surroundings of their youth and the graves of their fathers. They came covered with dust, with sweat, with grime, with rags— the strong men at the head of family parties, the lean old men pressing forward without hope of return; young boys with fearless eyes glancing curiously, shy little girls with tumbled long hair; the timid women muffled up and clasping to their breasts, wrapped in loose ends of soiled head-cloths, their sleeping babies, the unconscious pilgrims of an exacting belief.

"Look at dese cattle," said the German skipper to his new chief mate.

An Arab, the leader of that pious voyage, came last. He walked slowly aboard, handsome and grave in his white gown and large turban. A string of servants followed, loaded with his luggage; the *Patna* cast off and backed away from the wharf.

She was headed between two small islets, crossed obliquely the anchoring-ground of sailing ships, swung through half a circle in the shadow of a hill, then ranged close to a ledge of foaming reefs. The Arab, standing up aft, recited aloud the prayer of travellers by sea. He invoked the favour of the Most High upon that journey, implored His blessing on men's toil and on the secret purposes of their hearts; the steamer pounded in the dusk the calm water of the Strait; and far astern of the pilgrim ship a screw-pile lighthouse, planted by unbelievers on a treacherous shoal, seemed to wink at her its eye of flame, as if in derision of her errand of faith.

She cleared the Straits, crossed the bay, continued on her way through the "One-degree" passage. She held on straight for the Red Sea under a serene sky, under a sky scorching and unclouded, enveloped in a fulgor of sunshine that killed all thought, oppressed the heart, withered all impulses of strength and energy. And under the sinister splendour of that sky the sea, blue and profound, remained still, without a stir, without a ripple, without a wrinkle—viscous, stagnant, dead. The *Patna*, with a slight hiss, passed over that plain luminous and smooth, un-rolled a black ribbon of smoke across the sky, left behind her on the water a white ribbon of foam that vanished at once, like the phantom of a track drawn upon a lifeless sea by the phantom of a steamer.

Every morning the sun, as if keeping pace in his revolutions with the progress of the pilgrimage, emerged with a silent burst of light exactly at the same distance astern of the ship, caught up with her at noon, pouring the concentrated fire of his rays on the pious purposes of the men, glided past on his descent, and sank mys-teriously into the sea evening after evening, preserving the same distance ahead of her advancing bows. The five whites on board lived amidships, isolated from the human cargo. The awnings covered the deck with a white roof from stem to stern, and a faint hum, a low murmur of sad voices, alone revealed the presence of a crowd of people upon the great blaze of the ocean. Such were the days, still, hot, heavy, disappearing one by one into the past, as if falling into an abyss for ever open in the wake of the ship; and the ship, lonely under a wisp of smoke, held on her steadfast way black and smouldering in a luminous immensity, as if scorched by a flame flicked at her from a heaven without pity.

The nights descended on her like a benediction.

CHAPTER III.

A marvellous stillness pervaded the world, and the stars, together with the serenity of their rays, seemed to shed upon the earth the assurance of everlasting security. The young moon recurved, and shining low in the west, was like a slen-der shaving thrown up from a bar of gold, and the Arabian Sea, smooth and cool to the eye like a sheet of ice, extended its perfect level to the perfect circle of a dark horizon. The propeller turned without a check, as though its beat had been part of the scheme of a safe universe; and on each side of the *Patna* two deep folds of water, permanent and sombre on the unwrinkled shimmer, enclosed within their straight and diverging ridges a few white swirls of foam bursting in a low hiss, a few wavelets, a few ripples, a few undulations that, left behind, agitated the sur-face of the sea for an instant after the passage of the ship, subsided splashing gently, calmed down at last into the circular stillness of water and sky with the black speck of the moving hull remaining everlastingly in its centre.

Jim on the bridge was penetrated by the great certitude of unbounded safety and peace that could be read on the silent aspect of nature like the certitude of fos-

tering love upon the placid tenderness of a mother's face. Below the roof of awnings, surrendered to the wisdom of white men and to their courage, trusting the
power of their unbelief and the iron shell of their fire-ship, the pilgrims of an exacting faith slept on mats, on blankets, on bare planks, on every deck, in all the
dark corners, wrapped in dyed cloths, muffled in soiled rags, with their heads
resting on small bundles, with their faces pressed to bent forearms: the men, the
women, the children; the old with the young, the decrepit with the lusty—all
equal before sleep, death's brother.

A draught of air, fanned from forward by the speed of the ship, passed steadily through the long gloom between the high bulwarks, swept over the rows of
prone bodies; a few dim flames in globe-lamps were hung short here and there
under the ridge-poles, and in the blurred circles of light thrown down and trembling slightly to the unceasing vibration of the ship appeared a chin upturned, two
closed eyelids, a dark hand with silver rings, a meagre limb draped in a torn covering, a head bent back, a naked foot, a throat bared and stretched as if offering
itself to the knife. The well-to-do had made for their families shelters with heavy
boxes and dusty mats; the poor reposed side by side with all they had on earth tied
up in a rag under their heads; the lone old men slept, with drawn-up legs, upon
their prayer-carpets, with their hands over their ears and one elbow on each side
of the face: a father, his shoulders up and his knees under his forehead, dozed dejectedly by a boy who slept on his back with tousled hair and one arm commandingly extended; a woman covered from head to foot, like a corpse, with a piece of
white sheeting, had a naked child in the hollow of each arm; the Arab's belongings, piled right aft, made a heavy mound of broken outlines, with a cargo-lamp
swung above, and a great confusion of vague forms behind: gleams of paunchy
brass pots, the foot-rest of a deck-chair, blades of spears, the straight scabbard of
an old sword leaning against a heap of pillows, the spout of a tin coffee-pot. The
patent log on the taffrail periodically rang a single tinkling stroke for every mile
traversed on an errand of faith. Above the mass of sleepers a faint and patient sigh
at times floated, the exhalation of a troubled dream; and short metallic clangs
bursting out suddenly in the depths of the ship, the harsh scrape of a shovel, the
violent slam of a furnace-door, exploded brutally, as if the men handling the mysterious things below had their breasts full of fierce anger: while the slim high hull
of the steamer went on evenly ahead, without a sway of her bare masts, cleaving
continuously the great calm of the waters under the inaccessible serenity of the
sky.

Jim paced athwart, and his footsteps in the vast silence were loud to his own
ears, as if echoed by the watchful stars: his eyes roaming about the line of the horizon, seemed to gaze hungrily into the unattainable, and did not see the shadow
of the coming event. The only shadow on the sea was the shadow of the black
smoke pouring heavily from the funnel its immense streamer, whose end was constantly dissolving in the air. Two Malays, silent and almost motionless, steered,
one on each side of the wheel, whose brass rim shone fragmentarily in the oval of
light thrown out by the binnacle. Now and then a hand, with black fingers alternately letting go and catching hold of revolving spokes, appeared in the illumined
part; the links of wheel-chains ground heavily in the grooves of the barrel. Jim
would glance at the compass, would glance around the unattainable horizon,
would stretch himself till his joints cracked, with a leisurely twist of the body, in

the very excess of wellbeing; and, as if made audacious by the invincible aspect of the peace, he felt he cared for nothing that could happen to him to the end of his days. From time to time he glanced idly at a chart pegged out with four drawing-pins on a low three-legged table abaft the steering-gear case. The sheet of paper portraying the depths of the sea presented a shiny surface under the light of a bull's-eye lamp lashed to a stanchion, a surface as level and smooth as the glimmering surface of the waters. Parallel rulers with a pair of dividers reposed on it; the ship's position at last noon was marked with a small black cross, and the straight pencil-line drawn firmly as far as Perim figured the course of the ship—the path of souls towards the holy place, the promise of salvation, the reward of eternal life—while the pencil with its sharp end touching the Somali coast lay round and still like a naked ship's spar floating in the pool of a sheltered dock. "How steady she goes," thought Jim with wonder, with something like gratitude for this high peace of sea and sky. At such times his thoughts would be full of valorous deeds: he loved these dreams and the success of his imaginary achievements. They were the best parts of life, its secret truth, its hidden reality. They had a gorgeous virility, the charm of vagueness, they passed before him with a heroic tread; they carried his soul away with them and made it drunk with the divine philtre of an unbounded confidence in itself. There was nothing he could not face. He was so pleased with the idea that he smiled, keeping perfunctorily his eyes ahead; and when he happened to glance back he saw the white streak of the wake drawn as straight by the ship's keel upon the sea as the black line drawn by the pencil upon the chart.

The ash-buckets racketed, clanking up and down the stoke-hold ventilators, and this tin-pot clatter warned him the end of his watch was near. He sighed with content, with regret as well at having to part from that serenity which fostered the adventurous freedom of his thoughts. He was a little sleepy too, and felt a pleasurable languor running through every limb as though all the blood in his body had turned to warm milk. His skipper had come up noiselessly, in pyjamas and with his sleeping-jacket flung wide open. Red of face, only half awake, the left eye partly closed, the right staring stupid and glassy, he hung his big head over the chart and scratched his ribs sleepily. There was something obscene in the sight of his naked flesh. His bared breast glistened soft and greasy as though he had sweated out his fat in his sleep. He pronounced a professional remark in a voice harsh and dead, resembling the rasping sound of a wood-file on the edge of a plank; the fold of his double chin hung like a bag triced up close under the hinge of his jaw. Jim started, and his answer was full of deference; but the odious and fleshy figure, as though seen for the first time in a revealing moment, fixed itself in his memory for ever as the incarnation of everything vile and base that lurks in the world we love: in our own hearts we trust for our salvation, in the men that surround us, in the sights that fill our eyes, in the sounds that fill our ears, and in the air that fills our lungs.

The thin gold shaving of the moon floating slowly downwards had lost itself on the darkened surface of the waters, and the eternity beyond the sky seemed to come down nearer to the earth, with the augmented glitter of the stars, with the more profound sombreness in the lustre of the half-transparent dome covering the flat disc of an opaque sea. The ship moved so smoothly that her onward motion was imperceptible to the senses of men, as though she had been a crowded planet

speeding through the dark spaces of ether behind the swarm of suns, in the appalling and calm solitudes awaiting the breath of future creations. "Hot is no name
for it down below," said a voice.

Jim smiled without looking round. The skipper presented an unmoved
breadth of back: it was the renegade's trick to appear pointedly unaware of your
existence unless it suited his purpose to turn at you with a devouring glare before
he let loose a torrent of foamy, abusive jargon that came like a gush from a sewer.
Now he emitted only a sulky grunt; the second engineer at the head of the bridge-
ladder, kneading with damp palms a dirty sweat-rag, unabashed, continued the
tale of his complaints. The sailors had a good time of it up here, and what was the
use of them in the world he would be blowed if he could see. The poor devils of
engineers had to get the ship along anyhow, and they could very well do the rest
too; by gosh they— "Shut up!" growled the German stolidly. "Oh yes! Shut up—
and when anything goes wrong you fly to us, don't you?" went on the other. He
was more than half cooked, he expected; but anyway, now, he did not mind how
much he sinned, because these last three days he had passed through a fine
course of training for the place where the bad boys go when they die—b'gosh, he
had—besides being made jolly well deaf by the blasted racket below. The durned,
compound, surface-condensing, rotten scrap-heap rattled and banged down there
like an old deck-winch, only more so; and what made him risk his life every night
and day that God made amongst the refuse of a breaking-up yard flying round at
fifty-seven revolutions, was more than *he* could tell. He must have been born reckless, b'gosh. He . . . "Where did you get drink?" inquired the German, very savage, but motionless in the light of the binnacle, like a clumsy effigy of a man cut
out of a block of fat. Jim went on smiling at the retreating horizon; his heart was
full of generous impulses, and his thought was contemplating his own superiority.
"Drink!" repeated the engineer with amiable scorn: he was hanging on with both
hands to the rail, a shadowy figure with flexible legs. "Not from you, captain.
You're far too mean, b'gosh. You would let a good man die sooner than give him
a drop of shnaps. That's what you Germans call economy. Penny wise, pound
foolish." He became sentimental. The chief had given him a four-finger nip about
ten o'clock—"only one, s'elp me!"—good old chief; but as to getting the old fraud
out of his bunk—a five-ton crane couldn't do it. Not it. Not to-night anyhow. He
was sleeping sweetly like a little child, with a bottle of prime brandy under his pillow. From the thick throat of the commander of the *Patna* came a low rumble, on
which the sound of the word *schwein* fluttered high and low like a capricious
feather in a faint stir of air. He and the chief engineer had been cronies for a good
few years—serving the same jovial, crafty, old Chinaman, with horn-rimmed goggles and strings of red silk plaited into the venerable grey hairs of his pigtail. The
quay-side opinion in the *Patna's* home-port was that these two in the way of brazen
peculation "had done together pretty well everything you can think of." Outwardly they were badly matched: one dull-eyed, malevolent, and of soft fleshy
curves; the other lean, all hollows, with a head long and bony like the head of an
old horse, with sunken cheeks, with sunken temples, with an indifferent glazed
glance of sunken eyes. He had been stranded out East somewhere—in Canton, in
Shanghai, or perhaps in Yokohama; he probably did not care to remember himself
the exact locality, nor yet the cause of his shipwreck. He had been, in mercy to his
youth, kicked quietly out of his ship twenty years ago or more, and it might have
been so much worse for him that the memory of the episode had in it hardly a trace

of misfortune. Then, steam navigation expanding in these seas and men of his craft being scarce at first, he had "got on" after a sort. He was eager to let strangers know in a dismal mumble that he was "an old stager out here." When he moved a skeleton seemed to sway loose in his clothes; his walk was mere wandering, and he was given to wander thus around the engine room skylight, smoking, without relish, doctored tobacco in a brass bowl at the end of a cherrywood stem four feet long, with the imbecile gravity of a thinker evolving a system of philosophy from the hazy glimpse of a truth. He was usually anything but free with his private store of liquor; but on that night he had departed from his principles, so that his second, a weak-headed child of Wapping, what with the unexpectedness of the treat and the strength of the stuff, had become very happy, cheeky, and talkative. The fury of the New South Wales German was extreme; he puffed like an exhaust-pipe, and Jim, faintly amused by the scene, was impatient for the time when he could get below: the last ten minutes of the watch were irritating like a gun that hangs fire; those men did not belong to the world of heroic adventure; they weren't bad chaps though. Even the skipper himself . . . His gorge rose at the mass of panting flesh from which issued gurgling mutters, a cloudy trickle of filthy expressions; but he was too pleasurably languid to dislike actively this or any other thing. The quality of these men did not matter; he rubbed shoulders with them, but they could not touch him; he shared the air they breathed, but he was different. . . . Would the skipper go for the engineer? . . . The life was easy and he was too sure of himself—too sure of himself to . . . The line dividing his meditation from a surreptitious doze on his feet was thinner than a thread in a spider's web.

The second engineer was coming by easy transitions to the consideration of his finances and of his courage.

"Who's drunk? I? No, no, captain! That won't do. You ought to know by this time the chief ain't free-hearted enough to make a sparrow drunk, b'gosh. I've never been the worse for liquor in my life; the stuff ain't made yet that would make *me* drunk. I could drink liquid fire against your whiskey peg for peg, b'gosh, and keep as cool as a cucumber. If I thought I was drunk I would jump overboard—do away with myself, b'gosh. I would! Straight! And I won't go off the bridge. Where do you expect me to take the air on a night like this, eh? On deck amongst that vermin down there? Likely—ain't it! And I am not afraid of anything you can do."

The German lifted two heavy fists to heaven and shook them a little without a word.

"I don't know what fear is," pursued the engineer, with the enthusiasm of sincere conviction. "I am not afraid of doing all the bloomin' work in this rotten hooker, b'gosh! And a jolly good thing for you that there are some of us about the world that aren't afraid of their lives, or where would you be—you and this old thing here with her plates like brown paper—brown paper, s'elp me? It's all very fine for you—you get a power of pieces out of her one way and another; but what about me—what do I get? A measly hundred and fifty dollars a-month and find yourself. I wish to ask you respectfully—respectfully, mind—who wouldn't chuck a dratted job like this? 'Tain't safe, s'elp me, it ain't! Only I am one of them fearless fellows . . ."

He let go the rail and made ample gestures as if demonstrating in the air the shapes and extent of his valour; his thin voice darted in prolonged squeaks upon the sea, he tiptoed back and forth for the better emphasis of utterance, and suddenly pitched down head-first as though he had been clubbed from behind. He said "Damn!" as he tumbled; an instant of silence followed upon his screeching: Jim and the skipper staggered forward by common accord, and catching themselves up, stood very stiff and still gazing, amazed, at the undisturbed level of the sea. Then they looked upwards at the stars.

What had happened? The wheezy thump of the engines went on. Had the earth been checked in her course? They could not understand; and suddenly the calm sea, the sky without a cloud, appeared formidably insecure in their immobility, as it poised on the brow of yawning destruction. The engineer rebounded vertically full length and collapsed again into a vague heap. This heap said "What's that?" in the muffled accents of profound grief. A faint noise as of thunder, of thunder infinitely remote, less than a sound, hardly more than a vibration, passed slowly, and the ship quivered in response, as if the thunder had growled deep down in the water. The eyes of the two Malays at the wheel glittered towards the white men, but their dark hands remained closed on the spokes. The sharp hull driving on its way seemed to rise a few inches in succession through its whole length, as though it had become pliable, and settled down again rigidly to its work of cleaving the smooth surface of the sea. Its quivering stopped, and the faint noise of thunder ceased all at once, as though the ship had steamed across a narrow belt of vibrating water and of humming air.

CHAPTER IV.

A month or so afterwards, when Jim, in answer to pointed questions, tried to tell honestly the truth of this experience, he said, speaking of the ship: "She went over whatever it was as easy as a snake crawling over a stick." The illustration was good: the questions were aiming at facts, and the official Inquiry was being held in the police court of an Eastern port. He stood elevated in the witness-box, with burning cheeks in a cool lofty room: the big framework of punkahs moved gently to and fro high above his head, and from below many eyes were looking at him out of dark faces, out of white faces, out of red faces, out of faces attentive, spellbound, as if all these people sitting in orderly rows upon narrow benches had been enslaved by the fascination of his voice. It was very loud, it rang startling in his own ears, it was the only sound audible in the world, for the terribly distinct questions that extorted his answers seemed to shape themselves in anguish and pain within his breast,—came to him poignant and silent like the terrible questioning of one's conscience. Outside the court the sun blazed—within was the wind of great punkahs that made you shiver, the shame that made you burn, the attentive eyes whose glance stabbed. The face of the presiding magistrate, clean shaved and impassible, looked at him deadly pale between the red faces of the two nautical assessors. The light of a broad window under the ceiling fell from above on the heads and shoulders of the three men, and they were fiercely distinct in the half-light of the big court-room where the audience seemed composed of staring shadows. They wanted facts. Facts! They demanded facts from him, as if facts could explain anything!

"After you had concluded you had collided with something floating awash, say a water-logged wreck, you were ordered by your captain to go forward and ascertain if there was any damage done. Did you think it likely from the force of the blow?'' asked the assessor sitting to the left. He had a thin horseshoe beard, salient cheek-bones, and with both elbows on the desk clasped his rugged hands before his face, looking at Jim with thoughtful blue eyes; the other, a heavy, scornful man, thrown back in his seat, his left arm extended full length, drummed delicately with his finger-tips on a blotting-pad: in the middle the magistrate upright in the roomy arm-chair, his head inclined slightly on the shoulder, had his arms crossed on his breast and a few flowers in a glass vase by the side of his inkstand.

"I did not," said Jim. "I was told to call no one and to make no noise for fear of creating a panic. I thought the precaution reasonable. I took one of the lamps that were hung under the awnings and went forward. After opening the forepeak hatch I heard splashing in there. I lowered then the lamp the whole drift of its lanyard, and saw that the forepeak was more than half full of water already. I knew then there must be a big hole below the water-line." He paused.

"Yes," said the big assessor, with a dreamy smile at the blotting-pad; his fingers played incessantly, touching the paper without noise.

"I did not think of danger just then. I might have been a little startled: all this happened in such a quiet way and so very suddenly. I knew there was no other bulkhead in the ship but the collision bulkhead separating the forepeak from the forehold. I went back to tell the captain. I came upon the second engineer getting up at the foot of the bridge-ladder: he seemed dazed, and told me he thought his left arm was broken; he had slipped on the top step when getting down while I was forward. He exclaimed, 'My God! That rotten bulkhead'll give way in a minute, and the damned thing will go down under us like a lump of lead.' He pushed me away with his right arm and ran before me up the ladder, shouting as he climbed. His left arm hung by his side. I followed up in time to see the captain rush at him and knock him down flat on his back. He did not strike him again: he stood bending over him and speaking angrily but quite low. I fancy he was asking him why the devil he didn't go and stop the engines, instead of making a row about it on deck. I heard him say, 'Get up! Run, fly!' He swore also. The engineer slid down the starboard ladder and bolted round the skylight to the engine-room companion which was on the port-side. He moaned as he ran. . . ."

He spoke slowly; he remembered swiftly and with extreme vividness; he could have reproduced like an echo the moaning of the engineer for the better information of these men who wanted facts. After his first feeling of revolt he had come round to the view that only a meticulous precision of statement would bring out the true horror behind the appalling face of things. The facts those men were so eager to know had been visible, tangible, open to the senses, occupying their place in space and time, requiring for their existence a fourteen-hundred-ton steamer and twenty-seven minutes by the watch; they made a whole that had features, shades of expression, a complicated aspect that could be remembered by the eye, and something else besides, something invisible, a directing spirit of perdition that dwelt within, like a malevolent soul in a detestable body. He was anxious to make this clear. This had not been a common affair, everything in it had been of the utmost importance, and fortunately he remembered everything. He wanted to go on talking for truth's sake, perhaps for his own sake also; and while his utterance was deliberate, his mind positively flew round and round the serried circle of facts that had surged up all about him to cut him off from the rest of his kind: it was like a creature that, finding itself imprisoned within an enclosure of high stakes, dashes round and round, distracted in the night, trying to find a weak spot, a crevice, a place to scale, some opening through which it may squeeze itself and escape. This awful activity of mind made him hesitate at times in his speech. . . .

"The captain kept on moving here and there on the bridge; he seemed calm enough, only he stumbled several times; and once as I stood speaking to him he walked right into me as though he had been stone-blind. He made no definite answer to what I had to tell. He mumbled to himself; all I heard of it were a few words that sounded like 'confounded steam!' and 'infernal steam!'—something about steam. I thought . . ."

He was becoming irrelevant; a question to the point cut short his speech, like a pang of pain, and he felt extremely discouraged and weary. He was coming to that, he was coming to that—and now, checked brutally, he had to answer by yes or no. He answered truthfully by a curt "Yes, I did"; and fair of face, big of frame, with young, gloomy eyes, he held his shoulders upright above the box while his soul writhed within him. He was made to answer another question so much to the point and so useless, then waited again. His mouth was tastelessly dry, as though he had been eating dust, then salt and bitter as after a drink of sea-water. He wiped his damp forehead, passed his tongue over parched lips, felt a shiver run down his back. The big assessor had dropped his eyelids, and drummed on without a sound, careless and mournful; the eyes of the other above the sunburnt, clasped fingers seemed to glow with kindliness; the magistrate had swayed forward; his pale face hovered near the flowers, and then dropping sideways over the arm of his chair, he rested his temple in the palm of his hand. The wind of the punkahs eddied down on the heads, on the dark-faced natives wound about in voluminous draperies, on the Europeans sitting together very hot and in drill suits that seemed to fit them as close as their skins, and holding their round pith hats on their knees; while gliding along the walls the court peons, buttoned tight in long white coats, flitted rapidly to and fro, running on bare toes, red-sashed, red turban on head, as noiseless as ghosts, and on the alert like so many retrievers.

Jim's eyes, wandering in the intervals of his answers, rested upon a white man who sat apart from the others, with his face worn and clouded, but with quiet eyes that glanced straight, interested and clear. Jim answered another question and was tempted to cry out, "What's the good of this, what's the good!" He tapped with his foot slightly, bit his lip, and looked away over the heads. He met the eyes of the white man. The glance directed at him was not the fascinated stare of the others. It was an act of intelligent volition. Jim between two questions forgot himself so far as to find leisure for a thought. This fellow—ran the thought—looks at me as though he could see somebody or something past my shoulder. He had come across that man before—in the street perhaps. He was positive he had never spoken to him. For days, for many days, he had spoken to no one, but had held silent, incoherent, and endless converse with himself, like a prisoner alone in his cell or like a wayfarer lost in a wilderness. At present he was answering questions that did not matter though they had a purpose, but he doubted whether he would ever again speak out as long as he lived. The sound of his own truthful statements confirmed his deliberate opinion that speech was of no use to him any longer. That man there seemed to be aware of his hopeless difficulty. Jim looked at him, then turned away resolutely, as after a final parting.

And later on, many times, in distant parts of the world, Marlow showed himself willing to remember Jim, to remember him at length, in detail and audibly.

Perhaps it would be after dinner, on a verandah draped in motionless foliage and crowned with flowers, in the deep dusk speckled by fiery cigar-ends. The elongated bulk of each cane-chair harboured a silent listener. Now and then a small red glow would move abruptly, and expanding light up the fingers of a languid hand, part of a face in profound repose, or flash a crimson gleam into a pair of pensive eyes overshadowed by a fragment of an unruffled forehead: and with the very first word uttered Marlow's body, extended at rest in the seat, would become very still, as though his spirit had winged its way back into the lapse of time and were speaking through his lips from the past.

CHAPTER V.

"Oh yes. I attended the inquiry," he would say, "and to this day I haven't left off wondering why I went. I am willing to believe each of us has a guardian angel, if you fellows will concede to me that each of us has a familiar devil as well. I want you to own up, because I don't like to feel exceptional in any way, and I know I have him—the devil, I mean. I haven't seen him, of course, but I go upon circumstantial evidence. He is there right enough, and, being malicious, he lets me in for that kind of thing. What kind of thing, you ask? Why, the inquiry thing, the yellow-dog thing—you wouldn't think a mangy, native tyke would be allowed to trip up people in the verandah of a magistrate's court, would you?—the kind of thing that by devious, unexpected, truly diabolical ways causes me to run up against men with soft spots, with hard spots, with hidden plague spots, by Jove! and loosens their tongues at the sight of me for their infernal confidences; as though, forsooth, I had no confidences to make to myself, as though—God help me!—I didn't have enough confidential information about myself to harrow my own soul till the end of my appointed time. And what I have done to be thus favoured I want to know. I declare I am as full of my own concerns as the next man, and I have as much memory as the average pilgrim in this valley, so you see I am not particularly fit to be a receptacle of confessions. Then why? Can't tell—unless it be to make time pass away after dinner. Charley, my dear chap, your dinner was extremely good, and in consequence these men here look upon a quiet rubber as a tumultuous occupation. They wallow in your good chairs and think to themselves, 'Hang exertion. Let that Marlow talk.'

"Talk! So be it. And it's easy enough to talk of Master Jim, after a good spread, two hundred feet above the sea-level, with a box of decent cigars handy, on a blessed evening of freshness and starlight that would make the best of us forget we are only on sufferance here and got to pick our way in cross lights, watching every precious minute and every irremediable step, trusting we shall manage yet to go out decently in the end—but not so sure of it after all—and with dashed little help to expect from those we touch elbows with right and left. Of course there are men here and there to whom the whole of life is like an after-dinner hour with a cigar; easy, pleasant, empty, perhaps enlivened by some fable of strife to be forgotten before the end is told—before the end is told—even if there happens to be any end to it.

"My eyes met his for the first time at that inquiry. You must know that every-body connected in any way with the sea was there, because the affair had been notorious for days, ever since that mysterious cable message came from Aden to start us all cackling. I say mysterious, because it was so in a sense though it contained a naked fact, about as naked and ugly as a fact can well be. The whole waterside talked of nothing else. First thing in the morning as I was dressing in my state-room, I would hear through the bulkhead my Parsee Dubash jabbering about the *Patna* with the steward, while he drank a cup of tea, by favour, in the pantry. No sooner on shore I would meet some acquaintance, and the first remark would be, 'Did you ever hear of anything to beat this?' and according to his kind the man would smile cynically, or look sad, or let out a swear or two. Complete strangers would accost each other familiarly, just for the sake of easing their minds on the subject: every confounded loafer in the town came in for a harvest of drinks over this affair: you heard of it in the harbour office, at every ship-broker's, at your agent's, from whites, from natives, from half-castes, from the very boatmen squatting half-naked on the stone steps as you went up—by Jove! There was some indignation, not a few jokes, and no end of discussions as to what had become of them, you know. This went on for a couple of weeks or more, and the opinion that whatever was mysterious in this affair would turn out to be tragic as well, began to prevail, when one fine morning, as I was standing in the shade by the steps of the harbour office, I perceived four men walking towards me along the quay. I wondered for a while where that queer lot had sprung from, and suddenly, I may say, I shouted to myself, 'Here they are!'

"There they were, sure enough, three of them as large as life, and one much larger of girth than any living man has a right to be, just landed with a good break-fast inside of them from an outward bound Dale Lane steamer that had come in about an hour after sunrise. There could be no mistake; I spotted the jolly skipper of the *Patna* at the first glance: the fattest man in the whole blessed tropical belt clear round that good old earth of ours. Moreover, nine months or so before, I had come across him in Samarang. His steamer was loading in the Roads, and he was abusing the tyrannical institutions of the German empire, and soaking himself in beer all day long and day after day in De Jongh's back-shop, till De Jongh, who charged a guilder for every bottle without as much as the quiver of an eyelid, would beckon me aside, and, with his little leathery face all puckered up, declare confidentially, 'Business is business, but this man, captain, he make me very sick. Tfui!'

"I was looking at him from the shade. He was hurrying on a little in advance, and the sunlight beating on him brought out his bulk in a startling way. He made me think of a trained baby elephant walking on hind-legs. He was extravagantly gorgeous too—got up in a soiled sleeping suit, bright green and deep orange vertical stripes, with a pair of ragged straw slippers on his bare feet, and somebody's cast-off pith hat, very dirty and two sizes too small for him, tied up with a manilla rope-yarn on the top of his big head. You understand a man like that hasn't the ghost of a chance when it comes to borrowing clothes. Very well. On he came in hot haste, without a look right or left, passed within three feet of me, and in the innocence of his heart went on pelting up-stairs into the harbour-office to make his deposition, or report, or whatever you like to call it.

"It appears he addressed himself in the first instance to the principal shipping-master. Archie Ruthvel had just come in, and, as his story goes, was about to begin his arduous day by giving a dressing-down to his chief clerk. Some of you might have known him—an obliging little Portuguese half-caste with a miserably skinny neck, and always on the hop to get something from the shipmasters in the way of eatables—a piece of salt pork, a bag of biscuits, a few potatoes, or what not. One voyage, I recollect, I tipped him a live sheep out of the remnant of my sea-stock: not that I wanted him to do anything for me—he couldn't, you know—but because his childlike belief in the sacred right to perquisites quite touched my heart. It was so strong as to be almost beautiful. The race—the two races rather—and the climate . . . However, never mind. I know where I have a friend for life.

"Well, Ruthvel says he was giving him a severe lecture—on official morality, I suppose—when he heard a kind of subdued commotion at his back, and turning his head he saw, in his own words, something round and enormous, resembling a sixteen-hundred-weight sugar-hogshead wrapped in striped flannelette, up-ended in the middle of the large floor space in the office. He declares he was so taken aback that for quite an appreciable time he did not realise the thing was alive, and sat still wondering for what purpose and by what means that object had been transported in front of his desk. The archway from the anteroom was crowded with punkah-pullers, sweepers, police peons, the coxswain and crew of the harbour steam-launch, all craning their necks and almost climbing on each other's backs. Quite a riot. By that time the fellow had managed to tug and jerk his hat clear of his head, and advanced with slight bows at Ruthvel, who told me the sight was so discomposing that for some time he listened, quite unable to make out what that apparition wanted. It spoke in a voice harsh and lugubrious but in-trepid, and little by little it dawned upon Archie that this was a development of the *Patna* case. He says that as soon as he understood who it was before him he felt quite unwell,—Archie is so sympathetic and easily upset,—but pulled himself to-gether and shouted 'Stop! I can't listen to you. You must go to the Master Attend-ant. I can't possibly listen to you. Captain Elliot is the man you want to see. This way, this way.' He jumped up, ran round that long counter, pulled, shoved: the other let him, surprised but obedient at first, and only at the door of the private office some sort of animal instinct made him hang back and snort like a frightened bullock. 'Look here! what's up? Let go! Look here!' Archie flung open the door without knocking. 'The master of the *Patna*, sir,' he shouts. 'Go in, captain.' He saw the old man lift his head from some writing so sharp that his nose-nippers fell off, banged the door to, and fled to his desk, where he had some papers waiting for his signature: but he says the row that burst out in there was so awful that he couldn't collect his senses sufficiently to remember the spelling of his own name. Archie's the most sensitive shipping-master in the two hemispheres. He declares he felt as though he had thrown a man to a hungry lion. No doubt the noise was great. I heard it down below, and I have every reason to believe it was heard clear across the Esplanade as far as the band-stand. Old father Elliot had a great stock of words and could shout—and didn't mind who he shouted at either. He would have shouted at the Viceroy himself. As he used to tell me: 'I am as high as I can get; my pension is safe. I've a few pounds laid by, and if they don't like my notions of duty I would just as soon go home as not. I am an old man, and I have always spoken my mind. All I care for now is to see my girls married before I die.' He was a little crazy on that point. His three daughters were awfully nice, though they re-sembled him amazingly, and on the mornings he woke up with a gloomy view of their matrimonial prospects the office would read it in his eye and tremble, because, they said, he was sure to have somebody for breakfast. However, that morning he did not eat the renegade, but, if I may be allowed to carry on the metaphor, chewed him up very small, so to speak, and—ah! ejected him again.

"Thus in a very few moments I saw his monstrous bulk descend in haste and stand still on the outer steps. He had stopped close to me for the purpose of profound meditation: his large purple cheeks quivered. He was biting his thumb, and after a while noticed me with a sidelong vexed look. The other three chaps that had landed with him made a little group waiting at some distance. There was a sallow-faced, mean little chap with his arm in a sling, and a long individual in a blue flannel coat, as dry as a chip and no stouter than a broomstick, with drooping grey moustaches, who looked about him with an air of jaunty imbecility. The third was an upstanding, broad-shouldered youth, with his hands in his pockets, turning his back on the other two who appeared to be talking together earnestly. He stared across the empty Esplanade. A ramshackle gharry, all dust and venetian blinds, pulled up short opposite the group, and the driver, throwing up his right foot over his knee, gave himself up to the critical examination of his toes. The young chap, making no movement, not even stirring his head, just stared into the sunshine. This was my first view of Jim. He looked as unconcerned and unapproachable as only the young can look. There he stood, clean-limbed, clean-faced, firm on his feet, as promising a boy as the sun ever shone on; and, looking at him, knowing all he knew and a little more too, I was as angry as though I had detected him trying to get something out of me by false pretences. He had no business to look so sound. I thought to myself—well, if this sort can go wrong like that . . . and I felt as though I could fling down my hat and dance on it from sheer mortification, as I once saw the skipper of an Italian barque do because his duffer of a mate got into a mess with his anchors when making a flying moor in a roadstead full of ships. I asked myself, seeing him there apparently so much at ease—is he silly? is he callous? He seemed ready to start whistling a tune. And note, I did not care a rap about the behaviour of the other two. Their persons somehow fitted the tale that was public property, and was going to be the subject of an official inquiry. 'That old mad rogue up-stairs called me a hound,' said the captain of the *Patna*. I can't tell whether he recognised me—I rather think he did; but at any rate our glances met. He glared—I smiled; hound was the very mildest epithet that had reached me through the open window. 'Did he?' I said from some strange inability to hold my tongue. He nodded, bit his thumb again, swore under his breath: then lifting his head and looking at me with sullen and passionate impudence—'Bah! the Pacific is big, my friendt. You damned Englishmen can do your worst; I know where there's plenty room for a man like me: I am well aguaindt in Apia, in Honolulu, in . . .' He paused reflectively, while without effort I could depict to myself the sort of people he was 'aguaindt' within those places. I won't make a secret of it that I had been 'aguaindt' with not a few of that sort myself. There are times when a man must act as though life were equally sweet in any company. I've known such a time, and, what's more, I shan't now pretend to pull a long face over my necessity, because a good many of that bad company from want of moral—moral—what shall I say?—posture from some other equally profound cause, were twice as instructive and twenty times more amusing than the usual respectable thief of commerce you fellows ask to sit at your table without any real necessity—from habit, from cowardice, from good-nature, from a hundred sneaking and inadequate reasons.

"'You Englishmen are all rogues,' went on my patriotic Flensborg or Stettin Australian. I really don't recollect now what decent little port on the shores of the Baltic was defiled by being the nest of that precious bird. 'What are you to shout? Eh? You tell me? You no better than other people, and that old rogue he make Gottam fuss with me.' His thick carcass trembled on its legs that were like a pair of pillars; it trembled from head to foot. 'That's what you English always make— make a tam' fuss—for any little thing, because I was not born in your tam' country. Take away my certificate. Take it. I don't want the certificate. A man like me don't want your verfluchte certificate. I shpit on it.' He spat. 'I vill an Amerigan citizen begome,' he cried, fretting and fuming and shuffling his feet as if to free his ankles from some invisible and mysterious grasp that would not let him get away from that spot. He made himself so warm that the top of his bullet head positively smoked. Nothing mysterious prevented me from going away: curiosity is the most obvious of sentiments, and it held me there to see the effect of a full information upon that young fellow who, hands in pockets, and turning his back upon the sidewalk, gazed across the grass plots of the Esplanade at the yellow portico of the Malabar Hotel with the air of a man about to go for a walk as soon as his friend is ready. That's how he looked, and it was odious. I waited to see him overwhelmed, confounded, pierced through and through, squirming like an impaled beetle— and I was half-afraid to see it too—if you understand what I mean. Nothing more awful than to watch a man who has been found out, not in a crime but in a more than criminal weakness. The commonest sort of fortitude prevents us from becoming criminals in a legal sense; it is from weakness unknown, but perhaps suspected, as in some parts of the world you suspect a deadly snake in every bush,— from weakness that may lie hidden, watched or unwatched, prayed against or manfully scorned, repressed or maybe ignored more than half a lifetime, not one of us is safe. We are snared into doing things for which we get called names, and things for which we get hanged, and yet the spirit may well survive,—survive the condemnation, survive the halter, by Jove! And there are things—they look small enough sometimes too—by which some of us are totally and completely undone. I watched the youngster there. I liked his appearance; I knew his appearance; he came from the right place; he was one of us. He stood there for all the parentage of his kind, for men and women by no means clever or amusing, but whose very existence is based upon honest faith, and upon the instinct of courage. I don't mean military courage, or civil courage, or any special kind of courage. I mean just that inborn ability to look temptations straight in the face,—a readiness unintellectual enough, goodness knows, but without a pose,—a power of resistance, don't you see, ungracious if you like, but priceless—an unthinking and blessed stiffness before the outward and inward terrors, before the might of nature and the seductive corruption of men—backed by a faith invulnerable to the strength of facts, to the contagion of example, to the solicitation of ideas. Hang ideas! They are tramps, vagabonds, knocking at the backdoor of your mind, each taking a little of your substance, each carrying away some crumb of that belief in a few simple notions you must cling to if you want to live decently and would like to die easy!

"This has nothing to do with Jim, directly; only he was outwardly so typical of that good stupid kind we like to feel marching right and left of us in life, of the kind that is not disturbed by the vagaries of intelligence and the perversions of— of nerves, let us say. He was the kind of fellow you would, on the strength of his looks, leave in charge of the deck—figuratively and professionally speaking. I say

I would, and I ought to know. Haven't I turned out youngsters enough in my time, for the service of the Red Rag, to the craft of the sea, to the craft whose whole secret could be expressed in one short sentence, and yet must be driven afresh every day into young heads till it becomes the component part of every waking thought—till it is present in every dream of their young sleep! The sea has been good to me, but when I remember all these boys that passed through my hands, some grown up now and some drowned by this time, but all good stuff for the sea, I don't think I have done badly by it either. Were I to go home to-morrow, I bet that before two days passed over my head some sunburnt young chief mate would overtake me at some dock gateway or other, and a fresh deep voice speaking above my hat would ask: 'Don't you remember me, sir? Why! little So-and-so. Such and such a ship. It was my first voyage.' And I would remember a bewildered little shaver, no higher than the back of this chair, with a mother and perhaps a big sister on the quay, very quiet but too upset to wave their handkerchiefs at the ship that glides out gently between the pier-heads: or perhaps some decent middle-aged father who had come early with his boy to see him off, and stays all the morning, because he is interested in the windlass apparently, and stays too long, and has got to scramble ashore at last with no time at all to say good-bye. The mud pilot on the poop sings out to me in a drawl, 'Hold her with the check line for a moment, Mister Mate. There's a gentleman wants to get ashore. . . . Up with you, sir. Nearly got carried off to Talcahuano, didn't you? Now's your time; easy does it. . . . All right. Slack away again forward there.' The tugs, smoking like the pit of perdition, get hold and churn the old river into fury; the gentleman ashore is dusting his knees—the benevolent steward has shied his umbrella after him. All very proper. He has offered his bit of sacrifice to the sea, and now he may go home pretending he thinks nothing of it; and the little willing victim shall be very sea-sick before next morning. By-and-by, when he has learned all the little mysteries and the one great secret of the craft, he shall be fit to live or die as the sea may decree; and the man who had taken a hand in this fool game, in which the sea wins every toss, will be pleased to have his back slapped by a heavy young hand, and to hear a cheery sea-puppy voice: 'Do you remember me, sir? The little So-and-so.'

"I tell you this is good; it tells you that once in your life at least you had gone the right way to work. I have been thus slapped, and I have winced, for the slap was heavy, and I have glowed all day long and gone to bed feeling less lonely in the world by virtue of that hearty thump. Don't I remember the little So-and-so's! I tell you I ought to know the right kind of looks. I would have trusted the deck to that youngster on the strength of a single glance, and gone to sleep with both eyes—and, by Jove! it wouldn't have been safe. There are depths of horror in that thought. He looked as genuine as a new sovereign, but there was some infernal alloy in his metal. How much? The least thing—the least drop of something rare and accursed; the least drop!—but he made you—standing there with his don't-care-hang air—he made you wonder whether perchance he were nothing more rare than brass.

"I couldn't believe it. I tell you I wanted to see him squirm for the honour of the craft. The other two no-account chaps spotted their captain, and began to move slowly towards us. They chatted together as they strolled, and I did not care any more than if they had not been visible to the naked eye. They grinned at each other—might have been exchanging jokes, for all I know. I saw that with one of them it was a case of a broken arm; and as to the long individual with grey mous-

taches he was the chief engineer, and in various ways a pretty notorious personality. They were nobodies. They approached. The skipper gazed in an inanimate
way between his feet: he seemed to be swollen to an unnatural size by some awful
disease, by the mysterious action of an unknown poison. He lifted his head, saw
the two before him waiting, opened his mouth with an extraordinary, sneering
contortion of his puffed face—to speak to them, I suppose—and then a thought
seemed to strike him. His thick, purplish lips came together without a sound, he
went off in a resolute waddle to the gharry and began to jerk at the door-handle
with such a blind brutality of impatience that I expected to see the whole concern
overturned on its side, pony and all. The driver, shaken out of his meditation over
the sole of his foot, displayed at once all the signs of intense terror, and held with
both hands, looking round from his box at this vast carcass forcing its way into his
conveyance. The little machine shook and rocked tumultuously, and the crimson
nape of that lowered neck, the size of these straining thighs, the immense heaving
of that dingy, striped green-and-orange back, the whole burrowing effort of that
gaudy and sordid mass, troubled one's sense of probability with a droll and fearsome effect, like one of those grotesque and distinct visions that scare and fascinate one in a fever. He disappeared. I half expected the roof to split in two, the
little box on wheels to burst open in the manner of a ripe cotton-pod—but it only
sank with a click of flattened springs, and suddenly one venetian blind rattled
down. His shoulders reappeared, jammed in the small opening; his head hung
out, distended and tossing like a captive balloon, perspiring, furious, spluttering.
He reached for the gharry-wallah with vicious flourishes of a fist as dumpy and
red as a lump of raw meat. He roared at him to be off, to go on. Where? Into the
Pacific, perhaps. The driver lashed; the pony snorted, reared once, and darted off
at a gallop. Where? To Apia? to Honolulu? He had 6000 miles of tropical belt to
disport himself in, and I did not hear the precise address. A snorting pony
snatched him into 'ewigkeit' in the twinkling of an eye, and I never saw him again;
and, what's more, I don't know of anybody that ever had a glimpse of him after
he departed from my knowledge sitting inside a ramshackle little gharry that fled
round the corner in a white smother of dust. He departed, disappeared, vanished,
absconded; and absurdly enough it looked as though he had taken that gharry
with him, for never again did I come across a sorrel pony with a slit ear and a lack-
adaisical Tamil driver afflicted by a sore foot. The Pacific is indeed big; but whether
he found a place for a display of his talents in it or not, the fact remains he had
flown into space like a witch on a broomstick. The little chap with his arm in a sling
started to run after the carriage, bleating, 'Captain! I say, Captain! I sa-a-ay!'—but
after a few steps stopped short, hung his head, and walked back slowly. At the
sharp rattle of the wheels the young fellow spun round where he stood. He made
no other movement, no gesture, no sign, and remained facing in the new direction
after the gharry had swung out of sight.

"All this happened in much less time than it takes to tell, since I am trying to
interpret for you into slow speech the instantaneous effect of visual impressions.
Next moment the half-caste clerk, sent by Archie to look a little after the poor castaways of the *Patna*, came upon the scene. He ran out eager and bareheaded, looking right and left, and very full of his mission. It was doomed to be a failure as far
as the principal person was concerned, but he approached the others with fussy
importance, and, almost immediately, found himself involved in a violent altercation with the chap that carried his arm in a sling, and who turned out to be ex-

tremely anxious for a row. He wasn't going to be ordered about—'not he, b'gosh.'
He wouldn't be terrified with a pack of lies by a cocky half-bred little quill-driver.
He was not going to be bullied by 'no object of that sort,' if the story were true 'ever
so'! He bawled his wish, his desire, his determination to go to bed. 'If you weren't
a Godforsaken Portuguee,' I heard him yell, 'you would know that the hospital is
the right place for me.' He pushed the fist of his sound arm under the other's nose;
a crowd began to collect; the half-caste, flustered, but doing his best to appear dignified, tried to explain his intentions. I went away without waiting to see the end.

"But it so happened that I had a man in the hospital at the time, and going
there to see about him the day before the opening of the Inquiry, I saw in the white
men's ward that little chap tossing on his back, with his arm in splints, and quite
light-headed. To my great surprise the other one, the long individual with drooping white moustache, had also found his way there. I remembered I had seen him
slinking away during the quarrel, in a half prance, half shuffle, and trying very
hard not to look scared. He was no stranger to the port, it seems, and in his distress was able to make tracks straight for Mariani's billiard-room and grog-shop
near the bazaar. That unspeakable vagabond, Mariani, who had known the man
and had ministered to his vices in one or two other places, kissed the ground, in
a manner of speaking, before him, and shut him up with a supply of bottles in an
up-stairs room of his infamous hovel. It appears he was under some hazy apprehension as to his personal safety, and wished to be concealed. However, Mariani
told me a long time after (when he came on board one day to dun my steward for
the price of some cigars) that he would have done more for him without asking any
questions, from gratitude for some unholy favour received very many years ago—
as far as I could make out. He thumped twice his brawny chest, rolled enormous
black and white eyes glistening with tears: 'Antonio never forget—Antonio never
forget!' What was the precise nature of the immoral obligation I never learned, but
be it what it may, he had every facility given him to remain under lock and key,
with a chair, a table, a mattress in a corner, and a litter of fallen plaster on the floor,
in an irrational state of funk, and keeping up his pecker with such tonics as Mariani dispensed. This lasted till the evening of the third day, when, after letting out
a few horrible screams, he found himself compelled to seek safety in flight from a
legion of centipedes. He burst the door open, made one leap for dear life down the
crazy little stairway, landed bodily on Mariani's stomach, picked himself up, and
bolted like a rabbit into the streets. The police plucked him off a garbage-heap in
the early morning. At first he had a notion they were carrying him off to be
hanged, and fought for liberty like a hero, but when I sat down by his bed he had
been very quiet for two days. His lean bronzed head, with white moustaches,
looked fine and calm on the pillow, like the head of a war-worn soldier with a childlike soul, had it not been for a hint of spectral alarm that lurked in the blank glitter
of his glance, resembling a nondescript form of a terror crouching silently behind
a pane of glass. He was so extremely calm, that I began to indulge in the eccentric
hope of hearing something explanatory of the famous affair from his point of view.
Why I longed to go grubbing into the deplorable details of an occurrence which,
after all, concerned me no more than as a member of an obscure body of men held
together by a community of inglorious toil and by fidelity to a certain standard of
conduct, I can't explain. You may call it an unhealthy curiosity if you like; but I
have a distinct notion I wished to find something. Perhaps, unconsciously, I hoped
I would find that something, some profound and redeeming cause, some merciful

explanation, some convincing shadow of an excuse. I see well enough now that I hoped for the impossible—for the laying of what is the most obstinate ghost of man's creation, of the uneasy doubt uprising like a mist, secret and gnawing like a worm, and more chilling that the certitude of death—the doubt of the sovereign power enthroned in a fixed standard of conduct. It is the hardest thing to stumble against; it is the thing that breeds yelling panics and good little quiet villanies; it's the true shadow of calamity. Did I believe in a miracle? and why did I desire it so ardently? Was it for my own sake that I wished to find some shadow of an excuse for that young fellow whom I had never seen before, but whose appearance alone added a touch of personal concern to the thoughts suggested by the knowledge of his weakness—made it a thing of mystery and terror—like a hint of a destructive fate ready for us all whose youth—in its day—had resembled his youth? I fear that such was the secret motive of my prying. I was, and no mistake, looking for a miracle. The only thing that at this distance of time strikes me as miraculous is the extent of my imbecility. I positively hoped to obtain from that battered and shady invalid some exorcism against the ghost of doubt. I must have been pretty desperate too, for, without loss of time, after a few indifferent and friendly sentences which he answered with languid readiness, just as any decent sick man would do, I produced the word *Patna* wrapped up in a delicate question as in a wisp of floss silk. I was delicate selfishly; I did not want to startle him; I had no solicitude for him; I was not furious with him and sorry for him: his experience was of no importance, his redemption would have had no point for me. He had grown old in minor iniquities, and could no longer inspire aversion or pity. He repeated *Patna?* interrogatively, seemed to make a short effort of memory, and said: 'Quite right. I am an old stager out here. I saw her go down.' I made ready to vent my indignation at such a stupid lie, when he added smoothly, 'She was full of reptiles.'

"This made me pause. What did he mean? The unsteady phantom of terror behind his glassy eyes seemed to stand still and look into mine wistfully. 'They turned me out of my bunk in the middle watch to look at her sinking,' he pursued in a reflective tone. His voice sounded alarmingly strong all at once. I was sorry for my folly. There was no snowy-winged coiff of a nursing sister to be seen flitting in the perspective of the ward; but away in the middle of a long row of empty iron bedsteads an accident case from some ship in the Roads sat up brown and gaunt with a white bandage set rakishly on the forehead. Suddenly my interesting invalid shot out an arm thin like a tentacle and clawed my shoulder. 'Only my eyes were good enough to see. I am famous for my eyesight. That's why they called me, I expect. None of them was quick enough to see her go, but they saw that she was gone right enough, and sang out together—like this.' . . . A wolfish howl searched the very recesses of my soul. 'Oh! make 'im dry up,' whined the accident case irritably. 'You don't believe me, I suppose,' went on the other, with an air of ineffable conceit. 'I tell you there are no such eyes as mine this side of the Persian Gulf. Look under the bed.'

"Of course I stooped instantly. I defy anybody not to have done so. 'What can you see?' he asked. 'Nothing,' I said, feeling awfully ashamed of myself. He scrutinised my face with wild and withering contempt. 'Just so,' he said, 'but if I were to look I could see—there's no eyes like mine, I tell you.' Again he clawed, pulling at me downwards in his eagerness to relieve himself by a confidential communication. 'Millions of pink toads. There's no eyes like mine. Millions of pink toads. It's worse than seeing a ship sink. I could look at sinking ships and smoke my pipe all day long. Why don't they give me back my pipe? I would get a smoke while I watched these toads. The ship was full of them. They've got to be watched, you know.' He winked facetiously. The perspiration dripped on him off my head, my drill coat clung to my wet back: the afternoon breeze swept impetuously over the row of bedsteads, the stiff folds of curtains stirred perpendicularly, rattling on brass rods, the covers of empty beds blew about noiselessly near the bare floor all along the line, and I shivered to the very marrow. The soft wind of the tropics played in that naked ward as bleak as a winter's gale in an old barn at home. 'Don't you let him start his hollering, mister,' hailed from afar the accident case in a distressed angry shout that came ringing between the walls like a quavering call down a tunnel. The clawing hand hauled at my shoulders; he leered at me knowingly. 'The ship was full of them, you know, and we have to clear out on the strict Q.T.,' he whispered with extreme rapidity. 'All pink. All pink—as big as mastiffs, with an eye on the top of the head and claws all round their ugly mouths. Ough! Ough!' Quick jerks as of galvanic shocks disclosed under the flat coverlet the outlines of meagre and agitated legs; he let go my shoulder and reached after something in the air; his body trembled tensely like a released harp-string; and while I looked down, the spectral horror in him broke through his glassy gaze. Instantly his face of an old soldier, with its noble and calm outlines, became decomposed before my eyes by the corruption of stealthy cunning, of an abominable caution and of desperate fear. He restrained a cry—'Ssh; what are they doing now down there?' he asked, pointing to the floor with fantastic precautions of voice and gesture, whose meaning, borne upon my mind in a lurid flash, made me very sick of my cleverness. 'They are all asleep,' I answered, watching him narrowly. That was it. That's what he wanted to hear; these were the exact words that could calm him. He drew a long breath. 'Ssh! Quiet, steady. I am an old stager out here. I know them brutes. Bash in the head of the first that stirs. There's too many of them, and she won't swim more than ten minutes.' He panted again. 'Hurry up,' he yelled suddenly, and went on in a steady scream: 'They are all awake—millions of them. They are trampling on me! Wait! Oh, wait! I'll smash them in heaps like flies. Wait for me! Help! H-e-elp!' An interminable and sustained howl completed my discomfiture. I saw in the distance the accident case raise deplorably both his hands to his bandaged head; a dresser, aproned to the chin, showed himself in the vista of the ward, as if seen in the small end of a telescope. I confessed myself fairly routed, and without more ado, stepping out through one of the long windows, escaped into the outside gallery. The howl pursued me like a vengeance. I turned into a deserted landing, and suddenly all became very still and quiet around me, and I descended the bare and shiny staircase in a silence that enabled me to compose my distracted thoughts. Down below I met one of the resident surgeons who was crossing the courtyard and stopped me. 'Been to see your man, Captain? I think we may let him go to-morrow. These fools have no notion of taking care of themselves, though. I say, we've got the chief engineer of that pilgrim ship here. A curious case. D.T.'s of the worst kind. He has been drinking hard in that Greek's or Italian's grog-shop for three days. What can you expect? Four bottles of that kind of brandy a-day, I am told. Wonderful, if true. Sheeted with boiler-iron inside, I should think. The head, ah! the head, of course, but the curious part is there's some sort of method in his raving. I am trying to find out. Most unusual—that thread of logic in such a delirium. Traditionally, he ought to see snakes, but he doesn't. Good old tradition's at a discount nowadays. Eh! His—er—visions are batrachian. Ha! ha! No, seriously, I never remember being so interested in a case of jim-jams before. He ought to be dead, don't you know, after such a festive experiment. Oh! he is a tough object. Four-and-twenty years of the tropics too. You ought really to take a peep at him. Noble-looking old boozer. Most extraordinary man I ever met—medically, of course. Won't you?'

"I had been all along exhibiting the usual polite signs of interest, but now assuming an air of regret I murmured of want of time, and shook hands in a hurry. 'I say,' he cried after me, 'he can't attend that inquiry. Is his evidence material, you think?'

"'Not in the least,' I called back from the gateway."

CHAPTER VI.

"The authorities were evidently of the same opinion. The inquiry was not adjourned. It was held on the appointed day to satisfy the law, and it was well attended because of its human interest no doubt. There was no incertitude as to facts—as to the one material fact, I mean. How the *Patna* came by her hurt it was impossible to find out; the court did not expect to find out; and in the whole audience there was not a man who cared. Yet, as I've told you, all the sailors in the port attended, and the waterside business was fully represented. Whether they knew it or not, the interest that drew them there was purely psychological,—the expectation of some essential disclosure as to the strength, the power, the horror, of human emotions. Naturally nothing of the kind could be disclosed. The examination of the only man able and willing to face it was beating futilely round the well-known fact, and the play of questions upon it was as instructive as the tapping with a hammer on an iron box, were the object to find out what's inside. However, an official inquiry could not be any other thing. Its object was not the fundamental why, but the superficial how, of this affair.

"The young chap could have told them, and, though that very thing was the thing that interested the audience, the questions put to him necessarily led him away from what to me, for instance, would have been the only truth worth knowing. You can't expect the constituted authorities to inquire into the state of a man's soul—or is it only of his liver? Their business was to come down upon the consequences, and frankly, a casual police magistrate and two nautical assessors are not much good for anything else. I don't mean to imply these fellows were stupid. The magistrate was very patient. One of the assessors was a sailing-ship skipper with a reddish beard, and of a pious disposition. Brierly was the other. Big Brierly. Some of you must have heard of Big Brierly—the captain of the crack ship of the Blue Star line. That's the man.

"He seemed consumedly bored by the honour thrust upon him. He had never in his life made a mistake, never had an accident, never a mishap, never a check in his steady rise, and he seemed to be one of these lucky fellows who know nothing of indecision, much less of self-mistrust. At thirty-two he had one of the best commands going in the Eastern trade—and, what's more, he thought a lot of what he had. There was nothing like it in the world, and I suppose if you had asked him point-blank he would have confessed that in his opinion there was not such another commander. The choice had fallen upon the right man. The rest of mankind that did not command the sixteen-knot steel steamer *Ossa* were rather poor creatures. He had saved lives at sea, had rescued ships in distress, had a gold chronometer presented to him by the underwriters, and a pair of binoculars with a suitable inscription from some foreign Government, in commemoration of these services. He was acutely aware of his merits and of his rewards. I liked him well enough, though some I know—meek, friendly men at that—couldn't stand him at any price. I haven't the slightest doubt he considered himself vastly my superior—indeed, had you been Emperor of East and West, you could not have ignored your inferiority in his presence—but I couldn't get up any real sentiment of offence. He did not despise me for anything I could help, for anything I was—don't you know? I was a negligeable quantity simply because I was not *the* fortunate man of the earth, not Montague Brierly in command of the *Ossa*, not the owner of an inscribed gold chronometer and of silver-mounted binoculars testifying to the excellence of my seamanship and to my indomitable pluck; not possessed of an acute sense of my merits and of my rewards, besides the love and worship of a black retriever, the most wonderful of its kind—for never was such a man loved thus by such a dog. No doubt, to have all this forced upon you was exasperating enough; but when I reflected that I was associated in these fatal disadvantages with twelve hundred millions of other more or less human beings, I found I could bear my share of his good-natured and contemptuous pity for the sake of something indefinite and attractive in the man. I have never defined to myself this attraction, but there were moments when I envied him. The sting of life could do no more to his complacent soul than the scratch of a pin to the smooth face of a rock. This was enviable. As I looked at him, flanking on one side the unassuming pale-faced magistrate who presided at the inquiry, his self-satisfaction presented to me and to the world a surface as hard as granite. He committed suicide very soon after.

"No wonder Jim's case bored him, and while I thought with something akin to fear of the immensity of his contempt for the young man under examination, he was probably holding silent inquiry into his own case. The verdict must have been of unmitigated guilt, and he took the secret of the evidence with him in that leap into the sea. If I understand anything of men, the matter was no doubt of the gravest import, one of those trifles that awaken ideas—start into life some thought with which a man unused to such a companionship finds it impossible to live. I am in a position to know that it wasn't money, and it wasn't drink, and it wasn't woman. He jumped overboard at sea barely a week after the end of the inquiry, and less than three days after leaving port on his outward passage; as though on that exact spot in the midst of waters he had suddenly perceived the gates of the other world flung open wide for his reception.

"Yet it was not a sudden impulse. His grey-headed mate, a first-rate sailor and a nice old chap with strangers, but in his relations with his commander the surliest chief-officer I've ever seen, would tell the story with tears in his eyes. It appears that when he came on deck in the morning Brierly had been writing in the chart-room. 'It was ten minutes to four,' he said, 'and the middle watch was not relieved yet of course. He heard my voice on the bridge speaking to the second mate, and called me in. I was loth to go, and that's the truth, Captain Marlow,—I couldn't stand poor Captain Brierly, I tell you with shame; we never know what a man is made of. He had been promoted over too many heads, not counting my own, and he had a damnable trick of making you feel small, nothing but by the way he said "Good morning." I never addressed him, sir, but on matters of duty, and then it was as much as I could do to keep a civil tongue in my head.' (He flattered himself there. I often wondered how Brierly could put up with his manners for more than half a voyage.) 'I've a wife and children,' he went on, 'and I had been ten years in the Company, always expecting the next command—more fool I. Says he, just like this: "Come in here, Mr Jones," in that swagger voice of his—"Come in here, Mr Jones." In I went. "We'll lay down her position," says he, stooping over the chart, a pair of dividers in hand. By the standing orders, the officer going off duty would have done that at the end of his watch. However, I said nothing, and looked on while he marked off the ship's position with a tiny cross and wrote the date and the time. I can see him this moment writing his neat figures: seventeen, eight, four A.M. The year would be written in red ink at the top of the chart. He never used his charts more than a year, Captain Brierly didn't. I've the chart now. When he had done he stands looking down at the mark he had made and smiling to himself, then looks up at me. "Thirty-two miles more as she goes," says he, "and then we shall be clear, and you may alter the course twenty degrees to the southward."

"'We were passing to the north of the Hector Bank that voyage. I said, "All right sir," wondering what he was fussing about, since I had to call him before altering the course anyhow. Just then eight bells were struck: we came out on the bridge, and the second mate before going off mentions in the usual way—"Seventy-one on the log." Captain Brierly looks at the compass and then all round. It was dark and clear, and all the stars were out as plain as on a frosty night in high latitudes. Suddenly he says with a sort of a little sigh: "I am going aft, and shall set the log at zero for you myself, so that there can be no mistake. Thirty-two miles more on this course and then you are safe. Let's see—the correction on the log is six per cent additive; say, then, thirty by the dial to run, and you may come twenty degrees to starboard at once. No use losing any distance—is there?" I had never heard him talk so much at a stretch, and to no purpose as it seemed to me. I said nothing. He went down the ladder, and the dog, that was always at his heels whenever he moved, night or day, followed, sliding nose first, after him. I heard his boot-heels tap, tap on the after-deck, then he stopped and spoke to the dog— "Go back, Rover. On the bridge, boy! Go on—get." Then he calls out to me from the dark, "Shut that dog up in the chart-room, Mr Jones—will you?"

"'This was the last time I heard his voice, Captain Marlow. These are the last words he spoke in the hearing of any living human being, sir.' At this point the old chap's voice got quite unsteady. 'He was afraid the poor brute would jump after him, don't you see?' he pursued with a quaver. 'Yes, Captain Marlow. He set the log for me; he—would you believe it?—he put a drop of oil in it too. There was the oil-feeder where he left it near by. The boatswain's mate got the hose along aft to wash down at half-past five; by-and-by he knocks off and runs up on the bridge,— "Will you please come aft, Mr Jones," he says. "There's a funny thing. I don't like to touch it." It was Captain Brierly's gold chronometer watch carefully hung under the rail by its chain.

"'As soon as my eyes fell on it something struck me, and I knew, sir. My legs got soft under me. It was as if I had seen him go over; and I could tell how far behind he was left too. The taffrail-log marked eighteen miles and three-quarters, and four iron belaying-pins were missing round the mainmast. Put them in his pockets to help him down, I suppose; but, Lord! what's four iron pins to a pow-

erful man like Captain Brierly. Maybe his confidence in himself was just shook a
bit at the last. That's the only sign of fluster he gave in his whole life, I should
think; but I am ready to answer for him, that once over he did not try to swim a
stroke, the same as he would have had pluck enough to keep up all day long on
the bare chance had he fallen overboard accidentally. Yes, sir. He was second to
none—if he said so himself, as I heard him once. He had written two letters in the
middle watch, one to the Company and the other to me. He gave me a lot of instructions as to the passage—I had been in the trade before he was out of his
time—and no end of hints as to my conduct with our people in Shanghai, so that
I should keep the command of the *Ossa*. He wrote like a father would to a favourite
son, Captain Marlow, and I was five-and-twenty years his senior and had tasted
salt water before he was fairly breeched. In his letter to the owners—it was left
open for me to see—he said that he had always done his duty by them—up to that
moment—and even now he was not betraying their confidence, since he was leaving the ship to as competent a seaman as could be found—meaning me, sir, meaning me! He told them that if the last act of his life didn't take away all his credit
with them, they would give weight to my faithful service and to his warm recommendation, when about to fill the vacancy made by his death. And much more
like this, sir. I couldn't believe my eyes. It made me feel queer all over,' went on
the old chap, in great perturbation, and squashing something in the corner of his
eye with the end of a thumb as broad as a spatula. 'You would think, sir, he had
jumped overboard only to give an unlucky man a last show to get on. What with
the shock of him going in this awful rash way, and thinking myself a made man by
that chance, I was nearly off my chump for a week. But no fear. The captain of the
Pelion was shifted into the *Ossa*—came aboard in Shanghai—a little popinjay, sir,
in a grey check suit, with his hair parted in the middle. "Aw—I am—aw—your
new captain, Mister—Mister—aw—Jones." He was drowned in scent—fairly
stunk with it, Captain Marlow. I daresay it was the look I gave him that made him
stammer. He mumbled something about my natural disappointment—I had better
know at once that his chief officer got the promotion to the *Pelion*—he had nothing
to do with it, of course—supposed the office knew best—sorry. . . . Says I, "Don't
you mind old Jones, sir; dam' his soul, he's used to it." I could see directly I had
shocked his delicate ear, and while we sat at our first tiffin together he began to
find fault in a nasty manner with this and that in the ship. I never heard such a
voice out of a Punch and Judy show. I set my teeth hard, and glued my eyes to my
plate, and held my peace as long as I could; but at last I had to say something: up
he jumps tiptoeing, ruffling all his pretty plumes, like a little fighting cock. "You'll
find you have a different person to deal with than the late Captain Brierly." "I've
found it," says I, very glum, but pretending to be mighty busy with my steak. "You
are an old ruffian, Mr—aw—Jones; and what's more, you are known for an old
ruffian in the employ," he squeaks at me. The damned bottle-washers stood about
listening with their mouths stretched from ear to ear. "I may be a hard case," answers I, "but I ain't so far gone as to put up with the sight of you sitting in Captain
Brierly's chair." With that I lay down my knife and fork. "You would like to sit in
it yourself—that's where the shoe pinches," he sneers. I left the saloon, got my
rags together, and was on the quay with all my dunnage about my feet before the
stevedores had turned to again. Yes. Adrift—on shore—after ten years' service—
and with a poor woman and four children six thousand miles off depending on my
half-pay for every mouthful they ate. Yes, sir! I chucked it rather than hear Captain

Brierly abused. He left me his night-glasses—here they are; and he wished me to take care of the dog—here he is. Hallo, Rover, poor boy. Where's the captain, Rover?' The dog looked up at us with mournful yellow eyes, gave one desolate bark, and crept under the table.

"All this was taking place, more than two years afterwards, on board that nautical ruin the *Fire-Queen* this Jones had got charge of—quite by a funny accident, too—from Matherson—mad Matherson they generally called him—the same who used to hang out in Haï-phong, you know, before the occupation days. The old chap snuffled on—

"'Ay, sir, Captain Brierly will be remembered here, if there's no other place on earth. I wrote fully to his father and did not get a word in reply—neither Thank you, nor Go to the devil!—nothing! Perhaps they did not want to know.'

"The sight of that watery-eyed old Jones mopping his bald head with a red cotton handkerchief, the sorrowing yelp of the dog, the squalor of that fly-blown cuddy which was the only shrine of his memory, threw a veil of inexpressibly mean pathos over Brierly's remembered figure, the posthumous revenge of fate for that belief in his own splendour which had almost cheated his life of its legitimate terrors. Almost! Perhaps wholly. Who can tell what flattering view he had induced himself to take of his own suicide.

"'Why did he commit the rash act, Captain Marlow—can you think?' asked Jones, pressing his palms together. 'Why? It beats me! Why?' He slapped his low and wrinkled forehead. 'If he had been poor and old and in debt—and never a show—or else mad. But he wasn't of the kind that goes mad, not he. You trust me. What a mate don't know about his skipper isn't worth knowing. Young, healthy, well off, no cares. . . . I sit here sometimes thinking, thinking, till my head fairly begins to buzz. There was some reason.'

"'You may depend on it, Captain Jones,' said I, 'it wasn't anything that would have disturbed much either of us two,' I said; and then, as if a light had been flashed into the muddle of his brain, poor old Jones found a last word of amazing profundity. He blew his nose, nodding at me dolefully: 'Ay, ay! neither you nor I, sir, had ever thought so much of ourselves.'

"Of course the recollection of my last conversation with Brierly is tinged with the knowledge of his end that followed so close upon it. I spoke with him for the last time during the progress of the inquiry. It was after the first adjournment, and he came up with me in the street. He was in a state or irritation, which I noticed with surprise, his usual behaviour when he condescended to converse being perfectly cool, with a trace of amused tolerance, as if the existence of his interlocutor had been a rather good joke. 'They caught me for that inquiry, you see,' he began, and for a while enlarged complainingly upon the inconveniences of daily attendance in court. 'And goodness knows how long it will last. Three days, I suppose.' I heard him out in silence; in my then opinion it was a way as good as another of putting on side. 'What's the use of it? It is the stupidest set out you can imagine,' he pursued hotly. I remarked that there was no option. He interrupted me with a sort of pent-up violence. 'I feel like a fool all the time.' I looked up at him. This was going very far—for Brierly—when talking of Brierly. He stopped short, and seizing the lappel of my coat, gave it a slight tug. 'Why are we tormenting that young chap?' he asked. This question chimed in so well to the tolling of a certain thought of mine that, with the image of the absconding renegade in my eye, I answered at once, 'Hanged if I know, unless it be that he lets you.' I was astonished to see him fall into line, so to speak, with that utterance, which ought to have been tolerably cryptic. He said angrily, 'Why, yes. Can't he see that wretched skipper of his has cleared out? What does he expect to happen? Nothing can save him. He's done for.' We walked on in silence a few steps. 'Why eat all that dirt?' he exclaimed, with an oriental energy of expression—about the only sort of energy you can find a trace of east of the fiftieth meridian. I wondered greatly at the direction of his thoughts, but now I strongly suspect it was strictly in character: at bottom poor Brierly must have been thinking of himself. I pointed out to him that the skipper of the *Patna* was known to have feathered his nest pretty well, and could procure almost anywhere the means of getting away. With Jim it was otherwise: the Government was keeping him in the Sailors' Home for the time being, and probably he hadn't a penny in his pocket to bless himself with. It costs some money to run away. 'Does it? Not always,' he said, with a bitter laugh, and to some futher remark of mine—'Well, then, let him creep twenty feet underground and stay there! By heavens! *I* would.' I don't know why his tone provoked me, and I said, 'There is a kind of courage in facing it out as he does, knowing very well that if he went away nobody would trouble to run after him.' 'Courage be hanged!' growled Brierly. 'That sort of courage is of no use to keep a man straight, and I don't care a snap for such courage. If you were to say it was a kind of cowardice now—of softness. I tell you what, I will put up two hundred rupees if you put up another hundred and undertake to make the beggar clear out early to-morrow morning. The fellow's a gentleman if he ain't fit to be touched—he will understand. He must! This infernal publicity is too shocking: there he sits while all these confounded natives, serangs, lascars, quartermasters, are giving evidence that's enough to burn a man to ashes with shame. This is abominable. Why, Marlow, don't you think, don't you feel, that this is abominable; don't you now—come—as a seaman? If he went away all this would stop at once.' Brierly said these words with a most unusual animation, and made as if to reach after his pocketbook. I restrained him, and declared coldly that the cowardice of these four men did not seem to me a matter of such great importance. 'And you call yourself a seaman, I suppose,' he pronounced angrily. I said that's what I called myself, and I hoped I was too. He heard me out, and made a gesture with his big arm that seemed to deprive me of my individuality, to push me away into the crowd. 'The worst of it,' he said, 'is that all you fellows have no sense of dignity; you don't think enough of what you are supposed to be.'

"We had been walking slowly meantime, and now stopped opposite the harbour office, in the sight of the very spot from which the immense captain of the *Patna* had vanished as utterly as a tiny feather blown away in a hurricane. I smiled. Brierly went on: 'This is a disgrace. We've got all kinds amongst us—some anointed scoundrels in the lot; but, hang it, we must preserve professional decency or we become no better than so many tinkers going about loose. We are trusted. Do you understand?—trusted! Frankly, I don't care a snap for all the pilgrims that ever came out of Asia, but a decent man would not have behaved like this to a full cargo of old rags in bales. We aren't an organised body of men, and the only thing that holds us together is just the name for that kind of decency. Such an affair destroys one's confidence. A man may go pretty near through his whole sea-life without any call to show a stiff upper lip. But when the call comes. . . . Aha! . . . If I . . .'

"He broke off, and in a changed tone, 'I'll give you two hundred rupees now,

Marlow, and you just talk to that chap. Confound him! I wish he had never come out here. Fact is, I rather think some of my people know his. The old man's a parson, and I remember now I met him once when staying with my cousin in Essex last year. If I am not mistaken, the old chap seemed rather to fancy his sailor son. Horrible. I can't do it myself—but you. . . .'

"Thus, apropos of Jim, I had a glimpse of the real Brierly a few days before he committed his reality and his sham together to the keeping of the sea. Of course I declined to meddle. The tone of this last 'but you' (poor Brierly couldn't help it), that seemed to imply I was no more noticeable than an insect, caused me to look at the proposal with indignation, and on account of that provocation, or for some other reason, I became positive in my mind that the inquiry was a severe punishment to that Jim, and that his facing it—practically of his own freewill—was a redeeming feature in his abominable case. I hadn't been so sure of it before. Brierly went off in a huff. At the time his state of mind was more of a mystery to me than it is now.

"Next day, coming into court late, I sat by myself. Of course I could not forget the conversation I had with Brierly, and now I had them both under my eyes. The demeanour of one suggested gloomy impudence and of the other a contemptuous boredom; yet one attitude might not have been truer than the other, and I was aware that one was not true. Brierly was not bored—he was exasperated; and if so, then Jim might not have been impudent. According to my theory he was not. I imagined he was hopeless. Then it was that our glances met. They met, and the look he gave me was discouraging of any attention I might have had to speak to him. Upon either hypothesis—insolence or despair—I felt I could be of no use to him. This was the second day of the proceedings. Very soon after that exchange of glances the inquiry was adjourned again to the next day. The white men began to troop out at once. Jim had been told to stand down some time before, and was able to leave amongst the first. I saw his broad shoulders and his head outlined in the light of the door, and while I made my way slowly out talking with some one— some stranger who had addressed me casually—I could see him from within the court-room resting both elbows on the balustrade of the verandah and turning his back on the small stream of people trickling down the few steps. There was a murmur of voices and a shuffle of boots.

The next case was that of assault and battery committed upon a money-lender, I believe; and the defendant—a venerable villager with a straight white beard—sat on a mat just outside the door with his sons, daughters, sons-in-law, their wives, and, I should think, half the population of his village besides, squatting or standing around him. A slim dark woman, with part of her back and one black shoulder bared, and with a thin gold ring in her nose, suddenly began to talk in a high-pitched, shrewish tone. The man with me instinctively looked up at her. We were then just through the door, passing behind Jim's burly back.

"Whether those villagers had brought the yellow dog with them, I don't know. Anyhow, a dog was there, weaving himself in and out amongst people's legs in the mute stealthy way native dogs have, and my companion stumbled over him. The dog leaped away without a sound; the man, raising his voice a little, said with a low laugh, 'Look at that wretched cur,' and directly afterwards we became separated by a lot of people pushing in. I stood back for a moment against the wall while the stranger managed to get down the steps and disappeared. I saw Jim spin around. He made a step forward and barred my way. We were alone; he glared at me with an air of stubborn resolution. I became aware I was being held up, so to speak, as if in a wood. The verandah was empty by then, the noise and movement in the court had ceased: a great silence fell upon the building, in which, somewhere far within, an oriental voice began to whine abjectly. The dog, in the very act of trying to sneak in at the door, sat down hurriedly to hunt for fleas.

"'Did you speak to me?' asked Jim very low, and bending forward, not so much towards me but at me, if you know what I mean. I said 'No' at once. Something in the sound of that quiet tone of his warned me to be on my defence. I watched him. It was very much like a meeting in a wood, only more uncertain in its issue, since he could possibly want neither my money nor my life—nothing that I could simply give up or defend with a clear conscience. 'You say you didn't,' he said, very sombre. 'But I heard.' 'Some mistake,' I protested, utterly at a loss, and never taking my eyes off him. To watch his face was like watching a darkening sky before a clap of thunder, shade upon shade imperceptibly coming on, the gloom growing mysteriously intense in the calm of maturing violence.

"'As far as I know, I haven't opened my lips in your hearing,' I affirmed with perfect truth. I was getting a little angry, too, at the absurdity of this encounter. It strikes me now I have never in my life been so near a beating—I mean it literally; a beating with fists. I suppose I had some hazy prescience of that eventuality being in the air. Not that he was actively threatening me. On the contrary, he was strangely passive—don't you know? but he was lowering, and, though not exceptionally big, he looked generally fit to demolish a wall. The most reassuring symptom I noticed was a kind of slow and ponderous hesitation, which I took as a tribute to the evident sincerity of my manner and of my tone. We faced each other. In the court the assault case was proceeding. I caught the words: 'Well—buffalo—stick—in the greatness of my fear. . . .'

"'What did you mean be staring at me all the morning?' said Jim at last. He looked up and looked down again. 'Did you expect us all to sit with downcast eyes out of regard for your susceptibilities?' I retorted sharply. I was not going to submit meekly to any of his nonsense. He raised his eyes again, and this time continued to look me straight in the face. 'No. That's all right,' he pronounced with an air of deliberating with himself upon the truth of this statement—'that's all right. I am going through with that. Only'—and there he spoke a little faster—'I won't let any man call me names outside this court. There was a fellow with you. You spoke to him—oh yes—I know; 'tis all very fine. You spoke to him but you meant me to hear. . . .'

"I assured him he was under some extraordinary delusion. I had no conception how it came about. 'You thought I would be afraid to resent this,' he said, with just a faint tinge of bitterness. I was interested enough to discern the slightest shades of expression, but I was not in the least enlightened; yet I don't know what in these words, or perhaps just the intonation of that phrase, induced me suddenly to make all possible allowances for him. I ceased to be annoyed at my unexpected predicament. It was some mistake on his part; he was blundering, and I had an intuition that the blunder was of an odious, of an unfortunate nature. I was anxious to end this scene on grounds of decency, just as one is anxious to cut short some unprovoked and abominable confidence. The funniest part was, that in the midst of all these considerations of the higher order I was conscious of a certain trepidation as to the possibility—nay, likelihood—of this encounter ending in some disreputable brawl which could not possibly be explained, and would make me ridiculous. I did not hanker after a three days' celebrity as the man who got a black eye or something of the sort from the mate of the *Patna*. He, in all probability, did not care what he did, or at anyrate would be fully justified in his own eyes. It took no magician to see he was amazingly angry about something, for all his quiet and even torpid demeanour. I don't deny I was extremely desirous to pacify him at all costs, had I only known what to do. But I didn't know, as you may well imagine. It was a blackness without a single gleam. We confronted each other in silence. He hung fire for about fifteen seconds, then made a step nearer, and I made ready to ward off a blow, though I don't think I moved a muscle. 'If you were as big as two men and as strong as six,' he said very softly, 'I would tell you what I think of you. You . . .' 'Stop!' I exclaimed. This checked him for a second. 'Before you tell me what you think of me,' I went on quickly, 'will you kindly tell me what it is I've said or done?' During the pause that ensued he surveyed me with indignation, while I made supernatural efforts of memory, in which I was hindered by the oriental voice within the court-room expostulating with impassioned volubility against a charge of falsehood. Then we spoke almost together. 'I will soon show you I am not,' he said, in a tone suggestive of a crisis. 'I declare I don't know,' I protested earnestly at the same time. He tried to crush me by the scorn of his glance. 'Now that you see I am not afraid you try to crawl out of it,' he said. 'Who's a cur now—hey?' Then, at last, I understood.

"He had been scanning my features as though looking for a place where he would plant his fist. 'I will allow no man,' . . . he mumbled threateningly. It was, indeed, a hideous mistake; he had given himself away utterly. I can't give you an idea how shocked I was. I suppose he saw some reflection of my feelings in my face, because his expression changed just a little. 'Good God!' I stammered, 'you don't think I . . .' 'But I am sure I've heard,' he persisted, raising his voice for the first time since the beginning of this deplorable scene. Then with a shade of disdain he added, 'It wasn't you, then? Very well; I'll find the other.' 'Don't be a fool,' I cried in exasperation; 'it wasn't that at all.' 'I've heard,' he said again with an unshaken and sombre perseverance.

"There may be those who could have laughed at his pertinacity. I didn't. Oh, I didn't! There had never been a man so mercilessly shown up by his own natural impulse. A single word had stripped him of his discretion—of that discretion which is more necessary to the decencies of our inner being than clothing is to the decorum of our body. 'Don't be a fool,' I repeated. 'But the other man said it, you don't deny that?' he pronounced distinctly, and looking in my face without flinching. 'No, I don't deny,' said I, returning his gaze. At last his eyes followed downwards the direction of my pointing finger. He appeared at first uncomprehending, then confounded, and at last amazed and scared as though a dog had been a monster and he had never seen a dog before. 'Nobody dreamt of insulting you,' I said.

"He contemplated the wretched animal, that moved no more than an effigy: it sat with ears pricked and its sharp muzzle pointed into the doorway, and suddenly snapped at a fly like a piece of mechanism.

"I looked at him. The red of his fair sunburnt complexion deepened suddenly under the down of his cheeks, invaded his forehead, spread to the roots of his curly hair. His ears became intensely crimson, and even the clear blue of his eyes was darkened many shades by the rush of blood to his head. His lips pouted a little, trembling as though he had been on the point of bursting into tears. I perceived he was incapable of pronouncing a word from the excess of his humiliation. From disappointment too—who knows? Perhaps he looked forward to that hammering he was going to give me for rehabilitation, for appeasement? Who can tell what relief he expected from this chance of a row? He was naïve enough to expect anything; but he had given himself away for nothing in this case. He had been frank with himself—let alone with me—in the wild hope of arriving in that way at some effective refutation, and the stars had been ironically unpropitious. He made an inarticulate noise in his throat like a man imperfectly stunned by a blow on the head. It was pitiful.

"I didn't catch up again with him till well outside the gate. I had even to trot a bit at the last, but when, out of breath at his elbow, I taxed him with running away, he said, 'Never!' and at once turned at bay. I explained I never meant to say he was running away from *me*. 'From no man—from not a single man on earth,' he affirmed with a stubborn mien. I forbore to point out the one obvious exception which would hold good for the bravest of us; I thought he would find out by himself very soon. He looked at me patiently while I was thinking of something to say, but I could find nothing on the spur of the moment, and he began to walk on. I kept up, and anxious not to lose him, I said hurriedly that I couldn't think of leaving him under a false impression of my—of my—I stammered. The stupidity of the phrase appalled me while I was trying to finish it, but the power of sentences has nothing to do with their sense of the logic of their construction. My idiotic mumble seemed to please him. He cut it short by saying, with courteous placidity that argued an immense power of self-control or else a wonderful elasticity of spirits—'Altogether my mistake.' I marvelled greatly at this expression: he might have been alluding to some trifling occurrence. Hadn't he understood its deplorable meaning? 'You may well forgive me,' he continued, and went on a little moodily, 'All these staring people in court seemed such fools that—that it might have been as I supposed.'

"This opened suddenly a new view of him to my wonder. I looked at him curiously and met his unabashed and impenetrable eyes. 'I can't put up with this kind of thing,' he said, very simply, 'and I don't mean to. In court it's different; I've got to stand that—and I can do it too.'

"I don't pretend I understood him. The views he let me have of himself were like those glimpses through the shifting rents in a thick fog—bits of vivid and vanishing detail, giving no connected idea of the general aspect of a country. They fed one's curiosity without satisfying it; they were no good for purposes of orientation. Upon the whole he was misleading. That's how I summed him up to myself after he left me late in the evening. I had been staying at the Malabar House for a few days, and on my pressing invitation he dined with me there."

CHAPTER VII.

"An outward-bound mail-boat had come in that afternoon, and the big dining-room of the hotel was more than half full of people with a hundred pounds round-the-world tickets in their pockets. There were married couples looking domesticated and bored with each other in the midst of their travels; there were small parties and large parties, and lone individuals dining solemnly or feasting boisterously, but all thinking, conversing, joking, or scowling as was their wont at home; and just as intelligently receptive of new impressions as their trunks upstairs. Henceforth they would be labelled as having passed through this and that place, and so would be their luggage. They would cherish this distinction of their persons, and preserve the gummed tickets on their portmanteaus as documentary evidence, as the only permanent trace of their improving enterprise. The dark-faced servants tripped without noise over the vast and polished floor; now and then a girl's laugh would be heard, as innocent and empty as her mind, or, in a sudden hush of crockery, a few words in an affected drawl from some wit embroidering for the benefit of a grinning tableful the last funny story of shipboard scandal. Two nomadic old maids, dressed up to kill, worked acrimoniously through the bill of fare, whispering to each other with faded lips, wooden-faced and bizarre, like two sumptuous scarecrows. A little wine opened Jim's heart and loosened his tongue. His appetite was good, too, I noticed. He seemed to have buried somewhere the opening episode of our acquaintance. It was like a thing of which there would be no more question in this world. And all the time I had before me these blue, boyish eyes looking straight into mine, this young face, these capable shoulders, the open bronzed forehead with a white line under the roots of clustering fair hair, this appearance appealing at sight to all my sympathies: this frank aspect, the artless smile, the youthful seriousness. He was of the right sort; he was one of us. He talked soberly, with a sort of composed unreserve, and with a quiet bearing that might have been the outcome of manly self-control, of impudence, of callousness, of a colossal unconsciousness, of a gigantic deception. Who can tell! From our tone we might have been discussing a third person, a football match, last year's weather. My mind floated in a sea of conjectures till the turn of the conversation enabled me, without being offensive, to remark that, upon the whole, this inquiry must have been pretty trying to him. He darted his arm across the tablecloth, and clutching my hand by the side of my plate, glared fixedly. I *was* startled. 'It must be awfully hard,' I stammered, confused by this display of speechless feeling. 'It is—hell,' he burst out in a muffled voice.

"This movement and these words caused two well-grounded male globe-trotters at a neighbouring table to look up in alarm from their iced pudding. I rose, and we passed into the front gallery for coffee and cigars.

"On little octagon tables candles burned in glass globes; clumps of stiff-leaved plants separated sets of cosy wicker chairs; and between the pairs of columns, whose reddish shafts caught in a long row the sheen from the tall windows, the night, glittering and sombre, seemed to hang like a splendid drapery. The riding lights of ships winked afar like setting stars, and the hills across the roadstead resembled rounded black masses of arrested thunder-clouds.

"'I couldn't clear out,' Jim began. 'The skipper did—that's all very well for him. I couldn't, and I wouldn't. They all got out of it in one way or another, but it wouldn't do for me.'

"I listened with concentrated attention, not daring to stir in my chair; I wanted to know—and to this day I don't know, I can only guess. He would be confident and depressed all in the same breath, as if some conviction of innate blamelessness had checked the truth writhing within him at every turn. He began by saying, in the tone in which a man would admit his inability to jump a twenty-foot wall, that he could never go home now; and this declaration recalled to my mind what Brierly had said, 'that the old parson in Essex seemed to fancy his sailor son not a little.'

"I can't tell you whether Jim knew he was especially 'fancied' but the tone of his references to 'my Dad' was calculated to give me a notion that the good old rural dean was about the finest man that ever had been worried by the cares of a large family since the beginning of the world. This, though never stated, was implied with an anxiety that there should be no mistake about it, which was really very true and charming, but added a poignant sense of lives far off to the other elements of the story. 'He has seen it all in the home papers by this time,' said Jim. 'I can never face the poor old chap.' I did not dare to lift my eyes at this till I heard him add, 'I could never explain. He wouldn't understand.' Then I looked up. He was smoking reflectively, and after a moment, rousing himself, began to talk again. He discovered at once a desire that I should not confound him with his partners in—in crime, let us call it. He was not one of them; he was altogether of another sort. I gave no sign of dissent. I had no intention, for the sake of barren truth, to rob him of the smallest particle of any saving grace that would come in his way. I didn't know how much of it he believed himself. I didn't know what he was playing up to—if he was playing up to anything at all—and I suspect he did not know either; for it is my belief no man ever understands quite his own artful dodges to escape from the grim shadow of self-knowledge. I made no sound all the time he was wondering what he had better do after 'that stupid inquiry was over.'

"Apparently he shared Brierly's contemptuous opinion of these proceedings ordained by law. He would not know where to turn, he confessed, clearly thinking aloud rather than talking to me. Certificate gone, career broken, no money to get away, no work that he could obtain as far as he could see. At home he could perhaps get something; but it meant going to his people for help, and that he would not do. He saw nothing for it but ship before the mast—could get perhaps a quartermaster's billet in some steamer. Would do for a quartermaster. . . . 'Do you think you would?' I asked pitilessly. He jumped up, and going to the stone balustrade looked out into the night. In a moment he was back, towering above my chair with his youthful face clouded yet by the pain of a conquered emotion. He had understood very well I did not doubt his ability to steer a ship. In a voice that quavered a bit he asked me, 'Why did I say that? I had been "no end kind" to him. I had not even laughed at him when'—here he began to mumble—'that mistake, you know—made a confounded ass of myself.' I broke in by saying rather warmly that for me such a mistake was not a matter to laugh at. He sat down and drank deliberately some coffee, emptying the small cup to the last drop. 'That does not mean I admit for a moment the cap fitted,' he declared distinctly. 'No?' I said. 'No,' he affirmed with quiet decision. 'Do you know what *you* would have done? Do you? And you don't think yourself' . . . he gulped something . . . 'you don't think yourself a—a—cur?'

"And with this—upon my honour!—he looked up at me inquisitively. It was a question it appears—a *bonâ-fide* question! However, he didn't wait for an answer. Before I could recover he went on, with his eyes straight before him, as if reading off something written on the body of the night. 'It is all in being ready. I wasn't; not—not then. I don't want to excuse myself; but I would like to explain—I would like somebody to understand—somebody—one person at least! You! Why not you?'

"It was solemn, and a little ridiculous too, as they always are, those struggles of an individual trying to save from the fire his idea of what his moral identity should be, this precious notion of a convention, only one of the rules of the game, nothing more, but all the same so terribly effective by its assumption of unlimited power over natural instincts, by the awful penalties of its failure. He began his story quietly enough. On board that Dale Line steamer that had picked up these four floating in a boat upon the discreet sunset glow of the sea, they had been after the first day looked askance upon. The fat skipper told some story, the others had been silent, and at first it had been accepted. You don't cross-examine poor castaways you had the good luck to save, if not from cruel death, then at least from cruel suffering. Afterwards, with time to think it over, it might have struck the officers of the *Avondale* that there was 'something fishy' in the affair; but of course they would keep their doubts to themselves. They had picked up the captain, the mate, and two engineers of the steamer *Patna* sunk at sea, and that, very properly was enough for them. I did not ask Jim about the nature of his feelings during the ten days he spent on board. From the way he narrated that part I was at liberty to infer he was partly stunned by the discovery he had made—the discovery about himself—and no doubt was at work trying to explain it away to the only man who was capable of appreciating all its tremendous magnitude. You must understand he did not try to minimise its importance. Of that I am sure; and therein lies his distinction. As to what sensations he experienced when he got ashore and heard the unforeseen conclusion of the tale in which he had taken such a pitiful part, he told me nothing of them, and it is difficult to imagine. "I wonder whether he felt the ground cut from under his feet? I wonder? But no doubt he managed to get a fresh foothold very soon. He was ashore a whole fortnight waiting in the Sailors' Home, and as there were six or seven men staying there at the time, I had heard of him a little. Their languid opinion seemed to be that, in addition to his other shortcomings, he was a sulky brute. He had passed these days on the verandah, buried in a long chair, and coming out of his place of sepulture only at meal-times or late at night, when he wandered on the quays all by himself, detached from his surroundings, irresolute and silent, like a ghost without a home to haunt. 'I don't think I've spoken three words to a living soul in all that time,' he said, making me very sorry for him; and directly he added, 'One of these fellows would have been sure to blurt out something I had made up my mind not to put up with, and I didn't want a row. No! Not then. I was too—too . . . I had no heart for it.' 'So that bulkhead held out after all,' I remarked cheerfully. 'Yes,' he murmured, 'it held. And yet I swear to you I felt it bulge under my hand.' 'It's extraordinary what strains old iron will stand sometimes,' I said. Thrown back in his seat, his legs stiffy out and arms hanging down, he nodded slightly several times. You could not conceive a sadder spectacle. Suddenly he lifted his head; he sat up; he slapped his thigh. 'Ah! what a chance missed! My God! what a chance missed!' he blazed out, but the ring of the last 'missed' resembled a cry wrung out by pain.

"He was silent again with a still, far-away look of fierce yearning after that missed distinction, with his nostrils for an instant dilated, sniffing the intoxicating breath of that wasted opportunity. If you think I was either surprised or shocked you do me an injustice in more ways than one! Ah, he was an imaginative beggar! He would give himself away; he would give himself up. I could see in his glance darted into the night all his inner being carried on, projected headlong into the fanciful realm of recklessly heroic aspirations. He had no leisure to regret what he had lost, he was so wholly and naturally concerned for what he had failed to obtain. He was very far away from me who watched him across three feet of space. With every instant he was penetrating deeper into the impossible world of romantic achievements. He got to the heart of it at last! A strange look of beatitude overspread his features, his eyes sparkled in the light of the candle burning between us; he positively smiled! He had penetrated to the very heart—to the very heart. It was an ecstatic smile that your faces—or mine either—will never wear, my dear boys. I whisked him back by saying, 'If you had stuck to the ship, you mean!'

"He turned upon me, his eyes suddenly amazed and full of pain, with a bewildered, startled, suffering face, as though he had tumbled down from a star. Neither you nor I will ever look like this on any man. He shuddered profoundly, as if a cold finger-tip had touched his heart. Last of all he sighed.

"I was not in a merciful mood. He provoked one by his contradictory indiscretions. 'It is unfortunate you didn't know beforehand!' I said with every unkind intention; but the perfidious shaft fell harmless—dropped at his feet like a spent arrow, as it were, and he did not think of picking it up. Perhaps he had not even seen it. Presently, lolling at ease, he said, 'Dash it all! I tell you it bulged. I was holding up my lamp along the angle-iron in the lower desk when a flake of rust as big as the palm of my hand fell off the plate, all of itself.' He passed his hand over his forehead. 'The thing stirred and jumped off like something alive while I was looking at it.' 'That made you feel pretty bad,' I observed casually. 'Do you suppose,' he said, 'that I was thinking of myself, with a hundred and sixty people at my back, all fast asleep in that fore-'tween-deck alone—and more of them aft; more on the deck—sleeping—knowing nothing about it—three times as many as there were boats for, even if there had been time? I expected to see the iron open out as I stood there and the rush of water going over them as they lay. . . . What could I do—what?'

"I can easily picture him to myself in the peopled gloom of the cavernous place, with the light of the globe-lamp falling on a small portion of the bulkhead that had the weight of the ocean on the other side, and the breathing of unconscious sleepers in his ears. I can see him glaring at the iron, startled by the falling rust, overburdened by the knowledge of an imminent death. This, I gathered, was the second time he had been sent forward by that skipper of his, who, I rather think, wanted to keep him away from the bridge. He told me that his first impulse was to shout and straight away make all those people leap out of sleep into terror; but such an overwhelming sense of his helplessness came over him that he was not able to produce a sound. This is, I suppose, what people mean by the tongue cleaving to the roof of the mouth. 'Too dry,' was the concise expression he used in reference to this state. Without a sound, then, he scrambled out on deck through the number one hatch. A wind-sail rigged down there swung against him accidentally, and he remembered that the light touch of the canvas on his face nearly knocked him off the hatchway ladder.

"He confessed that his knees wobbled a good deal as he stood on the foredeck looking at another sleeping crowd. The engines having been stopped by that time, the steam was blowing off. Its deep rumble made the whole night vibrate like a bass string. The ship trembled to it.

"He saw here and there a head lifted off a mat, a vague form uprise in sitting posture, listen sleepily for a moment, sink down again into the billowy confusion of boxes, steam-winches, ventilators. He was aware all these people did not know enough to take intelligent notice of that strange noise. The ship of iron, the men with white faces, all the sights, all the sounds, everything on board to that ignorant and pious multitude was strange alike, and as trustworthy as it would for ever remain incomprehensible. It occurred to him that the fact was fortunate. The idea of it was simply terrible.

"You must remember he believed, as any other man would have done in his place, that the ship would go down at any moment; the bulging, rust-eaten plates that kept back the ocean, fatally must give way, all at once like an undermined dam, and let in a sudden and overwhelming flood. He stood still looking at these recumbent bodies, a doomed man aware of his fate, surveying the silent company of the dead. They *were* dead! Nothing could save them! There were boats enough for half of them perhaps, but there was no time. No time! No time! It did not seem worth while to open his lips, to stir hand or foot. Before he could shout three words, or make three steps, he would be floundering in a sea whitened awfully by the desperate struggles of human beings, clamorous with the distress of cries for help. There was no help. He imagined what would happen perfectly; he went through it all motionless by the hatchway with the lamp in his hand,—he went through it to the very last harrowing detail. I think he went through it again while he was telling me these things he could not tell the court.

"'I saw as clearly as I see you now that there was nothing I could do. It seemed to take all life out of my limbs. I thought I might just as well stand where I was and wait. I did not think I had many seconds . . .' Suddenly the steam ceased blowing off. The noise, he remarked, had been distracting, but the silence at once became intolerably oppressive.

"'I thought I would choke before I got drowned,' he said.

"He protested he did not think of saving himself. The only distinct thought formed, vanishing, and reforming in his brain, was: eight hundred people and seven boats; eight hundred people and seven boats.

"'Somebody was speaking aloud inside my head,' he said a little wildly. 'Eight hundred people and seven boats—and no time! Just think of it.' He leaned towards me across the little table, and I tried to avoid his stare. 'Do you think I was afraid of death?' he asked in a voice very fierce and low. He brought down his open hand with a bang that made the coffee-cups dance. 'I am ready to swear I was not—I was not . . . By God—no!' He hitched himself upright and crossed his arms; his chin fell on his breast.

"The soft clashes of crockery reached us faintly through the high windows. There was a burst of voices, and several men came out in high good-humour into the gallery. They were exchanging jocular reminiscences of the donkeys in Cairo. A pale anxious youth stepping softly on long legs was being chaffed by a strutting and rubicund globe-trotter about his purchases in the bazaar. 'No, really—do you think I've been done to that extent?' he inquired very earnest and deliberate. The band moved away, dropping into chairs as they went; matches flared, illuminating for a second faces without the ghost of an expression and the flat glaze of white shirt-fronts; the hum of many conversations animated with the ardour of feasting sounded to me absurd and infinitely remote.

"'Some of the crew were sleeping on the number one hatch within reach of my arm,' began Jim again.

"You must know they kept Kalashee watch in that ship, all hands sleeping through the night, and only the reliefs of quartermasters and look-out men being

called. He was tempted to grip and shake the shoulder of the nearest lascar, but
he didn't. Something held his arm down along his sides. He was not afraid—oh
no! only he just couldn't—that's all. He was not afraid of death perhaps, but I'll
tell you what, he was afraid of the emergency. His confounded imagination had
evoked for him all the horrors of panic, the trampling rush, the pitiful screams,
boats swamped—all the appalling incidents of a disaster at sea he had ever heard
of. He might have been resigned to die, but I suspect he wanted to die without
added terrors, quietly, in a sort of peaceful trance. A certain readiness to perish is
not so very rare, but it is seldom that you meet men whose souls, steeled in the
impenetrable armour of resolution, are ready to fight a losing battle to the last: the
desire of peace waxes stronger as hope declines, till at last it conquers the very desire of life. Which of us here has not observed this, or maybe experienced something of that feeling in his own person—this extreme weariness of emotions, the
vanity of effort, the yearning for rest? Those striving with unreasonable forces
know it well,—the shipwrecked castaways in boats, wanderers lost in a desert,
men battling against the unthinking might of nature, or the stupid brutality of
crowds."

CHAPTER VIII.

"How long he stood stock-still by the hatch expecting every moment to feel
the ship dip under his feet and the rush of water take him at the back and toss him
like a chip, I cannot say. Not very long—two minutes perhaps. A couple of men he
could not make out began to converse drowsily, and also, he could not tell where,
he detected a curious noise of shuffling feet. Above these faint sounds there was
that awful stillness preceding a catastrophe, that trying silence of the moment before the crash; then it came into his head that perhaps he would have time to rush
along and cut all the lanyards of the gripes, so that the boats would float off as the
ship went down.

"The *Patna* had a long bridge, and all the boats were up there, four on one side
and three on the other—the smallest of them on the port-side and nearly abreast
of the steering gear. He assured me, with evident anxiety to be believed, that he
had been most careful to keep them ready for instant service. He knew his duty.
I daresay he was a good enough mate as far as that went. 'I always believed in
being prepared for the worst,' he commented, staring anxiously in my face. I nodded my approval of the sound principle, averting my eyes before the subtle un-
soundness of the man.

"He started unsteadily to run. He had to step over legs, avoid stumbling
against the heads. Suddenly some one caught hold of his coat from below, and a
distressed voice spoke under his elbow. The light of the lamp he carried in his right
hand fell upon an upturned dark face whose eyes entreated him together with the
voice. He had picked up enough of the language to understand the word water,
repeated several times in a tone of insistence, of prayer, almost of despair. He gave
a jerk to get away, and felt an arm embrace his leg.

"'The beggar clung to me like a drowning man,' he said impressively. 'Water,

water! What water did he mean? What did he know? As calmly as I could I ordered him to let go. He was stopping me, time was pressing, other men began to stir; I wanted time—time to cut the boats adrift. He got hold of my hand now, and I felt that he would begin to shout. It flashed upon me it was enough to start a panic, and I hauled off with my free arm and slung the lamp in his face. The glass jingled, the light went out, but the blow made him let go, and I ran off—I wanted to get at the boats; I wanted to get at the boats. He leaped after me from behind. I turned on him. He would not keep quiet; he tried to shout; I had half throttled him before I made out what he wanted. He wanted some water—water to drink; they were on strict allowance, you know, and he had with him a young boy I had noticed several times. His child was sick—and thirsty. He had caught sight of me as I passed by, and was begging for a little water. That's all. We were under the bridge, in the dark. He kept on snatching at my wrists; there was no getting rid of him. I dashed into my berth, grabbed my water-bottle, and thrust it into his hands. He vanished. I didn't find out till then how much I was in want of a drink myself.' He leaned on one elbow with a hand over his eyes.

"I felt a creepy sensation all down my backbone; there was something peculiar in all this. The fingers of the hand that shaded his brow trembled slightly. He broke the short silence.

"'These things happen only once to a man and . . . Ah! well! When I got on the bridge at last the beggars were getting one of the boats off the chocks. A boat! I was running up the ladder when a heavy blow fell on my shoulder, just missing my head. It didn't stop me, and the chief engineer—they had got him out of his bunk by then—raised the boat-stretcher again. Somehow I had no mind to be surprised at anything. All this seemed natural—and awful—and awful. I dodged that miserable maniac, lifted him off the deck as though he had been a little child, and he started whispering in my arms: "Don't! don't! I thought you were one of them niggers." I flung him away, he skidded along the bridge and knocked the legs from under the little chap—the second. The skipper, busy about the boat, looked round and came at me head down, growling like a wild beast. I flinched no more than a stone. I was as solid standing there as this,' he tapped lightly with his knuckles the wall beside his chair. 'It was as though I had heard it all, seen it all, gone through it all twenty times already. I wasn't afraid of them. I drew back my fist and he stopped short, muttering—

"'"Ah! it's you. Lend a hand quick."

"'That's what he said. Quick! As if anybody could be quick enough. Aren't you going to do something,' I asked. '"Yes. Clear out," he snarled over his shoulder.

"'I don't think I understood then what he meant. The other two had picked themselves up by that time, and they rushed together to the boat. They tramped, they wheezed, they shoved, they cursed the boat, the ship, each other—cursed me. All in mutters. I didn't move, I didn't speak. I watched the slant of the ship. She was as still as if landed on the blocks in a dry dock—only she was like this.' He held up his hand, palm under, the tips of the fingers inclined downwards. 'Like this,' he repeated. 'I could see the line of the horizon before me, as clear as a bell, above her stem-head; I could see the water far off there black and sparkling, and still—still as a pond, deadly still, more still than ever sea was before—more still than I could bear to look at. Have you watched a ship floating head down, checked in sinking by a sheet of old iron too rotten to stand being shored up. Have you? Oh yes, shored up? I thought of that—I thought of every mortal thing; but can you shore up a bulkhead in five minutes—or in fifty for that matter? Where was I going to get men that would go down below? And the timber—the timber! Would you have had the courage to swing the maul for the first blow if you had seen that bulkhead? Don't say you would: you had not seen it; nobody would. Hang it—to do a thing like that you must believe there is a chance, one in a thousand, at least, some ghost of a chance; and you would not have believed. Nobody would have believed. You think me a cur for standing there, but what would you have done? What! You can't tell—nobody can tell. One must have time to turn round. What would you have me do? Where was the kindness in making crazy with fright all those people I could not save single-handed—that nothing could save? Look here! As true as I sit on this chair before you . . .'

"He drew quick breaths at every few words and shot quick glances at my face, as though in his anguish he were watchful of the effect. He was not speaking to me, he was only speaking before me, in a dispute with an invisible personality, an antagonistic and inseparable partner of his existence—another possessor of his soul. These were issues beyond the competency of a court of inquiry: it was a subtle and momentous quarrel as to the true essence of life, and did not want a judge. He wanted an ally, a helper, an accomplice. I felt the risk I ran of being circumvented, blinded, decoyed, bullied, perhaps, into taking a definite part in a dispute impossible of decision if one had to be fair to all the phantoms in possession—to the reputable that had its claims and to the disreputable that had its exigencies. I can't explain to you who haven't seen him and who hear his words only at second hand the mixed nature of my feelings. It seemed to me I was being made to comprehend the Inconceivable—and I know of nothing to compare with the discomfort of such a sensation. I was made to look at the convention that lurks in all truth and on the essential sincerity of falsehood. He appealed to all sides at once,—to the side turned perpetually to the light of day, and to that side of us which, like the other hemisphere of the moon, exists stealthily in perpetual darkness, with only a fearful ashy light falling at times on the edge. He swayed me. I own to it, I own up. The occasion was obscure, insignificant—what you will: a lost youngster, one in a million—but then he was one of us; an incident as completely devoid of importance as the flooding of an ant-heap, and yet the mystery of his attitude got hold of me as though he had been an individual in the forefront of his kind, as if the obscure truth involved were momentous enough to affect mankind's conception of itself. . . ."

Marlow paused to put new life into his expiring cheroot, seemed to forget all about the story, and abruptly began again.

"My fault of course. One has no business really to get interested. It's a weakness of mine. His was of another kind. My weakness consists in not having a discriminating eye for the incidental—for the externals,—no eye for the hod of the rag-picker or the fine linen of the next man. Next man—that's it. I have met so many men," he pursued, with momentary sadness—"met them too with a certain—certain—impact, let us say; like this fellow, for instance—and in each case all I could see was merely the human being. A confounded democratic quality of vision which may be better than total blindness, but has been of no advantage to me—I can assure you. Men expect one to take into account their fine linen. But I never could get up any enthusiasm about these things. Oh! It's a failing; it's a failing; and then comes a soft evening; a lot of men too indolent for whist—and a story. . . ."

He paused again to wait for an encouraging remark, perhaps, but nobody spoke; only the host, as if reluctantly performing a duty, murmured—

"You are so subtle, Marlow."

"Who? I?" said Marlow in a low voice. "Oh no! But *he* was; and try as I may for the success of this yarn I am missing innumerable shades—they were so fine, so difficult to render in colourless words. Because he complicated matters by being so simple, too—the simplest poor devil! . . . By Jove! he was amazing. There he sat telling me that just as I saw him before my eyes he wouldn't be afraid to face anything—and believing in it too. I tell you it was fabulously innocent and it was enormous, enormous! I watched him covertly, just as though I had suspected him of an intention to take a jolly good rise out of me. He was confident that, on the square, 'on the square, mind!' there was nothing he couldn't meet. Ever since he had been 'so high'—'quite a little chap,' he had been preparing himself for all the difficulties that can beset one on land and water. He confessed proudly to this kind of foresight. He had been elaborating dangers and defences, expecting the worst, rehearsing his best. He must have led a most exalted existence. Can you fancy it? A succession of adventures, so much glory, such a victorious progress! and the deep sense of his sagacity crowning every day of his inner life. He forgot himself; his eyes shone; and with every word my heart, searched by the light of his absurdity, was growing heavier in my breast. I had no mind to laugh, and lest I should smile I made for myself a stolid face. He gave signs of irritation.

"'It is always the unexpected that happens,' I said in a propitiatory tone. My obtuseness provoked him into a contemptuous 'Pshaw!' I suppose he meant that the unexpected couldn't touch him; nothing less than the unconceivable itself could get over his perfect state of preparation. He had been taken unawares—and he whispered to himself a malediction upon the waters and the firmament, upon the ship, upon the men. Everything had betrayed him! He had been tricked into that sort of high-minded resignation which prevented him lifting as much as his little finger, while these others who had a very clear perception of the actual necessity were tumbling against each other and sweating desperately over that boat business. Something had gone wrong there at the last moment. It appears that in their flurry they had contrived in some mysterious way to get the sliding bolt of the foremost boat-chock jammed tight, and forthwith had gone out of the remnants of their minds over the deadly nature of that accident. It must have been a pretty sight, the fierce industry of these beggars toiling on a motionless ship that floated quietly in the silence of a world asleep, fighting against time for the freeing of that boat, grovelling on all-fours, standing up in despair, tugging, pushing, snarling at each other venomously, ready to kill, ready to weep, and only kept from flying at each other's throats by the fear of death that stood silent behind them like an inflexible and cold-eyed taskmaster. Oh yes! It must have been a pretty sight. He saw it all, he could talk about it with scorn and bitterness; he had a minute knowledge of it by means of some sixth sense, I conclude, because he swore to me he had remained apart without a glance at them and at the boat—without one single glance. And I believe him. I should think he was too busy watching the threatening slant of the ship, the suspended menace discovered in the midst of the most perfect security—fascinated by the sword hanging by a hair over his imaginative head.

"Nothing in the world moved before his eyes, and he could depict to himself without hindrance the sudden swing upwards of the dark sky-line, the sudden tilt up of the vast plain of the sea, the swift still rise, the brutal fling, the grasp of the abyss, the struggle without hope, the starlight closing over his head for ever like the vault of a tomb—the revolt of his young life—the black end. He could! By Jove! who couldn't? And you must remember he was a finished artist in that peculiar way, he was a gifted poor devil with the faculty of swift and forestalling vision. The sights it showed him had turned him into cold stone from the soles of his feet to the nape of his neck; but there was a hot dance of thoughts in his head, a dance of lame, blind, mute thoughts—a whirl of awful cripples. Didn't I tell you he confessed himself before me as though I had the power to bind and to loose. He burrowed deep, deep, in the hope of my absolution, which would have been of no good to him. This was one of these cases which no solemn deception can palliate, where no man can help; where his very Maker seems to abandon a sinner to his own devices.

"He stood on the starboard side of the bridge, as far as he could get from the struggle for the boat, which went on with the agitation of madness and the stealthiness of a conspiracy. The two Malays had meantime remained holding to the wheel. Just picture to yourselves the actors in that, thank God! unique, episode of the sea, four beside themselves with fierce and secret exertions, and three looking on in complete immobility, above the awnings covering the profound ignorance of hundreds of human beings, with their weariness, with their dreams, with their hopes, arrested, held by an invisible hand on the brink of annihilation. For that they were so, makes no doubt to me: given the state of the ship, this was the deadliest possible description of accident that could happen. These beggars by the boat had every reason to go distracted with funk. Frankly, had I been there, I would not have given as much as a counterfeit farthing for the ship's chance to keep above water to the end of each successive second. And still she floated! These sleeping pilgrims were destined to accomplish their whole pilgrimage to the bitterness of some other end. It was as if the Omnipotence whose mercy they confessed had needed their humble testimony on earth for a while longer, and had looked down to make a sign, 'Thou shalt not!' to the ocean. Their escape would trouble me as a prodigiously inexplicable event, did I not know how tough old iron can be—as tough sometimes as the spirit of some men we meet now and then, worn to a shadow and breasting the weight of life. Not the least wonder of these twenty minutes, to my mind, is the behaviour of the two helmsmen. They were amongst the native batch of all sorts brought over from Aden to give evidence at the inquiry. One of them, labouring under intense bashfulness, was very young, and with his smooth, yellow, cheery countenance looked even younger than he was. I remember perfectly Brierly asking him, through the interpreter, what he thought of it at the time, and the interpreter, after a short colloquy, turning to the court with an important air—

"'He says he thought nothing.'

"The other with patient blinking eyes, a blue cotton handkerchief, faded with much washing, bound with a smart twist over a lot of grey wisps, his face shrunk into grim hollows, his brown skin made darker by a mesh of wrinkles, explained that he had a knowledge of some evil thing befalling the ship, but there had been no order; he could not remember an order; why should he leave the helm? To some further questions he jerked back his spare shoulders, and declared it never came into his mind then that the white men were about to leave the ship through fear of death. He did not believe it now. There might have been secret reasons. He wagged his old chin knowingly. Aha! secret reasons. He was a man of great experience, and he wanted *that* white Tuan to know—he turned towards Brierly, who didn't raise his head—that he had acquired a knowledge of many things by serving white men on the sea for a great number of years—and, suddenly, with shaky excitement he poured upon our spellbound attention a lot of queer-sounding names, names of dead-and-gone skippers, names of forgotten country ships, names of familiar and distorted sound, as if the hand of dumb time had been at work on them for ages. They stopped him at last. A silence fell upon the court,—a silence that remained unbroken for at least a minute, and passed gently into a deep murmur. This episode was *the* sensation of the second day's proceedings—affecting all the audience, affecting everybody except Jim, who was sitting moodily at the end of the first bench, and never looked up at this extraordinary and damning witness that seemed possessed of some mysterious theory of defence.

"So these two lascars stuck to the helm of that ship without steerage-way, where death would have found them if such had been their destiny. The whites did not give them half a glance, had probably forgotten their existence. Assuredly Jim did not remember it. He remembered he could do nothing; he could do nothing, now he was alone. There was nothing to do but to sink with the ship. No use making a disturbance about it. Was there? He waited upstanding, without a sound, stiffened in the idea of some sort of heroic discretion. The first engineer ran cautiously across the bridge to tug at his sleeve.

"'Come and help! For God's sake, come and help!'

"He ran back to the boat on the points of his toes, and returned directly to worry at his sleeve, begging and cursing at the same time.

"'I believe he would have kissed my hands,' said Jim savagely, 'and, next moment, he starts foaming and whispering in my face, "If I had the time I would like to crack your skull for you." I pushed him away. Suddenly he caught hold of me round the neck. Damn him! I hit him. I hit out without looking. "Won't you save your own life—you infernal coward," he sobs. Coward! He called me an infernal coward! Ha! ha! ha! ha! He called me—ha! ha! ha! . . .'

"He had thrown himself back and was shaking with laughter. I had never in my life heard anything so bitter as that noise. It fell like a blight on all the merriment about donkeys, pyramids, bazaars, or what not. Along the whole dim length of the gallery the voices dropped, the pale blotches of faces turned our way with one accord, and the silence became so profound that the clear tinkle of a teaspoon falling on the tesselated floor of the verandah rang out like a tiny and silvery scream.

"'You mustn't laugh like this, with all these people about,' I remonstrated. 'It isn't nice for them, you know.'

"He gave no sign of having heard at first, but after a while with a stare that, missing me altogether, seemed to probe the heart of some awful vision, he muttered carelessly—'Oh! they'll think I am drunk.'

"And after that you would have thought from his appearance he would never make a sound again. But—no fear! He could no more stop telling now than he could have stopped living by the mere exertion of his will.'"

CHAPTER IX.

"'I was saying to myself, "Sink—curse you! Sink!"' These were the words with which he began again. He wanted it over. He was severely left alone, and he formulated in his head this address to the ship in a tone of imprecation, while at the same time he enjoyed the privilege of witnessing scenes—as far as I can judge—of low comedy. They were still at that bolt. The skipper was ordering. 'Get under and try to lift;' and the others naturally shirked. You understand that to be squeezed flat under the keel of a boat wasn't a desirable position to be caught in if the ship went down suddenly. 'Why don't you—you the strongest?' whined the little engineer. 'Gott-for-dam! I am too thick,' spluttered the skipper in despair. It was funny enough to make angels weep. They stood idle for a moment, and suddenly the chief engineer rushed again at Jim.

"'Come and help, man! Are you mad to throw your only chance away? Come and help, man! Man! Look there—look!'

"And at last Jim looked astern where the other pointed with maniacal insistence. He saw a silent black squall which had eaten up already one-third of the sky. You know how these squalls come up there about that time of the year. First you see a darkening of the horizon—no more; then a cloud rises opaque like a wall. A straight edge of vapour lined with sickly whitish gleams flies up from the southwest, swallowing the stars in whole constellations; its shadow flies over the waters, and confounds sea and sky into one abyss of obscurity. And all is still. No thunder, no wind, no sound; not a flicker of lightning. Then in the tenebrous immensity a livid arch appears; a swell or two like undulations of the very darkness run past, and, suddenly, wind and rain strike together with a peculiar impetuosity as if they had burst through something solid. Such a cloud had come up while they weren't looking. They had just noticed it, and were perfectly justified in surmising that if in absolute stillness there was some chance for the ship to keep afloat a few minutes longer, the least disturbance of the sea would make an end of her instantly. Her first nod to the swell that precedes the burst of such a squall would be also her last, would become a plunge, would, so to speak, be prolonged into a long dive, down, down to the bottom. Hence, these new capers of their fright, these new antics in which they displayed their extreme aversion to die.

"'It was black, black,' pursued Jim with moody steadiness. 'It had sneaked upon us from behind. The infernal thing! I suppose there had been at the back of my head some hope yet. I don't know. But that was all over anyhow. It maddened me to see myself caught like this. I was angry, as though I had been trapped. I *was* trapped! The night was hot, too, I remember. Not a breath of air.'

"He remembered so well that, gasping in the chair, he seemed to sweat and choke before my eyes. No doubt it maddened him; it knocked him over afresh—in a manner of speaking—but it made him also remember that important purpose which had sent him rushing on that bridge only to slip clean out of his mind. He had intended to cut the life-boats clear of the ship. He whipped out his knife and went to work slashing as though he had seen nothing, had heard nothing, had known of no one on board. They thought him hopelessly wrong-headed and crazy, but dared not protest noisily against this useless loss of time. When he had done he returned to the very same spot from which he had started. The chief was there, ready with a clutch at him to whisper close to his head, scathingly, as though he wanted to bite his ear—

"'You silly fool! do you think you'll get the ghost of a show when all that lot of brutes is in the water? Why, they will batter your head for you from these boats.'

"He wrung his hands, ignored, at Jim's elbow. The skipper kept up a nervous shuffle in one place and mumbled, 'Hammer! hammer! Mein Gott! Get a hammer.'

"The little engineer whimpered like a child, but, broken arm and all, he turned out the least craven of the lot as it seems, and, actually, mustered enough pluck to run an errand to the engine-room. No trifle it must be owned in fairness to him. Jim told me he darted desperate looks like a cornered man, gave one low wail, and dashed off. He was back instantly clambering, hammer in hand, and without a pause flung himself at the bolt. The others gave up Jim at once and ran off to assist. He heard the tap, tap of the hammer, the sound of the released chock falling over. The boat was clear. Only then he turned to look—only then. But he kept his distance—he kept his distance. He wanted me to know he had kept his distance; that there was nothing in common between him and these men—who had the hammer. Nothing whatever. It is more than probable he thought himself cut off from them by a space that could not be traversed, by an obstacle that could not be overcome, by a chasm without bottom. He was as far as he could get from them—the whole breadth of the ship.

"His feet were glued to that remote spot and his eyes to their indistinct group bowed together and swaying strangely in the common torment of fear. A hand-lamp lashed to a stanchion above a little table rigged up on the bridge—the *Patna* had no chart-room amidships—threw a light on their labouring shoulders, on their arched and bobing backs. They pushed at the bow of the boat; they pushed out into the night; they pushed, and would no more look back at him. They had given him up as if indeed he had been too far, too hopelessly separated from themselves, to be worth an appealing word, a glance, or a sign. They had no leisure to look back upon his passive heroism, to feel the sting of his abstention. The boat was heavy; they pushed at the bow with no breath to spare for an encouraging word: but the turmoil of terror that had scattered their self-command like chaff before the wind, converted their desperate exertions into a bit of fooling, upon my word, fit for knockabout clowns in a farce. They pushed with their hands, with their heads, they pushed for dear life with all the weight of their bodies, they pushed with all the might of their souls—only no sooner had they succeeded in canting the stem clear of the davit than they would leave off like one man and start a wild scramble into her. As a natural consequence the boat would swing in abruptly, driving them back, helpless and jostling against each other. They would stand nonplussed for a while, exchanging in fierce whispers all the infamous names they could call to mind, and go at it again. Three times this occurred. He described it to me with morose thoughtfulness. He hadn't lost a single movement of that comic business. 'I loathed them. I hated them. I had to look at all that,' he said without emphasis, turning upon me a sombrely watchful glance. 'Was ever there any one so shamefully tried!'

"He took his head in his hands for a moment, like a man driven to distraction by some unspeakable outrage. These were things he could not explain to the court—and not even to me; but I would have been little fitted for the reception of his confidences had I not been able at times to understand the pauses between the words. In this assault upon his fortitude there was the jeering intention of a spiteful and vile vengeance; there was an element of burlesque in his ordeal—a degradation of funny grimaces in the approach of death or dishonour.

"He related facts which I have not forgotten, but at this distance of time I couldn't recall his very words: I only remember that he managed wonderfully to convey the brooding rancour of his mind into the bare recital of events. Twice, he told me, he shut his eyes in the certitude that the end was upon him already, and twice he had to open them again. Each time he noted the darkening of the great stillness. The shadow of the silent cloud had fallen upon the ship from the zenith, and seemed to have extinguished every sound of her teeming life. He could no longer hear the voices under the awnings. He told me that each time he closed his eyes a flash of thought showed him that crowd of bodies, laid out for death, as plain as daylight. When he opened them, it was to see the dim struggle of four men fighting like mad with a stubborn boat. 'They would fall back before it time after time, stand swearing at each other, and suddenly make another rush in a bunch. . . . Enough to make you die laughing,' he commented with downcast eyes; then raising them for a moment to my face with a dismal smile, 'I ought to have a merry life of it, by God! for I shall see that funny sight a good many times yet before I die.' His eyes fell again. 'See and hear. . . . See and hear,' he repeated twice, at long intervals, filled by vacant staring.

"He roused himself.

"'I made up my mind to keep my eyes shut,' he said, 'and I couldn't. I couldn't, and I don't care who knows it. Let them go through that kind of thing before they talk. Just let them—and do better—that's all. The second time my eyelids flew open and my mouth too. I had felt the ship move. She just dipped her bows—and lifted them gently—and slow! everlastingly slow; and ever so little. She hadn't done that much for days. The cloud had raced ahead, and this first swell seemed to travel upon a sea of lead. There was no life in that stir. It managed, though, to knock over something in my head. What would you have done? You are sure of yourself—aren't you? What would you do if you felt now—this minute—the house here move, just move a little under your chair. Leap! By heavens! you would take one spring from where you sit and land in that clump of bushes yonder.'

"He flung his arm out at the night beyond the stone balustrade. I held my peace. He looked at me very steadily, very severe. There could be no mistake: I was being bullied now, and it behoved me to make no sign lest by a gesture or a word I should be drawn into a fatal admission about myself which would have had some bearing on the case. I was not disposed to take any risk of that sort. Don't forget I had him before me, and really he was too much like one of us not to be dangerous. But if you want to know I don't mind telling you that I did, with a rapid glance, estimate the distance to the mass of denser blackness in the middle of the grass plot before the verandah. He exaggerated. I would have landed short by several feet—and that's the only thing of which I am fairly certain.

"The last moment had come, as he thought, and he did not move. His feet remained glued to the planks if his thoughts were knocking about loose in his head. It was at this moment too that he saw one of the men around the boat step backwards suddenly, clutch at the air with raised arms, totter and collapse. He didn't exactly fall, he only slid gently into a sitting posture, all hunched up, and with his shoulders propped against the side of the engine-room skylight. 'That was the donkey-man. A haggard, white-faced chap with a ragged moustache. Acted third engineer,' he explained.

"'Dead,' I said. We had heard something of that in court.

"'So they say,' he pronounced with sombre indifference. 'Of course I never knew. Weak heart. The man had been complaining of being out of sorts for some time before. Excitement. Over-exertion. Devil only knows. Ha! ha! ha! It was easy to see he did not want to die either. Droll, isn't it? May I be shot if he hadn't been fooled into killing himself! Fooled—neither more nor less. Fooled into it, by heavens! just as I . . . Ah! If he had only kept still; if he had only told them to go to the devil when they came to rush him out of his bunk because the ship was sinking! If he had only stood by with his hands in his pockets and called them names!'

"He got up, shook his fist, glared at me, and sat down.

"'A chance missed eh?' I murmured.

"'Why don't you laugh?' he said. 'A joke hatched in hell. Weak heart! . . . I wish sometimes mine had been.'

"This irritated me. 'Do you?' I exclaimed with deep-rooted irony. 'Yes! Can't *you* understand,' he cried. 'I don't know what more you could wish for,' I said angrily. He gave me an utterly uncomprehending glance. This shaft had also gone wide of the mark, and he was not the man to bother about stray arrows. Upon my word, he was too unsuspecting; he was not fair game. I was glad that my missile had been thrown away,—that he had not even heard the twang of the bow.

"Of course he could not know at the time the man was dead. The next minute—his last on board—was crowded with a tumult of events and sensations which beat about him like the sea upon a rock. I use the simile advisedly, because from his relation I am forced to believe he had preserved through it all a strange illusion of passiveness, as though he had not acted but had suffered himself to be handled by the infernal powers who had selected him for the victim of their practical joke. The first thing that came to him was the grinding surge of the heavy davits swinging out at last—a jar which seemed to enter his body from the deck through the soles of his feet, and travel up his spine to the crown of his head. Then, the squall being very near now, another and a heavier swell lifted the passive hull in a threatening heave that checked his breath, while his brain and his heart together were pierced as with daggers by panic-stricken screams. 'Let go! For God's sake, let go! Let go! She's going.' Following upon that the boat-falls ripped through the blocks, and a lot of men began to talk in startled tones under the awnings. 'When these beggars did break out, their yelps were enough to wake the dead,' he said. Next, after the splashing shock of the boat literally dropped in the water, came the hollow noises of stamping and tumbling in her, mingled with confused shouts: 'Unhook! Unhook! Shove! Unhook! Shove for your life! Here's the squall down on us. . . .' He heard, high above his head, the faint muttering of the wind; he heard below his feet a cry of pain. A lost voice alongside started cursing a swivel hook. The ship began to buzz fore and aft like a disturbed hive, and, as quietly as he was telling me of all this—because just then he was very quiet in attitude, in face, in voice—he went on to say without the slightest warning as it were, 'I stumbled over his legs.'

"This was the first I heard of his having moved at all. I could not restrain a grunt of surprise. Something had started him off at last, but of the exact moment, of the cause that tore him out of his immobility, he knew no more than the uprooted tree knows of the wind that laid it low. All this had come to him: the sounds, the sights, the legs of the dead man—by Jove! The infernal joke was being crammed devilishly down his throat, but—look you—he was not going to admit of any sort of swallowing motion in his gullet. It's extraordinary how he could cast upon you the spirit of his illusion. I listened as if to a tale of black magic at work upon a corpse.

"'He went over sideways, very gently, and this is the last thing I remember seeing on board,' he continued. 'I did not care what he did. It looked as though he were picking himself up: I thought he was picking himself up, of course: I expected him to bolt past me over the rail and drop into the boat after the others. I could hear them knocking about down there, and a voice as if crying up a shaft called out "George." Then three voices together raised a yell. They came to me separately: one bleated, another screamed, one howled. Ough!'

"He shivered a little, and I beheld him rise slowly as if a steady hand from above had been pulling him out of the chair by his hair. Up, slowly—to his full height, and when his knees had locked stiff the hand let him go, and he swayed a little on his feet. There was a suggestion of awful stillness in his face, in his movements, in his very voice when he said 'They shouted'—and involuntarily I pricked up my ears for the ghost of that shout that would be heard directly through the false effect of silence. 'There were eight hundred people in that ship,' he said, impaling me to the back of my seat with an awful blank stare. 'Eight hundred living people, and they were yelling after the one dead man to come down and be saved. "Jump, George! Jump! Oh, jump!" I stood by with my hand on the davit. I was very quiet. It had come over pitch dark. You could see neither sky nor sea. I heard the boat alongside go bump, bump, and not another sound down there for a while, but the ship under me was full of talking noises. Suddenly the skipper howled "Mein Gott! The squall! The squall! Shove off!" With the first hiss of rain, and the first gust of wind, they screamed, "Jump, George! We'll catch you! Jump!" The ship began a slow plunge; the rain swept over her like a broken sea; my cap flew off my head; my breath was driven back into my throat. I heard as if I had been on the top of a tower another wild screech, "Geo-o-o-orge! Oh jump!" She was going down, down, head first under me. . . .'

"He raised his hand deliberately to his face, and made picking motions with his fingers as though he had been bothered with cobwebs, and afterwards he looked into the open palm for quite half a second before he blurted out—

"'I had jumped . . .' He checked himself, averted his gaze. . . . 'It seems,' he added.

"His clear blue eyes turned to me with a piteous stare, and looking at him standing before me, dumfounded and hurt, I was oppressed by a sad sense of resigned wisdom, mingled with the amused and profound pity of an old man helpless before a childish disaster.

"'Looks like it,' I muttered.

"'I knew nothing about it till I looked up,' he explained hastily. And that's possible too. You had to listen to him as you would to a small boy in trouble. He didn't know. It had happened somehow. It would never happen again. He had landed partly on somebody and fallen across a thwart. He felt as though all his ribs on his left side must be broken; then he rolled over, and saw vaguely the ship he had deserted uprising above him, with the red side-light glowing large in the rain like a fire on the brow of a hill seen through a mist. 'She seemed higher than a wall; she loomed like a cliff over the boat, . . . I wished I could die,' he cried. 'There was no going back. It was as if I had jumped into a well—into an everlasting deep hole. . . .'"

CHAPTER X.

"He locked his fingers together and tore them apart. Nothing could be more true: he had indeed jumped into an everlasting deep hole. He had tumbled from a height he could never scale again. By that time the boat had gone driving forward past the bows. It was too dark just then for them to see each other, and, moreover, they were blinded and half drowned with rain. He told me it was like being swept by a flood through a cavern. They turned their backs to the squall; the skipper, it seems, got an oar over the stern to keep the boat before it, and for two or three minutes the end of the world had come through a deluge in a pitchy blackness. The sea hissed 'like twenty thousand kettles.' That's his simile, not mine. I fancy there was not much wind after the first gust; and he himself had admitted at the inquiry that the sea never got up that night to any extent. He crouched down in the bows and stole a furtive glance back. He saw just one yellow gleam of the mast-head light high up and blurred like a last star ready to dissolve. 'It terrified me to see it still there,' he said. That's what he said. What terrified him was the thought that the drowning was not over yet. No doubt he wanted to be done with that abomination as quickly as possible. Nobody in the boat made a sound. In the dark she seemed to fly, but of course she could not have had much way. Then the shower swept ahead, and the great, distracting, hissing noise followed the rain into distance and died out. There was nothing to be heard then but the slight wash about the boat's sides. Somebody's teeth were chattering violently. A hand touched his back. A faint voice said, 'You there?' Another cried out shakily, 'She's gone!' and they all stood up together to look astern. They saw no lights. All was black. A thin cold drizzle was driving into their faces. The boat lurched slightly. The teeth chattered faster, stopped, and began again twice before the man could master his shiver sufficiently to say, 'Ju-ju-st in ti-ti-me. . . . Brrrr.' He recognized the voice of the chief engineer saying surlily, 'I saw her go down. I happened to turn my head.' The wind had dropped almost completely.

"They watched in the dark with their heads half turned to windward as if expecting to hear cries. At first he was thankful the night had covered up the scene before his eyes, and then to know of it and yet to have seen and heard nothing appeared somehow the culminating-point of an awful misfortune. 'Strange isn't it?' he murmured, interrupting himself in his disjointed narrative.

"It did not seem so strange to me. He must have had an unconscious conviction that the reality could not be half as bad, not half as anguishing, appalling, and vengeful as the created terror of his imagination. I believe that, in this first moment, his heart was wrung with all the suffering, that his soul knew the accumulated savour of all the fear, all the horror, all the despair of eight hundred human beings pounced upon in the night by a sudden and violent death, else why should he have said, 'It seemed to me that I must jump out of that accursed boat and swim back to see—half a mile—more—any distance—to that very spot . . .'? Why this impulse? Do you see the significance? Why back to the very spot? Why not drown alongside—if he meant drowning—why back to the very spot, to see— as if his imagination had to be soothed by the assurance that all was over before death could bring relief? I defy any one of you to offer another explanation. It was one of those bizarre and exciting glimpses through the fog. It was an extraordinary disclosure. He let it out as the most natural thing one could say. He fought down that impulse and then he became conscious of the silence. He mentioned this to me. A silence of the sea, of the sky, merged into one indefinite immensity still as death around these saved, palpitating lives. 'You might have heard a pin drop in the boat,' he said with a queer contraction of his lips, like a man trying to master his sensibilities while relating some extremely moving fact. A silence! God alone, who had willed him as he was, knows what he made of it in his heart. 'I didn't think any spot on earth could be so still,' he said. 'You couldn't distinguish the sea from the sky; there was nothing to see and nothing to hear. Not a glimmer, not a shape, not a sound. You could have believed that every bit of dry land had gone to the bottom; that every man on earth but I and these beggars in the boat had got drowned.' He leaned over the table with his knuckles propped amongst coffee-cups, liqueur-glasses, cigar-ends. 'I seemed to believe it. Everything was gone and—all was over . . .' he fetched a deep sigh . . . 'with me.'"

Marlow sat up abruptly and flung away his cheroot with force. It made a darting red trail like a toy rocket fired through the drapery of creepers. Nobody stirred.

"Hey, what do you think of it?" he cried with sudden animation. "Wasn't he true to himself, wasn't he? His saved life was over for want of ground under his feet, for want of sights for his eyes, for want of voices in his ears. Annihilation—hey! And all the time it was only a clouded sky, a sea that did not break, the air that did not stir. Only a night; only a silence.

"It lasted for a while, and then they were suddenly and unanimously moved to make a noise over their escape. 'I knew from the first she would go.' 'Not a minute too soon.' 'A narrow squeak, b'gosh!' He said nothing, but the breeze that had dropped came back, a gentle draught freshened steadily, and the sea joined its murmuring voice to this talkative reaction succeeding the dumb moments of awe. She was gone! She was gone! Not a doubt of it. Nobody could have helped. They repeated the same words over and over again as though they couldn't stop themselves. Never doubted she would go. The lights were gone. No mistake. The lights were gone. Couldn't expect anything else. She had to go. . . . He noticed that they talked as though they had left behind them nothing but an empty ship. They concluded she would not have been long when she once started. It seemed to cause them some sort of satisfaction. They assured each other that she couldn't have been long about it—'Just shot down like a flat-iron.' The chief engineer declared that the mast-head light at the moment of sinking seemed to drop 'like a lighted match you throw down.' At this the second laughed hysterically. 'I am g-g-glad, I am gla-a-a-d.' His teeth went on 'like an electric rattle,' said Jim, 'and all at once he began to cry. He wept and blubbered like a child, catching his breath and sobbing "Oh dear! oh dear! oh dear!" He would be quiet for a while and start suddenly, "Oh, my poor arm! oh, my poor a-a-arm!" I felt I could knock him down. Some of them sat in the stern-sheets. I could just make out their shapes. Voices came to me, mumble, mumble, grunt, grunt. All this seemed very hard to bear. I was cold too. And I could do nothing. I thought that if I moved I would have to go over the side and— . . .'

"His hand groped stealthily, came in contact with a liqueur-glass, and was withdrawn suddenly as if it had touched a red-hot coal. I pushed the bottle slightly. 'Won't you have some more?' I asked. He looked at me angrily. 'Don't you think I can tell you what there is to tell without screwing myself up?' he asked. The squad of globetrotters had gone to bed. We were alone but for a vague white form erect in the shadow, that, being looked at, cringed forward, hesitated, backed away silently. It was getting late, but I did not hurry my guest.

"In the midst of his forlorn state he heard his companions begin to abuse some one. 'What kept you from jumping, you lunatic?' said a scolding voice. The chief engineer left the stern-sheets, and could be heard clambering forward as if with hostile intentions against 'the greatest idiot that ever was.' The skipper shouted with rasping effort offensive epithets from where he sat at the oar. He lifted his head at that uproar, and heard the name 'George,' while a hand in the dark struck him on the breast. 'What have you got to say for yourself, you fool?' queried somebody, with a sort of virtuous fury. 'They were after me,' he said. 'They were abusing me—abusing me . . . by the name of George.'

"He paused to stare, tried to smile, turned his eyes away and went on. 'That little second puts his head right under my nose, "Why, it's that blasted mate!"' "What!" howls the skipper from the other end of the boat. "No!" shrieks the chief. And he too stooped to look at my face.'

"The wind had left the boat suddenly. The rain began to fall again, and the soft, uninterrupted, a little mysterious sound with which the sea receives a shower arose on all sides in the night. 'They were too taken aback to say anything more at first,' he narrated steadily, 'and what could I have to say to them?' He faltered for a moment, and made an effort to go on. 'They called me horrible names.' His voice, sinking to a whisper, now and then would leap up suddenly, hardened by the passion of scorn, as though he had been talking of secret abominations. 'Never mind what they called me,' he said grimly. 'I could hear hate in their voices. A good thing too. They could not forgive me for being in that boat. They hated it. It made them mad. . . .' He laughed short. . . . 'But it kept me from—Look! I was sitting with my arms crossed, on the gunwale! . . .' He perched himself smartly on the edge of the table and crossed his arms. . . . 'Like this—see? One little tilt backwards and I would have been gone—after the others. One little tilt—the least bit— the least bit.' He frowned, and tapping his forehead with the tip of his middle finger, 'It was there all the time,' he said impressively. 'All the time—that notion. And the rain—cold, thick, cold as melted snow—colder—on my thin cotton clothes— I'll never be so cold again in my life, I know. And the sky was black too—all black. Not a star, not a light anywhere. Nothing outside that confounded boat and those two yapping before me like a couple of mean mongrels at a tree'd thief. Yap! yap! What you doing here? You're a fine sort! Too much of a bloomin' gentleman to put his hand to it. Come out of your trance, did you? To sneak in? Did you? Yap! yap! You ain't fit to live! Yap! yap! Two of them together trying to out-bark each other. The other would bay from the stern through the rain—couldn't see him—couldn't make out—some of his filthy jargon. Yap! yap! Bow-ow-ow-ow-ow! Yap! yap! It was sweet to hear them; it kept me alive—I tell you. It has saved my life. At it they went, as if trying to drive me overboard with the noise! . . . I wonder you had pluck enough to jump. You ain't wanted here. If I had known who it was, I would have tipped you over—you skunk. What have you done with the other? Where did you get the pluck to jump—you coward? What's to prevent us three from firing you overboard? . . . They were out of breath; the shower passed away upon the sea. Then nothing. There was nothing round the boat, not even a sound. Wanted to see me overboard, did they? Upon my soul! I think they would have had their wish if they had only kept quiet. Fire me overboard! Would they? "Try," I said. "I would for twopence." "Too good for you," they screeched together. It was so dark that it was only when one or the other of them moved that I was quite sure of seeing him. By heavens! I only wish they had tried.'

"I couldn't help exclaiming. 'What an extraordinary affair!'

"'Not bad—eh?' he said, as if in some sort astounded. 'They pretended to think I had done away with that donkey-man for some reason or other. Why should I? And how the devil was I to know? Didn't I get somehow into that boat? into that boat—I . . .' The muscles round his lips contracted into an unconscious grimace that tore through the mask of his usual expression—something violent, short-lived and illuminating like a twist of lightning that admits the eye for an instant into the secret convolutions of a cloud. 'I did. I was plainly there with them—wasn't I? Isn't it awful a man should be driven to do a thing like that—and be responsible? What did I know about their George they were howling after? I remembered I had seen him curled up on the deck. "Murdering coward!" the chief kept on calling me. He didn't seem able to remember any other two words. I didn't care, only his noise began to worry me. "Shut up," I said. At that he collected himself for a confounded screech. "You killed him. You killed him." "No," I shouted, "but I will kill you directly." I jumped up, and he fell backwards over a thwart with an awful loud thump. I don't know why. Too dark. Tried to step back, I suppose. I stood still facing aft, and the wretched little second began to whine, "You ain't going to hit a chap with a broken arm—and you call yourself a gentleman, too." I heard a heavy tramp—one—two—and wheezy grunting. The other beast was coming at me, clattering his oar over the stern. I saw him moving, big, big—as you see a man in a mist, in a dream. "Come on," I cried. I would have tumbled him over like a bale of shakings. He stopped, muttered to himself, and went back. Perhaps he had heard the wind. I didn't. It was the last heavy gust we had. He went back to his oar. I was sorry. I would have tried to—to . . .'

"He opened and closed his curved fingers, and his hands had an eager and cruel flutter. 'Steady, steady,' I murmured.

"'Eh? What? I am not excited,' he remonstrated, awfully hurt, and with a convulsive jerk of his elbow knocked over the cognac-bottle. I started forward, scraping my chair. He bounced off the table as if a mine had been exploded behind his back, and half turned before he alighted, crouching on his feet to show me a startled pair of eyes and a face white about the nostrils. A look of intense annoyance succeeded. 'Awfully sorry. How clumsy of me!' he mumbled, very vexed, while the pungent odour of spilt alcohol enveloped us suddenly with an atmosphere of a low drinking-bout in the cool, pure darkness of the night. The lights had been put out in the dining-hall; our candle glimmered solitary in the long gallery, and the columns had turned black from pediment to capital. On the vivid stars the high corner of the Harbour Office stood out distinct across the Esplanade, as though the sombre pile had glided nearer to see and hear.

"He assumed an air of indifference.

"'I daresay I am less calm now than I was then. I was ready for anything. These were trifles. . . .'

"'You had a lively time of it in that boat,' I remarked.

"'I was ready,' he repeated. 'After the ship's lights had gone, anything might have happened in that boat—anything in the world—and the world no wiser. I felt this, and I was pleased. It was just dark enough too. We were like men walled up quick in a roomy grave. No concern with anything on earth. Nobody to pass an opinion. Nothing mattered.' For the third time during this conversation he laughed harshly, but there was no one about to suspect him of being only drunk. 'No fear, no law, no sounds, no eyes—not even our own, till—till sunrise at least.'

"I was struck by the suggestive truth of his words. There is something peculiar in a small boat upon the wide sea. Over the lives borne from under the shadow of death there seems to fall the shadow of madness. When your ship fails you, your whole world seems to fail you; the world that made you, restrained you, taken care of you. It is as if the souls of men floating on an abyss and in touch with immensity had been set free for any excess of heroism, absurdity, or abomination. Of course, as with belief, thought, love, hate, conviction, or even the visual aspect of material things, there are as many shipwrecks as there are men, and in this one there was something abject which made the isolation more complete,—there was a villainy of circumstances that cut these men off more completely from the rest of mankind, whose ideal of conduct had never undergone the trial of a fiendish and appalling joke. They were exasperated with him for being a half-hearted shirker: he focussed on them his hate of the whole thing; he would have liked to take a signal revenge for the abhorrent opportunity they had put in his way. Trust a boat on the high seas to bring out the Irrational that lurks at the bottom of every thought, sentiment, sensation, emotion. It was part of the burlesque meanness pervading that particular disaster at sea that they did not come to blows. It was all threats, all a terribly effective feint, a sham from beginning to end, planned by the tremendous disdain of the Dark Powers whose real terrors, always on the verge of triumph, are perpetually foiled by the steadfastness of men. I asked, after waiting for a while, 'Well, what happened?' A futile question. I knew too much already to hope for the grace of a single uplifting touch, for the favour of hinted madness, of shadowed horror. 'Nothing,' he said. 'I meant business, but they meant noise only. Nothing happened.'

"And the rising sun found him just as he had jumped up first in the bows of the boat. What a persistence of readiness! He had been holding the tiller in his hand, too, all the night. They had dropped the rudder overboard while attempting to ship it, and I suppose the tiller got kicked forward somehow while they were rushing up and down that boat trying to do all sorts of things at once so as to get clear of the side. It was a long heavy piece of hard wood, and apparently he had been clutching it for six hours or so. If you don't call that being ready! Can you imagine him, silent and on his feet half the night, his face to the gusts of rain, staring at sombre forms, watchful of vague movements, straining his ears to catch rare low murmurs in the stern-sheets! Firmness of courage or effort of fear? What do you think? And the endurance is undeniable too. Six hours more or less on the defensive; six hours of alert immobility while the boat drove slowly or floated arrested according to the caprice of the wind; passed above his head'; while the sky from an immensity lustreless and black, diminished to a sombre and lustrous vault, scintillated with a greater brilliance, faded to the east, paled at the zenith; while the dark shapes blotting the low stars astern got outlines, relief; became shoulders, heads, faces, features,—confronted him with dreary stares, had dishevelled hair, torn clothes, blinked red eyelids at the white dawn. 'They looked as though they had been knocking about drunk in gutters for a week,' he described graphically; and then he muttered something about the sunrise being of a kind that foretells a calm day. You know that sailor habit of referring to the weather in every connection. And on my side his few mumbled words were enough to make me see the lower limb of the sun clearing the line of the horizon, the tremble of a vast ripple running over all the visible expanse of the sea, as if the waters had shuddered, giving birth to the globe of light, while the last puff of the breeze would stir in the air in a sigh of relief.

"'They sat in the stern shoulder to shoulder, with the skipper in the middle, like three dirty owls, and stared at me,' I heard him say with an intention of hate that distilled a corrosive virtue into the commonplace words like a drop of powerful poison falling into a glass of water; but my thoughts dwelt upon that sunrise. I could imagine under the pellucid emptiness of the sky these four men imprisoned in the solitude of the sea, the lonely sun, regardless of the speck of life, ascending the clear curve of the heaven as if to gaze ardently from a greater height at his own splendour reflected in the still ocean. 'They called out to me from aft,' said Jim, 'as though we had been chums together. I heard them. They were begging me to be sensible and drop that "blooming piece of wood." Why *would* I carry on so? They hadn't done me any harm—had they? There had been no harm. . . . No harm!'

"His face crimsoned as though he could not get rid of the air in his lungs.

"'No harm!' he burst out. 'I leave it to you. You can understand. Can't you? You see it—don't you? No harm! Good God! What more could they have done? Oh yes, I know very well—I jumped. Certainly. I jumped! I told you I jumped; but I tell you they were too much for any man. It was their doing as plainly as if they had reached up with a boat-hook and pulled me over. Can't you see it? You must see it. Come. Speak—straight out.'

"His uneasy eyes fastened upon mine, questioned, begged, challenged, entreated. For the life of me I couldn't help murmuring. 'You've been tried.' 'More than is fair,' he caught up swiftly. 'I wasn't given half a chance—with a gang like that. And now they were friendly—oh, so damnably friendly! Chums, shipmates. All in the same boat. Make the best of it. They hadn't meant anything. They didn't care a hang for George. George had gone back to his berth for something at the last moment and got caught. The man was a manifest fool. Very sad, of course. . . . Their eyes looked at me; their lips moved; they wagged their heads at the other end of the boat—three of them; they beckoned—to me. Why not? Hadn't I jumped? I said nothing. There are no words for the sort of things I wanted to say. If I had opened my lips just then I would have simply howled like an animal. I was asking myself when I would wake up. They urged me aloud to come aft and hear quietly what the skipper had to say. We were sure to be picked up before the evening— right in the track of all the Canal traffic; there was smoke to the north-west now.

"'It gave me an awful shock to see this faint, faint blur, this low trail of brown mist through which you could see the boundary of sea and sky. I called out to them that I could hear very well where I was. The skipper started swearing, as hoarse as a crow. He wasn't going to talk at the top of his voice for *my* accommodation. "Are you afraid they will hear you on shore?" I asked. He glared as if he would have liked to claw me to pieces. The chief engineer advised him to humour me. He said I wasn't right in my head yet. The other rose astern, like a thick pillar of flesh—and talked—talked. . . .'

"Jim remained thoughtful. 'Well?' I said. 'What did I care what story they agreed to make up?' he cried recklessly. 'They could tell what they jolly well liked. It was their business. I knew the story. Nothing they could make people believe could alter it for me. I let him talk, argue—talk, argue. He went on and on and on. Suddenly I felt my legs give way under me. I was sick, tired—tired to death. I let fall the tiller, turned my back on them, and sat down on the foremost thwart. I had enough. They called to me to know if I understood—wasn't it true, every word of it? It was true, by God! after their fashion. I did not turn my head. I heard them palavering together. "The silly ass won't say anything." "Oh, he understands well enough." "Let him be; he will be all right." "What can he do?" What could I do! Weren't we all in the same boat. I tried to be deaf. The smoke had disappeared to the northward. It was a dead calm. They had a drink from the water-breaker, and I drank too. Afterwards they made a great business of spreading the boat-sail over the gunwales. Would I keep a look-out? They crept under, out of my sight, thank God! I felt weary, weary, done up, as if I hadn't had one hour's sleep since the day I was born. I couldn't see the water for the glitter of the sunshine. From time to time one of them would creep out, stand up to take a look all round, and get under again. I could hear spells of snoring below the sail. Some of them could sleep. One of them at least. I couldn't! All was light, light, and the boat seemed to be falling through it. Now and then I would fell quite surprised to find myself sitting on a thwart. . . .'

"He began to walk with measured steps to and fro before my chair, one hand in his trousers-pocket, his head bent thoughtfully, and his right arm at long intervals raised for a gesture that seemed to put out of his way an invisible intruder.

"'I suppose you think I was going mad,' he began in a changed tone. 'And well you may, if you remember I had lost my cap. The sun crept all the way from east to west over my bare head, but that day I could not come to any harm, I suppose. The sun could not make me mad. . . .' His right arm put aside the idea of madness. . . . 'Neither could it kill me. . . .' Again his arm repulsed a shadow. . . . 'That rested with me.'

"'Did it?' I said, inexpressibly amazed at this new turn, and I looked at him with the same sort of feeling I might be fairly conceived to experience had he, after spinning round on his heel, presented an altogether new face.

"'I didn't get brain fever, I did not drop dead either,' he went on. 'I didn't bother myself at all about the sun over my head. I was thinking as coolly as any man that ever sat thinking in the shade. That greasy beast of a skipper poked his big cropped head from under the canvas and screwed his fishy eyes up at me. "Donnerwetter! you will die," he growled, and drew in like a turtle. I had seen him. I had heard him. He didn't interrupt me. I was thinking just then that I wouldn't.'

"He tried to sound my thought with an attentive glance dropped on me in passing. 'Do you mean to say you had been deliberating with yourself whether you would die?' I asked in as impenetrable a tone as I could command. He nodded without stopping. 'Yes, it had come to that as I sat there alone,' he said. He passed on a few steps to the imaginary end of his beat, and when he flung round to come back both his hands were thrust deep into his pockets. He stopped short in front of my chair and looked down. 'Don't you believe it?' he inquired with tense curiosity. I was moved to make a solemn declaration of my readiness to believe implicitly anything he thought fit to tell me."

CHAPTER XI.

"He heard me out with his head on one side, and I had another glimpse through a rent in the mist in which he moved and had his being. The dim candle spluttered within the ball of glass, and that was all I had to see him by; at his back was the dark night with the clear stars, whose distant glitter disposed in retreating planes lured the eye into the depths of a greater darkness; and yet a mysterious light seemed to show me his boyish head, as if in that moment the youth within him had, for a moment, gleamed and expired. 'You are an awful good sort to listen like this,' he said. 'It does me good. You don't know what it is to me. You don't . . .' words seemed to fail him. It was a distinct glimpse. He was a youngster of the sort you like to see about you; of the sort you like to imagine yourself to have been; of the sort whose appearance claims the fellowship of these illusions you had thought gone out, extinct, cold, and which, as if rekindled at the approach of another flame, give a flutter deep, deep down somewhere, give a flutter of light . . . of heat! . . . Yes; I had a glimpse of him then, . . . and it was not the last of that kind. . . . 'You don't know what it is for a fellow in my position to be believed—make a clean breast of it to an elder man. It is so difficult—so awfully unfair—so hard to understand.'

"The mists were closing again. I don't know how old I appeared to him—and how much wise? Not half as old as I felt just then; not half as uselessly wise as I knew myself to be. Surely in no other craft as in that of the sea do the hearts of those already launched to sink or swim go out so much to the youth on the brink, looking with shining eyes upon that glitter of the vast surface which is only a reflection of his own glances full of fire. There is such magnificent vagueness in the expectations that had driven each of us to sea, such a glorious indefiniteness, such a beautiful greed of adventures that are their own and only reward! What we get—well, we won't talk of that; but can one of us restrain a smile? In no other kind of life is the illusion more wide of reality—in no other is the beginning *all* illusion—the disenchantment more swift—the subjugation more complete. Hadn't we all commenced with the same desire, ended with the same knowledge, carried the memory of the same cherished glamour through the sordid days of imprecation? What wonder that when some heavy prod gets home the bond is found to be close; that besides the fellowship of the craft there is felt the strength of a wider feeling—the feeling that binds a man to a child. He was there before me, believing that age and wisdom can find a remedy against the pain of truth, giving me a glimpse of himself as a young fellow in a scrape that is the very devil of a scrape, the sort of scrape greybeards wag at solemnly while they hide a smile. And he had been deliberating upon death—confound him! He had found *that* to meditate about because he thought he had saved his life, while all its glamour had gone with the ship in the night. What more natural! It was tragic enough and funny enough in all conscience to call aloud for compassion, and in what was I better than the rest of us to refuse him my pity. And even as I looked at him the mists rolled into the rent, and his voice spoke—

"'I was so lost, you know. It was the sort of thing one does not expect to happen to one. It was not like a fight, for instance.'

"'It was not,' I admitted. He appeared changed, as if he had suddenly matured.

"'One couldn't be sure,' he muttered.

"'Ah! You were not sure,' I said, and was placated by the sound of a faint sigh that passed between us like the flight of a bird in the night.

"'Well, I wasn't,' he said courageously. 'It was something like that wretched story they made up. It was not a lie—but it wasn't truth all the same. It was something. . . . One knows a downright lie. There was not the thickness of a sheet of paper between the right and the wrong of this affair.'

"'How much more did you want?' I asked; but I think I spoke so low that he did not catch what I said. He had advanced his argument as though life had been a network of paths separated by chasms. His voice sounded reasonable.

"'Suppose I had not—I mean to say, suppose I had stuck to the ship? Well. How much longer? Say a minute—half a minute. Come. In thirty seconds, as it seemed certain then, I would have been overboard; and do you think I would not have laid hold of the first thing that came in my way—oar, life-buoy, grating—anything. Wouldn't you?'

"'And be saved,' I interjected.

"'I would have meant to be,' he retorted. 'And that's more than I meant when I' . . . he shivered as if about to swallow some nauseous drug . . . 'jumped,' he pronounced with a convulsive effort, whose stress, as if propagated by the waves of the air, made my body stir a little in the chair. He fixed me with lowering eyes. 'Don't you believe me?' he cried. 'I swear! . . . Confound it! You got me here to talk, and . . . You must! . . . You said you would believe.' 'Of course I do,' I protested, in a matter-of-fact tone which produced a calming effect. 'Forgive me,' he said. 'Of course I wouldn't have talked to you about all this if you had not been a gentleman. I ought to have known . . . I am—I am—a gentleman too . . .' 'Yes, yes,' I said hastily. He was looking me squarely in the face, and withdrew his gaze slowly. 'Now you understand why I didn't after all . . . didn't go out in that way. I wasn't going to be frightened at what I had done. And, anyhow, if I had stuck to the ship I would have done my best to be saved. Men have been known to float for hours—in the open sea—and be picked up not much the worse for it. I might have lasted it out better than many others. There's nothing the matter with *my* heart.' He withdrew his right fist from his pocket, and the blow he struck on his chest resounded like a muffled detonation in the night.

"'No,' I said. He meditated, with his legs slightly apart and his chin sunk. 'A hair's-breadth,' he muttered. 'Not the breadth of a hair between this and that. And at the time . . .'

"'It is difficult to see a hair at midnight,' I put in, a little viciously I fear. Don't you see what I mean by the solidarity of the craft? I was aggrieved against him, as though he had cheated me—me!—of a splendid opportunity to keep up the illusion of my beginnings, as though he had robbed our common life of the last spark of its glamour. 'And so you cleared out—at once.'

"'Jumped,' he corrected me incisively. 'Jumped—mind!' he repeated, and I wondered at the evident but obscure intention. 'Well, yes! Perhaps I could not see then. But I had plenty of time and any amount of light in that boat. And I could think too. Nobody would know, of course, but this did not make it any easier for me. You've got to believe that too. I did not want all this talk. . . . No . . . Yes . . . I won't lie . . . I wanted it: it is the very thing I wanted—there. Do you think you or anybody could have made me if I . . . I am—I am not afraid to tell. And I wasn't afraid to think either. I looked it in the face. I wasn't going to run away. At first—

at night, if it hadn't been for these fellows I might have . . . No! by heavens! I was not going to give them that satisfaction. They had done enough. They made up a story, and believed it for all I know. But I knew the truth, and I would live it down—alone, with myself. I wasn't going to give in to such a beastly unfair thing. What did it prove after all? I was confoundedly cut up. Sick of life—to tell you the truth; but what would have been the good to shirk it—in—in—that way? That was not the way. I believe—I believe it would have—it would have ended—nothing.'

"He had been walking up and down, but with the last word he turned short at me.

"'What do *you* believe?' he asked with violence. A pause ensued, and suddenly I felt myself overcome by a profound and hopeless fatigue, as though his voice had startled me out of a dream of wandering through empty spaces whose immensity had harassed my soul and exhausted my body.

"'. . . Would have ended nothing,' he muttered over me obstinately, after a little while. 'No! the proper thing was to face it out—alone before myself—wait for another chance—find out . . .'"

CHAPTER XII.

"All around everything was still as far as the ear could reach. The mist of his feelings shifted between us, as if disturbed by his struggles, and in the rifts of the immaterial veil he would appear to my staring eyes distinct of form and pregnant with vague appeal like a symbolic figure in a picture. The chill air of the night seemed to lie on my limbs as heavy as a slab of marble.

"'I see,' I murmured, more to prove to myself that I could break my state of numbness than for any other reason.

"'The *Avondale* picked us up just before sunset,' he remarked moodily. 'Steamed right straight for us. We had only to sit and wait.'

"After a long interval, he said, 'They told their story.' And again there was that oppressive silence. 'Then only I knew what it was I had made up my mind to,' he added.

"'You said nothing,' I whispered.

"'What could I say?' he asked, in the same low tone. . . . 'Shock slight. Stopped the ship. Ascertained the damage. Took measures to get the boats out without creating a panic. As the first boat was lowered ship went down in a squall. Sank like lead. . . . What could be more clear' . . . he hung his head . . . 'and more awful?' His lips quivered while he looked straight into my eyes. 'I had jumped—hadn't I?' he asked dismayed. 'That's what I had to live down. The story didn't matter.' . . . He clasped his hands for an instant, glanced right and left into the gloom: 'It was like cheating the dead,' he stammered.

"'And there were no dead,' I said.

"He went away from me at this. That is the only way I can describe it. In a moment I saw his back close to the balustrade. He stood there for some time, as if admiring the purity and the peace of the night. Some flowering-shrub in the garden below spread its powerful scent through the damp air. He returned to me with hasty steps.

"'And that did not matter,' he said, as stubbornly as you please.

"'Perhaps not,' I admitted. I began to have a notion he was too much for me. After all, what did I know?

"'Dead or not dead, I could not get clear,' he said. 'I had to live; hadn't I?'

"'Well, yes—if you take it in that way,' I mumbled.

"'I was glad of course,' he threw out carelessly, with his mind fixed on something else. 'The exposure,' he pronounced slowly, and lifted his head. 'Do you know what was my first thought when I heard? I was relieved. I was relieved to learn that those shouts—did I tell you I had heard shouts? No? Well, I did. Shouts for help, . . . blown along with the drizzle. Imagination, I suppose. And yet I can hardly . . . How stupid . . . The others did not. I asked them afterwards. They all said No. No? And I was hearing them even then! I might have known—but I didn't think—I only listened. Very faint screams—day after day. Then that little half-caste chap here came up and spoke to me. "The *Patna* . . . French gunboat . . . towed successfully to Aden . . . Investigation . . . Marine Office . . . Sailor's Home . . . arrangements made for your board and lodging!" I walked along with him, and I enjoyed the silence. So there had been no shouting. Imagination. I had to believe him. I could hear nothing any more. I wonder how long I could have stood it. It was getting worse, too . . . I mean—louder.'

"He fell into thought.

"'And I had heard nothing! Well—so be it. But the lights! The lights did go! We did not see them. They were not there. If they had been, I would have swam back—I would have gone back and shouted alongside—I would have begged them to take me on board. . . . I would have had my chance. . . . You doubt me? . . . How do you know how I felt? . . . What right have you to doubt? . . . I very nearly did it as it was—do you understand?' His voice fell. 'There was not a glimmer—not a glimmer,' he protested mournfully. 'Don't you understand that if there had been, you would not have seen me here? You see me—and you doubt.'

"I shook my head negatively. This question of the lights being lost sight of when the boat could not have been more than a quarter of a mile from the ship was a matter for much discussion. Jim stuck to it that there was nothing to be seen after the first shower had cleared away; and the others had affirmed the same thing to the officers of the *Avondale*. Of course people shook their heads and smiled. One old skipper who sat near me in court tickled my ear with his white beard to murmur, 'Of course they would lie.' As a matter of fact nobody lied; not even the chief engineer with his story of the mast-head light dropping like a match you throw down. Not consciously, at least. A man with his liver in such a state might very well have seen a floating spark in the corner of his eye when stealing a hurried glance over his shoulder. They had seen no light of any sort though they were well within range, and they could only explain this in one way: the ship had gone down. It was obvious and comforting. The foreseen fact coming so swiftly had justified their haste. No wonder they did not cast about for any other explanation. Yet the true one was very simple, and as soon as Brierly suggested it the court ceased to bother about the question. If you remember, the ship had been stopped, and was lying with her head on the course steered through the night, with her stern canted high and her bows brought low down in the water through the filling of the fore-compartment. Being thus out of trim, when the squall struck her a little on the quarter, she swung head to wind as sharply as though she had been at anchor. By this change in her position all her lights were in a very few moments shut off from the boat to leeward. It may very well be that, had they been seen, they would have had the effect of a mute appeal—that their glimmer lost in the darkness of the cloud would have had the mysterious power of the human glance that can awaken the feelings of remorse and pity. It would have said, 'I am here—still here' . . . and what more can the eye of the most forsaken of human beings say? But she turned her back on them as if in disdain of their fate: she had swung round, burdened, to glare stubbornly at the new danger of the open sea which she so strangely survived to end her days in a breaking-up yard, as if it had been her recorded fate to die obscurely under the blows of many hammers. What were the various ends their destiny provided for the pilgrims I am unable to say; but the immediate future brought, at about nine o'clock next morning, a French gunboat homeward bound from Réunion. The report of her commander was public property. He had swept a little out of his course to ascertain what was the matter with that steamer floating dangerously by the head upon a still and hazy sea. There was an ensign, union down, flying at her main gaff (the serang had the sense to make a signal of distress at daylight); but the cooks were preparing the food in the cooking-boxes forward as usual. The decks were packed as close as a sheep-pen: there were people perched all along the rails, jammed on the bridge in a solid mass; hundreds of eyes stared, and not a sound was heard when the gunboat ranged abreast, as if all that multitude of lips had been sealed by a spell.

"The Frenchman hailed, could get no intelligible reply, and after ascertaining through his binoculars that the crowd on deck did not look plague-stricken, decided to send a boat. Two officers came on board, listened to the serang, tried to talk with the Arab, couldn't make head or tail of it: but of course the nature of the emergency was obvious enough. They were also very much struck by discovering a white man, dead and curled up peacefully on the bridge. 'Fort intrigués par ce cadavre,' as I was informed a long time after by an elderly French lieutenant whom I came across one afternoon in Sydney, by the merest chance, in a sort of café, and who remembered the affair perfectly. Indeed this affair, I may notice in passing, had an extraordinary power of defying the shortness of memories and the length of time: it seemed to live, with a sort of uncanny vitality, in the minds of men, on the tips of their tongues. I've had the questionable pleasure of meeting it often, years afterwards, thousands of miles away, emerging from the remotest possible talk, coming to the surface of the most distant allusions. Has it not turned up tonight between us? And I am the only seaman here. I am the only one to whom it is a memory. And yet it has made its way out! But if two men who, unknown to each other, knew of this affair met accidentally on any spot of this earth, the thing would pop up between them as sure as fate, before they parted. I had never seen that Frenchman before, and at the end of an hour we had done with each other for life: he did not seem particularly talkative either; he was a quiet, massive chap in a creased uniform, sitting drowsily over a tumbler half full of some dark liquid. His shoulder-straps were a bit tarnished, his clean-shaved cheeks were large and sallow; he looked like a man who would be given to taking snuff—don't you know? I won't say he did; but the habit would have fitted that kind of man. It all began by his handing me a number of 'Home News,' which I didn't want, across the marble table. I said 'Merci.' We exchanged a few apparently innocent remarks, and suddenly, before I knew how it had come about, we were in the midst of it, and he was telling me how much they had been 'intrigued by that corpse.' It turned out he had been one of the boarding officers.

"In the establishment where we sat one could get a variety of foreign drinks which were kept for the visiting naval officers, and he took a sip of the dark medical-looking stuff, which probably was nothing more nasty than *cassis à l'eau*, and glancing with one eye into the tumbler, shook his head slightly. '*Impossible de comprendre—vous concevez,*' he said, with a curious mixture of unconcern and thoughtfulness. I could very easily conceive how impossible it had been for them to understand. Nobody in the gunboat knew enough English to get hold of the story as told by the serang. There was a good deal of noise, too, round the two officers. 'They crowded upon us. There was a circle round that dead man (*autour de ce mort*),' he described. 'One had to attend to the most pressing. These people were beginning to agitate themselves—*Parbleu!* A mob like that—don't you see?' he interjected with philosophic indulgence. As to the bulkhead, he had advised his commander that the safest thing was to leave it alone, it was so villainous to look at. They got two hawsers on board promptly (*en toute hâte*) and took the *Patna* in tow—stern foremost at that—which, under the circumstances, was not so foolish, since the rudder was too much out of the water to be of any great use for steering, and this manoeuvre eased the stain on the bulkhead, whose state, he expounded with stolid glibness, demanded the greatest care (*éxigeait les plus grands ménagements*). I could not help thinking that my new acquaintance must have had a voice in most of these arrangements: he looked a reliable officer, no longer very active, and he was seamanlike too, in a way, though as he sat there, with his thick fingers clasped lightly on his stomach, he reminded you of one of those snuffy, quiet village priests, into whose ears are poured the sins, the sufferings, the remorse of peasant generations, on whose faces the placid and simple expression is like a veil thrown over the mystery of pain and distress. He ought to have had a threadbare black *soutane* buttoned smoothly up to his ample chin, instead of a frock-coat with shoulder-straps and brass buttons. His broad bosom heaved regularly while he went on telling me that it had been the very devil of a job, as doubtless (*sans doute*) I could figure to myself in my quality of a seaman (*en votre qualité de marin*). At the end of the period he inclined his body slightly towards me, and, pursing his shaved lips, allowed the air to escape with a gentle hiss. 'Luckily,' he continued, 'the sea was level like this table, and there was no more wind than there is here.' . . . The place struck me as indeed intolerably stuffy, and very hot; my face burned as though I had been young enough to be embarrassed and blushing. They had directed their course, he pursued, to the nearest English port '*naturellement,*' where their responsibility ceased, '*Dieu merci.*' . . . He blew out his flat cheeks a little. . . . 'Because, mind you (*notez bien*), all the time of towing we had two quartermasters stationed with axes by the hawsers, to cut us clear of our tow in case she . . . ' He fluttered downwards his heavy eyelids, making his meaning as plain as possible. . . . 'What would you! One does what one can (*on fait ce qu'on peut*),' and for a moment he managed to invest his ponderous immobility with an air of resignation. 'Two quartermasters—thirty hours—always there. Two!' he repeated, lifting up his right hand a little, and exhibiting two fingers. This was absolutely the first gesture I saw him make. It gave me the opportunity to 'note' a starred scar on the back of his hand—effect of a gunshot clearly; and, as if my sight had been made more acute by this discovery, I perceived also the seam of an old wound, beginning a little below the temple and going out of sight under the short grey hair at the side of his head—the graze of a spear or the cut of a sabre. He clasped his hands on his stomach again. 'I remained on board that, that—my memory is going (*s'en va*). Ah! Patt-nà. *C'est bien ca.* Patt-nà. *Merci.* It is droll how one forgets. I stayed on that ship thirty hours. . . .'

"'You did!' I exclaimed. Still gazing at his hands, he pursed his lips a little, but this time made no hissing sound. 'It was judged proper,' he said, lifting his eyebrows dispassionately, 'that one of the officers should remain to keep an eye open (*pour ouvrir l'œil*)' . . . he sighed idly . . . 'and for communicating by signals with the towing ship—do you see—and so on. For the rest, it was my opinion too. We made our boats ready to drop over—and I also on that ship took measures. . . . *Enfin!* One has done one's possible. It was a delicate position. Thirty hours. They prepared me some food. As for the wine—go and whistle for it—not a drop.' In some extraordinary way, without any marked change in his inert attitude and in the placid expression of his face, he managed to convey the idea of profound disgust. 'I—you know—when it comes to eating without my glass of wine—I am nowhere.'

"I was afraid he would enlarge upon the grievance, for though he didn't stir a limb or twitch a feature, he made one aware how much he was irritated by the recollection. But he seemed to forget all about it. They delivered their charge to the 'port authorities,' as he expressed it. He was struck by the calmness with which it had been received. 'One might have thought they had such a droll find (*drôle de trouvaille*) brought them every day. You are extraordinary—you others,' he commented, with his back propped against the wall, and looking himself as incapable of an emotional display as a sack of meal. There happened to be a man-of-war and an Indian Marine steamer in the harbour at the time, and he did not conceal his admiration of the efficient manner in which the boats of these two ships cleared the *Patna* of her passengers. Indeed his torpid demeanour concealed nothing: it had that mysterious, almost miraculous, power of producing striking effects by means impossible of detection which is the last word of the highest art. 'Twenty-five minutes—watch in hand—twenty-five, no more.' . . . He unclasped and clasped again his fingers without removing his hands from his stomach, and made it infinitely more effective than if he had thrown up his arms to heaven in amazement. . . . 'All that lot (*tout ce monde*) on shore—with their little affairs—nobody left but a guard of seamen (*marins de l'État*) and that interesting corpse (*cet intéressant cadavre*). Twenty-five minutes.' . . . With downcast eyes and his head tilted slightly on one side he seemed to roll knowingly on his tongue the savour of a smart bit of work. He persuaded one without any further demonstration that his approval was eminently worth having, and resuming his hardly interrupted immobility, he went on to inform me that, being under orders to make the best of their way to Toulon, they left in two hours' time, 'so that (*de sorte que*) there are many things in this incident of my life (*dans cet épisode de ma vie*) which have remained obscure.'"

CHAPTER XIII.

"After these words, and without a change of attitude, he, so to speak, submitted himself passively to a state of silence. I kept him company; and suddenly, but not abruptly, as if the appointed time had arrived for his immobility, he pronounced, '*Mon Dieu!* how the time passes!' Nothing could have been more commonplace than his remark; but its utterance coincided for me with a moment of vision. It's extraordinary how we go through life with eyes half shut, with dull ears, with dormant thoughts. Perhaps it's just as well; and it may be that it is this very dulness that makes life to the incalculable majority so supportable and so welcome. Nevertheless, there can be but few of us who had never known one of these rare moments of awakening when we see, hear, understand ever so much—everything—in a flash—before we fall back again into our agreeable somnolence. I raised my eyes when he spoke, and I saw him as though I had never seen him before. I saw his chin sunk on his breast, the clumsy folds of his coat, his clasped hands, his motionless pose, so curiously suggestive of his having been simply left there. Time had passed indeed: it had overtaken him and gone ahead. It had left him hopelessly behind with a few poor gifts: the iron-grey hair, the heavy fatigue of the tanned face, two scars, a pair of tarnished shoulder-straps; one of those steady, reliable men who are the raw material of great reputations, one of those uncounted lives that are buried without drums and trumpets under the foundations of monumental successes. 'I am now third lieutenant of the *Victorieuse*' (she was the flagship of the French Pacific squadron at the time), he said, detaching his shoulders from the wall a couple of inches to introduce himself. I bowed slightly on my side of the table, and told him I commanded a merchant vessel at present anchored in Rushcutters' Bay. He had 'remarked' her,—a pretty little craft. He was very civil about it in his impassive way. I even fancy he went the length of tilting his head in compliment as he repeated, breathing visibly the while, 'Ah, yes. A little craft painted black—very pretty—very pretty (*très coquet*).' After a time he twisted his body slowly to face the glass door on our right. 'A dull town (*Triste ville*),' he observed, staring into the street. It was a brilliant day; a southerly buster was raging, and we could see the passersby, men and women, buffeted by the wind on the side-walks, the sunlit fronts of the houses across the road blurred by the tall whirls of dust. 'I descended on shore,' he said, 'to stretch my legs a little, but . . .' He didn't finish, and sank into the depths of his repose. 'Pray—tell me,' he began, coming up ponderously, 'what was there at the bottom of this affair—precisely (*au juste*)? It is curious. That dead man, for instance—and so on.'

"'There were living men too,' I said; 'much more curious.'

"'No doubt, no doubt,' he agreed half audibly, then, as if after mature consideration, murmured, 'Evidently.' I made no difficulty in communicating to him what had interested me most in this affair. It seemed as though he had a right to know: hadn't he spent thirty hours on board the *Patna*—had he not taken the succession, so to speak, had he not done 'his possible'? He listened to me, looking more priest-like than ever, and with what—probably on account of his downcast eyes—had the appearance of devout concentration. Once or twice he elevated his eyebrows (but without raising his eyelids), as one would say 'The devil!' Once he calmly exclaimed, 'Ah, bah!' under his breath, and when I had finished he pursed his lips in a deliberate way and emitted a sort of sorrowful whistle.

"In any one else it might have been an evidence of boredom, a sign of indifference; but he, in his occult way, managed to make his immobility appear profoundly responsive, and as full of valuable thoughts as an egg is of meat. What he said at last was nothing more than a 'very interesting,' pronounced politely, and not much above a whisper. Before I got over my disappointment he added, but as if speaking to himself, 'That's it. That *is* it.' His chin seemed to sink lower on his breast, his body to weigh heavier on his seat. I was about to ask him what he meant when a sort of preparatory tremor passed over his whole person, as a faint ripple may be seen upon stagnant water even before the wind is felt. 'And so that poor young man ran away along with the others,' he said, with grave tranquility.

"I don't know what made me smile: it is the only genuine smile of mine I can remember in connection with Jim's affair. But somehow this simple statement of the matter sounded funny in French. . . . 'S'est enfui avec les autres,' had said the lieutenant. And suddenly I began to admire the discrimination of the man. He had made out the point at once: he did get hold of the only thing I cared about. I felt as though I were taking professional opinion on the case. His imperturbable and mature calmness was that of an expert in possession of the facts, and to whom one's perplexities are mere child's-play. 'Ah! The young, the young,' he said indulgently. 'And after all, one does not die of it.' 'Die of what?' I asked swiftly. 'Of being afraid.' He elucidated his meaning and sipped his drink.

"I perceived that the three last fingers of his wounded hand were stiff and could not move independently of each other, so that he took up his tumbler with an ungainly clutch. 'One is always afraid. One may talk, but . . .' He put down the glass awkwardly. . . . 'The fear, the fear—look you—it is always there.' . . . He touched his breast near a brass button, on the very spot where Jim had given a thump to his own when protesting that there was nothing the matter with his heart. I suppose I made some sign of dissent, because he insisted, 'Yes! yes! One talks, one talks; this is all very fine; but at the end of the reckoning one is no cleverer than the next man—and no more brave. Brave! This is always to be seen. I have rolled my hump (roulé ma bosse),' he said, using the slang expression with imperturbable seriousness, 'in all parts of the world; I have known brave men—famous ones! Allez!' . . . He drank carelessly. . . . 'Brave—you conceive—in the Service—one has got to be—the trade demands it (le métier veux ça). Is it not so?' he appealed to me reasonably. 'Eh bien! Each of them—I say each of them, if he were an honest man—bien entendu—would confess that there is a point—there is a point—for the best of us—there is somewhere a point when you let go everything (vous lachez tout). And you have got to live with that truth—do you see? Given a certain combination of circumstances, fear is sure to come. Abominable funk (un trac épouvantable). And even for those who do not believe this truth there is fear all the same—the fear of themselves. Absolutely so. Trust me. Yes. Yes. . . . At my age one knows what one is talking about—que diable!' . . . He had delivered himself of all this as immovably as though he had been the mouthpiece of abstract wisdom, but at this point he heightened the effect of detachment by beginning to twirl his thumbs slowly. 'It's evident—parbleu!' he continued; 'for, make up your mind as much as you like, even a simple headache or a fit of indigestion (un dérangement d'estomac) is enough to . . . Take me, for instance—I have made my proofs. Eh Bien! I, who am speaking to you, once . . .'

"He drained his glass and returned to his twirling. 'No, no; one does not die of it,' he pronounced finally, and when I found he did not mean to proceed with the personal anecdote, I was extremely disappointed; the more so as it was not the sort of story, you know, one could very well press him for. I sat silent, and he too, as if nothing could please him better. Even his thumbs were still now. Suddenly his lips began to move. 'That is so,' he resumed placidly. 'Man is born a coward (L'homme est né poltron). It is a difficulty—parbleu! It would be too easy otherwise. But habit—habit—necessity—do you see?—the eye of others—voilà. One puts up with it. And then the example of others who are no better than yourself, and yet make good countenance. . . .'

"His voice ceased.

"'That young man—you will observe—had none of these inducements—at least at the moment,' I remarked.

"He raised his eyebrows forgivingly: 'I don't say; I don't say. The young man in question might have had the best dispositions—the best dispositions,' he repeated, wheezing a little.

"'I am glad to see you taking a lenient view,' I said. 'His own feeling in the matter was—ah!—hopeful, and . . .'

"The shuffle of his feet under the table interrupted me. He drew up his heavy eyelids. Drew up, I say—no other expression can describe the steady deliberation of the act—and at last was disclosed completely to me. I was confronted by two narrow grey circlets, like two tiny steel rings around the profound blackness of the pupils. The sharp glance, coming from that massive body, gave a notion of extreme efficiency, like a razor-edge on a battle-axe. 'Pardon,' he said punctiliously. His right hand went up, and he swayed forward. 'Allow me . . . I contended that one may get on knowing very well that one's courage does not come of itself (*ne vient pas tout seul*). There's nothing much in that to get upset about. One truth the more ought not to make life impossible. . . . But honour—the honour— monsieur! . . . The honour . . . that is real—that is! And what life may be worth when' . . . he got on his feet with a ponderous impetuosity, as a startled ox might scramble up from the grass . . . 'when the honour is gone—*ah ça! par exemple*—I can offer no opinion. I can offer no opinion—because—monsieur—I know nothing of it.'

"I had risen too, and, trying to throw infinite politeness into our attitudes, we faced each other mutely, like two china dogs on a mantelpiece. Hang the fellow! he had pricked the bubble. The blight of futility that lies in wait for men's speeches had fallen upon our conversation, and made it a thing of empty sounds. 'Very well,' I said, with a disconcerted smile; 'but couldn't it reduce itself to not being found out?' He made as if to retort readily, but when he spoke he had changed his mind. 'This, monsieur, is too fine for me—much above me—I don't think about it.' He bowed heavily over his cap, which he held before him by the peak, between the thumb and the forefinger of his wounded hand. I bowed too. We bowed together: we scraped our feet at each other with much ceremony, while a dirty specimen of a waiter looked on critically, as though he had paid for the performance. 'Serviteur,' said the Frenchman. Another scrape. 'Monsieur' . . . 'Monsieur.' . . . The glass door swung behind his burly back. I saw the southerly buster get hold of him and drive him down wind with his hand to his head, his shoulders braced, and the tails of his coat blown hard against his legs.

"I sat down again alone and discouraged—discouraged about Jim's case. If you wonder that after more than three years it had preserved its actuality, you must know that I had seen him only very lately. I had come straight from Samarang, where I had loaded a cargo for Sydney: an utterly uninteresting bit of business,—what Charley here would call one of my rational transactions—and in Samarang I had seen something of Jim. He was then working for De Jongh, on my recommendation. Water-clerk. 'My representative afloat,' as De Jongh called him. You can't imagine a mode of life more barren of consolation, less capable of being invested with a spark of glamour—unless it be the business of an insurance canvasser. Little Bob Stanton—Charley here knew him well—had gone through that experience. The same who got drowned afterwards trying to save a lady's-maid in the *Sephora* disaster. A case of collision on a hazy morning off the Spanish coast—

you may remember. All the passengers had been packed tidily into the boats and shoved clear of the ship, when Bob sheered alongside again and scrambled back on deck to fetch that girl. How she had been left behind I can't make out; anyhow, she had gone completely crazy—wouldn't leave the ship—held to the rail like grim death. The wrestling-match could be seen plainly from the boats; but poor Bob was the shortest chief mate in the merchant service, and the woman stood five feet ten in her shoes and was as strong as a horse, I've been told. So it went on, pull devil, pull baker, the wretched girl screaming all the time, and Bob letting out a yell now and then to warn his boat to keep well clear of the ship. One of the hands told me, hiding a smile at the recollection, 'It was for all the world, sir, like a naughty youngster fighting with his mother.' The same old chap said that 'At the last we could see that Mr Stanton had given up hauling at the gal, and just stood by looking at her, watchful like. We thought afterwards he must 've been reckoning that, maybe, the rush of water would tear her away from the rail by-and-by and give him a show to save her. We daren't come alongside for our life; and after a bit the old ship went down all on a sudden with a lurch to starboard—plop. The suck in was something awful. We never saw anything alive or dear come up.' Poor Bob's spell of shore-life had been one of the complications of a love affair, I believe. He fondly hoped he had done with the sea for ever, and made sure he had got hold of all the bliss on earth, but it came to canvassing in the end. Some cousin of his in Liverpool put him up to it. He used to tell us his experiences in that line. He made us laugh till we cried, and, not altogether displeased at the effect, undersized and bearded to the waist like a gnome, he would tiptoe amongst us and say, 'It's all very well for you beggars to laugh, but my immortal soul was shrivelled down to the size of a parched pea after a week of that work.' I don't know how Jim's soul accommodated itself to the new conditions of his life—I was kept too busy in getting him something to do that would keep body and soul together—but I am pretty certain his adventurous fancy was suffering all the pangs of starvation. It had certainly nothing to feed upon in this new calling. It was distressing to see him at it, though he tackled it with a stubborn serenity for which I must give him full credit. I kept my eye on his shabby plodding with a sort of notion that it was a punishment for the heroics of his fancy—an expiation for his craving after more glamour than he could carry. He had loved too well to imagine himself a glorious racehorse, and now he was condemned to toil without honour like a costermonger's donkey. He did it very well. He shut himself in, put his head down, said never a word. Very well; very well indeed—except for certain fantastic and violent outbreaks, on the deplorable occasions when the irrepressible *Patna* case cropped up. Unfortunately that scandal of the Eastern seas would not die out. And this is the reason why I could never feel I had done with Jim for good.

"I sat thinking of him after the French lieutenant had left, not, however, in connection with De Jongh's cool and gloomy backshop, where we had hurriedly shaken hands not very long ago, but as I had seen him years before in the last flickers of the candle, alone with me in the long gallery of the Malabar House, with the chill and the darkness of the night at his back. The respectable sword of his country's law was suspended over his head. To-morrow—or was it to-day? (midnight had slipped by long before we parted)—the marble-faced police magistrate, after distributing fines and terms of imprisonment in the assault-and-battery case, would take up the awful weapon and smite his bowed neck. Our communion in the night was uncommonly like a last vigil with a condemned man. He was guilty too. He was guilty—as I had told myself repeatedly, guilty and done for; never-theless, I wished to spare him the mere detail of a formal execution. I don't pre-tend to explain the reasons of my desire—I don't think I could; but if you haven't got a sort of notion by this time, then I must have been very obscure in my nar-rative, or you too sleepy to seize upon the sense of my words. I don't defend may morality. There was no morality in the impulse which induced me to lay before him Brierly's plan of evasion—I may call it—in all its primitive simplicity. There were the rupees—absolutely ready in my pocket and very much at his service. Oh! a loan; a loan of course—and if an introduction to a man (in Rangoon) who could put some work in his way. . . . Why! with the greatest pleasure. I had pen, ink, and paper in my room on the first floor. And even while I was speaking I was im-patient to begin the letter: day, month, year, 2.30 A.M. . . . for the sake of our old friendship I ask you to put some work in the way of Mr James So-and-so, in whom, &c., &c. . . . I was even ready to write in that strain about him. If he had not en-listed my sympathies he had done better for himself—he had gone to the very fount and origin of that sentiment, he had reached the secret sensibility of my ego-ism. I am concealing nothing from you, because were I to do so my action would appear more unintelligible than any man's action has the right to be, and—in the second place—to-morrow you shall forget my sincerity along with the other les-sons of the past. In this transaction, to speak grossly and precisely, I was the ir-reproachable man; but the subtle intentions of my immorality were defeated by the moral simplicity of the criminal. No doubt he was selfish too, but his selfishness had a higher origin, a more lofty aim. I discovered that, say what I would, he was eager to go through the ceremony of execution; and I didn't say much, for I felt that in argument his youth would tell against me heavily: he believed where I had al-ready ceased to doubt. There was something fine in the wildness of his unex-pressed, hardly formulated hope. 'Clear out! Couldn't think of it,' he said, with a shake of the head. 'I make you an offer for which I neither demand nor expect any sort of gratitude,' I said; 'you shall repay the money when convenient, and . . .' 'Awfully good of you,' he muttered without looking up. I watched him narrowly: the future must have appeared horribly uncertain to him; but he did not falter, as though indeed there had been nothing wrong with his heart. I felt angry—not for the first time that night. 'The whole wretched business,' I said, 'is bitter enough, I should think, for a man of your kind . . .' 'It is, it is,' he whispered twice, with his eyes fixed on the floor. It was heartrending. He towered above the light, and I could see the down on his cheek, the colour mantling warm under the smooth skin of his face. Believe me or not, I say it was outrageously heartrending. It provoked me to brutality. 'Yes,' I said; 'and allow me to confess that I am totally unable to imagine what advantage you can expect from this licking of the dregs.' 'Advan-tage!' he murmured out of his stillness. 'I am dashed if I do,' I said, enraged. 'I've been trying to tell you all there is in it,' he went on slowly, as if meditating some-thing unanswerable. 'But after all, it is *my* trouble.' I opened my mouth to retort, and discovered suddenly that I'd lost all confidence in myself; and it was as if he too had given up, for he mumbled like a man thinking half aloud. 'Went away . . . went into hospitals. . . . Not one of them would face it. . . . They! . . .' He moved his hand slightly to imply disdain. 'But I've got to get over this thing, and I mustn't shirk any of it or . . . I won't shirk any of it.' He was silent. He gazed as though he had been haunted. His unconscious face reflected the passing expressions of scorn, of despair, of resolution,—reflected them in turn, as a magic mirror would reflect the gliding passage of unearthly shapes. He lived surrounded by deceitful ghosts, by austere shades. 'Oh! nonsense, my dear fellow,' I began. He had a movement of impatience. 'You don't seem to understand,' he said incisively; then looking at me without a wink, 'I may have jumped, but I don't run away.' 'I meant no offence,' I said; and added stupidly, 'Better men than you have found it expedient to run, at times.' He coloured all over, while in my confusion I half-choked myself with my own tongue. 'Perhaps so,' he said at last; 'I am not good enough; I can't afford it. I am bound to fight this thing down—I am fighting it *now*.' I got out of my chair and felt stiff all over. The silence was embarrassing, and to put an end to it I imagined nothing better but to remark, 'I had no idea it was so late,' in an airy tone. . . . 'I daresay you have had enough of this,' he said brusquely: 'and to tell you the truth'—he began to look round for his hat—'so have I.'

"Well! he had refused this unique offer. He had struck aside my helping hand; he was ready to go now, and beyond the balustrade the night seemed to wait for him very still, as though he had been marked down for its prey. I heard his voice. 'Ah! here it is.' He had found his hat. For a few seconds we hung in the wind. 'What will you do after—after . . .' I asked very low. 'Go to the dogs as likely as not,' he answered in a gruff mutter. I had recovered my wits in a measure, and judged best to take it lightly. 'Pray remember,' I said, 'that I should like very much to see you again before you go.' 'I don't know what's to prevent you. The damned thing won't make me invisible,' he said with intense bitterness,—'no such luck.' And then at the moment of taking leave he treated me to a ghastly muddle of dubious stammers and movements, to an awful display of hesitations. God forgive him—me! He had taken it into his fanciful head that I was likely to make some difficulty as to shaking hands. It was too awful for words. I believe I shouted suddenly at him as you would bellow to a man you saw about to walk over a cliff; I remember our voices being raised, the appearance of a miserable grin on his face, a crushing clutch on my hand, a nervous laugh. The candle spluttered out, and the thing was over at last, with a groan that floated up to me in the dark. He got himself away somehow. The night swallowed his form. He was a horrible bungler. Horrible. I heard the quick crunch-crunch of the gravel under his boots. He was running. Absolutely running, with nowhere to go to. And he was not yet four-and-twenty."

CHAPTER XIV.

"I slept little, hurried over my breakfast, and after a slight hesitation gave up my early morning visit to my ship. It was really very wrong of me, because, though my chief mate was an excellent man all round, he was the victim of such black imaginings that if he did not get a letter from his wife at the expected time he would go quite distracted with rage and jealousy, lose all grip on the work, quarrel with all hands, and either weep in his cabin or develop such a ferocity of temper as all but drove the crew to the verge of mutiny. The thing had always seemed inexplicable to me: they had been married thirteen years; I had a glimpse of her once, and, honestly, I couldn't conceive a man abandoned enough to plunge into sin for the sake of such an unattractive person. I don't know whether I have not done wrong by refraining from putting that view before poor Selvin: the man made a little hell on earth for himself, and I also suffered indirectly, but some sort of, no doubt, false delicacy prevented me. The marital relations of seamen would make an interesting subject, and I could tell you instances. . . . However, this is not the place, nor the time, and we are concerned with Jim—who was unmarried. If his imaginative conscience or his pride; if all the extravagant ghosts and austere shades that were the disastrous familiars of his youth would not let him run away from the block, I, who of course can't be suspected of such familiars, was irresistibly impelled to go and see his head roll off. I wended my way towards the court. I didn't hope to be very much impressed or edified, or interested or even frightened—though, as long as there is any life before one, a jolly good fright now and then is a salutary discipline. But neither did I expect to be so awfully depressed. The bitterness of his punishment was in its chill and mean atmosphere. The real significance of crime is in its being a breach of faith with the community of mankind, and from that point of view he was no mean traitor, but his execution was a hole-and-corner affair. There was no high scaffolding, no scarlet cloth (did they have scarlet cloth on Tower Hill? They should have had), no awestricken multitude to be horrified at his guilt and be moved to tears at his fate—no air of sombre retribution. There was, as I walked along, the clear sunshine, a brilliance too passionate to be consoling, the streets full of jumbled bits of colour like a damaged kaleidoscope: yellow, green, blue, dazzling white, the brown nudity of an undraped shoulder, a bullock-cart with a red canopy, a company of native infantry in a drab body with dark heads marching in dusty laced boots, a native policeman in a sombre uniform of scanty cut and belted in patent leather, who looked up at me with orientally pitiful eyes as though his migrating spirit were suffering exceedingly from that unforeseen—what d'ye call 'em?—avatar—incarnation. Under the shade of a lonely tree in the courtyard, the villagers connected with the assault case sat in a picturesque group, looking like a chromo-lithograph of a camp in a book of Eastern travel. One missed the obligatory thread of smoke in the foreground and the pack-animals grazing. A blank yellow wall rose behind overtopping the tree, reflecting the glare. The court-room was sombre, seemed more vast. High up in the dim space the punkahs were swaying short to and fro, to and fro. Here and there a draped figure, dwarfed by the bare walls, remained without stirring amongst the rows of empty benches, as if absorbed in pious meditation. The plaintiff, who had been beaten, an obese chocolate-coloured man with shaved head, one fat breast bare and a bright yellow caste-mark above the bridge of his nose, sat in pompous immobility: only his eyes glittered, rolling in the gloom, and the nostrils dilated and collapsed violently as he breathed. Brierly dropped into his seat looking done up, as though he had spent the night in sprinting on a cinder-track. The pious sailing-ship skipper appeared excited and made uneasy movements, as if restraining with difficulty an impulse to stand up and exhort us earnestly to prayer and repentance. The head of the magistrate, delicately pale under the neatly arranged hair, resembled the head of a hopeless invalid after he had been washed and brushed and propped up in bed. He moved aside the vase of flowers—a bunch of purple with a few pink blossoms on long stalks—and seizing in both hands a long sheet of bluish paper, ran his eye over it, propped his forearms on the edge of the desk, and began to read aloud in an even, distinct, and careless voice.

"By Jove! For all my foolishness about scaffolds and heads rolling off—I assure you it was infinitely worse than a beheading. A heavy sense of finality brooded over all this, unrelieved by the hope of rest and safety following the fall of the axe. These proceedings had all the cold vengefulness of a death-sentence, and the cruelty of a sentence of exile. This is how I looked at it that morning—and even now I seem to see an undeniable vestige of truth in that exaggerated view of a common occurrence. You may imagine how strongly I felt this at the time. Perhaps it is for that reason that I could not bring myself to admit the finality. The thing was always with me, I was always eager to take opinion on it, as though it had not been practically settled: individual opinion—international opinion—by Jove! That Frenchman's, for instance. His own country's pronouncement was uttered in the passionless and definite phraseology a machine would use, if machines could speak. The head of the magistrate was half hidden by the paper, his brow was like alabaster.

"There were several questions before the Court. The first as to whether the ship was in every respect fit and seaworthy for the voyage. The Court found she was not. The next point, I remember, was, whether up to the time of the accident the ship had been navigated with proper and seamanlike care. They said Yes to that, goodness knows why, and then they declared that there was no evidence to show the exact cause of the accident. A floating derelict probably. I myself remember that a Norwegian barque bound out with a cargo of pitch-pine had been given up as missing about that time, and it was just the sort of craft that would capsize in a squall and float bottom up for months—a kind of maritime ghoul on the prowl to kill ships in the dark. Such wandering corpses are common enough in the North Atlantic, which is haunted by all the terrors of the sea,—fogs, icebergs, dead ships bent upon mischief, and long sinister gales that fasten upon one like a vampire till all the strength and the spirit and even hope are gone, and one feels like the empty shell of a man. But there—in those seas—the incident was rare enough to resemble a special arrangement of a malevolent providence, which, unless it had for its object the killing of a donkeyman and the bringing of worse than death upon Jim, appeared an utterly aimless piece of devilry. This view occurring to me took off my attention. For a time I was aware of the magistrate's voice as a sound merely; but in a moment it shaped itself into distinct words . . . 'in utter disregard of their plain duty,' it said. The next sentence escaped me somehow, and then . . . 'abandoning in the moment of danger the lives and property confided to their charge' . . . went on the voice evenly, and stopped. A pair of eyes under the white forehead shot darkly a glance above the edge of the paper. I looked for Jim hurriedly, as though I had expected him to disappear. He was very still—but he was there. He sat pink and fair and extremely attentive. 'Therefore, . . .' began the voice emphatically. He stared with parted lips, hanging upon the words of the man behind the desk. These came out into the stillness wafted on the wind made by the punkahs, and I, watching for their effect upon him, caught only the fragments of official language. . . . 'The Court . . . Gustav So-and-so master . . . native of Germany, . . . James So-and-so . . . mate . . . certificates cancelled.' A silence fell. The magistrate had dropped the paper, and, leaning sideways on the arm of his chair, began to talk with Brierly easily. People started to move out; others were pushing in, and I also made for the door. Outside I stood still, and when Jim passed me on his way to the gate, I caught at his arm and detained him. The look he gave discomposed me as though I had been responsible for his state: he looked at me as if I had been the embodied evil of life. 'It's all over,' I stammered. 'Yes,' he said thickly. 'And now let no man . . .' He jerked his arm out of my grasp. I watched his back as he went away. It was a long street, and he remained in sight for some time. He walked rather slow, and straddling his legs a little, as if he had found it difficult to keep a straight line. Just before I lost him I fancied he staggered a bit.

"'Man overboard,' said a deep voice behind me. Turning round, I saw a fellow I knew slightly, a West Australian; Chester was his name. He, too, had been look-ing after Jim. He was a man with an immense girth of chest, a rugged, clean-shaved face of mahogany colour, and two blunt tufts of iron-grey, thick, wiry hairs on his upper lip. He had been pearler, wrecker, trader, whaler too, I believe; in his own words—anything and everything a man may be at sea, but a pirate. The Pa-cific, north and south, was his proper hunting-ground; but he had wandered so far afield looking for a cheap steamer to buy. Lately he had discovered—so he said—a guano island somewhere, but its approaches were dangerous, and the an-chorage, such as it was, could not be considered safe, to say the least of it. 'As good as a gold-mine,' he would exclaim. 'Right bang in the middle of the Walpole Reefs, and if it's true enough that you can get no holding-ground anywhere in less than forty fathom, then what of that? There are the hurricanes, too. But it's a first-rate thing. As good as a gold-mine—better! Yet there's not a fool of them that will see it. I can't get a skipper or a shipowner to go near the place. So I made up my mind to cart the blessed stuff myself.' . . . This was what he required a steamer for, and I knew he was just then negotiating enthusiastically with a Parsee firm for an old, brig-rigged, sea-anachronism of ninety horse-power. We had met and spoken to-gether several times. He looked knowingly after Jim. 'Takes it to heart?' he asked scornfully. 'Very much,' I said. 'Then he's no good,' he opined. 'What's all the to-do about? A bit of ass's skin. That never yet made a man. You must see things ex-actly as they are—if you don't, you may just as well give in at once. You will never do anything in this world. Look at me. I made it a practice never to take anything to heart.' 'Yes,' I said, 'you see things as they are.' 'I wish I could see my partner coming along, that's what I wish to see,' he said. 'Know my partner? Old Robin-son. Yes; *the* Robinson. Don't *you* know? The notorious Robinson. The man who smuggled more opium and bagged more seals in his time than any loose Johnny now alive. They say he used to board the sealing-schooners up Alaska way when the fog was so thick that the Lord God, He alone, could tell one man from another. Holy-Terror Robinson. That's the man. He is with me in that guano thing. The best chance he ever came across in his life.' He put his lips to my ear. 'Cannibal?—well, they used to give him the name years and years ago. You remember the story? A shipwreck on the west side of Stewart Island; that's right; seven of them got ashore, and it seems they did not get on very well together. Some men are too can-tankerous for anything—don't know how to make the best of a bad job—don't see things as they are—as they *are*, my boy! And then what's the consequence? Ob-vious! Trouble, trouble; as likely as not a knock on the head; and serve 'em right too. That sort is the most useful when it's dead. The story goes that a boat of Her Majesty's ship *Wolverine* found him kneeling on the kelp, naked as the day he was born, and chanting some psalm-tune or other; light snow was falling at the time. He waited till the boat was an oar's length from the shore, and then up and away. They chased him for an hour up and down the boulders, till a marine flung a stone that took him behind the ear providentially and knocked him senseless. Alone? Of course. But that's like that tale of sealing-schooners; the Lord God knows the right and the wrong of that story. The cutter did not investigate much. They wrapped him in a boat-cloak and took him off as quick as they could, with a dark night coming on, the weather threatening, and the ship firing recall guns every five minutes. Three weeks afterwards he was as well as ever. He didn't allow any fuss that was made on shore to upset him; he just shut his lips tight, and let people screech. It was bad enough to have lost his ship, and all he was worth besides, without paying attention to the hard names they called him. That's the man for me.' He lifted his arm for a signal to some one down the street. 'He's got a little money, so I had to let him into my thing. Had to! It would have been sinful to throw away such a find, and I was cleaned out myself. It cut me to the quick, but I could see the matter just as it was, and if I *must* share—thinks I—with any man, then give me Robinson. I left him at breakfast in the hotel to come to court, because I've an idea. . . . Ah! Good morning, Captain Robinson. . . . Friend of mine, Captain Robinson.'

"An emaciated patriarch in a suit of white drill, a solah topi with a green-lined rim on a head trembling with age, joined us after crossing the street in a trotting shuffle, and stood propped with both hands on the handle of an umbrella. A white beard with amber streaks hung lumpily down to his waist. He blinked his creased eyelids at me in a bewildered way. 'How do you do? how do you do?' he piped amiably, and tottered. 'A little deaf,' said Chester aside. 'Did you drag him over six thousand miles to get a cheap steamer?' I asked. 'I would have taken him twice round the world as soon as look at him,' said Chester with immense energy. 'The steamer will be the making of us, my lad. Is it my fault that every skipper and shipowner in the whole of blessed Australasia turns out a blamed fool? Once I talked for three hours to a man in Auckland. "Send a ship," I said, "send a ship. I'll give you half of the first cargo for yourself, free gratis for nothing—just to make a good start." Says he, "I wouldn't do it if there was no other place on earth to send a ship to." Perfect ass, of course. Rocks, currents, no anchorage, sheer cliff to lay to, no insurance company would take the risk, didn't see how he could get loaded under three years. Ass! I nearly went on my knees to him. "But look at the thing as it is," says I. "Damn rocks and hurricanes. Look at it as it is. There's guano there, Queensland sugar-planters would fight for—fight for on the quay, I tell you." . . . What can you do with a fool? . . . "That's one of your little jokes, Chester," he says. . . . Joke! I could have wept. Ask Captain Robinson here. . . . And there was another shipowning fellow—a fat chap in a white waistcoat in Wellington, who seemed to think I was up to some swindle or other. "I don't know what sort of fool you're looking for," he says, "but I am busy just now. Good morning." I longed to take him in my two hands and smash him through the window of his own office. But I didn't. I was as mild as a curate. "Think of it," says I. "*Do* think it over. I'll call to-morrow." He grunted something about being "out all day." On the stairs I felt ready to beat my head against the wall from vexation. Captain Robinson here can tell you. It was awful to think of all that lovely stuff lying waste under the sun—stuff that would send the sugar-cane shooting sky-high. The making of Queensland! The making of Queensland! And in Brisbane, where I went to have a last try, they gave me the name of a lunatic. Idiots! The only sensible man I came across was the cabman who drove me about. A broken-down swell he was, I fancy. Hey! Captain Robinson? You remember I told you about my cabby in Brisbane—don't you? The chap had a wonderful eye for things. He saw it all in a jiffy. It was a real pleasure to talk with him. One evening after a devil of a day amongst shipowners I felt so bad that, says I, "I must get drunk. Come along; I must get drunk, or I'll go mad." "I am your man," he says; "go ahead." I don't know what I would have done without him. Hey! Captain Robinson.'

"He poked the ribs of his partner. 'He! he! he!' laughed the Ancient, looked aimlessly down the street, then peered at me doubtfully with sad, dim pupils. . . . 'He! he! he!' . . . He leaned heavier on the umbrella, and dropped his gaze on the ground. I needn't tell you I had tried to get away several times, but Chester had foiled every attempt by simply catching hold of my coat. 'One minute. I've a notion.' 'What's your infernal notion?' I exploded at last. 'If you think I am going in with you . . .' 'No, no, my boy. Too late, if you wanted ever so much. We've got a steamer.' 'You've got the ghost of a steamer,' I said. 'Good enough for a start—there's no superior nonsense about us. Is there, Captain Robinson?' 'No! no! no!' croaked the old man without lifting his eyes, and the senile tremble of his head became almost fierce with determination. 'I understand you know that young chap,' said Chester, with a nod at the street from which Jim had disappeared long ago. 'He's been having grub with you in the Malabar last night—so I was told.'

"I said that was true, and after remarking that he too liked to live well and in style, only that, for the present, he had to be saving of every penny—'none too many for the business! Isn't that so, Captain Robinson?'—he squared his shoulders and stroked his dumpy moustache, while the notorious Robinson, coughing at his side, clung more than ever to the handle of the umbrella, and seemed ready to subside passively into a heap of old bones. 'You see, the old chap has all the money,' whispered Chester confidentially. 'I've been cleaned out trying to engineer the dratted thing. But wait a bit, wait a bit. The good time is coming.' . . . He seemed suddenly astonished at the signs of impatience I gave. 'Oh crakee!' he cried; 'I am telling you of the biggest thing that ever was, and you . . .' 'I have an appointment,' I pleaded mildly. 'What of that?' he asked with genuine surprise; 'let it wait.' 'That's exactly what I am doing now,' I remarked; 'hadn't you better tell me what it is you want?' 'Buy twenty hotels like that,' he growled to himself; 'and every joker boarding in them too—twenty times over.' He lifted his head smartly. 'I want that young chap.' 'I don't understand,' I said. 'He's no good, is he?' said Chester crisply. 'I know nothing about it,' I protested. 'Why, you told me yourself he was taking it to heart,' argued Chester. 'Well, in my opinion a chap who . . . Anyhow, he can't be much good; but then you see I am on the look-out for somebody, and I've just got a thing that will suit him. I'll give him a job on my island.' He nodded significantly. 'I'm going to dump forty coolies there—if I've to steal 'em. Somebody must work the stuff. Oh! I mean to act square: wooden shed, corrugated-iron roof—I know a man in Hobart who will take my bill at six months for the materials. I do. Honour bright. Then there's the water-supply. I'll have to fly round and get somebody to trust me for half-a-dozen second-hand iron tanks. Catch rain-water, hey? Let him take charge. Make him supreme boss over the coolies. Good idea, isn't it? What do you say?' 'There are whole years when not a drop of rain falls on Walpole,' I said, too amazed to laugh. He bit his lip and seemed bothered. 'Oh, well, I will fix up something for them—or land a supply. Hang it all! That's not the question.'

"I said nothing. I had a rapid vision of Jim perched on a shadowless rock, up to his knees in guano, with the screams of sea-birds in his ears, the incandescent ball of the sun above his head; the empty sky and the empty ocean all a-quiver, simmering together in the heat as far as the eye could reach. 'I wouldn't advise my worst enemy . . .' I began. 'What's the matter with you?' cried Chester; 'I mean to give him a good screw—that is, as soon as the thing is set going, of course. It's as easy as falling off a log. Simply nothing to do; two six-shooters in his belt . . . Surely he wouldn't be afraid of anything forty coolies could do—with two six-shooters and he the only armed man too! It's much better than it looks. I want you to help me to talk him over.' 'No!' I shouted. Old Robinson lifted his bleared eyes dismally for a moment, Chester looked at me with infinite contempt. 'So you wouldn't advise him?' he uttered slowly. 'Certainly not,' I answered, as indignant as though he had requested me to help murder somebody; 'moreover, I am sure he wouldn't. He is badly cut up, but he isn't mad as far as I know.' 'He is no earthly good for anything,' Chester mused aloud. 'He would just have done for me. If you only could see a thing as it is, you would see it's the very thing for him. And besides . . . Why! it's the most splendid, sure chance . . .' He got angry suddenly. 'I must have a man. There! . . .' He stamped his foot and smiled unpleasantly. 'Anyhow, I could guarantee the island wouldn't sink under him—and I believe he is a bit particular on that point.' 'Good morning,' I said curtly. He looked at me as though I had been an incomprehensible fool. . . . 'Must be moving, Captain Robinson,' he yelled suddenly into the old man's ear. 'These Parsee Johnnies are waiting for us to clinch the bargain.' He took his partner under the arm with a firm grip, swung him round, and, unexpectedly, leered at me over his shoulder. 'I was trying to do him a kindness,' he asserted, with an air and tone that made my blood boil. 'Thank you for nothing—in his name,' I rejoined. 'Oh! you are devilish smart,' he sneered; 'but you are like the rest of them. Too much in the clouds. See what *you* will do with him.' 'I don't know that I want to do anything with him.' 'Don't you?' he spluttered; his grey moustache bristled with anger, and by his side the notorious Robinson, propped on the umbrella, stood with his back to me, as patient and still as a worn-out cab-horse. 'I haven't found a guano island,' I said. 'It's my belief you wouldn't know one if you were led right up to it by the hand,' he riposted quickly; 'and in this world you've got to see a thing first, before you can make use of it. Got to see it through and through at that, neither more nor less.' 'And get others to see it too,' I insinuated, with a glance at the bowed back by his side. Chester snorted at me. 'His eyes are right enough—don't you worry. He ain't a puppy.' 'Oh dear, no!' I said. 'Come along, Captain Robinson,' he shouted, with a sort of bullying deference under the rim of the old man's hat; the Holy Terror gave a submissive little jump. The ghost of a steamer was waiting for them, Fortune on that fair isle! They made a curious pair of Argonauts. Chester strode on leisurely, well set up, portly, and of conquering mien; the other, long, wasted, drooping, and hooked to his arm, shuffled his withered shanks with desperate haste."

CHAPTER XV.

"I did not start in search of Jim at once, only because I had really an appointment which I could not neglect. Then, as ill-luck would have it, in my agent's office I was fastened upon by a fellow fresh from Madagascar with a little scheme for a wonderful piece of business. It has something to do with cattle and cartridges and a Prince Ravonalo something; but the pivot of the whole affair was the stupidity of some admiral—Admiral Pierre, I think. Everything turned on that, and the chap couldn't find words strong enough to express his confidence. He had globular eyes starting out of his head with a fishy glitter, bumps on his forehead, and wore his long hair brushed back without a parting. He had a favourite phrase which he kept on repeating triumphantly, 'The minimum of risk with the maximum of profit is my motto. What?' He made my head ache, spoiled my tiffin, but got his own out of me all right; and as soon as I had shaken him off, I made straight for the water-side. I caught sight of Jim leaning over the parapet of the quay. Three native boat-men quarrelling over five annas were making an awful row at his elbow. He didn't hear me come up, but spun round as if the slight contact of my finger had released a catch. 'I was looking,' he stammered. I don't remember what I said, not much anyhow, but he made no difficulty in following me to the hotel.

"He followed me as manageable as a little child, with an obedient air, with no sort of manifestation, rather as though he had been waiting for me there to come along and carry him off. I need not have been so surprised as I was at his tracta-bility. On all the round earth, which to some seems so big and that others affect to consider as rather smaller than a mustard-seed, he had no place where he could—what shall I say?—where he could withdraw. That's it! Withdraw—be alone with his loneliness. He walked by my side very calm, glancing here and there, and once turned his head to look after a Sidiboy fireman in a cutaway coat and yellowish trousers, whose black face had silky gleams like a lump of anthracite coal. I doubt, however, whether he saw anything, or even remained all the time aware of my companionship, because if I had not edged him to the left here, or pulled him to the right there, I believe he would have gone straight before him in any direction till stopped by a wall or some other obstacle. I steered him into my bedroom, and sat down at once to write letters. This was the only place in the world (unless, perhaps, the Walpole Reef—but that was not so handy) where he could have it out with himself without being bothered by the rest of the universe. The damned thing—as he had expressed it—had not made him invisible, but I be-haved exactly as though he were. No sooner in my chair I bent over my writing-desk like a medieval scribe, and, but for the movement of the hand holding the pen, remained anxiously quiet. I can't say I was frightened; but I certainly kept as still as if there had been something dangerous in the room, that at the first hint of a movement on my part would be provoked to pounce upon me. There was not much in the room—you know how these bedrooms are—a sort of four-poster bed-stead under a mosquito-net, two or three chairs, the table I was writing at, a bare floor. A glass door opened on an upstairs verandah, and he stood with his face to it, having a hard time with all possible privacy. Dusk fell; I lit a candle with the greatest economy of movement and as much prudence as though it were an illegal proceeding. There is no doubt that he had a very hard time of it, and so had I, even to the point, I must own, of wishing him to the devil, or on Walpole Reef at least. It occurred to me once or twice that, after all, Chester was, perhaps, the man to deal effectively with such a disaster. That strange idealist had found a practical use for it at once—unerringly, as it were. It was enough to make one suspect that, maybe, he really could see the true aspect of things that appeared mysterious or utterly hopeless to less imaginative persons. I wrote and wrote; I liquidated all the arrears of my correspondence, and then went on writing to people who had no reason whatever to expect from me a gossipy letter about nothing at all. At times I stole a sidelong glance. He was rooted to the spot, but convulsive shudders ran down his back; his shoulders would heave suddenly. He was fighting, he was fighting—mostly for his breath, as it seemed. The massive shadows, cast all one way from the straight flame of the candle, seemed possessed of gloomy conscious-ness; the immobility of the furniture had to my furtive eye an air of attention. I was becoming fanciful in the midst of my industrious scribbling; and though, when the scratching of my pen stopped for a moment, there was complete silence and still-ness in the room, I suffered from that profound disturbance and confusion of thought which is caused by a violent and menacing uproar—of a heavy gale at sea, for instance. Some of you may know what I mean,—that mingled anxiety, distress, and irritation with a sort of craven feeling creeping in—not pleasant to acknowl-edge, but which gives a quiet special merit to one's endurance. I don't claim any merit for standing the stress of Jim's emotions; I could take refuge in the letters; I could have written to strangers if necessary. Suddenly, as I was taking up a fresh sheet of notepaper, I heard a low sound, the first sound that, since we had been shut up together, had come to my ears in the dim stillness of the room. I remained with my head down, with my hand arrested. Those who had kept vigil by a sickbed have heard such faint sounds in the stillness of the night watches, sounds wrung from a racked body, from a weary soul. He pushed the glass door with such force that all the panes rang: he stepped out, and I held my breath, straining my ears without knowing what else I expected to hear. He was really taking too much to heart an empty formality which to Chester's rigorous criticism seemed unwor-thy the notice of a man who could see things as they were. An empty formality; a piece of parchment. Well, well. As to an inaccessible guano deposit, that was an-other story altogether. One could intelligibly break one's heart over that. A feeble burst of many voices mingled with the tinkle of silver and glass floated up from the dining-room below; through the open door the outer edge of the light from my candle fell on his back faintly; beyond all was black; he stood on the brink of a vast obscurity, like a lonely figure by the shore of a sombre and hopeless ocean. There was the Walpole Reef in it—to be sure—a speck in the dark void, a straw for the drowning man. My compassion for him took the shape of the thought that I wouldn't have liked his people to see him at that moment. I found it trying myself. His back was no longer shaken by his gasps; he stood straight as an arrow, faintly visible and still; and the meaning of this stillness sank to the bottom of my soul like lead into the water, and made it so heavy that for a second I wished heartily that the only course left open for me were to pay for his funeral. Even the law had done with him. To bury him would have been such an easy kindness! It would have been so much in accordance with the wisdom of life, which consists in put-ting out of sight all the reminders of our folly, of our weakness, of our mortality; all that makes against our efficiency—the memory of our failures, the hints of our undying fears, the bodies of our dear friends. Perhaps he did take it too much to heart. And if so then—Chester's offer. . . . At this point I took up a fresh sheet and began to write resolutely. There was nothing but myself between him and the dark ocean. I had a sense of responsibility. If I spoke, would that motionless and suf-fering youth leap into the obscurity—clutch at the straw? I found out how difficult it may be sometimes to make a sound. There is a weird power in a spoken word. And why the devil not? I was asking myself persistently while I drove on with my writing. All at once, on the blank page, under the very point of the pen, the two figures of Chester and his antique partner, very distinct and complete, would dodge into view with stride and gestures, as if reproduced in the field of some optical toy. I would watch them for a while. No! They were too fantasmal and extravagant to enter into any one's fate. And a word carries far—very far—deals destruction through time as the bullets go flying through space. I said nothing; and he, out there with his back to the light, as if bound and gagged by all the invisible foes of man, made no stir and made no sound."

CHAPTER XVI.

"The time was coming when I should see him loved, trusted, admired, with a legend of strength and prowess forming round his names as though he had been the stuff of a hero. It's true—I assure you; as true as I'm sitting here talking about him in vain. He, on his side, had that faculty of beholding at a hint the face of his desire and the shape of his dream, without which the earth would know no lover and no adventurer. He captured much honour and an Arcadian happiness (I won't say anything about innocence) in the bush, and it was as good to him as the honour and the Arcadian happiness of the streets to another man. Felicity, felicity—how shall I say it?—is quaffed out of a golden cup in every latitude: the flavour is with you—with you alone, and you can make it as intoxicating as you please. He was of the sort that would drink deep, as you may guess from what went before. I found him, if not exactly intoxicated, then at least flushed with the elixir at his lips. He had not obtained it at once. There had been, as you know, a period of probation amongst infernal ship-chandlers, during which he had suffered and I had worried about—about—my trust—you may call it. I don't know that I am completely reassured now, after beholding him in all his brilliance. That was my last view of him—in a strong light, dominating, and yet in complete accord with his surroundings—with the life of the forests and with the life of men. I own that I was impressed, but I must admit to myself that after all this is not the lasting impression. He was protected by his isolation, alone of his own superior kind, in close touch with nature, that keeps faith on such easy terms with her lovers. But I cannot fix before my eye the image of his safety. I shall always remember him as seen through the open door of my room, taking, perhaps, too much to heart the mere consequences of his failure. I am pleased, of course, that some good—and even some splendour—came out of my endeavours; but at times it seems to me it would have been better for my peace of mind if I had not stood between him and Chester's confoundedly generous offer. I wonder what his exuberant imagination would have made of Walpole islet—that most hopelessly forsaken crumb of dry land on the face of the waters. It is not likely I would ever have heard, for, I must tell you, that Chester, after calling at some Australian port to patch up his brig-rigged sea-anachronism, steamed out into the Pacific with a crew of twenty-two hands all told, and the only news having a possible bearing upon the mystery of his fate was the news of a hurricane which is supposed to have swept in its course over the Walpole shoals, a month or so afterwards. Not a vestige of the Argonauts ever turned up; not a sound came out of the waste. Finis! The Pacific is the most discreet of live, hot-tempered oceans: the chilly Antarctic can keep a secret too, but more in the manner of a grave.

"And there is a sense of blessed finality in such discretion, which is what we all more or less sincerely are ready to admit—for what else is it that makes the idea of death supportable! End! Finis! the potent word that exorcises from the house of life the haunting shadow of fate. This is what—notwithstanding the testimony of my eyes and his own earnest assurances—I miss when I look back upon Jim's success. While there's life there is hope, truly; but there is fear too. I don't mean to say that I regret my action, nor will I pretend that I can't sleep o' nights in consequence; still the idea obtrudes itself that he made so much of his disgrace while it is the guilt alone that matters. He was not—if I may say so—clear to me. He was not clear. And there is a suspicion he was not clear to himself either. There were his fine sensibilities, his fine feelings, his fine longings—a sort of sublimated, idealised selfishness. He was—if you allow me to say so—very fine; very fine— and very unfortunate. A little coarser nature would not have borne the strain; it would have had to come to terms with itself—with a sigh, with a grunt, or even a guffaw; a still coarser one would have remained invulnerably ignorant and completely uninteresting.

"But he was too interesting or too unfortunate to be thrown to the dogs, or even to Chester. I felt this while I sat with my face over the paper and he fought and gasped, struggling for his breath in that terribly stealthy way, in my room; I felt it when he rushed out on the verandah as if to fling himself over—and didn't; I felt it more and more all the time he remained outside, faintly lighted on the background of night, as if standing on the shore of a sombre and hopeless sea.

"An abrupt heavy rumble made me lift my head. The noise seemed to roll away, and suddenly a searching and violent glare fell on the blind face of the night. The sustained and dazzling flickers seemed to last for an unconscionable time. The growl of the thunder increased steadily while I looked at him, distinct and black, planted solidly upon the shores of a sea of light. At the moment of greatest brilliance the darkness leaped back with a culminating crash, and he vanished before my dazzled eyes as utterly as though he had been blown to atoms. A blustering sigh passed; furious hands seemed to tear at the shrubs, shake the tops of the trees below, slam doors, break window-panes all along the front of the building. He stepped in, closing the door behind him, and found me bending over the table: my sudden anxiety as to what he would say was very great, and akin to a fright. 'May I have a cigarette?' he asked. I gave a push to the box without raising my head. 'I want—want—tobacco,' he muttered. I became extremely buoyant. 'Just a moment,' I grunted pleasantly. He took a few steps here and there. 'That's over,' I heard him say. A single distant clap of thunder came from the sea like a gun of distress. 'The monsoon breaks up early this year,' he remarked conversationally, somewhere behind me. This encouraged me to turn round, which I did as soon as I had finished addressing the last envelope. He was smoking greedily in the middle of the room, and though he heard the stir I made, he remained with his back to me for a time.

"'Come—I carried it off pretty well,' he said, wheeling suddenly. 'Something's paid off—not much. I wonder what's to come.' His face did not show any emotion, only it appeared a little darkened and swollen, as though he had been holding his breath. He smiled reluctantly as it were, and went on while I gazed up at him mutely. . . . 'Thank you, though—your room—jolly convenient—for a chap—badly hipped.' . . . The rain pattered and swished in the garden; a water-pipe (it must have had a hole in it) performed just outside the window a parody of blubbering woe with funny sobs and gurgling lamentations, interrupted by jerky spasms of silence. . . . 'A bit of shelter,' he mumbled and ceased.

"A flash of faded lightning darted in through the black framework of the windows and ebbed out without any noise. I was thinking how I had best approach him (I did not want to be flung off again) when he gave a little laugh. 'No better than a vagabond now' . . . the end of the cigarette smouldered between his fingers . . . 'without a single—single,' he pronounced slowly; 'and yet . . .' He paused; the rain fell with redoubled violence. 'Some day one's bound to come upon some sort of chance to get it all back again. Must!' he whispered distinctly, glaring at my boots.

"I did not even know what it was he wished so much to regain, what it was he had so terribly missed. It might have been so much that it was impossible to say. A piece of ass's skin, according to Chester. . . . He looked up at me inquisitively. 'Perhaps. If life's long enough,' I muttered through my teeth with unreasonable animosity. 'Don't reckon too much on it.'

"'Jove! I feel as if nothing could ever touch me,' he said in a tone of sombre conviction. 'If this business couldn't knock me over, then there's no fear of there being not enough time to—climb out, and . . .' He looked upwards.

"It struck me that it is from such as he that the great army of waifs and strays is recruited, the army that marches down, down into all the gutters of the earth. As soon as he left my room, that 'bit of shelter,' he would take his place in the ranks, and begin the journey toward the bottomless pit. I at least had no illusions; but it was I, too, who a moment ago had been so sure of the power of words, and now was afraid to speak, in the same way one dares not move for fear of losing a slippery hold. It is when we try to grapple with another man's intimate need that we perceive how incomprehensible, wavering, and misty are the beings that share with us the sight of the stars and the warmth of the sun. It is as if loneliness were a hard and absolute condition of existence; the envelope of flesh and blood on which our eyes are fixed melts before the outstretched hand, and there remains only the capricious, unconsolable, and elusive spirit that no eye can follow, no hand can grasp. It was the fear of losing him that kept me silent, for it was borne upon me suddenly and with unaccountable force that should I let him slip away into the darkness I would never forgive myself.

"'Well. Thanks—once more. You've been—er—uncommonly—really there's no word to . . . Uncommonly! I don't know why, I am sure. I am afraid I don't feel as grateful as I would if the whole thing hadn't been so brutally sprung on me. Because at bottom . . . you, yourself . . .' He stuttered.

"'Possibly,' I struck in. He frowned.

"'All the same, one is responsible.' He watched me like a hawk.

"'And that's true, too,' I said.

"'Well. I've gone with it to the end, and I don't intend to let any man cast it in my teeth without—without—resenting it.' He clenched his fist.

"'There's yourself,' I said with a smile—mirthless enough, God knows—but he looked at me menacingly. 'That's my business,' he said. An air of indomitable resolution came and went upon his face like a vain and passing shadow. Next moment he looked a dear good boy in trouble, as before. He flung away the cigarette. 'Good-bye,' he said, with the sudden haste of a man who had lingered too long in view of a pressing bit of work waiting for him; and then for a second or so he made not the slightest movement. The downpour fell with the heavy uninterrupted rush of a sweeping flood, with a sound of unchecked overwhelming fury that called to one's mind the images of collapsing bridges, of uprooted trees, of undermined mountains. No man could breast the colossal and headlong stream that seemed to break and swirl against the dim stillness in which we were precariously sheltered as if on an island. The perforated pipe gurgled, choked, spat, and splashed in odious ridicule of a swimmer fighting for his life. 'It is raining,' I remonstrated, 'and I . . .' 'Rain or shine,' he began brusquely, checked himself, and walked to the window. 'Perfect deluge,' he muttered after a while: he leaned his forehead on the glass. 'It's dark, too.'

"'Yes, it is very dark,' I said.

"He pivoted on his heels, crossed the room, and had actually opened the door leading into the corridor before I leaped up from my chair. 'Wait,' I cried, 'I want you to . . .' 'I can't dine with you again to-night,' he flung at me, with one leg out of the room already. 'I haven't the slightest intention to ask you,' I shouted. At this he drew back his foot, but remained mistrustfully in the very doorway. I lost no time in entreating him earnestly not to be absurd; to come in and shut the door."

CHAPTER XVII.

"He came in at last; but I believe it was mostly the rain that did it; it was falling just then with a devastating violence which quieted down gradually while we talked. His manner was very sober and set; his bearing was that of a naturally taciturn man possessed by an idea. My talk was of the material aspect of his position; it had the sole aim of saving him from the degradation, ruin, and despair that out there close so swiftly upon a friendless, homeless man; I pleaded with him to accept my help; I argued reasonably: and every time I looked up at that absorbed smooth face, so grave and youthful, I had a disturbing sense of being no help but rather an obstacle to some mysterious, inexplicable, impalpable striving of his wounded spirit.

"'I suppose you intend to eat and drink and to sleep under shelter in the usual way,' I remember saying with irritation. 'You say you won't touch the money that is due to you.' . . . He came as near as his sort can to making a gesture of horror. (There was three weeks and five days' pay owing him as mate of the *Patna*.) 'Well, that's too little to matter anyhow; but what will you do to-morrow? Where will you turn? You must live . . .' 'That isn't the thing,' was the comment that escaped him under his breath. I ignored it, and went on combating what I assumed to be the scruples of an exaggerated delicacy. 'On every conceivable ground,' I concluded, 'you must let me help you.' 'You can't,' he said very simply and gently, and holding fast to some deep idea which I could detect shimmering like a pool of water in the dark, but which I despaired of ever approaching near enough to fathom. I surveyed his well-proportioned bulk. 'At any rate,' I said, 'I am able to help what I can see of you. I don't pretend to do more.' He shook his head sceptically without looking at me. I got very warm. 'But I can,' I insisted. 'I can do even more. I *am* doing more. I am trusting you . . .' 'The money . . .' he began. 'Upon my word you deserve being told to go to the devil,' I cried, forcing the note of indignation. He was startled, smiled, and I pressed my attack home. 'It isn't a question of money at all. You are too superficial,' I said (and at the same time I was thinking to myself: Well, here goes! And perhaps he is, after all). 'Look at the letter I want you to take. I am writing to a man of whom I've never asked a favour, and I am writing about you in terms that one only ventures to use when speaking of an intimate friend. I make myself unreservedly responsible for you. That's what I am doing. And really if you will only reflect a little what that means . . .'

"He lifted his head. The rain had passed away; only the water-pipe went on shedding tears with an absurd drip, drip outside the window. It was very quiet in the room, whose shadows huddled together in corners, away from the still flame of the candle flaring upright in the shape of a dagger; his face after a while seemed suffused by a reflection of a soft light as if the dawn had broken already.

"'Jove!' he gasped out. 'It is noble of you!'

"Had he suddenly put out his tongue at me in derision, I could not have felt more humiliated. I thought to myself—Serve me right for a sneaking humbug. . . . His eyes shone straight into my face, but I perceived it was not a mocking brightness. All at once he sprang into jerky agitation, like one of these flat wooden figures that are worked by a string. His arms went up, then came down with a slap. He became another man altogether. 'And I had never seen,' he shouted; then suddenly bit his lip and frowned. 'What a bally ass I've been,' he said very slow in an awed tone. . . . 'You are a brick,' he cried next in a muffled voice. He snatched my hand as though he had just then seen it for the first time, and dropped it at once. 'Why! this is what I—you—I . . .' he stammered, and then with a return of his old stolid, I may say mulish, manner he began heavily, 'I would be a brute now if I . . .' and then his voice seemed to break. 'That's all right,' I said. I was almost alarmed by this display of feeling, through which pierced a strange elation. I had pulled the string accidentally, as it were; I did not fully understand the working of the toy. 'I must go now,' he said. 'Jove! You *have* helped me. Can't sit still. The very thing . . .' He looked at me with puzzled admiration. 'The very thing . . .'

"Of course it was the thing. It was ten to one that I had saved him from starvation—of that peculiar sort that is almost invariably associated with drink. This was all. I had not a single illusion on that score, but looking at him, I allowed myself to wonder at the nature of the one he had, within the last three minutes, so evidently taken unto his bosom. I had forced into his hand the means to carry on decently the serious business of life, to get food, drink, and shelter of the customary kind, while his wounded spirit, like a bird with a broken wing, might hop and flutter into some hole, to die quietly of inanition there. This is what I had thrust upon him: a definitely small thing; and—behold!—by the manner of its reception it loomed in the dim light of the candle like a big, indistinct, perhaps a dangerous shadow. 'You don't mind me not saying anything appropriate,' he burst out. 'There isn't anything one could say. Last night already you have done me no end of good. Listening to me—you know. I give you my word I've thought more than once the top of my head would fly off . . .' He darted—positively darted—here and there, rammed his hands into his pockets, jerked them out again, flung his cap on his head. I had no idea it was in him to be so airily brisk. I thought of a dry leaf imprisoned in an eddy of wind, while a mysterious apprehension, a load of indefinite doubt, weighed me down in my chair. He stood stock-still, as if struck motionless by a discovery. 'You have given me confidence,' he declared soberly. 'Oh! for God's sake, my dear fellow—don't!' I entreated, as though he had hurt me. 'All right. I'll shut up now and henceforth. Can't prevent me thinking though. . . . Never mind! . . . I'll show yet . . .' He went to the door in a hurry, paused with his head down, and came back, stepping deliberately. 'I always thought that if a fellow could begin with a clean slate. . . . And now you . . . in a measure . . . yes . . . clean slate.' I waved my hand, and he marched out without looking back; the sound of his footfalls died out gradually behind the closed door—the unhesitating tread of a man walking in broad daylight.

"But as to me, left alone with the solitary candle, I remained strangely unenlightened. I was no longer young enough to behold at every turn the magnificence that besets our significant footsteps in good and in evil. I smiled to think that, after all, it was yet he, of us two, who had the light. And I felt sad. A clean slate, did he say? As if the initial word of each our destiny were not graven in imperishable characters upon the face of a rock."

CHAPTER XVIII.

"Six months afterwards my friend (he was a cynical, more than middle-aged bachelor, with a reputation for eccentricity, and owned a rice-mill) wrote to me, and judging, from the warmth of my recommendation, that I would like to hear, enlarged a little upon Jim's perfections. These were apparently of a quiet and effective sort. 'Not having been able so far to find more in my heart than a resigned toleration for any individual of my kind, I have lived till now alone in a house that even in this steaming climate could be considered as too big for one man. I have had him to live with me for some time past. It seems I haven't made a mistake.' It seemed to me on reading this letter that my friend had found in his heart more than tolerance for Jim,—that there were the beginnings of active liking. Of course he stated his grounds in a characteristic way. For one thing, Jim kept his freshness in the climate. Had he been a girl—my friend wrote—one could have said he was blooming—blooming modestly—like a violet, not like some of these blatant tropical flowers. He had been in the house for six weeks, and had not as yet attempted to slap him on the back, or address him as 'old boy,' or try to make him feel a superannuated fossil. He had nothing of the exasperating young man's chatter. He was good-tempered, had not much to say for himself, was not clever by any means, thank goodness—wrote my friend. It appeared, however, that Jim was clever enough to be quietly appreciative of his wit, while, on the other hand, he amused him by his naïveness. 'The dew is yet on him, and since I had the bright idea of giving him a room in the house and having him at meals I feel less withered myself. The other day he took it into his head to cross the room with.no other purpose but to open a door for me; and I felt more in touch with mankind than I had been for years. Ridiculous, isn't it? Of course I guess there is something—some awful little scrape—which you know all about—but if I am sure that it is terribly heinous, I fancy one could manage to forgive it. For my part, I declare I am unable to imagine him guilty of anything much worse than robbing an orchard. *Is it* much worse? Perhaps you ought to have told me; but it is such a long time since we both turned saints that you may have forgotten we too had sinned in our time? It may be that some day I shall have to ask you, and then I shall expect to be told. I don't care to question him myself till I have some idea what it is. Moreover, it's too soon as yet. Let him open the door a few times more for me. . . .' Thus my friend. I was trebly pleased—at Jim's shaping so well, at the tone of the letter, at my own cleverness. Evidently I had known what I was doing. I had read characters aright, and so on. And what if something unexpected and wonderful were to come of it? That evening, reposing in a deck-chair under the shade of my own poop awning (it was in Hong-Kong harbour), I laid on Jim's behalf the first stone of a castle in Spain.

"I made a trip to the northward, and when I returned I found another letter from my friend waiting for me. It was the first envelope I tore open. 'There are no spoons missing, as far as I know,' ran the first line; 'I haven't been interested enough to inquire. He is gone, leaving on the breakfast-table a formal little note of apology, which is either silly or heartless. Probably both—and it's all one to me. Allow me to say, lest you should have some more mysterious young men in reserve, that I have shut up shop, definitely and for ever. This is the last eccentricity I shall be guilty of. Do not imagine for a moment that I care a hang; but he is very much regretted at tennis-parties, and for my own sake I've told a plausible lie at the club. . . .' I flung the letter aside and started looking through the batch on my table, till I came upon Jim's handwriting. Would you believe it? One chance in a hundred! But it is always that hundredth chance! That little second engineer of the *Patna* had turned up in a more or less destitute state and got a temporary job of looking after the machinery of the mill. 'I couldn't stand the familiarity of the little beast,' Jim wrote from a seaport seven hundred miles south of the place where he should have been in clover. 'I am now for the time with Egström & Blake, ship-chandlers, as their—well—runner, to call the thing by its right name. For reference I gave them your name, which they know of course, and if you could write a word in my favour it would be a permanent employment.' I was utterly crushed under the ruins of my castle, but of course I wrote as desired. Before the end of the year my new charter took me that way, and I had an opportunity of seeing him.

"He was still with Egström & Blake, and we met in what they called 'our parlour' opening out of the store. He had that moment come in from boarding a ship, and confronted me head down, ready for a tussle. 'What have you got to say for yourself?' I began as soon as we had shaken hands. 'What I wrote you—nothing more,' he said stubbornly. 'Did the fellow blab—or what?' I asked. He looked up at me with a troubled smile. 'Oh no! He didn't. He made it a kind of confidential business between us. He was most damnably mysterious whenever I came over to the mill; he would wink at me in a respectful manner—as much as to say we know what we know. Infernally fawning and familiar—and that sort of thing . . .' He threw himself into a chair and stared down his legs. 'One day we happened to be alone and the fellow had the cheek to say, "Well, Mr James"—I was called Mr James there as if I had been the son—"Here we are together once more. This is better than the old ship—ain't it?" . . . Wasn't it appalling, eh? I looked at him, and he put on a knowing air. "Don't you be uneasy, sir," he says. "I know a gentleman when I see one, and I know how a gentleman feels. I hope, though, you will be keeping me on this job. I had a hard time of it too, along of that rotten old *Patna* racket." Jove! It was awful. I don't know what I should have said or done if I had not just then heard Mr. Denver calling me in the passage. It was tiffin-time, and we walked together across the yard and through the garden to the bungalow. He began to chaff me in his kindly way . . . I believe he liked me . . .

"Jim was silent for a while.

"'I know he liked me. That's what made it so hard. Such a splendid man! . . . That morning he slipped his hand under my arm. . . . He, too, was familiar with me.' He burst into a short laugh, and dropped his chin on his breast. 'Pah! When I remembered how that mean little beast had been talking to me,' he began suddenly in a vibrating voice, 'I couldn't bear to think of myself . . . I suppose you know . . .' I nodded . . . 'More like a father,' he cried; his voice sank. 'I would have had to tell him. I couldn't let it go on—could I?' 'Well?' I murmured, after waiting a while. 'I preferred to go,' he said slowly; 'this thing must be buried.'

"We could hear in the shop Blake upbraiding Egström in an abusive, strained voice. They had been associated for many years, and every day from the moment the doors were opened to the last minute before closing, Blake, a little man with sleek, jetty hair and unhappy, beady eyes, could be heard rowing his partner incessantly with a sort of scathing and plaintive fury. The sound of that everlasting scolding was part of the place like the other fixtures; even strangers would very soon come to disregard it completely unless it be perhaps to mutter. 'Nuisance,' or to get up suddenly and shut the door of the 'parlour.' Egström himself, a raw-boned, heavy Scandinavian, with a busy manner and immense blonde whiskers, went on directing his people, checking parcels, making out bills or writing letters at a stand-up desk in the shop, and comported himself in that clatter exactly as though he had been stone-deaf. Now and again he would emit a bothered perfunctory 'Sssh,' which neither produced nor was expected to produce the slightest effect. 'They are very decent to me here,' said Jim. 'Blake's a little cad, but Egström all right.' He stood up quickly, and walking with measured steps to a tripod telescope standing in the window and pointed at the roadstead, he applied his eye to it. 'There's that ship which had been becalmed outside all the morning has got a breeze now and is coming in,' he remarked patiently; 'I must go and board.' We shook hands in silence, and he turned to go. 'Jim!' I cried. He looked round with his hand on the lock. 'You—you have thrown away something like a fortune.' He came back to me all the way from the door. 'Such a splendid old chap,' he said. 'How could I? How could I?' His lips twitched. 'Here it does not matter.' 'Oh! you—you—' I began, and had to cast about for a suitable word, but before I became aware that there was no name that would just do, he was gone. I heard outside Egström's deep gentle voice saying cheerily, 'That's the Sarah W. Granger, Jimmy. You must manage to be first aboard;' and directly Blake struck in, screaming after the manner of an outraged cockatoo, 'Tell the captain we've got some of his mail here. That'll fetch him. D'ye hear, Mister What's-your-name?' And there was Jim answering Egström with something boyish in his tone. 'All right. I'll make a race of it.' He seemed to take refuge in the boat-sailing part of that sorry business.

"I did not see him again that trip, but on my next (I had a six months' charter) I went up to the store. Ten yards away from the door Blake's scolding met my ears, and when I came in he gave me a glance of utter wretchedness; Egström, all smiles, advanced, extending a large bony hand. 'Glad to see you, Captain. . . . Sssh. . . . Been thinking you were about due back here. What did you say, sir? . . . Sssh. . . . Oh! him! he has left us. Come into the parlour.' . . . After the slam of the door Blake's strained voice became faint, as the voice of one scolding desperately in a wilderness. . . . 'Put us to a great inconvenience, too. Used us badly—I must say . . .' 'Where's he gone to? Do you know?' I asked. 'No. It's no use asking either,' said Egström, standing bewhiskered and obliging before me with his arms hanging down his sides clumsily, and a thin silver watch-chain looped very low on a rucked-up blue serge waistcoat. 'A man like that don't go anywhere in particular.' I was too concerned at the news at ask for the explanation of that pronouncement, and he went on. 'He left—let's see—the very day a steamer with returning pilgrims from the Red Sea put in here with two blades of her propeller gone. Three weeks ago now.' 'Wasn't there something said about the *Patna* case?' I asked, fearing the worst. He gave a start, and looked at me as if I had been a sorcerer. 'Why, yes! How do you know? Some of them were talking about it here. There was a captain or two, the manager of Vanlo's engineering shop at the harbour, two or three others, and myself. Jim was in here too, having a sandwich and a glass of beer; when we are busy—you see, captain—there's no time for a proper tiffin. He was standing by this table eating sandwiches, and the rest of us were round the telescope watching that steamer come in; and by-and-by Vanlo's manager began to talk about the chief of the *Patna*; he had done some repairs for him once, and from that he went on to tell us what an old ruin she was, and the money that had been made out of her. He came to mention her last voyage, and then we all struck in. Some said one thing and some another—not much—what you or any other man might say; and there was some laughing. Captain O'Brien of the *Sarah W. Granger,* a large, noisy old man with a stick—he was sitting listening to us in this arm-chair here—he let drive suddenly with his stick at the floor, and roars out, "Skunks!" . . . Made us all jump. Vanlo's manager winks at us and asks, "What's the matter, Captain O'Brien?" "Matter! matter!" the old man began to shout; "what are you Injuns laughing at? It's no laughing matter. It's a disgrace to human natur'—that's what it is. I would despise being seen in the same room with one of those men. Yes, sir!" He seemed to catch my eye like, and I had to speak out of civility. "Skunks!" says I, "of course, Captain O'Brien, and I wouldn't care to have them here myself, so you're quite safe in this room, Captain O'Brien. Have a little something cool to drink." "Dam' your drink, Egström," says he, with a twinkle in his eye; "when I want a drink I will shout for it. I am going to quit. It stinks here now." At this all the others burst out laughing, and out they go after the old man. And then, sir, that blasted Jim he puts down the sandwich he had in his hand and walks round the table to me; there was his glass of beer poured out quite full. "I am off," he says—just like this. "It isn't half-past one yet," says I; "you might snatch a smoke first." I thought he meant it was time for him to go down to his work. When I understood what he was up to, my arms fell—so! Can't get a man like that every day, you know, sir; a regular devil for sailing a boat; ready to go out miles to sea to meet ships in any sort of weather. More than once a captain would come in here full of it, and the first thing he would say would be, "That's a reckless sort of a lunatic you've got for water-clerk, Egström. I was feeling my way in at daylight under short canvas when there comes flying out of the mist right under my forefoot a boat half under water, sprays going over the masthead, two frightened niggers on the bottom boards, a yelling fiend at the tiller. Hey! hey! Ship ahoy! ahoy! Captain! Hey! hey! Egström & Blake's man first to speak to you! Hey! hey! Egström & Blake! Hallo! hey! whoop! Kick the niggers—out reefs—a squall on at the time—shoots ahead whooping and yelling to me to make sail and he would give me a lead in—more like a demon than a man. Never saw a boat handled like that in all my life. Couldn't have been drunk—was he? Such a quiet, soft-spoken chap too—blush like a girl when he came on board.

. . . " I tell you, Captain Marlow, nobody had a chance against us with a strange ship when Jim was out. The other ship-chandlers just kept their old customers, and . . .'

"Egström appeared overcome with emotion.

"'Why, sir—it seemed as though he wouldn't mind going a hundred miles out to sea in an old shoe to nab a ship for the firm. If the business had been his own and all to make yet, he couldn't have done more in that way. And now . . . all at once . . . like this! Thinks I to myself: "Oho! a rise in the screw—that's the trouble—is it? All right," says I, "no need of all that fuss with me, Jimmy. Just mention your figure. Anything in reason." He looks at me as if he wanted to swallow something that stuck in his throat. "I can't stop with you." "What's that blooming joke?" I asks. He shakes his head, and I could see in his eye he was as good as gone already, sir. So I turned to him and slanged him till all was blue. "What is it you're running away from?" I asks. "Who has been getting at you? What scared you? You haven't as much sense as a rat; they don't clear out from a good ship. Where do you expect to get a better berth?—you this and you that." I made him look sick, I can tell you. "This business ain't going to sink," says I. He gave a big jump. "Good-bye," he says, nodding at me like a lord; "you ain't half a bad chap, Egström. I give you my word that if you knew my reasons you wouldn't care to keep me." "That's the biggest lie you ever told in your life," says I; "I know my own mind." He made me so mad that I had to laugh. "Can't you really stop long enough to drink this glass of beer here, you funny beggar, you?" I don't know what came over him; he didn't seem able to find the door; something comical, I can tell you, captain. I drank the beer myself. "Well, if you're in such a hurry, here's luck to you in your own drink," says I; "only, you mark my words, if you keep up this game you'll very soon find that the earth ain't big enough to hold you—that's all." He gave me one black look, and out he rushed with a face fit to scare little children.'

"Egström snorted bitterly, and combed one auburn whisker with knotty fingers. 'Haven't been able to get a man that was any good since. It's nothing but worry, worry, worry in business. And where might you have come across him, captain, if it's fair to ask?'

"'He was the mate of the *Patna* that voyage,' I said, feeling that I owed some explanation. For a time Egström remained very still, with his fingers plunged in the hair at the side of his face, and then exploded. 'And who the devil cares about that?' 'I daresay no one,' I began . . . 'And what the devil is he—anyhow—for to go on like this?' He stuffed suddenly his left whisker into his mouth and stood amazed. 'Jee!' he exclaimed, 'I told him the earth wouldn't be big enough to hold his caper.'"

CHAPTER XIX.

"I have told you these two episodes at length to show his manner of dealing with himself under the new conditions of his life. There were many others of the sort, more than I could count on the fingers of my two hands. They were all equally tinged by a high-minded absurdity of intention which made their futility profound and touching. To fling away your daily bread so as to get your hands free for a grapple with a ghost may be an act of prosaic heroism. Men had done it before (though we who have lived know full well that it is not the haunted soul but the hungry body that makes an outcast), and men who had eaten and meant to eat every day had applauded the creditable folly. He was indeed unfortunate, for all his recklessness could not carry him out from under the shadow. There was always a doubt of his courage. The truth seems to be that it is impossible to lay the ghost of a fact. You can face it or shirk it—and I have come across a man or two who could wink at their familiar shades. Obviously Jim was not of the winking sort; but what I could never make up my mind about was whether his line of conduct amounted to shirking his ghost or to facing him out.

"I strained my mental eyesight only to discover that, as with the complexion of all our actions, the shade of difference was so delicate that it was impossible to say. It might have been flight and it might have been a mode of combat. To the common mind he became known as a rolling stone, because this was the funniest part: he did after a time become perfectly known, and even notorious, within the circle of his wanderings (which had a diameter of, say, three thousand miles), in the same way as an eccentric character is known to a whole countryside. For instance, in Bankok, where he found employment with Yucker Brothers, charterers and teak merchants, it was almost pathetic to see him go about in sunshine hugging his secret, which was known to the very up-country logs on the river. Schomberg, the keeper of the hotel where he boarded, a hirsute Alsatian of manly bearing and an irrepressible retailer of all the scandalous gossip of the place, would, with both elbows on the table, impart an adorned version of the story to any guest who cared to imbibe knowledge along with the more costly liquors. 'And, mind you, the nicest fellow you could meet,' would be his generous conclusion; 'quite superior.' It says a lot for the casual crowd that frequented Schomberg's establishment that Jim managed to hang out in Bankok for a whole six months. I remarked that people, perfect strangers, took to him as one takes to a nice child. His manner was reserved, but it was as though his personal appearance, his hair, his eyes, his smile, made friends for him wherever he went. And, of course, he was no fool. I heard Siegmund Yucker (native of Switzerland), a gentle creature ravaged by a cruel dyspepsia, and so frightfully lame that his head swung through a quarter of a circle at every step he took, declare appreciatively that for one so young he was 'of great gabasidy,' as though it had been a mere question of cubic contents. 'Why not send him up country?' I suggested anxiously. (Yucker Brothers had concessions and teak forests in the interior.) 'If he has capacity, as you say, he will soon get hold of the work. And physically he is very fit. His health is always excellent.' 'Ach! It's a great ting in dis goundry to be vree vrom tispep-shia,' sighed poor Yucker enviously, casting a stealthy glance at the pit of his ruined stomach. I left him drumming pensively on his desk and muttering, 'Es ist ein idee. Es ist ein idee.' Unfortunately, that very evening an unpleasant affair took place in the hotel.

"I don't know that I blame Jim very much, but it was a truly regrettable incident. It belonged to the lamentable species of bar-room scuffles, and the other party to it was a cross-eyed Dane of sorts whose visiting-card recited under his misbegotten name: first lieutenant in the Royal Siamese Navy. The fellow, of course, was utterly hopeless at billiards, but did not like to be beaten, I suppose. He had had enough to drink to turn nasty after the sixth game, and make some scornful remark at Jim's expense. Most of the people there didn't hear what was said, and those who had heard seemed to have had all precise recollection scared out of them by the appalling nature of the consequences that immediately ensued. It was very lucky for the Dane that he could swim, because the room opened on a verandah and the Menam flowed below very wide and black. A boat-load of Chinamen, bound, as likely as not, on some thieving expedition, fished out the officer of the King of Siam, and Jim turned up at about midnight on board my ship without a hat. 'Everybody in the room seemed to know,' he said, gasping yet from the contest, as it were. He was rather sorry, on general principles, for what had happened, though in this case there had been, he said, 'no option.' But what dismayed him was to find the nature of his burden as well known to everybody as though he had gone about all that time carrying it on his shoulders. Naturally after this he couldn't remain in the place. He was universally condemned for the brutal violence, so unbecoming a man in his delicate position; some maintained he had been disgracefully drunk at the time; others criticised his want of tact. Even Schomberg was very much annoyed. 'He is a very nice young man,' he said argumentatively to me, 'but the lieutenant is a first-rate fellow too. He dines every night at my *table d'hôte*, you know. And there's a billiard-cue broken. I can't allow that. First thing this morning I went over with my apologies to the lieutenant, and I think I've made it all right for myself; but only think, captain, if everybody started such games! Why, the man might have been drowned! And here I can't run out into the next street and buy a new cue. I've got to write to Europe for them. No, no! A temper like that won't do!' . . . He was extremely sore on the subject.

"This was the worst incident of all in his—his retreat. Nobody could deplore it more than myself; for if, as somebody said hearing him mentioned, 'Oh yes! I know. He has knocked about a good deal out here,' yet he had somehow avoided being battered and chipped in the process. This last affair, however, made me seriously uneasy, because if his exquisite sensibilities were to go the length of involving him in pot-house shindies, he would lose his name of an inoffensive, if aggravating, fool, and acquire that of a common loafer. For all my confidence in him I could not help reflecting that in such cases from the name to the thing itself is but a step. I suppose you will understand that by that time I could not think of washing my hands of him. I took him away from Bankok in my ship, and we had a longish passage. It was pitiful to see how he shrank within himself. A seaman, even if a mere passenger, takes an interest in a ship, and looks at the sea-life around him with the critical enjoyment of a painter, for instance, looking at another man's work. In every sense of the expression he is 'on deck'; but my Jim, for the most part, skulked down below as though he had been a stowaway. He infecte⁴ me so that I avoided speaking on professional matters, such as would suggest themselves naturally to two sailors during a passage. For whole days we did not exchange a word; I felt extremely unwilling to give orders to my officers in his presence. Often, when alone with him on deck or in the cabin, we didn't know what to do with our eyes.

"I placed him with De Jongh, as you know, glad enough to dispose of him in any way, yet persuaded that his position was now growing intolerable. He had lost some of that elasticity which had enabled him to rebound back into his uncompromising position after every overthrow. One day, coming ashore, I saw him standing on the quay; the water of the roadstead and the sea in the offing made one smooth ascending plane, and the outermost ships at anchor seemed to ride motionless in the sky. He was waiting for his boat, which was being loaded at our feet with packages of small stores for some vessel ready to leave. After exchanging greetings, we remained silent—side by side. 'Jove!' he said suddenly, 'this is killing work.'

"He smiled at me; I must say he generally could manage a smile. I made no reply. I knew very well he was not alluding to his duties; he had an easy time of it with De Jongh. Nevertheless, as soon as he had spoken I became completely convinced that the work was killing. I did not even look at him. 'Would you like,' said I, 'to leave this part of the world altogether; try California or the West Coast? I'll see what I can do . . .' He interrupted me a little scornfully. 'What difference would it make?' . . . I felt at once convinced that he was right. It would make no difference; it was not relief he wanted; I seemed to perceive dimly that what he wanted, what he was, as it were, waiting for, was something not easy to define— something in the nature of an opportunity. I had given him many opportunities, but they had been merely opportunities to earn his bread. Yet what more could any man do? The position struck me as hopeless, and poor Brierly's saying recurred to me, 'Let him creep twenty feet underground and stay there.' Better that, I thought, than this waiting above ground for the impossible. Yet one could not be sure even of that. There and then, before his boat was three oars' lengths away from the quay, I had made up my mind to go and consult Stein in the evening.

"This Stein was a wealthy and respected merchant. His 'house' (because it was a house, Stein & Co., and there was some sort of partner who, as Stein said, 'looked after the Moluccas') had a large inter-island business, with a lot of trading posts established in the most out-of-the-way places for collecting the produce. His wealth and his respectability were not exactly the reasons why I was anxious to seek his advice. I desired to confide my difficulty to him because he was one of the most trustworthy men I had ever known. The gentle light of a simple, unwearied, as it were, and intelligent good-nature illumined his long hairless face. It had deep downward folds, and was pale as of a man who had always led a sedentary life— which was indeed very far from being the case. His hair was thin, and brushed back from a massive and lofty forehead. One fancied that at twenty he must have looked very much like what he was now at threescore. It was a student's face; only the eyebrows nearly all white, thick and bushy, together with the resolute searching glance that came from under them, were not in accord with his, I may say, learned appearance. He was tall and loose-jointed; his slight stoop, together with an innocent smile, made him appear benevolently ready to lend you his ear; his long arms with pale big hands had rare deliberate gestures of a pointing out, demonstrating kind. I speak of him at length, because under this exterior, and in conjunction with an upright and indulgent nature, this man possessed an intrepidity of spirit and a physical courage that could have been called reckless had it not been like a natural function of the body—say good digestion, for instance—completely unconscious of itself. It is sometimes said of a man that he carries his life in his hand. Such a saying would have been inadequate if applied to him; during the early part of his existence in the East he had been playing ball with it. All this was in the past, but I knew the story of his life and the origin of his fortune. He was also a naturalist of some distinction, or perhaps I should say a learned collector. Entomology was his special study. His collection of *Buprestidæ* and *Longicorns*— beetles all—horrible miniature monsters, looking malevolent in death and immobility, and his cabinet of butterflies, beautiful and hovering under the glass of cases of lifeless wings, had spread his fame far over the earth. The name of this merchant, adventurer, sometime adviser of a Malay sultan (to whom he never alluded otherwise than as 'my poor Mohammed Bonso'), had, on account of a few bushels of dead insects, become known to learned persons in Europe, who could have had no conception, and certainly would not have cared to know anything, of his life or character. I, who knew, considered him an eminently suitable person to receive my confidences about Jim's difficulties as well as my own."

CHAPTER XX.

"Late in the evening I entered his study, after traversing an imposing but empty dining-room very dimly lit. The house was silent. I was preceded by an elderly grim Javanese servant in a sort of livery of white jacket and yellow sarong, who, after throwing the door open, exclaimed low, 'O master!' and stepping aside, vanished in a mysterious way as though he had been a ghost only momentarily embodied for that particular service. Stein turned round with the chair, and in the same movement his spectacles seemed to get pushed up on his forehead. He welcomed me in his quiet and humorous voice. Only one corner of the vast room, the corner in which stood his writing-desk, was strongly lighted by a shaded reading-lamp, and the rest of the spacious apartment melted into shapeless gloom like a cavern. Narrow shelves filled with dark boxes of uniform shape and colour ran round the walls, not from floor to ceiling, but in a sombre belt about four feet broad. Catacombs of beetles. Wooden tablets were hung above at irregular intervals. The light reached one of them, and the word *Coleoptera* written in gold letters glittered mysteriously upon a vast dimness. The glass cases containing the collection of butterflies were ranged in three long rows upon slender-legged little tables. One of these cases had been removed from its place and stood on the desk, which was bestrewn with oblong slips of paper blackened with minute handwriting.

"'So you see me—so,' he said. His hand hovered over the case where a butterfly in solitary grandeur spread out dark bronze wings, seven inches or more across, with exquisite white veinings and a gorgeous border of yellow spots. 'Only one specimen like this they have in *your* London, and then—no more. To my small native town this my collection I shall bequeath. Something of me. The best.'

"He bent forward in the chair and gazed intently, his chin over the front of the case. I stood at his back. 'Marvellous,' he whispered, and seemed to forget my presence. His history was curious. He had been born in Bavaria, and when a youth of twenty-two had taken an active part in the revolutionary movement of 1848. Heavily compromised, he managed to make his escape, and at first found a refuge with a poor republican watchmaker in Trieste. From there he made his way to Tripoli with a stock of cheap watches to hawk about,—not a very great opening truly, but it turned out lucky enough, because it was there he came upon a Dutch traveller—a rather famous man, I believe, but I don't remember his name. It was that naturalist who, engaging him as a sort of assistant, took him to the East. They travelled in the Archipelago together and separately, collecting insects and birds, for four years or more. Then the naturalist went home, and Stein, having no home to go to, remained with an older trader he had come across in his journeys in the interior of Celebes—if Celebes may be said to have an interior. This old Scotsman, the only white man allowed to reside in the country at the time, was a privileged friend of the chief ruler of Wajo States, who was a woman. I often heard Stein relate how that chap, who was slightly paralysed on one side, had introduced him to the native court a short time before another stroke carried him off. He was a heavy man with a patriarchal white beard, and of imposing stature. He came into the council-hall where all the rajahs, pangerans, and headmen were assembled, with the queen, a fat wrinkled woman (very free in her speech, Stein said), reclining on a high couch under a canopy. He dragged his leg, thumping with his stick, and grasped Stein's arm, leading him right up to the couch. 'Look, queen, and you rajahs, this is my son,' he proclaimed in a stentorian voice. 'I have traded with your fathers, and when I die he shall trade with you and your sons.'

"By means of this simple formality Stein inherited the Scotsman's privileged position and all his stock-in-trade, together with a fortified house on the banks of the only navigable river in the country. Shortly afterwards the old queen, who was so free in her speech, died, and the country became disturbed by various pretenders to the throne. Stein joined the party of a younger son, the one of whom thirty years later he never spoke otherwise but as 'my poor Mohammed Bonso.' They both became the heroes of innumerable exploits; they had wonderful adventures, and once stood a siege in the Scotsman's house for a month, with only a score of followers against a whole army. I believe the natives talk of that war to this day. Meantime, it seems, Stein never failed to annex on his own account every butterfly or beetle he could lay hands on. After some eight years of war, negotiations, false truces, sudden outbreaks, reconciliation, treachery, and so on, and just as peace seemed at last permanently established; his 'poor Mohammed Bonso' was assassinated at the gate of his own royal residence while dismounting in the highest spirits on his return from a successful deer-hunt. This event rendered Stein's position extremely insecure, but he would have stayed perhaps had it not been that a short time afterwards he lost Mohammed's sister ('my dear wife the princess,' he used to say solemnly), by whom he had had a daughter—mother and child both dying within three days of each other from some infectious fever. He left the country, which this cruel loss had made unbearable to him. Thus ended the first and adventurous part of his existence. What followed was so different that, but for the reality of sorrow which remained with him, this strange past must have resembled a dream. He had a little money; he started life afresh, and in the course of years acquired a considerable fortune. At first he had travelled a good deal amongst the islands, but age had stolen upon him, and of late he seldom left his spacious house three miles out of town, with an extensive garden, and surrounded by stables, offices, and bamboo cottages for his servants and dependants, of whom he had many. He drove in his buggy every morning to town, where he had an office with white and Chinese clerks. He owned a small fleet of schooners and native craft, and dealt in island produce on a large scale. For the rest he lived solitary, but not misanthropic, with his books and his collection, classing and arranging specimens, corresponding with entomologists in Europe, writing up a descriptive catalogue of his treasures. Such was the history of the man whom I had come to consult upon Jim's case without any definite hope. Simply to hear what he would have to say would have been a relief. I was very anxious, but I respected, the intense, almost passionate, absorption with which he looked at a butterfly, as though on the bronze sheen of these frail wings, in the white tracings, in the gorgeous markings, he could see other things, an image of something as perishable and defying destruction as these delicate and lifeless tissues displaying a splendour unmarred by death.

"'Marvellous!' he repeated, looking up at me. 'Look! The beauty—but that is nothing—look at the accuracy, the harmony. And so fragile! And so strong! And so exact! This is Nature—the balance of colossal forces. Every star is so—and every blade of grass stands so—and the mighty Kosmos in perfect equilibrium produces—this. This wonder; this masterpiece of Nature—the great artist.'

"'Never heard an entomologist go on like this,' I observed cheerfully. 'Masterpiece! And what of man?'

"'Man is amazing, but he is not a masterpiece,' he said, keeping his eyes fixed on the glass case. 'Perhaps the artist was a little mad. Eh? What do you think? Sometimes it seems to me that man is come where he is not wanted, where there is no place for him; for if not, why should he want all the place? Why should he run about here and there making a great noise about himself, talking about the stars, disturbing the blades of grass? . . .

"'Catching butterflies,' I chimed in.

"He smiled, threw himself back in his chair, and stretched his legs. 'Sit down,' he said. 'I captured this rare specimen myself one very fine morning. And I had a very big emotion. You don't know what it is for a collector to capture such a rare specimen. You can't know.'

"I smiled at my ease in a rocking-chair. His eyes seemed to look far beyond the wall at which they stared; and he narrated how, one night, a messenger arrived from his 'poor Mohammed,' requiring his presence at the 'residenz'—as he called it—which was distant some nine or ten miles by a bridle-path over a cultivated plain, with patches of forest here and there. Early in the morning he started from his fortified house, after embracing his little Emma, and leaving the 'princess,' his wife, in command. He described how she came with him as far as the gate, walking with one hand on the neck of his horse; she had on a white jacket, gold pins in her hair, and a brown leather belt over her left shoulder with a revolver in it. 'She talked as women will talk,' he said, 'telling me to be careful, and to try to get back before dark, and what a great wickedness it was for me to go alone. We were at war, and the country was not safe; my men were putting up bullet-proof shutters to the house and loading their rifles, and she begged me to have no fear for her. She could defend the house against anybody till I returned. And I laughed with pleasure a little. I liked to see her so brave and young and strong. I too was young then. At the gate she caught hold of my hand and gave it one squeeze and fell back. I made my horse stand still outside till I heard the bars of the gate put up behind me. There was a great enemy of mine, a great noble—and a great rascal too—roaming with a band in the neighbourhood. I cantered for four or five miles; there had been rain in the night, but the mists had gone up, up—and the face of the earth was clean; it lay smiling to me, so fresh and innocent—like a little child. Suddenly somebody fires a volley—twenty shots at least it seemed to me. I hear bullets sing in my ear, and my hat jumps to the back of my head. It was a little intrigue, you understand. They got my poor Mohammed to send for me and then laid that ambush. I see it all in a minute, and I think— This wants a little management. My pony snort, jump, and stand, and I fall slowly forward with my head on his mane.

He begins to walk, and with one eye I could see over his neck a faint cloud of smoke hanging in front of a clump of bamboos to my left. I think— Aha! my friends, why you not wait long enough before you shoot? This is not yet *gelungen*. Oh no! I get hold of my revolver with my right hand—quiet—quiet. After all, there were only seven of these rascals. They get up from the grass and start running with their sarongs tucked up, waving spears above their heads, and yelling to each other to look out and catch the horse, because I was dead. I let them come as close as the door here, and then bang, bang, bang—take aim each time too. One more shot I fire at a man's back, but I miss. Too far already. And then I sit alone on my horse with the clean earth smiling at me, and there are the bodies of three men lying on the ground. One was curled up like a dog, another on his back had an arm over his eyes as if to keep off the sun, and the third man he draws up his leg very slowly and makes it with one kick straight again. I watch him very carefully from my horse, but there is no more—*bleibt ganz ruhig*—keep still, so. And as I looked at his face for some sign of life I observed something like a faint shadow pass over his forehead. It was the shadow of this butterfly. Look at the form of the wing. This species fly high with a strong flight. I raised my eyes and I saw him fluttering away. I think— Can it be possible? And then I lost him. I dismounted and went on very slow, leading my horse and holding my revolver with one hand and my eyes darting up and down and right and left, everywhere! At last I saw him sitting on a small heap of dirt ten feet away. At once my heart began to beat quick. I let go my horse, keep my revolver in one hand, and with the other snatch my soft felt hat off my head. One step. Steady. Another step. Flop! I got him! When I got up I shook like a leaf with excitement, and when I opened these beautiful wings and made sure what a rare and so extraordinary perfect specimen I had, my head went round and my legs became so weak with emotion that I had to sit on the ground. I had greatly desired to possess myself of a specimen of that species when collecting for the professor. I took long journeys and underwent great privations; I had dreamed of him in my sleep, and here suddenly I had him in my fingers— for myself! In the words of the poet' (he pronounced it 'boet')—

> "'So halt' ich's endlich denn in meinen Händen,
>   Und nenn' es in gewissem Sinne mein.'"

He gave to the last word the emphasis of a suddenly lowered voice, and withdrew his eyes slowly from my face. He began to charge a long-stemmed pipe busily and in silence, then, pausing with his thumb on the orifice of the bowl, looked again at me significantly.

"'Yes, my good friend. On that day I had nothing to desire; I had greatly annoyed my principal enemy; I was young, strong; I had friendship; I had the love' (he said 'lof') 'of woman, a child I had, to make my heart very full—and even what I had once dreamed in my sleep had come into my hand too!

"He struck a match, which flared violently. His thoughtful placid face twitched once.

"'Friend, wife, child,' he said slowly, gazing at the small flame—'phoo!' The match was blown out. He sighed and turned again to the glass case. The frail and beautiful wings quivered faintly, as if his breath had for an instant called back to life that gorgeous object of his dreams.

"'The work,' he began suddenly, pointing to the scattered slips, and in his usual gentle and cheery tone, 'is making great progress. I have been this rare specimen describing. . . . Na! And what is your good news?'

"'To tell you the truth, Stein,' I said with an effort that surprised me, 'I came here to describe a specimen. . . .'

"'Butterfly?' he asked, with an unbelieving and humorous eagerness.

"'Nothing so perfect,' I answered, feeling suddenly dispirited with all sorts of doubts. 'A man!'

"'Ach so!' he murmured, and his smiling countenance, turned to me, became grave. Then after looking at me for a while he said slowly, 'Well—I am a man too.'

"Here you have him as he was; he knew how to be so generously encouraging as to make a scrupulous man hesitate on the brink of confidence; but if I did hesitate it was not for long.

"He heard me out, sitting with crossed legs. Sometimes his head would disappear completely in a great eruption of smoke, and a sympathetic growl would come out from the cloud. When I finished he uncrossed his legs, laid down his pipe, leaned forward towards me earnestly with his elbows on the arms of his chair, the tips of his fingers together.

"'I understand very well. He is romantic.'

"He had diagnosed the case for me, and at first I was quite startled to find how simple it was; and indeed our conference resembled so much a medical consultation—Stein, of learned aspect sitting in an arm-chair before his desk; I, anxious, in another, facing him, but a little to one side—that it seemed natural to ask—

"'What's good for it?'

"'He lifted up a long forefinger.

"'There is only one remedy! One thing alone can us from being ourselves cure!' The finger came down on the desk with a smart rap. The case which he had made to look so simple before became if possible still simpler—and altogether hopeless. There was a pause. 'Yes,' said I, 'strictly speaking, the question is not how to get cured, but how to live.'

"He approved with his head, a little sadly as it seemed. 'Ja! ja! In general, adapting the words of your great poet: That is the question. . . .' He went on nodding sympathetically. . . . 'How to be! Ach! How to be.'

"He stood up with the tips of his fingers resting on the desk.

"'We want in so many different ways to be,' he began again. 'This magnificent butterfly finds a little heap of dirt and sits still on it; but man he will never on his heap of mud keep still. He want to be so, and again he want to be so.' . . . He moved his hand up, then down. . . . 'He wants to be a saint, and he wants to be a devil—and every time he shuts his eyes he sees himself as a very fine fellow—so fine as he can never be. . . . In a dream. . . .'

"He lowered the glass lid, the automatic lock clicked sharply, and taking up the case in both hands he bore it religiously away to its place, passing out of the bright circle of the lamp into the ring of fainter light—into shapeless dusk at last. It had an odd effect—as if these few steps had carried him out of this concrete and perplexed world. His tall form, as though robbed of its substance, hovered noiselessly over invisible things with stooping and indefinite movements; his voice, heard in that remoteness where he could be glimpsed mysteriously busy with immaterial cares, was no longer incisive, seemed to roll voluminous and grave—mellowed by distance.

"'And because you not always can keep your eyes shut there comes the real trouble—the heart pain—the world pain. I tell you, my friend, it is not good for you to find you cannot make your dream come true, for the reason that you not strong enough are, or not clever enough. *Ja!* . . . And all the time you are such a fine fellow too! *Wie? Was? Gott in Himmel!* How can that be? Ha! ha! ha!'

"The shadow prowling amongst the graves of butterflies laughed boisterously.

"'Yes! Very funny this terrible thing is. A man that is born falls into a dream like a man who falls into the sea. If he tries to climb out into the air as inexperienced people endeavour to do, he drowns—*nicht wahr?* . . . No! I tell you! The way is to the destructive element submit yourself, and with the exertions of your hands and feet in the water make the deep, deep sea keep you up. So if you ask me—how to be?'

"His voice leaped up extraordinarily strong, as though away there in the dusk he had been inspired by some whisper of knowledge. 'I will tell you! For that too there is only one way.'

"With a hasty swish swish of his slippers he loomed up in the ring of faint light, and suddenly appeared in the bright circle of the lamp. His extended hand aimed at my breast like a pistol; his deep-set eyes seemed to pierce through me, but his twitching lips uttered no word, and the austere exaltation of a certitude seen in the dusk vanished from his face. The hand that had been pointing at my breast fell, and by-and-by, coming a step nearer, he laid it gently on my shoulder. There were things, he said mournfully, that perhaps could never be told, only he had lived so much alone that sometimes he forgot—he forgot. The light had destroyed the assurance which had inspired him in the distant shadows. He sat down and, with both elbows on the desk, rubbed his forehead. 'And yet it is true—it is true. In the destructive element immerse.' . . . He spoke in a subdued tone, without looking at me, one hand on each side of his face. 'That was the way. To follow the dream, and again to follow the dream—and so—*ewig*—*usque ad finem*. . . .' The whisper of his conviction seemed to open before me a vast and uncertain expanse, as of a crepuscular horizon on a plain at dawn—or was it, perchance, at the coming of the night? One had not the courage to decide; but it was a charming and deceptive light, throwing the impalpable poesy of its dimness over pitfalls—over graves. His life had begun in sacrifice, in enthusiasm for generous ideas; he had travelled very far, on various ways, on strange paths, and whatever he followed it had been without faltering, and therefore without shame and without regret. In so far he was right. That was the way, no doubt. Yet for all that the great plain on which men wander amongst graves and pitfalls remained very desolate under the impalpable poesy of its crepuscular light, overshadowed in the centre, circled with a bright edge as if surrounded by an abyss full of flames. When at last I broke the silence it was to express the opinion that no one could be more romantic than himself.

"He shook his head slowly, and afterwards looked at me with a patient and inquiring glance. It was a shame, he said. There we were sitting and talking like two boys, instead of putting our heads together to find something practical—a practical remedy—for the evil—for the great evil—he repeated, with a humorous and indulgent smile. For all that, our talk did not grow more practical. We avoided pronouncing Jim's name as though we had tried to keep flesh and blood out of our discussion, or he were nothing but an erring spirit, a suffering and nameless shade. 'Na!' said Stein, rising. 'To-night you sleep here, and in the morning we shall do something practical—practical. . . .' He lit a two-branched candlestick and led the way. We passed through empty dark rooms, escorted by gleams from the lights Stein carried. They glided along the waxed floors, sweeping here and there over the polished surface of a table, leaped upon a fragmentary curve of a piece of furniture, or flashed perpendicularly in and out of distant mirrors, while the forms of two men and the flicker of two flames could be seen for a moment stealing silently across the depths of a crystalline void. He walked slowly a pace in advance with stooping courtesy; there was a profound, as it were a listening, quietude on his face; the long flaxen locks mixed with white threads were scattered thinly upon his slightly bowed neck.

"'He is romantic—romantic,' he repeated. 'And that is very bad—very bad. . . . Very good, too,' he added. 'But is he?' I queried.

"'Gewiss,' he said, and stood still holding up the candelabrum, but without looking at me. 'Evident! What is it that by inward pain makes him know himself? What is it that for you and me makes him—exist?'

"At that moment it was difficult to believe in Jim's existence—starting from a country parsonage, blurred by crowds of men as by clouds of dust, silenced by the clashing claims of life and death in a material world—but his imperishable reality came to me with a convincing, with an irresistable force! I saw it vividly, as though in our progress through the lofty silent rooms amongst fleeting gleams of light and the sudden revelations of human figures stealing with flickering flames within unfathomable and pellucid depths, we had approached nearer to absolute Truth, which, like Beauty itself, floats elusive, obscure, half submerged, in the silent still waters of mystery. 'Perhaps he is,' I admitted with a slight laugh, whose unexpectedly loud reverberation made me lower my voice directly; 'but I am sure you are.' With his head dropping on his breast and the light held high he began to walk again. 'Well—I exist too,' he said.

"He preceded me. My eyes followed his movements, but what I did see was not the head of the firm, the welcome guest at afternoon receptions, the correspondent of learned societies, the entertainer of stray naturalists; I saw only the reality of his destiny, which he had known how to follow with unfaltering footsteps, that life began in humble surroundings, rich in generous enthusiasms, in friendship, love, war—in all the exalted elements of romance. At the door of my room he faced me. 'Yes,' I said, as though carrying on a discussion, 'and amongst other things you dreamed foolishly of a certain butterfly; but when one fine morning your dream came in your way you did not let the splendid opportunity escape. Did you? Whereas he . . .' Stein lifted his hand. 'And do you know how many opportunities I let escape; how many dreams I had lost that had come in my way?' He shook his head regretfully. 'It seems to me that some would have been very fine—if I had made them come true. Do you know how many? Perhaps I myself don't know.' 'Whether his were fine or not,' I said, 'he knows of one which he certainly did not catch.' 'Everybody knows of one or two like that,' said Stein; 'and that is the trouble—the great trouble. . . .'

"He shook hands on the threshold, peered into my room under his raised arm. 'Sleep well. And to-morrow we must do something practical—practical. . . .'

"Though his own room was beyond mine I saw him return the way he came. He was going back to his butterflies."

CHAPTER XXI.

"I don't suppose any of you had ever heard of Patusan?" Marlow resumed, after a silence occupied in the careful lighting of a cigar. "It does not matter; there's many a heavenly body in the lot crowding upon us of a night that mankind had never heard of, it being outside the sphere of its activitives and of no earthly importance to anybody but to the astronomers who are paid to talk learnedly about its composition, weight, path—the irregularities of its conduct, the aberrations of its light,—a sort of scientific scandal-mongering. Thus with Patusan. It was referred to knowingly in the inner government circles in Batavia, especially as to its irregularities and aberrations, and it was known by name to some few, very few, in the mercantile world. Nobody, however, had been there, and I suspect no one desired to go there in person, just as an astronomer, I should fancy, would strongly object to being transported into a distant heavenly body, where, parted from his earthly emoluments, he would be bewildered by the view of an unfamiliar heavens. However, neither heavenly bodies nor astronomers have anything to do with Patusan. It was Jim who went there. I only meant you to understand that had Stein arranged to send him into a star of the fifth magnitude the change could not have been greater. He left his earthly failings behind him and that sort of reputation he had, and there was a totally new set of conditions for his imaginative faculty to work upon. Entirely new, entirely remarkable. And he got hold of them in a remarkable way.

"Stein was the man who knew more about Patusan than anybody else. More than was known in the government circles I suspect. I have no doubt he had been there, either in his butterfly-hunting days or later on, when he tried in his incorrigible way to season with a pinch of romance the fattening dishes of his commercial kitchen. There were very few places in the Archipelago he had not seen in the original dusk of their being, before light (and even electric light) had been carried into them for the sake of better morality and—and—well—the greater profit too. It was at breakfast of the morning following our talk about Jim that he mentioned the place, after I had quoted poor Brierly's remark: "Let him creep twenty feet underground and stay there.' He looked up at me with interested attention as though I had been a rare insect. 'This could be done too,' he remarked, sipping his coffee. 'Bury him in some sort,' I explained. 'One doesn't like to do it of course, but it would be the best thing, seeing what he is.' 'Yes; he is young,' Stein mused. 'The youngest human being now in existence,' I affirmed. 'Schön. There's Patusan,' he went on in the same tone. . . . 'And the woman is dead now,' he added incomprehensibly.

"Of course I don't know that story; I can only guess that once before Patusan had been used as a grave for some sin, transgression, or misfortune. It is impossible to suspect Stein. The only woman that had ever existed for him was the Malay girl he called 'My wife the princess,' or, more rarely, in moments of expansion, 'the mother of my Emma.' Who was the woman he had mentioned in connection with Patusan I can't say; but from his allusions I understand she had been an educated and very good-looking Dutch-Malay girl, with a tragic or perhaps only a pitiful history, whose most painful part no doubt was her marriage with a Malacca Portuguese who had been clerk in some commercial house in the Dutch colonies.

I gathered from Stein that this man was an unsatisfactory person in more ways than one, all being more or less indefinite and offensive. It was solely for his wife's sake that Stein had appointed him manager of Stein & Co.'s trading post in Patusan; but commercially the arrangement was not a success, at any rate for the firm, and now the woman had died, Stein was disposed to try another agent there. The Portuguese, whose name was Cornelius, considered himself a very deserving but ill-used person, entitled by his abilities to a better position. This man Jim would have to relieve. 'But I don't think he will go away from the place,' remarked Stein. 'That has nothing to do with me. It was only for the sake of the woman that I . . . But as I think there is a daughter left, I shall let him, if he likes to stay, keep the old house.

"Patusan is a remote district of a native-ruled State, and the chief settlement bears the same name. At a point on the river about forty miles from the sea, where the first houses come into view, there can be seen rising above the level of the forests the summits of two steep hills very close together, and separated by what looks like a deep fissure, the cleavage of some mighty stroke. As a matter of fact, the valley between is nothing but a narrow ravine; the appearance from the settlement is of one irregularly conical hill split in two, and with the two halves leaning slightly apart. On the third day after the full, the moon, as seen from the open space in front of Jim's house (he had a very fine house in the native style when I visited him), rose exactly behind these hills, its diffused light at first throwing the two masses into intensely black relief, and then the nearly perfect disc, glowing ruddily, appeared, gliding upwards between the sides of the chasm, till it floated away above the summits, as if escaping from a yawning grave in gentle triumph. 'Wonderful effect,' said Jim by my side. 'Worth seeing. Is it not?'

"And this question was put with a note of personal pride that made me smile, as though he had had a hand in regulating that unique spectacle. He had regulated so many things in Patusan! Things that would have appeared as much beyond his control as the motions of the moon and the stars.

"It was inconceivable. That was the distinctive quality of the part into which Stein and I had tumbled him unwittingly, with no other notion than to get him out of the way; out of his own way, be it understood. That was our main purpose, though, I own, I might have had another motive which had influenced me a little. I was about to go home for a time; and it may be I desired, more than I was aware of myself, to dispose of him—to dispose of him, you understand—before I left. I was going home, and he had come to me from there, with his miserable trouble and his shadowy claim, like a man panting under a burden in a mist. I cannot say I had ever seen him distinctly—not even to this day, after I had my last view of him; but it seemed to me that the less I understood the more I was bound to him in the name of that doubt which is the inseparable part of our knowledge. I did not know so much more about myself. And then, I repeat, I was going home—to that home distant enough for all its hearthstones to be like one hearthstone, by which the humblest of us has the right to sit. We wander in our thousands over the face of the earth, the illustrious and the obscure, earning beyond the seas our fame, our money, or only a crust of bread; but it seems to me that for each of us going home must be like going to render an account. We return to face our superiors, our kindred, our friends—those whom we obey, and those whom we love; but even they who have neither, the most free, lonely, irresponsible and bereft of ties,— even those for whom home holds no dear face, no familiar voice,—even they have to meet the spirit that dwells within the land, under its sky, in its air, in its valleys, and on its rises, in its fields, in its waters and its trees—a mute friend, judge, and inspirer. Say what you like, to get its joy, to breathe its peace, to face its truth, one must return with a clear conscience. All this may seem to you sheer sentimentalism; and indeed very few of us have the will or the capacity to look consciously under the surface of familiar emotions. There are the girls we love, the men we look up to, the tenderness, the friendships, the opportunities, the pleasures! But the fact remains that you must touch your reward with clean hands, lest it turn to dead leaves, to thorns, in your grasp. I think it is the lonely, without a fireside or an affection they may call their own, those who return not to a dwelling but to the land itself, to meet its disembodied, eternal, and unchangeable spirit—it is those who understand best its severity, its saving power, the grace of its secular right to our fidelity, to our obedience. Yes! few of us understand, but we all feel it though, and I say *all* without exception, because those who do not feel do not count. Each blade of grass has its spot on earth whence it draws its life, its strength; and so is man rooted to the land from which he draws his faith together with his life. I don't know how much Jim understood; but I know he felt confusedly but powerfully, the demand of some such truth or some such illusion—I don't care how you call it, there is so little difference, and the difference means so little. The thing is that in virtue of his feeling he mattered. He would never go home now. Not he. Never. Had he been capable of picturesque manifestations he would have shuddered at the thought and made you shudder too. But he was not of that sort, though he was expressive enough in his way. Before the idea of going home he would grow desperately stiff and immovable, with lowered chin and pouted lips, and with those candid blue eyes of his glowering darkly under a frown, as if before something unbearable, as if before something revolting. There was imagination in that hard skull of his, over which the thick clustering hair fitted like a cap. As to me, I have no imagination (I would be more certain about him today, if I had), and I do not mean to imply that I figured to myself the spirit of the land uprising above the white cliffs of Dover, to ask me what I—returning with no bones broken, so to speak—had done with my very young brother. I could not make such a mistake. I knew very well he was of those about whom there is no inquiry; I had seen better men go out, disappear, vanish utterly, without provoking a sound of curiosity or sorrow. The spirit of the land, as becomes the ruler of great enterprises, is careless of innumerable lives. Woe to the stragglers! We exist only in so far as we hang together. He had straggled in a way; he had not hung on; but he was aware of it with an intensity that made him touching, just as man's more intense life makes his death more touching than the death of a tree. I happened to be handy, and I happened to be touched. That's all there is to it. I was concerned as to the way he would go out. It would have hurt me if, for instance, he had taken to drink. The earth is so small that I was afraid of, some day, being waylaid by a blear-eyed, swollen-faced, besmirched loafer, with no soles to his canvas shoes, and with a flutter of rags about the elbows, who, on the strength of old acquaintance, would ask for a loan of five dollars. You know the awful jaunty bearing of these scarecrows coming to you from a decent past, the rasping careless voice, the half-averted impudent glances—those meetings more trying to a man who believes in the solidarity of our lives than the sight of an impenitent death-bed to a priest. That, to tell you the truth, was the only danger I could see for him and for me; but I also mistrusted my want of imagination. It might even come to something worse, in some way it was beyond my powers of fancy to foresee. He wouldn't let me forget how imaginative he was, and your imaginative people swing farther in any direction, as if given a longer scope of cable in the uneasy anchorage of life. They do. They take to drink too. It may be I was belittling him by such a fear. How could I tell? Even Stein could say no more than that he was romantic. I only knew he was one of us. And what business had he to be romantic? I am telling you so much about my own instinctive feelings and bemused reflections because there remains so little to be told of him. He existed for me, and after all it is only through me that he exists for you. I've led him out by the hand; I have paraded him before you. Were my commonplace fears unjust? I won't say—not even now. You may be able to tell better, since the proverb has it that the onlookers see most of the game. At any rate, they were superfluous. He did not go out, not at all; on the contrary, he came on wonderfully, came on straight as a die and in excellent form, which showed that he could stay as well as spurt. I ought to be delighted, for it is a victory in which I had taken my part; but I am not so pleased as I would have expected to be. I ask myself whether his rush had really carried him out of that mist in which he loomed interesting if not very big, with floating outlines—a straggler yearning inconsolably for his humble place in the ranks. And besides, the last word is not said,—probably shall never be said. Are not our lives too short for that full utterance which through all our stammerings is of course our only and abiding intention? I have given up expecting those last words, whose ring, if they could only be pronounced, would shake both heaven and earth. There is never time to say our last word—the last word of our love, of our desire, faith, remorse, submission, revolt. The heaven and the earth must not be shaken, I suppose—at least, not by us who know so many truths about either. My last words about Jim shall be few. I affirm he had achieved greatness; but the thing would be dwarfed in the telling, or rather in the hearing. Frankly, it is not my words that I mistrust but your minds. I could be eloquent were I not afraid you fellows had starved your imaginations to feed your bodies. I do not mean to be offensive; it is respectable to have no illusions—and safe—and profitable—and dull. Yet you too in your time must have known the intensity of life, that light of glamour created in the shock of trifles, as amazing as the glow of sparks struck from a cold stone—and as short-lived, alas!"

CHAPTER XXII.

"The conquest of love, honour, men's confidence—the pride of it, the power of it, are fit materials for a heroic tale; only our minds are struck by the externals of such a success, and to Jim's successes there were no externals. Thirty miles of forest shut it off from the sight of an indifferent world, and the noise of the white surf along the coast overpowered the voice of fame. The stream of civilisation, as if divided on a headland a hundred miles north of Patusan, branches east and south-east, leaving its plains and valleys, its old trees and its old mankind, neglected and isolated, such as an insignificant and crumbling islet between the two branches of a mighty, devouring stream. You find the name of the country pretty often in collections of old voyages. The seventeenth-century traders went there for pepper, because the passion for pepper seemed to burn like a flame of love in the breast of Dutch and English adventurers about the time of James the First. Where wouldn't they go for pepper! For a bag of pepper they would cut each other's throats without hesitation, and would forswear their souls, of which they were so careful otherwise: the bizarre obstinacy of that desire made them defy death in a thousand shapes; the unknown seas, the loathsome and strange diseases; wounds, captivity, hunger, pestilence, and despair. It made them great! By heavens! it made them heroic; and it made them pathetic too in their craving for trade with the inflexible death levying its toll on young and old. It seems impossible to believe that mere greed could hold men to such a steadfastness of purpose, to such a blind persistence in endeavour and sacrifice. And indeed those who adventured their persons and lives risked all they had for a slender reward. They left their bones to lie bleaching on distant shores, so that wealth might flow to the living at home. To us, their less tried successors, they appear magnified, not as agents of trade but as instruments of a recorded destiny, pushing out into the unknown in obedience to an inward voice, to an impulse beating in the blood, to a dream of the future. They were wonderful; and it must be owned they were ready for the wonderful. They recorded it complacently in their sufferings, in the aspect of the seas, in the customs of strange nations, in the glory of splendid rulers.

"In Patusan they had found lots of pepper, and had been impressed by the magnificence and the wisdom of the Sultan; but somehow, after a century of checkered intercourse, the country seems to drop gradually out of the trade. Perhaps the pepper had given out. Be it as it may, nobody cares for it now; the glory has departed, the Sultan is an imbecile youth with two thumbs on his left hand and an uncertain and beggarly revenue extorted from a miserable population and stolen from him by his many uncles.

"This of course I have from Stein. He gave me their names and a short sketch of life and character of each. He was as full of information about native States as an official report, but infinitely more amusing. He *had* to know. He traded in so many, and in some districts—as in Patusan, for instance—his firm was the only one to have an agency by special permit from the Dutch authorities. The Government trusted his discretion, and it was understood that he took all the risks. The men he employed understood that too, but he made it worth their while apparently. He was perfectly frank with me over the breakfast-table in the morning. As far as he was aware (the last news were thirteen months old he stated precisely), utter insecurity for life and property was the normal condition. There were in Patusan antagonistic forces, and one of them was Rajah Allang, the worst of the Sultan's uncles, the governor of the river, who did the extorting and the stealing, and ground down to the point of extinction the country-born Malays, who, utterly defenceless, had not even the resource of emigrating,—'for indeed,' as Stein remarked, 'where could they go, and how could they get away?' No doubt they did not even desire to get away. The world (which is circumscribed by lofty impassable mountains) has been given into the hand of the high-born, and *this* Rajah they knew: he was of their own royal house. I had the pleasure of meeting the gentleman later on. He was a dirty, little, used-up old man with evil eyes and a weak mouth, who swallowed an opium pill every two hours, and in defiance of common decency wore his hair uncovered and falling in wild stringy locks about his wizened grimy face. When giving audience he would clamber upon a sort of narrow stage erected in a hall like a ruinous barn with a rotten bamboo floor, through the cracks of which you could see twelve or fifteen feet below the heaps of refuse and garbage of all kinds lying under the house. That is where and how he received us when, accompanied by Jim, I paid him a visit of ceremony. There were about forty people in the room, and perhaps three times as many in the great courtyard below. There was constant movement, coming and going, pushing and murmuring, at our backs. A few youths in gay silks glared from the distance; the majority, slaves and humble dependents, were half naked, in ragged sarongs, dirty with ashes and mud-stains. I had never seen Jim look so grave, so self-possessed, in an impenetrable, impressive way. In the midst of these dark-faced men, his stalwart figure in white apparel, the gleaming clusters of his fair hair, seemed to catch all the sunshine that trickled through the cracks in the closed shutters of that dim hall, with its walls of mats and a roof of thatch. He appeared like a creature not only of another kind but of another essence. Had they not seen him come up in a canoe they might have thought he had descended upon them from the clouds. He did, however, come in a crazy dug-out, sitting (very still and with his knees together, for fear of overturning the thing)—sitting on a tin box—which I had lent him—nursing on his lap a revolver of the navy pattern—presented by me on parting—which, through an interposition of Providence, or through some wrong-headed notion, that was just like him, or else from sheer instinctive sagacity, he had decided to carry unloaded. That's how he ascended the Patusan river. Nothing could have been more prosaic and more unsafe, more extravagantly casual, more lonely. Strange, this fatality that would cast the complexion of a flight upon all his acts, of impulsive unreflecting desertion—of a jump into the unknown.

"It is precisely the casualness of it that strikes me most. Neither Stein nor I had a clear conception of what might be on the other side when we, metaphorically speaking, took him up and hove him over the wall with scant ceremony. At the moment I merely wished to achieve his disappearance; Stein characteristically enough had a sentimental motive. He had a notion of paying off (in kind, I suppose) the old debt he had never forgotten. Indeed he had been all his life especially friendly to anybody from the British Isles. His late benefactor, it is true, was a Scot—even to the length of being called Alexander M'Neil—and Jim came from a long way south of the Tweed; but at the distance of six or seven thousand miles Great Britain, though never diminished, looks foreshortened enough even to its own children to rob such details of their importance. Stein was excusable, and his hinted intentions were so generous that I begged him most earnestly to keep them secret for a time. I felt that no consideration of personal advantage should be allowed to influence Jim; that not even the risk of such influence should be run. We had to deal with another sort of reality. He wanted a refuge, and a refuge at the cost of danger should be offered him—nothing more.

"Upon every other point I was perfectly frank with him, and I even (as I believed at the time) exaggerated the danger of the undertaking. As a matter of fact I did not do it justice; his first day in Patusan was nearly his last—would have been his last if he had not been so reckless or so hard on himself and had condescended to load that revolver. I remember, as I unfolded our precious scheme for his retreat, how his stubborn but weary resignation was gradually replaced by surprise, interest, wonder, and by boyish eagerness. This was a chance he had been dreaming of. He couldn't think how he merited that I . . . He would be shot if he could see to what he owed . . . And it was Stein, Stein the merchant, who . . . but of course it was me he had to . . . " I cut him short. He was not articulate, and his gratitude caused me inexplicable pain. I told him that if he owed this chance to any one especially, it was to an old Scot of whom he had never heard, who had died many years ago, of whom little was remembered besides a roaring voice and a rough sort of honesty. There was really no one to receive his thanks. Stein was passing on to a young man the help he had received in his own young days, and I had done no more than to mention his name. Upon this he coloured, and, twisting a bit of paper in his fingers, he remarked bashfully that I had always trusted him.

"I admitted that such was the case, and added after a pause that I wished he had been able to follow my example. 'You think I don't?' he asked uneasily, and remarked in a mutter that one had to get some sort of show first; then brightening up, and in a loud voice he protested he would give me no occasion to regret my confidence, which—which . . .

"'Do not misapprehend,' I interrupted. 'It is not in your power to make me regret anything.' There would be no regrets; but if there were, it would be altogether my own affair: on the other hand, I wished him to understand clearly that this arrangement, this—this—experiment, was his own doing; he was responsible for it and no one else. 'Why? Why!' he stammered, 'this is the very thing that I' . . . I begged him not to be dense, and he looked more puzzled than ever. He was in a fair way to make life intolerable to himself. . . . 'Do you think so?' he asked disturbed; but in a moment added confidently, 'I was going on though. Was I not?' It was impossible to be angry with him: I could not help a smile, and told him that in the old days people who went on like this were on the way of becoming hermits in a wilderness. 'Hermits be hanged!' he commented with engaging impulsiveness. Of course he didn't mind a wilderness. . . . 'I was glad of it,' I said. That was where he would be going to. He would find it lively enough, I ventured to promise. 'Yes, yes,' he said keenly. He had shown a desire, I continued inflexibly, to go out and shut the door after him. . . . 'Did I?' he interrupted in a strange access of gloom that seemed to envelop him from head to foot like the shadow of a passing cloud. He was wonderfully expressive after all. Wonderfully! 'Did I?' he repeated bitterly. 'You can't say I made much noise about it. And I can keep it up too—only, confound it! you show me a door.' . . . 'Very well. Pass on,' I struck in. I could make him a solemn promise that it would be shut behind him with a vengeance. His fate, whatever it was, would be ignored, because the country, for all its rotten state, was not judged ripe for interference. Once he got in, it would be for the outside world as though he had never existed. He would have nothing but the soles of his two feet to stand upon, and he would have first to find his ground at that. 'Never existed—that's it, by Jove,' he murmured to himself. His eyes, fastened upon my lips, sparkled. If he had thoroughly understood the conditions, I concluded, he had better jump into the first gharry he could see and drive on to Stein's house for his final instructions. He flung out of the room before I had fairly finished speaking."

CHAPTER XXIII.

"He did not return till next morning. He had been kept to dinner and for the night. There never had been such a wonderful man as Mr Stein. He had in his pocket a letter for Cornelius ('the Johnnie who's going to get the sack,' he explained with a momentary drop in his elation), and he exhibited with glee a silver ring, such as natives use, worn down very thin and showing faint traces of chasing.

"This was his introduction to an old chap called Doramin—one of the principal men out there—a big pot—who had been Mr Stein's friend in that country where he had all these adventures. Mr Stein called him 'war-comrade.' War-comrade was good. Wasn't it? And didn't Mr Stein speak English wonderfully well? Said he had learned it in Celebes—of all places! That was awfully funny. Was it not? He did speak with an accent—a twang—did I notice? That chap Doramin had given him the ring. They had exchanged presents when they parted for the last time. Sort of promising eternal friendship. He called it fine—did I not? They had to make a dash for dear life out of the country when that Mohammed—Mohammed—What's-his-name had been killed. I knew the story, of course. Seemed a beastly shame, didn't it? . . .

"He ran on like this, forgetting his plate, with a knife and fork in hand (he had found me at tiffin), slightly flushed, and with his eyes darkened many shades, which was with him a sign of excitement. The ring was a sort of credential. ('It's like something you read of in books,' he threw in appreciatively), and Doramin would do his best for him. Mr Stein had been the means of saving that chap's life on some occasion; purely by accident, Mr Stein had said, but he—Jim—had his own opinion about that. Mr Stein was just the man to look out for such accidents. No matter. Accident or purpose, this would serve his turn immensely. Hoped to goodness the jolly old beggar had not gone off the hooks meantime. Mr Stein could not tell. There had been no news for more than a year; they were kicking up no end of an all-fired row amongst themselves, and the river was closed. Jolly awkward, this; but, no fear; he would manage to find a crack to get in.

"He impressed, almost frightened, me with his elated rattle. He was voluble like a youngster on the eve of a long holiday with a prospect of delightful scrapes, and such an attitude of mind in a grown man and in this connection had in it something phenomenal, a little mad, dangerous, unsafe. I was on the point of entreating him to take things seriously when he dropped his knife and fork (he had begun eating, or rather swallowing food, as it were, unconsciously), and began a search all round his plate. The ring! The ring! Where the devil . . . Ah! Here it was . . . He closed his big hand on it, and tried all his pockets one after another. Jove! wouldn't do to lose the thing. He meditated gravely over his fist. Had it? Would hang the bally affair round his neck! And he proceeded to do this immediately, producing a string (which looked like a bit of a cotton shoe-lace) for the purpose. There! That would do the trick! It would be the deuce if . . . He seemed to catch sight of my face for the first time, and it steadied him a little. I probably didn't realise, he said with a naïve gravity, how much importance he attached to that token. It meant a friend; and it is a good thing to have a friend. He knew something about that. He nodded at me expressively, but before my disclaiming gesture he leaned his head on his hand and for a while sat silent, playing thoughtfully with the bread-crumbs on the cloth . . . 'Slam the door—that was jolly well put,' he cried, and jumping up, began to pace the room, reminding me by the set of the shoulders, the turn of his head, the headlong and uneven stride, of that night when he had paced thus, confessing, explaining—what you will—but, in the last instance, living—living before me, under his own little cloud, with all his unconscious subtlety which could draw consolation from the very source of sorrow. It was the same mood, the same and different, like a fickle companion that to-day guiding you on the true path, with the same eyes, the same step, the same impulse, to-morrow will lead you hopelessly astray. His tread was assured, his straying, darkened eyes seemed to search the room for something. One of his footfalls somehow sounded louder than the other—the fault of his boots probably—and gave a curious impression of an invisible halt in his gait. One of his hands was rammed deep into his trousers' pocket, the other waved suddenly above his head. 'Slam the door!' he shouted. 'I've been waiting for that. I'll show yet . . . I'll . . . I'm ready for any confounded thing . . . I've been dreaming of it . . . Jove! Get out of this. Jove! This is luck at last . . . You wait. I'll . . .'

"He tossed his head fearlessly, and I confess that for the first and last time in our acquaintance I perceived myself unexpectedly to be thoroughly sick of him. Why these vapourings? He was stumping about the room flourishing his arm absurdly, and now and then feeling on his breast for the ring under his clothes. Where was the sense of such exaltation in a man appointed to be a trading-clerk, and in a place where there was no trade—at that? Why hurl defiance at the universe? This was not a proper frame of mind to approach any undertaking; an improper frame of mind not only for him, I said, but for any man. He stood still over me. Did I think so? he asked, by no means subdued, and with a smile in which I seemed to detect suddenly something insolent. But then I am twenty years his senior. Youth *is* insolent; it is its right—its necessity; it has got to assert itself, and all assertion in this world of doubts is a defiance, is an insolence. He went off into a far corner, and coming back, he, figuratively speaking, turned to rend me. I spoke like that because I—even I, who had been no end kind to him—even I remembered—remembered—against him—what—what had happened. And what about others—the—the—world. Where's the wonder he wanted to get out, meant to get out, meant to stay out—by heavens! And I talked about proper frames of mind!

"'It is not I or the world who remember,' I shouted. 'It is you—you, who remember.'

"He did not flinch, and went on with heat, 'Forget everything, everybody, everybody.' . . . His voice fell . . . 'But you,' he added.

"'Yes—me too—if it would help,' I said, also in a low tone. After this we remained silent and languid for a time as if exhausted. Then he began again, composedly, and told me that Mr Stein had instructed him to wait for a month or so, to see whether it was possible for him to remain, before he began building a new house for himself, so as to avoid 'vain expense.' He did make use of funny expressions—Stein did. 'Vain expense' was good. . . . Remain? Why! of course. He would hang on. Let him only get in—that's all; he would answer for it he would remain. Never get out. It was easy enough to remain.

"'Don't be foolhardy,' I said, rendered uneasy by his threatening tone. 'If you only live long enough you will want to come back.'

"'Come back to what?' he asked absently, with his eyes fixed upon the face of a clock on the wall.

"I was silent for a while. 'Is it to be never, then?' I said. 'Never,' he repeated dreamily without looking at me, and then flew into sudden activity. 'Jove! Two o'clock, and I sail at four?'

"It was true. A brigantine of Stein's was leaving for the westward that afternoon, and he had been instructed to take his passage in her, only no orders to delay the sailing had been given. I suppose Stein forgot. He made a rush to get his things while I went aboard my ship, where he promised to call on his way to the outer roadstead. He turned up accordingly in a great hurry and with a small leather valise in his hand. This wouldn't do, and I offered him an old tin trunk of mine supposed to be water-tight, or at least damp-tight. He effected the transfer by the simple process of shooting out the contents of his valise as you would empty a sack of wheat. I saw three books in the tumble; two small, in dark covers, and a thick green-and-gold volume—a half-crown complete Shakespeare. 'You read this?' I asked. 'Yes. Best thing to cheer up a fellow,' he said hastily. I was struck by this appreciation, but there was no time for Shakespearian talk. A heavy revolver and two small boxes of cartridges were lying on the cuddy-table. 'Pray take this,' I said. 'It may help you to remain.' No sooner were these words out of my mouth than I perceived what grim meaning they could bear. 'May help you to get in,' I corrected myself remorsefully. He however was not troubled by obscure meanings; he thanked me effusively and bolted out, calling Good-bye over his shoulder. I heard his voice through the ship's side urging his boatmen to give way, and look-ing out of the stern-port I saw the boat rounding under the counter. He sat in her leaning forward, exciting his men with voice and gestures; and as he had kept the revolver in his hand and seemed to be presenting it at their heads, I shall never forget the scared faces of the four Javanese, and the frantic swing of their stroke which snatched that vision from under my eyes. Then turning away, the first thing I saw were the two boxes of cartridges on the cuddy-table. He had forgotten to take them.

"I ordered my gig manned at once; but Jim's rowers, under the impression that their lives hung on a thread while they had that madman in the boat, made such excellent time that before I had traversed half the distance between the two vessels I caught sight of him clambering over the rail, and of his box being passed up. All the brigantine's canvas was loose, her mainsail was set, and the windlass was just beginning to clink as I stepped upon her deck: her master, a dapper little half-caste of forty or so, in a blue flannel suit, with lively eyes, his round face the colour of lemon-peel, and with a thin little black moustache drooping on each side of his thick, dark lips, came forward smirking. He turned out, notwithstanding his self-satisfied and cheery exterior, to be of a careworn temperament. In answer to a remark of mine (while Jim had gone below for a moment) he said, 'Oh yes. Pa-tusan.' He was going to carry the gentleman to the mouth of the river, but would 'never ascend.' His flowing English seemed to be derived from a dictionary com-piled by a lunatic. Had Mr Stein desired him to 'ascend,' he would have 'rever-entially'—(I think he wanted to say respectfully—but devil only knows)—'reverentially made objects for the safety of properties.' If disregarded, he would have presented 'resignation to quit.' Twelve months ago he had made his last voy-age there, and though Mr Cornelius 'propitiated many offertories' to Mr Rajah Al-lang and the 'principal populations,' on conditions which made the trade 'a snare and ashes in the mouth,' yet his ship had been fired upon from the woods by 'ir-responsive parties' all the way down the river; which causing his crew 'from ex-posure to limb to remain silent in hidings,' the brigantine was nearly stranded on a sandbank at the bar, where she 'would have been perishable beyond the act of man.' The angry disgust at the recollection, the pride of his fluency, to which he turned an attentive ear, struggled for the possession of his broad simple face. He scowled and beamed at me, and watched with satisfaction the undeniable effect of his phraseology. Dark frowns ran swiftly over the placid sea, and the brigantine, with her fore-topsail to the mast and her main-boom amidships, seemed bewildered amongst the cat's-paws. He told me further, gnashing his teeth, that the Rajah was a 'laughable hyæna' (can't imagine how he got hold of hyænas); while somebody else was many times falser than the 'weapons of a crocodile.' Keeping one eye on the movements of his crew forward, he let loose his volubility—comparing the place to a 'cage of beasts made ravenous by long impenitence.' I fancy he meant impunity. He had no intention, he cried, to 'exhibit himself to be made attached purposefully to robbery.' The long-drawn wails, giving the time for the pull of the men catting the anchor, came to an end, and he lowered his voice. 'Plenty too much enough of Patusan,' he concluded, with energy.

"I heard afterwards he had been so indiscreet as to get himself tied up by the neck with a rattan halter to a post planted in the middle of a mud-hole before the Rajah's house. He spent the best part of a day and a whole night in that unwholesome situation, but there is every reason to believe the thing had been meant as a sort of joke. He brooded for a while over that horrid memory, I suppose, and then addressed in a quarrelsome tone the man coming aft to the helm. When he turned to me again it was to speak judicially, without passion. He would take the gentleman to the mouth of the river at Batu Kring (Patusan town 'being situated internally,' he remarked, 'thirty miles'). But in his eyes, he continued—a tone of bored, weary conviction replacing his previous voluble delivery—the gentleman was already 'in the similitude of a corpse.' 'What? What do you say?' I asked. He assumed a startlingly ferocious demeanour, and imitated to perfection the act of stabbing from behind. 'Already like the body of one deported,' he explained, with the insufferably conceited air of his kind after what they imagine a display of cleverness. Behind him I perceived Jim smiling silently at me, and with a raised hand checking the exclamation on my lips.

"Then, while the half-caste, bursting with importance, shouted his orders, while the yards swung creaking and the heavy boom came surging over, Jim and I, alone as it were, to leeward of the mainsail, clasped each other's hands and exchanged the last hurried words. My heart was freed from that dull resentment which had existed side by side with interest in his fate. The absurd chatter of the half-caste had given more reality to the miserable dangers of his path than Stein's careful statements. On that occasion the sort of formality that had been always present in our intercourse vanished from our speech; I believe I called him 'dear boy,' and he tacked on the words 'old man' to some half-uttered expression of gratitude, as though his risk set off against my years had made us more equal in age and in feeling. There was a moment of real and profound intimacy, unexpected and short-lived like a glimpse of some everlasting, of some saving truth. He exerted himself to soothe me as though he had been the more mature of the two. 'All right, all right,' he said rapidly and with feeling. 'I promise to take care of myself. Yes; I won't take any risks. Not a single blessed risk. Of course not. I mean to hang out. Don't you worry; Jove! I feel as if nothing could touch me. Why! this is luck from the word Go. I wouldn't spoil such a magnificent chance!' . . . A magnificent chance! Well, it *was* magnificent, but chances are what men make them, and how was I to know. As he had said, even I—even I remembered—his—his misfortune against him. It was true. And the best thing for him was to go.

"My gig had dropped in the wake of the brigantine, and I saw him aft detached upon the light of the westering sun, raising his cap high above his head. I heard an indistinct shout, 'You—shall—hear—of—me.' Of me, or from me, I don't know which. I think it must have been *of* me. My eyes were too dazzled by the glitter of the sea below his feet to see him clearly; I am fated never to see him clearly; but I can assure you no man could have appeared less 'in the similitude of a corpse,' as that half-caste croaker had put it. I could see the little wretch's face, the shape and colour of a ripe pumpkin, poked out somewhere under Jim's elbow. He too raised his arm as if for a downward thrust, *Absit omen!*"

CHAPTER XXIV.

"The coast of Patusan (I saw it nearly two years afterwards) is straight and sombre, and faces a misty ocean. Red trails are seen like cataracts of rust streaming under the dark-green foliage of bushes and creepers clothing the low cliffs. Swampy plains open out at the mouth of rivers, with a view of jagged blue peaks beyond the vast forests. In the offing a chain of islands, dark, crumbling shapes, stand out in the everlasting sunlit haze like the remnants of a wall breached by the sea.

"There is a village of fisher-folk at the mouth of the Batu Kring branch of the estuary. The river, which had been closed so long, was open then, and Stein's little schooner, in which I had my passage, worked her way up in three tides without being exposed to a fusilade from 'irresponsive parties.' Such a state of affairs belonged already to ancient history, if I could believe the elderly headman of the fishing village who came on board to act as a sort of pilot. He talked to me (the second white man he had ever seen) with confidence, and most of his talk was about the first white man he had ever seen. He called him Tuan Jim, and the tone of his references was made remarkable by a strange mixture of familiarity and awe. They, in the village, were under that lord's special protection, which showed that Jim bore no grudge. If he had warned me that I would hear of him it was perfectly true. I was hearing of him. There was already a story that the tide had turned two hours before its time to help him on his journey up the river. The talkative old man himself had steered the canoe and had marvelled at the phenomenon. Moreover, all the glory was in his family. His son and his son-in-law had paddled; but they were only youths without experience, who did not notice the speed of the canoe till he pointed out to them the amazing fact.

"Jim's coming to that fishing village was a blessing; but to them, as to many of us, the blessing came heralded by terrors. So many generations had been released since the last white man had visited the river that the very tradition had been lost. The appearance of the being that descended upon them and demanded inflexibly to be taken up to Patusan was discomposing; his insistance was alarming; his generosity more than suspicious. It was an unheard-of request. There was no precedent. What would the Rajah say to this? What would he do to them? The best part of the night was spent in consultation; but the immediate risk from the anger of that strange man seemed so great that at last a cranky dug-out was got ready. The women shrieked with grief as it put off. A fearless old hag cursed the stranger.

"He sat in it, as I've told you, on his tin box, nursing the unloaded revolver on his lap. He sat with precaution—than which there is nothing more fatiguing—and thus entered the land he was destined to fill with the fame of his virtues, from the blue peaks inland to the white ribbon of surf on the coast. At the first bend he lost sight of the sea with its labouring waves for ever rising, sinking, and vanishing to rise again—the very image of struggling mankind,—and faced the immovable forests rooted deep in the soil, soaring towards the sunshine, everlasting in the shadowy might of their tradition, like life itself. And his opportunity sat veiled by his side like an Eastern bride waiting to be uncovered by the hand of the master. He too was the heir of a shadowy and mighty tradition! He told me, however, that he had never in his life felt so depressed and tired as in that canoe. All the movement he dared to allow himself was to reach, as it were by stealth, after the shell of half a cocoanut floating between his shoes, and bale some of the water out with a carefully restrained action. He discovered how hard the lid of a block-tin case was to sit upon. He had heroic health; but several times during that journey he experienced fits of giddiness, and between whiles he speculated hazily as to the size of the blister the sun was raising on his back. For amusement he tried by looking ahead to decide whether the muddy object he saw lying on the water's edge was a log of wood or an alligator. Only very soon he had to give that up. No fun in it. Always alligator. One of them flopped into the river and all but capsized the canoe. But this excitement was over directly. Then in a long empty reach he was very grateful to a troop of monkeys who came right down on the bank and made an insulting hullabaloo on his passage. Such was the way in which he was approaching greatness as genuine as any man ever achieved. Principally, he longed for sunset; and meantime his three paddlers were preparing to put into execution their plan of delivering him up to the Rajah.

"'I suppose I must have been stupid with fatigue, or perhaps I did doze off for a time,' he said. The first thing he knew was his canoe coming to the bank. He became instantaneously aware of the forest having been left behind, of the first houses being visible higher up, of a stockade on his left, and of his boatmen leaping out together upon a low point of land and taking to their heels. Instinctively he leaped out after them. At first he thought himself deserted for some inconceivable reason, but he heard excited shouts, a gate swung open, and a lot of people poured out, making towards him. At the same time a boat full of armed men appeared on the river and came alongside his empty canoe, thus shutting off his retreat.

"'I was too startled to be quite cool—don't you know? and if that revolver had been loaded I would have shot somebody—perhaps two, three bodies, and that would have been the end of me. But it wasn't. . . .' 'Why not?' I asked. 'Well, I couldn't fight the whole population, and I wasn't coming to them as if I were afraid of my life,' he said, with just a faint hint of his stubborn sulkiness in the glance he gave me. I refrained from pointing out to him that they could not have known the chambers were actually empty. He had to satisfy himself in his own way. . . . 'Anyhow it wasn't,' he repeated good-humouredly, 'and so I just stood still and asked them what was the matter. That seemed to strike them dumb. I saw some of these thieves going off with my box. That long-legged old scoundrel Kassim (I'll show him to you to-morrow) ran out fussing to me about the Rajah wanting to see me. I said, "All right"; I too wanted to see the Rajah, and I simply walked in through the gate and—and—here I am.' He laughed, and then with unexpected emphasis, 'And do you know what's the best in it?' he asked. 'I'll tell you. It's the knowledge that had I been wiped out it is this place that would have been the loser.'

"He spoke thus to me before his house on that evening I've mentioned—after we had watched the moon float away above the chasm between the hills like an ascending spirit out of a grave; its sheen descended, cold and pale, like the ghost of dead sunlight. There is something haunting in the light of the moon; it has all the dispassionateness of a disembodied soul, and something of its inconceivable mystery. It is to our sunshine which—say what you like—is all we have to live by, what the echo is to the sound: misleading and confusing whether the note be mocking or sad. It robs all forms of matter—which, after all, is our domain—of their substance, and gives a sinister reality to shadows alone. And the shadows were very real around us, but Jim by my side looked very stalwart, as though nothing—not even the occult power of moonlight—could rob him of his reality in my eyes. Perhaps, indeed, nothing could touch him since he had survived the assault of the dark powers. All was silent, all was still; even on the river the moonbeams slept as on a pool. It was the moment of high water, a moment of immobility that accentuated the utter isolation of this lost corner of the earth. The houses crowding along the wide shining sweep without ripple or glitter, stepping into the water in a line of jostling, vague, grey, silvery forms mingled with black masses of shadow, were like a spectral herd of shapeless creatures pressing forward to drink in a spectral and lifeless stream. Here and there a red gleam twinkled within the bamboo walls, warm, like a living spark, significant of human affections, of shelter, of repose.

"He confessed to me that he often watched these tiny warm gleams go out one by one, that he loved to see people go to sleep under his eyes, confident in the security of to-morrow. 'Peaceful here, hey?' he asked. He was not eloquent, but there was a deep meaning in the words that followed. 'Look at these houses; there's not one where I am not trusted. Jove! I told you I would hang on. Ask any man, woman, or child . . .' He paused. 'Well, I am all right anyhow.'

"I observed quickly that he had found that out in the end. I had been sure of it, I added. He shook his head. 'Were you?' He pressed my arm lightly above the elbow. 'Well, then—you were right.'

"There was elation and pride, there was awe almost, in that low exclamation. 'Jove!' he cried, 'only think what it is to me.' Again he pressed my arm. 'And you asked me whether I thought of leaving. Good God! I! want to leave! Especially now after what you told me of Mr Stein's . . . Leave! Why! That's what I was afraid of. It would have been—it would have been harder than dying. No—on my word. Don't laugh. I must feel—every day, every time I open my eyes—that I am trusted—that nobody has a right—don't you know? Leave! For where? What for? To get what?'

"I had told him (indeed it was the main object of my visit) that it was Stein's intention to present him at once with the house and the stock of trading goods, on certain easy conditions which would make the transaction perfectly regular and valid. He began to snort and plunge at first. 'Confound your delicacy!' I shouted. 'It isn't Stein at all. It's giving you what you had made for yourself. And in any case keep your remarks for M'Neil—when you meet him in the other world. I hope it won't happen soon. . . .' He had to give in to my arguments; because all his conquests, the trust, the fame, the friendships, the love,—all these things that made him master had made him a captive too. He looked with an owner's eye at the peace of the evening, at the river, at the houses, at the everlasting life of the forests, at the life of the old mankind, at the secrets of the land, at the pride of his own heart; but it was they that possessed him and made him their own to the innermost thought, to the slightest stir of blood, to his last breath.

"It was something to be proud of. I too was proud—for him, if not so certain of the fabulous value of the bargain. It was wonderful. It was not so much of his fearlessness that I thought. It is strange how little account I took of it: as if it had been something too conventional to be at the root of the matter. No. I was more struck by the other gifts he had displayed. He had proved his grasp of the unfamiliar situation, his intellectual alertness in that field of thought. There was his readiness too! Amazing. And all this had come to him in a manner like keen scent to a well-bred hound. He was not eloquent, but there was a dignity in this constitutional reticence, there was a high seriousness in his stammerings. He had still his old trick of stubborn blushing. Now and then, though, a word, a sentence, would escape him that showed how deeply, how solemnly, he felt about that work which had given him the certitude of rehabilitation. That is why he seemed to love the land and the people with a sort of fierce egoism, with a contemptuous tenderness."

CHAPTER XXV.

"'This is where I was prisoner for three days,' he murmured to me (it was on the occasion of our visit to the Rajah), while we were making our way slowly through a kind of awestruck riot of dependants across Tunku Allang's courtyard. 'Filthy place, isn't it? And I couldn't get anything to eat either, unless I made a row about it, and then it was only a small plate of rice and a fried fish not much bigger than a stickleback—confound them! Jove! I've been hungry prowling inside this stinking enclosure with some of these vagabonds shoving their mugs right under my nose. I had given up that famous revolver of yours at the first demand. Glad to get rid of the bally thing. Look like a fool walking about with an empty shooting-iron in my hand.' At that moment we came into the presence, and he became unflinchingly grave and complimentary with his late captor. Oh! magnificent! I want to laugh when I think of it. But I was impressed too. The old disreputable Tunku Allang could not help showing his fear (he was no hero, for all the tales of his hot youth he was fond of telling); and at the same time there was a wistful confidence in his manner towards his late prisoner. Note! Even where he would be most hated he was still trusted. Jim—as far as I could follow the conversation—was improving the occasion by the delivery of a lecture. Some poor villagers had been waylaid and robbed while on their way to Doramin's house with a few pieces of gum or bee's-wax which they wished to exchange for rice. 'It was Doramin who was a thief,' burst out the Rajah. A shaking fury seemed to enter that old frail body. He writhed weirdly on his mat, gesticulating with his hands and feet, tossing the tangled strings of his mop—an impotent incarnation of rage. There were staring eyes and dropping jaws all around us. Jim began to speak. Resolutely, coolly, and for some time he enlarged upon the text that no man should be prevented from getting his food and his children's food honestly. The other sat like a tailor at his board, one palm on each knee, his head low, and fixing Jim through the grey hair that fell over his very eyes. When Jim had done there was a great stillness. Nobody seemed to breathe even; no one made a sound till the old Rajah sighed faintly, and looking up, with a toss of his head, said quickly, 'You hear, my people! No more of these little games.' This decree was received in profound silence. A rather heavy man, evidently in a position of confidence, with intelligent eyes, a bony, broad, very dark face, and a cheerily officious manner (I learned later on he was the executioner), presented to us two cups of coffee on a brass tray, which he took from the hands of an inferior attendant. 'You needn't drink,' muttered Jim very rapidly. I didn't perceive the meaning at first, and only looked at him. He took a good sip and sat composedly, holding the saucer in his left hand. In a moment I felt excessively annoyed. 'Why the devil,' I whispered, smiling at him amiably, 'do you expose me to such a stupid risk?' I drank, of course, there was nothing for it, while he gave no sign, and almost immediately afterwards we took our leave. While we were going down the courtyard to our boat, escorted by the intelligent and cheery executioner, Jim said he was very sorry. It was the barest chance, of course. Personally he thought nothing of poison. The remotest chance. He was—he assured me—considered to be infinitely more useful than dangerous, and so . . . 'But the Rajah is afraid of you abominably. Anybody can see that,' I argued with, I own, a certain peevishness, and all the time watching anxiously for the first twist of some sort of ghastly colic. I was awfully disgusted. 'If I am to do any good here and preserve my position,' he said, taking his seat by my side in the boat, 'I must stand the risk: I take it once every month, at least. Many people trust me to do that—for them. Afraid of me. That's just it. Most likely he is afraid of me because I am not afraid of his coffee.' Then showing me a place on the north front of the stockade where the pointed tops of several stakes were broken, 'This is where I leaped over on my third day in Patusan. They haven't put new stakes there yet. Good leap, eh?' A moment later we passed the mouth of a muddy creek. 'This is my second leap. I had a bit of a run and took this one flying, but fell short. Thought I would leave my skin there. Lost my shoes struggling. And all the time I was thinking to myself how beastly it would be to get a jab with a bally long spear while sticking in the mud like this. I remember how sick I felt wriggling in that slime. I mean really sick—as if I had bitten something rotten.'

"That's how it was—and the opportunity ran by his side, leaped over the gap, floundered in the mud . . . still veiled. The unexpectedness of his coming was the only thing, you understand, that saved him from being at once despatched with krises and flung into the river. They had him, but it was like getting hold of an apparition, a wraith, a portent. What did it mean? What to do with it? Was it too late to conciliate him? Hadn't he better be killed without more delay? But what would happen then? Wretched old Allang went nearly mad with apprehension and through the difficulty of making up his mind. Several times the council was broken up, and the advisers made a break helter-skelter for the door and out on to the verandah. One—it is said—even jumped down to the ground—fifteen feet, I should judge—and broke his leg. The royal governor of Patusan had bizarre mannerisms, and one of them was to introduce boastful rhapsodies into every arduous discussion, when, getting gradually excited, he would end by flying off his perch with a kris in his hand. But, barring such interruptions, the deliberations upon Jim's fate went on night and day.

"Meanwhile he wandered about the courtyard, shunned by some, glared at by others, but watched by all, and practically at the mercy of the first casual ragamuffin with a chopper, in there. He took possession of a small tumble-down shed to sleep in; the effluvia of filth and rotten matter incommoded him greatly: it seems he had not lost his appetite though, because—he told me—he had been hungry all the blessed time. Now and again 'some fussy ass' deputed from the council-room would come out running to him, and in honeyed tones would administer amazing interrogatories. 'Were the Dutch coming to take the country? Would the white man like to go back down the river? What was the object of coming to such a miserable country? The Rajah wanted to know whether the white man could repair a watch?' They did actually bring out to him a nickel clock of New England make, and out of sheer unbearable boredom he busied himself in trying to get the alarum to work. It was apparently when thus occupied in his shed that the true perception of his extreme peril dawned upon him. He dropped the thing—he says—'like a hot potato,' and walked out hastily, without the slightest idea of what he would, or indeed could, do. He only knew that the position was intolerable. He strolled aimlessly beyond a sort of ramshackle little granary on posts, and his eyes fell on the broken stakes of the palisade; and then—he says—at once, without any mental process as it were, without any stir of emotion, he set about his escape as if executing a plan matured for a month. He walked off carelessly to give himself a good run, and when he faced about there was some dignitary with two spearmen in attendance close at his elbow ready with a question. He started off 'from under his very nose,' went over 'like a bird,' and landed on the other side with a fall that jarred all his bones and seemed to split his head. He picked himself up instantly. He never thought of anything at the time; all he could remember—he said—was a great yell; the first houses of Patusan were before him four hundred yards away; he saw the creek, and as it were mechanically put on more pace. The earth seemed fairly to fly backwards under his feet. He took off from the last dry spot, felt himself flying through the air, felt himself, without any shock, planted upright in an extremely soft and sticky mudbank. It was only when he tried to move his legs and found he couldn't that, in his own words, 'he came to himself.' He began to think of the 'bally long spears.' As a matter of fact, considering that the people inside the stockade had to run to the gate, then get down to the landing-place, get into boats, and pull round a point of land, he had more advance than he imagined. Besides, it being low water, the creek was without water—you couldn't call it dry,—and practically he was safe for a time from everything but a very long shot perhaps. The higher firm ground was about six feet in front of him. 'I thought I would have to die there all the same,' he said. He reached and grabbed desperately with his hands, and only succeeded in gathering a horrible cold shiny heap of slime against his breast—up to his very chin. It seemed to him he was burying himself alive, and then he struck out madly, scattering the mud with his fists. It fell on his head, on his face, over his eyes, into his mouth. He told me that he remembered suddenly the courtyard, as you remember a place where you had been very happy years ago. He longed—so he said—to be back there again, mending the clock. Mending the clock—that was the idea. He made efforts, tremendous sobbing gasping efforts, efforts that seemed to burst his eyeballs in their sockets and make him blind, and culminating into one mighty supreme effort in the darkness to crack the earth asunder, to throw it off his limbs—and he felt himself creeping feebly up the bank. He lay full length on the firm ground and saw the light, the sky. Then as a sort of happy thought the notion came

to him that he would go to sleep. He will have it that he *did* actually go to sleep;
that he slept—perhaps for a minute, perhaps for twenty seconds, or only for one
second, but he recollects distinctly the violent convulsive start of awakening. He
remained lying still for a while, and then he arose muddy from head to foot and
stood there, thinking he was alone of his kind for hundreds of miles, alone, with
no help, no sympathy, no pity to expect from any one, like a hunted animal. The
first houses were not more than twenty yards from him; and it was the desperate
screaming of a frightened woman trying to carry off a child that started him again.
He pelted straight on in his socks, beplastered with filth out of all semblance to a
human being. He traversed more than half the length of the settlement. The nim-
bler women fled right and left, the slower men just dropped whatever they had in
their hands, and remained petrified with dropping jaws. He was a flying terror.
He says he noticed the little children trying to run for life, falling on their little
stomachs and kicking. He swerved between two houses up a slope, clambered in
desperation over a barricade of felled trees (there wasn't a week without some
fight in Patusan at that time), burst through a fence into a maize-patch, where a
scared boy flung a stick at him, blundered upon a path, and ran all at once into the
arms of several startled men. He just had breath enough to gasp out, 'Doramin!
Doramin!' He remembers being half-carried, half-rushed to the top of the slope,
and in a vast enclosure with palms and fruit-trees being run up to a large man sitting massively in a chair in the midst of the greatest possible commotion and excitement. He fumbled in mud and clothes to produce the ring, and, finding
himself suddenly on his back, wondered who had knocked him down. They had
simply let him go—don't you know?—but he couldn't stand. At the foot of the
slope random shots were fired, and above the roofs of the settlement there rose a
dull roar of amazement. But he was safe. Doramin's people were barricading the
gate and pouring water down his throat; Doramin's old wife, full of business and
commiseration, was issuing shrill orders to her girls. 'The old woman,' he said
softly, 'made a to-do over me as if I had been her own son. They put me into an
immense bed—her state bed—and she ran in and out wiping her eyes to give me
pats on the back. I must have been a pitiful object. I just lay there like a log for I
don't know how long.'

"He seemed to have a great liking for Doramin's old wife. She on her side had
taken a motherly fancy to him. She had a round, nut-brown, soft face, all fine
wrinkles, large, bright red lips (she chewed betel assiduously), and screwed up,
winking, benevolent eyes. She was constantly in movement, scolding busily and
ordering unceasingly a troop of young women with clear brown faces and big
grave eyes, her daughters, her servants, her slave-girls. You know how it is in
these households: it's generally impossible to tell the difference. She was very
spare, and even her ample outer garment, fastened in front with jewelled clasps,
had somehow a skimpy effect. Her dark bare feet were thrust into yellow straw
slippers of Chinese make. I have seen her myself flitting about with her extremely
thick, long, grey hair falling about her shoulders. She uttered homely shrewd sayings, was of noble birth, and was eccentric and arbitrary. In the afternoon she
would sit in a very roomy armchair, opposite her husband, gazing steadily
through a wide opening in the wall which gave an extensive view of the settlement
and the river.

"She invariably tucked up her feet under her, but old Doramin sat squarely,
sat imposingly as a mountain sits on a plain. He was only of the *nakhoda* or merchant class, but the respect shown to him and the dignity of his bearing were very

striking. He was the chief of the second power in Patusan. The immigrants from Celebes (about sixty families that, with dependants and so on, could muster some two hundred men 'wearing the kris') had elected him years ago for their head. The men of that race are intelligent, enterprising, revengeful, but with a more frank courage than the other Malays, and restless under oppression. They formed the party opposed to the Rajah. Of course the quarrels were for trade. This was the primary cause of faction fights, of the sudden outbreaks that would fill this or that part of the settlement with smoke, flame, the noise of shots and shrieks. Villages were burnt, men were dragged into the Rajah's stockade to be killed or tortured for the crime of trading with anybody else but himself. Only a day or two before Jim's arrival several heads of households in the very fishing village that was afterwards taken under his especial protection had been driven over the cliffs by a party of Rajah's spearmen, on suspicion of having been collecting edible birds' nests for a Celebes trader. Rajah Allang pretended to be the only trader in his country, and the penalty for the breach of the monopoly was death; but his idea of trading was indistinguishable from the commonest forms of robbery. His cruelty and rapacity had no other bounds than his cowardice, and he was afraid of the organised power of the Celebes men, only—till Jim came—he was not afraid enough to keep quiet. He struck at them through his subjects, and thought himself pathetically in the right. The situation was complicated by a wandering stranger, an Arab half-bred, who, I believe, on purely religious grounds, had incited the tribes in the interior (the bush-folk, as Jim himself called them) to rise, and had established himself in a fortified camp on the summit of one of the twin hills. He hung over the town of Patusan like a hawk over a poultry-yard, but he devastated the open country. Whole villages, deserted, rotted on their blackened posts over the banks of clear streams, dropping piecemeal into the water the grass of their walls, the leaves of their roofs, with a curious effect of natural decay as if they had been a form of vegetation stricken by a blight at its very root. The two parties in Patusan were not sure which one this partisan most desired to plunder. The Rajah intrigued with him feebly. Some of the Bugis settlers, weary with endless insecurity, were half inclined to call him in. The younger spirits amongst them, chaffing, advised to 'get Sherif Ali with his wild men and drive the Rajah Allang out of the country.' Doramin restrained them with difficulty. He was growing old, and, though his influence had not diminished, the situation was getting beyond him. This was the state of affairs when Jim, bolting from the Rajah's stockade, appeared before the chief of the Bugis, produced the ring, and was received, in a manner of speaking, into the heart of the community."

CHAPTER XXVI.

"Doramin was one of the most remarkable men of his race I had ever seen. His bulk for a Malay was immense, but he did not look merely fat; he looked imposing, monumental. This motionless body clad in rich stuffs, coloured silks, gold embroideries; this huge head, enfolded in a red-and-gold headkerchief; the flat, big, round face, wrinkled, furrowed, with two semicircular heavy folds starting on each side of wide, fierce nostrils, and enclosing a thick-lipped mouth; the throat like a bull; the vast corrugated brow overhanging the staring proud eyes,—made a whole that, once seen, can never be forgotten. His impassive repose (he seldom stirred a limb when once he sat down) was like a display of dignity. He was never known to raise his voice. It was a hoarse and powerful murmur, slightly veiled as if heard from a distance. When he walked, two short, sturdy young fellows, naked to the waist, in white sarongs and with black skull-caps on the backs of their heads, sustained his elbows: they would ease him down and stand behind his chair till he wanted to rise, when he would turn his head slowly, as if with difficulty, to the right and to the left, and then they would catch him under his armpits and help him up. For all that, there was nothing of a cripple about him: on the contrary, all his ponderous movements were like manifestations of a mighty deliberate force. It was generally believed he consulted his wife as to public affairs; but nobody, as far as I know, had ever heard them exchange a single word. When they sat in state by the wide opening it was in silence. They could see below them in the declining light the vast expanse of the forest country, a dark sleeping sea of sombre green undulating as far as the violet and purple range of mountains; the shining sinuosity of the river like an immense letter S of beaten silver; the brown ribbon of houses following the sweep of both banks, overtopped by the twin-hills uprising above the nearer tree-tops. They were wonderfully contrasted: she, light, delicate, spare, quick, a little witch-like, with a touch of motherly fussiness in her repose; he, facing her, immense and heavy, like a figure of a man roughly fashioned of stone, with something magnanimous and ruthless in his immobility. The son of these old people was a most distinguished youth.

"They had him late in life. Perhaps he was not really so young as he looked. Four- or five-and-twenty is not so young when a man is already father of a family at eighteen. When he entered the large room, lined and carpeted with fine mats, and with a high ceiling of white sheeting, where the couple sat in state surrounded by a most deferential retinue, he would make his way straight to Doramin, to kiss his hand—which the other abandoned to him, majestically—and then would step across to stand by his mother's chair. I suppose I may say they idolised him, but I never caught them giving him an overt glance. Those, it is true, were public functions. The room was generally thronged. The solemn formality of greetings and leave-takings, the profound respect expressed in gestures, on the faces, in the low whispers, is simply indescribable. 'It's well worth seeing,' Jim had assured me while we were crossing the river, on our way back. 'They are like people in a book, aren't they?' he said triumphantly. 'And Dain Waris—their son—is the best friend (barring you) I ever had. What Mr Stein would call a good "war-comrade." I was in luck. Jove! I was in luck when I tumbled amongst them at my last gasp.' He meditated with bowed head, then rousing himself he added—

"'Of course I didn't go to sleep over it, but . . .' He paused again. 'It seemed to come to me,' he murmured. 'All at once I saw what I had to do . . .'

"There was no doubt that it had come to him; and it had come through war, too, as is natural, since this power that came to him was the power to make peace. It is in this sense alone that might so often *is* right. You must not think he had seen his way at once. When he arrived the Bugis community was in a most critical position. 'They were all afraid,' he said to me—'each man afraid for himself; while I could see as plain as possible that they must do something at once if they did not want to go under one after another, what between the Rajah and that vagabond Sherif.' But to see that was nothing. When he got his idea he had to drive it into reluctant minds, through the bulwarks of fear, of selfishness. He drove it in at last.

And that was nothing. He had to devise the means. He devised them—an audacious plan; and his task was only half done. He had to inspire with his own confidence a lot of people who had hidden and absurd reasons to hang back; he had
to conciliate imbecile jealousies, and argue away all sorts of senseless mistrusts.
Without the weight of Doramin's authority, and his son's fiery enthusiasm, he
would have failed. Dain Waris, the distinguished youth, was the first to believe in
him; theirs was one of these strange, profound, rare friendships between brown
and white, in which the very difference of race seems to draw two human beings
closer by some mystic element of sympathy. Of Dain Waris, his own people said
with pride that he knew how to fight like a white man. This was true; he had that
sort of courage—the courage in the open, I may say,—but he had also a European
mind. You meet them sometimes like that, and are surprised to discover unexpectedly a familiar turn of thought, an unobscured vision, a tenacity of purpose,
a touch of altruism. Of small stature, but admirably well proportioned, Dain Waris
had a proud carriage, a polished, easy bearing, a temperament like a clear flame.
His dusky face, with big black eyes, was in action expressive, and in repose
thoughtful. He was of a silent disposition; a firm glance, an ironic smile, a courteous deliberation of manner seemed to hint at great reserves of intelligence and
power. Such beings open to the Western eye, so often concerned with mere surfaces, the hidden possibilities of races and lands over which hangs the mystery of
unrecorded ages. He not only trusted Jim, he understood him, I firmly believe. I
speak of him because he had captivated me. His—if I may say so—his caustic placidity, and, at the same time, his intelligent sympathy with Jim's aspirations, appealed to me. I seemed to behold the very origin of friendship. If Jim took the lead,
the other had captivated his leader. In fact, Jim the leader was a captive in every
sense. The land, the people, the friendship, the love, were like the jealous guard-
ians of his body. Every day added a link to the fetters of that strange freedom. I felt
convinced of it, as from day to day I learned more of the story.

"The story! Haven't I heard the story? I've heard it on the march, in camp (he
made me scour the country after invisible game); I've listened to a good part of it
on one of the twin-summits, after climbing the last hundred feet or so on my
hands and knees. Our escort (we had volunteer followers from village to village)
had camped meantime on a bit of level ground half-way up the slope, and in the
still breathless evening the smell of wood-smoke reached our nostrils from below
with the penetrating delicacy of some choice scent. Voices also ascended, wonderful in their distinct and immaterial clearness. Jim sat on the trunk of a felled
tree, and pulling out his pipe began to smoke. A new growth of grass and bushes
was springing up; there were traces of an earthwork under a mass of thorny twigs.
'It all started from here,' he said, after a long and meditative silence. On the other
hill, two hundred yards across a sombre precipice, I saw a line of high blackened
stakes, showing here and there ruinously—the remnants of Sherif Ali's impreg-
nable camp.

"But it had been taken though. That had been his idea. He had mounted Doramin's old ordnance on the top of that hill; two rusty iron 7-pounders, a lot of
small brass cannon—currency cannon. But if the brass guns represent wealth,
they can also, when crammed recklessly to the muzzle, send a solid shot to some
little distance. The thing was to get them up there. He showed me where he had
fastened the cables, explained how he had improvised a rude capstan out of a hollowed log turning upon a pointed stake, indicated with the bowl of his pipe the
outline of the earthwork. The last hundred feet of the ascent had been the most

difficult. He had made himself responsible for success on his own head. He had induced the war party to work hard all night. Big fires lighted at intervals blazed all down the slope, 'but up here,' he explained, 'the hoisting gang had to fly around in the dark.' From the top he saw men moving on the hillside like ants at work. He himself on that night had kept on rushing down and climbing up like a squirrel, directing, encouraging, watching all along the line. Old Doramin had himself carried up the hill in his arm-chair. They put him down on the level place upon the slope, and he sat there in the light of one of the big fires—'amazing old chap—real old chieftain,' said Jim, 'with his little fierce eyes—a pair of immense flintlock pistols on his knees. Magnificent things, ebony, silver-mounted, with beautiful locks and a calibre like an old blunderbuss. A present from Stein, it seems—in exchange for that ring, you know. Used to belong to good old M'Neil. God only knows how *he* came by them. There he sat, moving neither hand nor foot, a flame of dry brushwood behind him, and lots of people rushing about, shouting and pulling round him—the most solemn, imposing old chap you can imagine. *He* wouldn't have had much chance if Sherif Ali had let his infernal crew loose at us and stampeded my lot. Eh? Anyhow, he had come up there to die if anything went wrong. No mistake! Jove! It thrilled me to see him there—like a rock. But the Sherif must have thought us mad, and never troubled to come and see how we got on. Nobody believed it could be done. Why! I think the very chaps who pulled and shoved and sweated over it did not believe it could be done! Upon my word I don't think they did. . . .'

"He stood erect, the smouldering brier-wood in his clutch, with a smile on his lips and a sparkle in his boyish eyes. I sat on the stump of a tree at his feet, and below us stretched the land, the great expanse of the forests, sombre under the sunshine, rolling like a sea, with glints of winding rivers, the grey spots of villages, and here and there a clearing, like an islet of light amongst the dark waves of continuous tree-tops. A brooding gloom lay over this vast and monotonous landscape; the light fell on it as if into an abyss. The land devoured the sunshine; only far off, along the coast, the empty ocean, smooth and polished within the faint haze, seemed to rise up to the sky in a wall of steel.

"And there I was with him, high in the sunshine on the top of that historic hill of his. He dominated the forest, the secular gloom, the old mankind. He was like a figure set up on a pedestal, to represent in his persistent youth the power, and perhaps the virtues, of races that never grow old, that have emerged from the gloom. I don't know why he should always have appeared to me symbolic. Perhaps this is the real cause of my interest in his fate. I don't know whether it was exactly fair to him to remember the incident which had given a new direction to his life, but at that very moment I remembered very distinctly. It was like a shadow in the light."

CHAPTER XXVII.

"Already the legend had gifted him with super-natural powers. Yes, it was said, there had been many ropes cunningly disposed, and a strange contrivance that turned by the efforts of many men, and each gun went up tearing slowly

through the bushes, like a wild pig rooting its way in the undergrowth, but,
. . . and the wisest shook their heads. There was something occult in all this, no
doubt; for what is the strength of ropes and of men's arms? There is a rebellious
soul in things which must be overcome by powerful charms and incantations.
Thus old Sura—a very respectable householder of Patusan—with whom I had a
quiet chat one evening. However, Sura was a professional sorcerer also, who attended all the rice sowings and reapings for miles around for the purpose of sub-
duing the stubborn soul of things. This occupation he seemed to think a most
arduous one, and perhaps the souls of things are more stubborn than the souls of
men. As to the simple folk of outlying villages, they believed and said (as the most
natural thing in the world) that Jim had carried the guns up the hill on his back—
two at a time.

"This would make Jim stamp his foot in vexation and exclaim with an exasperated little laugh, 'What can you do with such silly beggars? They will sit up half
the night talking bally rot, and the greater the lie the more they seem to like it.' You
could trace the subtle influence of his surroundings in this irritation. It was part of
his captivity. The earnestness of his denials was amusing, and at last I said, 'My
dear fellow, you don't suppose I believe this.' He looked at me quite startled. 'Well,
no! I suppose not,' he said, and burst into a Homeric peal of laughter. 'Well, anyhow the guns were there, and went off all together at sunrise. Jove! You should
have seen the splinters fly,' he cried. By his side Dain Waris, listening with a quiet
smile, dropped his eyelids and shuffled his feet a little. It appears that the success
in mounting the guns had given Jim's people such a feeling of confidence that he
ventured to leave the battery under charge of two elderly Bugis who had seen
some fighting in their day, and went to join Dain Waris and the storming-party
who were concealed in the ravine. In the small hours they began creeping up, and
when two-thirds of the way up, lay in the wet grass waiting for the appearance of
the sun, which was the agreed signal. He told me with what impatient anguishing
emotion he watched the swift coming of the dawn; how, heated with the work and
the climbing, he felt the cold dew chilling his very bones; how afraid he was he
would begin to shiver and shake like a leaf before the time came for the advance.
'It was the slowest half-hour in my life,' he declared. Gradually the silent stockade
came out on the sky above him. Men scattered all down the slope were crouching
amongst the dark stones and dripping bushes. Dain Waris was lying flattened by
his side. 'We looked at each other,' Jim said, resting a gentle hand on his friend's
shoulder. 'He smiled at me as cheery as you please, and I dared not stir my lips for
fear I would break out into a shivering fit. 'Pon my word, it's true! I had been
streaming with perspiration when we took cover—so you may imagine . . .' He declared, and I believe him, that he had no fears as to the result. He was only anxious
as to his ability to repress these shivers. He didn't bother about the result. He was
bound to get to the top of that hill and stay there, whatever might happen. There
could be no going back for him. Those people had trusted him implicitly. Him
alone! His bare word. . . .

"I remember how, at this point, he paused with his eyes fixed upon me. 'As
far as he knew, they never had an occasion to regret it yet,' he said. 'Never. He
hoped to God they never would. Meantime—worse luck!—they had got into the
habit of taking his word for anything and everything. I could have no idea! Why?
Only the other day an old fool he had never seen in his life came from some village
miles away to find out if he should divorce his wife. Fact. Solemn word. That's the
sort of thing . . . He wouldn't have believed it. Would I? Squatted on the verandah

chewing betel-nut, sighing and spitting all over the place for more than an hour, and as glum as an undertaker before he came out with that dashed conundrum. That's the kind of thing that isn't so funny as it looks. What was a fellow to say?—Good wife?—Yes. Good wife—old though; started a confound long story about some brass pots. Been living together for fifteen years—twenty years—could not tell. A long, long time. Good wife. Beat her a little—not much—just a little, when she was young. Had to—for the sake of his honour. Suddenly in her old age she goes and lends three brass pots to her sister's son's wife, and begins to abuse him every day in a loud voice. His enemies jeered at him; his face was utterly black-ened. Pots totally lost. Awfully cut up about it. Impossible to fathom a story like that; told him to go home, and promised to come along myself and settle it all. It's all very well to grin, but it was the dashedest nuisance! A day's journey through the forest, another day lost in coaxing a lot of silly villagers to get at the rights of the affair. There was the making of a sanguinary shindy in the thing. Every bally idiot took sides with one family or the other, and one-half of the village was ready to go for the other half with anything that came handy. Honour bright! No joke! . . . Instead of attending to their bally crops. Got him the infernal pots back of course—and pacified all hands. No trouble to settle it. Of course not. Could settle the deadliest quarrel in the country by crooking his little finger. The trouble was to get at the truth of anything. Was not sure to this day whether he had been fair to all parties. It worried him. And the talk! Jove! There didn't seem to be any head or tail to it. Rather storm a twenty-foot-high old stockade any day. Much! Child's play to that other job. Wouldn't take so long either. Well, yes; a funny set out, upon the whole—the fool looked old enough to be his grandfather. But from another point of view it was no joke. His word decided everything—ever since the smash-ing of Sherif Ali. An awful responsibility,' he repeated. 'No, really—joking apart, had it been three lives instead of three rotten brass pots it would have been the same. . . .'

"Thus he illustrated the moral effect of his victory in war. It was in truth im-mense. It had led him from strife to peace, and through death into the innermost life of the people; but the gloom of the land spread out under the sunshine pre-served its appearance of inscrutable, of secular repose. The sound of his fresh young voice (it's extraordinary how very few signs of wear he showed) floated lightly, and passed away over the unchanged face of the forests like the sound of the big guns on that cold dewy morning when he had no other concern on earth but the proper control of the chills in his body. With the first slant of sun-rays along these immovable tree-tops the summit of one hill wreathed itself, with heavy re-ports, in white clouds of smoke, and the other burst into an amazing noise of yells, war-cries, shouts of anger, of surprise, of dismay. Jim and Dain Waris were the first to lay their hands on the stakes. The popular story has it that Jim with a touch of one finger had thrown down the gate. He was, of course, anxious to disclaim this achievement. The whole stockade—he would insist on explaining to you—was a poor affair (Sherif Ali trusted mainly to the inaccessible position); and, anyway, the thing had been already knocked to pieces and only hung together by a miracle. He put his shoulder to it like a little fool and went in head over heels. Jove! If it hadn't been for Dain Waris, a pock-marked tattooed vagabond would have pinned him with his spear to a baulk of timber like one of Stein's beetles. The third man in, it seems, had been Tamb' Itam, Jim's own servant. This was a Malay from the north, a stranger who had wandered into Patusan, and had been forcibly detained by Rajah Allang as paddler of one of the state boats. He had made a bolt of it at the first opportunity, and finding a precarious refuge (but very little to eat) amongst the Bugis settlers, had attached himself to Jim's person. His complexion was very dark, his face flat, his eyes prominent and injected with bile. There was something excessive, almost fanatical, in his devotion to his 'white lord.' He was inseparable from Jim like a morose shadow. On state occasions he would tread on his master's heels, one hand on the haft of his kris, keeping the common people at a distance by his truculent brooding glances. Jim had made him the headman of his establishment, and all Patusan respected and courted him as a person of much influence. At the taking of the stockade he had distinguished himself greatly by the methodical ferocity of his fighting. The storming-party had come on so quick—Jim said—that notwithstanding the panic of the garrison, there was a 'hot five minutes hand-to-hand inside that stockade, till some bally ass set fire to the shelters of boughs and dry grass, and we all had to clear out for dear life.'

"The rout, it seems, had been complete. Doramin waiting immovably in his chair on the hillside, with the smoke of the guns spreading slowly above his big head, received the news with a deep grunt. When informed that his son was safe and leading the pursuit, he, without another sound, made a mighty effort to rise; his attendants hurried to his help, and, held up reverently, he shuffled with great dignity into a bit of shade, where he laid himself down to sleep covered entirely with a piece of white sheeting. In Patusan the excitement was intense. Jim told me that from the hill, turning his back on the stockade with its embers, black ashes, and half-consumed corpses, he could see time after time the open spaces between the houses on both sides of the stream fill suddenly with a seething rush of people and get empty in a moment. His ears caught feebly from below the tremendous din of gongs and drums; the wild shouts of the crowd reached him in bursts of faint roaring. A lot of streamers made a flutter as of little white, red, yellow birds amongst the brown ridges of roofs. 'You must have enjoyed it,' I murmured, feeling the stir of sympathetic emotion.

"'It was . . . it was immense! Immense!' he cried aloud, flinging his arms open. The sudden movement startled me as though I had seen him bare the secrets of his breast to the sunshine, to the brooding forests, to the steely sea. Below us the town reposed in easy curves upon the banks of a stream whose current seemed to sleep. 'Immense!' he repeated for a third time, speaking in a whisper, for himself alone.

"Immense! No doubt it was immense; the seal of success upon his words, the conquered ground for the soles of his feet, the blind trust of men, the belief in himself snatched from the fire, the solitude of his achievement. All this, as I've warned you, gets dwarfed in the telling. I can't with mere words convey to you the impression of his total and utter isolation. I know, of course, he was in every sense alone of his kind there, but the unsuspected qualities of his nature had brought him in such close touch with his surroundings that this isolation seemed only the effect of his power. His loneliness added to his stature. There was nothing within sight to compare him with, as though he had been one of these exceptional men who can be only measured by the greatness of their fame; and his fame, remember, was the greatest thing around for many a day's journey. You would have to paddle, pole, or track a long weary way through the jungle before you passed beyond the reach of its voice. Its voice was not the trumpeting of the disreputable goddess we all know—not blatant—not brazen. It took its tone from the stillness and gloom of the land without a past, where his word was the one truth of every passing day. It shared something of the nature of that silence through which it accompanied you into unexplored depths, heard continuously by your side, penetrating, far-reaching—tinged with wonder and mystery on the lips of whispering men."

CHAPTER XXVIII.

"The defeated Sherif Ali fled the country without making another stand, and when the miserable hunted villagers began to crawl out of the jungle back to their rotting houses, it was Jim who, in consultation with Dain Waris, appointed the headmen. Thus he became the virtual rule of the land. As to old Tunku Allang, his fears at first had known no bounds. It is said that at the intelligence of the successful storming of the hill he flung himself, face down, on the bamboo floor of his audience-hall, and lay motionless for a whole night and a whole day, uttering stifled sounds of such an appalling nature that no man dared approach his prostrate form nearer than a spear's length. Already he could see himself driven ignominiously out of Patusan, wandering, abandoned, stripped, without opium, without his women, without followers, a fair game for the first comer to kill. After Sherif Ali his turn would come, and who could resist an attack led by such a devil? And indeed he owed his life and such authority as he still possessed at the time of my visit to Jim's idea of what was fair alone. The Bugis had been extremely anxious to pay off old scores, and the impassive old Doramin cherished the hope of yet seeing his son ruler of Patusan. During one of our interviews he deliberately allowed me to get a glimpse of this secret ambition. Nothing could be finer in its way than the dignified wariness of his approaches. He himself—he began by declaring—had used his strength in his young days, but now he had grown old and tired. . . . With his imposing bulk and haughty little eyes darting sagacious, inquisitive glances, he reminded one irresistibly of a cunning old elephant; the slow rise and fall of his vast breast went on powerful and regular, like the heave of a calm sea. He too, as he protested, had an unbounded confidence in Tuan Jim's wisdom. If he could only obtain a promise! One word would be enough! . . . His breathing silences, the low rumblings of his voice, recalled the last efforts of a spent thunderstorm.

"I tried to put the subject aside. It was difficult, for there could be no question that Jim had the power; in his new sphere there did not seem to be anything that was not his to hold or to give. But that, I repeat, was nothing in comparison with the notion, which occurred to me, while I listened with a show of attention, that he seemed to have come very near at last to mastering his fate. Doramin was anxious about the future of the country, and I was struck by the turn he gave to the argument. The land remains where God had put it, but white men—he said—they come to us and in a little while they go. They go away. Those they leave behind do not know when to look for their return. They go to their own land, to their people,

and so this white man too would. . . . I don't know what induced me to commit
myself at this point by a vigorous 'No, no.' The whole extent of this indiscretion
became apparent when Doramin, turning full upon me his face, whose expression, fixed in rugged deep folds, remained unalterable, like a huge brown mask,
said that this was good news indeed, reflectively; and then wanted to know why.

"His little, motherly witch of a wife sat on my other hand, with her head covered and her feet tucked up, gazing through the great shutter-hole. I could only
see a straying lock of grey hair, a high cheek-bone, the slight masticating motion
of the sharp chin. Without removing her eyes from the vast prospect of forests
stretching as far as the hills, she asked me in a pitying voice why was it that he so
young had wandered from his home, coming so far, through so many dangers?
Had he no household there, no kinsmen in his own country? Had he no old
mother, who would always remember his face? . . .

"I was completely unprepared for this. I could only mutter and shake my head
vaguely. Afterwards I am perfectly aware I cut a very poor figure trying to extricate
myself out of this difficulty. From that moment, however, the old *nakhoda* became
taciturn. He was not very pleased, I fear, and evidently I had given him food for
thought. Strangely enough, on the evening of that very day (which was my last in
Patusan) I was once more confronted with the same question, with the unanswerable why of Jim's fate. And this brings me to the story of his love.

"I suppose you think it is a story that you can imagine for yourselves. We have
heard so many such stories, and the majority of us don't believe them to be stories
of love at all. For the most part we look upon them as stories of opportunities: episodes of passion at best, or perhaps only of youth and temptation, doomed to forgetfulness in the end, even if they pass through the reality of tenderness and
regret. This view mostly is right, and perhaps in this case too. . . . Yet I don't
know. To tell this story is by no means so easy as it should be—were the ordinary
standpoint adequate. Apparently it is a story very much like the others: for me,
however, there is visible in its background the melancholy figure of a woman, the
shadow of a cruel wisdom buried in a lonely grave, looking on wistfully, helplessly,
with sealed lips. The grave itself, as I came upon it during an early morning stroll,
was a rather shapeless brown mound, with an inlaid neat border of white lumps
of coral at the base, and enclosed within a circular fence made of split saplings,
with the bark left on. A garland of leaves and flowers was woven about the heads
of the slender posts—and the flowers were fresh.

"Thus, whether the shadow is of my imagination or not, I can at all events
point out the significant fact of an unforgotten grave. When I tell you besides that
Jim with his own hands had worked at the rustic fence, you will perceive directly
the difference, the individual side of the story. There is in his espousal of memory
and affection belonging to another human being something characteristic of his seriousness. He had a conscience, and it was a romantic conscience. Through her
whole life the wife of the unspeakable Cornelius had no other companion, confidant, and friend but her daughter. How the poor woman had come to marry the
awful little Malacca Portuguese—after the separation from the father of her girl—
and how that separation had been brought about, whether by death, which can be
sometimes merciful, or by the merciless pressure of conventions, is a mystery to
me. From the little which Stein (who knew so many stories) had let drop in my
hearing, I am convinced that she was no ordinary woman. Her own father had

been a white; a high official; one of the brilliantly endowed men who are not dull
enough to nurse a success, and whose careers so often end under a cloud. I suppose she too must have lacked the saving dulness—and her career ended in Patusan. Our common fate . . . for where is the man—I mean a real sentient man—
who does not remember vaguely having been deserted in the fulness of possession by some one or something more precious than life? . . . our common fate fastens upon the women with a peculiar cruelty. It does not punish like a master, but
inflicts lingering torment, as if to gratify a secret, unappeasable spite. One would
think that, appointed to rule on earth, it seeks to revenge itself upon the beings
that come nearest to rising above the trammels of earthly caution; for it is only
women who manage to put at times into their love an element just palpable
enough to give one a fright—an extra-terrestrial touch. I ask myself with wonder—
how the world can look to them—whether it has the shape and substance *we*
know, the air *we* breathe! Sometimes I fancy it must be a region of unreasonable
sublimities seething with the excitement of their adventurous souls, lighted by the
glory of all possible risks and renunciations. However, I suspect there are very few
women in the world, though of course I am aware of the multitudes of mankind
and of the equality of sexes in point of numbers—that is. But I am sure that the
mother was as much of a woman as the daughter seemed to be. I cannot help pic-
turing to myself these two, at first the young woman and the child, then the old
woman and the young girl, the awful sameness and the swift passage of time, the
barrier of forest, the solitude and the turmoil round these two lonely lives, and
every word spoken between them penetrated with sad meaning. There must have
been confidences, not so much of fact, I suppose, as of innermost feeling—regrets—fears—warnings, no doubt: warnings that the younger did not fully understand till the elder was dead—and Jim came along. Then I am sure she
understood much—not everything—the fear mostly it seems. Jim called her by a
word that means precious, in the sense of a precious gem—jewel. Pretty, isn't it?
But he was capable of anything. He was equal to his fortune, as he—after all—
must have been equal to his misfortune. Jewel he called her; and he would say this
as he might have said 'Jane,' don't you know, with a marital, homelike, peaceful
effect. I heard the name for the first time ten minutes after I had landed in his
courtyard, when, after nearly shaking my arm off, he darted up the steps and began to make a joyous, boyish disturbance at the door under the heavy eaves.
'Jewel! O! Jewel. Quick! Here's a friend come,' . . . and suddenly peering at me in
the dim verandah, he mumbled earnestly, 'You know—this—no confounded nonsense about it—can't tell you how much I owe to her—and so—you understand—
I—exactly as if . . .' His hurried, anxious whispers were cut short by the flitting of
a white form within the house, a faint exclamation, and a child-like but energetic
little face with delicate features and a profound attentive glance peeped out of the
inner gloom, like a bird out of the recess of a nest. I was struck by the name, of
course; but it was not till later on that I connected it with an astonishing rumour
that had met me on my journey, at a little place on the coast about 230 miles south
of Patusan river. Stein's schooner, in which I had my passage, put in there, to collect some produce, and, going ashore, I found to my great surprise that the
wretched locality could boast of a third-class deputy-assistant resident, a big, fat,
greasy, blinking fellow of mixed descent, with turned out, shiny lips. I found him
lying extended on his back in a cane chair, odiously unbuttoned, with a large

green leaf of some sort on the top of his steaming head, and another in his hand which he used lazily as a fan. . . . Going to Patusan? Oh yes. Stein's Trading Company. He knew. Had a permission. No business of his. It was not so bad there now, he remarked negligently, and, he went on drawling, 'there's some sort of white vagabond had got in there, I hear. . . . Eh? What you say? Friend of yours? So! . . . Then it was true there was one of these *vordamte* —What was he up to? Found his way in, the rascal. Eh? I had not been sure. Patusan—they cut throats there—no business of ours.' He interrupted himself to groan. 'Phoo! Almighty! The heat! The heat! Well, then, there might be something in the story too, after all, and . . .' He shut one of his beastly glassy eyes (the eyelid went on quivering), while he leered at me atrociously with the other. 'Look here,' says he mysteriously, 'if—do you understand?—if he has really got hold of something fairly good—none of your bits of green glass—understand?—I am a government official—you tell the rascal . . . Eh? What? Friend of yours?' . . . He continued wallowing calmly in the chair . . . 'You said so; that's just it; and I am pleased to give you the hint. I suppose you too would like to get something out of it? Don't interrupt. You just tell him I've heard the tale, but to my government I have made no report. Not yet. See? Why make a report? Eh? Tell him to come to me if they let him get alive out of the country. He had better look out for himself. Eh? I promise to ask no questions. On the quiet—you understand? You too—you shall get something from me. Small commission for the trouble. Don't interrupt. I am a government official, and make no report. That's business. Understand? I know some good people that will buy anything worth having, and can give him more money than the scoundrel ever saw in his life. I know his sort.' He fixed me steadfastly with both his eyes open, while I stood over him utterly amazed, and asking myself whether he was mad or drunk. he perspired, puffed, moaning feebly, and scratching himself with such horrible composure that I could not bear the sight long enough to find out. Next day, talking casually with the people of the little native court of the place, I discovered that a story was travelling slowly down the coast about a mysterious white man in Patusan who had got hold of an extraordinary gem—namely, an emerald of an enormous size, and altogether priceless. The emerald seems to appeal more to the Eastern imagination than any other precious stone. The white man had obtained it, I was told, partly by the exercise of his wonderful strength and partly by cunning, from the ruler of a distant country, whence he had fled instantly, arriving in Patusan in utmost distress, but frightening the people by his extreme ferocity, which nothing seemed able to subdue. Most of my informants were of the opinion that the stone was probably unlucky,—like the famous stone of the Sultan of Succadana, which in the old times had brought wars and untold calamities upon that country. Perhaps it was the same stone—one couldn't say. Indeed the story of a fabulously large emerald is as old as the arrival of the first white men in the Archipelago; and the belief in it is so persistent that less than forty years ago there had been an official Dutch inquiry into the truth of it. Such a jewel—it was explained to me by the old fellow from whom I heard most of this amazing Jim-myth—a sort of scribe to the wretched little Rajah of the place;—such a jewel, he said, cooking his poor purblind eye up at me (he was sitting on the cabin floor out of respect), is best preserved by being concealed about the person of a woman. Yet it is not every woman that would do. She must be young—he sighed deeply—and insensible to the seductions of love. He shook his head sceptically. But such a woman seemed to be actually in existence. He had been told of a tall girl, whom the white man treated with great respect and care, and who never went forth from the house unattended. People said the white man could be seen with her almost any day; they walked side by side, openly, he holding her arm under his—pressed to his side—thus—in a most extraordinary way. This might be a lie, he conceded, for it was indeed a strange thing for any one to do: on the other hand, there could be no doubt she wore the white man's jewel concealed upon her bosom."

CHAPTER XXIX.

"This was the theory of Jim's marital evening walks. I made a third on more than one occasion, unpleasantly aware every time of Cornelius, who nursed the aggrieved sense of his legal paternity, slinking in the neighbourhood with that peculiar twist of his mouth as if he were perpetually on the point of gnashing his teeth. But do you notice how, three hundred miles beyond the end of telegraph cables and mail-boat lines, the haggard utilitarian lies of our civilisation wither and die, to be replaced by pure exercises of imagination, that have the futility, often the charm, and sometimes the deep hidden truthfulness, of works of art? Romance had singled Jim for its own—and that was the true part of the story, which otherwise was all wrong. He did not hide his jewel. In fact, he was extremely proud of it.

"It comes to me now that I had, on the whole, seen very little of her. What I remember best is the even, olive pallor of her complexion, and the intense blue-black gleams of her hair, flowing abundantly from under a small crimson cap she wore far back on her shapely head. Her movements were free, assured, and she blushed a dusky red. While Jim and I were talking, she would come and go with rapid glances at us, leaving on her passage an impression of grace and charm and a distinct suggestion of watchfulness. Her manner presented a curious combination of shyness and audacity. Every pretty smile was succeeded swiftly by a look of silent, repressed anxiety, as if put to flight by the recollection of some abiding danger. At times she would sit down with us and, with her soft cheek dimpled by the knuckles of her little hand, she would listen to our talk; her big clear eyes would remain fastened on our lips, as though each pronounced word had a visible shape. Her mother had taught her to read and write; she had learned a good bit of English from Jim, and she spoke it most amusingly, with his own clipping, boyish intonation. Her tenderness hovered over him like a flutter of wings. She lived so completely in his contemplation that she had acquired something of his outward aspect, something that recalled him in her movements, in the way she stretched her arm, turned her head, directed her glances. Her vigilant affection had an intensity that made it almost perceptible to the senses; it seemed actually to exist in the ambient matter of space, to envelope him like a peculiar fragrance, to dwell in the sunshine like a tremulous, subdued, and impassioned note. I suppose you think that I too am romantic, but it is a mistake. I am relating to you the sober impressions of a bit of youth, of a strange uneasy romance that had come in my way. I observed with interest the work of his—well—good fortune. He was jealously loved, but why she should be jealous, and of what, I could not tell. The land, the people, the forests were her accomplices, guarding him with vigilant accord, with an air of seclusion, of mystery, of invincible possession. There was no appeal, as it were; he was imprisoned within the very freedom of his power, and she, though ready to make a footstool of her head for his feet, guarded her conquest inflexibly—as though he were hard to keep. The very Tamb' Itam, marching on our journeys upon the heels of his white lord, with his head thrown back, truculent and be-weaponed like a janissary, with kris, chopper, and lance (besides carrying Jim's gun); even Tamb' Itam allowed himself to put on the airs of uncompromising guardianship, like a surly devoted jailer ready to lay down his life for his captive. On the evenings when we sat up late his silent, indistinct form would pass and repass under the verandah, with noiseless footsteps, or lifting my head I would unexpectedly make him out standing rigidly erect in the shadow. As a general rule he would vanish after a time, without a sound; but when we rose he would spring up close to us as if from the ground, ready for any orders Jim might wish to give. The girl too, I believe, never went to sleep till we had separated for the night. More than once I saw her and Jim through the window of my room come out together quietly and lean on the rough balustrade—two white forms very close, his arm about her waist, her head on his shoulder. Their soft murmurs reached me, penetrating, tender, with a calm sad note in the stillness of the night; like a self-communion of one being carried on in two tones. Later on, tossing on my bed under the mosquito-net, I was sure to hear slight creakings, faint breathing, a throat cleared cautiously—and I would know that Tamb' Itam was still on the prowl. Though he had (by the favour of the white lord) a house in the compound, had 'taken wife,' and had lately been blessed with a child, I believe that, during my stay at all events, he slept on the verandah every night. It was very difficult to make this faithful and grim retainer talk. Even Jim himself was answered in jerky short sentences, under protest as it were. Talking, he seemed to imply, was no business of his. The longest speech I heard him volunteer was one morning when, suddenly extending his hand towards the courtyard, he pointed at Cornelius and said, 'Here comes the Nazarene.' I don't think he was addressing me, though I stood at his side; his object seemed rather to awaken the indignant attention of the universe. Some muttered allusions, which followed, to dogs and the smell of roast-meat, struck me as singularly felicitous. The courtyard, a large square space, was one torrid blaze of sunshine, and, bathed in intense light, Cornelius was creeping across in full view with an inexpressible effect of stealthiness, of dark and secret slinking. He reminded one of everything that is unsavoury. His slow laborious walk resembled the creeping of a repulsive beetle, the legs alone moving with horrid industry while the body glided evenly. I suppose he made straight enough for the place where he wanted to get to, but his progress with one shoulder carried forward seemed oblique. He was often seen circling slowly amongst the sheds, as if following a scent; passing before the verandah with upward stealthy glances; disappearing without haste round the corner of some hut. That he seemed free of the place demonstrated Jim's absurd carelessness or else his infinite disdain, for Cornelius had played a very dubious part (to say the least of it) in a certain episode which might have ended fatally for Jim. As a matter of fact, it had redounded to his glory. But everything redounded to his glory; and it was the irony of his good fortune that he, who had been too careful of it once, seemed to bear a charmed life.

"You must know he had left Doramin's place very soon after his arrival—much too soon, in fact, for his safety, and of course a long time before the war. In this he was actuated by a sense of duty; he had to look after Stein's business, he said. Hadn't he? To that end, with an utter disregard of his personal safety, he crossed the river and took up his quarters with Cornelius. How the latter had managed to exist through the troubled times I can't say. As Stein's agent, after all, he must have had Doramin's protection in a measure; and in one way or another he had managed to wriggle through all the deadly complications, while I have no doubt that his conduct, whatever line he was forced to take, was marked by that abjectness which was like the stamp of the man. That was his characteristic; he was fundamentally and outwardly abject, as other men are markedly of a gener-ous, distinguished, or venerable appearance. It was the element of his nature which permeated all his acts and passions and emotions; he raged abjectly, smiled abjectly, was abjectly sad; his civilities and his indignations were alike abject. I am sure his love would have been the most abject of sentiments—but can one imagine a loathsome insect in love? And his loathsomeness too was abject, so that a simply disgusting person would have appeared noble by his side. He has his place neither in the background nor in the foreground of the story; he is simply seen skulking on its outskirts, enigmatical and unclean, tainting the fragrance of its youth and of its naïveness.

"His position in any case could not have been other than extemely miserable, yet it may very well be that he found some advantages in it. Jim told me he had been received at first with an abject display of the most amicable sentiments. 'The fellow apparently couldn't contain himself for joy,' said Jim with disgust. 'He flew at me every morning to shake both my hands—confound him! but I could never tell whether there would be any breakfast. If I got three meals in two days I con-sidered myself jolly lucky, and he made me sign a chit for ten dollars every week. Said he was sure Mr Stein did not mean him to keep me for nothing. Well—he kept me on nothing as near as possible. Put it down to the unsettled state of the coun-try, and made as if to tear his hair out, begging my pardon twenty times a-day, so that I had at last to entreat him not to worry. It made me sick. Half the roof of his house had fallen in, and the whole place had a mangy look, with wisps of dry grass sticking out and the corners of broken mats flapping on every wall. He did his best to make out that Mr Stein owed him money on the last three years' trad-ing, but his books were all torn, and some were missing. He tried to hint it was his late wife's fault. Disgusting scoundrel! At last I had to forbid him to mention his late wife at all. It made Jewel cry. I couldn't discover what became of all the trade-goods; there was nothing in the store but rats, having a high old time amongst a litter of brown paper and old sacking. I was assured on every hand that he had a lot of money buried somewhere, but of course could get nothing out of him. It was the most miserable existence I led there in that wretched house. I tried to do my duty by Stein, but I had also other matters to think of. When I escaped to Doramin old Tunku Allang got frightened and returned all my things. It was done in a roun-dabout way, and with no end of mystery, through a Chinaman who keeps a small shop here; but as soon as I left the Bugis quarter and went to live with Cornelius it began to be said openly that the Rajah had made up his mind to have me killed before long. Pleasant, wasn't it? And I couldn't see what was there to prevent him if he really *had* made up his mind. The worst of it was, I couldn't help feeling I wasn't doing any good either for Stein or for myself. Oh! it was beastly—the whole six weeks of it.'"

CHAPTER XXX.

"He told me further that he didn't know what made him hang on—but of course we may guess. He sympathised deeply with the defenceless girl, at the mercy of that 'mean, cowardly scoundrel.' It appears Cornelius led her an awful life, stopping only short of actual ill-usage, for which he had not the pluck, I suppose. He insisted upon her calling him father—'and with respect too—with respect,' he would scream, shaking a little yellow fist in her face. 'I am a respectable man, and what are you? Tell me—what are you? You think I am going to bring up somebody else's child and not be treated with respect? You ought to be glad I let you. Come—say Yes, father. . . . No? . . . You wait a bit.' Thereupon he would begin to abuse the dead woman, till the girl would run off with her hands to her head. He pursued her, dashing in and out and round the house and amongst the sheds, would drive her into some corner, where she would fall on her knees stopping her ears, and then he would stand at a distance and declaim filthy denunciations at her back for half an hour at a stretch. 'Your mother was a devil, a deceitful devil—and you too are a devil,' he would shriek in a final outburst, pick up a bit of dry earth or a handful of mud (there was plenty of mud around the house), and fling it into her hair. Sometimes, though, she would hold out full of scorn, confronting him in silence, her face sombre and contracted, and only now and then uttering a word or two that would make the other jump and writhe with the sting. Jim told me these scenes were terrible. It was indeed a strange thing to come upon in a wilderness. The endlessness of such a subtly cruel situation was appalling—if you think of it. The respectable Cornelius (Inchi 'Nelyus the Malays called him, with a grimace that meant many things) was a much-disappointed man. I don't know what he had expected would be done for him in consideration of his marriage; but evidently the liberty to steal, and embezzle, and appropriate to himself for many years and in any way that suited him best, the goods of Stein's Trading Co. (Stein kept the supply up unfalteringly as long as he could get his skippers to take it there) did not seem to him a fair equivalent for the sacrifice of his honourable name. Jim would have enjoyed exceedingly thrashing Cornelius within an inch of his life; on the other hand, the scenes were of so painful a character, so abominable, that his impulse would be to get out of earshot, in order to spare the girl's feelings. They left her agitated, speechless, clutching her bosom now and then with a stony, desperate face, and then Jim would lounge up and say unhappily, 'Now—come—really—what's the use—you must try to eat a bit,' or give some such mark of sympathy. Cornelius would keep on slinking through the doorways, across the verandah and back again, as mute as a fish, and with malevolent, mistrustful, underhand glances. 'I can stop his game,' Jim said to her once. 'Just say the word.' And do you know what she answered? She said—Jim told me impressively—that if she had not been sure he was intensely wretched himself, she would have found the courage to kill him with her own hands. 'Just fancy that! The poor devil of a girl, almost a child, being driven to talk like that,' he exclaimed in horror. It seemed impossible to save her not only from that mean rascal but even from herself! It wasn't that he pitied her so much, he affirmed; it was more than pity; it was as if he had something on his conscience, while that life went on. To leave the house would have appeared a base desertion. He had understood at last that there was nothing to expect from a longer stay, neither accounts nor money, nor truth of any sort, but he stayed on, exasperating Cornelius to the verge, I won't say of insanity, but almost of courage. Meantime he felt all sorts of dangers gathering obscurely about him. Doramin had sent over twice a trusty servant to tell him seriously that he could do nothing for his safety unless he would recross the river again and live amongst the Bugis as at first. People of every condition used to call, often in the dead of night, in order to disclose to him plots for his assassination. He was to be poisoned. He was to be stabbed in the bath-house. Arrangements were being made to have him shot from a boat on the river. Each of these informants professed himself to be his very good friend. It was enough—he told me—to spoil a fellow's rest for ever. Something of the kind was extremely possible—nay, probable—but the lying warnings gave him only the sense of deadly scheming going on all around him, on all sides, in the dark. Nothing more calculated to shake the best of nerve. Finally, one night, Cornelius himself, with a great apparatus of alarm and secrecy, unfolded in solemn wheedling tones a little plan wherein for one hundred dollars—or even for eighty; let's say eighty—he, Cornelius, would procure a trustworthy man to smuggle Jim out of the river, all safe. There was nothing else for it now—if Jim cared a pin for his life. What's eighty dollars? A trifle. An insignificant sum. While he, Cornelius, who had to remain behind, was absolutely courting death by this proof of devotion to Mr Stein's young friend. The sight of his abject grimacing was—Jim told me—very hard to bear: he clutched at his hair, beat his breast, rocked himself to and fro with his hands pressed to his stomach, and actually pretended to shed tears. 'Your blood be on your own head,' he squeaked at last, and rushed out. It is a curious question how far Cornelius was sincere in that performance. Jim confessed to me that he did not sleep a wink after the fellow had gone. He lay on his back on a thin mat spread over the bamboo flooring, trying idly to make out the bare rafters, and listening to the rustlings in the torn thatch. A star suddenly twinkled through a hole in the roof. His brain was in a whirl; but, nevertheless, it was on that very night that he matured his plan for overcoming Sherif Ali. It had been the thought of all the moments he could spare from the hopeless investigation into Stein's affairs, but the notion—he says—came to him then all at once. He could see, as it were, the guns mounted on the top of the hill. He got very hot and excited lying there; sleep was out of the question more than ever. He jumped up, and went out barefooted on the verandah. Walking silently, he came upon the girl, motionless against the wall, as if on the watch. In his then state of mind it did not surprise him to see her up, nor yet to hear her ask in an anxious whisper where Cornelius could be. He simply said he did not know. She moaned a little, and peered into the *campong*. Everything was very quiet. He was possessed by his new idea, and so full of it that he could not help telling the girl all about it at once. She listened, clapped her hands lightly, whispered softly her admiration, but was evidently on the alert all the time. It seems he had been used to make a confident of her all along—and that she on her part could and did give him a lot of useful hints as to Patusan affairs there is no doubt. He assured me more than once that he had never found himself the worse for her advice. At any rate, he was proceeding to explain his plan fully to her there and then, when she pressed his arm once, and vanished from his side. Then Cornelius appeared from somewhere, and, perceiving Jim, ducked sideways, as though he had been shot at, and afterwards stood very still in the dusk. At last he came forward prudently, like a suspicious cat. 'There were some fish-

ermen there—with fish,' he said in a shaky voice. 'To sell fish—you understand.'
. . . It must have been then two o'clock in the morning—a likely time for anybody
to hawk fish about!

"Jim, however, let the statement pass, and did not give it a single thought.
Other matters occupied his mind, and besides he had neither seen nor heard anything. He contented himself by saying, 'Oh!' absently, got a drink of water out of
a pitcher standing there, and leaving Cornelius a prey to some inexplicable emotion—that made him embrace with both arms the worm-eaten rail of the verandah
as if his legs had failed—went in again and lay down on his mat to think. By-and-
by he heard stealthy footsteps. They stopped. A voice whispered tremulously
through the wall, 'Are you asleep?' 'No! What is it?' he answered briskly, and there
was an abrupt movement outside, and then all was still, as if the whisperer had
been startled. Extremely annoyed at this, Jim came out impetuously, and Cornelius with a faint shriek fled along the verandah as far as the steps, where he hung
on to the broken banister. Very puzzled, Jim called out to him from the distance
to know what the devil he meant. 'Have you given your consideration to what I
spoke to you about?' asked Cornelius, pronouncing the words with difficulty, like
a man in the cold fit of a fever. 'No!' shouted Jim in a passion. 'I did not, and I don't
intend to. I am going to live here, in Patusan.' 'You shall d-d-die h-h-here,' answered Cornelius, still shaking violently, and in a sort of expiring voice. The whole
performance was so absurd and provoking that Jim didn't know whether he ought
to be amused or angry. 'Not till I had seen you tucked away, you bet,' he called out,
exasperated yet ready to laugh. Half seriously (being excited with his own
thoughts, you know) he went on shouting, 'Nothing can touch me! You can do
your damnedest.' Somehow the shadowy Cornelius far off there seemed to be the
hateful embodiment of all the annoyances and difficulties he had found in his
path. He let himself go—his nerves had been over-wrought for days—and called
him many pretty names,—swindler, liar, sorry rascal: in fact, carried on in an extraordinary way. He admits he passed all bounds, that he was quite beside himself—defied all Patusan to scare him away—declared he would make them all
dance to his own tune yet, and so on, in a menacing, boasting strain. Perfectly
bombastic and ridiculous, he said. His ears burned at the bare recollection. Must
have been off his chump in some way. . . . The girl, who was sitting with us, nodded her little head at me quickly, frowned faintly, and said, 'I heard him,' with
childlike solemnity. He laughed and blushed. What stopped him at last, he said,
was the silence, the complete deathlike silence, of the indistinct figure far over
there, that seemed to hang collapsed, doubled over the rail in a weird immobility.
He came to his senses, and ceasing suddenly, wondered greatly at himself. He
watched for a while. Not a stir, not a sound. 'Exactly as if the chap had died while
I had been making all that noise,' he said. He was so ashamed of himself that he
went indoors in a hurry without another word, and flung himself down again. The
row seemed to have done him good though, because he went to sleep for the rest
of the night like a baby. Hadn't slept like that for weeks. 'But I didn't sleep,' struck
in the girl, one elbow on the table and nursing her cheek. 'I watched.' Her big eyes
flashed, rolling a little, and then she fixed them on my face intently."

CHAPTER XXXI.

"You may imagine with what interest I listened. All these details were perceived to have some significance twenty-four hours later. In the morning Cornelius made no allusion to the events of the night. 'I suppose you will come back to my poor house,' he muttered surlily, slinking up just as Jim was entering the canoe to go over to Doramin's *campong*. Jim only nodded, without looking at him. 'You find it good fun, no doubt,' muttered the other in a sour tone. Jim spent the day with the old *nakhoda*, preaching the necessity of vigorous action to the principal men of the Bugis community, who had been summoned for a big talk. He remembered with pleasure how very eloquent and persuasive he had been. 'I managed to put some backbone into them that time, and no mistake,' he said. Sherif Ali's last raid had swept the outskirts of the settlement, and some women belonging to the town had been carried off to the stockade. Sherif Ali's emissaries had been seen in the marketplace the day before, strutting about haughtily in white cloaks, and boasting of the Rajah's friendship for their master. One of them stood forward in the shade of a tree, and, leaning on the long barrel of a rifle, exhorted the people to prayer and repentance, advising them to kill all the strangers in their midst, some of whom, he said, were infidels and others even worse—children of Satan in the guise of Moslems. It was reported that several of the Rajah's people amongst the listeners had loudly expressed their approbation. The terror amongst the common people was intense. Jim, immensely pleased with his day's work, crossed the river again before sunset.

"As he had got the Bugis irretrievably committed to action, and had made himself responsible for success on his own head, he was so elated that in the lightness of his heart he absolutely tried to be civil with Cornelius. But Cornelius became wildly jovial in response, and it was almost more than he could stand, he says, to hear his little squeaks of false laughter, to see him wriggle and blink, and suddenly catch hold of his chin and crouch low over the table with a distracted stare. The girl did not show herself, and Jim retired early. When he rose to say good-night, Cornelius jumped up, knocking his chair over, and ducked out of sight as if to pick up something he had dropped. His good-night came huskily from under the table. Jim was amazed to see him emerge out with a dropping jaw, and staring, stupidly frightened eyes. He clutched the edge of the table. 'What's the matter? Are you unwell?' asked Jim. 'Yes, yes, yes. A great colic in my stomach,' says the other; and it is Jim's opinion that it was perfectly true. If so, it was, in view of his contemplated action, an abject sign of a still imperfect callousness for which he must be given all due credit.

"Be it as it may, Jim's slumbers were disturbed by a dream of heavens like brass resounding with a great voice, which called upon him to Awake! Awake! so loud that, notwithstanding his desperate determination to sleep on, he did wake up in reality. The glare of a red spluttering conflagration going on in mid-air fell on his eyes. Coils of black thick smoke curved round the head of some apparition, some unearthly being, all in white, with a severe, drawn, anxious face. After a second or so he recognised the girl. She was holding a dammar torch at arm's-length aloft, and in a persistent, urgent monotone she was repeating, 'Get up! Get up! Get up!'

"Suddenly he leaped to his feet; at once she put into his hand a revolver; his own revolver, which had been hanging on a nail, but loaded this time. He gripped it in silence, bewildered, blinking in the light. He wondered what he could do for her.

"She asked rapidly and very low, 'Can you face four men with this?' He laughed while narrating this part at the recollection of his polite alacrity. It seems he made a great display of it. 'Certainly—of course—certainly—command me.' He was not properly awake, and had a notion of being very civil in these extraordinary circumstances, of showing his unquestioning, devoted readiness. She left the room, and he followed her; in the passage they disturbed an old hag who did the casual cooking of the household, though she was so decrepit as to be hardly able to understand human speech. She got up and hobbled behind them, mumbling toothlessly. On the verandah a hammock of sail-cloth, belonging to Cornelius, swayed lightly to the touch of Jim's elbow. It was empty.

"The Patusan establishment, like all the posts of Stein's Trading Company, had originally consisted of four buildings. Two of them were represented by two heaps of sticks, broken bamboos, rotten thatch, over which the four corner-posts of hardwood leaned sadly at different angles: the principal storeroom, however, stood yet, facing the agent's house. It was an oblong hut, built of mud and clay: it had at one end a wide door of stout planking, which so far had not come off the hinges, and in one of the side walls there was a square aperture, a sort of window, with three wooden bars. Before descending the few steps the girl turned her face over her shoulder and said quickly. 'You were to be set upon while you slept.' Jim tells me he experienced a sense of deception. It was the old story. He was weary of these attempts upon his life. He had had his fill of these alarms. He was sick of them. He assured me he was angry with the girl for deceiving him. He had followed her under the impression that it was she who wanted his help, and now he had half a mind to turn on his heel and go back in disgust. 'Do you know,' he commented profoundly; 'I rather think I was not quite myself for whole weeks on end about that time?' 'Oh yes. You were though,' I couldn't help contradicting.

"But she moved on swiftly, and he followed her into the courtyard. All its fences had fallen in a long time ago; the neighbours' buffaloes would pace in the morning across the open space, snorting profoundly, without haste; the very jungle was invading it already. Jim and the girl stopped in the rank grass. The light in which they stood made a dense blackness all round, and only above their heads there was an opulent glitter of stars. He told me it was a beautiful night—quite cool, with a little stir of breeze from the river. It seems he noticed its friendly beauty. Remember this is a love-story I am telling you now. A lovely night that seemed to breathe on them a soft caress. The flame of the torch streamed now and then with a fluttering noise like a flag, and for a time this was the only sound. 'They are in the storeroom waiting,' whispered the girl; 'they are waiting for the signal.' 'Who's to give it?' he asked. She shook the torch, which blazed up after a shower of sparks. 'Only you have been sleeping so restlessly,' she continued in a murmur. 'I watched your sleep, too.' 'You!' he exclaimed, craning his neck to look about him. 'You think I watched on this night only!' she said, with a sort of despairing indignation.

"He says it was as if he had received a blow on the chest. He gasped. He thought he had been an awful brute somehow, and he felt remorseful, touched, happy, elated. This, let me remind you again, is a love-story; you can see it by the imbecility, not a repulsive imbecility, the exalted imbecility of these proceedings, this station in torchlight, as if they had come there on purpose to have it out for the edification of concealed murderers. If Sherif Ali's emissaries had been possessed—as Jim remarked—of a pennyworth of spunk, this was the time to make a rush. His heart was thumping—not with fear—but he seemed to hear the grass rustle, and he stepped smartly out of the light. Something dark, imperfectly seen, flitted rapidly out of sight. He called out in a strong voice, 'Cornelius! O Cornelius!' A profound silence succeeded: his voice did not seem to have carried twenty feet. Again the girl was by his side. 'Fly!' she said. The old woman was coming up; her broken figure hovered in crippled little jumps on the edge of the light; they heard her mumbling, and a light, moaning sigh. 'Fly!' repeated the girl excitedly. 'They are frightened now—this light—the voices. They know you are awake now—they know you are big, strong, fearless . . .' 'If I am all that,' he began, but she interrupted him. 'Yes—to-night! But what of to-morrow night? Of the next night? Of the night after—of all the many, many nights? Can I be always watching?' A sobbing catch of her breath affected him beyond the power of words.

"He told me that he had never felt so small, so powerless—and as to courage, what was the good of it, he thought. He was so helpless that even flight seemed of no use; and though she kept on whispering, 'Go to Doramin, go to Doramin,' with feverish insistence, he realised that for him there was no refuge from that loneliness which centupled all his dangers except—in her. 'I thought,' he said to me, 'that if I went away from her it would be the end of everything somehow. Only as they couldn't stop there for ever in the middle of that courtyard, he made up his mind to go and look into the storehouse. He let her follow him without thinking of any protest, as if they had been indissolubly united. 'I am fearless—am I?' he muttered through his teeth. She restrained his arm. 'Wait till you hear my voice,' she said, and, torch in hand, ran lightly round the corner. He remained alone in the darkness, his face to the door: not a sound, not a breath came from the other side. The old hag let out a dreary groan somewhere behind his back. He heard a high-pitched almost screaming call from the girl. 'Now! Push!' He pushed violently; the door swung with a creak and a clatter, disclosing to his intense astonishment the low dungeon-like interior illuminated by a lurid, wavering glare. A turmoil of smoke eddied down upon an empty wooden crate in the middle of the floor, a litter of rags and straw tried to soar, but only stirred feebly in the draught. She had thrust the light through the bars of the window. He saw her bare round arm extended and rigid, holding up the torch with the steadiness of an iron bracket. A conical ragged heap of old mats cumbered a distant corner almost to the ceiling, and that was all.

"He explained to me that he was bitterly disappointed at this. His fortitude had been tried by so many warnings, he had been for weeks surrounded by so many hints of danger, that he wanted the relief of some reality, of something tangible that he could meet. 'It would have cleared the air for a couple of hours at least, if you know what I mean,' he said to me. 'Jove! I had been living for days with a stone on my chest.' Now at last he had thought he would get hold of something, and—nothing! Not a trace, not a sign of anybody. He had raised his weapon as the door flew open, but now his arm fell. 'Fire! Defend yourself,' the girl outside cried in an agonising voice. She, being in the dark and with her arm thrust in to the shoulder through the small hole, couldn't see what was going on, and she dared not withdraw the torch now to run round. 'There's nobody here!' yelled Jim contemptuously, but his impulse to burst into a resentful exasperated laugh died without a sound: he had perceived in the very act of turning away that he was exchanging glances with a pair of eyes in the heap of mats. He saw a shifting gleam of whites. 'Come out!' he cried in a fury, a little doubtful, and a dark-faced head, a head without a body, shaped itself in the rubbish, a strangely detached head, that looked at him with a steady scowl. Next moment the whole mound stirred, and with a low grunt a man emerged swiftly, and bounded towards Jim. Behind him the mats as it were jumped and flew, his right arm was raised with a crooked elbow, and the dull blade of a *kriss* protruded from his fist held off, a little above his head. A cloth wound tight round his loins seemed dazzlingly white on his bronze skin; his naked body glistened as if wet.

"Jim noted all this. He told me he was experiencing a feeling of unutterable relief, of vengeful elation. He held his shot, he says, deliberately. He held it for the tenth part of a second, for three strides of the man—an unconscionable time. He held it for the pleasure of saying to himself, That's a dead man! He was absolutely positive and certain. He let him come on because it did not matter. A dead man, anyhow. He noticed the dilated nostrils, the wide eyes, the intent, eager stillness of the face, and then he fired.

"The explosion in that confined space was stunning. He stepped back a pace. He saw the man jerk his head up, fling his arms forward, and drop the *kriss*. He ascertained afterwards that he had shot him through the mouth, a little upwards, the bullet coming out high at the back of the skull. With the impetus of his rush the man drove straight on, his face suddenly gaping disfigured, with his hands open before him gropingly, as though blinded, and landed with terrific violence on his forehead, just short of Jim's bare toes. Jim says he didn't lose the smallest detail of all this. He found himself calm, appeased, without rancour, without uneasiness, as if the death of that man had atoned for everything. The place was getting very full of sooty smoke from the torch, in which the unswaying flame burned blood-red without a flicker. He walked in resolutely, striding over the dead body, and covered with his revolver another naked figure outlined vaguely at the other end. As he was about to pull the trigger, the man threw away with force a short heavy spear, and squatted submissively on his hams, his back to the wall and his clasped hands between his legs. 'You want your life?' Jim said. The other made no sound. 'How many more of you?' asked Jim again. 'Two more, Tuan,' said the man very softly, looking with big fascinated eyes into the muzzle of the revolver. Accordingly two more crawled from under the mats, holding out ostentatiously their empty hands."

CHAPTER XXXII.

"Jim took up an advantageous position and shepherded them out in a bunch through the doorway: all that time the torch had remained vertical in the grip of a little hand, without so much as a tremble. The three men obeyed him, perfectly mute, moving automatically. He ranged them in a row. 'Link arms!' he ordered.

They did so. 'The first who withdraws his arm or turns his head is a dead man,' he said. 'March!' They stepped out together, rigidly; he followed, and at the side the girl, in a trailing white gown, her black hair falling as low as her waist, bore the light. Erect and swaying, she seemed to glide without touching the earth; the only sound was the silky swish and rustle of the long grass. 'Stop!' cried Jim.

"The river-bank was steep; a great freshness ascended, the light fell on the edge of smooth dark water frothing without a ripple; right and left the shapes of the houses ran together below the sharp outlines of the roofs. 'Take my greetings to Sherif Ali—till I come myself,' said Jim. Not one head of the three budged. 'Jump!' he thundered. The three splashes made one splash, a shower flew up, black heads bobbed convulsively, and disappeared; but a great blowing and spluttering went on, growing faint, for they were diving industriously, in great fear of a parting shot. Jim turned to the girl, who had been a silent and attentive observer. His heart seemed suddenly to grow too big for his breast and choke him in the hollow of his throat. This probably made him speechless for so long, and after returning his gaze she flung the burning torch with a wide sweep of the arm into the river. The ruddy fiery glare, taking a long flight through the night, sank with a vicious hiss, and the calm soft starlight descended upon them, unchecked.

"He did not tell me what it was he said when at last he recovered his voice. I don't suppose he could be very eloquent. The world was still, the night breathed on them, one of those nights that seem created for the sheltering of tenderness, and there are moments when our souls, as if freed from their dark envelope, glow with an exquisite sensibility that makes certain silences more lucid than speeches. As to the girl, he told me, 'She broke down a bit. Excitement—don't you know. Reaction. Deucedly tired she must have been—and all that kind of thing. And—and—hang it all—she was fond of me, don't you see. . . . I too . . . didn't know, of course . . . never entered my head . . .'

"There he got up and began to walk about in some agitation. 'I—I love her dearly. More than I could tell. Of course one cannot tell. You take a different view of your actions when you come to understand, when you are *made* to understand every day that your existence is necessary—you see, absolutely necessary—to another person. I am made to feel that. Wonderful. But only try to think what her life had been. It is too extravagantly awful! Isn't it? And me finding her here like this— as you may go out for a stroll and come suddenly upon somebody drowning in a lonely dark place. Jove! No time to lose. Well, it is a trust too . . . I believe I am equal to it . . .'

"I must tell you the girl had left us to ourselves some time before. He slapped his chest. 'Yes! I feel that, but I believe I am equal to all my luck!' He had the gift of finding a special meaning in everything that happened to him. This was the view he took of his love-affair; it was idyllic, a little solemn, and also true, since his belief had all the unshakable seriousness of youth. Some time after, on another occasion, he said to me, 'I've been only two years here, and now, upon my word, I can't conceive being able to live anywhere else. The very thought of the world outside is enough to give me a fright; because, don't you see,' he continued, with downcast eyes watching the action of his boot busied in squashing thoroughly a tiny bit of dried mud (we were strolling on the river-bank)—'Because I have not forgotten why I came here. Not yet!'

"I refrained from looking at him, but I think I heard a short sigh; we took a turn or two in silence. 'Upon my soul and conscience,' he began again, 'if such a thing can be forgotten, then I think I have a right to dismiss it from my mind. Ask any man here' . . . his voice changed. 'Is it not strange,' he went on in a gentle, almost yearning tone, 'that all these people, all these people who would do anything for me, can never be made to understand? Never! If you disbelieved me I could not call them up. It seems hard, somehow. I am stupid, am I not? What more can I want? If you ask them who is brave—who is true—who is just—who is it they would trust with their lives?—they would say, Tuan Jim. And yet they can never know the real, real truth . . .'

"That's what he said to me on my last day with him. I did not let a murmur escape me: I felt he was going to say more, and come no nearer to the root of the matter. The sun, whose concentrated glare dwarfs the earth into a restless mote of dust, had sunk behind the forest, and the diffused light from an opal sky seemed to cast upon a world without shadows and without brilliance the illusion of a calm and pensive greatness. I don't know why, listening to him, I should have noted so distinctly the gradual darkening of the river, of the air; the irresistible slow work of the night settling silently on all the visible forms, effacing the outlines, burying the shapes deeper and deeper, like a steady fall of impalpable black dust.

"'Jove!' he began abruptly, 'there are days when a fellow is too absurd for anything; only I know I can tell you what I like. I talk about being done with it—with the bally thing at the back of my head . . . Forgetting . . . Hang me if I know! I can think of it quietly. After all, what has it proved? Nothing. I suppose you don't think so . . .'

"I made a protesting murmur.

"'No matter,' he said. 'I am satisfied . . . nearly. I've got to look only at the face of the first man that comes along, to regain my confidence. They can't be made to understand what is going on in me. What of that? Come! I haven't done so badly.'

"'Not so badly,' I said.

"'But all the same, you wouldn't like to have me aboard your own ship—hey?'

"'Confound you!' I cried. 'Stop this.'

"'Aha! You see,' he said, crowing, as it were, over me placidly. 'Only,' he went on, 'you just try to tell this to any of them here. They would think you a fool, a liar, or worse. And so I can stand it. I've done a thing or two for them, but this is what they have done for me.'

"'My dear chap,' I cried, 'you shall always remain for them an insoluble mystery.' Thereupon we were silent.

"'Mystery,' he repeated, before looking up. 'Well, then let me always remain here.'

"After the sun had set, the darkness seemed to drive upon us, borne in every faint puff of the breeze. In the middle of a hedged path I saw the arrested, gaunt, watchful, and apparently one-legged silhouette of Tamb' Itam; and across the dusky space my eye detected something white moving to and fro behind the supports of the roof. As soon as Jim, with Tamb' Itam at his heels, had started upon his evening rounds, I went up to the house alone, and, unexpectedly, found myself waylaid by the girl, who had been clearly waiting for this opportunity.

"It is hard to tell you what it was precisely she wanted to wrest from me. Obviously it would be something very simple—the simplest impossibility in the world; as, for instance, the exact description of the form of a cloud. She wanted an assurance, a statement, a promise, an explanation—I don't know how to call it: the thing has no name. It was dark under the projecting roof, and all I could see were the flowing lines of her gown, the pale small oval of her face, with the white flash of her teeth, and, turned towards me, the big sombre orbits of her eyes, where there seemed to be a faint stir, such as you may fancy you can detect when you plunge your gaze to the bottom of an immensely deep well. What is it that moves there? you ask yourself. Is it a blind monster or only a lost gleam from the universe? It occurred to me—don't laugh—that all things being dissimilar, she was more inscrutable in her childish ignorance than the sphinx propounding childish riddles to wayfarers. She had been carried off to Patusan before her eyes were open. She had grown up there; she had seen nothing, she had known nothing, she had no conception of anything. I ask myself whether she were sure that anything else existed. What notions she may have formed of the outside world is to me inconceivable: all that she knew of its inhabitants were a betrayed woman and a sinister pantaloon. Her lover also came to her from there, gifted with irresistible seductions; but what would become of her if he should return to these inconceivable regions that seemed always to claim back their own? Her mother had warned her of this with tears, before she died . . .

"She had caught hold of my arm firmly, and as soon as I had stopped she had withdrawn her hand in haste. She was audacious and shrinking. She feared nothing, but she was checked by the profound incertitude and the extreme strangeness—a brave person groping in the dark. I belonged to this Unknown that might claim Jim for its own at any moment. I was, as it were, in the secret of its nature and of its intentions;—the confidant of a threatening mystery;—armed with its power perhaps! I believe she supposed I could with a word whisk Jim away out of her very arms: it is my sober conviction she went through agonies of apprehension during my long talks with Jim; through a real and intolerable anguish that might have conceivably driven her into plotting my murder, had the fierceness of her soul been equal to the tremendous situation it had created. This is my impression, and it is all I can give you: the whole thing dawned gradually upon me, and as it got clearer and clearer I was overwhelmed by a slow incredulous amazement. She made me believe her, but there is no word that on my lips could render the effect of the headlong and vehement whisper, of the soft, passionate tones, of the sudden breathless pause and the appealing movement of the white arms extended swiftly. They fell; the ghostly figure swayed like a slender tree in the wind, the pale oval of the face drooped; it was impossible to distinguish her features, the darkness of the eyes was unfathomable; two wide sleeves uprose in the dark like unfolding wings, and she stood silent, holding her head in her hands."

CHAPTER XXXIII.

"I was immensely touched: her youth, her ignorance, her pretty beauty, which had the simple charm and the delicate vigour of a wild-flower, her pathetic pleading, her helplessness, appealed to me with almost the strength of her own unreasonable and natural fear. She feared the unknown as we all do, and her ignorance made the unknown infinitely vast. I stood for it, for myself, for you fellows, for all the world that neither cared for Jim nor needed him in the least. I would have been ready enough to answer for the indifference of the teeming earth but for the reflection that he too belonged to this mysterious unknown of her fears, and that, however much I stood for, I did not stand for him. This made me hesitate. A murmur of hopeless pain unsealed my lips. I began by protesting that I at least had come with no intention to take Jim away.

"Why did I come, then? After a slight movement she was as still as a marble statue in the night. I tried to explain briefly: friendship, business; if I had any wish in the matter it was rather to see him stay. . . . 'They always leave us,' she murmured. The breath of sad wisdom from the grave which her piety wreathed with flowers seemed to pass in a faint sigh. . . . Nothing, I said, could separate Jim from her.

"It is my firm conviction now; it was my conviction at the time; it was the only possible conclusion from the facts of the case. It was not made more certain by her whispering in a tone in which one speaks to oneself, 'He swore this to me.' 'Did you ask him?' I said.

"She made a step nearer. 'No. Never!' She had asked him only to go away. It was that night on the river-bank, after he had killed the man—after she had flung the torch in the water because he was looking at her so. There was too much light, and the danger was over then—for a little time—for a little time. He said then he would not abandon her to Cornelius. She had insisted. She wanted him to leave her. He said that he could not—that it was impossible. He trembled while he said this. She had felt him tremble. . . . One does not require much imagination to see the scene, almost to hear their whispers. She was afraid for him too. I believe that then she saw in him only a predestined victim of dangers which she understood better than himself. Though by nothing but his mere presence he had mastered her heart, had filled all her thoughts, and had possessed himself of all her affections, she underestimated his chances of success. It is obvious that at about that time everybody was inclined to underestimate his chances. Strictly speaking he didn't seem to have any. I know this was Cornelius's view. He confessed that much to me in extenuation of the shady part he had played in Sherif Ali's plot to do away with the infidel. Even Sherif Ali himself, as it seems certain now, had nothing but contempt for the white man. Jim was to be murdered mainly on religious grounds, I believe. A simple act of piety (and so far infinitely meritorious), but otherwise without much importance. In the last part of this opinion Cornelius concurred. 'Honourable sir,' he argued abjectly on the only occasion he managed to have me to himself—'Honourable sir, how was I to know? Who was he? What could he do to make people believe him? What did Mr Stein mean sending a boy like that to talk big to an old servant? I was ready to save him for eighty dollars. Only eighty dollars. Why didn't the fool go? Was I to get stabbed myself for the sake of a stranger?' He grovelled in spirit before me, with his body doubled up insinuatingly and his hands hovering about my knees, as though he were ready to embrace my legs. 'What's eighty dollars? An insignificant sum to give to a defenceless old man ruined for life by a deceased she-devil.' Here he wept. But I anticipate. I didn't that night chance upon Cornelius till I had had it out with the girl.

"She was unselfish when she urged Jim to leave her, and even to leave the country. It was his danger that was foremost in her thoughts—even if she wanted to save herself too—perhaps unconsciously: but then look at the warning she had, look at the lesson that could be drawn from every moment of the recently ended life in which all her memories were centred. She fell at his feet—she told me so—there by the river, in the discreet light of stars which showed nothing except great masses of silent shadows, indefinite open spaces, and trembling faintly upon the broad stream made it appear as wide as the sea. He had lifted her up. He lifted her up, and then she would struggle no more. Of course not. Strong arms, a tender voice, a stalwart shoulder to rest her poor lonely little head upon. The need—the infinite need—of all this for the aching heart, for the bewildered mind;—the promptings of youth—the necessity of the moment. What would you have? One understands—unless one is incapable of understanding anything under the sun. And so she was content to be lifted up—and held. 'You know—Jove! this is serious—no nonsense in it!' as Jim had whispered hurriedly with a troubled concerned face on the threshold of his house. I don't know so much about nonsense, but there was nothing light-hearted in their romance: they came together under the shadow of a life's disaster, like knight and maiden meeting to exchange vows amongst haunted ruins. The starlight was good enough for that story, a light so faint and remote that it cannot resolve shadows into shapes, and show the other shore of a stream. I did look upon the stream that night and from the very place; it rolled silent and as black as Styx: the next day I went away, but I am not likely to forget what it was she wanted to be saved from when she entreated him to leave her while there was time. She told me what it was, calmed—she was now too passionately interested for mere excitement—in a voice as quiet in the obscurity as her white half-lost figure. She told me, 'I didn't want to die weeping.' I thought I had not heard aright.

'"You did not want to die weeping?' I repeated after her. 'Like my mother,' she added readily. The outlines of her white shape did not stir in the least. 'My mother had wept bitterly before she died,' she explained. An inconceivable calmness seemed to have risen from the ground around us, imperceptibly, like the still rise of a flood in the night, obliterating the familiar landmarks of emotions. There came upon me, as though I had felt myself losing my footing in the midst of waters, a sudden dread, the dread of the unknown depths. She went on explaining that, during the last moments, being alone with her mother, she had to leave the side of the couch to go and set her back against the door, in order to keep Cornelius out. He desired to get in, and kept on drumming with both fists, only desisting now and again to shout huskily, 'Let me in! Let me in! Let me in!' In a far corner upon a few mats the moribund woman, already speechless and unable to lift her arm, rolled her head over, and with a feeble movement of her hand seemed to command—No! No! and the obedient daughter, setting her shoulders with all her strength against the door, was looking on: 'The tears fell from her eyes—and then she died,' concluded the girl in an imperturbable monotone, which more than anything else, more than the white statuesque immobility of her person, more than mere words could do, troubled my mind profoundly with the passive, irremediable horror of the scene. It had the power to drive me out of my conception of existence, out of that shelter each of us makes for himself to creep under in moments of danger, as a tortoise withdraws within its shell. For a moment I had a view of a world that seemed to wear a vast and dismal aspect of disorder, while, in truth, thanks to our unwearied efforts, it is as sunny an arrangement of small conveniences as the mind of man can conceive. But still—it was only a moment: I went back into my shell directly. One *must*—don't you know?—though I seemed to have lost all my words in the chaos of dark thoughts I had contemplated for a second or two beyond the pale. These came back too very soon, for words also belong to the sheltering conception of light and order which is our refuge. I had them ready at my disposal before she whispered softly, 'He swore he would never leave me, when we stood there alone! He swore to me!' . . . 'And is it possible that you—you! do not believe him?' I asked, sincerely reproachful, genuinely shocked. Why couldn't she believe? Wherefore this craving for incertitude, this clinging to fear, as if incertitude and fear had been the safeguards of her love. It was monstrous. She should have made for herself a shelter of inexpugnable peace out of that honest affection. She had not the knowledge—not the skill perhaps. The night had come on apace; it had grown pitch-dark where we were, so that without stirring she had faded like the intangible form of a wistful and perverse spirit. And suddenly I heard her quiet whisper again, 'Other men had sworn the same thing.' It was like a meditative comment on some thoughts full of sadness, of awe. And she added, still lower if possible, 'My father did.' She paused the time to draw an inaudible breath. 'Her father too.' . . . These were the things she knew! At once I said, 'Ah! but he is not like that.' This, it seemed, she did not intend to dispute; but after a time the strange still whisper wandering dreamily in the air stole into my ears. 'Why is he different? Is he better? Is he . . .' 'Upon my word of honour,' I broke in, 'I believe he is.' We subdued our tones to a mysterious pitch. Amongst the huts of Jim's workmen (they were mostly liberated slaves from the Sherif's stockade) somebody started a shrill, drawling song. Across the river a big fire (at Doramin's, I think) made a glowing ball, completely isolated in the night. 'Is he more true?' she murmured. 'Yes,' I said.

More true than any other man,' she repeated in lingering accents. 'Nobody here I said, 'would dream of doubting his word—nobody would dare—except you.

"I think she made a movement at this. 'More brave,' she went on in a changed tone. 'Fear shall never drive him away from you,' I said a little nervously. The song stopped short on a shrill note, and was succeeded by several voices talking in the distance. Jim's voice too. I was struck by her silence. 'What has he been telling you? He has been telling you something?' I asked. There was no answer. 'What is it he told you?' I insisted.

"'Do you think I can tell you? How am I to know? How am I to understand? she cried at last. There was a stir. I believe she was wringing her hands. 'There is something he can never forget.'

"'So much the better for you,' I said gloomily.

"'What is it? What is it?' She put an extraordinary force of appeal into her supplicating tone. 'He says he had been afraid. How can I believe this? Am I a mad woman to believe this? You all remember something! You all go back to it. What is it? You tell me! What is this thing? Is it alive?—is it dead? I hate it. It is cruel. Has it got a face and a voice—this calamity? Will he see it—will he hear it? In his sleep perhaps when he cannot see me—and then arise and go. Ah! I shall never forgive him. My mother had forgiven—but I, never! Will it be a sign—a call . . .'

"It was a wonderful experience. She mistrusted his very slumbers—and she seemed to think I could tell her why! Thus a poor mortal seduced by the charm of an apparition might have tried to wring from another ghost the tremendous secret of the claim the other world holds over a disembodied soul astray amongst the passions of this earth. The very ground on which I stood seemed to melt under my feet. And it was so simple too; but if the spirits evoked by our fears and our unrest have ever to vouch for each other's constancy before the forlorn magicians that we are, then I—I alone of us dwellers in the flesh—have shuddered in the hopeless chill of such a task. A sign, a call! How telling in its expression was her ignorance. A few words! How she came to know them, how she came to pronounce them, I can't imagine. Women find their inspiration in the stress of moments that for us are merely awful, absurd, or futile. To discover that she had a voice at all was enough to strike awe into the heart. Had a spurned stone cried out in pain it could not have appeared a greater and more pitiful miracle. These few sounds wandering in the dark had made their two benighted lives tragic to my mind. It was impossible to make her understand. I chafed silently at my impotence. And Jim, too—poor devil! Who would need him? Who would remember him? He had what he wanted. His very existence probably had been forgotten by this time. They had mastered their fates. They were tragic.

"Her immobility before me was clearly expectant, and my part was to speak for my brother from the realm of forgetful shades. I was deeply moved at my responsibility and at her distress. I would have given anything for the power to soothe her frail soul, tormenting itself in its invincible ignorance like a small bird beating about the cruel wires of a cage. Nothing easier than to say, Have no fear! Nothing more difficult. How does one kill fear, I wonder? How do you shoot a spectre through the heart, slash off its spectral head, take it by its spectral throat? It is an enterprise you rush into while you dream, and are glad to make your escape with wet hair and every limb shaking. The bullet is not run, the blade not forged, the man not born; even the winged words of truth drop at your feet like lumps of lead. You require for such a desperate encounter an enchanted and poisoned shaft dipped in a lie too subtle to be found on earth. An enterprise for a dream, my masters!

"I began my exorcism with a heavy heart, with a sort of sullen anger in it too. Jim's voice, suddenly raised with a stern intonation, carried across the courtyard, reproving the carelessness of some dumb sinner by the river-side. Nothing—I said, speaking in a distinct murmur—there could be nothing, in that unknown world she fancied so eager to rob her of her happiness, there was nothing neither living nor dead, there was no face, no voice, no power, that could tear Jim from her side. I drew breath and she whispered softly, 'He told me so.' 'He told you the truth,' I said. 'Nothing,' she sighed out, and abruptly turned upon me with a barely audible intensity of tone. 'Why did you come to us from out there? He speaks of you too often. You make me afraid. Do you—do you want him?' A sort of stealthy fierceness had crept into our hurried mutters. 'I shall never come again,' I said bitterly. 'And I don't want him. No one wants him.' 'No one,' she repeated in a tone of doubt. 'No one,' I affirmed, feeling myself swayed by some strange excitement. 'You think him strong, wise, courageous, great—why not believe him to be true too? I shall go to-morrow—and that is the end. You shall never be troubled by a voice from there again. This world you don't know is too big to miss him. You understand? Too big. You've got his heart in your hand. You must feel that. You must know that.' 'Yes, I know that,' she breathed out, hard and still, as a statue might whisper.

"I felt I had done nothing. And what is it that I had wished to do? I am not sure now. At the time I was animated by an inexplicable ardour, as if before some great and necessary task—the influence of the moment upon my mental and emotional state. There are in all our lives such moments, such influences, coming from the outside, as it were, irresistible, incomprehensible—as if brought about by the mysterious conjunctions of the planets. She owned, as I had put it to her, his heart. She had that and everything else—if she could only believe it. What I had to tell her was that in the whole world there was no one who ever would need his heart, his mind, his hand. It was a common fate, and yet it seemed an awful thing to say of any man. She listened without a word, and her stillness now was like the protest of an invincible unbelief. What need she care for the world beyond the forests? I asked. From all the multitudes that peopled the vastness of that unknown there would come, I assured her, as long as he lived, neither a call nor a sign for him. Never. I was carried away. Never! Never! I remember with wonder the sort of dogged fierceness I displayed. I had the illusion of having got the spectre by the throat at last. Indeed the whole real thing has left behind the detailed and amazing impression of a dream. Why should she fear? She knew him to be strong, true, wise, brave. He was all that. Certainly. He was more. He was great—invincible— and the world did not want him, it had forgotten him, it would not even know him.

"I stopped; the silence over Patusan was profound, and the feeble dry sound of a paddle striking the side of a canoe somewhere in the middle of the river seemed to make it infinite. 'Why?' she murmured. I felt that sort of rage one feels during a hard tussle. The spectre was trying to slip out of my grasp. 'Why?' she repeated louder; 'tell me!' And as I remained confounded, she stamped with her foot like a spoilt child. 'Why? Speak.' 'You want to know,' I asked in a fury. 'Yes!' she cried. 'Because he is not good enough,' I said brutally. During the moment's pause I noticed the fire on the other shore blaze up, dilating the circle of its glow like an amazed stare, and contract suddenly to a red pin-point. I only knew how close to me she had been when I felt the clutch of her fingers on my forearm. With- out raising her voice, she threw into it an infinity of scathing contempt, bitterness, and despair.

"'This is the very thing he said. . . . You lie!'

"The last two words she cried at me in the native dialect. 'Hear me out!' I en- treated; she caught her breath tremulously, flung my arm away. 'Nobody, nobody is good enough,' I began with the greatest earnestness. I could hear the sobbing labour of her breath frightfully quickened. I hung my head. What was the use? Footsteps were approaching; I slipped away without another word. . . ."

CHAPTER XXXIV.

Marlow swung his legs out, got up quickly, and staggered a little, as though he had been set down after a rush through space. He leaned his back against the balustrade and faced a disordered array of long cane-chairs. The bodies prone in them seemed startled out of their torpor by his movement. One or two sat up as if alarmed; here and there a cigar glowed yet; Marlow looked at them all with the eyes of a man returning from the excessive remoteness of a dream. A throat was cleared; a calm voice encouraged negligently, "Well."

"Nothing," said Marlow with a slight start. "He had told her—that's all. She did not believe him—nothing more. As to myself, I do not know whether it be just, proper, decent for me to rejoice or to be sorry. For my part, I cannot say what I believed—indeed I don't know to this day, and never shall probably. But what did the poor devil believe himself? Truth shall prevail—don't you know. *Magna est veritas et . . .* Yes, when it gets a chance. There is a law, no doubt—and likewise a law regulates your luck in the throwing of dice. It is not Justice the servant of men, but accident, hazard, Fortune—the ally of patient Time—that holds an even and scrupulous balance. Both of us had said the very same thing. Did we both speak the truth—or one of us did—or neither? . . ."

Marlow paused, crossed his arms on his breast, and in a changed tone—

"She said we lied. Poor soul. Well—let's leave it to chance, whose ally is Time, that cannot be hurried, and whose enemy is Death, that will not wait. I had retreated—a little cowed, I must own. I had tried a fall with fear itself and got thrown—of course. I had only succeeded in adding to her anguish the hint of some mysterious collusion, of an inexplicable and incomprehensible conspiracy to keep her for ever in the dark. And it had come easily, naturally, unavoidably, by his act, by her own act! It was as though I had been shown the working of the implacable destiny of which we are the victims—and the tools. It was appalling to think of the girl whom I had left standing there motionless; Jim's footsteps had a fateful sound as he tramped by, without seeing me, in his heavy laced boots. What? No lights!' he said in a loud, surprised voice. 'What are you doing in the dark—you two?' Next moment he caught sight of her, I suppose. 'Hallo, girl!' he cried cheerily. 'Hallo, boy!' she answered at once, with amazing pluck.

"This was their usual greeting to each other, and the bit of swagger she would put into her rather high but sweet voice was very droll, pretty, and childlike. It delighted Jim greatly. This was the last occasion on which I heard them exchange this familiar hail, and it struck a chill into my heart. There was the high sweet voice, the pretty effort, the swagger; but it all seemed to die out prematurely, and the playful call sounded like a moan. It was too confoundedly awful. 'What have you done with Marlow?' Jim was asking; and then, 'Gone down—has he? Funny I didn't meet him. . . . You there, Marlow?'

"I didn't answer. I wasn't going in—not yet at any rate. I really couldn't. While he was calling me I was engaged in making my escape through a little gate leading out upon a stretch of newly cleared ground. No; I couldn't face them yet. I walked hastily with lowered head along a trodden path. The ground rose gently, the few big trees had been felled, the undergrowth had been cut down and the grass fired. He had a mind to try a coffee-plantation there. The big hill, rearing its double summit coal-black in the clear yellow glow of the rising moon, seemed to cast its shadow upon the ground prepared for that experiment. He was going to try ever so many experiments; I had admired his energy, his enterprise, and his shrewdness. Nothing on earth seemed less real now than his plans, his energy, and his enthusiasm; and raising my eyes, I saw part of the moon glittering through the bushes at the bottom of the chasm. For a moment it looked as though the smooth disc, falling from its place in the sky upon the earth, had rolled to the bottom of that precipice: its ascending movement was like a leisurely rebound; it disengaged itself from the tangle of twigs; the bare contorted limb of some tree, growing on the slope, made a black crack right across its face. It threw its level rays afar as if from a cavern, and in this mournful eclipse-like light the stumps of felled trees uprose very dark, the heavy shadows fell at my feet on all sides, my own moving shadow, and across my path the shadow of the solitary grave perpetually garlanded with flowers. In the darkened moonlight the interlaced blossoms took on shapes foreign to one's memory and colours indefinable to the eye, as though they had been special flowers gathered by no man, grown not in this world, and destined for the use of the dead, alone. Their powerful scent hung in the warm air, making it thick and heavy like the fumes of incense. The lumps of white coral shone round the dark mound like a chaplet of bleached skulls, and everything around was so quiet that when I stood still all sound and all movement in the world seemed to come to an end.

"It was a great peace, as if the earth had been one grave, and for a time I stood there thinking mostly of the living who, buried in remote places out of the knowledge of mankind, still are fated to share in its tragic or grotesque miseries. In its noble struggles too—who knows? The human heart is vast enough to contain all the world. It is valiant enough to bear the burden, but where is the courage that would cast it off?

"I suppose I must have fallen into a sentimental mood; I only know that I stood there long enough for the sense of utter solitude to get hold of me so completely that all I had lately seen, all I had heard, and the very human speech itself, seemed to have passed away out of existence, living only for a while longer in my memory, as though I had been the last of mankind. It was a strange and melancholy illusion, evolved half-consciously like all our illusions, which I suspect only to be visions of remote unattainable truth, seen dimly. This was, indeed, one of the lost, forgotten, unknown places of the earth; I had looked under its obscure surface; and I felt that when to-morrow I had left it for ever, it would slip out of existence, to live only in my memory till I myself passed into oblivion. I have that feeling about me now; perhaps it is that feeling which had incited me to tell you the story, to try to hand over to you, as it were, its very existence, its reality—the truth disclosed in a moment of illusion.

"Cornelius broke upon it. He bolted out, verminlike, from the long grass growing in a depression of the ground. I believe his house was rotting somewhere near by, though I've never seen it, not having been far enough in that direction. He ran towards me upon the path; his feet, shod in dirty white shoes, twinkled on the dark earth; he pulled himself up, and began to whine and cringe under a tall stove-pipe hat. His dried-up little carcass was swallowed up, totally lost, in a suit of black broadcloth. That was his costume for holidays and ceremonies, and it reminded me that this was the fourth Sunday I had spent in Patusan. All the time of my stay I had been vaguely aware of his desire to confide in me, if he only could get me all to himself. He hung about with an eager craving look on his sour yellow little face; but his timidity had kept him back as much as my natural reluctance to have anything to do with such an unsavoury creature. He would have succeeded, nevertheless, had he not been so ready to slink off as soon as you looked at him. He would slink off before Jim's severe gaze, before my own, which I tried to make indifferent, even before Tamb' Itam's surly, superior glance. He was perpetually slinking away; whenever seen he was seen moving off deviously, his face over his shoulder, with either a mistrustful snarl or a woe-begone, piteous, mute aspect; but no assumed expression could conceal this innate irremediable abjectness of his nature, any more than an arrangement of clothing can conceal some monstrous deformity of the body.

"I don't know whether it was the demoralisation of my utter defeat in my encounter with a spectre of fear less than an hour ago, but I let him capture me without even a show of resistance. I was doomed to be the recipient of confidences, and to be confronted with unanswerable questions. It was trying; but the contempt, the unreasoned contempt, the man's appearance provoked, made it easier to bear. He couldn't possibly matter. Nothing mattered, since I had made up my mind that Jim, for whom alone I cared, had at last mastered his fate. He had told me he was satisfied . . . nearly. This is going further than most of us dare. I—who have the right to think myself good enough—dare not. Neither does any of you here, I suppose? . . ."

Marlow paused, as if expecting an answer. Nobody spoke.

"Quite right," he began again. "Let no soul know, since the truth can be wrung out of us only by some cruel, little, awful catastrophe. But he is one of us, and he could say he was satisfied . . . nearly. Just fancy this! Nearly satisfied. One could almost envy him his catastrophe. Nearly satisfied. After this nothing could matter. It did not matter who suspected him, who trusted him, who loved him, who hated him—especially as it was Cornelius who hated him.

"Yet after all this was a kind of recognition. You shall judge of a man by his foes as well as by his friends, and this enemy of Jim was such as no decent man would be ashamed to own, without, however, making too much of him. This was the view Jim took, and in which I shared; but Jim disregarded him on general grounds. 'My dear Marlow,' he said, 'I feel that if I go straight nothing can touch me. Indeed I do. Now you have been long enough here to have a good look round—and, frankly, don't you think I am pretty safe. It all depends upon me, and, by Jove! I have lots of confidence in myself. The worst thing he could do would be to kill me, I suppose. I don't think for a moment he would. He couldn't, you know—not if I were myself to hand him a loaded rifle for the purpose, and then turn my back on him. That's the sort of thing he is. And suppose he would—suppose he could? Well—what of that? I didn't come here flying for my life—did I? I came here to set my back against the wall, and I am going to stay here . . .'

"'Till you are *quite* satisfied,' I struck in.

"We were sitting at the time under the roof in the stern of his boat; twenty paddles flashed like one, ten on a side, striking the water with a single splash, while behind our backs Tamb' Itam dipped silently right and left, and stared right down the river, attentive to keep the long canoe in the greatest strength of the current. Jim bowed his head, and our last talk seemed to flicker out for good. He was seeing me off as far as the mouth of the river. The schooner had left the day before, working down and drifting on the ebb, while I had prolonged my stay overnight. And now he was seeing me off.

"Jim had been a little angry with me for mentioning Cornelius at all. I had not, in truth, said much. The man was too insignificant to be dangerous, though he was as full of hate as he could hold. He had called me 'honourable sir' at every second sentence, and had whined at my elbow as he followed me from the grave of his 'late wife' to the gate of Jim's compound. He declared himself the most unhappy of men, a victim, crushed like a worm; he entreated me to look at him. I wouldn't turn my head to do so; but I could see out of the corner of my eye his obsequious shadow gliding after mine, while the moon, suspended on our right hand, seemed to gloat serenely upon the spectacle. He tried to explain—as I've told you—his share in the events of the memorable night. It was a matter of expediency. How could he know who was going to get the upper hand? 'I would have saved him, honourable sir! I would have saved him for eighty dollars,' he protested in dulcet tones, keeping a pace behind me. 'He has saved himself,' I said, 'and he has forgiven you.' I heard a sort of tittering, and turned upon him; at once he appeared ready to take to his heels. 'What are you laughing at?' I asked, standing still. 'Don't be deceived, honourable sir!' he shrieked, seemingly losing all control over his feelings. '*He* save himself! He knows nothing, honourable sir—nothing whatever. Who is he? What does he want here—the big thief? What does he want here? He throws dust into everybody's eyes; he throws dust into your eyes, honourable sir; but he can't throw dust into my eyes. He is a big fool, honourable sir.' I laughed contemptuously, and, turning on my heel, began to walk on again. He ran up to my elbow and whispered forcibly, 'He's no more than a little child here—like a little child—a little child.' Of course I didn't take the slightest notice, and seeing the time pressed, because we were approaching the bamboo fence that glittered over the blackened ground of the clearing, he came to the point. He commenced by being abjectly lachrymose. His great misfortunes had affected his head. He hoped I would kindly forget what nothing but his troubles made him say. He didn't mean anything by it; only the honourable sir did not know what it was to be ruined, broken down, trampled upon. After this introduction he approached the matter near his heart, but in such a rambling, ejaculatory, craven fashion, that for a long time I couldn't make out what he was driving at. He wanted me to intercede with Jim in his favour. It seemed, too, to be some sort of money affair. I heard time and again the words, 'Moderate provision—suitable present.' He seemed to be claiming value for something, and he even went the length of saying with some warmth that life was not worth having if a man were to be robbed of everything. I did not breathe a word, of course, but neither did I stop my ears. The gist of the affair, which became clear to me gradually, was in this, that he regarded himself as entitled to some money in exchange for the girl. He had brought her up. Somebody else's child. Great trouble and pains—old man now—suitable present. If the honourable sir would say a word. . . . I stood still to look at him with curiosity, and fearful lest I should think him extortionate, I suppose, he hastily brought himself to make a concession. In consideration of a 'suitable present' given at once, he would, he declared, be willing to undertake the charge of the girl, 'without any other provision—when the time came for the gentleman to go home.' His little yellow face, all crumpled as though it had been squeezed together, expressed the most anxious, eager avarice. His voice whined coaxingly, 'No more trouble—natural guardian—a sum of money . . .'

"I stood there and marvelled. That kind of thing, with him, was evidently a vocation. I discovered suddenly in his cringing attitude a sort of assurance, as though he had been all his life dealing in certitudes. He must have thought I was dispassionately considering his proposal, because he became as sweet as honey. 'Every gentleman made a provision when the time came to go home,' he began insinuatingly. I slammed the little gate. 'In this case, Mr Cornelius,' I said, 'the time shall never come.' He took a few seconds to gather this in. 'What!' he fairly squealed. 'Why,' I continued from my side of the gate, 'haven't you heard him say so himself? He will never go home.' 'Oh! this is too much,' he shouted. He would not address me as 'honoured sir' any more. He was very still for a time, and then without a trace of humility began very low. 'Never go—ah! He—he—he comes here devil knows from where—comes here—devil knows why—to trample on me till I die—ah—trample' (he stamped softly with both feet), 'trample like this—nobody knows why—till I die. . . .' His voice became quite extinct; he was bothered by a little cough; he came up close to the fence and told me, dropping into a con-

fidential and piteous tone, that he would *not* be trampled upon. 'Patience—patience,' he muttered, striking his breast. I had done laughing at him, but unexpectedly he treated me to a wild cracked burst of it. 'Ha! ha! ha! We shall see! We
shall see! What? Steal from me? Steal from me everything. Everything! Everything!' His head dropped on one shoulder, his hands were hanging before him
lightly clasped. One would have thought he had cherished the girl with surpassing
love, that his spirit had been crushed and his heart broken by the most cruel of
spoliations. Suddenly he lifted his head and shot out an infamous word. 'Like her
mother—she is like her deceitful mother. Exactly. In her face too. In her face. The
devil!' He leaned his forehead against the fence, and in that position uttered
threats and horrible blasphemies in Portuguese in very weak ejaculations, mingled
with miserable plaints and groans, coming out with a heave of the shoulders as
though he had been overtaken by a deadly fit of sickness. It was an inexpressibly
grotesque and vile performance, and I hastened away. He tried to shout something
after me. Some disparagement of Jim, I believe—not too loud though, we were too
near the house. All I heard distinctly was, 'No more than a little child—a little
child.'"

CHAPTER XXXV.

"But next morning, at the first bend of the river shutting off the houses of Patusan, all this dropped out of my sight bodily, with its colour, its design, and its
meaning, like a picture created by fancy on a canvas, upon which, after long contemplation, you turn your back for the last time. It remains in the memory motionless, unfaded, with its life arrested, in an unchanging light. There are the
ambitions, the fears, the hate, the hopes, and they remain in my mind just at I had
seen them—intense and as if for ever suspended in their expression. I had turned
away from the picture and was going back to the world where events move, men
change, light flickers, life flows in a clear stream, no matter whether over mud or
over stones. I wasn't going to dive into it; I would have enough to do to keep my
head above the surface. But as to what I was leaving behind, I cannot imagine any
alteration. The immense and magnanimous Doramin and his little motherly witch
of a wife, gazing together upon the land and nursing secretly their dreams of pa-
rental ambition; Tunku Allang, wizened and greatly perplexed; Dain Waris, intelligent and brave, with his faith in Jim, with his firm glance and his ironic
friendliness; the girl, absorbed in her frightened, suspicious adoration; Tamb'
Itam, surly and faithful; Cornelius, leaning his forehead against the fence under
the moonlight—I am certain of them. They exist as if under an enchanter's wand.
But the figure round which all these are grouped—that one lives, and I am not
certain of him. No magician's wand can immobilise him under my eyes. He is one
of us.

"Jim, as I've told you, accompanied me on the first stage of my journey back
to the world he had renounced, and the way at times seemed to lead through the
very heart of untouched wilderness. The empty reaches sparkled under the high
sun; between the high walls of vegetation the heat drowsed upon the water, and

the boat, impelled vigorously, cut her way through the air that seemed to have settled dense and warm under the shelter of lofty trees.

"The shadow of the impending separation had already put an immense space between us, and when we spoke it was with an effort, as if to force our low voices across a vast and increasing distance. The boat fairly flew; we sweltered side by side in the stagnant superheated air; the smell of mud, of marsh, the primeval smell of fecund earth, seemed to sting our faces; till suddenly at a bend it was as if a great hand far away had lifted a heavy curtain, had flung open an immense portal. The light itself seemed to stir, the sky above our heads widened, a far off murmur reached our ears, a freshness enveloped us, filled our lungs, quickened our thoughts, our blood, our regrets—and, straight ahead, the forests sank down against the dark-blue ridge of the sea.

"I breathed deeply, I revelled in the vastness of the opened horizon, in the different atmosphere that seemed to vibrate with the toil of life, with the energy of an impeccable world. This sky and this sea were open to me. The girl was right—there was a sign, a call in them—something to which I responded with every fibre of my being. I let my eyes roam through space, like a man released from bonds who stretches his cramped limbs, runs, leaps, responds to the inspiring elation of freedom. 'This is glorious!' I cried, and then I looked at the sinner by my side. He sat with his head sunk on his breast and said 'Yes,' without raising his eyes, as if afraid to see writ large on the clear sky of the offing the reproach of his romantic conscience.

"I remember the smallest details of that afternoon. We landed on a bit of white beach. It was backed by a low cliff wooded on the brow, draped in creepers to the very foot. Below us the plain of the sea, of a serene and intense blue, stretched with a slight upward tilt to the thread-like horizon drawn at the height of our eyes. Great waves of glitter blew lightly along the pitted dark surface, as swift as feathers chased by the breeze. A chain of islands sat broken and massive facing the wide estuary, displayed in a sheet of pale glassy water reflecting faithfully the contour of the shore. High in the colourless sunshine a solitary bird, all black, hovered, dropping and soaring above the same spot with a slight rocking motion of the wings. A ragged, sooty bunch of flimsy mat hovels was perched over its own inverted image upon a crooked multitude of high piles the colour of ebony. A tiny black canoe put off from amongst them with two tiny men, all black, who toiled exceedingly, striking down at the pale water: and the canoe seemed to slide painfully on a mirror. This bunch of miserable hovels was the fishing village that boasted of the white lord's especial protection, and the two men crossing over were the old headman and his son-in-law. They landed and walked up to us on the white sand, lean, dark-brown as if dried in smoke, with ashy patches on the skin of their naked shoulders and breasts. Their heads were bound in dirty but carefully folded headkerchiefs, and the old man began at once to state a complaint, voluble, stretching a lank arm, screwing up at Jim his old bleared eyes confidently. The Rajah's people would not leave them alone; there had been some trouble about a lot of turtles' eggs his people had collected on the islets there—and leaning at arm's-length upon his paddle, he pointed with a brown skinny hand over the sea. Jim listened for a time without looking up, and at last told him gently to wait. He would hear him by-and-by. They withdrew obediently to some little distance, and sat on their heels, with their paddles lying before them on the sand; the silvery gleams in their eyes followed our movements patiently: and the immensity of the outspread sea, the stillness of the coast, passing north and south beyond the limits of my vision, made up one colossal Presence watching us four dwarfs isolated on a strip of glistening sand.

"'The trouble is,' remarked Jim moodily, 'that for generations these beggars of fishermen in that village there had been considered as the Rajah's personal slaves—and the old rip can't get it into his head that . . .'

"He paused. 'That you have changed all that,' I said.

"'Yes. I've changed all that,' he muttered in a gloomy voice.

"'You have had your opportunity,' I pursued.

"'Had I?' he said. 'Well, yes. I suppose so. Yes. I have got back my confidence in myself—a good name—yet sometimes I wish . . . No! I shall hold what I've got. Can't expect anything more.' He flung his arm out towards the sea. 'Not out there anyhow.' He stamped his foot upon the sand. 'This is my limit, because nothing less will do.'

"We continued pacing the beach. 'Yes, I've changed all that,' he went on, with a sidelong glance at the two patient squatting fishermen; 'but only try to think what it would be if I went away. Jove! can't you see it? Hell loose. No! To-morrow I shall go and take my chance of drinking that silly old Tunku Allang's coffee, and I shall make no end of fuss over these rotten turtles' eggs. No. I can't say—enough. Never. I must go on, go on for ever holding up my end, to feel sure that nothing can touch me. I must stick to their belief in me to feel safe and to—to' . . . He cast about for a word, seemed to look for it on the sea . . . 'to keep in touch with' . . . His voice sank suddenly to a murmur . . . 'with those whom, perhaps, I shall never see any more. With—with—you, for instance.'

"I was profoundly humbled by his words. 'For God's sake,' I said, 'don't set me up, my dear fellow; just look to yourself.' I felt a gratitude, an affection, for that straggler whose eyes had singled me out, keeping my place in the ranks of an insignificant multitude. How little that was to boast of, after all! I turned my burning face away; under the low sun, glowing, darkened and crimson, like an ember snatched from the fire, the sea lay outspread, offering all its immense stillness to the approach of the fiery orb. Twice he was going to speak, but checked himself: at last, as if he had found a formula—

"'I shall be faithful,' he said quietly. 'I shall be faithful,' he repeated, without looking at me, but for the first time letting his eyes wander upon the waters, whose blueness had changed to a gloomy purple under the fires of sunset. Ah! he was romantic, romantic. I recalled some words of Stein's. . . . 'In the destructive element immerse! . . . To follow the dream, and again to follow the dream—and so— always—*usque ad finem* . . .' He was romantic, but none the less true. Who could tell what forms, what visions, what faces, what forgiveness he could see in the glow of the west! . . . A small boat, leaving the schooner, moved slowly, with a regular beat of two oars, towards the sandbank to take me off. 'And then there's Jewel,' he said, out of the great silence of earth, sky, and sea, which had mastered my very thoughts so that his voice made me start. 'There's Jewel.' 'Yes,' I murmured. 'I need not tell you what she is to me,' he pursued. 'You've seen. In time she will come to understand . . .' 'I hope so,' I interrupted. 'She trusts me, too,' he mused, and then changed his tone. 'When shall we meet next, I wonder?' he said.

"'Never—unless you come out,' I answered, avoiding his glance. He didn't seem to be surprised; he kept very quiet for a while.

"'Good-bye, then,' he said, after a pause. 'Perhaps it's just as well.'

"We shook hands, and I walked to the boat, which waited with her nose on the beach. The schooner, her mainsail set and jib-sheet to windward, curveted on the purple sea; there was a rosy tinge on her sails. 'Will you be going home again soon?' asked Jim, just as I swung my leg over the gunwale. 'In a year or so if I live,' I said. The forefoot grated on the sand, the boat floated, the wet oars flashed and dipped once, twice. Jim, at the water's edge, raised his voice, 'Tell them . . .' he began. I signed to the men to cease rowing, and waited in wonder. Tell who? The half-submerged sun faced him; I could see its red gleam in his eyes that looked dumbly at me. . . . 'No—nothing,' he said, and with a slight wave of his hand motioned the boat away. I did not look again at the shore till I had clambered on board the schooner.

"By that time the sun had set. The twilight lay over the east, and the coast, turned black, extended infinitely its sombre wall that seemed the very stronghold of the night; the western horizon was one great blaze of gold and crimson in which a big detached cloud floated dark and still, casting a slaty shadow on the water beneath, and I saw Jim on the beach watching the schooner fall off and gather headway.

"The two half-naked fishermen had arisen as soon as I had gone; they were no doubt pouring the plaint of their trifling, miserable, oppressed lives into the ears of the white lord, and no doubt he was listening to it, making it his own, for was it not a part of his luck—the luck 'from the word Go'—the luck to which he had assured me he was so completely equal. They too, I should think, were in luck, and I was sure their pertinacity would be equal to it. Their dark-skinned bodies vanished on the dark background long before I had lost sight of their protector. He was white from head to foot, and remained persistently visible with the stronghold of the night at his back, the sea at his feet, the opportunity by his side—still veiled. What do you say? Was it still veiled? I don't know. For me that white figure in the stillness of coast and sea seemed to stand at the heart of a vast enigma. The twilight was ebbing fast from the sky above his head, the strip of sand had sunk already under his feet, he himself appeared no bigger than a child—then only a speck, a tiny white speck, that seemed to catch all the light left in a darkened world. . . . And, suddenly, I lost him. . . ."

CHAPTER XXXVI.

With these words Marlow had ended his narrative, and his audience had broken up forthwith, under his abstract, pensive gaze. Men drifted off the verandah in pairs or alone without loss of time, without offering a remark, as if the last image of that incomplete story, its incompleteness itself, and the very tone of the speaker, had made discussion vain and comment impossible. Each of them seemed to carry away his own impression, to carry it away with him like a secret; but there was only one man of all these listeners who was ever to hear the last word of the story. It came to him at home, more than two years later, and it came contained in a thick packet addressed in Marlow's upright and angular handwriting.

The privileged man opened the packet, looked in, then, laying it down, went to the window. His rooms were in the highest flat of a lofty building, and his glance could travel afar beyond the clear panes of glass, as though he were looking out of the lantern of a lighthouse. The slopes of the roofs glistened, the dark broken ridges succeeded each other without end like sombre, uncrested waves, and from the depths of the town under his feet ascended a confused and unceasing mutter. The spires of churches, numerous, scattered haphazard, uprose like beacons on a maze of shoals without a channel; the driving rain mingled with the falling dusk of a winter's evening; and the booming of a big clock on a tower striking the hour, rolled past in voluminous, austere bursts of sound, with a shrill vibrating cry at the core. He drew the heavy curtains.

The light of his shaded reading-lamp slept like a sheltered pool, his footfalls made no sound on the carpet, his wandering days were over. No more horizons as boundless as hope, no more twilights within the forests as solemn as temples, in the hot quest for the Ever-undiscovered Country over the hill, across the stream, beyond the wave. The hour was striking! No more! No more!—but the opened packet under the lamp brought back the sounds, the visions, the very savour of the past—a multitude of fading faces, a tumult of low voices, dying away upon the shores of distant seas under a passionate and unconsoling sunshine. He sighed and sat down to read.

At first he saw three distinct enclosures. A good many pages closely blackened and pinned together; a loose square sheet of greyish paper with a few words traced in a handwriting he had never seen before, and an explanatory letter from Marlow. From this last fell another letter, yellowed by time and frayed on the folds. He picked it up and, laying it aside, turned to Marlow's message, ran swiftly over the opening lines, and, checking himself, thereafter read on deliberately, like one approaching with slow feet and alert eyes the glimpse of an undiscovered country.

". . . I don't suppose you've forgotten," went on the letter. "You alone have showed an interest in him that survived the telling of his story, though I remember well you would not admit he had mastered his fate. You prophesied for him the disaster of weariness and of disgust with acquired honour, with the self-appointed task, with the love sprung from pity and youth. You had said you knew so well 'that kind of thing,' its illusory satisfaction, its unavoidable deception. You said also—I call to mind—that 'giving your life up to them' (*them* meaning all of mankind with skins brown, yellow, or black in colour) 'was like selling your soul to a brute.' You contended that 'that kind of thing' was only endurable and enduring when based on a firm conviction in the truth of ideas racially our own, in whose name are established the order, the morality of an ethical progress. 'We want its strength at our backs,' you had said. 'We want a belief in its necessity and its justice, to make a worthy and conscious sacrifice of our lives. Without it the sacrifice is only forgetfulness, the way of offering is no better than the way to perdition.' In other words, you maintained that we must fight in the ranks or our lives don't count. Possibly! You ought to know—be it said without malice—you who have rushed into one or two places single-handed and came out cleverly, without singeing your wings. The point, however, is that of all mankind Jim had no dealings but with himself, and the question is whether at the last he had not confessed to a faith mightier than the laws of order and progress.

"I affirm nothing. Perhaps you may pronounce—after you've read. There is much truth—after all—in the common expression 'under a cloud.' It is impossible to see him clearly—especially as it is through the eyes of others that we take our last look at him. I have no hesitation in imparting to you all I know of the last episode that, as he used to say, had 'come to him.' One wonders whether this was perhaps that supreme opportunity, that last and satisfying test for which I had always suspected him to be waiting, before he could frame a message to the impeccable world. You remember that when I was leaving him for the last time he had asked whether I would be going home soon, and suddenly cried after me, 'Tell them!' . . . I had waited—curious I'll own, and hopeful too—only to hear him shout, 'No. Nothing.' That was all then—and there shall be nothing more; there shall be no message, unless such as each of us can interpret for himself from the language of facts, that are so often more enigmatic than the craftiest arrangement of words. He made, it is true, one more attempt to deliver himself; but that too failed, as you may perceive if you look at the sheet of greyish foolscap enclosed here. He had tried to write; do you notice the commonplace hand? It is headed 'The Fort, Patusan.' I suppose he had carried out his intention of making out of his house a place of defence. It was an excellent plan: a deep ditch, an earth wall topped by a palisade, and at the angles guns mounted on platforms to sweep each side of the square. Doramin had agreed to furnish him the guns; and so each man of his party would know there was a place of safety, upon which every faithful partisan could rally in case of some sudden danger. All this showed his judicious foresight, his faith in the future. What he called 'my own people'—the liberated captives of the Sherif—were to make a distinct quarter of Patusan, with their huts and little plots of ground under the walls of the stronghold. Within he would be an invincible host in himself. 'The Fort, Patusan.' No date, as you observe. What is a number and a name to a day of days? It is also impossible to say whom he had in his mind when he seized the pen: Stein—myself—the world at large—or was this only the aimless startled cry of a solitary man confronted by his fate? 'An awful thing has happened,' he wrote before he flung the pen down for the first time; look at the ink blot resembling the head of an arrow under these words. After a while he had tried again, scrawling heavily, as if with a hand of lead, another line. 'I must now at once . . .' The pen had spluttered, and that time he gave it up. There's nothing more; he had seen a broad gulf that neither eye nor voice could span. I can understand this. He was overwhelmed by the inexplicable; he was overwhelmed by his own personality—the gift of that destiny which he had done his best to master.

"I send you also an old letter—a very old letter. It was found carefully preserved in his writing-case. It is from his father, and by the date you can see he must have received it a few days before he joined the *Patna*. Thus it must be the last letter he ever had from home. He had treasured it all these years. The good old parson fancied his sailor-son. I've looked in at a sentence here and there. There is nothing in it except just affection. He tells his 'dear James' that the last long letter from him was very 'honest and entertaining.' He would not have him 'judge men harshly or hastily.' There are four pages of it, easy morality and family news. Tom had 'taken orders.' Carrie's husband had 'money losses.' The old chap goes on equably trusting Providence and the established order of the universe, but alive to its small dangers and its small mercies. One can almost see him, grey-haired and serene in the inviolable shelter of his book-lined, faded, and comfortable study, where for forty years he had conscientiously gone over and over again the round of his little thoughts about faith and virtue, about the conduct of life and the only proper manner of dying; where he had written so many sermons, where he sits talking to his boy, over there, on the other side of the earth. But what of the distance. Virtue is one all over the world, and there is only one faith, one conceivable conduct of life, one manner of dying. He hopes his 'dear James' will never forget that 'who once gives way to temptation, in the very instant hazards his total depravity and everlasting ruin. Therefore resolve fixedly never, through any possible motives, to do anything which you believe to be wrong.' There is also some news of a favourite dog; and a pony, 'which all you boys used to ride,' had gone blind from old age and had to be shot. The old chap invokes Heaven's blessing; the mother and all the girls then at home send their love. . . . No, there is nothing much in that yellow frayed letter fluttering out of his cherishing grasp after so many years. It was never answered, but who can say what converse he may have held with all these placid, colourless forms of men and women peopling that quiet corner of the world as free of danger or strife as a tomb, and breathing equably the air of undisturbed rectitude. It seems amazing that he should belong to it, he to whom so many things 'had come.' Nothing ever came to them; they would never be taken unawares, and never be called upon to grapple with fate. Here they all are, evoked by the mild gossip of the father, all these brothers and sisters, bone of his bone and flesh of his flesh, gazing with clear unconscious eyes, while I seem to see him, returned at last, no longer a mere white speck at the heart of an immense mystery, but of full stature, standing disregarded amongst their untroubled shapes, with a stern and romantic aspect, but always mute, dark—under a cloud.

"The story of the last events you shall find in the few pages enclosed here. You must admit that it is romantic beyond the wildest dreams of his boyhood, and yet there is to my mind a sort of profound and terrifying logic in it, as if it were our imagination alone that could set loose upon us the might of an overwhelming destiny. The imprudence of our thoughts recoils upon our heads; who toys with the sword shall perish by the sword. This astounding adventure, of which the most astounding part is that it is true, comes on as an unavoidable consequence. Something of the sort had to happen. You repeat this to yourself while you marvel that such a thing could happen in the year of grace before last. But it has happened— and there is no disputing its logic.

"I put it down here for you as though I had been an eyewitness. My information was fragmentary, but I've fitted the pieces together, and there is enough of them to make an intelligible picture. I wonder how he would have related it himself. He has confided so much in me that at times it seems as though he must come in presently and tell the story in his own words, in his careless yet feeling voice, with his offhand manner, a little puzzled, a little bothered, a little hurt, but now and then by a word or a phrase giving one of these glimpses of his very own self that were never any good for purposes of orientation. It's difficult to believe he will never come. I shall never hear his voice again, nor shall I see his smooth tan-and-pink face with a white line on the forehead, and the youthful eyes darkened by excitement to a profound, unfathomable blue."

CHAPTER XXXVII.

"It all begins with a remarkable exploit of a man called Brown, who stole with complete success a Spanish schooner out of a small bay near Zamboanga. Till I discovered the fellow my information was incomplete, but most unexpectedly I did come upon him a few hours before he gave up his arrogant ghost. Fortunately he was willing and able to talk between the choking fits of asthma, and his racked body writhed with malicious exultation at the bare thought of Jim. He exulted thus at the idea that he had 'paid out the stuck-up beggar after all.' He gloated over his action. I had to bear the sunken glare of his fierce crow-footed eyes if I wanted to know; and so I bore it, reflecting how much certain forms of evil are akin to madness, derived from intense egoism, inflamed by resistance, tearing the soul to pieces, and giving factitious vigour to the body. The story also reveals unsuspected depths of cunning in the wretched Cornelius, whose abject and intense hate acts like a subtle inspiration, pointing out an unerring way towards revenge.

"'I could see directly I set my eyes on him what sort of a fool he was,' gasped the dying Brown. 'He a man! Hell! He was a hollow sham. As if he couldn't have said straight out, "Hands off my plunder!" blast him! That would have been like a man! Rot his superior soul! He had me there—but he hadn't devil enough in him to make an end of me. Not he! A thing like that letting me off as if I wasn't worth a kick! . . .' Brown struggled desperately for breath. . . . 'Fraud. . . . Letting me off. . . . And so I did make an end of him after all. . . .' He choked again. . . . 'I expect this thing'll kill me, but I shall die easy now. You . . . you here. . . . I don't know your name—I would give you a five-pound note if—if I had it—for the news—or my name's not Brown. . . .' He grinned horribly. . . . 'Gentleman Brown.'

"He said all these things in profound gasps, staring at me with his yellow eyes out of a long, ravaged brown face; he jerked his left arm; a pepper-and-salt matted beard hung almost into his lap; a dirty ragged blanket covered his legs. I had found him out in Bankok through that busy-body Schomberg, the hotelkeeper, who had, confidentially, directed me where to look. It appears that a sort of loafing, fuddled vagabond—a white man living amongst the natives with a Siamese woman—had considered it a great privilege to give a shelter to the last days of the famous Gentleman Brown. While he was talking to me in the wretched hovel, and, as it were, fighting for every minute of his life, the Siamese woman with big bare legs and a stupid coarse face, sat in a dark corner chewing betel stolidly. Now and then she would get up for the purpose of shooing a chicken away from the door. The whole hut shook when she walked. An ugly yellow child, naked and pot-bellied like a little heathen god, stood at the foot of the couch, finger in mouth, lost in a profound and calm contemplation of the dying man.

"He talked feverishly; but in the middle of a word, perhaps, an invisible hand would take him by the throat, and he would look at me dumbly with an expression of doubt and anguish. He seemed to fear that I would get tired of waiting and go away, leaving him with his tale untold, with his exultation unexpressed. He died during the night, I believe, but by that time I had nothing more to learn.

"So much as to Brown, for the present.

"Eight months before this, coming into Samarang, I went as usual to see Stein. On the garden side of the house a Malay on the verandah greeted me shyly, and I remembered that I had seen him in Patusan, in Jim's house, amongst other

Bugis men who used to come in the evening to talk interminably over their war reminiscences and to discuss State affairs. Jim had pointed him out to me once as a respectable petty trader owning a small seagoing native craft, who had showed himself 'one of the best at the taking of the stockade.' I was not very surprised to see him, since any Patusan trader venturing as far as Samarang would naturally find his way to Stein's house. I returned his greeting and passed on. At the door of Stein's room I came upon another Malay in whom I recognised Tamb' Itam.

"I asked him at once what he was doing there; it occurred to me that Jim might have come on a visit. I own I was pleased and excited at the thought. Tamb' Itam looked as if he did not know what to say. 'Is Tuan Jim inside?' I asked impatiently. 'No,' he mumbled, hanging his head for a moment, and then with sudden earnestness, 'He would not fight. He would not fight,' he repeated twice. As he seemed unable to say anything else, I pushed him aside and went in.

"Stein, tall and stooping, stood alone in the middle of the room between the rows of butterfly cases. 'Ach! is it you, my friend?' he said sadly, peering through his glasses. A drab sack-coat of alpaca hung, unbuttoned, down to his knees. He had a Panama hat on his head, and there were deep furrows on his pale cheeks. 'What's the matter now?' I asked nervously. 'There's Tamb' Itam there. . . .' 'Come and see the girl. Come and see the girl. She is here,' he said, with a half-hearted show of activity. I tried to detain him, but with gentle obstinacy he would take no notice of my eager questions. 'She is here, she is here,' he repeated, in great perturbation. 'They came here two days ago. An old man like me, a stranger—*sehen sie*—can not do much. . . . Come this way. . . . Young hearts are unforgiving. . . .' I could see he was in utmost distress. . . . 'The strength of life in them, the cruel strength of life. . . .' He mumbled, leading me round the house; I followed him, lost in dismal and angry conjectures. At the door of the drawing-room he barred my way. 'He loved her very much,' he said interrogatively, and I only nodded, feeling so bitterly disappointed that I would not trust myself to speak. 'Very frightful,' he murmured. 'She can't understand me. I am only a strange old man. Perhaps you . . . she knows you. Talk to her. We can't leave it like this. Tell her to forgive him. It was very frightful.' 'No doubt,' I said, exasperated at being in the dark; 'but have *you* forgiven him?' He looked at me queerly. 'You shall hear,' he said, and opening the door, absolutely pushed me in.

"You know Stein's big house and the two immense reception-rooms, uninhabited and uninhabitable, clean, full of solitude and of shining things that look as if never beheld by the eye of man? They are cool on the hottest days, and you enter them as you would a scrubbed cave underground. I passed through one, and in the other I saw the girl sitting at the end of a big mahogany table, on which she rested her head, the face hidden in her arms. The waxed floor reflected her dimly as though it had been a sheet of frozen water. The rattan screens were down, and through the strange greenish gloom made by the foliage of the trees outside, a strong wind blew in gusts, swaying the long draperies of windows and doorways. Her white figure seemed shaped in snow; the pendent crystals of a great chandelier clicked above her head like glittering icicles. She looked up and watched my approach. I was chilled as if these vast apartments had been the cold abode of despair.

"She recognised me at once, and as soon as I had stopped looking down at her: 'He has left me,' she said quietly; 'you always leave us—for your own ends.' Her face was set. All the heat of life seemed withdrawn within some inaccessible spot in her breast. 'It would have been easy to die with him,' she went on, and made a slight weary gesture as if giving up the incomprehensible. 'He would not! It was like a blindness—and yet it was I who was speaking to him; it was I who stood before his eyes; it was at me that he looked all the time! Ah! you are hard, treacherous, without truth, without compassion. What makes you so wicked? Or is it that you are all mad?'

"I took her hand; it did not respond, and when I dropped it, it hung down to the floor. That indifference, more awful than tears, cries, and reproaches, seemed to defy time and consolation. You felt that nothing you could say would reach the seat of the still and benumbing pain.

"Stein had said, 'You shall hear.' I did hear. I heard it all, listening with amazement, with awe, to the tones of her inflexible weariness. She could not grasp the real sense of what she was telling me, and her resentment filled me with pity for her—for him too. I stood rooted to the spot after she had finished. Leaning on her arm, she stared with hard eyes, and the wind passed in gusts, the crystals kept on clicking in the greenish gloom. She went on whispering to herself: 'And yet he was looking at me! He could see my face, hear my voice, hear my grief! When I used to sit at his feet, with my cheek against his knee and his hand on my head, the curse of cruelty and madness was already within him, waiting for the day. The day came! . . . and before the sun had set he could not see me any more— he was made blind and deaf and without pity, as you all are. He shall have no tears from me. Never, never. Not one tear. I will not! He went away from me as if I had been worse than death. He fled as if driven by some accursed thing he had heard or seen in his sleep. . . .'

"Her steady eyes seemed to strain after the shape of a man torn out of her arms by the strength of a dream. She made no sign to my silent bow. I was glad to escape.

"I saw her once again, the same afternoon. On leaving her I had gone in search of Stein, whom I could not find indoors; and I wandered out, pursued by distressful thoughts, into the gardens, these famous gardens of Stein, in which you can find every plant and tree of tropical lowlands. I followed the course of the canalised stream, and sat for a long time on a shaded bench near the ornamental pond, where some waterfowl with clipped wings were diving and splashing nois- ily. The branches of casuarina-trees behind me swayed lightly, incessantly, re- minding me of the soughing of fir-trees at home.

"This mournful and restless sound was a fit accompaniment to my medita- tions. She had said he had been driven away from her by a dream,—and there was no answer one could make her—there seemed to be no forgiveness for such a transgression. And yet is not mankind itself, pushing on its blind way, driven by a dream of its greatness and its power upon the dark paths of excessive cruelty and of excessive devotion? And what is the pursuit of truth—after all?

"When I rose to get back to the house I caught sight of Stein's drab coat through a gap in the foliage, and very soon at a turn of the path I came upon him walking with the girl. Her little hand rested on his forearm, and under the broad, flat rim of his Panama hat he bent over her, grey-haired, paternal, with compas- sionate and chivalrous deference. I stood aside, but they stopped, facing me. His gaze was bent on the ground at his feet; the girl, erect and slight on his arm, stared sombrely beyond my shoulder with black, clear, motionless eyes. 'Schrecklich,' he murmured. 'Terrible! Terrible! What can one do?' He seemed to be appealing to me, but her youth, the length of the days suspended over her head, appealed to me more; and suddenly, even as I realised that nothing could be said, I found myself pleading his cause for her sake. 'You must forgive him.' I concluded, and my own voice seemed to me muffled, lost in an irresponsive deaf immensity. 'We all want to be forgiven,' I added after a while.

"'What have I done?' she asked with her lips only.

"'You always mistrusted him,' I said.

"'He was like the others,' she pronounced slowly.

"'Not like the others,' I protested, but she continued evenly, without any feeling—

"'He was false.' And suddenly Stein broke in. 'No! no! no! My poor child! . . .' He patted her hand lying passively on his sleeve. 'No! no! Not false! True! true! true!' He tried to look into her stony face. 'You don't understand. Ach! Why you do not understand? . . . Terrible,' he said to me. 'Some day she *shall* understand.'

"'Will *you* explain?' I asked, looking hard at him. They moved on.

"I watched them. Her gown trailed on the path, her black hair fell loose. She walked upright and light by the side of the tall man, whose long shapeless coat hung in perpendicular folds from the stooping shoulders, whose feet moved slowly. They disappeared beyond that spinney (you may remember) where sixteen different kinds of bamboo grow together, all distinguishable to the learned eye. For my part, I was fascinated by the exquisite grace and beauty of that fluted grove, crowned with pointed leaves and feathery heads, the lightness, the vigour, the charm as distinct as a voice of that unperplexed luxuriating life. I remember staying to look at it for a long time, as one would linger within reach of a consoling whisper. The sky was pearly grey. It was one of these overcast days so rare in the tropics, in which memories crowd upon one, memories of other shores, of other faces.

"I drove back to town the same afternoon, taking with me Tamb' Itam and the other Malay, in whose seagoing craft they had escaped in the bewilderment, fear, and gloom of the disaster. The shock of it seemed to have changed their natures. It had turned her passion into stone, and it made the surly taciturn Tamb' Itam almost loquacious. His surliness, too, was subdued into puzzled humility, as though he had seen the failure of a potent charm in a supreme moment. The Bugis trader, a shy hesitating man, was very clear in the little he had to say. Both were evidently overawed by a sense of deep inexpressible wonder, by the touch of an inscrutable mystery."

There with Marlow's signature the letter proper ended. The privileged reader screwed up his lamp, and solitary above the billowy roofs of the town, like a light-house-keeper above the sea, he turned to the pages of the story.

CHAPTER XXXVIII.

"It all begins, as I've told you, with the man called Brown," ran the opening sentence of Marlow's narrative. "You who have knocked about the Western Pacific must have heard of him. He was the show ruffian on the Australian coast—not that he was often to be seen there, but because he was always trotted out in the stories of lawless life a visitor from home is treated to; and the mildest of these stories which were told about him from Cape York to Eden Bay was more than enough to hang a man if told in the right place. They never failed to let you know, too, that he was supposed to be the son of a baronet. Be it as it may, it is certain he had deserted from a home ship in the early gold-digging days, and in a few years became talked about as the terror of this or that group of islands in Polynesia. He would kidnap natives, he would strip some lonely white trader to the very pyjamas he stood in, and after he had robbed the poor devil, he would as likely as not invite him to fight a duel with shot-guns on the beach—which would have been fair enough as these things go, if the other man hadn't been by that time already half-dead with fright. Brown was a latter-day buccaneer, sorry enough, like his more celebrated prototypes; but what distinguished him from his contemporary brother ruffians, like Bully Hayes or the mellifluous Pease, or that perfumed, Dundreary-whiskered, dandified scoundrel known as Dirty Dick, was the arrogant temper of his misdeeds and a vehement scorn for mankind at large and for his victims in particular. The others were merely vulgar and greedy brutes, but he seemed moved by some complex intention. He would rob a man as if only to demonstrate his poor opinion of the creature, and he would bring to the shooting or maiming of some quiet, unoffending stranger a savage and vengeful earnestness fit to terrify the most reckless of desperadoes. In the days of his greatest glory he owned an armed barque, manned by a mixed crew of Kanakas and runaway whalers, and boasted, I don't know with what truth, of being financed on the quiet by a most respectable firm of copra merchants. Later on he ran off—it was reported—with the wife of a missionary, a very young girl from Clapham way, who had married the mild, flat-footed fellow in a moment of enthusiasm, and suddenly transplanted to Melanesia, lost her bearings somehow. It was a dark story. She was ill at the time he carried her off, and died on board his ship. It is said—as the most wonderful part of the tale—that over her body he gave way to an outburst of sombre and violent grief. His luck left him, too, very soon after. He lost his ship on some rocks off Malaita, and disappeared for a time as though he had gone down with her. He is heard of next at Nuka-Hiva, where he bought an old French schooner out of Government service. What creditable enterprise he might have had in view when he made that purchase I can't say, but it is evident that what with High Commissioners, consuls, men-of-war, and international control, the South Seas were getting too hot to hold gentlemen of his kidney. Clearly he must have shifted the scene of his operations farther west, because a year later he plays an incredibly audacious, but not a very profitable part, in a serio-comic business in Manila Bay, in which a peculating governor and an absconding treasurer are the principal figures; thereafter he seems to have hung around the Philippines in his rotten schooner, battling with an adverse fortune, till at last, running his appointed course, he sails into Jim's history, a blind accomplice of the Dark Powers.

"His tale goes that when a Spanish patrol cutter captured him he was simply trying to run a few guns for the insurgents. If so, then I can't understand what he was doing off the south coast of Mindanao. My belief, however, is that he was blackmailing the native villages along the coast. The principal thing is that the cutter, throwing a guard on board, made him sail in company towards Zamboanga. On the way, for some reason or other, both vessels had to call at one of these new Spanish settlements—which never came to anything in the end—where there was not only a civil official in charge on shore, but a good stout coasting schooner lying at anchor in the little bay; and this craft, in every way much better than his own, Brown made up his mind to steal.

"He was down on his luck—as he told me himself. The world he had bullied for twenty years with fierce, aggressive disdain, had yielded him nothing in the way of material advantage except a small bag of silver dollars, which was concealed in his cabin so that 'the devil himself couldn't smell it out.' And that was all—absolutely all. He was tired of his life, and not afraid of death. But this man, who would stake his existence on a whim with a bitter and jeering recklessness, stood in mortal fear of imprisonment. He had an unreasoning cold-sweat, nerve-shaking, blood-to-water-turning sort of horror at the bare possibility of being locked up—the sort of terror a superstitious man would feel at the thought of being embraced by a spectre. Therefore the civil official who came on board to make a preliminary investigation into the capture, investigated arduously all day long, and only went ashore after dark, muffled up in a cloak, and taking great care not to let Brown's little all clink in its bag. Afterwards, being a man of his word, he contrived (the very next evening, I believe) to send off the Government cutter on some urgent bit of special service. As her commander could not spare a prize crew, he contented himself by taking away before he left all the sails of Brown's schooner to the very last rag, and took good care to tow his two boats on to the beach a couple of miles off.

"But in Brown's crew there was a Solomon Islander, kidnapped in his youth and devoted to Brown, who was the best man of the whole gang. That fellow swam off to the coaster—five hundred yards or so—with the end of a warp made up of all the running gear unrove for the purpose. The water was smooth, and the bay dark, 'like the inside of a cow,' as Brown described it. The Solomon Islander clambered over the bulwarks with the end of the rope in his teeth. The crew of the coaster—all Tagals—were ashore having a jollification in the native village. The two shipkeepers left on board woke up suddenly and saw the devil. It had glittering eyes and leaped quick as lightening about the deck. They fell on their knees, paralysed with fear, crossing themselves and mumbling prayers. With a long knife he found in the caboose the Solomon Islander, without interrupting their orisons, stabbed first one, then the other; with the same knife he set to sawing patiently at the coir cable till suddenly it parted under the blade with a splash. Then in the silence of the bay he let out a cautious shout, and Brown's gang, who meantime had been peering and straining their hopeful ears in the darkness, began to pull gently at their end of the wrap. In less than five minutes the two schooners came together with a slight shock and a creak of spars.

"Brown's crowd transferred themselves without losing an instant, taking with them their firearms and a large supply of ammunition. They were sixteen in all: two runaway blue-jackets, a lanky deserter from a Yankee man-of-war, a couple of simple, blond Scandinavians, a mulatto of sorts, one bland Chinaman who cooked—and the rest of the nondescript spawn of the South Seas. None of them cared; Brown bent them to his will, and Brown, indifferent to gallows, was running away from the spectre of a Spanish prison. He didn't give them the time to trans-ship enough provisions; the weather was calm, the air was charged with dew, and when they cast off the ropes and set sail to a faint off-shore draught there was no flutter in the damp canvas; their old schooner seemed to detach itself gently from the stolen craft and slip away silently, together with the black mass of the coast, into the night.

"They got clear away. Brown related to me in detail their passage down the Straits of Macassar. It is a harrowing and desperate story. They were short of food and water; they boarded several native craft and got a little from each. With a stolen ship Brown did not dare to put into any port, of course. He had no money to buy anything, no papers to show, and no lie plausible enough to get him out again. An Arab barque, under the Dutch flag, surprised one night at anchor off Poulo Laut, yielded a little dirty rice, a bunch of bananas, and a cask of water; three days of squally, misty weather from the north-east shot the schooner across the Java Sea. The yellow muddy waves drenched that collection of hungry ruffians. They sighted mail-boats moving on their appointed routes; passed well-found home ships with rusty iron sides anchored in the shallow sea waiting for a change of weather or the turn of the tide; an English gunboat, white and trim, with two slim masts, crossed their bows one day in the distance; and on another occasion a Dutch corvette, black and heavily sparred, loomed up on their quarter, steaming dead slow in the mist. They slipped through unseen or disregarded, a wan, sallow-faced band of utter outcasts, enraged with hunger and hunted by fear. Brown's idea was to make for Madagascar, where he expected, on grounds not altogether illusory, to sell the schooner in Tamatave, and no questions asked, or perhaps obtain some more or less forged papers for her. Yet before he could face the long passage across the Indian Ocean food was wanted—water too.

"Perhaps he had heard of Patusan—or perhaps he just only happened to see the name written in small letters on the chart—probably that of a largish village up a river in a native state, perfectly defenceless, far from the beaten tracks of the sea and from the ends of submarine cables. He had done that kind of thing before—in the way of business; and this now was an absolute necessity, a question of life and death—or rather of liberty. Of liberty! He was sure to get provisions— bullocks—rice—sweet-potatoes. The sorry gang licked their chops. A cargo of produce for the schooner perhaps could be extorted—and, who knows—some real ringing coined money! Some of these chiefs and village headmen can be made to part freely. He told me he would have roasted their toes rather than be baulked. I believe him. His men believed him too. They didn't cheer aloud, being a dumb pack, but made ready wolfishly.

"Luck served him as to weather. A few days of calm would have brought unmentionable horrors on board that schooner, but with the help of land and sea breezes, in less than a week after clearing the Sunda Straits, he anchored off the Batu Kring mouth within a pistol-shot of the fishing village.

"Fourteen of them packed into the schooner's long-boat (which was big, having been used for cargo-work) and started up the river, while two remained in charge of the schooner with food enough to keep starvation off for ten days. The tide and wind helped, and early one afternoon the big white boat under a ragged sail shouldered its way before the sea breeze into Patusan Reach, manned by fourteen assorted scarecrows glaring hungrily ahead, and fingering the breach-blocks of cheap rifles. Brown calculated upon the terrifying surprise of his appearance. They sailed in with the last of the flood; the Rajah's stockade gave no sign; the first houses on both sides of the stream seemed deserted. A few canoes were seen up the reach in full flight. Brown was astonished at the size of the place. A profound silence reigned. The wind dropped between the houses; two oars were got out and the boat held on upstream, the idea being to effect a lodgment in the centre of the town before the inhabitants could think of resistance.

"It seems, however, that the headman of the fishing village at Batu Kring had managed to send off a timely warning. When the long-boat came abreast of the mosque (which Doramin had built: a structure with gables and roof finials of

carved coral) the open space before it was full of people. A shout went up, and was
followed by a clash of gongs all up the river. From a point above two little brass 6-
pounders were discharged, and the round-shot came skipping down the empty
reach, spirting glittering jets of water in the sunshine. In front of the mosque a
shouting lot of men began firing in volleys that whipped athwart the current of the
river; an irregular, rolling fusilade was opened on the boat from both banks, and
Brown's men replied with a wild, rapid fire. The oars had been got in.

"The turn of the tide at high water comes on very quick in that river, and the
boat in mid-stream, nearly hidden in smoke, began to drift back stern foremost.
Along both shores the smoke thickened also, lying below the roofs in a level streak
as you may see a long cloud cutting the slope of a mountain. A tumult of war-cries,
the vibrating clang of gongs, the deep snoring of drums, yells of rage, crashes of
volley-firing, made an awful din, in which Brown sat confounded but steady at the
tiller, working himself into a fury of hate and rage against those people who dared
to defend themselves. Two of his men had been wounded, and he saw his retreat
cut off below the town by some boats that had put off from Tunku Allang's stockade. There were six of them full of men. While he was thus beset he perceived the
entrance of the narrow creek (the same which Jim had jumped at low water). It
was then brim full. Steering the long-boat in, they landed, and, to make a long
story short, they established themselves on a little knoll about 900 yards from the
stockade, which, in fact, they commanded from that position. The slopes of the
knoll were bare, but there were a few trees on the summit. They went to work cutting these down for a breastwork, and were fairly intrenched before dark; meantime the Rajah's boats remained in the river with curious neutrality. When the sun
set the glare of many brushwood blazes lighted on the river-front, and between the
double line of houses on the land side threw into black relief the roofs, the groups
of slender palms, the heavy clumps of fruit-trees. Brown ordered the grass round
his position to be fired; a low ring of thin flames under the slow ascending smoke
wriggled rapidly down the slopes of the knoll; here and there a dry bush caught
with a tall, vicious roar. The conflagration made a clear zone of fire for the rifles of
the small party, and expired smouldering on the edge of the forests and along the
muddy bank of the creek. A strip of jungle luxuriating in a damp hollow between
the knoll and the Rajah's stockade stopped it on that side with a great crackling
and detonations of bursting bamboo stems. The sky was sombre, velvety, and
swarming with stars. The blackened ground smoked quietly with low creeping
wisps, till a little breeze came on and blew everything away. Brown expected an
attack to be delivered as soon as the tide had flowed enough again to enable the
war-boats which had cut off his retreat to enter the creek. At any rate he was sure
there would be an attempt to carry off his long-boat, which lay below the hill, a
dark high lump on the feeble sheen of a wet mud-flat. But no move of any sort was
made by the boats in the river. Over the stockade and the Rajah's buildings Brown
saw their lights on the water. They seemed to be anchored across the stream.
Other lights afloat were moving in the reach, crossing and recrossing from side to
side. There were also lights twinkling motionless upon the long walls of houses
up the reach, as far as the bend, and more still beyond, others isolated inland. The
loom of the big fires disclosed buildings, roofs, black piles as far as he could see.
It was an immense place. The fourteen desperate invaders lying flat behind the
felled trees raised their chins to look over at the stir of that town that seemed to
extend up-river for miles and swarm with thousands of angry men. They did not
speak to each other. Now and then they would hear a loud yell, or a single shot

rang out, fired very far somewhere. But round their position everything was still, dark, silent. They seemed to be forgotten, as if the excitement keeping awake all the population had nothing to do with them, as if they had been dead already."

CHAPTER XXXIX.

"All the events of that night have a great importance, since they brought about a situation which remained unchanged till Jim's return. Jim had been away in the interior for more than a week, and it was Dain Waris who had directed the first repulse. That brave and intelligent youth ('who knew how to fight after the manner of white men') wished to settle the business off-hand, but his people were too much for him. He had not Jim's racial prestige and the reputation of invincible, supernatural power. He was not the visible, tangible incarnation of unfailing truth and of unfailing victory. Beloved, trusted, and admired as he was, he was still one of *them*, while Jim was one of *us*. Moreover, the white man, a tower of strength in himself, was invulnerable, while Dain Waris could be killed. Those unexpressed thoughts guided the opinions of the chief men of the town who elected to assemble in Jim's fort for deliberation upon the emergency as if expecting to find wisdom and courage in the dwelling of the absent white man. The shooting of Brown's ruffians was so far good or lucky that there had been half-a-dozen casualties amongst the defenders. The wounded were lying on the verandah tended by their women-folk. The women and children from the lower part of the town had been sent into the fort at the first alarm. There Jewel was in command, very efficient and high-spirited, obeyed by Jim's 'own people,' who, quitting in a body their little settle-ment under the stockade, had gone in to form the garrison. The refugees crowded round her; and through the whole affair, to the very disastrous last, she showed an extraordinary martial ardour. It was to her that Dain Waris had gone at once at the first intelligence of danger, for you must know that Jim was the only one in Patusan who possessed a store of gunpowder. Stein, with whom he had kept up intimate relations by letters, had obtained from the Dutch Government a special authorisation to export five hundred kegs of it to Patusan. The powder-magazine was a small hut of rough logs covered entirely with earth, and in Jim's absence the girl had the key. In the council, held at eleven o'clock in the evening in Jim's din-ing-room, she backed up Waris's advice for immediate and vigorous action. I am told that she stood up by the side of Jim's empty chair at the head of the long table and made a warlike impassioned speech, which for the moment extorted murmurs of approbation from the assembled headmen. Old Doramin, who had not showed himself outside his own gate for more than a year, had been brought across with great difficulty. He was, of course, the chief man there. The temper of the council was very unforgiving, and the old man's word would have been decisive; but it is my opinion that, well aware of his son's fiery courage, he dared not pronounce the word. More dilatory counsels prevailed. A certain Haji Saman pointed out at great length that 'these tyrannical and ferocious men had delivered themselves to a cer-tain death in any case. They would stand fast on their hill and starve, or they would try to regain their boat and be shot from ambushes across the creek, or they would break and fly into the forest and perish singly there.' He argued that by the use of proper stratagems these evil-minded strangers could be destroyed without the risk of a battle, and his words had a great weight, especially with the Patusan men proper. What unsettled the minds of the townfolk was the failure of the Rajah's boats to act at the decisive moment. It was the diplomatic Kassim who represented the Rajah at the council. He spoke very little, listened smilingly, very friendly and impenetrable. During the sitting messengers kept arriving every few minutes almost, with reports of the invaders' proceedings. Wild and exaggerated rumours were flying: there was a large ship at the mouth of the river with big guns and many more men—some white, others with black skins and of bloodthirsty appearance. They were coming with many more boats to exterminate every living thing. A sense of near, incomprehensible danger affected the common people. At one moment there was a panic in the courtyard amongst the women; shrieking; a rush; children crying—Haji Saman went out to quiet them. Then a fort sentry fired at something moving on the river, and nearly killed a villager bringing in his women-folk in a canoe together with the best of his domestic utensils and a dozen fowls. This caused more confusion. Meantime the palaver inside Jim's house went on in the presence of the girl. Doramin sat fierce-faced, heavy, looking at the speakers in turn, and breathing slow like a bull. He didn't speak till the last, after Kassim had declared that the Rajah's boats would be called in because the men were required to defend his master's stockade. Dain Waris in his father's presence would offer no opinion, though the girl entreated him in Jim's name to speak out. She offered him Jim's own men in her anxiety to have these intruders driven out at once. He only shook his head, after a glance or two at Doramin. Finally, when the council broke up it had been decided that the houses nearest the creek should be strongly occupied to obtain the command of the enemy's boat. The boat itself was not to be interfered with openly, so that the robbers on the hill should be tempted to embark, when a well-directed fire would kill most of them, no doubt. To cut the escape of those who might survive, and to prevent more of them coming up, Dain Waris was ordered by Doramin to take an armed party of Bugis down the river to a certain spot ten miles below Patusan, and there form a camp on the shore and blockade the stream with the canoes. I don't believe for a moment that Doramin feared the arrival of fresh forces. My opinion is that his conduct was guided solely by his wish to keep his son out of harm's way. To prevent a rush being made into the town the construction of a stockade was to be commenced at daylight at the end of the street on the left bank. The old Nakhoda declared his intention to command there himself. A distribution of powder, bullets, and percussion-caps was made immediately under the girl's supervision. Several messengers were to be despatched in different directions after Jim, whose exact whereabouts were unknown. These men started at dawn, but before that time Kassim had managed to open communications with the besieged Brown.

"That accomplished diplomatist and confidant of the Rajah, on leaving the fort to go back to his master, took into his boat Cornelius, whom he found slinking mutely amongst the people in the courtyard. Kassim had a little plan of his own and wanted him for an interpreter. Thus it came about that towards morning Brown, reflecting upon the desperate nature of his position, heard from the marshy overgrown hollow an amicable, quavering, strained voice crying—in English—for permission to come up, under a promise of personal safety and on a very important errand. He was overjoyed. If he was spoken to he was no longer a hunted wild beast. These friendly sounds took off at once the awful stress of vigilant watchfulness as of so many blind men not knowing whence the deathblow might come. He pretended a great reluctance. The voice declared itself 'a white man. A poor, ruined, old man who had been living here for years.' A mist, wet and chilly, lay on the slopes of the hill, and after some more shouting from one to the other, Brown called out, 'Come on, then, but alone, mind!' As a matter of fact—he told me, writhing with rage at the recollection of his helplessness—it made no difference. They couldn't see more than a few yards before them, and no treachery could make their position worse. By-and-by Cornelius, in his week-day attire of a ragged dirty shirt and pants, barefooted, with a broken-rimmed pith hat on his head, was made out vaguely, sidling up to the defences, hesitating, stopping to listen in a peering posture. 'Come along! You are safe,' yelled Brown, while his men stared. All their hopes of life became suddenly centered in that dilapidated, mean new-comer, who in profound silence clambered clumsily over a felled tree-trunk, and shivering, with his sour mistrustful face, looked about at the knot of bearded, anxious, sleepless desperadoes.

"Half an hour's confidential talk with Cornelius opened Brown's eyes as to the home affairs of Patusan. He was on the alert at once. There were possibilities, immense possibilities; but before he would talk over Cornelius's proposals he demanded that some food should be sent up as a guarantee of good faith. Cornelius went off, creeping sluggishly down the hill on the side of the Rajah's place, and after some delay a few of Tunku Allang's men came up, bringing a scanty supply of rice, chillies, and dried fish. This was immeasurably better than nothing. Later on Cornelius returned accompanying Kassim, who stepped out with an air of perfect good-humoured trustfulness, in sandals, and muffled up from neck to ankles in dark-blue sheeting. He shook hands with Brown discreetly, and the three drew aside for a conference. Brown's men, recovering their confidence, were slapping each other on the back, and cast knowing glances at their captain while they busied themselves with preparations for cooking.

"Kassim disliked Doramin and his Bugis very much, but he hated the new order of things still more. It had occurred to him that these whites, together with the Rajah's followers, could attack and defeat the Bugis before Jim's return. Then, he reasoned, general defection of the townfolk was sure to follow, and the reign of the white man who protected poor people would be over. Afterwards the new allies could be dealt with. They would have no friends. The fellow was perfectly able to perceive the difference of character, and had seen enough of white men to know that these new-comers were outcasts, men without country. Brown preserved a stern and inscrutable demeanour. When he first heard Cornelius's voice demanding admittance, it brought merely the hope of a loophole for escape. In less than an hour other thoughts were seething in his head. Urged by an extreme necessity, he had come there to steal food, a few tons of rubber or gum may be, perhaps a handful of dollars, and had found himself enmeshed by deadly dangers. Now in consequence of these overtures from Kassim he began to think of stealing the whole country. Some confounded fellow had apparently accomplished something of the kind—single-handed at that. Couldn't have done it very well though. Perhaps they could work together—squeeze everything dry and then go out quietly. In the course of his negotiations with Kassim he became aware that he was supposed to have a big ship with plenty of men outside. Kassim begged him earnestly to have his big ship with his many guns and men brought up the river without delay for the Rajah's service. Brown professed himself willing, and on this basis the negotiation was carried on with mutual distrust. Three times in the course of the morning the courteous and active Kassim went down to consult the Rajah and came up busily with his long stride. Brown, while bargaining, had a sort of grim enjoyment in thinking of his wretched schooner, with nothing but a heap of dirt in her hold, that stood for an armed ship, and a Chinaman and a lame ex-beach-comber of Levuka on board, who represented all his many men. In the afternoon he obtained further doles of food, a promise of some money, and a supply of mats for his men to make shelters for themselves. They lay down and snored, protected from the burning sunshine; but Brown, sitting fully exposed on one of the felled trees, feasted his eyes upon the view of the town and the river. There was much loot there. Cornelius, who had made himself at home in the camp, talked at his elbow, pointing out the localities, imparting advice, giving his own version of Jim's character, and commenting in his own fashion upon the events of the last three years. Brown, who, apparently indifferent and gazing away, listened with atten-tion to every word, could not make out clearly what sort of man this Jim could be. 'What's his name? Jim! Jim! That's not enough for a man's name.' 'They call him,' said Cornelius scornfully, 'Tuan Jim here. As you may say Lord Jim.' 'What is he? Where does he come from?' inquired Brown. 'What sort of man is he? Is he an Englishman?' 'Yes, yes, he's an Englishman. I am an Englishman too. From Ma-lacca. He is a fool. All you have to do is to kill him and then you are king here. Everything belongs to him,' explained Cornelius. 'It strikes me he may be made to share with somebody before very long,' commented Brown half aloud. 'No, no. The proper way is to kill him the first chance you get, and then you can do what you like,' Cornelius would insist earnestly. 'I have lived for many years here, and I am giving you a friend's advice.'

"In such converse and in gloating over the view of Patusan, which he had de-termined in his mind should become his prey, Brown whiled away most of the afternoon, his men, meantime, resting. On that day Dain Waris's fleet of canoes stole one by one under the shore farthest from the creek, and went down to close the river against his retreat. Of this Brown was not aware, and Kassim, who came up the knoll an hour before sunset, took good care not to enlighten him. He wanted the white man's ship to come up the river, and this news, he feared, would be discouraging. He was very pressing with Brown to send the 'order,' offering at the same time a trusty messenger, who for greater secrecy (as he explained) would make his way by land to the mouth of the river and deliver the 'order' on board. After some reflection Brown judged it expedient to tear a page out of his pocket-book, on which he simply wrote, 'We are getting on. Big job. Detain the man.' The stolid youth selected by Kassim for that service performed it faithfully, and was rewarded by being suddenly tipped, head first, into the schooner's empty hold by the ex-beach-comber and the Chinaman, who thereupon hastened to put on the hatches. What became of him afterwards Brown did not say."

CHAPTER XL.

"Brown's object was to gain time by fooling with Kassim's diplomacy. For doing a real stroke of business he could not help thinking the white man was the person to work with. He could not imagine such a chap (who must be confound-edly clever after all to get hold of the natives like that) refusing a help that would

do away with the necessity for slow, cautious, risky cheating, that imposed itself
as the only possible line of conduct for a single-handed man. He, Brown, would
offer him the power. No man could hesitate. Everything was in coming to a clear
understanding. Of course they would share. The idea of there being a fort—all
ready to his hand—a real fort, with artillery (he knew this from Cornelius), excited
him. Let him only once get in and . . . He would impose modest conditions. Not
too low, though. The man was no fool, it seemed. They would work like brothers
till, . . . till the time came for a quarrel and a shot that would settle all accounts.
With grim impatience of plunder he wished himself to be talking with the man
now. The land already seemed to be his to tear to pieces, squeeze, and throw away.
Meantime Kassim had to be fooled for the sake of food first—and for a second
string. But the principal thing was to get something to eat from day to day. Besides,
he was not averse to begin fighting on that Rajah's account, and teach a lesson to
those people who had received him with shots. The lust of battle was upon him.

"I am sorry that I can't give you this part of the story, which of course I have
mainly from Brown, in Brown's own words. There was in the broken, violent
speech of that man, unveiling before me his thoughts with the very hand of Death
upon his throat, an undisguised ruthlessness of purpose, a strange vengeful attitude towards his own past, and a blind belief in the righteousness of his will
against all mankind, something of that feeling which could induce the leader of a
horde of wandering cut-throats to call himself proudly the Scourge of God. No
doubt the natural senseless ferocity which is the basis of such a character was exasperated by failure, ill-luck, and the recent privations, as well as by the desperate
position in which he found himself; but what was most remarkable of all was this,
that while he planned treacherous alliances, had already settled in his own mind
the fate of the white man, and intrigued in an overbearing, offhand manner with
Kassim, one could perceive that what he had really desired, almost in spite of himself, was to play havoc with that jungle town which had defied him, to see it
strewn over with corpses and enveloped in flames. Listening to his pitiless, panting voice, I could imagine how he must have looked at it from the hillock, peopling
it with images of murder and rapine. The part nearest to the creek wore an abandoned aspect, though as a matter of fact every house concealed a few armed men
on the alert. Suddenly beyond the stretch of waste ground, interspersed with
small patches of low dense bush, excavations, heaps of rubbish, with trodden
paths between, a man, solitary and looking very small, strolled out into the deserted opening of the street between the shut-up, dark, lifeless buildings at the
end. Perhaps one of the inhabitants, who had fled to the other bank of the river,
coming back for some object of domestic use. Evidently he supposed himself quite
safe at that distance from the hill on the other side of the creek. A light stockade,
set up hastily, was just round the turn of the street, full of his friends. He moved
leisurely. Brown saw him, and instantly called to his side the Yankee deserter, who
acted as a sort of second in command. This lanky, loose-jointed fellow came forward, wooden-faced, trailing his rifle lazily. When he understood what was
wanted from him a homicidal and conceited smile uncovered his teeth, making
two deep folds down his sallow, leathery cheeks. He prided himself on being a
dead shot. He dropped on one knee, and taking aim from a steady rest through
the unlopped branches of a felled tree, fired, and at once stood up to look. The
man, far away, turned his head to the report, made another step forward, seemed
to hesitate, and abruptly got down on his hands and knees. In the silence that fell
upon the sharp crack of the rifle, the dead shot, keeping his eyes fixed upon the

quarry, guessed that 'this there coon's health would never be a source of anxiety to his friends any more.' The man's limbs were seen to move rapidly under his body in an endeavour to run on all-fours. In that empty space arose a multitudinous shout of dismay and surprise. The man sank flat, face down, and moved no more. 'That showed them what we could do,' said Brown to me. 'Struck the fear of sudden death into them. That was what we wanted. They were two hundred to one, and this gave them something to think over for the night. Not one of them had an idea of such a long shot before. That beggar belonging to the Rajah scouted down-hill with his eyes hanging out of his head.'

"As he was telling me this he tried with a shaking hand to wipe the thin foam on his blue lips. 'Two hundred to one. Two hundred to one . . . strike terror, . . . terror, terror, I tell you. . . .' His own eyes were starting out of their sockets. He fell back, clawing the air with skinny fingers, sat up again, bowed and hairy, glared at me sideways like some man-beast of folk-lore, with open mouth in his miserable and awful agony before he got his speech back after that fit. There are sights one never forgets.

"Furthermore, to draw the enemy's fire and locate such parties as might have been hiding in the bushes along the creek, Brown ordered the Solomon Islander to go down to the boat and bring an oar, as you send a spaniel after a stick into the water. This failed, and the fellow came back without a single shot having been fired at him from anywhere. 'There's nobody,' opined some of the men. It is 'onnatural,' remarked the Yankee. Kassim had gone, by that time, very much impressed, pleased too, and also uneasy. Pursuing his tortuous policy, he had despatched a message to Dain Waris warning him to look out for the white men's ship, which, he had had information, was about to come up the river. He minimised its strength and exhorted him to oppose its passage. This double-dealing answered his purpose, which was to keep the Bugis forces divided and to weaken them by fighting. On the other hand, he had in the course of that day sent word to the assembled Bugis chiefs in town, assuring them that he was trying to induce the invaders to retire; his messages to the fort asked earnestly for powder for the Rajah's men. It was a long time since Tunku Allang had had ammunition for the score or so of old muskets rusting in their arm-racks in the audience-hall. The open intercourse between the hill and the palace unsettled all the minds. It was already time for men to take sides, it began to be said. There would soon be much bloodshed, and thereafter great trouble for many people. The social fabric of orderly, peaceful life, when every man was sure of to-morrow, the edifice raised by Jim's hands, seemed on that evening ready to collapse into a ruin reeking with blood. The poorer folk were already taking to the bush or flying up the river. A good many of the upper class judged it necessary to go and pay their court to the Rajah. The Rajah's youths jostled them rudely. Old Tunku Allang, almost out of his mind with fear and indecision, either kept a sullen silence or abused them violently for daring to come with empty hands: they departed very much frightened; only old Doramin kept his countrymen together and pursued his tactics inflexibly. Enthroned in a big chair behind the improvised stockade, he issued his orders in a deep veiled rumble, unmoved, like a deaf man, in the flying rumours.

"Dusk fell, hiding first the body of the dead man, which had been left lying with arms outstretched as if nailed to the ground, and then the revolving sphere of the night rolled smoothly over Patusan and came to a rest, showering the glitter of countless worlds upon the earth. Again, in the exposed part of the town big fires blazed along the only street, revealing from distance to distance upon their glares the falling straight lines of roofs, the fragments of wattled walls jumbled in confusion, here and there a whole hut elevated in the glow upon the vertical black stripes of a group of high piles; and all this line of dwellings, revealed in patches by the swaying flames, seemed to flicker tortuously away up-river into the gloom at the heart of the land. A great silence, in which the looms of successive fires played without noise, extended into the darkness at the foot of the hill; but the other bank of the river, all dark save for a solitary bonfire at the river-front before the fort, sent out into the air an increasing tremor that might have been the stamping of a multitude of feet, the hum of many voices, or the fall of an immensely distant waterfall. It was then, Brown confessed to me, while, turning his back on his men, he sat looking at it all, that notwithstanding his disdain, his ruthless faith in himself, a feeling came over him that at last he had run his head against a stone wall. Had his boat been afloat at the time, he believed he would have tried to steal away, taking his chances of a long chase down the river and of starvation at sea. It is very doubtful whether he would have succeeded in getting away. However he didn't try this. For another moment he had a passing thought of trying to rush the town, but he perceived very well that in the end he would find himself in the lighted street, where they would be shot down like dogs from the houses. They were two hundred to one—he thought, while his men, huddling round two heaps of smouldering embers, munched that last of the bananas and roasted the few yams they owed to Kassim's diplomacy. Cornelius sat amongst them dozing sulkily.

"Then one of the whites remembered that some tobacco had been left in the boat, and, encouraged by the impunity of the Solomon Islander, said he would go to fetch it. At this all the others shook off their despondency. Brown applied to, said, 'Go, and be d—d to you,' scornfully. He didn't think there was any danger in going to the creek in the dark. The man threw a leg over the tree-trunk and disappeared. A moment later he was heard clambering into the boat and then clambering out. 'I've got it,' he cried. A flash and a report at the very foot of the hill followed. 'I am hit,' yelled the man. 'Look out, look out—I am hit,' and instantly all the rifles went off. The hill squirted fire and noise into the night like a little volcano, and when Brown and the Yankee with curses and cuffs stopped the panic-stricken firing, a profound, weary groan floated up from the creek, succeeded by a plaint whose heartrending sadness was like some poison turning the blood cold in the veins. Then a strong voice pronounced several distinct incomprehensible words somewhere beyond the creek. 'Let no one fire,' shouted Brown. 'What does it mean?' . . . 'Do you hear on the hill? Do you hear? Do you hear?' repeated the voice three times. Cornelius translated, and then prompted the answer. 'Speak,' cried Brown, 'we hear.' Then the voice, declaiming in the sonorous inflated tone of a herald, and shifting continually on the edge of the vague waste-land, proclaimed that between the men of the Bugis nation living in Patusan and the white men on the hill and those with them, there would be no faith, no compassion, no speech, no peace. A bush rustled; a haphazard volley rang out. 'Dam' foolishness,' muttered the Yankee, vexedly grounding the butt. Cornelius translated. The wounded man below the hill, after crying out twice, 'Take me up! take me up!' went on complaining in moans. While he had kept on the blackened earth of the slope, and afterwards crouching in the boat, he had been safe enough. It seems that in his joy at finding the tobacco he forgot himself and jumped out on her off-side, as it were. The white boat, lying high and dry, showed him up; the creek was no more than seven yards wide in that place, and there happened to be a man crouching in the bush on the other bank.

"He was a Bugis of Tondano only lately come to Patusan, and a relation of the man shot in the afternoon. That famous long shot had indeed appalled the beholders. The man in utter security had been struck down, in full view of his friends, dropping with a joke on his lips, and they seemed to see in the act an atrocity which had stirred a bitter rage. That relation of his, Si-Lapa by name, was then with Doramin in the stockade only a few feet away. You who know these chaps must admit that the fellow showed an unusual pluck by volunteering to carry the message, alone, in the dark. Creeping across the open ground, he had deviated to the left and found himself opposite the boat. He was startled when Brown's man shouted. He came to a sitting position with his gun to his shoulder, and when the other jumped out, exposing himself, he pulled the trigger and lodged three jagged slugs point-blank into the poor wretch's stomach. Then, lying flat on his face, he gave himself up for dead, while a thin hail of lead chopped and swished the bushes close on his right hand; afterwards he delivered his speech shouting, bent double, dodging all the time in cover. With the last word he leaped sideways, lay close for a while, and afterwards got back to the houses unharmed, having achieved on that night such a renown as his children will not willingly allow to die.

"And on the hill the forlorn band let the two little heaps of embers go out under their bowed heads. They sat dejected on the ground with compressed lips and downcast eyes, listening to their comrade below. He was a strong man and died hard, with moans now loud, now sinking to a strange confidential note of pain. Sometimes he shrieked, and again, after a period of silence, he could be heard muttering deliriously a long and unintelligible complaint. Never for a moment did he cease.

"'What's the good?' Brown had said unmoved once, seeing the Yankee, who had been swearing under his breath, prepare to go down. 'That's so,' assented the deserter, reluctantly desisting. 'There's no encouragement for wounded men here. Only his noise is calculated to make all the others think too much of the hereafter, cap'n.' 'Water!' cried the wounded man in an extraordinary clear vigorous voice, and then went off moaning feebly. 'Ay, water. Water will do it,' muttered the other to himself, resignedly. 'Plenty by-and-by. The tide is flowing.'

"At last the tide flowed, silencing the plaint and the cries of pain, and the dawn was near when Brown, sitting with his chin in the palm of his hand before Patusan, as one might stare at the unscalable side of a mountain, heard the brief ringing bark of a brass 6-pounder far away in town somewhere. 'What's this?' he asked of Cornelius, who hung about him. Cornelius listened. A muffled roaring shout rolled down-river over the town; a big drum began to throb, and others responded, pulsating and droning. Tiny scattered lights began to twinkle in the dark half of the town, while the part lighted by the loom of fires hummed with a deep and prolonged murmur. 'He has come,' said Cornelius. 'What? Already? Are you sure?' Brown asked. 'Yes! yes! Sure. Listen to the noise.' 'What are they making that row about?' pursued Brown. 'For joy,' snorted Cornelius; 'he is a very great man, but all the same, he knows no more than a child, and so they make a great noise to please him, because they know no better.' 'Look here,' said Brown, 'How is one to get at him?' 'He shall come to talk to you,' Cornelius declared. 'What do you mean? Come down here strolling as it were?' Cornelius nodded vigorously in the dark. 'Yes. He will come straight here and talk to you. He is just like a fool. You shall see what a fool he is.' Brown was incredulous. 'You shall see; you shall see,' repeated Cornelius. 'He is not afraid—not afraid of anything. He will come and order you to leave his people alone. Everybody must leave his people alone. He is like a little child. He will come to you straight.' Alas! he knew Jim well—that 'mean little skunk,' as Brown called him to me. 'Yes, certainly,' he pursued with ardour, 'and then, captain, you tell that tall man with a gun to shoot him. Just you kill him, and you shall frighten everybody so much that you can do anything you like with them afterwards—get what you like—go away when you like. Ha! ha! ha! Fine . . .' He almost danced with impatience and eagerness; and Brown, looking over his shoulder at him, could see, shown up by the pitiless dawn, his men drenched with dew, sitting amongst the cold ashes and the litter of the camp, haggard, cowed, and in rags."

CHAPTER XLI.

"To the very last moment, till the full day came upon them with a spring, the fires on the west bank blazed bright and clear; and then Brown saw in a knot of coloured figures motionless between the advanced houses a man in European clothes, in a helmet, all white. 'That's him; look! look!' Cornelius said excitedly. All Brown's men had sprung up and crowded at his back with lustreless eyes. The group of vivid colours and dark faces with the white figure in their midst were observing the knoll. Brown could see naked arms being raised to shade the eyes and other brown arms pointing. What should he do? He looked around, and the forests that faced him on all sides walled the cock-pit of an unequal contest. He looked once more at his men. A contempt, a weariness, the desire of life, the wish to try for one more chance—for some other grave—struggled in his breast. From the outline the figure presented it seemed to him that the white man there, backed up by all the power of the land, was examining his position through binoculars. Brown jumped up on the log, throwing his arms up, the palms outwards. The coloured group closed round the white man, and fell back twice before he got clear of them, walking slowly alone. Brown remained standing on the log till Jim, appearing and disappearing between the patches of thorny scrub, had nearly reached the creek; then Brown jumped off and went down to meet him on his side.

"They met, I should think, not very far from the place, perhaps on the very spot, where Jim took the second desperate leap of his life—the leap that landed him into the life of Patusan, into the trust, the love, the confidence of the people. They faced each other across the creek, and with steady eyes tried to understand each other before they opened their lips. Their antagonism must have been expressed in their glances; I know that Brown hated Jim at first sight. Whatever hopes he might have had vanished at once. This was not the man he had expected to see. He hated him for this—and in a checked flannel shirt with sleeves cut off at the elbows, grey bearded, with a sunken, sunblackened face—he cursed in his heart the other's youth and assurance, his clear eyes and his untroubled bearing. That fellow had got in a long way before him! He did not look like a man who would be willing to give anything for assistance. He had all the advantages on his side—possession, security, power; he was on the side of an overwhelming force! He was not hungry and desperate, and he did not seem in the least afraid. And there was something in the very neatness of Jim's clothes, from the white helmet to the canvas leggings and the pipeclayed shoes, which in Brown's sombre irritated eyes seemed to belong to things he had in the very shaping of his life contemned and flouted.

"'Who are you?' asked Jim at last, speaking in his usual voice. 'My name's Brown,' answered the other loudly. 'Captain Brown. What's yours?' and Jim after a little pause went on quietly, as if he had not heard: 'What made you come here?' 'You want to know,' said Brown bitterly. 'It's easy to tell. Hunger. And what made you?'

"'The fellow started at this,' said Brown, relating to me the opening of this strange conversation between those two men, separated only by the muddy bed of a creek, but standing on the opposite poles of that conception of life which includes all mankind—'The fellow started at this and got very red in the face. Too big to be questioned, I suppose. I told him that if he looked upon me as a dead man with whom you may take liberties, he himself was not a whit better off really. I had a fellow up there who had a bead drawn on him all the time, and only waited for a sign from me. There was nothing to be shocked at in this. He had come down of his own freewill. "Let us agree," said I, "that we are both dead men, and let us talk on that basis, as equals. We are all equal before death," I said. I admitted I was there like a rat in a trap, but we had been driven to it, and even a trapped rat can give a bite. He caught me up in a moment. "Not if you don't go near the trap till the rat is dead." I told him that sort of game was good enough for these native friends of his, but I would have thought him too white to serve even a rat so. Yes, I had wanted to talk with him. Not to beg for my life, though. My fellows were—well—what they were—men like himself, anyhow. All we wanted from him was to come on in the devil's name and have it out. "God d—n it," said I, while he stood there as still as a wooden post, "you don't want to come out here every day with your glasses to count how many of us are left on our feet. Come. Either bring your infernal crowd along or let us go out and starve in the open sea, by God! You have been white once, for all your tall talk of this being your own people and you being one with them. Are you? And what the devil do you get for it; what is it you've found here that is so d—d precious? Hey? You don't want us to come down here perhaps—do you? You are two hundred to one. You don't want us to come down into the open. Ah! I promise you we shall give you some sport before you've done. You talk about me making a cowardly set upon unoffending people. What's that to me that they are unoffending when I am starving for next to no offence? But I am not a coward. Don't you be one. Bring them along or, by all the fiends, we shall yet manage to send half of your unoffending town to heaven with us in smoke!"'

"He was terrible—relating this to me—this tortured skeleton of a man drawn up together with his face over his knees, upon a miserable bed in that wretched hovel, and lifting his head to look at me with malignant triumph.

"'That's what I told him—I knew what to say,' he began again, feebly at first, but working himself up with incredible speed into a fiery utterance of his scorn. 'We aren't going into the forest to wander like a string of living skeletons dropping one after another for ants to go to work upon us before we are fairly dead. Oh no!

. . . "You don't deserve a better fate," he said. "And what do you deserve," I shouted at him, "you that I find skulking here with your mouth full of your responsibility, of innocent lives, of your infernal duty? What do you know more of me than I know of you? I came here for food. D'ye hear?—food to fill our bellies. And what did *you* come for? What did you ask for when you came here? We don't ask you for anything but to give us a fight or a clear road to go back whence we came. . . ." "I would fight with you now," says he, pulling at his little moustache. "And I would let you shoot me, and welcome," I said. "This is as good a jumping-off place for me as another. I am sick of my infernal luck. But it would be too easy. There are my men in the same boat—and, by God, I am not the sort to jump out of trouble and leave them in a d—d lurch," I said. He stood thinking for a while and then wanted to know what I had done ("out there" he says, tossing his head down-stream) to be hazed about so. "Have we met to tell each other the story of our lives?" I asked him. "Suppose you begin. No? Well, I am sure I don't want to hear. Keep it to yourself. I know it is no better than mine. I've lived—and so did you, though you talk as if you were one of those people that should have wings so as to go about without touching the dirty earth. Well—it is dirty. I haven't got any wings. I am here because I was afraid once in my life. Want to know what of? Of a prison. That scares me, and you may know it—if it's any good to you. I won't ask you what scared you into this infernal hole, where you seem to have found pretty pickings. That's your luck and this is mine—the privilege to beg for the favour of being shot quickly, or else kicked out to go free and starve in my own way." . . .'

"His debilitated body shook with an exultation so vehement, so assured, and so malicious that it seemed to have driven off the death waiting for him in that hut. The corpse of his mad self-love uprose from rags and destitution as from the dark horrors of a tomb. It is impossible to say how much he lied to Jim then, how much he lied to me now—and to himself always. Vanity plays lurid tricks with our memory, and the truth of every passion wants some pretence to make it live. Standing at the gate of the other world in the guise of a beggar, he had slapped this world's face, he had spat on it, he had thrown upon it an immensity of scorn and revolt at the bottom of his misdeeds. He had overcome them all—men, women, savages, traders, ruffians, missionaries—and Jim—that beefy-faced beggar. I did not begrudge him this triumph in *articulo mortis*, this almost posthumous illusion of having trampled all the earth under his feet. While he was boasting to me, in his sordid and repulsive agony, I couldn't help thinking of the chuckling talk relating to the time of his greatest splendour when, during a year or more, Gentleman Brown's ship was to be seen, for many days on end, hovering off an islet befringed with green upon azure, with the dark dot of the mission-house on a white beach; while Gentleman Brown, ashore, was casting his spells over a romantic girl for whom Melanesia had been too much, and giving hopes of a remarkable conversion to her husband. The poor man, some time or other, had been heard to express the intention of winning 'Captain Brown to a better way of life.' . . . 'Bag Gentleman Brown for Glory'—as a leery-eyed loafer expressed it once—'just to let them see up above what a Western Pacific trading skipper looks like.' And this was the man, too, who had run off with a dying woman, and had shed tears over her body. 'Carried on like a big baby,' his then mate was never tired of telling, 'and where the fun came in may I be kicked to death by diseased Kanakas if I know. Why, gents! She was too far gone when he brought her aboard to know him; she just lay there on her back in his bunk staring at the beam with awful shining eyes—and then she died. Dam' bad sort of fever, I guess. . . .' I remembered all these stories while, wiping his matted lump of a beard with a livid hand, he was telling me from his noisome couch how he got round, got in, got home, on that confounded, immaculate, don't-you-touch-me sort of fellow. He admitted that he couldn't be scared, but there was a way, 'as broad as a turnpike, to get in and shake his twopenny soul around and inside out and upside down—by God!'"

CHAPTER XLII.

"I don't think he could do more than perhaps look upon that straight path. He seemed to have been puzzled by what he saw, for he interrupted himself in his narrative more than once to exclaim, 'He nearly slipped from me there. I could not make him out. Who was he?' And after glaring at me widly he would go on, jubilating and sneering. To me the conversation of these two across the creek appears now as the deadliest kind of duel on which Fate looked on with her cold-eyed knowledge of the end. No, he didn't turn Jim's soul inside out, but I am much mistaken if the spirit so utterly out of his reach had not been made to taste to the full the bitterness of that contest. These were the emissaries with whom the world he had renounced was pursuing him in his retreat. White men from 'out there' where he did not think himself good enough to live. This was all that came to him—a menace, a shock, a danger to his work. I suppose it is this sad, half-resentful, half-resigned feeling, piercing through the few words Jim said now and then, that puzzled Brown so much in the reading of his character. Some great men owe most of their greatness to the ability of detecting in those they destine for their tools the exact quality of strength that matters for their work; and Brown, as though he had been really great, had a satanic gift of finding out the best and the weakest spot in his victims. He admitted to me that Jim wasn't of the sort that can be got over by truckling, and accordingly he took care to show himself as a man confronting without dismay ill-luck, censure, and disaster. The smuggling of a few guns was no great crime, he pointed out. As to coming to Patusan, who had the right to say he hadn't come to beg? The infernal people here let loose at him from both banks without staying to ask questions. He made the point brazenly, for, in truth, Dain Waris's energetic action has prevented the greatest calamities: because Brown told me distinctly that, perceiving the size of the place, he had resolved instantly in his mind that as soon as he had gained a footing he would set fire right and left, and begin by shooting down everything living in sight, in order to cow and terrify the population. The disproportion of forces was so great that this was the only way giving him the slightest chance of attaining his ends—he argued in a fit of coughing. But he didn't tell Jim this. As to the hardships and starvation they had gone through, these had been very real; it was enough to look at his band. He made, at the sound of a shrill whistle, all his men appear standing in a row on the logs in full view, so that Jim could see them. For the killing of the man, it had been done—well, it had—but was not this war, bloody war—in a corner? and the fellow had been killed cleanly, shot through the chest, not like that poor devil of his lying now in the creek. They had to listen to him dying for six hours, with his entrails torn with slugs. At any rate this was a life for a life. . . . And all this was said with the weariness, with the recklessness of a man spurred on and on by ill-luck till he cares not where he runs. When he asked Jim, with a sort of brusque despairing frankness, whether he himself—straight now—didn't understand that when 'it came to saving one's life in the dark, one didn't care who else went—three, thirty, three hundred people'—it was as if a demon had been whispering advice in his ear. 'I made him wince,' boasted Brown to me. 'He very soon left off coming the righteous over me. He just stood there with nothing to say, and looking as black as thunder—not to me—on the ground.' He asked Jim whether he had nothing fishy in his life to remember that he was so damnedly hard upon a man trying to get out of a deadly hole by the first means that came to hand—and so on, and so on. And there ran through the rough talk a vein of subtle reference to their common blood, an assumption of common experience; a sickening suggestion of common guilt, of secret knowledge that was like a bond of their minds and of their hearts.

"At last Brown threw himself down full length and watched Jim out of the corners of his eyes. Jim on his side of the creek stood thinking and switching his leg. The houses in view were silent as if a pestilence had swept them clean of every breath of life; but many invisible eyes were turned, from within, upon the two men with the creek between them, a stranded white boat, and the body of the third man half sunk in the mud. On the river canoes were moving again, for Patusan was recovering its belief in the stability of earthly institutions since the return of the white lord. The right bank, the platforms of the houses, the rafts moored along the shores, even the roofs of bathing-huts, were covered with people that, far away out of earshot and almost out of sight, were straining their eyes towards the knoll beyond the Rajah's stockade. Within the wide irregular ring of forests, broken in two places by the sheen of the river there was a silence. 'Will you promise to leave the coast?' Jim asked. Brown lifted and let fall his hand, giving everything up as it were—accepting the inevitable. 'And surrender your arms?' Jim went on. Brown sat up and glared across. 'Surrender our arms! Not till you come to take them out of our stiff hands. You think I am gone crazy with funk? Oh no! That and the rags I stand in is all I have got in the world, besides a few more breech-loaders on board; and I expect to sell the lot in Madagascar, if I ever get so far,— begging my way from ship to ship.'

"Jim said nothing to this. At last, throwing away the switch he held in his hand, he said, as if speaking to himself, 'I don't know whether I have the power. . . .' 'You don't know! And you wanted me just now to give up my arms! That's good, too,' cried Brown. 'Suppose they say one thing to you, and do the other thing to me.' He calmed down markedly. 'I daresay you have the power, or what's the meaning of all this talk?' he continued. 'What did you come down here for? To pass the time of day?

"'Very well,' said Jim, lifting his head suddenly after a long silence. 'You shall have a clear road or else a clear fight.' He turned on his heel and walked away.

"Brown got up at once, but he did not go up the hill till he had seen Jim disappear between the first houses. He never set his eyes on him again. On his way back he met Cornelius slouching down with his head between his shoulders. He stopped before Brown. 'Why didn't you kill him?' he demanded in a sour, discontented voice. 'Because I could do better than that,' Brown said with an amused smile. 'Never! never!' protested Cornelius with energy. 'Couldn't. I have lived here for many years.' Brown looked up at him curiously. There were many sides to the life of that place in arms against him; things he would never find out. Cornelius slunk past dejectedly in the direction of the river. He was now leaving his new friends; he accepted the disappointing course of events with a sulky obstinacy which seemed to draw more together his little yellow old face; and as he went down he glanced askant here and there, never giving up his fixed idea.

"Henceforth events move fast without a check, flowing from the very hearts of men like a stream from a dark source, and we see Jim amongst them, mostly through Tamb' Itam's eyes. The girl's eyes had watched him too, but her life is too much entwined with his: there is her passion, her wonder, her anger, and, above all, her fear and her unforgiving love. Of the faithful servant, uncomprehending as the rest of them, it is the fidelity alone that comes into play; a fidelity and a belief in his lord so strong that even amazement is subdued to a sort of saddened acceptance of a mysterious failure. He has eyes only for one figure, and through all the mazes of bewilderment he preserves his air of guardianship, of obedience, of care.

"His master came back from his talk with the white men, walking slowly towards the stockade in the street. Everybody was rejoiced to see him return, for while he was away every man had been afraid not only of him being killed, but also of what would come after. Jim went into one of the houses, where old Doramin had retired, and remained alone for a long time with the head of the Bugis settlers. No doubt he discussed the course to follow with him then, but no man was present at the conversation. Only Tamb' Itam, keeping as close to the door as he could, heard his master say, 'Yes. I shall let all the people know that such is my wish; but I spoke to you, O Doramin, before all the others, and alone; for you know my heart as well as I know yours and its greatest desire. And you know well also that I have no thought but for the people's good.' Then his master, lifting the sheeting in the doorway, went out, and he, Tamb' Itam, had a glimpse of old Doramin within, sitting in the chair with his hands on his knees, and looking between his feet. Afterwards he followed his master to the fort, where all the principal Bugis and Patusan inhabitants had been summoned for a talk. Tamb' Itam himself hoped there would be some fighting. 'What was it but the taking of another hill?' he exclaimed regretfully. However, in the town many hoped that the rapacious strangers would be induced, by the sight of so many brave men making ready to fight, to go away. It would be a good thing if they went away. Since Jim's arrival had been made known before daylight by the gun fired from the fort and the beating of the big drum there, the fear that had hung over Patusan had broken and subsided like a wave on a rock, leaving the seething foam of excitement, curiosity, and endless speculation. Half of the population had been ousted out of their homes for purposes of defence, and were living in the street on the left side of the river, crowding round the fort, and in momentary expectation of seeing their abandoned dwellings on the threatened bank burst into flames. The general anxiety was to see the matter settled quickly. Food, through Jewel's care, had been served out to the refugees. Nobody knew what their white man would do. Some remarked that it was worse than in Sherif Ali's war. Then many people did not care; now everybody had something to lose. The movements of canoes passing to and fro between the two parts of the town were watched with interest. A couple of Bugis war-boats lay anchored in the middle of the stream to protect the river, and a thread of smoke stood at the bow of each; the men in them were cooking their midday rice when Jim, after his interviews with Brown and Doramin, crossed the river and entered by the water-gate of his fort. The people inside crowded round him so that he could hardly make his way to the house. They had not seen him before, because on his arrival during the night he had only exchanged a few words with the girl, who had come down to the landing-stage for the purpose, and had then gone on at once to join the chiefs and the fighting men on the other bank. People shouted greetings after him. One old woman raised a laugh by pushing her way to the front madly and enjoining him in a scolding voice to see to it that her two sons who were with Doramin did not come to harm at the hands of the robbers. Several of the bystanders tried to pull her away, but she struggled and cried, 'Let me go. What is this, O Muslims? This laughter is unseemly. Are they not cruel, bloodthirsty robbers bent on killing?' 'Let her be,' said Jim, and as a silence fell suddenly, he said slowly, 'Everybody shall be safe.' He entered the house before the great sigh, and the loud murmurs of satisfaction, had died out.

"There's no doubt his mind was made up that Brown should have his way clear back to the sea. His fate, revolted, was forcing his hand. He had for the first time to affirm his will in the face of outspoken opposition. 'There was much talk, and at first my master was silent,' Tamb' Itam said. 'Darkness came, and then I lit the candles on the long table. The chiefs sat on each side, and the lady remained by my master's right hand.'

"When he began to speak the unaccustomed difficulty seemed only to fix his resolve more immovably. The white men were now waiting for his answer on the hill. Their chief had spoken to him in the language of his own people, making clear many things difficult to explain in any other speech. They were erring men whom suffering had made blind to right and wrong. It is true that lives had been lost already, but why lose more? He declared to his hearers, the assembled heads of the people, that their welfare was his welfare, their losses his losses, their mourning his mourning. He looked round at the grave listening faces and told them to remember that they had fought and worked side by side. They knew his courage . . . Here a murmur interrupted him . . . And that he had never deceived them. For many years they had dwelt together. He loved the land and the people living in it with a very great love. He was ready to answer with his life for any harm that should come to them if the white men with beards were allowed to retire. They were evil-doers, but their destiny had been evil too. Had he ever advised them ill? Had his words ever brought suffering to the people? he asked. He believed that it would be best to let these whites and their followers go with their lives. It would be a small gift. 'I whom you have tried and found always true ask you to let them go.' He turned to Doramin. The old Nakhoda made no movement. 'Then,' said Jim, 'call in Dain Waris, your son, my friend, for in this business I shall not lead.'"

CHAPTER XLIII.

"Tamb' Itam behind his chair was thunderstruck. The declaration produced an immense sensation. 'Let them go because this is best in my knowledge, which has never deceived you,' Jim insisted. There was a silence. In the darkness of the courtyard could be heard the subdued whispering, shuffling noise of many people. Doramin raised his heavy head and said that there was no more reading of hearts than touching the sky with the hand, but—he consented. The others gave their opinion in turn. 'It is best,' 'Let them go,' and so on. But most of them simply said that they 'believed Tuan Jim.'

"In this simple form of assent to his will lies the whole gist of the situation; their creed, his truth; and the testimony to that faithfulness which made him in his own eyes the equal of the impeccable men who never fall out of the ranks. Stein's words, 'Romantic!—Romantic!' seem to ring over those distances that will never give him up now to a world indifferent to his failing and his virtues, and to that ardent and clinging affection that refuses him the dole of tears in the bewilderment of a great grief and of eternal separation. From the moment the sheer truthfulness of his last three years of life carries the day against the ignorance, the fear, and the anger of men, he appears no longer to me as I saw him last—a white speck catching all the dim light left upon a sombre coast and the darkened sea—but greater and more pitiful in the loneliness of his soul, that remains even for her who loved him best a cruel and insoluble mystery.

"It is evident that he did not mistrust Brown; there was no reason to doubt the story, whose truth seemed warranted by the rough frankness, by a sort of virile sincerity in accepting the morality and the consequences of his acts. But Jim did not know the almost inconceivable egotism of the man which made him, when resisted and foiled in his will, mad with the indignant and revengeful rage of a thwarted autocrat. But if Jim did not mistrust Brown, he was evidently anxious that some misunderstanding should not occur, ending perhaps in collision and bloodshed. It was for this reason that directly the Malay chiefs had gone he asked Jewel to get him something to eat, as he was going out of the fort to take command in the town. On her remonstrating against this on the score of his fatigue, he said that something might happen for which he would never forgive himself. 'I am responsible for every life in the land,' he said. He was moody at first; she served him with her own hands, taking the plates and dishes (of the dinner-service presented him by Stein) from Tamb' Itam. He brightened up after a while; told her she would be again in command of the fort for another night. 'There's no sleep for us, old girl,' he said, 'while our people are in danger.' Later on he said jokingly that she was the best man of them all. 'If you and Dain Waris had done what you wanted, not one of these poor devils would be alive to-day.' 'Are they very bad?' she asked, leaning over his chair. 'Men act badly sometimes without being much worse than others,' he said after some hesitation.

"Tamb' Itam followed his master to the landing-stage outside the fort. The night was clear but without a moon, and the middle of the river was dark, while the water under each bank reflected the light of many fires 'as on a night of Ramadan,' Tamb' Itam said. War-boats drifted silently in the dark lane or, anchored, floated motionless with a loud ripple. That night there was much paddling in a canoe and walking at his master's heels for Tamb' Itam: up and down the street they tramped, where the fires were burning, inland on the outskirts of the town where small parties of men kept guard in the fields. Tuan Jim gave his orders and was obeyed. Last of all they went to the Rajah's stockade, which a detachment of Jim's people manned on that night. The old Rajah had fled early in the morning with most of his women to a small house he had near a jungle village on a tributary stream. Kassim, left behind, had attended the council with his air of diligent activity to explain away the diplomacy of the day before. He was considerably cold-shouldered, but managed to preserve his smiling, quiet alertness, and professed himself highly delighted when Jim told him sternly that he proposed to occupy the stockade on that night with his own men. After the council broke up he was heard outside accosting this and that departing chief, and speaking in a loud, gratified tone of the Rajah's property being protected in the Rajah's absence.

"About ten or so Jim's men marched in. The stockade commanded the mouth of the creek, and Jim meant to remain there till Brown had passed below. A small fire was lit on the flat, grassy point outside the wall of stakes, and Tamb' Itam placed a little folding-stool for his master. Jim told him to try and sleep. Tamb' Itam got a mat and lay down a little way off; but he could not sleep, though he knew he had to go on an important journey before the night was out. His master walked to and fro before the fire with bowed head and with his hands behind his back. His face was sad. Whenever his master approached him Tamb' Itam pretended to sleep, not wishing his master to know he had been watched. At last his master stood still, looking down on him as he lay, and said softly, 'It is time.'

"Tamb' Itam arose directly and made his preparations. His mission was to go down the river, preceding Brown's boat by an hour or more, to tell Dain Waris finally and formally that the whites were to be allowed to pass out unmolested. Jim would not trust anybody else with that service. Before starting Tamb' Itam, more as a matter of form (since his position about Jim made him perfectly known), asked for a token. 'Because, Tuan,' he said, 'the message is important, and these are thy very words I carry.' His master first put his hand into one pocket, then into another, and finally took off his forefinger Stein's silver ring, which he habitually wore, and gave it to Tamb' Itam. When Tamb' Itam left on his mission, Brown's camp on the knoll was dark but for a single small glow shining through the branches of one of the trees the white men had cut down.

"Early in the evening Brown had received from Jim a folded piece of paper on which was written, 'You get the clear road. Start as soon as your boat floats on the morning tide. Let your men be careful. The bushes on both sides of the creek and the stockade at the mouth are full of well-armed men. You would have no chance, but I don't believe you want bloodshed.' Brown read it, tore the paper into small pieces, and, turning to Cornelius, who had brought it, said jeeringly, 'Good-bye, my excellent friend.' Cornelius had been in the fort, and had been sneaking around Jim's house during the afternoon. Jim chose him to carry the note because he could speak English, was known to Brown, and was not likely to be shot by some nervous mistake of one of the men as a Malay, approaching in the dusk, perhaps might have been.

"Cornelius didn't go away after delivering the paper. Brown was sitting up over a tiny fire; all the others were lying down. 'I could tell you something you would like to know,' Cornelius mumbled crossly. Brown paid no attention. 'You did not kill him,' went on the other, 'and what do you get for it? You might have had money from the Rajah, besides the loot of all the Bugis houses, and now you get nothing.' 'You had better clear out from here,' growled Brown, without even looking at him. But Cornelius let himself drop by his side and began to whisper very fast, touching his elbow from time to time. What he had to say made Brown sit up at first, with a curse. He had simply informed him of Dain Waris's armed party down the river. At first Brown saw himself completely sold and betrayed, but a moment's reflection convinced him that there could be no treachery intended. He said nothing, and after a while Cornelius remarked, in a tone of complete indifference, that there was another way out of the river which he knew very well. 'A good thing to know, too,' said Brown, pricking up his ears; and Cornelius began to talk of what went on in town and repeated all that had been said in council, gossiping in an even undertone at Brown's ear as you talk amongst sleeping men you do not wish to wake. 'He thinks he has made me harmless, does he? mumbled Brown very low. . . . 'Yes. He is a fool. A little child. He came here and robbed me,' droned on Cornelius, 'and he made all the people believe him. But if something happened that they did not believe him any more, where would he be? And the Bugis Dain who is waiting for you down the river there, captain, is the very man who chased you up here when you first came.' Brown observed nonchalantly that it would be just as well to avoid him, and with the same detached, musing air Cornelius declared himself acquainted with a backwater broad enough to take Brown's boat past Waris's camp. 'You will have to be quiet,' he said as an afterthought, 'for in one place we pass close behind his camp. Very close. They are camped ashore with their boats hauled up.' 'Oh, we know how to be as quiet as mice. Never fear,' said Brown. Cornelius stipulated that in case he were to pilot Brown out, his canoe should be towed. 'I'll have to get back quick,' he explained.

"It was two hours before the dawn when word was passed to the stockade from outlying watchers that the white robbers were coming down to their boat. In a very short time every armed man from one end of Patusan to the other was on the alert, yet the banks of the river remained so silent that but for the fires burning with sudden blurred flares the town might have been asleep as if in peace-time. A heavy mist lay very low on the water, making a sort of illusive grey light that showed nothing. When Brown's long-boat glided out of the creek into the river, Jim was standing on the low point of land before the Rajah's stockade—on the very spot where for the first time he put his foot on Patusan shore. A shadow loomed up, moving in the greyness, solitary, very bulky, and yet constantly eluding the eye. A murmur of low talking came out of it. Brown at the tiller heard Jim speak calmly: 'A clear road. You had better trust to the current while the fog lasts; but this will lift presently.' 'Yes, presently we shall see clear,' replied Brown.

"The thirty or forty men standing with muskets at ready outside the stockade held their breath. The Bugis owner of the prau, whom I saw on Stein's verandah, and who was amongst them, told me that the boat, shaving the low point close, seemed for a moment to grow big and hang over it like a mountain. 'If you think it worth your while to wait a day outside,' called out Jim, 'I'll try to send you down something—a bullock, some yams—what I can.' The shadow went on moving. 'Yes. Do,' said a voice, blank and muffled out of the fog. Not one of the many attentive listeners understood what the words meant; and then Brown and his men in their boat floated away, fading spectrally without the slightest sound.

"Thus Brown, invisible in the mist, goes out of Patusan elbow to elbow with Cornelius in the stern-sheets of the long-boat. 'Perhaps you shall get a small bullock,' said Cornelius. 'Oh yes. Bullock. Yam. You'll get it if *he* said so. He always speaks the truth. He stole everything I had. I suppose you like a small bullock better than the loot of many houses.' 'I would advise you to hold your tongue, or somebody here may fling you overboard into this damned fog,' said Brown. The boat seemed to be standing still; nothing could be seen, not even the river alongside, only the water-dust flew and trickled, condensed, down their beards and faces. It was weird, Brown told me. Every individual man of them felt as though he were adrift alone in a boat, haunted by an almost imperceptible suspicion of sighing, muttering ghosts. 'Throw me out, would you? But I would know where I was,' mumbled Cornelius surlily. 'I've lived many years here.' 'Not long enough to see through a fog like this,' Brown said, lolling back with his arm swinging to and fro on the useless tiller. 'Yes. Long enough for that,' snarled Cornelius. 'That's very useful,' commented Brown. 'Am I to believe you could find that backway you spoke of blind-fold, like this?' Cornelius grunted. 'Are you too tired to row?' he asked after a silence. 'No, by God!' shouted Brown suddenly. 'Out with your oars there.' There was a great knocking in the fog, which after a while settled into a regular grind of invisible sweeps against invisible tholepins. Otherwise nothing was changed, and but for the slight splash of a dipped blade it was like rowing a balloon car in a cloud, said Brown. Thereafter Cornelius did not open his lips except to ask querulously for somebody to bale out his canoe, which was towing behind the long-boat. Gradually the fog whitened and became luminous ahead. To the left Brown saw a darkness as though he had been looking at the back of the departing night. All at once a big bough covered with leaves appeared above his head, and ends of twigs, dripping and still, curved slenderly close alongside. Cornelius, without a word, took the tiller from his hand.''

CHAPTER XLIV.

"I don't think they spoke together again. The boat entered a narrow by-channel, where it was pushed by the oar-blades set into crumbling banks, and there was a gloom as if enormous black wings had been outspread above the mist that filled its depth to the summits of the trees. The branches overhead showered big drops through the gloomy fog. At a mutter from Cornelius, Brown ordered his men to load. 'I'll give you a chance to get even with them before we're done, you dismal cripples, you,' he said to his gang. 'Mind you don't throw it away—you hounds.' Low growls answered that speech. Cornelius showed much fussy concern for the safety of his canoe.

"Meantime Tamb' Itam had reached the end of his journey. The fog had delayed him a little, but he had paddled steadily, keeping in touch with the south bank. By-and-by daylight came like a glow in a ground glass globe. The shores made on each side of the river a dark smudge, in which one could detect hints of columnar forms and shadows of twisted branches high up. The mist was still thick on the water, but a good watch was being kept, for as Tamb' Itam approached the camp the figures of two men emerged out of the white vapour, and voices spoke to him boisterously. He answered, and presently a canoe lay alongside, and he exchanged news with the paddlers. All was well. The trouble was over. Then the men in the canoe let go their grip on the side of his dug-out and incontinently fell out of sight. He pursued his way till he heard voices coming to him quietly over the water, and saw, under the now lifting, swirling mist, the glow of many little fires burning on a sandy stretch, backed by lofty thin timber and bushes. There again a look-out was kept, for he was challenged. He shouted his name as the two last sweeps of his paddle ran his canoe up on the strand. It was a big camp. Men crouched in many little knots under a subdued murmur of early morning talk.

Many thin threads of smoke curled slowly on the white mist. Little shelters, elevated above the ground, had been built for the chiefs. Muskets were stacked in
small pyramids, and long spears were stuck singly into the sand near the fires.

"Tamb' Itam, assuming an air of importance, demanded to be led to Dain
Waris. He found the friend of his white lord lying on a raised couch made of bamboo, and sheltered by a sort of shed of sticks covered with mats. Dain Waris was
awake, and a bright fire was burning before his sleeping place, which resembled
a rude shrine. The only son of Nakhoda Doramin answered his greeting kindly.
Tamb' Itam began by handing him the ring which vouched for the truth of the messenger's words. Dain Waris, reclining on his elbow, bade him speak and tell all the
news. Beginning with the consecrated formula, 'The news is good,' Tamb' Itam
delivered Jim's own words. The white men, departing with the consent of all the
chiefs, were to be allowed to pass down the river. In answer to a question or two
Tamb' Itam then reported the proceedings of the last council. Dain Waris listened
attentively to the end, toying with the ring which ultimately he slipped on the forefinger of his right hand. After hearing all he had to say he dismissed Tamb' Itam
to have food and rest. Orders for the return in the afternoon were given immediately. Afterwards Dain Waris lay down again, open-eyed, while his personal attendants were preparing his food at the fire, by which Tamb' Itam also sat talking
to the men who lounged up to hear the latest intelligence from the town. The sun
was eating up the mist. A good watch was kept upon the reach of the main stream
where the boat of the whites was expected to appear every moment.

"It was then that Brown took his revenge upon the world which, after twenty
years of contemptuous and reckless bullying, refused him the tribute of a common
robber's success. It was an act of cold-blooded ferocity, and it consoled him on his
death-bed like a memory of an indomitable defiance. Stealthily he landed his men
on the other side of the island opposite to the Bugis camp, and led them across.
After a short but quite silent scuffle Cornelius, who had tried to slink away at the
moment of landing, resigned himself to show the way where the undergrowth was
most sparse. Brown held both his skinny hands together behind his back in the
grip of one vast fist, and now and then impelled him forward with a fierce push.
Cornelius remained as mute as a fish, abject but faithful to his purpose, whose
accomplishment loomed before him dimly. At the edge of the patch of forest
Brown's men spread themselves out in cover and waited. The camp was plain
from end to end before their eyes, and no one looked their way. Nobody even
dreamed that the white men could have any knowledge of the narrow channel at
the back of the island. When he judged the moment come, Brown yelled, 'Let
them have it,' and fourteen shots rang out like one.

"Tamb' Itam told me the surprise was so great that, except for those who fell
dead or wounded, not a soul of them moved for quite an appreciable time after the
first discharge. Then a man screamed, and after that scream a great yell of amazement and fear went up from all the throats. A blind panic drove these men in a
surging swaying mob to and fro along the shore like a herd of cattle afraid of the
water. Some few jumped into the river then, but most of them did so only after the
last discharge. Three times Brown's men fired into the ruck, Brown, the only one
in view, cursing and yelling, 'Aim low! aim low!'

"Tamb' Itam says that, as for him, he understood at the first volley what had
happened. Though untouched he fell down and lay as if dead, but with his eyes
open. At the sound of the first shots Dain Waris, reclining on the couch, jumped

up and ran out upon the open shore, just in time to receive a bullet in his forehead at the second discharge. Tamb' Itam saw him fling his arms wide open before he fell. Then, he says, a great fear came upon him—not before. The white men retired as they had come—unseen.

"Thus Brown balanced his account with the evil fortune. Notice that even in this awful outbreak there is a superiority as of a man who carries right—the abstract thing—within the envelope of his common desires. It was not a vulgar and treacherous massacre; it was a lesson, a retribution—a demonstration of some obscure and awful attribute of our nature which, I am afraid, is not so very far under the surface as we like to think.

"Afterwards the whites depart unseen by Tamb' Itam, and seem to vanish from before men's eyes altogether; and the schooner, too, vanishes after the manner of stolen goods. But a story is told of a white long-boat picked up a month later in the Indian Ocean by a cargo-steamer. Two parched, yellow, glassy-eyed, whispering skeletons in her recognised the authority of a third, who declared that his name was Brown. His schooner, he reported, bound south with a cargo of Java sugar, had sprung a bad leak and sank under his feet. He and his companions were the survivors of a crew of six. The two died on board the steamer which rescued them. Brown lived to be seen by me, and I can testify that he played his part to the last.

"It seems, however, that in going away they had neglected to cast off Cornelius's canoe. Cornelius himself Brown had let go at the beginning of the shooting, with a kick for a parting benediction. Tamb' Itam, after arising from amongst the dead, saw the Nazarene running up and down the shore amongst the corpses and the expiring fires. He uttered little cries. Suddenly he rushed to the water, and made frantic efforts to get one of the Bugis boats into the water. 'Afterwards, till he had seen me,' related Tamb' Itam, 'he stood looking at the heavy canoe and scratching his head.' 'What became of him?' I asked. Tamb' Itam, staring hard at me, made an expressive gesture with his right arm. 'Twice I struck, Tuan,' he said. 'When he beheld me approaching he cast himself violently on the ground and made a great outcry, kicking. He screeched like a frightened hen till he felt the point; then he was still, and lay staring at me while his life went out of his eyes.'

"This done, Tamb' Itam did not tarry. He understood the importance of being the first with the awful news at the fort. There were, of course, many survivors of Dain Waris's party; but in the extremity of panic some had swam across the river, others had bolted into the bush. The fact is that they did not know really who struck that blow—whether more white robbers were not coming, whether they had not already got hold of the whole land. They imagined themselves to be the victims of a vast treachery, and utterly doomed to destruction. It is said that some small parties did not come in till three days afterwards. However, a few tried to make their way back to Patusan at once, and one of the canoes that were patrolling the river that morning was in sight of the camp at the very moment of the attack. It is true that at first the men in her leaped overboard and swam to the opposite bank, but afterwards they returned to their boat and started fearfully up-stream. Of these Tamb' Itam had an hour's advance."

CHAPTER XLV.

"When Tamb' Itam, paddling madly, came into the town-reach, the women, thronging the platforms before the houses, were looking out for the return of Dain Waris's little fleet of boats. The town had a festive air; here and there men, still with spears or guns in their hands, could be seen moving or standing on the shore in groups. Chinamen's shops had been opened early; but the market-place was empty, and a sentry, still posted at the corner of the fort, made out Tamb' Itam, and shouted to those within. The gate was wide open. Tamb' Itam jumped ashore and ran in headlong. The first person he met was the girl coming down from the house.

"Tamb' Itam, disordered, panting, with trembling lips and wild eyes, stood for a time before her as if a sudden spell had been laid on him. Then he broke out very quickly: 'They have killed Dain Waris and many more.' She clapped her hands, and her first words were, 'Shut the gates.' Most of the fortmen had gone back to their houses, but Tamb' Itam hurried on the few who remained for their turn of duty within. The girl stood in the middle of the courtyard while the others ran about. 'Doramin,' she cried despairingly as Tamb' Itam passed her. Next time he went by he answered her thought rapidly, 'Yes. But we have all the powder in Patusan.' She caught him by the arm, and, pointing at the house, 'Call him out,' she whispered, trembling.

"Tamb' Itam ran up the steps. His master was sleeping. 'It is I, Tamb' Itam,' he cried at the door, 'with tidings that cannot wait.' He saw Jim turn over on the pillow and open his eyes, and he burst out at once. 'This, Tuan, is a day of evil, an accursed day.' His master raised himself on his elbow to listen—just as Dain Waris had done. And then Tamb' Itam began his tale, trying to relate the story in order, calling Dain Waris Panglima, and saying, 'The Panglima then called out to the chief of his own boatmen, "Give Tamb' Itam something to eat"'—when his master put his feet to the ground and looked at him with such a discomposed face that the words remained in his throat.

"'Speak out,' said Jim. 'Is he dead?' 'May you live long,' cried Tamb' Itam. 'It was a most cruel treachery. He ran out at the first shots and fell.' . . . His master walked to the window and with his fist struck at the shutter. The room was made light; and then in a steady voice, but speaking fast, he began to give him orders to assemble a fleet of boats for immediate pursuit, go to this man, to the other—send messengers; and as he talked he sat down on the bed, stooping to lace his boots hurriedly, and suddenly looked up. 'Why do you stand here?' he asked very red-faced. 'Waste no time.' Tamb' Itam did not move. 'Forgive me, Tuan, but . . . but,' he began to stammer. 'What?' cried his master aloud, looking terrible, leaning forward with his hands gripping the edge of the bed. 'It is not safe for thy servant to go out amongst the people,' said Tamb' Itam, after hesitating a moment.

"Then Jim understood. He had retreated from one world, for a small matter of an impulsive jump, and now the other, the work of his own hands, had fallen in ruins upon his head. It was not safe for his servant to go out amongst his own people! I believe that in that very moment he had decided to defy the disaster in the only way it occurred to him such a disaster could be defied; but all I know is that without a word he came out of his room and sat before the long table, at the head of which he was accustomed to regulate the affairs of his world, proclaiming daily the truth that surely lived in his heart. The dark powers should not rob him twice of his peace. He sat like a stone figure. Tamb' Itam, deferential, hinted at preparations for defence. The girl he loved came in and spoke to him, but he made a sign with his hand, and she was awed by the dumb appeal for silence in it. She went out on the verandah and sat on the threshold, as if to guard him with her body from dangers outside.

"What thoughts passed through his head—what memories? Who can tell. Everything was gone, and he who had been once unfaithful to his trust had lost again all men's confidence. It was then, I believe, he tried to write—to somebody—and gave it up. Loneliness was closing on him. People had trusted him with their lives—only for that; and yet they could never, as he had said, never be made to understand him. Those without did not hear him make a sound. Later, towards the evening, he came to the door and called for Tamb' Itam. 'Well,' he asked. 'There is much weeping. Much anger too,' said Tamb' Itam. Jim looked up at him. 'You know,' he murmured. 'Yes, Tuan,' said Tamb' Itam. 'Thy servant does know, and the gates are closed. We shall have to fight.' 'Fight! What for?' he asked. 'For our lives.' 'I have no life,' he said. Tamb' Itam heard a cry from the girl at the door. 'Who knows?' said Tamb' Itam. 'By audacity and cunning we may even escape. There is much fear in men's hearts too.' He went out, thinking vaguely of boats and of open sea, leaving Jim and the girl together.

"I haven't the heart to set down here such glimpses as she had given me of the hour or more she has passed in there wrestling with him for the possession of her happiness. Whether he had any hope—what he expected, what he imagined—it is impossible to say. He was inflexible, and with the growing loneliness of his obstinacy his spirit seemed to rise above the ruins of his existence. She cried 'Fight!' into his ear. She could not understand. There was nothing to fight for. He was going to prove his power in another way and conquer the fatal destiny itself. He came out into the courtyard, and behind him, with streaming hair, wild of face, breathless, she staggered out and leaned on the side of the doorway. 'Open the gates,' he ordered. Afterwards turning to those of his men who were inside, he gave them leave to depart to their homes. 'For how long, Tuan?' asked one of them timidly. 'For all life,' he said, in a sombre tone.

"A hush had fallen upon the town after the outburst of wailing and lamentation that had swept over the river, like a gust of wind from the opened abode of sorrow. But rumours flew in whispers, filling the hearts with consternation and horrible doubts. The robbers were coming back, bringing many others with them, in a great ship, and there would be no refuge in the land for any one. A sense of utter insecurity as during an earthquake pervaded the minds of men, who whispered their suspicions, looking at each other as if in the presence of some awful portent.

"The sun was sinking towards the forests when Dain Waris's body was brought into Doramin's *campong*. Four men carried it in, covered decently with a white sheet which the old mother had sent out down to the gate to meet her son on his return. They laid him at Doramin's feet, and the old man sat still for a long time, one hand on each knee, looking down. The fronds of palms swayed gently, and the foliage of fruit-trees stirred above his head. Every single man of his people was there, fully armed, when the old Nakhoda at last raised his eyes. He moved them slowly over the crowd, as if seeking for a missing face. Again his chin sank on his breast. The whispers of many men mingled with the slight rustling of the leaves.

"The Malay who had brought Tamb' Itam and the girl to Samarang was there too. 'Not so angry as many,' he said to me, but struck with a great awe and wonder at the 'suddenness of men's fate, which hangs over their heads like a cloud charged with thunder.' He told me that when Dain Waris's body was uncovered at a sign of Doramin's, he whom they often called the white lord's friend was disclosed lying unchanged with his eyelids a little open as if about to wake. Doramin leaned forward a little more, like one looking for something fallen on the ground. His eyes searched the body from its feet to its head, for the wound maybe. It was in the forehead and small; and there was no word spoken while one of the bystanders, stooping, took off the silver ring from the cold stiff hand. In silence he held it up before Doramin. A murmur of dismay and horror ran through the crowd at the sight of that familiar token. The old Nakhoda stared at it, and suddenly let out one great fierce cry, deep from the chest, a roar of pain and fury, as mighty as the bellow of a wounded bull, bringing great fear into men's hearts, by the magnitude of his anger and his sorrow that could be plainly discerned without words. There was a great stillness afterwards for a space, while the body was being borne aside by four men. They laid it down under a tree, and on the instant, with one long shriek, all the women of the household began to wail together; they mourned with shrill cries; the sun was setting, and in the intervals of screamed lamentations the high sing-song voices of two old men intoning the Koran chanted alone.

"About this time Jim, leaning on a gun-carriage, looked at the river, and turned his back on the house; and the girl, in the doorway, panting as if she had run herself to a standstill, was looking at him across the yard. Tamb' Itam stood not far from his master, waiting patiently for what might happen. All at once Jim, who seemed to be lost in quiet thought, turned to him and said, 'Time to finish this.'

"'Tuan?' said Tamb' Itam, advancing with alacrity. He did not know what his master meant, but as soon as Jim made a movement the girl started too and walked down into the open space. It seems that no one else of the people of the house was in sight. She tottered slightly, and about half-way down called out to Jim, who had apparently resumed his peaceful contemplation of the river. He turned round, setting his back against the gun. 'Will you fight?' she cried. 'There is nothing to fight for,' he said; 'nothing is lost.' Saying this he made a step towards her. 'Will you fly?' she cried again. 'There is no escape,' he said, stopping short, and she stood still also, silent, devouring him with her eyes. 'And you shall go?' she said slowly. He bent his head. 'Ah!' she exclaimed, peering at him as it were, 'you are mad or false. Do you remember the night I prayed you to leave me, and you said that you could not? That it was impossible! Impossible! Do you remember you said you would never leave me? Why? I asked you for no promise. You promised unasked—remember.' 'Enough, poor girl,' he said. 'I should not be worth having.'

"Tamb' Itam said that while they were talking she would laugh loud and senselessly like one under the visitation of God. His master put his hands to his head. He was fully dressed as for every day, but without a hat. She stopped laughing suddenly. 'For the last time,' she cried menacingly, 'will you defend yourself?' 'Nothing can touch me,' he said in a last flicker of superb egoism. Tamb' Itam saw her lean forward where she stood, open her arms, and run at him swiftly. She flung herself upon his breast and clasped him round the neck.

"'Ah! but I shall hold thee thus,' she cried. . . . 'Thou art mine!'

"She sobbed on his shoulder. The sky over Patusan was blood-red, immense, streaming like an open vein. An enormous sun nestled crimson amongst the tree-tops, and the forest below had a black and forbidding face.

"Tamb' Itam tells me that on that evening the aspect of the heavens was angry and frightful. I may well believe it, for I know that on that very day a cyclone passed within sixty miles of the coast, though there was hardly more than a languid stir of air in the place.

"Suddenly Tamb' Itam saw Jim catch her arms, trying to unclasp her hands. She hung on them with her head fallen back; her hair touched the ground. 'Come here!' his master called, and Tamb' Itam helped to ease her down. It was difficult to separate her fingers. Jim, bending over her, looked earnestly upon her face, and all at once ran to the landing-stage. Tamb' Itam followed him, but turning his head, he saw that she had struggled up to her feet. She ran after them a few steps, then fell down heavily on her knees. 'Tuan! Tuan!' called Tamb' Itam, 'look back;' but Jim was already in a canoe, standing up paddle in hand. He did not look back. Tamb' Itam had just time to scramble in after him when the canoe floated clear. The girl was then on her knees, with clasped hands, at the water-gate. She remained thus for a time in a supplicating attitude before she sprang up. 'You are false!' she screamed out after Jim. 'Forgive me,' he cried. 'Never! Never!' she called back.

"Tamb' Itam took the paddle from Jim's hands, it being unseemly that he should sit while his lord paddled. When they reached the other shore his master forbade him to come any farther; but Tamb' Itam did follow him at a distance, walking up the slope to Doramin's *campong*.

"It was beginning to grow dark. Torches twinkled here and there. Those they met seemed awestruck, and stood aside hastily to let Jim pass. The wailing of women came from above. The courtyard was full of armed Bugis with their followers, and of Patusan people.

"I do not know what this gathering really meant. Were these preparations for war, or for vengeance, or to repulse a threatened invasion? Many days elapsed before the people had ceased to look out, quaking, for the return of the white men with long beards and in rags, whose exact relation to their own white man they could never understand. Even for those simple minds poor Jim remains under a cloud.

"Doramin, alone, immense and desolate, sat in his armchair with the pair of flintlock pistols on his knees, faced by an armed throng. When Jim appeared, at somebody's exclamation, all the heads turned round together, and then the mass opened right and left, and he walked up a lane of averted glances. Whispers followed him; murmurs: 'He has worked all the evil.' 'He hath a charm.' . . . He heard them—perhaps!

"When he came up into the light of torches the wailing of the women ceased suddenly. Doramin did not lift his head, and Jim stood silent before him for a time. Then he looked to the left, and moved in that direction with measured steps. Dain Waris's mother crouched at the head of the body, and the grey dishevelled hair concealed her face. Jim came up slowly, looked at his dead friend, lifting the sheet, then dropped it without a word. Slowly he walked back.

"'He came! He came,' was running from lip to lip, making a murmur to which he moved. 'He hath taken it upon his own head,' a voice said aloud. He heard this and turned to the crowd. 'Yes. Upon my head.' A few people recoiled. Jim waited awhile before Doramin, and then said gently, 'I am come in sorrow.' He waited again. 'I am come ready and unarmed,' he repeated.

"The unwieldy old man, lowering his big forehead like an ox under a yoke, made an effort to rise, clutching at the flintlock pistols on his knees. From his throat came gurgling, choking, inhuman sounds, and his two attendants helped him from behind. People remarked that the ring which he had dropped on his lap fell and rolled against the foot of the white man, and that poor Jim glanced down at the talisman that had opened for him the door of fame, love, and success within the wall of forests fringed with white foam, within the coast that under the western sun looks like the very strong-hold of the night. Doramin, struggling to keep his feet, made with his two supporters a swaying, tottering group; his little eyes stared with an expression of mad pain, of rage, with a ferocious glitter, which the bystanders noticed, and then, while Jim stood stiffened and with bared head in the light of torches; looking him straight in the face, he clung heavily with his left arm round the neck of a bowed youth, and lifting deliberately his right, shot his son's friend through the chest.

"The crowd, which had fallen apart behind Jim as soon as Doramin had raised his hand, rushed tumultuously forward after the shot. They say that the white man sent right and left at all those faces a proud and unflinching glance. Then with his hand over his lips he fell forward, dead.

"And that's the end. He passes away under a cloud, inscrutable at heart, forgotten, unforgiven, and excessively romantic. Not in the wildest days of his boyish visions could he have seen the alluring shape of such an extraordinary success! For it may very well be that in the short moment of his last proud and unflinching glance, he had beheld the face of that opportunity which, like an Eastern bride, had come veiled to his side.

"But we can see him, an obscure conqueror of fame, tearing himself out of the arms of a jealous love at the sign, at the call of his exalted egoism. He goes away from a living woman to celebrate his pitiless wedding with a shadowy ideal of conduct. Is he satisfied—quite, now, I wonder? We ought to know. He is one of us—and have I not stood up once, like an evoked ghost, to answer for his eternal constancy? Was I so very wrong after all? Now, he is no more, there are days when the reality of his existence comes to me with an immense, with an overwhelming force; and yet upon my honour there are moments too when he passes from my eyes like a disembodied spirit astray amongst the passions of this earth, ready to surrender himself faithfully to the claim of his own world of shades.

"Who knows? He is gone, inscrutable at heart, and the poor girl is leading a sort of soundless, inert life in Stein's house. Stein has aged greatly of late. He feels it himself, and says often that he is 'preparing to leave all this; preparing to leave, . . .' while he waves his hand sadly at his butterflies."

TYPHOON

I

Captain MacWhirr, of the steamer *Nan-Shan*, had a physiognomy that, in the order of material appearances, was the exact counterpart of his mind: it presented no marked characteristics of firmness or stupidity; it had no pronounced characteristics whatever; it was simply ordinary, irresponsive, and unruffled.

The only thing his aspect might have been said to suggest, at times, was bashfulness; because he would sit, in business offices ashore, sunburnt and smiling faintly, with downcast eyes. When he raised them, they were perceived to be direct in their glance and of blue colour. His hair was fair and extremely fine, clasping from temple to temple the bald dome of his skull in a clamp as of fluffy silk. The hair of his face, on the contrary, carroty and flaming, resembled a growth of copper wire clipped short to the line of the lip; while, no matter how close he shaved, fiery metallic gleams passed, when he moved his head, over the surface of his cheeks. He was rather below the medium height, a bit round-shouldered, and so sturdy of limb that his clothes always looked a shade too tight for his arms and legs. As if unable to grasp what is due to the difference of latitudes, he wore a brown bowler hat, a complete suit of a brownish hue, and clumsy black boots. These harbour togs gave to his thick figure an air of stiff and uncouth smartness. A thin silver watch-chain looped his waistcoat, and he never left his ship for the shore without clutching in his powerful, hairy fist an elegant umbrella of the very best quality, but generally unrolled. Young Jukes, the chief mate, attending his commander to the gangway, would sometimes venture to say, with the greatest gentleness, "Allow me, sir,"—and possessing himself of the umbrella deferentially, would elevate the ferule, shake the folds, twirl a neat furl in a jiffy, and hand it back; going through the performance with a face of such portentous gravity, that Mr. Solomon Rout, the chief engineer, smoking his morning cigar over the skylight, would turn away his head in order to hide a smile. "Oh! aye! The blessed gamp.... Thank 'ee, Jukes, thank 'ee," would mutter Captain MacWhirr heartily, without looking up.

Having just enough imagination to carry him through each successive day, and no more, he was tranquilly sure of himself; and from the very same cause he was not in the least conceited. It is your imaginative superior who is touchy, overbearing, and difficult to please; but every ship Captain MacWhirr commanded was the floating abode of harmony and peace. It was, in truth, as impossible for him to take a flight of fancy as it would be for a watchmaker to put together a chronometer with nothing except a two-pound hammer and a whip-saw in the way of tools. Yet the uninteresting lives of men so entirely given to the actuality of the bare existence have their mysterious side. It was impossible in Captain MacWhirr's case, for instance, to understand what under heaven could have induced that perfectly satisfactory son of a petty grocer in Belfast to run away to sea. And yet he had done that very thing at the age of fifteen. It was enough, when you thought it over, to give you the idea of an immense, potent, and invisible hand thrust into the ant-heap of the earth, laying hold of shoulders, knocking heads together, and setting the unconscious faces of the multitude towards inconceivable goals and in undreamt-of directions.

His father never really forgave him for this undutiful stupidity. "We could have got on without him," he used to say later on, "but there's the business. And he an only son too!" His mother wept very much after his disappearance. As it had never occurred to him to leave word behind, he was mourned over for dead till, after eight months, his first letter arrived from Talcahuano. It was short, and contained the statement: "We had very fine weather on our passage out." But evidently, in the writer's mind, the only important intelligence was to the effect that his captain had, on the very day of writing, entered him regularly on the ship's articles as ordinary Seaman. "Because I can do the work," he explained. The mother again wept copiously, while the remark, "Tom's an ass," expressed the emotions of the father. He was a corpulent man, with a gift for sly chaffing, which to the end of his life he exercised in his intercourse with his son, a little pityingly, as if upon a half-witted person.

MacWhirr's visits to his home were necessarily rare, and in the course of years he despatched other letters to his parents, informing them of his successive promotions and of his movements upon the vast earth. In these missives could be found sentences like this: "The heat here is very great." Or: "On Christmas day at 4 P.M. we fell in with some icebergs." The old people ultimately became acquainted with a good many names of ships, and with the names of the skippers who commanded them—with the names of Scots and English shipowners—with the names of seas, oceans, straits, promontories—with outlandish names of lumber-ports, of rice-ports, of cotton-ports—with the names of islands—with the name of their son's young woman. She was called Lucy. It did not suggest itself to him to mention whether he thought the name pretty. And then they died.

The great day of MacWhirr's marriage came in due course, following shortly upon the great day when he got his first command.

All these events had taken place many years before the morning when, in the chart-room of the steamer Nan-Shan, he stood confronted by the fall of a barometer he had no reason to distrust. The fall—taking into account the excellence of the instrument, the time of the year, and the ship's position on the terrestrial globe—was of a nature ominously prophetic; but the red face of the man betrayed no sort of inward disturbance. Omens were as nothing to him, and he was unable to discover the message of a prophecy till the fulfilment had brought it home to his very door. "That's a fall, and no mistake," he thought. "There must be some uncommonly dirty weather knocking about."

The Nan-Shan was on her way from the southward to the treaty port of Fu-chau, with some cargo in her lower holds, and two hundred Chinese coolies returning to their village homes in the province of Fo-kien, after a few years of work in various tropical colonies. The morning was fine, the oily sea heaved without a sparkle, and there was a queer white misty patch in the sky like a halo of the sun. The fore-deck, packed with Chinamen, was full of sombre clothing, yellow faces, and pigtails, sprinkled over with a good many naked shoulders, for there was no wind, and the heat was close. The coolies lounged, talked, smoked, or stared over the rail; some, drawing water over the side, sluiced each other; a few slept on hatches, while several small parties of six sat on their heels surrounding iron trays with plates of rice and tiny teacups; and every single Celestial of them was carrying with him all he had in the world— a wooden chest with a ringing lock and brass on the corners, containing the savings of his labours: some clothes of ceremony, sticks of incense, a little opium maybe, bits of nameless rubbish of conventional value, and a small hoard of silver dollars, toiled for in coal lighters, won in gambling-houses or in petty trading, grubbed out of earth, sweated out in mines, on railway lines, in deadly jungle, under heavy burdens—amassed patiently, guarded with care, cherished fiercely.

A cross swell had set in from the direction of Formosa Channel about ten o'clock, without disturbing these passengers much, because the *Nan-Shan*, with her flat bottom, rolling chocks on bilges, and great breadth of beam, had the reputation of an exceptionally steady ship in a sea-way. Mr. Jukes, in moments of expansion on shore, would proclaim loudly that the "old girl was as good as she was pretty." It would never have occurred to Captain MacWhirr to express his favourable opinion so loud or in terms so fanciful.

She was a good ship, undoubtedly, and not old either. She had been built in Dumbarton less than three years before, to the order of a firm of merchants in Siam—Messrs. Sigg and Son. When she lay afloat, finished in every detail and ready to take up the work of her life, the builders contemplated her with pride.

"Sigg has asked us for a reliable skipper to take her out," remarked one of the partners; and the other, after reflecting for a while, said: "I think MacWhirr is ashore just at present." "Is he? Then wire him at once. He's the very man," declared the senior, without a moment's hesitation.

Next morning MacWhirr stood before them unperturbed, having travelled from London by the midnight express after a sudden but undemonstrative parting with his wife. She was the daughter of a superior couple who had seen better days.

"We had better be going together over the ship, Captain," said the senior partner; and the three men started to view the perfections of the *Nan-Shan* from stem to stern, and from her keelson to the trucks of her two stumpy pole-masts.

Captain MacWhirr had begun by taking off his coat, which he hung on the end of a steam windlass embodying all the latest improvements.

"My uncle wrote of you favourably by yesterday's mail to our good friends— Messrs. Sigg, you know—and doubtless they'll continue you out there in command," said the junior partner. "You'll be able to boast of being in charge of the handiest boat of her size on the coast of China, Captain," he added.

"Have you? Thank 'ee," mumbled vaguely MacWhirr, to whom the view of a distant eventuality could appeal no more than the beauty of a wide landscape to a purblind tourist; and his eyes happening at the moment to be at rest upon the lock of the cabin door, he walked up to it, full of purpose, and began to rattle the handle vigorously, while he observed, in his low, earnest voice, "You can't trust the workmen nowadays. A brand-new lock, and it won't act at all. Stuck fast. See? See?"

As soon as they found themselves alone in their office across the yard: "You praised that fellow up to Sigg. What is it you see in him?" asked the nephew, with faint contempt.

"I admit he has nothing of your fancy skipper about him, if that's what you mean," said the elder man curtly. "Is the foreman of the joiners on the *Nan-Shan* outside?.... Come in, Bates. How is it that you let Tait's people put us off with a defective lock on the cabin door? The Captain could see directly he set eye on it. Have it replaced at once. The little straws, Bates... the little straws...."

The lock was replaced accordingly, and a few days afterwards the *Nan-Shan* steamed out to the East, without MacWhirr having offered any further remark as to her fittings, or having been heard to utter a single word hinting at pride in his ship, gratitude for his appointment, or satisfaction at his prospects.

With a temperament neither loquacious nor taciturn, he found very little occasion to talk. There were matters of duty, of course—directions, orders, and so on; but the past being to his mind done with, and the future not there yet, the more general actualities of the day required no comment—because facts can speak for themselves with overwhelming precision.

Old Mr. Sigg liked a man of few words, and one that "you could be sure would not try to improve upon his instructions." MacWhirr satisfying these requirements, was continued in command of the *Nan-Shan*, and applied himself to the careful navigation of his ship in the China seas. She had come out on a British register, but after some time Messrs. Sigg judged it expedient to transfer her to the Siamese flag.

At the news of the contemplated transfer Jukes grew restless, as if under a sense of personal affront. He went about grumbling to himself, and uttering short scornful laughs. "Fancy having a ridiculous Noah's Ark elephant in the ensign of one's ship," he said once at the engine-room door. "Dash me if I can stand it: I'll throw up the billet. Don't it make *you* sick, Mr. Rout?" The chief engineer only cleared his throat with the air of a man who knows the value of a good billet.

The first morning the new flag floated over the stern of the *Nan-Shan* Jukes stood looking at it bitterly from the bridge. He struggled with his feelings for a while, and then remarked, "Queer flag for a man to sail under, sir."

"What's the matter with the flag?" inquired Captain MacWhirr. "Seems all right to me." And he walked across to the end of the bridge to have a good look.

"Well, it looks queer to me," burst out Jukes, greatly exasperated, and flung off the bridge.

Captain MacWhirr was amazed at these manners. After a while he stepped quietly into the chart-room, and opened his International Signal Code-book at the plate where the flags of all the nations are correctly figured in gaudy rows. He ran his finger over them, and when he came to Siam he contemplated with great attention the red field and the white elephant. Nothing could be more simple; but to make sure he brought the book out on the bridge for the purpose of comparing the coloured drawing with the real thing at the flag-staff astern. When next Jukes, who was carrying on the duty that day with a sort of suppressed fierceness, happened on the bridge, his commander observed:

"There's nothing amiss with that flag."

"Isn't there?" mumbled Jukes, falling on his knees before a deck-locker and jerking therefrom viciously a spare lead-line.

"No. I looked up the book. Length twice the breadth and the elephant exactly in the middle. I thought the people ashore would know how to make the local flag. Stands to reason. You were wrong, Jukes. . . ."

"Well, sir," began Jukes, getting up excitedly, "all I can say—" He fumbled for the end of the coil of line with trembling hands.

"That's all right." Captain MacWhirr soothed him, sitting heavily on a little canvas folding-stool he greatly affected. "All you have to do is to take care they don't hoist the elephant upside-down before they get quite used to it."

Jukes flung the new lead-line over on the fore-deck with a loud "Here you are, bo'ss'en—don't forget to wet it thoroughly," and turned with immense resolution towards his commander; but Captain MacWhirr spread his elbows on the bridge-rail comfortably.

"Because it would be, I suppose, understood as a signal of distress," he went on. "What do you think? That elephant there, I take it, stands for something in the nature of the Union Jack in the flag. . . ."

"Does it!" yelled Jukes, so that every head on the Nan-Shan's decks looked towards the bridge. Then he sighed, and with sudden resignation: "It would certainly be a dam' distressful sight," he said meekly.

Later in the day he accosted the chief engineer with a confidential "Here, let me tell you the old man's latest."

Mr. Solomon Rout (frequently alluded to as Long Sol, Old Sol, or Father Rout), from finding himself almost invariably the tallest man on board every ship he joined, had acquired the habit of a stooping, leisurely condescension. His hair was scant and sandy, his flat cheeks were pale, his bony wrists and long scholarly hands were pale too, as though he had lived all his life in the shade.

He smiled from on high at Jukes, and went on smoking and glancing about quietly, in the manner of a kind uncle lending an ear to the tale of an excited schoolboy. Then, greatly amused but impassive, he asked:

"And did you throw up the billet?"

"No," cried Jukes, raising a weary, discouraged voice above the harsh buzz of the Nan-Shan's friction winches. All of them were hard at work, snatching slings of cargo, high up, to the end of long derricks, only, as it seemed, to let them rip down recklessly by the run. The cargo chains groaned in the gins, clinked on coamings, rattled over the side; and the whole ship quivered, with her long grey flanks smoking in wreaths of steam. "No," cried Jukes, "I didn't. What's the good? I might just as well fling my resignation at this bulkhead. I don't believe you can make a man like that understand anything. He simply knocks me over."

At that moment Captain MacWhirr, back from the shore, crossed the deck, umbrella in hand, escorted by a mournful, self-possessed Chinaman, walking behind in paper-soled silk shoes, and who also carried an umbrella.

The master of the Nan-Shan, speaking just audibly and gazing at his boots as his manner was, remarked that it would be necessary to call at Fu-chau this trip, and desired Mr. Rout to have steam up to-morrow afternoon at one o'clock sharp. He pushed back his hat to wipe his forehead, observing at the same time that he hated going ashore anyhow; while overtopping him Mr. Rout, without deigning a word, smoked austerely, nursing his right elbow in the palm of his left hand. Then Jukes was directed in the same subdued voice to keep the forward 'tween-deck clear of cargo. Two hundred coolies were going to be put down there. The Bun Hin Company were sending that lot home. Twenty-five bags of rice would be coming off in a sampan directly, for stores. All seven-years'-men they were, said Captain MacWhirr, with a camphor-wood chest to every man. The carpenter should be set to work nailing three-inch battens along the deck below, fore and aft, to keep these boxes from shifting in a sea-way. Jukes had better look to it at once. "D'ye hear, Jukes?" This Chinaman here was coming with the ship as far as Fu-chau,—a sort of interpreter he would be. Bun Hin's clerk he was, and wanted to have a look at the space. Jukes had better take him forward. "D'ye hear, Jukes?"

Jukes took care to punctuate these instructions in proper places with the obligatory "Yes, sir," ejaculated without enthusiasm. His brusque "Come along John; make look see" set the Chinaman in motion at his heels.

"Wanchee look see, all same look see can do," said Jukes, who having no talent for foreign languages mangled the very pidgin-English cruelly. He pointed at the open hatch. "Catchee number one piecie place to sleep in. Eh?"

He was gruff, as became his racial superiority, but not unfriendly. The Chinaman, gazing sad and speechless into the darkness of the hatchway, seemed to stand at the head of a yawning grave.

"No catchee rain down there—savee?" pointed out Jukes. "Suppose all 'ee same fine weather, one piecie coolie-man come topside," he pursued, warming up imaginatively. "Make so—Phooooo!" He expanded his chest and blew out his cheeks. "Savee, John? Breathe—fresh air. Good. Eh? Washee him piecie pants, chow-chow top-side—see, John?"

With his mouth and hands he made exuberant motions of eating rice and washing clothes; and the Chinaman, who concealed his distrust of this panto-mime under a collected demeanour tinged by a gentle and refined melancholy, glanced out of his almond eyes from Jukes to the hatch and back again. "Velly good," he murmured, in a disconsolate undertone, and hastened smoothly along the decks, dodging obstacles in his course. He disappeared, ducking low under a sling of ten dirty gunny-bags full of some costly merchandise and exhaling a repulsive smell.

Captain MacWhirr meantime had gone on the bridge, and into the chart-room, where a letter, commenced two days before, awaited termination. These long letters began with the words, "My darling wife," and the steward, between the scrubbing of the floors and the dusting of chronometer-boxes, snatched at every opportunity to read them. They interested him much more than they possibly could the woman for whose eye they were intended; and this for the reason that they related in minute detail each successive trip of the *Nan-Shan*.

Her master, faithful to facts, which alone his consciousness reflected, would set them down with painstaking care upon many pages. The house in a northern suburb to which these pages were addressed had a bit of garden before the bow-windows, a deep porch of good appearance, coloured glass with imitation lead frame in the front door. He paid five-and-forty pounds a year for it, and did not think the rent too high, because Mrs. MacWhirr (a pretentious person with a scraggy neck and a disdainful manner) was admittedly ladylike, and in the neighbourhood considered as "quite superior." The only secret of her life was her abject terror of the time when her husband would come home to stay for good. Under the same roof there dwelt also a daughter called Lydia and a son, Tom. These two were but slightly acquainted with their father. Mainly, they knew him as a rare but privileged visitor, who of an evening smoked his pipe in the dining-room and slept in the house. The lanky girl, upon the whole, was rather ashamed of him; the boy was frankly and utterly indifferent in a straight-forward, delightful, unaffected way manly boys have.

And Captain MacWhirr wrote home from the coast of China twelve times every year, desiring queerly to be "remembered to the children," and subscribing himself "your loving husband," as calmly as if the words so long used by so many men were, apart from their shape, worn-out things, and of a faded mean-ing.

The China seas north and south are narrow seas. They are seas full of every-day, eloquent facts, such as islands, sand-banks, reefs, swift and changeable currents—tangled facts that nevertheless speak to a seaman in clear and definite language. Their speech appealed to Captain MacWhirr's sense of realities so forcibly that he had given up his state-room below and practically lived all his days on the bridge of his ship, often having his meals sent up, and sleeping at night in the chart-room. And he indited there his home letters. Each of them, without exception, contained the phrase, "The weather has been very fine this trip," or some other form of a statement to that effect. And this statement, too, in its wonderful persistence, was of the same perfect accuracy as all the others they contained.

Mr. Rout likewise wrote letters; only no one on board knew how chatty he could be pen in hand, because the chief engineer had enough imagination to keep his desk locked. His wife relished his style greatly. They were a childless couple, and Mrs. Rout, a big, high-bosomed, jolly woman of forty, shared with Mr. Rout's toothless and venerable mother a little cottage near Teddington. She would run over her correspondence, at breakfast, with lively eyes, and scream out interesting passages in a joyous voice at the deaf old lady, prefacing each extract by the warning shout, "Solomon says!" She had the trick of firing off Solomon's utterances also upon strangers, astonishing them easily by the un-familiar text and the unexpectedly jocular vein of these quotations. On the day the new curate called for the first time at the cottage, she found occasion to remark, "As Solomon says: 'the engineers that go down to the sea in ships behold the wonders of sailor nature';" when a change in the visitor's countenance made her stop and stare.

"Solomon . . . Oh! . . . Mrs. Rout," stuttered the young man, very red in the face, "I must say . . . I don't . . ."

"He's my husband," she announced in a great shout, throwing herself back in the chair. Perceiving the joke, she laughed immoderately with a handkerchief to her eyes, while he sat wearing a forced smile, and, from his inexperience of jolly women, fully persuaded that she must be deplorably insane. They were excellent friends afterwards; for, absolving her from irreverent intention, he came to think she was a very worthy person indeed; and he learned in time to receive without flinching other scraps of Solomon's wisdom.

"For my part," Solomon was reported by his wife to have said once, "give me the dullest ass for a skipper before a rogue. There is a way to take a fool; but a rogue is smart and slippery." This was an airy generalisation drawn from the particular case of Captain MacWhirr's honesty, which, in itself, had the heavy obviousness of a lump of clay. On the other hand, Mr. Jukes, unable to generalise, unmarried, and unengaged, was in the habit of opening his heart after another fashion to an old chum and former shipmate, actually serving as second officer on board an Atlantic liner.

First of all he would insist upon the advantages of the Eastern trade, hinting at its superiority to the Western ocean service. He extolled the sky, the seas, the ships, and the easy life of the Far East. The *Nan-Shan*, he affirmed, was second to none as a sea-boat.

"We have no brass-bound uniforms, but then we are like brothers here," he wrote. "We all mess together and live like fighting-cocks. . . . All the chaps of the black-squad are as decent as they make that kind, and old Sol, the Chief, is a dry stick. We are good friends. As to our old man, you could not find a quieter skipper. Sometimes you would think he hadn't sense enough to see anything wrong. And yet it isn't that. Can't be. He has been in command for a good few years now. He doesn't do anything actually foolish, and gets his ship along all right without worrying anybody. I believe he hasn't brains enough to enjoy kicking up a row. I don't take advantage of him. I would scorn it. Outside the routine of duty he doesn't seem to understand more than half of what you tell him. We get a laugh out of this at times; but it is dull, too, to be with a man like this—in the long-run. Old Sol says he hasn't much conversation. Conversation! O Lord! He never talks. The other day I had been yarning under the bridge with one of the engineers, and he must have heard us. When I came up to take my watch, he steps out of the chart-room and has a good look all round, peeps over at the sidelights, glances at the compass, squints upwards at the stars. That's his regular performance. By-and-by he says: 'Was that you talking just now in the port alleyway?' 'Yes, sir.' 'With the third engineer?' 'Yes, sir.' He walks off to starboard, and sits under the dodger on a little campstool of his, and for half an hour perhaps he makes no sound, except that I heard him sneeze once. Then after a while I hear him getting up over there, and he strolls across to port, where I was. 'I can't understand what you can find to talk about,' says he. 'Two solid hours. I am not blaming you. I see people ashore at it all daylong, and then in the evening they sit down and keep at it over the drinks. Must be saying the same things over and over again. I can't understand.'

"Did you ever hear anything like that? And he was so patient about it. It made me quite sorry for him. But he is exasperating too sometimes. Of course one would not do anything to vex him even if it were worth while. But it isn't. He's so jolly innocent that if you were to put your thumb to your nose and wave your fingers at him he would only wonder gravely to himself what got into you. He told me once quite simply that he found it very difficult to make out what made people always act so queerly. He's too dense to trouble about, and that's the truth."

Thus wrote Mr. Jukes to his chum in the Western ocean trade, out of the fulness of his heart and the liveliness of his fancy.

He had expressed his honest opinion. It was not worth while trying to impress a man of that sort. If the world had been full of such men, life would have probably appeared to Jukes an unentertaining and unprofitable business. He was not alone in his opinion. The sea itself, as if sharing Mr. Jukes' good-natured forbearance, had never put itself out to startle the silent man, who seldom looked up, and wandered innocently over the waters with the only visible purpose of getting food, raiment, and house-room for three people ashore. Dirty weather he had known, of course. He had been made wet, uncomfortable, tired in the usual way, felt at the time and presently forgotten. So that upon the whole he had been justified in reporting fine weather at home. But he had never been given a glimpse of immeasurable strength and of immoderate wrath, the wrath that passes exhausted but never appeased—the wrath and fury of the passionate sea. He knew it existed, as we know that crime and abominations exist; he had heard of it as a peaceable citizen in a town hears of battles, famines, and floods, and yet knows nothing of what these things mean—though, indeed, he may have been mixed up in a street row, have gone without his dinner once, or been soaked to the skin in a shower. Captain MacWhirr had sailed over the surface of the oceans as some men go skimming over the years of existence to sink gently into a placid grave, ignorant of life to the last, without ever having been made to see all it may contain of perfidy, of violence, and of terror. There are on sea and land such men thus fortunate—or thus disdained by destiny or by the sea.

II

Observing the steady fall of the barometer, Captain MacWhirr thought, "There's some dirty weather knocking about." This is precisely what he thought. He had had an experience of moderately dirty weather—the term dirty as applied to the weather implying only moderate discomfort to the seaman. Had he been informed by an indisputable authority that the end of the world was to be finally accomplished by a catastrophic disturbance of the atmosphere, he would have assimilated the information under the simple idea of dirty weather, and no other, because he had no experience of cataclysms, and belief does not necessarily imply comprehension. The wisdom of his country had pronounced by means of an Act of Parliament that before he could be considered as fit to take charge of a ship he should be able to answer certain simple questions on the subject of circular storms such as hurricanes, cyclones, typhoons; and apparently he had answered them, since he was now in command of the Nan-Shan in the China seas during the season of typhoons. But if he had answered he remembered nothing of it. He was, however, conscious of being made uncomfortable by the clammy heat. He came out on the bridge, and found no relief to this oppression. The air seemed thick. He gasped like a fish, and began to believe himself greatly out of sorts.

The Nan-Shan was ploughing a vanishing furrow upon the circle of the sea that had the surface and the shimmer of an undulating piece of grey silk. The sun, pale and without rays, poured down leaden heat in a strangely indecisive light, and the Chinamen were lying prostrate about the decks. Their bloodless, pinched, yellow faces were like the faces of bilious invalids. Captain MacWhirr noticed two of them especially, stretched out on their backs below the bridge. As soon as they had closed their eyes they seemed dead. Three others, however, were quarrelling barbarously away forward; and one big fellow, half naked, with herculean shoulders, was hanging limply over a winch; another, sitting on the deck, his knees up and his head drooping sideways in a girlish attitude, was plaiting his pigtail with infinite languor depicted in his whole person and in the very movement of his fingers. The smoke struggled with difficulty out of the funnel, and instead of streaming away spread itself out like an infernal sort of cloud, smelling of sulphur and raining soot all over the decks.

"What the devil are you doing there, Mr. Jukes?" asked Captain MacWhirr.

This unusual form of address, though mumbled rather than spoken, caused the body of Mr. Jukes to start as though it had been prodded under the fifth rib. He had had a low bench brought on the bridge, and sitting on it, with a length of rope curled about his feet and a piece of canvas stretched over his knees, was pushing a sail-needle vigorously. He looked up, and his surprise gave to his eyes an expression of innocence and candour.

"I am only roping some of that new set of bags we made last trip for whipping up coals," he remonstrated gently. "We shall want them for the next coaling, sir."

"What became of the others?"

"Why, worn out of course, sir."

Captain MacWhirr, after glaring down irresolutely at his chief mate, disclosed the gloomy and cynical conviction that more than half of them had been lost overboard, "if only the truth was known," and retired to the other end of the bridge. Jukes, exasperated by this unprovoked attack, broke the needle at the second stitch, and dropping his work got up and cursed the heat in a violent undertone.

The propeller thumped, the three Chinamen forward had given up squabbling very suddenly, and the one who had been plaiting his tail clasped his legs and stared dejectedly over his knees. The lurid sunshine cast faint and sickly shadows. The swell ran higher and swifter every moment, and the ship lurched heavily in the smooth, deep hollows of the sea.

"I wonder where that beastly swell comes from," said Jukes aloud, recovering himself after a stagger.

"North-east," grunted the literal MacWhirr, from his side of the bridge. "There's some dirty weather knocking about. Go and look at the glass."

When Jukes came out of the chart-room, the cast of his countenance had changed to thoughtfulness and concern. He caught hold of the bridge-rail and stared ahead.

The temperature in the engine-room had gone up to a hundred and seventeen degrees. Irritated voices were ascending through the skylight and through the fiddle of the stokehold in a harsh and resonant uproar, mingled with angry clangs and scrapes of metal, as if men with limbs of iron and throats of bronze had been quarrelling down there. The second engineer was falling foul of the stokers for letting the steam go down. He was a man with arms like a blacksmith, and generally feared; but that afternoon the stokers were answering him back recklessly, and slammed the furnace doors with the fury of despair. Then the noise ceased suddenly, and the second engineer appeared, emerging out of the stokehold streaked with grime and soaking wet like a chimney-sweep coming out of a well. As soon as his head was clear of the fiddle he began to scold Jukes for not trimming properly the stokehold ventilators; and in answer Jukes made with his hands deprecatory soothing signs meaning: No wind—can't be helped— you can see for yourself. But the other wouldn't hear reason. His teeth flashed angrily in his dirty face. He didn't mind, he said, the trouble of punching their blanked heads down there, blank his soul, but did the condemned sailors think you could keep steam up in the God-forsaken boilers simply by knocking the blanked stokers about? No, by George! You had to get some draught too—may he be everlastingly blanked for a swab-headed deck-hand if you didn't! And the chief, too, rampaging before the steam-gauge and carrying on like a lunatic up and down the engine-room ever since noon. What did Jukes think he was stuck up there for, if he couldn't get one of his decayed, good-for-nothing deck-cripples to turn the ventilators to the wind?

The relations of the "engine-room" and the "deck" of the *Nan-Shan* were, as is known, of a brotherly nature; therefore Jukes leaned over and begged the other in a restrained tone not to make a disgusting ass of himself; the skipper was on the other side of the bridge. But the second declared mutinously that he didn't care a rap who was on the other side of the bridge, and Jukes, passing in a flash from lofty disapproval into a state of exaltation, invited him in unflattering terms to come up and twist the beastly things to please himself, and catch such wind as a donkey of his sort could find. The second rushed up to the fray. He flung himself at the port ventilator as though he meant to tear it out bodily and toss it overboard. All he did was to move the cowl round a few inches, with an enormous expenditure of force, and seemed spent in the effort. He leaned against the back of the wheel-house, and Jukes walked up to him.

"Oh, Heavens!" ejaculated the engineer in a feeble voice. He lifted his eyes to the sky, and then let his glassy stare descend to meet the horizon that, tilting up to an angle of forty degrees, seemed to hang on a slant for a while and settled down slowly. "Heavens! Phew! What's up, anyhow?"

Jukes, straddling his long legs like a pair of compasses, put on an air of superiority. "We're going to catch it this time," he said. "The barometer is tumbling down like anything, Harry. And you trying to kick up that silly row..."

The word "barometer" seemed to revive the second engineer's mad animosity. Collecting afresh all his energies, he directed Jukes in a low and brutal tone to shove the unmentionable instrument down his gory throat. Who cared for his crimson barometer? It was the steam—the steam—that was going down; and what between the firemen going faint and the chief going silly, it was worse than a dog's life for him; he didn't care a tinker's curse how soon the whole show was blown out of the water. He seemed on the point of having a cry, but after regaining his breath he muttered darkly, "I'll faint them," and dashed off. He stopped upon the fiddle long enough to shake his fist at the unnatural daylight, and dropped into the dark hole with a whoop.

When Jukes turned, his eyes fell upon the rounded back and the big red ears of Captain MacWhirr, who had come across. He did not look at his chief officer, but said at once, "That's a very violent man, that second engineer."

"Jolly good second, anyhow," grunted Jukes. "They can't keep up steam," he added rapidly, and made a grab at the rail against the coming lurch.

Captain MacWhirr, unprepared, took a run and brought himself up with a jerk by an awning stanchion.

"A profane man," he said obstinately. "If this goes on, I'll have to get rid of him the first chance."

"It's the heat," said Jukes. "The weather's awful. It would make a saint swear. Even up here I feel exactly as if I had my head tied up in a woollen blanket."

Captain MacWhirr looked up. "D'ye mean to say, Mr. Jukes, you ever had your head tied up in a blanket? What was that for?"

"It's a manner of speaking, sir," said Jukes stolidly.

"Some of you fellows do go on! What's that about saints swearing? I wish you wouldn't talk so wild. What sort of saint would that be that would swear? No more saint than yourself, I expect. And what's a blanket got to do with it— or the weather either... The heat does not make me swear—does it? It's filthy bad temper. That's what it is. And what's the good of your talking like this?"

Thus Captain MacWhirr expostulated against the use of images in speech, and at the end electrified Jukes by a contemptous snort, followed by words of passion and resentment: "Damme! I'll fire him out of the ship if he don't look out."

And Jukes, incorrigible, thought: "Goodness me! Somebody's put a new inside to my old man. Here's temper, if you like. Of course it's the weather; what else? It would make an angel quarrelsome—let alone a saint."

All the Chinamen on deck appeared at their last gasp.

At its setting the sun had a diminished diameter and an expiring brown, rayless glow, as if millions of centuries elapsing since the morning had brought it near its end. A dense bank of cloud became visible to the northward; it had a sinister dark olive tint, and lay low and motionless upon the sea, resembling a solid obstacle in the path of the ship. She went floundering towards it like an exhausted creature driven to its death. The coppery twilight retired slowly, and the darkness brought out overhead a swarm of unsteady, big stars, that, as if blown upon, flickered exceedingly and seemed to hang very near the earth. At eight o'clock Jukes went into the chart-room to write up the ship's log.

He copied neatly out of the rough-book the number of miles, the course of the ship, and in the column for "wind" scrawled the word "calm" from top to bottom of the eight hours since noon. He was exasperated by the continuous, monotonous rolling of the ship. The heavy inkstand would slide away in a manner that suggested perverse intelligence in dodging the pen. Having written in the large space under the head of "Remarks" "Heat very oppressive," he stuck the end of the penholder in his teeth, pipe fashion, and mopped his face carefully.

"Ship rolling heavily in a high cross swell," he began again, and commented to himself, "Heavily is no word for it." Then he wrote: "Sunset threatening, with a low bank of clouds to N. and E. Sky clear over-head."

Sprawling over the table with arrested pen, he glanced out of the door, and in that frame of his vision he saw all the stars flying upwards between the teak-wood jambs on a black sky. The whole lot took flight together and disappeared, leaving only a blackness flecked with white flashes, for the sea was as black as the sky and speckled with foam afar. The stars that had flown to the roll came back on the return swing of the ship, rushing downwards in their glittering multitude, not of fiery points, but enlarged to tiny discs brilliant with a clear wet sheen.

Jukes watched the flying big stars for a moment, and then wrote: "8 P.M. Swell increasing. Ship labouring and taking water on her decks. Battened down the coolies for the night. Barometer still falling." He paused, and thought to himself, "Perhaps nothing whatever'll come of it." And then he closed resolutely his entries: "Every appearance of a typhoon coming on."

On going out he had to stand aside, and Captain MacWhirr strode over the doorstep without saying a word or making a sign.

"Shut the door, Mr. Jukes, will you?" he cried from within.

Jukes turned back to do so, muttering ironically: "Afraid to catch cold, I suppose." It was his watch below, but he yearned for communion with his kind; and he remarked cheerily to the second mate: "Doesn't look so bad, after all— does it?"

The second mate was marching to and fro on the bridge, tripping down with small steps one moment, and the next climbing with difficulty the shifting slope of the deck. At the sound of Juke's voice he stood still, facing forward, but made no reply.

"Hallo! That's a heavy one," said Jukes, swaying to meet the long roll till his lowered hand touched the planks. This time the second mate made in his throat a noise of an unfriendly nature.

He was an oldish, shabby little fellow, with bad teeth and no hair on his face. He had been shipped in a hurry in Shanghai, that trip when the second officer brought from home had delayed the ship three hours in port by contriving (in some manner Captain MacWhirr could never understand) to fall overboard into an empty coal-lighter lying alongside, and had to be sent ashore to the hospital with concussion of the brain and a broken limb or two.

Jukes was not discouraged by the unsympathetic sound. "The Chinamen must be having a lovely time of it down there," he said. "It's lucky for them the old girl has the easiest roll of any ship I've ever been in. There now! This one wasn't so bad."

"You wait," snarled the second mate.

With his sharp nose, red at the tip, and his thin pinched lips, he always looked as though he were raging inwardly; and he was concise in his speech to the point of rudeness. All his time off duty he spent in his cabin with the door shut, keeping so still in there that he was supposed to fall asleep as soon as he had disappeared; but the man who came in to wake him for his watch on deck would invariably find him with his eyes wide open, flat on his back in the bunk, and glaring irritably from a soiled pillow. He never wrote any letters, did not seem to hope for news from anywhere; and though he had been heard once to mention West Hartlepool, it was with extreme bitterness, and only in connection with the extortionate charges of a boarding-house. He was one of those men who are picked up at need in the ports of the world. They are competent enough, appear hopelessly hard up, show no evidence of any sort of vice, and carry about them all the signs of manifest failure. They come aboard on an emergency, care for no ship afloat, live in their own atmosphere of casual connection amongst their shipmates who know nothing of them, and make up their minds to leave at inconvenient times. They clear out with no words of leave-taking in some God-forsaken port other men would fear to be stranded in, and go ashore in company of a shabby sea-chest, corded like a treasure-box, and with an air of shaking the ship's dust off their feet.

"You wait," he repeated, balanced in great swings with his back to Jukes, motionless and implacable.

"Do you mean to say we are going to catch it hot?" asked Jukes with boyish interest.

"Say? . . . I say nothing. You don't catch me," snapped the little second mate, with a mixture of pride, scorn, and cunning, as if Jukes' question had been a trap cleverly detected. "Oh no! None of you here shall make a fool of me if I know it," he mumbled to himself.

Jukes reflected rapidly that this second mate was a mean little beast, and in his heart he wished poor Jack Allen had never smashed himself up in the coal-lighter. The far-off blackness ahead of the ship was like another night seen through the starry night of the earth—the starless night of the immensities beyond the created universe, revealed in its appalling stillness through a low fissure in the glittering sphere of which the earth is the kernel.

"Whatever there might be about," said Jukes, "we are steaming straight into it."

"*You've* said it," caught up the second mate, always with his back to Jukes. "You've said it, mind—not I."

"Oh, go to Jericho!" said Jukes frankly; and the other emitted a triumphant little chuckle.

"You've said it," he repeated.

"And what of that?"

"I've known some real good men get into trouble with their skippers for saying a dam' sight less," answered the second mate feverishly. "Oh no! You don't catch me."

"You seem deucedly anxious not to give yourself away," said Jukes, completely soured by such absurdity. "I wouldn't be afraid to say what I think."

"Aye, to me! That's no great trick. I am nobody, and well I know it."

The ship, after a pause of comparative steadiness, started upon a series of rolls, one worse than the other, and for a time Jukes, preserving his equilibrium, was too busy to open his mouth. As soon as the violent swinging had quieted down somewhat, he said: "This is a bit too much of a good thing. Whether anything is coming or not I think she ought to be put head on to that swell. The old man is just gone in to lie down. Hang me if I don't speak to him."

But when he opened the door of the chart-room he saw his captain reading a book. Captain MacWhirr was not lying down: he was standing up with one hand grasping the edge of the bookshelf and the other holding open before his face a thick volume. The lamp wriggled in the gimbals, the loosened books toppled from side to side on the shelf, the long barometer swung in jerky circles, the table altered its slant every moment. In the midst of all this stir and movement Captain MacWhirr, holding on, showed his eyes above the upper edge, and asked, "What's the matter?"

"Swell getting worse, sir."

"Noticed that in here," muttered Captain MacWhirr. "Anything wrong?"

Jukes, inwardly disconcerted by the seriousness of the eyes looking at him over the top of the book, produced an embarrassed grin.

"Rolling like old boots," he said sheepishly.

"Aye! Very heavy—very heavy. What do you want?"

At this Jukes lost his footing and began to flounder.

"I was thinking of our passengers," he said, in the manner of a man clutching at a straw.

"Passengers?" wondered the Captain gravely. "What passengers?"

"Why, the Chinamen, sir," explained Jukes, very sick of this conversation.

"The Chinamen! Why don't you speak plainly? Couldn't tell what you meant. Never heard a lot of coolies spoken of as passengers before. Passengers, indeed! What's come to you?"

Captain MacWhirr, closing the book on his fore-finger, lowered his arm and looked completely mystified. "Why are you thinking of the Chinamen, Mr. Jukes?" he inquired.

Jukes took a plunge, like a man driven to it. "She's rolling her decks full of water, sir. Thought you might put her head on perhaps—for a while. Till this goes down a bit—very soon, I dare say. Head to the eastward. I never knew a ship roll like this."

He held on in the doorway, and Captain MacWhirr, feeling his grip on the shelf inadequate, made up his mind to let go in a hurry, and fell heavily on the couch.

"Head to the eastward?" he said, struggling to sit up. "That's more than four points off her course."

"Yes, sir. Fifty degrees... Would just bring her head far enough round to meet this..."

Captain MacWhirr was now sitting up. He had not dropped the book, and he had not lost his place.

"To the eastward?" he repeated, with dawning astonishment. "To the ... Where do you think we are bound to? You want me to haul a full-powered steamship four points off her course to make the Chinamen comfortable! Now, I've heard more than enough of mad things done in the world—but this... If I didn't know you, Jukes, I would think you were in liquor. Steer four points off... And what afterwards? Steer four points over the other way, I suppose, to make the course good. What put it into your head that I would start to tack a steamer as if she were a sailing ship?"

"Jolly good thing she isn't," threw in Jukes, with bitter readiness. "She would have rolled every blessed stick out of her this afternoon."

"Aye! And you just would have had to stand and see them go," said Captain MacWhirr, showing a certain animation. "It's a dead calm, isn't it?"

"It is, sir. But there's something out of the common coming, for sure."

"Maybe. I suppose you have a notion I should be getting out of the way of that dirt," said Captain MacWhirr, speaking with the utmost simplicity of manner and tone, and fixing the oilcloth on the floor with a heavy stare. Thus he noticed neither Jukes' discomfiture nor the mixture of vexation and astonished respect on his face.

"Now, here's this book," he continued with deliberation, slapping his thigh with the closed volume. "I've been reading the chapter on the storms there."

This was true. He had been reading the chapter on the storms. When he had entered the chart-room, it was with no intention of taking the book down. Some influence in the air—the same influence, probably, that caused the steward to bring without orders the Captain's sea-boots and oilskin coat up to the chart-room—had as it were guided his hand to the shelf; and without taking the time to sit down he had waded with a conscious effort into the terminology of the subject. He lost himself amongst advancing semi-circles, left- and right-hand quadrants, the curves of the tracks, the probable bearing of the centre, the shifts of wind and the readings of barometer. He tried to bring all these things into a definite relation to himself, and ended by becoming contemptuously angry with such a lot of words and with so much advice, all head-work and supposition, without a glimmer of certitude.

"It's the damnedest thing, Jukes," he said. "If a fellow was to believe all that's in there, he would be running most of his time all over the sea trying to get behind the weather."

Again he slapped his leg with the book; and Jukes opened his mouth, but said nothing.

"Running to get behind the weather! Do you understand that, Mr. Jukes? It's the maddest thing!" ejaculated Captain MacWhirr, with pauses, gazing at the floor profoundly. "You would think an old woman had been writing this. It passes me. If that thing means anything useful, then it means that I should at once alter the course away, away to the devil somewhere, and come booming down on Fu-chau from the northward at the tail of this dirty weather that's supposed to be knocking about in our way. From the north! Do you understand, Mr. Jukes? Three hundred extra miles to the distance, and a pretty coal bill to show. I couldn't bring myself to do that if every word in there was gospel truth, Mr. Jukes. Don't you expect me . . ."

And Jukes, silent, marvelled at this display of feeling and loquacity.

"But the truth is that you don't know if the fellow is right anyhow. How can you tell what a gale is made of till you get it? He isn't aboard here, is he? Very well. Here he says that the centre of them things bears eight points off the wind; but we haven't got any wind, for all the barometer falling. Where's his centre now?"

"We will get the wind presently," mumbled Jukes.

"Let it come, then," said Captain MacWhirr, with dignified indignation. "It's only to let you see, Mr. Jukes, that you don't find everything in books. All these rules for dodging breezes and circumventing the winds of heaven, Mr. Jukes, seem to me the maddest thing, when you come to look at it sensibly."

He raised his eyes, saw Jukes gazing at him dubiously, and tried to illustrate his meaning.

"About as queer as your extraordinary notion of dodging the ship head to sea, for I don't know how long, to make the Chinamen comfortable; whereas all we've got to do is to take them to Fu-chau, being timed to get there before noon on Friday. If the weather delays me—very well. There's your log-book to talk straight about the weather. But suppose I went swinging off my course and came in two days late, and they asked me: 'Where have you been all that time, Captain?' What could I say to that? 'Went around to dodge the bad weather,' I would say. 'It must've been dam' bad,' they would say. 'Don't know,' I would have to say; 'I've dodged clear of it.' See that, Jukes? I have been thinking it all out this afternoon."

He looked up again in his unseeing, unimaginative way. No one had ever heard him say so much at one time. Jukes, with his arms open in the doorway, was like a man invited to behold a miracle. Unbounded wonder was the intellectual meaning of his eye, while incredulity was seated in his whole countenance.

"A gale is a gale, Mr. Jukes," resumed the Captain, "and a full-powered steam-ship has got to face it. There's just so much dirty weather knocking about the world, and the proper thing is to go through it with none of what old Captain Wilson of the *Melita* calls 'storm strategy.' The other day ashore I heard him hold forth about it to a lot of shipmasters who came in and sat at a table next to mine. It seemed to me the greatest nonsense. He was telling them how he— out-manœuvred, I think he said, a terrific gale, so that it never came nearer than fifty miles to him. A neat piece of head-work he called it. How he knew there was a terrific gale fifty liles off beats me altogether. It was like listening to a crazy man. I would have thought Captain Wilson was old enough to know better."

Captain MacWhirr ceased for a moment, then said, "It's your watch below, Mr. Jukes?"

Jukes came to himself with a start. "Yes, sir."

"Leave orders to call me at the slightest change," said the Captain. He reached up to put the book away, and tucked his legs upon the couch. "Shut the door so that it don't fly open, will you? I can't stand a door banging. They've put a lot of rubbishy locks into this ship, I must say."

Captain MacWhirr closed his eyes.

He did so to rest himself. He was tired, and he experienced that state of mental vacuity which comes at the end of an exhaustive discussion that had liberated some belief matured in the course of meditative years. He had indeed been making his confession of faith, had he only known it; and its effect was to make Jukes, on the other side of the door, stand scratching his head for a good while.

Captain MacWhirr opened his eyes.

He thought he must have been asleep. What was that loud noise? Wind? Why had he not been called? The lamp wriggled in its gimbals, the barometer swung in circles, the table altered its slant every moment; a pair of limp seaboots with collapsed tops went sliding past the couch. He put out his hand instantly, and captured one.

Jukes' face appeared in a crack of the door: only his face, very red, with staring eyes. The flame of the lamp leaped, a piece of paper flew up, a rush of air enveloped Captain MacWhirr. Beginning to draw on the boot, he directed an expectant gaze at Jukes' swollen, excited features.

"Came on like this," shouted Jukes, "five minutes ago . . . all of a sudden."

The head disappeared with a bang, and a heavy splash and patter of drops swept past the closed door as if a pailful of melted lead had been flung against the house. A whistling could be heard now upon the deep vibrating noise outside. The stuffy chart-room seemed as full of draughts as a shed. Captain MacWhirr collared the other sea-boot on its violent passage along the floor. He was not flustered, but he could not find at once the opening for inserting his foot. The shoes he had flung off were scurrying from end to end of the cabin, gambolling playfully over each other like puppies. As soon as he stood up he kicked at them viciously, but without effect.

He threw himself into the attitude of a lunging fencer, to reach after his oilskin coat; and afterwards he staggered all over the confined space while he jerked himself into it. Very grave, straddling his legs far apart, and stretching his neck, he started to tie deliberately the strings of his sou'-wester under his chin, with thick fingers that trembled slightly. He went through all the movements of a woman putting on her bonnet before a glass, with a strained, listening attention, as though he had expected every moment to hear the shout of his name in the confused clamour that had suddenly beset his ship. Its increase filled his ears while he was getting ready to go out and confront whatever it might mean. It was tumultuous and very loud—made up of the rush of the wind, the crashes of the sea, with that prolonged deep vibration of the air, like the roll of an immense and remote drum beating the charge of the gale.

He stood for a moment in the light of the lamp, thick, clumsy, shapeless in his panoply of combat, vigilant and red-faced.

"There's a lot of weight in this," he muttered.

As soon as he attempted to open the door the wind caught it. Clinging to the handle, he was dragged out over the doorstep, and at once found himself engaged with the wind in a sort of personal scuffle whose object was the shutting of that door. At the last moment a tongue of air scurried in and licked out the flame of the lamp.

Ahead of the ship he perceived a great darkness lying upon a multitude of white flashes; on the starboard beam a few amazing stars drooped, dim and fitful, above an immense waste of broken seas, as if seen through a mad drift of smoke.

On the bridge a knot of men, indistinct and toiling, were making great efforts in the light of the wheel-house windows that shone mistily on their heads and backs. Suddenly darkness closed upon one pane, then on another. The voices of the lost group reached him after the manner of men's voices in a gale, in shreds and fragments of forlorn shouting snatched past the ear. All at once Jukes appeared at his side, yelling, with his head down.

"Watch—put in—wheelhouse shutters—glass—afraid—blow in."

Jukes heard his commander upbraiding.

"This—come—anything—warning—call me."

He tried to explain, with the uproar pressing on his lips.

"Light air—remained—bridge—sudden—north-east—could turn—thought—you—sure—hear."

They had gained the shelter of the weather-cloth, and could converse with raised voices, as people quarrel.

"I got the hands along to cover up all the ventilators. Good job I had remained on deck I didn't think you would be asleep, and so . . . What did you say, sir? What?"

"Nothing," cried Captain MacWhirr. "I said—all right."

"By all the powers! We've got it this time," observed Jukes in a howl.

"You haven't altered her course?" inquired Captain MacWhirr, straining his voice.

"No, sir. Certainly not. Wind came out right ahead. And here comes the head sea."

A plunge of the ship ended in a shock as if she had landed her forefoot upon something solid. After a moment of stillness a lofty flight of sprays drove hard with the wind upon their faces.

"Keep her at it as long as we can," shouted Captain MacWhirr.

Before Jukes had squeezed the salt water out of his eyes all the stars had disappeared.

III

Jukes was as ready a man as any half-dozen young mates that may be caught by casting a net upon the waters; and though he had been somewhat taken aback by the startling viciousness of the first squall, he had pulled himself together on the instant, had called out the hands and had rushed them along to secure such openings about the deck as had not been already battened down earlier in the evening. Shouting in his fresh, stentorian voice, "Jump, boys, and bear a hand!" he led in the work, telling himself the while that he had "just expected this."

But at the same time he was growing aware that this was rather more than he had expected. From the first stir of the air felt on his cheek the gale seemed to take upon itself the accumulated impetus of an avalanche. Heavy sprays enveloped the *Nan-Shan* from stem to stern, and instantly in the midst of her regular rolling she began to jerk and plunge as though she had gone mad with fright.

Jukes thought, "This is no joke." While he was exchanging explanatory yells with his captain, a sudden lowering of the darkness came upon the night, falling before their vision like something palpable. It was as if the masked lights of the world had been turned down. Jukes was uncritically glad to have his captain at hand. It relieved him as though that man had, by simply coming on deck, taken most of the gale's weight upon his shoulders. Such is the prestige, the privilege, and the burden of command.

Captain MacWhirr could expect no relief of that sort from any one on earth. Such is the loneliness of command. He was trying to see, with that watchful manner of a seaman who stares into the wind's eye as if into the eye of an adversary, to penetrate the hidden intention and guess the aim and force of the thrust. The strong wind swept at him out of a vast obscurity; he felt under his feet the uneasiness of his ship, and he could not even discern the shadow of her shape. He wished it were not so; and very still he waited, feeling stricken by a blind man's helplessness.

To be silent was natural to him, dark or shine. Jukes, at his elbow, made himself heard yelling cheerily in the gusts, "We must have got the worst of it at once, sir." A faint burst of lightning quivered all round, as if flashed into a cavern—into a black and secret chamber of the sea, with a floor of foaming crests.

It unveiled for a sinister, fluttering moment a ragged mass of clouds hanging low, the lurch of the long outlines of the ship, the black figures of men caught on the bridge heads forward, as if petrified in the act of butting. The darkness palpitated down upon all this, and then the real thing came at last.

It was something formidable and swift, like the sudden smashing of a vial of wrath. It seemed to explode all round the ship with an overpowering concussion and a rush of great waters, as if an immense dam had been blown up to windward. In an instant the men lost touch of each other. This is the disintegrating power of a great wind: it isolates one from one's kind. An earthquake, a landslip, an avalanche, overtake a man incidentally, as it were—without passion. A furious gale attacks him like a personal enemy, tries to grasp his limbs, fastens upon his mind, seeks to rout his very spirit out of him.

Jukes was driven away from his commander. He fancied himself whirled a great distance through the air. Everything disappeared—even, for a moment, his power of thinking; but his hand had found one of the rail-stanchions. His distress was by no means alleviated by an inclination to disbelieve the reality of this experience. Though young, he had seen some bad weather, and had never doubted his ability to imagine the worst; but this was so much beyond his powers of fancy that it appeared incompatible with the existence of any ship whatever. He would have been incredulous about himself in the same way, perhaps, had he not been so harassed by the necessity of exerting a wrestling effort against a force trying to tear him away from his hold. Moreover, the conviction of not being utterly destroyed returned to him through the sensations of being half-drowned, bestially shaken, and partly choked.

It seemed to him he remained there precariously alone with the stanchion for a long, long time. The rain poured on him, flowed, drove in sheets. He breathed in gasps; and sometimes the water he swallowed was fresh and sometimes it was salt. For the most part he kept his eyes shut tight, as if suspecting his sight might be destroyed in the immense flurry of the elements. When he ventured to blink hastily, he derived some moral support from the green gleam of the starboard light shining feebly upon the flight of rain and sprays. He was actually looking at it when its ray fell upon the uprearing sea which put it out. He saw the head of the wave topple over, adding the mite of its crash to the tremendous uproar raging around him, and almost at the same instant the stanchion was wrenched away from his embracing arms. After a crushing thump on his back he found himself suddenly afloat and borne upwards. His first irresistible notion was that the whole China Sea had climbed on the bridge. Then, more sanely, he concluded himself gone overboard. All the time he was being tossed, flung, and rolled in great volumes of water, he kept on repeating mentally, with the utmost precipitation, the words: "My God! My God! My God! My God!"

All at once, in a revolt of misery and despair, he formed the crazy resolution to get out of that. And he began to thresh about with his arms and legs. But as soon as he commenced his wretched struggles he discovered that he had become somehow mixed up with a face, an oilskin coat, somebody's boots. He clawed ferociously all these things in turn, lost them, found them again, lost them once more, and finally was himself caught in the firm clasp of a pair of stout arms. He returned the embrace closely round a thick solid body. He had found his captain.

They tumbled over and over, tightening their hug. Suddenly the water let them down with a brutal bang; and, stranded against the side of the wheelhouse, out of breath and bruised, they were left to stagger up in the wind and hold on where they could.

Jukes came out of it rather horrified, as though he had escaped some unparalleled outrage directed at his feelings. It weakened his faith in himself. He started shouting aimlessly to the man he could feel near him in that fiendish blackness, "Is it you, sir? Is it you, sir?" till his temples seemed ready to burst. And he heard in answer a voice, as if crying far away, as if screaming to him fretfully from a very great distance, the one word "Yes!" Other seas swept again over the bridge. He received them defencelessly right over his bare head, with both his hands engaged in holding.

The motion of the ship was extravagant. Her lurches had an appalling helplessness: she pitched as if taking a header into a void, and seemed to find a wall to hit every time. When she rolled she fell on her side head-long, and she would be righted back by such a demolishing blow that Jukes felt her reeling as a clubbed man reels before he collapses. The gale howled and scuffled about gigantically in the darkness, as though the entire world were one black gully. At certain moments the air streamed against the ship as if sucked through a tunnel with a concentrated solid force of impact that seemed to lift her clean out of the water and keep her up for an instant with only a quiver running through her from end to end. And then she would begin her tumbling again as if dropped back into a boiling cauldron. Jukes tried hard to compose his mind and judge things coolly.

The sea, flattened down in the heavier gusts, would uprise and overwhelm both ends of the *Nan-Shan* in snowy rushes of foam, expanding wide, beyond both rails, into the night. And on this dazzling sheet, spread under the blackness of the clouds and emitting a bluish glow, Captain MacWhirr could catch a desolate glimpse of a few tiny specks black as ebony, the tops of the hatches, the battened companions, the heads of the covered winches, the foot of a mast. This was all he could see of his ship. Her middle structure, covered by the bridge which bore him, his mate, the closed wheelhouse where a man was steering shut up with the fear of being swept overboard together with the whole thing in one great crash—her middle structure was like a half-tide rock awash upon a coast. It was like an outlying rock with the water boiling up, streaming over, pouring off, beating round—like a rock in the surf to which shipwrecked people cling before they let go—only it rose, it sank, it rolled continuously, without respite and rest, like a rock that should have miraculously struck adrift from a coast and gone wallowing upon the sea.

The *Nan-Shan* was being looted by the storm with a senseless, destructive fury: trysails torn out of the extra gaskets, double-lashed awnings blown away, bridge swept clean, weather-cloths burst, rails twisted, light-screens smashed— and two of the boats had gone already. They had gone unheard and unseen, melting, as it were, in the shock and smother of the wave. It was only later, when upon the white flash of another high sea hurling itself amidships, Jukes had a vision of two pairs of davits leaping black and empty out of the solid blackness, with one overhauled fall flying and an iron-bound block capering in the air, that he became aware of what had happened within about three yards of his back.

He poked his head forward, groping for the ear of his commander. His lips touched it—big, fleshy, very wet. He cried in an agitated tone, "Our boats are going now, sir."

And again he heard that voice, forced and ringing feebly, but with a pen-etrating effect of quietness in the enormous discord of noises, as if sent out from some remote spot of peace beyond the black wastes of the gale; again he heard a man's voice—the frail and indomitable sound that can be made to carry an infinity of thought, resolution and purpose, that shall be pronouncing confident words on the last day, when heavens fall, and justice is done—again he heard it, and it was crying to him, as if from very, very far—"All right."

He thought he had not managed to make himself understood. "Our boats— I say boats—the boats, sir! Two gone!"

The same voice, within a foot of him and yet so remote, yelled sensibly, "Can't be helped."

Captain MacWhirr had never turned his face, but Jukes caught some more words on the wind.

"What can—expect—when hammering through—such—Bound to leave— something behind—stands to reason."

Watchfully Jukes listened for more. No more came. This was all Captain MacWhirr had to say; and Jukes could picture to himself rather than see the board squat back before him. An impenetrable obscurity pressed down upon the ghostly glimmers of the sea. A dull conviction seized upon Jukes that there was nothing to be done.

If the steering-gear did not give way, if the immense volumes of water did not burst the deck in or smash one of the hatches, if the engines did not give up, if way could be kept on the ship against this terrific wind, and she did not bury herself in one of these awful seas, of whose white crests alone, topping high above her bows, he could now and then get a sickening glimpse—then there was a chance of her coming out of it. Something within him seemed to turn over, bringing uppermost the feeling that the *Nan-Shan* was lost.

"She's done for," he said to himself, with a surprising mental agitation, as though he had discovered an unexpected meaning in this thought. One of these things was bound to happen. Nothing could be prevented now, and nothing could be remedied. The men on board did not count, and the ship could not last. This weather was too impossible.

Jukes felt an arm thrown heavily over his shoulders; and to this overture he responded with great intelligence by catching hold of his captain round the waist.

They stood clasped thus in the blind night, bracing each other against the wind, cheek to cheek and lip to ear, in the manner of two hulks lashed stem to stern together.

And Jukes heard the voice of his commander hardly any louder than before, but nearer, as though, starting to march athwart the prodigious rush of the hurricane, it had approached him, bearing that strange effect of quietness like the serene glow of a halo.

"D'ye know where the hands got to?" it asked, vigorous and evanescent at the same time, overcoming the strength of the wind, and swept away from Jukes instantly.

Jukes didn't know. They were all on the bridge when the real force of the hurricane struck the ship. He had no idea where they had crawled to. Under the circumstances they were nowhere, for all the use that could be made of them. Somehow the Captain's wish to know distressed Jukes.

"Want the hands, sir?" he cried apprehensively.

"Ought to know," asserted Captain MacWhirr. "Hold hard."

They held hard. An outburst of unchained fury, a vicious rush of the wind absolutely steadied the ship; she rocked only, quick and light like a child's cradle, for a terrific moment of suspense, while the whole atmosphere, as it seemed, streamed furiously past her, roaring away from the tenebrous earth.

It suffocated them, and with eyes shut they tightened their grasp. What from the magnitude of the shock might have been a column of water running upright in the dark, butted against the ship, broke short, and fell on her bridge, crushingly, from on high, with a dead burying weight.

A flying fragment of that collapse, a mere splash, enveloped them in one swirl from their feet over their heads, filling violently their ears, mouths and nostrils with salt water. It knocked out their legs, wrenched in haste at their arms, seethed away swiftly under their chins; and opening their eyes, they saw the piled-up masses of foam dashing to and fro amongst what looked like the fragments of a ship. She had given way as if driven straight in. Their panting hearts yielded too before the tremendous blow; and all at once she sprang up again to her desperate plunging, as if trying to scramble out from under the ruins.

The seas in the dark seemed to rush from all sides to keep her back where she might perish. There was hate in the way she was handled, and a ferocity in the blows that fell. She was like a living creature thrown to the rage of a mob: hustled terribly, struck at, borne up, flung down, leaped upon. Captain MacWhirr and Jukes kept hold of each other, deafened by the noise, gagged by the wind; and the great physical tumult beating about their bodies, brought, like an unbridled display of passion, a profound trouble to their souls. One of these wild and appalling shrieks that are heard at times passing mysteriously overhead in the steady roar of a hurricane, swooped, as if borne on wings, upon the ship, and Jukes tried to outscream it.

"Will she live through this?"

The cry was wrenched out of his breast. It was as unintentional as the birth of a thought in the head, and he heard nothing of it himself. It all became extinct at once—thought, intention, effort—and of his cry the inaudible vibration added to the tempest waves of the air.

He expected nothing from it. Nothing at all. For indeed what answer could be made? But after a while he heard with amazement the frail and resisting voice in his ear, the dwarf sound, unconquered in the giant tumult.

"She may!"

It was a dull yell, more difficult to seize than a whisper. And presently the voice returned again, half submerged in the vast crashes, like a ship battling against the waves of an ocean.

"Let's hope so!" it cried—small, lonely and unmoved, a stranger to the visions of hope or fear; and it flickered into disconnected words: "Ship ... This ... Never—Anyhow ... for the best." Jukes gave it up.

Then, as if it had come suddenly upon the one thing fit to withstand the power of a storm, it seemed to gain force and firmness for the last broken shouts:

"Keep on hammering ... builders ... good men ... And chance it ... engines ... Rout ... good man."

Captain MacWhirr removed his arm from Jukes' shoulders, and thereby ceased to exist for his mate, so dark it was; Jukes, after a tense stiffening of every muscle, would let himself go limp all over. The gnawing of profound discomfort existed side by side with an incredible disposition to somnolence, as though he had been buffeted and worried into drowsiness. The wind would get hold of his head and try to shake it off his shoulders; his clothes, full of water, were as heavy as lead, cold and dripping like an armour of melting ice: he shivered—it lasted a long time; and with his hands closed hard on his hold, he was letting himself sink slowly into the depths of bodily misery. His mind became concentrated upon himself in an aimless, idle way, and when something pushed lightly at the back of his knees he nearly, as the saying is, jumped out of his skin.

In the start forward he bumped the back of Captain MacWhirr, who didn't move; and then a hand gripped his thigh. A lull had come, a menacing lull of the wind, the holding of a stormy breath—and he felt himself pawed all over. It was the boatswain. Jukes recognised these hands, so thick and enormous that they seemed to belong to some new species of man.

The boatswain had arrived on the bridge, crawling on all fours against the wind, and had found the chief mate's legs with the top of his head. Immediately he crouched and began to explore Jukes' person upwards, with prudent, apologetic touches, as became an inferior.

He was an ill-favoured, undersized, gruff sailor of fifty, coarsely hairy, short-legged, long-armed, resembling an elderly ape. His strength was immense; and in his great lumpy paws, bulging like boxing gloves on the end of furry forearms,

the heaviest objects were handled like playthings. Apart from the grizzled pelt
on his chest, the menacing demeanour and the hoarse voice, he had none of
the classical attributes of his rating. His good nature almost amounted to imbecility: the men did what they liked with him, and he had not an ounce of
initiative in his character, which was easy-going and talkative. For these reasons
Jukes disliked him; but Captain MacWhirr, to Jukes' scornful disgust, seemed
to regard him as a first-rate petty officer.

He pulled himself up by Jukes' coat, taking that liberty with the greatest
moderation, and only so far as it was forced upon him by the hurricane.

"What is it, boss'n, what is it?" yelled Jukes, impatiently. What could that
fraud of a boss'n want on the bridge? The typhoon had got on Jukes' nerves.
The husky bellowings of the other, though unintelligible, seemed to suggest a
state of lively satisfaction. There could be no mistake. The old fool was pleased
with something.

The boatswain's other hand had found some other body, for in a changed
tone he began to inquire: "Is it you, sir? Is it you, sir?" The wind strangled his
howls.

"Yes!" cried Captain MacWhirr.

IV

All that the boatswain, out of a superabundance of yells, could make clear to
Captain MacWhirr was the bizarre intelligence that "All them Chinamen in the
fore 'tween deck have fetched away, sir."

Jukes to leeward could hear these two shouting within six inches of his face,
as you may hear on a still night half a mile away two men conversing across a
field. He heard Captain MacWhirr's exasperated "What? What?" and the strained
pitch of the other's hoarseness. "In a lump ... seen them myself ... Awful sight,
sir ... thought ... tell you."

Jukes remained indifferent, as if rendered irresponsible by the force of the
hurricane, which made the very thought of action utterly vain. Besides, being
very young, he had found the occupation of keeping his heart completely steeled
against the worst so engrossing that he had come to feel an overpowering dislike
towards any other form of activity whatever. He was not scared; he knew this
because, firmly believing he would never see another sunrise, he remained calm
in that belief.

These are the moments of do-nothing heroics to which even good men
surrender at times. Many officers of ships can no doubt recall a case in their
experience when just a trance of confounded stoicism would come all at once
over a whole ship's company. Jukes, however, had no wide experience of men
or storms. He conceived himself to be calm—inexorably calm; but as a matter
of fact he was daunted; not abjectly, but only so far as a decent man may,
without becoming loathsome to himself.

It was rather like a forced-on numbness of spirit. The long, long stress of
a gale does it; the suspense of the interminably culminating catastrophe; and

there is a bodily fatigue in the mere holding on to existence within the excessive tumult; a searching and insidious fatigue that penetrates deep into a man's breast to cast down and sadden his heart, which is incorrigible, and of all the gifts of the earth—even before life itself—aspires to peace.

Jukes was benumbed much more than he supposed. He held on—very wet, very cold, stiff in every limb; and in a momentary hallucination of swift visions (it is said that a drowning man thus reviews all his life) he beheld all sorts of memories altogether unconnected with his present situation. He remembered his father, for instance: a worthy business man, who at an unfortunate crisis in his affairs went quietly to bed and died forthwith in a state of resignation. Jukes did not recall these circumstances, of course, but remaining otherwise unconcerned he seemed to see distinctly the poor man's face; a certain game of nap played when quite a boy in Table Bay on board a ship, since lost with all hands; the thick eyebrows of his first skipper; and without any emotion, as he might years ago have walked listlessly into her room and found her sitting there with a book, he remembered his mother—dead, too, now—the resolute woman, left badly off, who had been very firm in his bringing up.

It could not have lasted more than a second, perhaps not so much. A heavy arm had fallen about his shoulders; Captain MacWhirr's voice was speaking his name into his ear.

"Jukes! Jukes!"

He detected the tone of deep concern. The wind had thrown its weight on the ship, trying to pin her down amongst the seas. They made a clean breach over her, as over a deep-swimming log; and the gathered weight of crashes menaced monstrously from afar. The breakers flung out of the night with a ghostly light on their crests—the light of sea-foam that in a ferocious, boiling-up pale flash showed upon the slender body of the ship the toppling rush, the downfall, and the seething mad scurry of each wave. Never for a moment could she shake herself clear of the water; Jukes, rigid, perceived in her motion the ominous sign of haphazard floundering. She was no longer struggling intelligently. It was the beginning of the end; and the note of busy concern in Captain MacWhirr's voice sickened him like an exhibition of blind and pernicious folly.

The spell of the storm had fallen upon Jukes. He was penetrated by it, absorbed by it; he was rooted in it with a rigour of dumb attention. Captain MacWhirr persisted in his cries, but the wind got between them like a solid wedge. He hung round Jukes' neck as heavy as a millstone, and suddenly the sides of their heads knocked together.

"Jukes! Mr. Jukes, I say!"

He had to answer that voice that would not be silenced. He answered in the customary manner: " . . . Yes, sir."

And directly, his heart, corrupted by the storm that breeds a craving for peace, rebelled against the tyranny of training and command.

Captain MacWhirr had his mate's head fixed firm in the crook of his elbow, and pressed it to his yelling lips mysteriously. Sometimes Jukes would break in, admonishing hastily: "Look out, sir!" or Captain MacWhirr would bawl an earnest exhortation to "Hold hard, there!" and the whole black universe seemed to reel together with the ship. They paused. She floated yet. And Captain MacWhirr would resume his shouts. " . . . Says . . . whole lot . . . fetched away . . . Ought to see . . . what's the matter."

Directly the full force of the hurricane had struck the ship, every part of her deck became untenable; and the sailors, dazed and dismayed, took shelter in the port alleyway under the bridge. It had a door aft, which they shut; it was very black, cold, and dismal. At each heavy fling of the ship they would groan all together in the dark, and tons of water would be heard scuttling about as if trying to get them from above. The boatswain had been keeping up a gruff talk, but a more unreasonable lot of men, he said afterwards, he had never been with. They were snug enough there, out of harm's way, and not wanted to do anything, either; and yet they did nothing but grumble and complain peevishly like so many sick kids. Finally, one of them said that if there had been at least some light to see each other's noses by, it wouldn't be so bad. It was making him crazy, he declared, to lie there in the dark waiting for the blamed hooker to sink.

"Why don't you step outside, then, and be done with it at once?" the boatswain turned on him.

This called up a shout of execration. The boatswain found himself overwhelmed with reproaches of all sorts. They seemed to take it ill that a lamp was not instantly created for them out of nothing. They would whine after a light to get drowned by—anyhow! And though the unreason of their revilings was patent—since no one could hope to reach the lamp-room, which was forward—he became greatly distressed. He did not think it was decent of them to be nagging at him like this. He told them so, and was met by general contumely. He sought refuge, therefore, in an embittered silence. At the same time their grumbling and sighing and muttering worried him greatly, but by-and-by it occurred to him that there were six globe lamps hung in the 'tween-deck, and that there could be no harm in depriving the coolies of one of them.

The *Nan-Shan* had an athwartship coal-bunker, which, being at times used as cargo space, communicated by an iron door with the fore 'tween-deck. It was empty then, and its manhole was the foremost one in the alleyway. The boatswain could get in, therefore, without coming out on deck at all; but to his great surprise he found he could induce no one to help him in taking off the manhole cover. He groped for it all the same, but one of the crew lying in his way refused to budge.

"Why, I only want to get you that blamed light you are crying for," he expostulated, almost pitifully.

Somebody told him to go and put his head in a bag. He regretted he could not recognise the voice, and that it was too dark to see, otherwise, as he said, he would have put a head on *that* son of a sea-cook, anyway, sink or swim. Nevertheless, he had made up his mind to show them he could get a light, if he were to die for it.

Through the violence of the ship's rolling, every movement was dangerous. To be lying down seemed labour enough. He nearly broke his neck dropping into the bunker. He fell on his back, and was sent shooting helplessly from side to side in the dangerous company of a heavy iron bar—a coal rimmer's slice probably—left down there by somebody. This thing made him as nervous as though it had been a wild beast. He could not see it, the inside of the bunker coated with coal-dust being perfectly and impenetrably black; but he heard it sliding and clattering, and striking here and there, always in the neighbourhood of his head. It seemed to make an extraordinary noise, too—to give heavy thumps as though it had been as big as a bridge girder. This was remarkable enough for him to notice while he was flung from port to starboard and back again, and clawing desperately the smooth sides of the bunker in the endeavour to stop himself. The door into the 'tween-deck not fitting quite true, he saw a thread of dim light at the bottom.

Being a sailor, and a still active man, he did not want much of a chance to regain his feet; and as luck would have it, in scrambling up he put his hand on the iron slice, picking it up as he rose. Otherwise he would have been afraid of the thing breaking his legs, or at least knocking him down again. At first he stood still. He felt unsafe in this darkness that seemed to make the ship's motion unfamiliar, unforeseen, and difficult to counteract. He felt so much shaken for a moment that he dared not move for fear of "taking charge again." He had no mind to get battered to pieces in that bunker.

He had struck his head twice; he was dazed a little. He seemed to hear yet so plainly the clatter and bangs of the iron slice flying about his ears that he tightened his grip to prove to himself he had it there safely in his hand. He was vaguely amazed at the plainness with which down there he could hear the gale raging. Its howls and shrieks seemed to take on, in the emptiness of the bunker, something of the human character, of human rage and pain—being not vast but infinitely poignant. And there were, with every roll, thumps too—profound, ponderous thumps, as if a bulky object of five-ton weight or so had got play in the hold. But there was no such thing in the cargo. Something on deck? Impossible. Or alongside? Couldn't be.

He thought all this quickly, clearly, competently, like a seaman, and in the end remained puzzled. This noise, though, came deadened from outside, together with the washing and pouring of water on deck above his head. Was it the wind? Must be. It made down there a row like the shouting of a big lot of crazed men. And he discovered in himself a desire for a light too—if only to get drowned by—and a nervous anxiety to get out of that bunker as quickly as possible.

He pulled back the bolt: the heavy iron plate turned on its hinges; and it was though he had opened the door to the sounds of the tempest. A gust of hoarse yelling met him: the air was still; and the rushing of water overhead was covered by a tumult of strangled, throaty shrieks that produced an effect of desperate confusion. He straddled his legs the whole width of the doorway and stretched his neck. And at first he perceived only what he had come to seek: six small yellow flames swinging violently on the great body of the dusk.

It was stayed like the gallery of a mine, with a row of stanchions in the middle, and cross-beams overhead, penetrating into the gloom ahead—indefinitely. And to port there loomed, like the caving in of one of the sides, a bulky mass with a slanting outline. The whole place, with the shadows and the shapes, moved all the time. The boatswain glared: the ship lurched to starboard, and a great howl came from that mass that had the slant of fallen earth.

Pieces of wood whizzed past. Planks, he thought, inexpressibly startled, and flinging back his head. At his feet a man went sliding over, open-eyed, on his back, straining with uplifted arms for nothing: and another came bounding like a detached stone with his head between his legs and his hands clenched. His pigtail whipped in the air; he made a grab at the boatswain's legs, and from his opened hand a bright white disc rolled against the boatswain's foot. He recognised a silver dollar, and yelled at it with astonishment. With a precipitated sound of trampling and shuffling of bare feet, and with guttural cries, the mound of writhing bodies piled up to port detached itself from the ship's side and shifted to starboard, sliding, inert and struggling, to a dull, brutal thump. The cries ceased. The boatswain heard a long moan through the roar and whistling of the wind; he saw an inextricable confusion of heads and shoulders, naked soles kicking upwards, fists raised, tumbling back, legs, pigtails, faces.

"Good Lord!" he cried, horrified, and banged-to the iron door upon this vision.

This was what he had come on the bridge to tell. He could not keep it to himself; and on board ship there is only one man to whom it is worth while to unburden yourself. On his passage back the hands in the alleyway swore at him for a fool. Why didn't he bring that lamp? What the devil did the coolies matter to anybody? And when he came out, the extremity of the ship made what went on inside of her appear of little moment.

At first he thought he had left the alleyway in the very moment of her sinking. The bridge ladders had been washed away, but an enormous sea filling the after-deck floated him up. After that he had to lie on his stomach for some time, holding to a ring-bolt, getting his breath now and then, and swallowing salt water. He struggled farther on his hands and knees, too frightened and distracted to turn back. In this way he reached the after-part of the wheelhouse. In that comparatively sheltered spot he found the second mate. The boatswain was pleasantly surprised—his impression being that everybody on deck must have been washed away a long time ago. He asked eagerly where the captain was.

The second mate was lying low, like a malignant little animal under a hedge.

"Captain? Gone overboard, after getting us into this mess." The mate, too, for all he knew or cared. Another fool. Didn't matter. Everybody was going by-and-by.

The boatswain crawled out again into the strength of the wind; not because he much expected to find anybody, he said, but just to get away from "that man." He crawled out as outcasts go to face an inclement world. Hence his great joy at finding Jukes and the Captain. But what was going on in the 'tween-deck was to him a minor matter by that time. Besides, it was difficult to make yourself heard. But he managed to convey the idea that the Chinamen had broken adrift together with their boxes, and that he had come up on purpose to report this. As to the hands, they were all right. Then, appeased, he subsided on the deck in a sitting posture, hugging with his arms and legs the stand of the engine-room telegraph—an iron casting as thick as a post. When that went, why, he expected he would go too. He gave no more thought to the coolies.

Captain MacWhirr had made Jukes understand that he wanted him to go down below—to see.

"What am I to do then, sir?" And the trembling of his whole wet body caused Jukes' voice to sound like bleating.

"See first ... Boss'n ... says ... adrift."

"That boss'n is a confounded fool," howled Jukes shakily.

The absurdity of the demand made upon him revolted Jukes. He was unwilling to go as if the moment he had left the deck of the ship were sure to sink.

"I must know ... can't leave ... "

"They'll settle, sir."

"Fight ... boss'n says they fight ... Why? Can't have ... fighting ... board ship...Much rather keep you here...case...I should...washed overboard myself...Stop it...some way. You see and tell me...through engine-room tube. Don't want you...come up here...too often. Dangerous...moving about...deck."

Jukes, held with his head in chancery, had to listen to what seemed horrible suggestions.

"Don't want...you get lost...so long...ship isn't...Rout...Good man...Ship...may...through this...all right yet."

All at once Jukes understood he would have to go.

"Do you think she may?" he screamed.

But the wind devoured the reply, out of which Jukes heard only the one word, pronounced with great energy "...Always..."

Captain MacWhirr released Jukes, and bending over the boatswain, yelled "Get back with the mate." Jukes only knew that the arm was gone off his shoulders. He was dismissed with his orders—to do what? He was exasperated into letting go his hold carelessly, and on the instant was blown away. It seemed to him that nothing could stop him from being blown right over the stern. He flung himself down hastily, and the boatswain, who was following, fell on him.

"Don't you get up yet, sir," cried the boatswain. "No hurry!"

A sea swept over. Jukes understood the boatswain to splutter that the bridge ladders were gone. "I'll lower you down, sir, by your hands," he screamed. He shouted also something about the smoke-stack being as likely to go overboard as not. Jukes thought it very possible, and imagined the fires out, the ship helpless.... The boatswain by his side kept on yelling. "What? What is it?" Jukes cried distressfully; and the other repeated. "What would my old woman say if she saw me now?"

In the alleyway, where a lot of water had got in and splashed in the dark, the men were still as death, till Jukes stumbled against one of them and cursed him savagely for being in the way. Two or three voices then asked, eager and weak, "Any chance for us, sir?"

"What's the matter with you fools?" he said brutally. He felt as though he could throw himself down amongst them and never move any more. But they seemed cheered; and in the midst of obsequious warnings, "Look out! Mind that manhole lid, sir, they lowered him into the bunker. The boatswain tumbled down after him, and as soon as he had picked himself up he remarked, "She would say, 'Serve you right, you old fool, for going to sea.'"

The boatswain had some means, and made a point of alluding to them frequently. His wife—a fat woman—and two grown-up daughters kept a green-grocer's shop in the East-end of London.

In the dark, Jukes, unsteady on his legs, listened to a faint thunderous patter. A deadened screaming went on steadily at his elbow, as it were; and from above the louder tumult of the storm descended upon these near sounds. His head swam. To him, too, in that bunker, the motion of the ship seemed novel and menacing, sapping his resolution as though he had never been afloat before.

He had half a mind to scramble out again; but the remembrance of Captain MacWhirr's voice made this impossible. His orders were to go and see. What was the good of it, he wanted to know. Enraged, he told himself he would see—of course. But the boatswain, staggering clumsily, warned him to be careful how he opened that door; there was a blamed fight going on. And Jukes, as if in great bodily pain, desired irritably to know what the devil they were fighting for.

"Dollars! Dollars, sir. All their rotten chests got burst open. Blamed money skipping all over the place, and they are tumbling after it head over heels—tearing and biting like anything. A regular little hell in there."

Jukes convulsively opened the door. The short boatswain peered under his arm.

One of the lamps had gone out, broken perhaps. Rancorous, guttural cries burst out loudly on their ears, and a strange panting sound, the working of all these straining breasts. A hard blow hit the side of the ship: water fell above with a stunning shock, and in the forefront of the gloom, where the air was reddish and thick, Jukes saw a head bang the deck violently, two thick calves waving on high, muscular arms twined round a naked body, a yellow-face, open-mouthed and with a set wild stare, look up and slide away. An empty chest clattered turning over; a man fell head first with a jump, as if lifted by a kick; and farther off, indistinct, others streamed like a mass of rolling stones down a bank, thumping the deck with their feet and flourishing their arms wildly. The hatchway ladder was loaded with coolies swarming on it like bees on a branch. They hung on the steps in a crawling, stirring cluster, beating madly with their fists the underside of the battened hatch, and the headlong rush of the water above was heard in the intervals of their yelling. The ship heeled over more, and they began to drop off: first one, then two, then all the rest went away together, falling straight off with a great cry.

Jukes was confounded. The boatswain, with gruff anxiety, begged him, "Don't you go in there, sir."

The whole place seemed to twist upon itself, jumping incessantly the while; and when the ship rose to a sea Jukes fancied that all these men would be shot upon him in a body. He backed out, swung the door to, and with trembling hands pushed at the bolt. . . .

As soon as his mate had gone Captain MacWhirr, left alone on the bridge, sidled and staggered as far as the wheel-house. Its door being hinged forward, he had to fight the gale for admittance, and when at last he managed to enter, it was with an instantaneous clatter and a bang, as though he had been fired through the wood. He stood within, holding on to the handle.

The steering-gear leaked steam, and in the confined space the glass of the binnacle made a shiny oval of light in a thin white fog. The wind howled, hummed, whistled, with sudden booming gusts that rattled the doors and shutters in the vicious patter of sprays. Two coils of lead-line and a small canvas bag hung on a long lanyard, swung wide off, and came back clinging to the bulkheads. The gratings underfoot were nearly afloat; with every sweeping blow of a sea, water squirted violently through the cracks all round the door, and the man at the helm had flung down his cap, his coat, and stood propped against the gear-casing in a stripped cotton shirt open on his breast. The little brass wheel in his hands had the appearance of a bright and fragile toy. The cords of his neck stood hard and lean, a dark patch lay in the hollow of his throat, and his face was still and sunken as in death.

Captain MacWhirr wiped his eyes. The sea that had nearly taken him overboard had, to his great annoyance, washed his sou'-wester hat off his bald head.

The fluffy, fair hair, soaked and darkened, resembled a mean skein of cotton threads festooned round his bare skull. His face, glistening with sea-water, had been made crimson with the wind, with the sting of sprays. He looked as though he had come off sweating from before a furnace.

"You here?" he muttered heavily.

The second mate had found his way into the wheel-house some time before. He had fixed himself in a corner with his knees up, a fist pressed against each temple; and this attitude suggested rage, sorrow, resignation, surrender, with a sort of concentrated unforgiveness. He said mournfully and defiantly, "Well, it's my watch below now: ain't it?"

The steam gear clattered, stopped, clattered again; and the helmsman's eyeballs seemed to project out of a hungry face as if the compass card behind the binnacle glass had been meat. God knows how long he had been left there to steer, as if forgotten by all his shipmates. The bells had not been struck; there had been no reliefs; the ship's routine had gone down wind; but he was trying to keep her head north-north-east. The rudder might have been gone for all he knew, the fires out, the engines broken down, the ship ready to roll over like a corpse. He was anxious not to get muddled and lose control of her head, because the compass-card swung far both ways, wriggling on the pivot, and sometimes seemed to whirl right round. He suffered from mental stress. He was horribly afraid, also, of the wheelhouse going. Mountains of water kept on tumbling against it. When the ship took one of her desperate dives the corners of his lips twitched.

Captain MacWhirr looked up at the wheelhouse clock. Screwed to the bulk-head, it had a white face on which the black hands appeared to stand quite still. It was half-past one in the morning.

"Another day," he muttered to himself.

The second mate heard him, and lifting his head as one grieving amongst ruins, "You won't see it break," he exclaimed. His wrists and his knees could be seen to shake violently. "No, by God! You won't..."

He took his face again between his fists.

The body of the helmsman had moved slightly, but his head didn't budge on his neck,—like a stone head fixed to look one way from a column. During a roll that all but took his booted legs from under him, and in the very stagger to save himself, Captain MacWhirr said austerely, "Don't you pay any attention to what that man says." And then, with an indefinable change of tone, very grave, he added, "He isn't on duty."

The sailor said nothing.

The hurricane boomed, shaking the little place, which seemed air-tight; and the light of the binnacle flickered all the time.

"You haven't been relieved," Captain MacWhirr went on, looking down. "I want you to stick to the helm, though, as long as you can. You've got the hang of her. Another man coming here might make a mess of it. Wouldn't do. No child's play. And the hands are probably busy with a job down below.... Think you can?"

The steering gear leaped into an abrupt short clatter, stopped smouldering like an ember; and the still man, with a motionless gaze, burst out, as if all the passion in him had gone into his lips: "By Heavens, sir! I can steer for ever if nobody talks to me."

"Oh! aye! All right, . . . " The Captain lifted his eyes for the first time to the man, " . . . Hackett."

And he seemed to dismiss this matter from his mind. He stooped to the engine-room speaking-tube, blew in, and bent his head. Mr. Rout below answered, and at once Captain MacWhirr put his lips to the mouthpiece.

With the uproar of the gale around him he applied alternately his lips and his ear, and the engineer's voice mounted to him, harsh and as if out of the heat of an engagement. One of the stokers was disabled, the others had given in, the second engineer and the donkey-man were firing-up. The third engineer was standing by the steam-valve. The engines were being tended by hand. How was it above?

"Bad enough. It mostly rests with you," said Captain MacWhirr. Was the mate down there yet? No? Well, he would be presently. Would Mr. Rout let him talk through the speaking-tube?—through the deck speaking-tube, because he—the Captain—was going out again on the bridge directly. There was some trouble amongst the Chinamen. They were fighting, it seemed. Couldn't allow fighting anyhow. . . .

Mr. Rout had gone away, and Captain MacWhirr could feel against his ear the pulsation of the engines, like the beat of the ship's heart. Mr. Rout's voice down there shouted something distantly. The ship pitched headlong, the pulsation leaped with a hissing tumult, and stopped dead. Captain MacWhirr's face was impassive, and his eyes were fixed aimlessly on the crouching shape of the second mate. Again Mr. Rout's voice cried out in the depths, and the pulsating beats recommenced, with slow strokes—growing swifter.

Mr. Rout had returned to the tube. "It don't matter much what they do," he said hastily; and then, with irritation, "She takes these dives as if she never meant to come up again."

"Awful sea," said the Captain's voice from above.

"Don't let me drive her under," barked Solomon Rout up the pipe.

"Dark and rain. Can't see what's coming," uttered the voice. "Must—keep—her—moving—enough to steer—and chance it," it went on to state distinctly.

"I am doing as much as I dare."

"We are—getting—smashed up—a good deal up here," proceeded the voice mildly. "Doing—fairly well—though. Of course, if the wheelhouse should go . . ."

Mr. Rout, bending an attentive ear, muttered peevishly something under his breath.

But the deliberate voice up there became animated to ask: "Jukes turned up yet?" Then, after a short wait, "I wish he would bear a hand. I want him to be done and come up here in case of anything. To look after the ship. I am all alone. The second mate's lost. . . ."

"What?" shouted Mr. Rout into the engine-room, taking his head away. Then up the tube he cried, "Gone overboard?" and clapped his ear to.

"Lost his nerve," the voice from above continued in a matter-of-fact tone. "Damned awkward circumstance."

Mr. Rout, listening with bowed neck, opened his eyes wide at this. However, he heard something like the sounds of a scuffle and broken exclamations coming down to him. He strained his hearing; and all the time Beale, the third engineer, with his arms uplifted, held between the palms of his hands the rim of a little black wheel projecting at the side of a big copper pipe. He seemed to

be poising it above his head, as though it were a correct attitude in some sort
of game.

To steady himself, he pressed his shoulder against the white bulkhead, one
knee bent, and a sweat-rag tucked in his belt hanging on his hip. His smooth
cheek was begrimed and flushed, and the coal dust on his eyelids, like the black
pencilling of a make-up, enhanced the liquid brilliance of the whites, giving to
his youthful face something of a feminine, exotic and fascinating aspect. When
the ship pitched he would with hasty movements of his hands screw hard at
the little wheel.

"Gone crazy," began the Captain's voice suddenly in the tube. "Rushed at
me.... Just now. Had to knock him down..... This minute. You heard, Mr.
Rout?"

"The devil!" muttered Mr. Rout. "Look out, Beale!"

His shout rang out like the blast of a warning trumpet, between the iron
walls of the engine-room. Painted white, they rose high into the dusk of the
skylight, sloping like a roof; and the whole lofty space resembled the interior
of a monument, divided by floors of iron grating, with lights flickering at different levels, and a mass of gloom lingering in the middle, within the columnar
stir of machinery under the motionless swelling of the cylinders. A loud and
wild resonance, made up of all the noises of the hurricane, dwelt in the still
warmth of the air. There was in it the smell of hot metal, of oil, and a slight
mist of steam. The blows of the sea seemed to traverse it in an unringing,
stunning shock, from side to side.

Gleams, like pale long flames, trembled upon the polish of metal; from the
flooring below the enormous crank-heads emerged in their turns with a flash
of brass and steel—going over; while the connecting-rods, big-jointed, like skeleton limbs, seemed to thrust them down and pull them up again with an irresistible precision. And deep in the half-light other rods dodged deliberately
to and fro, crossheads nodded, discs of metal rubbed smoothly against each
other, slow and gentle, in a commingling of shadows and gleams.

Sometimes all those powerful and unerring movements would slow down
simultaneously, as if they had been the functions of a living organism, stricken
suddenly by the blight of languor; and Mr. Rout's eyes would blaze darker in
his long sallow face. He was fighting this fight in a pair of carpet slippers. A
short shiny jacket barely covered his loins, and his white wrists protruded far
out of the tight sleeves, as though the emergency had added to his stature, had
lengthened his limbs, augmented his pallor, hollowed his eyes.

He moved, climbing high up, disappearing low down, with a restless,
purposeful industry, and when he stood still, holding the guard-rail in front of
the starting-gear, he would keep glancing to the right at the steam-gauge, at
the water-gauge, fixed upon the white wall in the light of a swaying lamp. The
mouths of two speaking-tubes gaped stupidly at his elbow, and the dial of the
engine-room telegraph resembled a clock of large diameter, bearing on its face
curt words instead of figures. The grouped letters stood out heavily black, around
the pivot-head of the indicator, emphatically symbolic of loud exclamations:
AHEAD, ASTERN, SLOW, HALF, STAND BY; and the fat black hand pointed downwards to the word FULL, which, thus singled out, captured the eye as a sharp
cry secures attention.

The wood-encased bulk of the low-pressure cylinder, frowning portly from
above, emitted a faint wheeze at every thrust, and except for that low hiss the

engines worked their steel limbs headlong or slow with a silent, determined smoothness. And all this, the white walls, the moving steel, the floor plates under Solomon Rout's feet, the floors of iron grating above his head, the dusk and the gleams, uprose and sank continuously, with one accord, upon the harsh wash of the waves against the ship's side. The whole loftiness of the place, booming hollow to the great voice of the wind, swayed at the top like a tree, would go over bodily, as if borne down this way and that by the tremendous blasts.

"You've got to hurry up," shouted Mr. Rout, as soon as he saw Jukes appear in the stokehold doorway.

Jukes' glance was wandering and tipsy; his red face was puffy, as though he had overslept himself. He had had an arduous road, and had travelled over it with immense vivacity, the agitation of his mind corresponding to the exertions of his body. He had rushed up out of the bunker, stumbling in the dark alleyway amongst a lot of bewildered men who, trod upon, asked "What's up, sir?" in awed mutters all round him;—down the stokehold ladder, missing many iron rungs in his hurry, down into a place deep as a well, black as Tophet, tipping over back and forth like a see-saw. The water in the bilges thundered at each roll, and lumps of coal skipped to and fro, from end to end, rattling like an avalanche of pebbles on a slope of iron.

Somebody in there moaned with pain, and somebody else could be seen crouching over what seemed the prone body of a dead man; a lusty voice blasphemed; and the glow under each fire-door was like a pool of flaming blood radiating quietly in a velvety blackness.

A gust of wind struck upon the nape of Jukes' neck, and next moment he felt it streaming about his wet ankles. The stokehold ventilators hummed: in front of the six fire-doors two wild figures, stripped to the waist, staggered and stooped, wrestling with two shovels.

"Hallo! Plenty of draught now," yelled the second engineer at once, as though he had been all the time looking out for Jukes. The donkeyman, a dapper little chap with a dazzling fair skin and a tiny, gingery moustache, worked in a sort of mute transport. They were keeping a full head of steam, and a profound rumbling, as of an empty furniture van trotting over a bridge, made a sustained bass to all the other noises of the place.

"Blowing off all the time," went on yelling the second. With a sound as of a hundred scoured saucepans, the orifice of a ventilator spat upon his shoulder a sudden gush of salt water, and he volleyed a stream of curses upon all things on earth including his own soul, ripping and raving, and all the time attending to his business. With a sharp clash of metal the ardent pale glare of the fire opened upon his bullet head, showing his spluttering lips, his insolent face, and with another clang closed like the white-hot wink of an iron eye.

"Where's the blooming ship? Can you tell me? blast my eyes! Under water— or what? It's coming down here in tons. Are the condemned cowls gone to Hades? Hey? Don't you know anything—you jolly sailor-man you ...?"

Jukes, after a bewildered moment, had been helped by a roll to dart through; and as soon as his eyes took in the comparative vastness, peace and brilliance of the engine-room, the ship, setting her stern heavily in the water, sent him charging head down upon Mr. Rout.

The chief's arm, long like a tentacle, and straightening as if worked by a spring, went out to meet him, and deflected his rush into a spin towards the speaking-tubes. At the same time Mr. Rout repeated earnestly: "You've got to hurry up, whatever it is."

Jukes yelled "Are you there, sir?" and listened. Nothing. Suddenly the roar of the wind fell straight into his ear, but presently a small voice shoved aside the shouting hurricane quietly.

"You, Jukes?—Well?"

Jukes was ready to talk: it was only time that seemed to be wanting. It was easy enough to account for everything. He could perfectly imagine the coolies battened down in the reeking 'tween-deck, lying sick and scared between the rows of chests. Then one of these chests—or perhaps several at once—breaking loose in a roll, knocking out others, sides splitting, lids flying open, and all these clumsy Chinamen rising up in a body to save their property. Afterwards every fling of the ship would hurl that tramping, yelling mob here and there, from side to side, in a whirl of smashed wood, torn clothing, rolling dollars. A struggle once started, they would be unable to stop themselves. Nothing could stop them now except main force. It was a disaster. He had seen it, and that was all he could say. Some of them must be dead, he believed. The rest would go on fighting. . . .

He sent up his words, tripping over each other, crowding the narrow tube. They mounted as if into a silence of an enlightened comprehension dwelling alone up there with a storm. And Jukes wanted to be dismissed from the face of that odious trouble intruding on the great need of the ship.

V

He waited. Before his eyes the engines turned with slow labour, that in the moment of going off into a mad fling would stop dead at Mr. Rout's shout, "Look out, Beale!" They paused in an intelligent immobility, stilled in mid-stroke, a heavy crank arrested on the cant, as if conscious of danger and the passage of time. Then, with a "Now, then!" from the chief, and the sound of a breath expelled through clenched teeth, they would accomplish the interrupted revolution and begin another.

There was the prudent sagacity of wisdom and the deliberation of enormous strength in their movements. This was their work—this patient coaxing of a distracted ship over the fury of the waves and into the very eye of the wind. At times Mr. Rout's chin would sink on his breast, and he watched them with knitted eyebrows as if lost in thought.

The voice that kept the hurricane out of Jukes' ear began: "Take the hands with you . . .," and left off unexpectedly.

"What could I do with them, sir?"

A harsh, abrupt, imperious clang exploded suddenly. The three pairs of eyes flew up to the telegraph dial to see the hand jump from FULL to STOP, as if snatched by a devil. And then these three men in the engine-room had the intimate sensation of a check upon the ship, of a strange shrinking, as if she had gathered herself for a desperate leap.

"Stop her!" bellowed Mr. Rout.

Nobody—not even Captain MacWhirr, who alone on deck had caught sight of a white line of foam coming on at such a height that he couldn't believe his eyes—nobody was to know the steepness of that sea and the awful depth of the hollow the hurricane had scooped out behind the running wall of water.

It raced to meet the ship, and, with a pause, as of girding the loins, the *Nan-Shan* lifted her bows and leaped. The flames in all the lamps sank, darkening the engine-room. One went out. With a tearing crash and a swirling, raving tumult, tons of water fell upon the deck, as though the ship had darted under the foot of a cataract.

Down there they looked at each other, stunned.

"Swept from end to end, by God!" bawled Jukes.

She dipped into the hollow straight down, as if going over the edge of the world. The engine-room toppled forward menacingly, like the inside of a tower nodding in an earthquake. An awful racket, of iron things falling, came from the stokehold. She hung on this appalling slant long enough for Beale to drop on his hands and knees and begin to crawl as if he meant to fly on all fours out of the engine-room, and for Mr. Rout to turn his head slowly, rigid, cavernous, with the lower jaw dropping. Jukes had shut his eyes, and his face in a moment became hopelessly blank and gentle, like the face of a blind man.

At last she rose slowly, staggering, as if she had to lift a mountain with her bows.

Mr. Rout shut his mouth; Jukes blinked; and little Beale stood up hastily.

"Another one like this, and that's the last of her," cried the chief.

He and Jukes looked at each other, and the same thought came into their heads. The Captain! Everything must have been swept away. Steering gear gone—ship like a log. All over directly.

"Rush!" ejaculated Mr. Rout thickly, glaring with enlarged, doubtful eyes at Jukes, who answered him by an irresolute glance.

The clang of the telegraph gong soothed them instantly. The black hand dropped in a flash from STOP to FULL.

"Now then, Beale!" cried Mr. Rout.

The steam hissed low. The piston-rods slid in and out. Jukes put his ear to the tube. The voice was ready for him. It said: "Pick up all the money. Bear a hand now. I'll want you up here." And that was all.

"Sir?" called up Jukes. There was no answer.

He staggered away like a defeated man from the field of battle. He had got, in some way or other, a cut above his left eyebrow—a cut to the bone. He was not aware of it in the least: quantities of the China Sea, large enough to break his neck for him, had gone over his head, had cleaned, washed, and salted that wound. It did not bleed, but only gaped red; and this gash over the eye, his dishevelled hair, the disorder of his clothes, gave him the aspect of a man worsted in a fight with fists.

"Got to pick up the dollars." He appealed to Mr. Rout, smiling pitifully at random.

"What's that?" asked Mr. Rout wildly. "Pick up . . . ? I don't care. . . ." Then, quivering in every muscle, but with an exaggeration of paternal tone, "Go away now, for God's sake. You deck people'll drive me silly. There's that second mate been going for the old man. Don't you know? You fellows are going wrong for want of something to do. . . ."

At these words Jukes discovered in himself the beginnings of anger. Want of something to do—indeed.... Full of hot scorn against the chief, he turned to go the way he had come. In the stokehold the plump donkeyman toiled with his shovel mutely, as if his tongue had been cut out; but the second was carrying on like a noisy, undaunted maniac, who had preserved his skill in the art of stoking under a marine boiler.

"Hallo, you wandering officer! Hey! Can't you get some of your slush-slingers to wind up a few of them ashes? I am getting choked with them here. Curse it! Hallo! Hey! Remember the articles: *Sailors and firemen to assist each other.* Hey! D'ye hear?"

Jukes was climbing out frantically, and the other, lifting up his face after him, howled, "Can't you speak? What are you poking about here for? What's your game, anyhow?"

A frenzy possessed Jukes. By the time he was back amongst the men in the darkness of the alleyway, he felt ready to wring all their necks at the slightest sign of hanging back. The very thought of it exasperated him. *He* couldn't hang back. They shouldn't.

The impetuosity with which he came amongst them carried them along. They had already been excited and startled at all his comings and goings—by the fierceness and rapidity of his movements; and more felt than seen in his rushes, he appeared formidable—busied with matters of life and death that brooked no delay. At his first word he heard them drop into the bunker one after another obediently, with heavy thumps.

They were not clear as to what would have to be done. "What is it?" What is it?" they were asking each other. The boatswain tried to explain; the sounds of a great scuffle surprised them: and the mighty shocks, reverberating awfully in the black bunker, kept them in mind of their danger. When the boatswain threw open the door it seemed that an eddy of the hurricane, stealing through the iron sides of the ship, had set all these bodies whirling like dust: there came to them a confused uproar, a tempestuous tumult, a fierce mutter, gusts of screams dying away, and the tramping of feet mingling with the blows of the sea.

For a moment they glared amazed, blocking the doorway. Jukes pushed through them brutally. He said nothing, and simply darted in. Another lot of coolies on the ladder, struggling suicidally to break through the battened hatch to a swamped deck, fell off as before, and he disappeared under them like a man overtaken by a landslide.

The boatswain yelled excitedly: "Come along. Get the mate out. He'll be trampled to death. Come on."

They charged in, stamping on breasts, on fingers, on faces, catching their feet in heaps of clothing, kicking broken wood; but before they could get hold of him Jukes emerged waist deep in a multitude of clawing hands. In the instant he had been lost to view, all the buttons of his jacket had gone, its back had got split up to the collar, his waistcoat had been torn open. The central struggling mass of Chinamen went over to the roll, dark, indistinct, helpless, with a wild gleam of many eyes in the dim light of the lamps.

"Leave me alone—damn you. I am all right," screeched Jukes. "Drive them forward. Watch your chance when she pitches. Forward with 'em. Drive them against the bulkhead. Jam 'em up."

The rush of the sailors into the seething 'tween-deck was like a splash of cold water into a boiling cauldron. The commotion sank for a moment.

The bulk of Chinamen were locked in such a compact scrimmage that, linking their arms and aided by an appalling dive of the ship, the seamen sent it forward in one great shove, like a solid block. Behind their backs small clusters and loose bodies tumbled from side to side.

The boatswain performed prodigious feats of strength. With his long arms open, and each great paw clutching at a stanchion, he stopped the rush of seven entwined Chinamen rolling like a boulder. His joints cracked; he said, "Ha!" and they flew apart. But the carpenter showed the greater intelligence. Without saying a word to anybody he went back into the alleyway, to fetch several coils of cargo gear he had seen there—chain and rope. With these life-lines were rigged.

There was really no resistance. The struggle, however it began, had turned into a scramble of blind panic. If the coolies had started up after their scattered dollars they were by that time fighting only for their footing. They took each other by the throat merely to save themselves from being hurled about. Whoever got a hold anywhere would kick at the others who caught at his legs and hung on, till a roll sent them flying together across the deck.

The coming of the white devils was a terror. Had they come to kill? The individuals torn out of the ruck became very limp in the seamen's hands: some, dragged aside by the heels, were passive, like dead bodies, with open, fixed eyes. Here and there a coolie would fall on his knees as if begging for mercy; several, whom the excess of fear made unruly, were hit with hard fists between the eyes, and cowered; while those who were hurt submitted to rough handling, blinking rapidly without a plaint. Faces streamed with blood; there were raw places on the shaven heads, scratches, bruises, torn wounds, gashes. The broken porcelain out of the chests was mostly responsible for the latter. Here and there a Chinaman, wild-eyed, with his tail unplaited, nursed a bleeding sole.

They had been ranged closely, after having been shaken into submission, cuffed a little to allay excitement, addressed in gruff words of encouragement that sounded like promises of evil. They sat on the deck in ghastly, drooping rows, and at the end the carpenter, with two hands to help him, moved busily from place to place, setting taut and hitching the life-lines. The boatswain, with one leg and one arm embracing a stanchion, struggled with a lamp pressed to his breast, trying to get a light, and growling all the time like an industrious gorilla. The figures of seamen stooped repeatedly, with the movements of gleaners, and everything was being flung into the bunker: clothing, smashed wood, broken china, and the dollars too, gathered up in men's jackets. Now and then a sailor would stagger towards the doorway with his arms full of rubbish; and dolorous, slanting eyes followed his movements.

With every roll of the ship the long rows of sitting Celestials would sway forward brokenly, and her head-long dives knocked together the line of shaven polls from end to end. When the wash of water rolling on the deck died away for a moment, it seemed to Jukes, yet quivering from his exertions, that in his mad struggle down there he had overcome the wind somehow: that a silence had fallen upon the ship, a silence in which the sea struck thunderously at her sides.

Everything had been cleared out of the 'tween-deck—all the wreckage, as the men said. They stood erect and tottering above the level of heads and drooping shoulders. Here and there a coolie sobbed for his breath. Where the high light fell, Jukes could see the salient ribs of one, the yellow, wistful face of another; bowed necks; or would meet a dull stare directed at his face. He was amazed that there had been no corpses; but the lot of them seemed at their last gasp, and they appeared to him more pitiful than if they had been all dead.

Suddenly one of the coolies began to speak. The light came and went on his lean, straining face; he threw his head up like a baying hound. From the bunker came the sounds of knocking and the tinkle of some dollars rolling loose; he stretched out his arm, his mouth yawned black, and the incomprehensible guttural hooting sounds, that did not seem to belong to a human language, penetrated Jukes with a strange emotion as if a brute had tried to be eloquent.

Two more started mouthing what seemed to Jukes fierce denunciations; the others stirred with grunts and growls. Jukes ordered the hands out of the 'tween-decks hurriedly. He left last himself, backing through the door, while the grunts rose to a loud murmur and hands were extended after him as after a malefactor. The boatswain shot the bolt, and remarked uneasily, "Seems as if the wind had dropped, sir."

The seamen were glad to get back into the alleyway. Secretly each of them thought that at the last moment he could rush out on deck—and that was a comfort. There is something horribly repugnant in the idea of being drowned under a deck. Now they had done with the Chinamen, they again became conscious of the ship's position.

Jukes on coming out of the alleyway found himself up to the neck in the noisy water. He gained the bridge, and discovered he could detect obscure shapes as if his sight had become preternaturally acute. He saw faint outlines. They recalled not the familiar aspect of the *Nan-Shan*, but something remembered—an old dismantled steamer he had seen years ago rotting on a mudbank. She recalled that wreck.

There was no wind, not a breath, except the faint currents created by the lurches of the ship. The smoke tossed out of the funnel was settling down upon her deck. He breathed it as he passed forward. He felt the deliberate throb of the engines, and heard small sounds that seemed to have survived the great uproar: the knocking of broken fittings, the rapid tumbling of some piece of wreckage on the bridge. He perceived dimly the squat shape of his captain holding on to a twisted bridge-rail, motionless and swaying as if rooted to the planks. The unexpected stillness of the air oppressed Jukes.

"We have done it, sir," he gasped.

"Thought you would," said Captain MacWhirr.

"Did you?" murmured Jukes to himself.

"Wind fell all at once," went on the Captain.

Jukes burst out: "If you think it was an easy job—"

But his captain, clinging to the rail, paid no attention. "According to the books the worst is not over yet."

"If most of them hadn't been half dead with sea-sickness and fright, not one of us would have come out of that 'tween-deck alive," said Jukes.

"Had to do what's fair by them," mumbled MacWhirr stolidly. "You don't find everything in books."

"Why, I believe they would have risen on us if I hadn't ordered the hands out of that pretty quick," continued Jukes with warmth.

After the whisper of their shouts, their ordinary tones, so distinct, rang out very loud to their ears in the amazing stillness of the air. It seemed to them they were talking in a dark and echoing vault.

Through a jagged aperture in the dome of clouds the light of a few stars fell upon the black sea, rising and falling confusedly. Sometimes the head of a watery cone would topple on board and mingle with the rolling flurry of foam on the swamped deck; and the *Nan-Shan* wallowed heavily at the bottom of a circular cistern of clouds. This ring of dense vapours, gyrating madly round the calm of the centre, encompassed the ship like a motionless and unbroken wall of an aspect inconceivably sinister. Within, the sea, as if agitated by an internal commotion, leaped in peaked mounds that jostled each other, slapping heavily against her sides; and a low moaning sound, the infinite plaint of the storm's fury, came from beyond the limits of the menacing calm. Captain MacWhirr remained silent, and Jukes' ready ear caught suddenly the faint, long-drawn roar of some immense wave rushing unseen under that thick blackness, which made the appalling boundary of his vision.

"Of course," he started resentfully, "they thought we had caught at the chance to plunder them. Of course! You said—pick up the money. Easier said than done. They couldn't tell what was in our heads. We came in, smash— right into the middle of them. Had to do it by a rush."

"As long as it's done...," mumbled the Captain, without attempting to look at Jukes. "Had to do what's fair."

"We shall find yet there's the devil to pay when this is over," said Jukes, feeling very sore. "Let them only recover a bit, and you'll see. They will fly at our throats, sir. Don't forget, sir, she isn't a British ship now. These brutes know it well, too. The damn'd Siamese flag."

"We are on board, all the same," remarked Captain MacWhirr.

"The trouble's not over yet," insisted Jukes prophetically, reeling and catching on. "She's a wreck," he added faintly.

"The trouble's not over yet," assented Captain MacWhirr, half aloud.... "Look out for her a minute."

"Are you going off the deck, sir?" asked Jukes hurriedly, as if the storm were sure to pounce upon him as soon as he had been left alone with the ship.

He watched her, battered and solitary, labouring heavily in a wild scene of mountainous black waters lit by the gleams of distant worlds. She moved slowly, breathing into the still core of the hurricane the excess of her strength in a white cloud of steam—and the deep-toned vibration of the escape was like the defiant trumpeting of a living creature of the sea impatient for the renewal of the contest. It ceased suddenly. The still air moaned. Above Jukes' head a few stars shone into the pit of black vapours. The inky edge of the cloud-disc frowned upon the ship under the patch of glittering sky. The stars too seemed to look at her intently, as if for the last time, and the cluster of their splendour sat like a diadem on a lowering brow.

Captain MacWhirr had gone into the chart-room. There was no light there; but he could feel the disorder of that place where he used to live tidily. His armchair was upset. The books had tumbled out on the floor: he scrunched a piece of glass under his boot. He groped for the matches, and found a box on a shelf with a deep ledge. He struck one, and puckering the corners of his eyes, held out the little flame towards the barometer whose glittering top of glass and metals nodded at him continuously.

It stood very low—incredibly low, so low that Captain MacWhirr grunted. The match went out, and hurriedly he extracted another, with thick, stiff fingers.

Again a little flame flared up before the nodding glass and metal of the top. His eyes looked at it, narrowed with attention, as if expecting an imperceptible sign. With his grave face he resembled a booted and mis-shapen pagan burning incense before the oracle of a Joss. There was no mistake. It was the lowest reading he had ever seen in his life.

Captain MacWhirr emitted a low whistle. He forgot himself till the flame diminished to a blue spark, burnt his fingers and vanished. Perhaps something had gone wrong with the thing!

There was an aneroid glass screwed above the couch. He turned that way, struck another match, and discovered the white face of the other instrument looking at him from the bulkhead, meaningly, not to be gainsaid, as though the wisdom of men were made unerring by the indifference of matter. There was no room for doubt now. Captain MacWhirr pshawed at it, and threw the match down.

The worst was to come, then—and if the books were right this worst would be very bad. The experience of the last six hours had enlarged his conception of what heavy weather could be like. "It'll be terrific," he pronounced mentally. He had not consciously looked at anything by the light of the matches except at the barometer; and yet somehow he had seen that his water-bottle and the two tumblers had been flung out of their stand. It seemed to give him a more intimate knowledge of the tossing the ship had gone through. "I wouldn't have believed it," he thought. And his table had been cleared too; his rulers, his pencils, the inkstand—all the things that had their safe appointed places—they were gone, as if a mischievous hand had plucked them out one by one and flung them on the wet floor. The hurricane had broken in upon the orderly arrangements of his privacy. This had never happened before, and the feeling of dismay reached the very seat of his composure. And the worst was to come yet! He was glad the trouble in the 'tween-deck had been discovered in time. If the ship had to go after all, then, at least, she wouldn't be going to the bottom with a lot of people in her fighting teeth and claw. That would have been odious. And in that feeling there was a humane intention and a vague sense of the fitness of things.

These instantaneous thoughts were yet in their essence heavy and slow, partaking of the nature of the man. He extended his hand to put back the matchbox in its corner of the shelf. There were always matches there—by his order. The steward had his instructions impressed upon him long before. "A box...just there, see? Not so very full...where I can put my hand on it, steward. Might want a light in a hurry. Can't tell on board ship *what* you might want in a hurry. Mind, now."

And of course on his side he would be careful to put it back in its place scrupulously. He did so now, but before he removed his hand it occurred to him that perhaps he would never have occasion to use that box any more. The vividness of the thought checked him, and for an infinitesimal fraction of a second his fingers closed again on the small object as though it had been the symbol of all these little habits that chain us to the weary round of life. He released it at last, and letting himself fall on the settee, listened for the first sounds of returning wind.

Not yet. He heard only the wash of water, the heavy splashes, the dull shocks of the confused seas boarding his ship from all sides. She would never have a chance to clear her decks.

But the quietude of the air was startlingly tense and unsafe, like a slender hair holding a sword suspended over his head. By this awful pause the storm penetrated the defences of the man and unsealed his lips. He spoke out in the solitude and the pitch darkness of the cabin, as if addressing another being awakened within his breast.

"I shouldn't like to lose her," he said half aloud.

He sat unseen, apart from the sea, from his ship, isolated, as if withdrawn from the very current of his own existence, where such freaks as talking to himself surely had no place. His palms reposed on his knees, he bowed his short neck and puffed heavily, surrendering to a strange sensation of weariness he was not enlightened enough to recognise for the fatigue of mental stress.

From where he sat he could reach the door of a washstand locker. There should have been a towel there. There was. Good. . . . He took it out, wiped his face, and afterwards went on rubbing his wet head. He towelled himself with energy in the dark, and then remained motionless with the towel on his knees. A moment passed, of a stillness so profound that no one could have guessed there was a man sitting in that cabin. Then a murmur arose.

"She may come out of it yet."

When Captain MacWhirr came out on deck, which he did brusquely, as though he had suddenly become conscious of having stayed away too long, the calm had lasted already more than fifteen minutes—long enough to make itself intolerable even to his imagination. Jukes, motionless on the forepart of the bridge, began to speak at once. His voice, blank and forced as though he were talking through hard-set teeth, seemed to flow away on all sides into the darkness, deepening again upon the sea.

"I had the wheel relieved. Hackett began to sing out that he was done. He's lying in there alongside the steering gear with a face like death. At first I couldn't get anybody to crawl out and relieve the poor devil. That boss'en's worse than no good, I always said. Thought I would have had to go myself and haul out one of them by the neck."

"Ah, well," muttered the Captain. He stood watchful by Jukes' side.

"The second mate's in there too, holding his head. Is he hurt, sir?"

"No—crazy," said Captain MacWhirr, curtly.

"Looks as if he had a tumble, though."

"I had to give him a push," explained the Captain.

Jukes gave an impatient sigh.

"It will come very sudden," said Captain MacWhirr, "and from over there, I fancy. God only knows, though. These books are only good to muddle your head and make you jumpy. It will be bad, and there's an end. If we only can steam her round in time to meet it . . ."

A minute passed. Some of the stars winked rapidly and vanished.

"You left them pretty safe?" began the Captain abruptly, as though the silence were unbearable.

"Are you thinking of the coolies, sir? I rigged life-lines all ways across that 'tween-deck."

"Did you? Good idea, Mr. Jukes."

"I didn't . . . think you cared to . . . know," said Jukes—the lurching of the ship cut his speech as though somebody had been jerking him around while he talked—"how I got on with . . . that infernal job. We did it. And it may not matter in the end."

"Had to do what's fair, for all—they are only Chinamen. Give them the same chance with ourselves—hang it all. She isn't lost yet. Bad enough to be shut up below in a gale—"

"That's what I thought when you gave me the job, sir," interjected Jukes modily.

"—without being battered to pieces," pursued Captain MacWhirr with rising vehemence. "Couldn't let that go on in my ship, if I knew she hadn't five minutes to live. Couldn't bear it, Mr. Jukes."

A hollow echoing noise, like that of a shout rolling in a rocky chasm, approached the ship and went away again. The last star, blurred, enlarged, as if returning to the fiery mist of its beginning, struggled with the colossal depth of blackness hanging over the ship—and went out.

"Now for it!" muttered Captain MacWhirr. "Mr. Jukes."

"Here, sir."

"The two men were growing indistinct to each other.

"We must trust her to go through it and come out on the other side. That's plain and straight. There's no room for Captain Wilson's storm-strategy here."

"No, sir."

"She will be smothered and swept again for hours," mumbled the Captain. "There's not much left by this time above deck for the sea to take away—unless you or me."

"Both, sir," whispered Jukes breathlessly.

"You are always meeting trouble half way, Jukes," Captain MacWhirr remonstrated quaintly. "Though it's a fact that the second mate is no good. D'ye hear, Mr. Jukes? You would be left alone if . . ."

Captain MacWhirr interrupted himself, and Jukes, glancing on all sides, remained silent.

"Don't you be put out by anything," the Captain continued, mumbling rather fast. "Keep her facing it. They may say what they like, but the heaviest seas run with the wind. Facing it—always facing it—that's the way to get through. You are a young sailor. Face it. That's enough for any man. Keep a cool head."

"Yes, sir," said Jukes, with a flutter of the heart.

In the next few seconds the Captain spoke to the engine-room and got an answer.

For some reason Jukes experienced an access of confidence, a sensation that came from outside like a warm breath, and made him feel equal to every demand. The distant muttering of the darkness stole into his ears. He noted it unmoved, out of that sudden belief in himself, as a man safe in a shirt of mail would watch a point.

The ship laboured without intermission amongst the black hills of water, paying with this hard tumbling the price of her life. She rumbled in her depths, shaking a white plummet of steam into the night, and Jukes' thought skimmed like a bird through the engine-room, where Mr. Rout—good man—was ready. When the rumbling ceased it seemed to him that there was a pause of every sound, a dead pause in which Captain MacWhirr's voice rang out startlingly.

"What's that? A puff of wind?"—it spoke much louder than Jukes had ever heard it before—"On the bow. That's right. She may come out of it yet."

The mutter of the winds drew near apace. In the forefront could be distinguished a drowsy waking plaint passing on, and far off the growth of a multiple clamour, marching and expanding. There was the throb as of many drums in it, a vicious rushing note, and like the chant of a tramping multitude.

Jukes could no longer see his captain distinctly. The darkness was absolutely piling itself upon the ship. At most he made out movements, a hint of elbows spread out, of a head thrown up.

Captain MacWhirr was trying to do up the top button of his oilskin coat with unwonted haste. The hurricane, with its power to madden the seas, to sink ships, to uproot trees, to overturn strong walls and dash the very birds of the air to the ground, had found this taciturn man in its path, and, doing its utmost, had managed to wring out a few words. Before the renewed wrath of winds swooped on his ship, Captain MacWhirr was moved to declare, in a tone of vexation, as it were: "I wouldn't like to lose her."

He was spared that annoyance.

VI

On a bright sunshiny day, with the breeze chasing her smoke far ahead, the *Nan-Shan* came into Fu-chau. Her arrival was at once noticed on shore, and the seamen in harbour said: "Look! Look at that steamer. What's that? Siamese—isn't she? Just look at her!"

She seemed, indeed, to have been used as a running target for the secondary batteries of a cruiser. A hail of minor shells could not have given her upper works a more broken, torn, and devastated aspect: and she had about her the worn, weary air of ships coming from the far ends of the world—and indeed with truth, for in her short passage she had been very far; sighting, verily, even the coast of the Great Beyond, whence no ship ever returns to give up her crew to the dust of the earth. She was incrusted and grey with salt to the trucks of her masts and to the top of her funnel; as though (as some facetious seaman said) "the crowd on board had fished her out somewhere from the bottom of the sea and brought her in here for salvage." And further, excited by the felicity of his own wit, he offered to give five pounds for her—"as she stands."

Before she had been quite an hour at rest, a meagre little man, with a red-tipped nose and a face cast in an angry mould, landed from a sampan on the quay of the Foreign Concession, and incontinently turned to shake his fist at her.

A tall individual, with legs much too thin for a rotund stomach, and with watery eyes, strolled up and remarked, "Just left her—eh? Quick work."

He wore a soiled suit of blue flannel with a pair of dirty cricketing shoes; a dingy grey moustache drooped from his lip, and daylight could be seen in two places between the rim and the crown of his hat.

"Hallo! what are you doing here?" asked the ex-second-mate of the *Nan-Shan*, shaking hands hurriedly.

"Standing by for a job—chance worth taking—got a quiet hint," explained the man with the broken hat, in jerky, apathetic wheezes.

The second shook his fist again at the *Nan-Shan*. "There's a fellow there that ain't fit to have the command of a scow," he declared, quivering with passion, while the other looked about listlessly.

"Is there?"

But he caught sight on the quay of a heavy seaman's chest, painted brown under a fringed sailcloth cover, and lashed with new manila line. He eyed it with awakened interest.

"I would talk and raise trouble if it wasn't for that damned Siamese flag. Nobody to go to—or I would make it hot for him. The fraud! Told his chief engineer—that's another fraud for you—I had lost my nerve. The greatest lot of ignorant fools that ever sailed the seas. No! You can't think..."

"Got your money all right?" inquired his seedy acquaintance suddenly.

"Yes. Paid me off on board," raged the second mate. " 'Get your breakfast on shore,' says he."

"Mean skunk!" commented the tall man vaguely, and passed his tongue on his lips. "What about having a drink of some sort?"

"He struck me," hissed the second mate.

"No! Struck! You don't say?" The man in blue began to bustle about sympathetically. "Can't possibly talk here. I want to know all about it. Struck—eh? Let's get a fellow to carry your chest. I know a quiet place where they have some bottled beer...."

Mr. Jukes, who had been scanning the shore through a pair of glasses, informed the chief engineer afterwards that "our late second mate hasn't been long in finding a friend. A chap looking uncommonly like a bummer. I saw them walk away together from the quay."

The hammering and banging of the needful repairs did not disturb Captain MacWhirr. The steward found in the letter he wrote, in a tidy chart-room, passages of such absorbing interest that twice he was nearly caught in the act. But Mrs. MacWhirr, in the drawing-room of the forty-pound house, stifled a yawn—perhaps out of self-respect—for she was alone.

She reclined in a plush-bottomed and gilt hammock-chair near a tiled fireplace, with Japanese fans on the mantel and a glow of coals in the grate. Lifting her hands, she glanced wearily here and there into the many pages. It was not her fault they were so prosy, so completely uninteresting—from "My darling wife" at the beginning, to "Your loving husband" at the end. She couldn't be really expected to understand all these ship affairs. She was glad, of course, to hear from him, but she had never asked herself why, precisely.

"... They are called typhoons... The mate did not seem to like it... Not in books... Couldn't think of letting it go on...."

The paper rustled sharply. ".... A calm that lasted over twenty minutes," she read perfunctorily; and the next words her thoughtless eyes caught, on the top of another page, were: "see you and the children again. . . ." She had a movement of impatience. He was always thinking of coming home. He had never had such a good salary before. What was the matter now!

It did not occur to her to turn back overleaf to look. She would have found it recorded there that between 4 and 6 A.M. on December 25th, Captain MacWhirr did actually think that his ship could not possibly live another hour in such a sea, and that he would never see his wife and children again. Nobody was to know this (his letters got mislaid so quickly)—nobody whatever but the steward, who had been greatly impressed by that disclosure. So much so, that he tried to give the cook some idea of the "narrow squeak we all had" by saying solemnly, "The old man himself had a dam' poor opinion of our chance."

"How do you know?" asked contemptuously the cook, an old soldier, "He hasn't told you, maybe?"

"Well, he did give me a hint to that effect," the steward brazened it out.

"Get along with you! He will be coming to tell *me* next," jeered the old cook over his shoulder.

Mrs. MacWhirr glanced farther, on the alert. " . . . Do what's fair. . . . Miserable objects. . . . Only three, with a broken leg each, and one . . . Thought had better keep the matter quiet . . . hope to have done the fair thing. . . . "

She let fall her hands. No: there was nothing more about coming home. Must have been merely expressing a pious wish. Mrs. MacWhirr's mind was set at ease, and a black marble clock, priced by the local jeweller at £3 18s. 6d., had a discreet stealthy tick.

The door flew open, and a girl in the long-legged, short-frocked period of existence, flung into the room. A lot of colourless, rather lanky hair was scattered over her shoulders. Seeing her mother, she stood still, and directed her pale prying eyes upon the letter.

"From father," murmured Mrs. MacWhirr. "What have you done with your ribbon?"

The girl put her hands up to her head and pouted.

"He's well," continued Mrs. MacWhirr languidly. "At least I think so. He never says." She had a little laugh. The girl's face expressed a wandering indifference, and Mrs. MacWhirr surveyed her with fond pride.

"Go and get your hat," she said after a while. "I am going out to do some shopping. There is a sale at Linom's."

"Oh, how jolly!" uttered the child impressively, in unexpectedly grave vibrating tones, and bounded out of the room.

It was a fine afternoon, with a grey sky and dry sidewalks. Outside the draper's Mrs. MacWhirr smiled upon a woman in a black mantle of generous proportions, armoured in jet and crowned with flowers blooming falsely above a bilious matronly countenance. They broke into a swift little babble of greetings and exclamations both together, very hurried, as if the street were ready to yawn open and swallow all that pleasure before it could be expressed.

Behind them the high glass doors were kept on the swing. People couldn't pass, men stood aside waiting patiently, and Lydia was absorbed in poking the end of her parasol between the stone flags. Mrs. MacWhirr talked rapidly.

"Thank you very much. He's not coming home yet. Of course it's very sad to have him away, but it's such a comfort to know he keeps so well." Mrs. MacWhirr drew breath. "The climate there agrees with him," she added beamingly, as if poor MacWhirr had been away touring in China for the sake of his health.

Neither was the chief engineer coming home yet. Mr. Rout knew too well the value of a good billet.

"Solomon says wonders will never cease," cried Mrs. Rout joyously at the old lady in her armchair by the fire. Mr. Rout's mother moved slightly, her withered hands lying in black half-mittens on her lap.

The eyes of the engineer's wife fairly danced on the paper. "That captain of the ship he is in—a rather simple man, you remember, mother?—has done something rather clever, Solomon says."

"Yes, my dear," said the old woman meekly, sitting with bowed silvery head, and that air of inward stillness characteristic of very old people who seem lost in watching the last flickers of life. "I think I remember."

Solomon Rout, Old Sol, Father Sol, The Chief, "Rout, good man"—Mr. Rout, the condescending and paternal friend of youth, had been the baby of her many children—all dead by this time. And she remembered him best as a boy of ten—long before he went away to serve his apprenticeship in some great engineering works in the North. She had seen so little of him since, she had gone through so many years, that she had now to retrace her steps very far back to recognise him plainly in the mist of time. Sometimes it seemed that her daughter-in-law was talking of some strange man.

Mrs. Rout junior was disappointed. "H'm. H'm." She turned the page. "How provoking! He doesn't say what it is. Says I couldn't understand how much there was in it. Fancy! What could it be so very clever? What a wretched man not to tell us!"

She read on without further remark soberly, and at last sat looking into the fire. The chief wrote just a word or two of the typhoon; but something had moved him to express an increased longing for the companionship of the jolly woman. "If it hadn't been that mother must be looked after, I would send you your passage-money to-day. You could set up a small house out here. I would have a chance to see you sometimes then. We are not growing younger. . . ."

"He's well, mother," sighed Mrs. Rout, rousing herself.

"He always was a strong healthy boy," said the old woman placidly.

But Mr. Jukes' account was really animated and very full. His friend in the Western Ocean trade imparted it freely to the other officers of his liner. "A chap I know writes to me about an extraordinary affair that happened on board his ship in that typhoon—you know—that we read of in the papers two months ago. It's the funniest thing! Just see for yourself what he says. I'll show you his letter."

There were phrases in it calculated to give the impression of light-hearted, indomitable resolution. Jukes had written them in good faith, for he felt thus when he wrote. He described with lurid effect the scenes in the 'tween-deck. ". . . It struck me in a flash that those confounded Chinamen couldn't tell we weren't a desperate kind of robbers. 'Tisn't good to part the Chinaman from his money if he is the stronger party. We need have been desperate indeed to go thieving in such weather, but what could these beggars know of us? So, without thinking of it twice, I got the hands away in a jiffy. Our work was done—that the old man had set his heart on. We cleared out without staying to inquire how they felt. I am convinced that if they had not been so unmercifully shaken, and afraid—each individual one of them—to stand up, we would have been torn to pieces. Oh! It was pretty complete, I can tell you; and you may run to and fro across the Pond to the end of time before you find yourself with such a job on your hands."

After this he alluded professionally to the damage done to the ship, and went on thus:

"It was when the weather quieted down that the situation became confoundedly delicate. It wasn't made any better by us having been lately transferred to the Siamese flag; though the skipper can't see that it makes any difference— 'as long as *we* are on board'—he says. There are feelings that this man simply hasn't got—and there's an end of it. You might just as well try to make a bedpost understand. But apart from this it is an infernally lonely state for a ship to be going about the China seas with no proper consuls, not even a gunboat of her own anywhere, nor a body to go to in case of some trouble.

"My notion was to keep these Johnnies under hatches for another fifteen hours or so; as we weren't much farther than that from Fu-chau. We would find there, most likely, some sort of a man-of-war, and once under her guns we were safe enough; for surely any skipper of a man-of-war—English, French or Dutch— would see white men through as far as row on board goes. We could get rid of them and their money afterwards by delivering them to their Mandarin or Taotai, or whatever they call these chaps in goggles you see being carried about in sedan-chairs through their stinking streets.

"The old man wouldn't see it somehow. He wanted to keep the matter quiet. He got that notion into his head, and a steam windlass couldn't drag it out of him. He wanted as little fuss made as possible, for the sake of the ship's name and for the sake of the owners—'for the sake of all concerned,' says he, looking at me very hard. It made me angry hot. Of course you couldn't keep a thing like that quiet; but the chests had been secured in the usual manner and were safe enough for any earthly gale, while this had been an altogether fiendish business I couldn't give you even an idea of.

"Meantime, I could hardly keep on my feet. None of us had a spell of any sort for nearly thirty hours, and there the old man sat rubbing his chin, rubbing the top of his head, and so bothered he didn't even think of pulling his long boots off.

"'I hope, sir,' says I, 'you won't be letting them out on deck before we make ready for them in some shape or other.' Not, mind you, that I felt very sanguine about controlling these beggars if they meant to take charge. A trouble with a cargo of Chinamen is no child's play. I was dam' tired too. 'I wish,' said I, 'you would let us throw the whole lot of these dollars down to them and leave them to fight it out amongst themselves, while we get a rest.'

"'Now you talk wild, Jukes,' says he, looking up in his slow way that makes you ache all over, somehow. 'We must plan out something that would be fair to all parties.'

"I had no end of work on hand, as you may imagine, so I set the hands going, and then I thought I would turn in a bit. I hadn't been asleep in my bunk ten minutes when in rushes the steward and begins to pull at my leg.

"'For God's sake, Mr. Jukes, come out! Come on deck quick, sir. Oh, do come out!'

"The fellow scared all the sense out of me. I didn't know what had happened: another hurricane—or what. Could hear no wind.

"'The Captain's letting them out. Oh, he is letting them out! Jump on deck, sir, and save us. The chief engineer has just run below for his revolver.'

"That's what I understood the fool to say. However, Father Rout swears he went in there only to get a clean pocket-handkerchief. Anyhow, I made one jump into my trousers and flew on deck aft. There was certainly a good deal of noise going on forward of the bridge. Four of the hands with the boss'en were at work abaft. I passed up to them some of the rifles all the ships on the China coast carry in the cabin, and led them on the bridge. On the way I ran against Old Sol, looking startled and sucking at an unlighted cigar.

"'Come along,' I shouted to him.

"We charged, the seven of us, up to the chart-room. All was over. There stood the old man with his sea-boots still drawn up to the hips and in shirt-sleeves—got warm thinking it out, I suppose. Bun-hin's dandy clerk at his elbow, as dirty as a sweep, was still green in the face. I could see directly I was in for something.

"'What the devil are these monkey tricks, Mr. Jukes?' asks the old man, as angry as ever he could be. I tell you frankly it made me lose my tongue. 'For God's sake, Mr. Jukes,' says he, 'do take away these rifles from the men. Somebody's sure to get hurt before long if you don't. Damme, if this ship isn't worse than Bedlam! Look sharp now. I want you up here to help me and Bun-hin's Chinaman to count that money. You wouldn't mind lending a hand too, Mr. Rout, now you are here. The more of us the better.

"He had settled it all in his mind while I was having a snooze. Had we been an English ship, or only going to land our cargo of coolies in an English port, like Hong-Kong, for instance, there would have been no end of inquiries and bother, claims for damages and so on. But these Chinamen know their officials better than we do.

"The hatches had been taken off already, and they were all on deck after a night and a day down below. It made you feel queer to see so many gaunt, wild faces together. The beggars stared about at the sky, at the sea, at the ship, as though they had expected the whole thing to have been blown to pieces. And no wonder! They had had a doing that would have shaken the soul out of a white man. But then they say a Chinaman has no soul. He has, though, something about him that is deuced tough. There was a fellow (amongst others of the badly hurt) who had had his eye all but knocked out. It stood out of his head the size of half a hen's egg. This would have laid out a white man on his back for a month: and yet there was that chap elbowing here and there in the crowd and talking to the others as if nothing had been the matter. They made a great hubbub amongst themselves, and whenever the olf man showed his bald head on the foreside of the bridge, they would all leave off jawing and look at him from below.

"It seems that after he had done his thinking he made that Bun-hin's fellow go down and explain to them the only way they could get their money back. He told me afterwards that, all the coolies having worked in the same place and for the same length of time, he reckoned he would be doing the fair thing by them as near as possible if he shared all the cash we had picked up equally among the lot. You couldn't tell one man's dollars from another's, he said, and if you asked each man how much money he brought on board he was afraid they would lie, and he would find himself a long way short. I think he was right there. As to giving up the money to any Chinese official he could scare up in Fu-chau, he said he might just as well put the lot in his own pocket at once for all the good it would be to them. I suppose they thought so too.

"We finished the distribution before dark. It was rather a sight: the sea running high, the ship a wreck to look at, these Chinamen staggering up on the bridge one by one for their share, and the old man still booted, and in his shirt-sleeves, busy paying out at the chart-room door, perspiring like anything, and now and then coming down sharp on myself or Father Rout about one thing or another not quite to his mind. He took the share of those who were disabled himself to them on the No.2 hatch. There were three dollars left over, and these went to the three most damaged coolies, one to each. We turned-to afterwards, and shovelled out on deck heaps of wet rags, all sorts of fragments of things without shape, and that you couldn't give a name to, and let them settle the ownership themselves.

"This certainly is coming as near as can be to keeping the thing quiet for the benefit of all concerned. What's your opinion, you pampered mail-boat swell? The old chief says that this was plainly the only thing that could be done. The skipper remarked to me the other day, 'There are things you find nothing about in books.' I think that he got out of it very well for such a stupid man."

AMY
FOSTER

Kennedy is a country doctor, and lives in Colebrook, on the shores of Eastbay. The high ground rising abruptly behind the red roofs of the little town crowds the quaint High Street against the wall which defends it from the sea. Beyond the sea-wall there curves for miles in a vast and regular sweep the barren beach of shingle, with the village of Brenzett standing out darkly across the water, a spire in a clump of trees; and still further out the perpendicular column of a lighthouse, looking in the distance no bigger than a lead-pencil, marks the vanishing-point of the land. The country at the back of Brenzett is low and flat; but the bay is fairly well sheltered from the seas, and occasionally a big ship, windbound or through stress of weather, makes use of the anchoring ground a mile and a half due north from you as you stand at the back door of the "Ship Inn" in Brenzett. A dilapidated windmill near by lifting its shattered arms from a mound no loftier than a rubbish-heap, and a Martello tower squatting at the water's edge half a mile to the south of the Coastguard cottages, are familiar to the skippers of small craft. These are the official seamarks for the patch of trustworthy bottom represented on the Admirality charts by an irregular oval of dots enclosing several figures six, with a tiny anchor engraved among them, and the legend "mud and shells" over all.

The brow of the upland overtops the square tower of the Colebrook Church. The slope is green and looped by a white road. Ascending along this road, you open a valley broad and shallow, a wide green trough of pastures and hedges merging inland into a vista of purple tints and flowing lines closing the view.

In the valley down to Brenzett and Colebrook and up to Darnford, the market town fourteen miles away, lies the practice of my friend Kennedy. He had begun life as surgeon in the Navy, and afterwards had been the companion of a famous traveller, in the days when there were continents with unexplored interiors. His papers on the fauna and flora made him known to scientific societies. And now he had come to a country practice—from choice. The penetrating power of his mind, acting like a corrosive fluid, had destroyed his ambition, I fancy. His intelligence is of a scientific order, of an investigating habit, and of that unappeasable curiosity which believes that there is a particle of a general truth in every mystery.

A good many years ago now, on my return from abroad, he invited me to stay with him. I came readily enough, and as he could not neglect his patients to keep me company, he took me on his rounds—thirty miles or so of an afternoon, sometimes. I waited for him on the roads; the horse reached after

247

the leafy twigs, and, sitting high in the dogcart, I could hear Kennedy's laugh through the half-open door of some cottage. He had a big, hearty laugh that would have fitted a man twice his size, a brisk manner, a bronzed face, and a pair of grey, profoundly attentive eyes. He had the talent of making people talk to him freely, and an inexhaustible patience in listening to their tales.

One day, as we trotted out of a large village into a shady bit of road, I saw on our left hand a low, black cottage, with diamond panes in the windows, a creeper on the end wall, a roof of shingle, and some roses climbing on the rickety trellis-work of the tiny porch. Kennedy pulled up to a walk. A woman, in full sunlight, was throwing a dripping blanket over a line stretched between two old apple-trees. And as the bobtailed, long-necked chestnut, trying to get his head, jerked the left hand, covered by a thick dogskin glove, the doctor raised his voice over the hedge: "How's your child, Amy?"

I had the time to see her dull face, red, not with a mantling blush, but as if her flat cheeks had been vigorously slapped, and to take in the squat figure, the scanty, dusty brown hair drawn into a tight knot at the back of the head. She looked quite young. With a distinct catch in her breath, her voice sounded low and timid.

"He's well, thank you."

We trotted again. "A young patient of yours," I said; and the doctor, flicking the chestnut absently, muttered, "Her husband used to be."

"She seems a dull creature," I remarked listlessly.

"Precisely," said Kennedy. "She is very passive. It's enough to look at the red hands hanging at the end of those short arms, at those slow, prominent brown eyes, to know the inertness of her mind—an inertness that one would think made it everlastingly safe from all the surprises of imagination. And yet which of us is safe? At any rate, such as you see her, she had enough imagination to fall in love. She's the daughter of one Isaac Foster, who from a small farmer has sunk into a shepherd, the beginning of his misfortunes dating from his runaway marriage with the cook of his widowed father—a well-to-do, apoplectic grazier, who passionately struck his name off his will, and had been heard to utter threats against his life. But this old affair, scandalous enough to serve as a motive for a Greek tragedy, arose from the similarity of their characters. There are other tragedies, less scandalous and of a subtler poignancy, arising from irreconcilable differences and from that fear of the Incomprehensible that hangs over all our heads—over all our heads. . . ."

The tired chestnut dropped into a walk; and the rim of the sun, all red in a speckless sky, touched familiarly the smooth top of a ploughed rise near the road as I had seen it times innumerable touch the distant horizon of the sea. The uniform brownness of the harrowed field glowed with a rosy tinge, as though the powdered clods had sweated out in minute pearls of blood the toil of uncounted ploughmen. From the edge of a copse a waggon with two horses was rolling gently along the ridge. Raised above our heads upon the sky-line, it loomed up against the red sun, triumphantly big, enormous, like a chariot of giants drawn by two slow-stepping steeds of legendary proportions. And the clumsy figure of the man plodding at the head of the leading horse projected itself on the background of the Infinite with a heroic uncouthness. The end of his carter's whip quivered high up in the blue. Kennedy discoursed

"She's the eldest of a large family. At the age of fifteen they put her out to service at the New Barns Farm. I attended Mrs. Smith, the tenant's wife, and saw that girl there for the first time. Mrs. Smith, a genteel person with a sharp nose, made her put on a black dress every afternoon. I don't know what induced me to notice her at all. There are faces that call your attention by a curious want of definiteness in their whole aspect, as, walking in a mist, you peer attentively at a vague shape which, after all, may be nothing more curious or strange than a signpost. The only peculiarity I perceived in her was a slight hesitation in her utterance, a sort of preliminary stammer which passes away with the first word. When sharply spoken to, she was apt to lose her head at once; but her heart was of the kindest. She had never been heard to express a dislike for a single human being, and she was tender to every living creature. She was devoted to Mrs. Smith, to Mr. Smith, to their dogs, cats, canaries; and as to Mrs. Smith's grey parrot, its peculiarities exercised upon her a positive fascination. Nevertheless, when that outlandish bird, attacked by the cat, shrieked for help in human accents, she ran out into the yard stopping her ears, and did not prevent the crime. For Mrs. Smith this was another evidence of her stupidity; on the other hand, her want of charm, in view of Smith's well-known frivolousness, was a great recommendation. Her short-sighted eyes would swim with pity for a poor mouse in a trap, and she had been seen once by some boys on her knees in the wet grass helping a toad in difficulties. If it's true, as some German fellow has said, that without phosphorus there is no thought, it is still more true that there is no kindness of heart without a certain amount of imagination. She had some. She had even more than is necessary to understand suffering and to be moved by pity. She fell in love under circumstances that leave no room for doubt in the matter; for you need imagination to form a notion of beauty at all, and still more to discover your ideal in an unfamiliar shape.

"How this aptitude came to her, what it did feed upon, is an inscrutable mystery. She was born in the village, and had never been further away from it than Colebrook or perhaps Darnford. She lived for four years with the Smiths. New Barns is an isolated farmhouse a mile away from the road, and she was content to look day after day at the same fields, hollows, rises; at the trees and the hedgerows; at the faces of the four men about the farm, always the same— day after day, month after month, year after year. She never showed a desire for conversation, and, as it seemed to me, she did not know how to smile. Sometimes of a fine Sunday afternoon she would put on her best dress, a pair of stout boots, a large grey hat trimmed with a black feather (I've seen her in that finery), seize an absurdly slender parasol, climb over two stiles, tramp over three fields and along two hundred yards of road—never further. There stood Foster's cottage. She would help her mother to give their tea to the younger children, wash up the crockery, kiss the little ones, and go back to the farm. That was all. All the rest, all the change, all the relaxation. She never seemed to wish for anything more. And then she fell in love. She fell in love silently, obstinately—perhaps helplessly. It came slowly, but when it came it worked like a powerful spell; it was love as the Ancients understood it: an irresistible and fateful impulse—a possession! Yes, it was in her to become haunted and possessed by a face, by a presence, fatally, as though she had been a pagan worshipper of form under a joyous sky—and to be awakened at last from that mysterious forgetfulness of self, from that enchantment, from that transport, by a fear resembling the unaccountable terror of a brute......"

With the sun hanging low on its western limit, the expanse of the grass-lands framed in the counter-scarps of the rising ground took on a gorgeous and sombre aspect. A sense of penetrating sadness, like that inspired by a grave strain of music, disengaged itself from the silence of the fields. The men we met walked past, slow, unsmiling, with downcast eyes, as if the melancholy of an over-burdened earth had weighted their feet, bowed their shoulders, borne down their glances.

"Yes," said the doctor to my remark, "one would think the earth is under a curse, since of all her children these that cling to her the closest are uncouth in body and as leaden of gait as if their very hearts were loaded with chains. But here on this same road you might have seen amongst these heavy men a being lithe, supple and long-limbed, straight like a pine, with something striving upwards in his appearance as though the heart within him had been buoyant. Perhaps it was only the force of the contrast, but when he was passing one of these villagers here, the soles of his feet did not seem to me to touch the dust of the road. He vaulted over the stiles, paced these slopes with a long elastic stride that made him noticeable at a great distance, and had lustrous black eyes. He was so different from the mankind around that, with his freedom of move-ment, his soft—a little startled, glance, his olive complexion and graceful bear-ing, his humanity suggested to me the nature of a woodland creature. He came from there."

The doctor pointed with his whip, and from the summit of the descent seen over the rolling tops of the trees in a park by the side of the road, appeared the level sea far below us, like the floor of an immense edifice inlaid with bands of dark ripple, with still trails of glitter, ending in a belt of glassy water at the foot of the sky. The light blurr of smoke, from an invisible steamer, faded on the great clearness of the horizon like the mist of a breath on a mirror; and, inshore, the white sails of a coaster, with the appearance of disentangling themselves slowly from under the branches, floated clear of the foliage of the trees.

"Shipwrecked in the bay?" I said.

"Yes; he was a castaway. A poor emigrant from Central Europe bound to America and washed ashore here in a storm. And for him, who knew nothing of the earth, England was an undiscovered country. It was some time before he learned its name; and for all I know he might have expected to find wild beasts or wild men here, when, crawling in the dark over the sea-wall, he rolled down the other side into a dyke, where it was another miracle he didn't get drowned. But he struggled instinctively like an animal under a net, and this blind struggle threw him out into a field. He must have been, indeed, of a tougher fibre than he looked to withstand without expiring such buffetings, the violence of his exertions, and so much fear. Later on, in his broken English that resembled curiously the speech of a young child, he told me himself that he put his trust in God, believing he was no longer in this world. And truly—he would add—how was he to know? He fought his way against the rain and the gale on all fours, and crawled at last among some sheep huddled close under the lee of a hedge. They ran off in all directions, bleating in the darkness, and he welcomed the first familiar sound he heard on these shores. It must have been two in the morning then. And this is all we know of the manner of his landing, though he did not arrive unattended by any means. Only his grisly company did not begin to come ashore till much later in the day. . . ."

The doctor gathered the reins, clicked his tongue; we trotted down the hill. Then turning, almost directly, a sharp corner into the High Street, we rattled over the stones and were home.

Late in the evening Kennedy, breaking a spell of moodiness that had come over him, returned to the story. Smoking his pipe, he paced the long room from end to end. A reading-lamp concentrated all its light upon the papers on his desk; and, sitting by the open window, I saw, after the windless, scorching day, the frigid splendour of a hazy sea lying motionless under the moon. Not a whisper, not a splash, not a stir of the shingle, not a footstep, not a sigh came up from the earth below—never a sign of life but the scent of climbing jasmine: and Kennedy's voice, speaking behind me, passed through the wide casement, to vanish outside in a chill and sumptuous stillness.

". . . .The relations of shipwrecks in the olden time tell us of much suffering. Often the castaways were only saved from drowning to die miserably from starvation on a barren coast; others suffered violent death or else slavery, passing through years of precarious existence with people to whom their strangeness was an object of suspicion, dislike or fear. We read about these things, and they are very pitiful. It is indeed hard upon a man to find himself a lost stranger, helpless, incomprehensible, and of a mysterious origin, in some obscure corner of the earth. Yet amongst all the adventurers shipwrecked in all the wild parts of the world, there is not one, it seems to me, that ever had to suffer a fate so simply tragic as the man I am speaking of, the most innocent of adventurers cast out by the sea in the bight of this bay, almost within sight from this very window.

"He did not know the name of his ship. Indeed, in the course of time we discovered he did not even know that ships had names—'like Christian people'; and when, one day, from the top of the Talfourd Hill, he beheld the sea lying open to his view, his eyes roamed afar, lost in an air of wild surprise, as though he had never seen such a sight before. And probably he had not. As far as I could make out, he had been hustled together with many others on board an emigrant-ship lying at the mouth of the Elbe, too bewildered to take note of his surroundings, too weary to see anything, too anxious to care. They were driven below into the 'tween-deck and battened down from the very start. It was a low timber dwelling—he would say—with wooden beams overhead, like the houses in his country, but you went into it down a ladder. It was very large, very cold, damp and sombre, with places in the manner of wooden boxes where people had to sleep one above another, and it kept on rocking all ways at once all the time. He crept into one of these boxes and lay down there in the clothes in which he had left his home many days before, keeping his bundle and his stick by his side. People groaned, children cried, water dripped, the lights went out, the walls of the place creaked, and everything was being shaken so that in one's little box one dared not lift one's head. He had lost touch with his only companion (a young man from the same valley, he said), and all the time a great noise of wind went on outside and heavy blows fell—boom! boom! An awful sickness overcame him, even to the point of making him neglect his prayers. Besides, one could not tell whether it was morning or evening. It seemed always to be night in that place.

"Before that he had been travelling a long, long time on the iron track. He looked out of the window, which had a wonderfully clear glass in it, and the trees, the houses, the fields, and the long roads seemed to fly round and round about him till his head swam. He gave me to understand that he had on his passage beheld uncounted multitudes of people—whole nations—all dressed in such clothes as the rich wear. Once he was made to get out of the carriage, and slept through a night on a bench in a house of bricks with his bundle under his head; and once for many hours he had to sit on a floor of flat stones dozing, with his knees up and with his bundle between his feet. There was a roof over him, which seemed made of glass, and was so high that the tallest mountain-pine he had ever seen would have had room to grow under it. Steam-machines rolled in at one end and out at the other. People swarmed more than you can see on a feast-day round the miraculous Holy Image in the yard of the Carmelite Convent down in the plains where, before he left his home, he drove his mother in a wooden cart:—a pious old woman who wanted to offer prayers and make a vow for his safety. He could not give me an idea of how large and lofty and full of noise and smoke and gloom, and clang of iron, the place was, but some one had told him it was called Berlin. Then they rang a bell, and another steam-machine came in, and again he was taken on and on through a land that wearied his eyes by its flatness without a single bit of a hill to be seen anywhere. One more night he spent shut up in a building like a good stable with a litter of straw on the floor, guarding his bundle amongst a lot of men, of whom not one could understand a single word he said. In the morning they were all led down to the stony shores of an extremely broad muddy river, flowing not between hills but between houses that seemed immense. There was a steam-machine that went on the water, and they all stood upon it packed tight, only now there were with them many women and children who made much noise. A cold rain fell, the wind blew in his face; he was wet through, and his teeth chattered. He and the young man from the same valley took each other by the hand.

"They thought they were being taken to America straight away, but suddenly the steam-machine bumped against the side of a thing like a great house on the water. The walls were smooth and black, and there uprose, growing from the roof as it were, bare trees in the shape of crosses, extremely high. That's how it appeared to him then, for he had never seen a ship before. This was the ship that was going to swim all the way to America. Voices shouted, everything swayed; there was a ladder dipping up and down. He went up on his hands and knees in mortal fear of falling into the water below, which made a great splashing. He got separated from his companion, and when he descended into the bottom of that ship his heart seemed to melt suddenly within him.

"It was then also, as he told me, that he lost contact for good and all with one of those three men who the summer before had been going about through all the little towns in the foothills of his country. They would arrive on market-days driving in a peasant's cart, and would set up an office in an inn or some other Jew's house. There were three of them, of whom one with a long beard looked venerable; and they had red cloth collars round their necks and gold lace on their sleeves like Government officials. They sat proudly behind a long table; and in the next room, so that the common people shouldn't hear, they kept a cunning telegraph machine, through which they could talk to the Emperor of America. The fathers hung about the door, but the young men of the mountains would crowd up to the table asking many questions, for there was work to be got all the year round at three dollars a day in America, and no military service to do.

"But the American Kaiser would not take everybody. Oh no! He himself had a great difficulty in getting accepted, and the venerable man in uniform had to go out of the room several times to work the telegraph on his behalf. The American Kaiser engaged him at last at three dollars, he being young and strong. However, many able young men backed out, afraid of the great distance; besides, those only who had some money could be taken. There were some who sold their huts and their land because it cost a lot of money to get to America; but then, once there, you had three dollars a day, and if you were clever you could find places where true gold could be picked up on the ground. His father's house was getting over full. Two of his brothers were married and had children. He promised to send money home from America by post twice a year. His father sold an old cow, a pair of piebald mountain ponies of his own raising, and a cleared plot of fair pasture land on the sunny slope of a pine-clad pass to a Jew inn-keeper, in order to pay the people of the ship that took men to America to get rich in a short time.

"He must have been a real adventurer at heart, for how many of the greatest enterprises in the conquest of the earth had for their beginning just such a bargaining away of the paternal cow for the mirage or true gold far away! I have been telling you more or less in my own words what I learned fragmentarily in the course of two or three years, during which I seldom missed an opportunity of a friendly chat with him. He told me this story of his adventure with many flashes of white teeth and lively glances of black eyes, at first in a sort of anxious baby-talk, then, as he acquired the language, with great fluency, but always with that singing, soft, and at the same time vibrating intonation that instilled a strangely penetrating power into the sound of the most familiar English words, as if they had been the words of an unearthly language. And he always would come to an end, with many emphatic shakes of his head, upon that awful sensation of his heart melting within him directly he set foot on board that ship. Afterwards there seemed to come for him a period of blank ignorance, at any rate as to facts. No doubt he must have been abominably seasick and abominably unhappy—this soft and passionate adventurer, taken thus out of his knowledge, and feeling bitterly as he lay in his emigrant bunk his utter loneliness; for his was a highly sensitive nature. The next thing we know of him for certain is that he had been hiding in Hammond's pig-pound by the side of the road to Norton, six miles, as the crow flies, from the sea. Of these experiences he was unwilling to speak: they seemed to have seared into his soul a sombre sort of wonder and indignation. Through the rumours of the country-side, which lasted for a good many days after his arrival, we know that the fishermen of West Colebrook had been disturbed and startled by heavy knocks against the walls of weatherboard cottages, and by a voice crying piercingly strange words in the night. Several of them turned out even, but, no doubt, he had fled in sudden alarm at their rough angry tones hailing each other in the darkness. A sort of frenzy must have helped him up the steep Norton hill. It was he, no doubt, who early the following morning had been seen lying (in a swoon, I should say) on the roadside grass by the Brenzett carrier, who actually got down to have a nearer look, but drew back intimidated by the perfect immobility, and by something queer in the aspect of that tramp, sleeping so still under the showers. As the day advanced, some children came dashing into school at Norton in such a fright that the schoolmistress went out and spoke indignantly to a 'horrid-looking man' on the road. He edged away, hanging his head, for a few steps, and then suddenly ran off with extraordinary fleetness. The driver of Mr. Bradley's milk-cart made no secret of it that he had lashed with his whip at a hairy sort of gipsy fellow who, jumping up at a turn of the road by the Vents, made a snatch at the pony's bridle. And he caught him a good one too, right over the face, he said, that made him drop down in the mud a jolly sight quicker than he had jumped up; but it was a good half a mile before he could stop the pony. Maybe that in his desperate endeavours to get help, and in his need to get in touch with some one, the poor devil had tried to stop the cart. Also three boys confessed afterwards to throwing stones at a funny tramp, knocking about all wet and muddy, and, it seemed, very drunk, in the narrow deep lane by the lime-kilns. All this was the talk of three villages for days; but we have Mrs. Finn's (the wife of Smith's waggoner) unimpeachable testimony that she saw him get over the low wall of Hammond's pig-pound and lurch straight at her, babbling aloud in a voice that was enough to make one die of fright. Having the baby with her in a perambulator, Mrs. Finn called out to him to go away, and as he persisted in coming nearer, she hit him courageously with her umbrella over the head, and, without once looking back, ran like the wind with the perambulator as far as the first house in the village. She stopped then, out of breath, and spoke to old Lewis, hammering there at a heap of stones; and the old chap, taking off his immense black wire goggles, got up on his shaky legs to look where she pointed. Together they followed with their eyes the figure of the man running over a field; they saw him fall down, pick himself up, and run on again, staggering and waving his long arms above his head, in the direction of the New Barns Farm. From that moment he is plainly in the toils of his obscure and touching destiny. There is no doubt after this of what happened to him. All is certain now: Mrs. Smith's intense terror; Amy Foster's stolid conviction held against the other's nervous attack, that the man 'meant no harm'; Smith's exasperation (on his return from Darnford Market) at finding the dog barking himself into a fit, the back-door locked, his wife in hysterics; and all for an unfortunate dirty tramp, supposed to be even then lurking in his stackyard. Was he? He would teach him to frighten women.

"Smith is notoriously hot-tempered, but the sight of some nondescript and miry creature sitting cross-legged amongst a lot of loose straw, and swinging itself to and fro like a bear in a cage, made him pause. Then this tramp stood up silently before him, one mass of mud and filth from head to foot. Smith, alone amongst his stacks with this apparition, in the stormy twilight ringing with the infuriated barking of the dog, felt the dread of an inexplicable strangeness. But when that being, parting with his black hands the long matted locks that hung before his face, as you part the two halves of a curtain, looked out at him with glistening, wild, black-and-white eyes, the weirdness of this silent encounter fairly staggered him. He had admitted since (for the story has been a legitimate subject of conversation about here for years) that he made more than one step backwards. Then a sudden burst of rapid, senseless speech persuaded him at once that he had to do with an escaped lunatic. In fact, that impression never wore off completely. Smith has not in his heart given up his secret conviction of the man's essential insanity to this very day.

"As the creature approached him, jabbering in a most discomposing manner, Smith (unaware that he was being addressed as 'gracious lord,' and adjured in God's name to afford food and shelter) kept on speaking firmly but gently to it, and retreating all the time into the other yard. At last, watching his chance, by a sudden charge he bundled him headlong into the wood-lodge, and instantly shot the bolt. Thereupon he wiped his brow, though the day was cold. He had done his duty to the community by shutting up a wandering and probably dangerous maniac. Smith isn't a hard man at all, but he had room in his brain only for that one idea of lunacy. He was not imaginative enough to ask himself whether the man might not be perishing with cold and hunger. Meantime, at first, the maniac made a great deal of noise in the lodge. Mrs. Smith was screaming upstairs, where she had locked herself in her bedroom; but Amy Foster sobbed piteously at the kitchen-door, wringing her hands and muttering, 'Don't! don't!' I daresay Smith had a rough time of it that evening with one noise and another, and this insane, disturbing voice crying obstinately through the door only added to his irritation. He couldn't possibly have connected this troublesome lunatic with the sinking of a ship in Eastbay, of which there had been a rumour in the Darnford market-place. And I daresay the man inside had been very near to insanity on that night. Before his excitement collapsed and he became unconscious he was throwing himself violently about in the dark, rolling on some dirty sacks, and biting his fists with rage, cold, hunger, amazement, and despair.

"He was a mountaineer of the eastern range of the Carpathians, and the vessel sunk the night before in Eastbay was the Hamburg emigrant-ship *Herzogin Sophia-Dorothea*, of appalling memory.

"A few months later we could read in the papers the accounts of the bogus 'Emigration Agencies' among the Sclavonian peasantry in the more remote provinces of Austria. The object of these scoundrels was to get hold of the poor ignorant people's homesteads, and they were in league with the local usurers. They exported their victims through Hamburg mostly. As to the ship, I had watched her out of this very window, reaching close-hauled under short canvas into the bay on a dark, threatening afternoon. She came to an anchor, correctly by the chart, off the Brenzett Coastguard station. I remember before the night fell looking out again at the outlines of her spars and rigging that stood out dark and pointed on a background of ragged, slaty clouds like another and a slighter spire to the left of the Brenzett church-tower. In the evening the wind rose. At midnight I could hear in my bed the terrific gusts and the sounds of a driving deluge.

"About that time the Coastguardmen thought they saw the lights of a steamer over the anchoring-ground. In a moment they vanished; but it is clear that another vessel of some sort had tried for shelter in the bay on that awful, blind night, had rammed the German ship amidships (a breach—as one of the divers told me afterwards—'that you could sail a Thames barge through') and then had gone out either scathless or damaged, who shall say; but had gone out, unknown, unseen, and fatal, to perish mysteriously at sea. Of her nothing ever came to light, and yet the hue and cry that was raised all over the world

would have found her out if she had been in existence anywhere on the face
of the waters.

"A completeness without a clue, and a stealthy silence as of a neatly executed
crime, characterise this murderous disaster, which, as you may remember, had
its gruesome celebrity. The wind would have prevented the loudest outcries
from reaching the shore; there had been evidently no time for signals of distress.
It was death without any sort of fuss. The Hamburg ship, filling all at once,
capsized as she sank, and at daylight there was not even the end of a spar to
be seen above water. She was missed, of course, and at first the Coastguardmen
surmised that she had either dragged her anchor or parted her cable some time
during the night, and had been blown out to sea. Then, after the tide turned,
the wreck must have shifted a little and released some of the bodies, because a
child—a little fair-haired child in a red frock—came ashore abreast of the Martello tower. By the afternoon you could see along three miles of beach dark
figures with bare legs dashing in and out of the tumbling foam, and rough-
looking men, women with hard faces, children, mostly fair-haired, were being
carried, stiff and dripping, on stretchers, on wattles, on ladders, in a long
procession past the door of the "Ship Inn," to be laid out in a row under the
north wall of the Brenzett Church.

"Officially, the body of the little girl in the red frock is the first thing that
came ashore from that ship. But I have patients amongst the seafaring population
of West Colebrook, and, unofficially, I am informed that very early that morning
two brothers, who went down to look after their cobble hauled up on the beach,
found, a good way from Brenzett, an ordinary ship's hencoop lying high and
dry on the shore, with eleven drowned ducks inside. Their families ate the birds,
and the hencoop was split into firewood with a hatchet. It is possible that a
man (supposing he happened to be on deck at the time of the accident) might
have floated ashore on that hencoop. He might. I admit it is improbable, but
there was the man—and for days, nay, for weeks—it didn't enter our heads
that we had amongst us the only living soul that had escaped from that disaster.
The man himself, even when he learned to speak intelligibly, could tell us very
little. He remembered he had felt better (after the ship had anchored, I suppose),
and that the darkness, the wind, and the rain took his breath away. This looks
as if he had been on deck some time during that night. But we mustn't forget
he had been taken out of his knowledge, that he had been sea-sick and battened
down below for four days, that he had no general notion of a ship or of the
sea, and therefore could have no definite idea of what was happening to him.
The rain, the wind, the darkness he knew; he understood the bleating of the
sheep, and he remembered the pain of his wretchedness and misery, his heart-
broken astonishment that it was neither seen nor understood, his dismay at
finding all the men angry and all the women fierce. He had approached them
as a beggar, it is true, he said; but in his country, even if they gave nothing,
they spoke gently to beggars. The children in his country were not taught to
throw stones at those who asked for compassion. Smith's strategy overcame
him completely. The wood-lodge presented the horrible aspect of a dungeon.
What would be done to him next?.....No wonder that Amy Foster appeared
to his eyes with the aureole of an angel of light. The girl had not been able to
sleep for thinking of the poor man, and in the morning, before the Smiths were
up, she slipped out across the back yard. Holding the door of the wood-lodge

ajar, she looked in and extended to him half a loaf of white bread—'such bread as the rich eat in my country,' he used to say.

"At this he got up slowly from amongst all sorts of rubbish, stiff, hungry, trembling, miserable, and doubtful. 'Can you eat this?' she asked in her soft and timid voice. He must have taken her for a 'gracious lady.' He devoured ferociously, and tears were falling on the crust. Suddenly he dropped the bread, seized her wrist, and imprinted a kiss on her hand. She was not frightened. Through his forlorn condition she had observed that he was good-looking. She shut the door and walked back slowly to the kitchen. Much later on, she told Mrs. Smith, who shuddered at the bare idea of being touched by that creature.

"Through this act of impulsive pity he was brought back again within the pale of human relations with his new surroundings. He never forgot it—never.

"That very same morning old Mr. Swaffer (Smith's nearest neighbour) came over to give his advice, and ended by carrying him off. He stood, unsteady on his legs, meek, and caked over in half-dried mud, while the two men talked around him in an incomprehensible tongue. Mrs. Smith had refused to come downstairs till the madman was off the premises; Amy Foster, far from within the dark kitchen, watched through the open back door; and he obeyed the signs that were made to him to the best of his ability. But Smith was full of mistrust. 'Mind, sir! It may be all his cunning,' he cried repeatedly in a tone of warning. When Mr. Swaffer started the mare, the deplorable being sitting humbly by his side, through weakness, nearly fell out over the back of the high two-wheeled cart. Swaffer took him straight home. And it is then that I come upon the scene.

"I was called in by the simple process of the old man beckoning to me with his forefinger over the gate of his house as I happened to be driving past. I got down, of course.

"'I've got something here,' he mumbled, leading the way to an outhouse at a little distance from his other farm-buildings.

"It was there that I saw him first, in a long low room taken upon the space of that sort of coach-house. It was bare and whitewashed, with a small square aperture glazed with one cracked, dusty pane at its further end. He was lying on his back upon a straw pallet; they had given him a couple of horse-blankets, and he seemed to have spent the remainder of his strength in the exertion of cleaning himself. He was almost speechless; his quick breathing under the blankets pulled up to his chin, his glittering, restless black eyes reminded me of a wild bird caught in a snare. While I was examining him, old Swaffer stood silently by the door, passing the tips of his fingers along his shaven upper lip. I gave some directions, promised to send a bottle of medicine, and naturally made some inquiries.

"'Smith caught him in the stackyard at New Barns,' said the old chap in his deliberate, unmoved manner, and as if the other had been indeed a sort of wild animal, 'That's how I came by him. Quite a curiosity, isn't he? Now tell me, doctor—you've been all over the world—don't you think that's a bit of a Hindoo we've got hold of here.'

"I was greatly surprised. His long black hair scattered over the straw bolster contrasted with the olive pallor of his face. It occurred to me he might be a Basque. It didn't necessarily follow that he should understand Spanish; but I tried him with the few words I know, and also with some French. The whispered sounds I caught by bending my ear to his lips puzzled me utterly. That afternoon the young ladies from the Rectory (one of them read Goethe with a dictionary, and the other had struggled with Dante for years), coming to see Miss Swaffer, tried their German and Italian on him from the doorway. They retreated, just the least bit scared by the flood of passionate speech which, turning on his pallet, he let out at them. They admitted that the sound was pleasant, soft, musical—but, in conjunction with his looks perhaps, it was startling—so excitable, so utterly unlike anything one had ever heard. The village boys climbed up the bank to have a peep through the little square aperture. Everybody was wondering what Mr. Swaffer would do with him.

"He simply kept him.

"Swaffer would be called eccentric were he not so much respected. They will tell you that Mr. Swaffer sits up as late as ten o'clock at night to read books, and they will tell you also that he can write a cheque for two hundred pounds without thinking twice about it. He himself would tell you that the Swaffers had owned land between this and Darnford for these three hundred years. He must be eighty-five to-day, but he does not look a bit older than when I first came here. He is a great breeder of sheep, and deals extensively in cattle. He attends market days for miles around in every sort of weather, and drives sitting bowed low over the reins, his lank grey hair curling over the collar of his warm coat, and with a green plaid rug round his legs. The calmness of advanced age gives a solemnity to his manner. He is clean-shaved; his lips are thin and sensitive; something rigid and monachal in the set of his features lends a certain elevation to the character of his face. He has been known to drive miles in the rain to see a new kind of rose in somebody's garden, or a monstrous cabbage grown by a cottager. He loves to hear tell of or to be shown something what he calls 'outlandish.' Perhaps it was just that outlandishness of the man which influenced old Swaffer. Perhaps it was only an inexplicable caprice. All I know is that at the end of three weeks I caught sight of Smith's lunatic digging in Swaffer's kitchen garden. They had found out he could use a spade. He dug barefooted.

"His black hair flowed over his shoulders. I suppose it was Swaffer who had given him the striped old cotton shirt; but he wore still the national brown cloth trousers (in which he had been washed ashore) fitting to the leg almost like tights; was belted with a broad leathern belt studded with little brass discs; and had never yet ventured into the village. The land he looked upon seemed to him kept neatly, like the grounds round a landowner's house; the size of the cart-horses struck him with astonishment; the roads resembled garden walks, and the aspect of the people, especially on Sundays, spoke of opulence. He wondered what made them so hardhearted and their children so bold. He got his food at the back door, carried it in both hands, carefully, to his outhouse, and, sitting alone on his pallet, would make the sign of the cross before he began. Beside the same pallet, kneeling in the early darkness of the short days, he recited aloud the Lord's Prayer before he slept. Whenever he saw old Swaffer he would bow with veneration from the waist, and stand erect while the old man, with his fingers over his upper lip, surveyed him silently. He bowed also to Miss Swaffer, who kept house frugally for her father—a broad-shouldered, big-boned woman of forty-five, with the pocket of her dress full of keys, and a grey, steady eye. She was Church—as people said (while her father was one of the trustees of the Baptist Chapel)—and wore a little steel cross at her waist. She dressed severely in black, in memory of one of the innumerable Bradleys of the neighbourhood, to whom she had been engaged some twenty-five years ago—a young farmer who broke his neck out hunting on the eve of the wedding-day. She had the unmoved countenance of the deaf, spoke very seldom, and her lips, thin like her father's, astonished one sometimes by a mysteriously ironic curl.

"These were the people to whom he owed allegiance, and an overwhelming loneliness seemed to fall from the leaden sky of that winter without sunshine. All the faces were sad. He could talk to no one, and had no hope of ever understanding anybody. It was as if these had been the faces of people from the other world—dead people—he used to tell me years afterwards. Upon my word, I wonder he did not go mad. He didn't know where he was. Somewhere very far from his mountains—somewhere over the water. Was this America, he wondered?

"If it hadn't been for the steel cross at Miss Swaffer's belt he would not, he confessed, have known whether he was in a Christian country at all. He used to cast stealthy glances at it, and feel comforted. There was nothing here the same as in his country! The earth and the water were different; there were no images of the Redeemer by the roadside. The very grass was different, and the trees. All the trees but the three old Norway pines on the bit of lawn before Swaffer's house, and these reminded him of his country. He had been detected once, after dusk, with his forehead against the trunk of one of them, sobbing, and talking to himself. They had been like brothers to him at that time, he affirmed. Everything else was strange. Conceive you the kind of an existence over-shadowed, oppressed, by the everyday material appearances, as if by the visions of a nightmare. At night, when he could not sleep, he kept on thinking of the girl who gave him the first piece of bread he had eaten in this foreign land. She had been neither fierce nor angry, nor frightened. Her face he re-membered as the only comprehensible face amongst all these faces that were as closed, as mysterious, and as mute as the faces of the dead who are possessed of a knowledge beyond the comprehension of the living. I wonder whether the memory of her compassion prevented him from cutting his throat. But there! I suppose I am an old sentimentalist, and forget the instinctive love of life which it takes all the strength of an uncommon despair to overcome.

"He did the work which was given him with an intelligence which surprised old Swaffer. By-and-by it was discovered that he could help at the ploughing, could milk the cows, feed the bullocks in the cattle-yard, and was of some use with the sheep. He began to pick up words, too, very fast; and suddenly, one fine morning in spring, he rescued from an untimely death a grand-child of old Swaffer.

"Swaffer's younger daughter is married to Willcox, a solicitor and the Town Clerk of Colebrook. Regularly twice a year they come to stay with the old man for a few days. Their only child, a little girl not three years old at the time, ran out of the house alone in her little white pinafore, and, toddling across the grass of a terraced garden, pitched herself over a low wall head first into the horsepond in the yard below.

"Our man was out with the waggoner and the plough in the field nearest to the house, and as he was leading the team round to begin a fresh furrow, he saw, through the gap of a gate, what for anybody else would have been a mere flutter of something white. But he had straight-glancing, quick, far-reach-ing eyes, that only seemed to flinch and lose their amazing power before the immensity of the sea. He was barefooted, and looking as outlandish as the heart of Swaffer could desire. Leaving the horses on the turn, to the inexpressible disgust of the waggoner he bounded off, going over the ploughed ground in long leaps, and suddenly appeared before the mother, thrust the child into her arms, and strode away.

"The pond was not very deep; but still, if he had not had such good eyes, the child would have perished—miserably suffocated in the foot or so of sticky mud at the bottom. Old Swaffer walked out slowly into the field, waited till the plough came over to his side, had a good look at him, and without saying a word went back to the house. But from that time they laid out his meals on the kitchen table; and at first, Miss Swaffer, all in black and with an inscrutable face, would come and stand in the doorway of the living-room to see him make a big sign of the cross before he fell to. I believe that from that day, too, Swaffer began to pay him regular wages.

"I can't follow step by step his development. He cut his hair short, was seen in the village and along the road going to and fro to his work like any other man. Children ceased to shout after him. He became aware of social differences, but remained for a long time surprised at the bare poverty of the churches among so much wealth. He couldn't understand either why they were kept shut up on week-days. There was nothing to steal in them. Was it to keep people from praying too often? The rectory took much notice of him about that time, and I believe the young ladies attempted to prepare the ground for his conversion. They could not, however, break him of his habit of crossing himself, but he went so far as to take off the string with a couple of brass medals the size of a sixpence, a tiny metal cross, and a square sort of scapulary which he wore round his neck. He hung them on the wall by the side of his bed, and he was still to be heard every evening reciting the Lord's Prayer, in incomprehensible words and in a slow, fervent tone, as he had heard his old father do at the head of all the kneeling family, big and little, on every evening of his life. And though he wore corduroys at work, and a slop-made pepper-and-salt suit on Sundays, strangers would turn round to look after him on the road. His foreignness had a peculiar and indelible stamp. At last people became used to see him. But they never became used to him. His rapid, skimming walk; his swarthy complexion; his hat cocked on the left ear; his habit, on warm evenings, of wearing his coat over one shoulder, like a hussar's dolman; his manner of leaping over the stiles, not as a feat of agility, but in the ordinary course of progression—all these peculiarities were, as one may say, so many causes of scorn and offense to the inhabitants of the village. They wouldn't in their dinner hour lie flat on their backs on the grass to stare at the sky. Neither did they go about the fields screaming dismal tunes. Many times have I heard his high-pitched voice from behind the ridge of some sloping sheep-walk, a voice light and soaring, like a lark's, but with a melancholy human note, over our fields that hear only the song of birds. And I should be startled myself. Ah! He was different: innocent of heart, and full of good will, which nobody wanted, this castaway, that, like a man transplanted into another planet, was separated by an immense space from his past and by an immense ignorance from his future. His quick, fervent utterance positively shocked everybody. "An excitable devil," they called him. One evening, in the tap-room of the Coach and Horses, (having drunk some whisky), he upset them all by singing a love-song of his country. They hooted him down, and he was pained; but Preble, the lame wheelwright, and Vincent, the fat blacksmith, and the other notables too, wanted to drink their evening beer in peace. On another occasion he tried to show them how to dance. The dust rose in clouds from the sanded floor; he leaped straight up amongst the deal tables, struck his heels together, squatted on one heel in front of old Preble, shooting out the other leg, uttered wild and exulting cries, jumped up to whirl on one foot, snapping his fingers above his head—and a strange carter who was having a drink in there began to swear, and cleared out with his half-pint in his hand into the bar. But when suddenly he sprang upon a table and continued to dance among the glasses, the landlord interfered. He didn't want any "accrobat tricks in the tap-room." They laid their hands on him. Having had a glass or two, Mr. Swaffer's foreigner tried to expostulate: was ejected forcibly: got a black eye.

"I believe he felt the hostility of his human surroundings. But he was tough—tough in spirit, too, as well as in body. Only the memory of the sea frightened him, with that vague terror that is left by a bad dream. His home was far away; and he did not want now to go to America. I had often explained to him that there is no place on earth where true gold can be found lying ready and to be got for the trouble of the picking up. How then, he asked, could he ever return home with empty hands when there had been sold a cow, two ponies, and a bit of land to pay for his going? His eyes would fill with tears, and, averting them from the immense shimmer of the sea, he would throw himself face down on the grass. But sometimes, cocking his hat with a little conquering air, he would defy my wisdom. He had found his bit of true gold. That was Amy Foster's heart; which was "a golden heart, and soft to people's misery," he would say in the accents of overwhelming conviction.

"He was called Yanko. He had explained that this meant Little John; but as he would also repeat very often that he was a mountaineer (some word sounding in the dialect of his country like Goorall) he got it for his surname. And this is the only trace of him that the succeeding ages may find in the marriage register of the parish. There it stands—Yanko Goorall—in the rector's handwriting. The crooked cross made by the cast-away, a cross whose tracing no doubt seemed to him the most solemn part of the whole ceremony, is all that remains now to perpetuate the memory of his name.

"His courtship had lasted some time—ever since he got his precarious footing in the community. It began by his buying for Amy Foster a green satin ribbon in Darnford. This was what you did in his country. You bought a ribbon at a Jew's stall on a fair-day. I don't suppose the girl knew what to do with it, but he seemed to think that his honourable intentions could not be mistaken.

"It was only when he declared his purpose to get married that I fully understood how, for a hundred futile and inappreciable reasons, how—shall I say odious?—he was to all the countryside. Every old woman in the village was up in arms. Smith, coming upon him near the farm, promised to break his head for him if he found him about again. But he twisted his little black moustache with such a bellicose air and rolled such big, black fierce eyes at Smith that this promise came to nothing. Smith, however, told the girl that she must be mad to take up with a man who was surely wrong in his head. All the same, when she heard him in the gloaming whistle from beyond the orchard a couple of bars of a weird and mournful tune, she would drop whatever she had in her hand—she would leave Mrs. Smith in the middle of a sentence—and she would run out to his call. Mrs. Smith called her a shameless hussy. She answered nothing. She said nothing at all to anybody, and went on her way as if she had been deaf. She and I alone all in the land, I fancy, could see his very real beauty. He was very good-looking, and most graceful in his bearing, with that something wild as of a woodland creature in his aspect. Her mother moaned over her dismally whenever the girl came to see her on her day out. The father was surly, but pretended not to know; and Mrs. Finn once told her plainly that 'this man, my dear, will do you some harm some day yet.' And so it went on. They could be seen on the roads, she tramping stolidly in her finery—grey dress, black feather, stout boots, prominent white cotton gloves that caught your eye a hundred yards away; and he, his coat slung picturesquely over one shoulder, pacing by her side, gallant of bearing and casting tender glances upon the girl with the golden heart. I wonder whether he saw how plain she was. Perhaps among types so different from what he had ever seen, he had not the power to judge; or perhaps he was seduced by the divine quality of her pity.

"Yanko was in great trouble meantime. In his country you get an old man for an ambassador in marriage affairs. He did not know how to proceed. However, one day in the midst of sheep in a field (he was now Swaffer's under-shepherd with Foster) he took off his hat to the father and declared himself humbly. 'I daresay she's fool enough to marry you,' was all Foster said. 'And then,' he used to relate, 'he puts his hat on his head, looks black at me as if he wanted to cut my throat, whistles the dog, and off he goes, leaving me to do the work.' The Fosters, of course, didn't like to lose the wages the girl earned: Amy used to give all her money to her mother. But there was in Foster a very genuine aversion to that match. He contended that the fellow was very good with sheep, but was not fit for any girl to marry. For one thing, he used to go along the hedges muttering to himself like a dam' fool; and then, these foreigners behave very queerly to women sometimes. And perhaps he would want to carry her off somewhere—or run off himself. It was not safe. He preached it to his daughter that the fellow might ill-use her in some way. She made no answer. It was, they said in the village, as if the man had done something to her. People discussed the matter. It was quite an excitement, and the two went on "walking out" together in the face of opposition. Then something unexpected happened.

"I don't know whether old Swaffer ever understood how much he was regarded in the light of a father by his foreign retainer. Anyway the relation was curiously feudal. So when Yanko asked formally for an interview—'and the Miss too' (he called the severe, deaf Miss Swaffer simply *Miss*)—it was to obtain their permission to marry. Swaffer heard him unmoved, dismissed him by a nod, and then shouted the intelligence into Miss Swaffer's best ear. She showed no surprise, and only remarked grimly, in a veiled blank voice, 'He certainly won't get any other girl to marry him.'

"It is Miss Swaffer who has all the credit of the munificence: but in a very few days it came out that Mr. Swaffer had presented Yanko with a cottage (the cottage you've seen this morning) and something like an acre of ground—had made it over to him in absolute property. Willcox expedited the deed, and I remember him telling me he had a great pleasure in making it ready. It recited: 'In consideration of saving the life of my beloved grandchild, Bertha Willcox.'

"Of course, after that no power on earth could prevent them from getting married.

"Her infatuation endured. People saw her going out to meet him in the evening. She stared with unblinking, fascinated eyes up the road where he was expected to appear, walking freely, with a swing from the hip, and humming one of the love-tunes of his country. When the boy was born, he got elevated at the 'Coach and Horses,' essayed again a song and a dance, and was again ejected. People expressed their commiseration for a woman married to that Jack-in-the-box. He didn't care. There was a man now (he told me boastfully) to whom he could sing and talk in the language of his country, and show how to dance by-and-by.

"But I don't know. To me he appeared to have grown less springy of step, heavier in body, less keen of eye. Imagination, no doubt; but it seems to me now as if the net of fate had been drawn closer round him already.

"One day I met him on the footpath over the Talfourd Hill. He told me that 'women were funny.' I had heard already of domestic differences. People were saying that Amy Foster was beginning to find out what sort of man she had married. He looked upon the sea with indifferent, unseeing eyes. His wife had snatched the child out of his arms one day as he sat on the doorstep crooning to it a song such as the mothers sing to babies in his mountains. She seemed to think he was doing it some harm. Women are funny. And she had objected to him praying aloud in the evening. Why? He expected the boy to repeat the prayer aloud after him by-and-by, as he used to do after his old father when he was a child—in his own country. And I discovered he longed for their boy to grow up so that he could have a man to talk with in that language that to our ears sounded so distrubing, so passionate, and so bizarre. Why his wife should dislike the idea he couldn't tell. But that would pass, he said. And tilting his head knowingly, he tapped his breastbone to indicate that she had a good heart: not hard, not fierce, open to compassion, charitable to the poor!

"I walked away thoughtfully; I wondered whether his difference, his strangeness, were not penetrating with repulsion that dull nature they had begun by irresistibly attracting. I wondered . . ."

The Doctor came to the window and looked out at the frigid splendour of the sea, immense in the haze, as if enclosing all the earth with all the hearts lost among the passions of love and fear.

"Physiologically, now," he said, turning away abruptly, "it was possible. It was possible."

He remained silent. Then went on—

"At all events, the next time I saw him he was ill—lung trouble. He was tough, but I daresay he was not acclimatised as well as I had supposed. It was a bad winter; and, of course, these mountaineers do get fits of home sickness; and a state of depression would make him vulnerable. He was lying half dressed on a couch downstairs.

"A table covered with a dark oilcloth took up all the middle of the little room. There was a wicker cradle on the floor, a kettle spouting steam on the hob, and some child's linen lay drying on the fender. The room was warm, but the door opens right into the garden, as you noticed perhaps.

"He was very feverish, and kept on muttering to himself. She sat on a chair and looked at him fixedly across the table with her brown, blurred eyes. 'Why don't you have him upstairs?' I asked. With a start and a confused stammer she said, 'Oh! ah! I couldn't sit with him upstairs, sir?'

"I gave her certain directions; and going outside, I said again that he ought to be in bed upstairs. She wrung her hands. 'I couldn't. I couldn't. He keeps on saying something—I don't know what.' With the memory of all the talk against the man that had been dinned into her ears, I looked at her narrowly. I looked into her short-sighted eyes, at her dumb eyes that once in her life had seen an enticing shape, but seemed, staring at me, to see nothing at all now. But I saw she was uneasy.

"'What's the matter with him?' she asked in a sort of vacant trepidation. 'He doesn't look very ill. I never did see anybody look like this before....'

"'Do you think,' I asked indignantly, 'he is shamming?'

"'I can't help it, sir,' she said stolidly. And suddenly she clapped her hands and looked right and left. 'And there's the baby. I am so frightened. He wanted me just now to give him the baby. I can't understand what he says to it.'

"'Can't you ask a neighbour to come in to-night?' I asked.

"'Please, sir, nobody seems to care to come,' she muttered, dully resigned all at once.

"I impressed upon her the necessity of the greatest care, and then had to go. There was a good deal of sickness that winter. 'Oh, I hope he won't talk!' she exclaimed softly just as I was going away.

"I don't know how it is I did not see—but I didn't. And yet, turning in my trap, I saw her lingering before the door, very still, and as if meditating a flight up the miry road.

"Towards the night his fever increased.

"He tossed, moaned, and now and then muttered a complaint. And she sat with the table between her and the couch, watching every movement and every sound, with the terror, the unreasonable terror, of that man she could not understand creeping over her. She had drawn the wicker cradle close to her feet. There was nothing in her now but the maternal instinct and that unaccountable fear.

"Suddenly coming to himself, parched, he demanded a drink of water. She did not move. She had not understood, though he may have thought he was speaking in English. He waited, looking at her, burning with fever, amazed at her silence and immobility, and then he shouted impatiently, 'Water! Give me water!'

"She jumped to her feet, snatched up the child, and stood still. He spoke to her, and his passionate remonstrances only increased her fear of that strange man. I believe he spoke to her for a long time, entreating, wondering, pleading, ordering, I suppose. She says she bore it as long as she could. And then a gust of rage came over him.

"He sat up and called out terribly one word—some word. Then he got up as though he hadn't been ill at all, she says. And as in fevered dismay, indignation, and wonder he tried to get to her round the table, she simply opened the door and ran out with the child in her arms. She heard him call twice after her down the road in a terrible voice—and fled.... Ah! but you should have seen stirring behind the dull, blurred glance of these eyes the spectre of the fear which had hunted her on that night three miles and a half to the door of Foster's cottage! I did the next day.

"And it was I who found him lying face down and his body in a puddle, just outside the little wicker-gate.

"I had been called out that night to an urgent case in the village, and on my way home at daybreak passed by the cottage. The door stood open. My man helped me to carry him in. We laid him on the couch. The lamp smoked, the fire was out, the chill of the stormy night oozed from the cheerless yellow paper on the wall. 'Amy!' I called aloud, and my voice seemed to lose itself in the emptiness of this tiny house as if I had cried in a desert. He opened his eyes. 'Gone!' he said distinctly. 'I had only asked for water—only for a little water. . . .'

"He was muddy. I covered him up and stood waiting in silence, catching a painfully gasped word now and then. They were no longer in his own language. The fever had left him, taking with it the heat of life. And with his panting breast and lustrous eyes he reminded me again of a wild creature under the net; of a bird caught in a snare. She had left him. She had left him—sick—helpless—thirsty. The spear of the hunter had entered his very soul. 'Why?' he cried in the penetrating and indignant voice of a man calling to a responsible Maker. A gust of wind and a swish of rain answered.

"And as I turned away to shut the door he pronounced the word 'Merciful!' and expired.

"Eventually I certified heart-failure as the immediate cause of death. His heart must have indeed failed him, or else he might have stood this night of storm and exposure, too. I closed his eyes and drove away. Not very far from the cottage I met Foster walking sturdily between the dripping hedges with his collie at his heels.

"'Do you know where your daughter is?' I asked.

"'Don't I!' he cried. 'I am going to talk to him a bit. Frightening a poor woman like this.'

"'He won't frighten her any more,' I said. 'He is dead.'

"He struck with his stick at the mud.

"'And there's the child.'

"Then, after thinking deeply for a while—

"'I don't know that it isn't for the best.'

"That's what he said. And she says nothing at all now. Not a word of him. Never. Is his image as utterly gone from her mind as his lithe and striding figure, his carolling voice are gone from our fields? He is no longer before her eyes to excite her imagination into a passion of love or fear; and his memory seems to have vanished from her dull brain as a shadow passes away upon a white screen. She lives in the cottage and works for Miss Swaffer. She is Amy Foster for everybody, and the child is 'Amy Foster's boy.' She calls him Johnny—which means Little John.

"It is impossible to say whether this name recalls anything to her. Does she ever think of the past? I have seen her hanging over the boy's cot in a very passion of maternal tenderness. The little fellow was lying on his back, a little frightened at me, but very still, with his big black eyes, with his fluttered air of a bird in a snare. And looking at him I seemed to see again the other one—the father, cast out mysteriously by the sea to perish in the supreme disaster of loneliness and despair."

FALK—
A REMINISCENCE

Several of us, all more or less connected with the sea, were dining in a small river-hostelry not more than thirty miles from London, and less than twenty from that shallow and dangerous puddle to which our coasting men give the grandiose name of "German Ocean." And through the wide windows we had a view of the Thames; an enfilading view down the Lower Hope Reach. But the dinner was execrable, and all the feast was for the eyes.

That flavour of salt-water which for so many of us had been the very water of life permeated our talk. He who hath known the bitterness of the Ocean shall have its taste for ever in his mouth. But one or two of us, pampered by the life of the land, complained of hunger. It was impossible to swallow any of that stuff. And indeed there was a strange mustiness in everything. The wooden dining-room stuck out over the mud of the shore like a lacustrine dwelling; the planks of the floor seemed rotten; a decrepid old waiter tottered pathetically to and fro before an antediluvian and worm-eaten sideboard; the chipped plates might have been disinterred from some kitchen midden near an inhabited lake; and the chops recalled times more ancient still. They brought forcibly to one's mind the night of ages when the primeval man, evolving the first rudiments of cookery from his dim consciousness, scorched lumps of flesh at a fire of sticks in the company of other good fellows; then, gorged and happy, sat him back among the gnawed bones to tell his artless tales of experience—the tales of hunger and hunt—and of women, perhaps!

But luckily the wine happened to be as old as the waiter. So, comparatively empty, but upon the whole fairly happy, we sat back and told our artless tales. We talked of the sea and all its works. The sea never changes, and its works for all the talk of men are wrapped in mystery. But we agreed that the times were changed. And we talked of old ships, of sea-accidents, of break-downs, dismastings; and of a man who brought his ship safe to Liverpool all the way from the River Platte under a jury rudder. We talked of wrecks, of short rations and of heroism—or at least of what the newspapers would have called heroism at sea—a manifestation of virtues quite different from the heroism of primitive times. And now and then falling silent all together we gazed at the sights of the river.

A P. & O. boat passed bound down. "One gets jolly good dinners on board these ships," remarked one of our band. A man with sharp eyes read out the name on her bows: *Arcadia*. "What a beautiful model of a ship!" murmured some of us. She was followed by a small cargo-steamer, and the flag they hauled down aboard while we were looking showed her to be a Norwegian. She made an awful lot of smoke; and before it had quite blown away, a high-sided, short, wooden barque, in ballast and towed by a paddle-tug, appeared in front of the windows. All her hands were forward busy setting up the headgear; and aft a woman in a red hood, quite alone with the man at the wheel, paced the length of the poop back and forth, with the grey wool of some knitting work in her hands.

"German I should think," muttered one. "The skipper has his wife on board," remarked another; and the light of the crimson sunset all ablaze behind the London smoke, throwing a glow of Bengal light upon the barque's spars, faded away from the Hope Reach.

Then one of us, who had not spoken before, a man of over fifty, that had commanded ships for a quarter of a century, looking after the barque now gliding far away, all black on the lustre of the river, said:

This reminds me of an absurd episode in my life, now many years ago, when I got first the command of an iron barque, loading then in a certain Eastern seaport. It was also the capital of an Eastern kingdom, lying up a river as might be London lies up this old Thames of ours. No more need be said of the place; for this sort of thing might have happened anywhere where there are ships, skippers, tugboats, and orphan nieces of indescribable splendour. And the absurdity of the episode concerns only me, my enemy Falk, and my friend Hermann.

There seemed to be something like peculiar emphasis on the words "My friend Hermann," which caused one of us (for we had just been speaking of heroism at sea) to say idly and nonchalantly:

"And was this Hermann a hero?"

Not at all, said our grizzled friend. No hero at all. He was a Schiff-führer: Ship-conductor. That's how they call a Master Mariner in Germany. I prefer our way. The alliteration is good, and there is something in the nomenclature that gives to us as a body the sense of corporate existence: Apprentice, Mate, Master, in the ancient and honourable craft of the sea. As to my friend Hermann, he might have been a consummate master of the honourable craft, but he was called officially Schiff-führer, and had the simple, heavy appearance of a well-to-do farmer, combined with the good-natured shrewdness of a small shopkeeper. With his shaven chin, round limbs, and heavy eyelids he did not look like a toiler, and even less like an adventurer of the sea. Still, he toiled upon the seas, in his own way, much as a shopkeeper works behind his counter. And his ship was the means by which he maintained his growing family.

She was a heavy, strong, blunt-bowed affair, awakening the ideas of primitive solidity, like the wooden plough of our forefathers. And there were, about her, other suggestions of a rustic and homely nature. The extraordinary timber projections which I have seen in no other vessel made her square stern resemble the tail end of a miller's waggon. But the four stern ports of her cabin, glazed with six little greenish panes each, and framed in wooden sashes painted brown, might have been the windows of a cottage in the country. The tiny white curtains and the greenery of flower-pots behind the glass completed the resemblance. On one or two occasions when passing under her stern I had detected from my boat a round arm in the act of tilting a watering-pot, and the bowed sleek head of a maiden whom I shall always call Hermann's niece, because as a matter of fact I've never heard her name, for all my intimacy with the family.

This, however, sprang up later on. Meantime in common with the rest of the shipping in that Eastern port, I was left in no doubt as to Hermann's notions of hygienic clothing. Evidently he believed in wearing good stout flannel next his skin. On most days little frocks and pinafores could be seen drying in the mizzen rigging of his ship, or a tiny row of socks fluttering on the signal halyards; but once a fortnight the family washing was exhibited in force. It covered the poop entirely. The afternoon breeze would incite to a weird and flabby activity all that crowded mass of clothing, with its vague suggestions of drowned, mutilated and flattened humanity. Trunks without heads waved at you arms without hands; legs without feet kicked fantastically with collapsible flourishes; and there were long white garments, that taking the wind fairly through their neck openings edged with lace, became for a moment violently distended as by the passage of obese and invisible bodies. On these days you could make out that ship at a great distance by the multi-coloured grotesque riot going on abaft her mizzen-mast.

She had her berth just ahead of me, and her name was *Diana*,—Diana not of Ephesus but of Bremen. This was proclaimed in white letters a foot long spaced widely across the stern (somewhat like the lettering of a shop-sign) under the cottage windows. This ridiculously unsuitable name struck one as an impertinence towards the memory of the most charming of goddesses; for, apart from the fact that the old craft was physically incapable of engaging in any sort of chase, there was a gang of four children belonging to her. They peeped over the rail at passing boats and occasionally dropped various objects into them. Thus, sometime before I knew Hermann to speak to, I received on my hat a horrid rag-doll belonging to Hermann's eldest daughter. However, these youngsters were upon the whole well behaved. They had fair heads, round eyes, round little knobby noses, and they resembled their father a good deal.

This *Diana* of Bremen was a most innocent old ship, and seemed to know nothing of the wicked sea, as there are on shore households that know nothing of the corrupt world. And the sentiments she suggested were unexceptionable and mainly of a domestic order. She was a home. All these dear children had learned to walk on her roomy quarter-deck. In such thoughts there is something pretty, even touching. Their teeth, I should judge, they had cut on the ends of her running gear. I have many times observed the baby Hermann (Nicholas) engaged in gnawing the whipping of the fore-royal brace. Nicholas' favourite place of residence was under the main fife-rail. Directly he was let loose he would crawl off there, and the first seaman who came along would bring him, carefully held aloft in tarry hands, back to the cabin door. I fancy there must have been a standing order to that effect. In the course of these transportations the baby, who was the only peppery person in the ship, tried to smite these stalwart young German sailors on the face.

Mrs. Hermann, an engaging, stout housewife, wore on board baggy blue dresses with white dots. When, as happened once or twice I caught her at an elegant little wash-tub rubbing hard on white collars, baby's socks, and Hermann's summer neck-ties, she would blush in girlish confusion, and raising her wet hands greet me from afar with many friendly nods. Her sleeves would be rolled up to the elbows, and the gold hoop of her wedding ring glittered among the soap-suds. Her voice was pleasant, she had a serene brow, smooth bands of very fair hair, and a good-humoured expression of the eyes. She was motherly and moderately talkative. When this simple matron smiled, youthful dimples broke out on her fresh broad cheeks. Hermann's niece on the other hand, an orphan and very silent, I never saw attempt a smile. This, however, was not gloom on her part but the restraint of youthful gravity.

They had carried her about with them for the last three years, to help with the children and be company for Mrs. Hermann, as Hermann mentioned once to me. It had been very necessary while they were all little, he had added in a vexed manner. It was her arm and her sleek head that I had glimpsed one morning, through the stern-windows of the cabin, hovering over the pots of fuchsias and migonette; but the first time I beheld her full length I surrendered to her proportions. They fix her in my mind, as great beauty, great intelligence, quickness of wit or kindness of heart might have made some other woman equally memorable.

With her it was form and size. It was her physical personality that had this imposing charm. She might have been witty, intelligent, and kind to an exceptional degree. I don't know, and this is not to the point. All I know is that she was built on a magnificent scale. Built is the only word. She was constructed, she was erected, as it were, with a regal lavishness. It staggered you to see this reckless expenditure of material upon a chit of a girl. She was youthful and also perfectly mature, as though she had been some fortunate immortal. She was heavy too, perhaps, but that's nothing. It only added to that notion of permanence. She was barely nineteen. But such shoulders! Such round arms! Such a shadowing forth of mighty limbs when with three long strides she pounced across the deck upon the overturned Nicholas—it's perfectly indescribable! She seemed a good, quiet girl, vigilant as to Lena's needs, Gustav's tumbles, the state of Carl's dear little nose—conscientious, hardworking, and all that. But what magnificent hair she had! Abundant, long, thick, of a tawny colour. It had the sheen of precious metals. She wore it plaited tightly into one single tress hanging girlishly down her back; and its end reached down to her waist. The massiveness of it surprised you. On my word it reminded one of a club. Her face was big, comely, of an unruffled expression. She had a good complexion, and her blue eyes were so pale that she appeared to look at the world with the empty white candour of a statue. You could not call her good-looking. It was something much more impressive. The simplicity of her apparel, the opulence of her form, her imposing stature, and the extraordinary sense of vigorous life that seemed to emanate from her like a perfume exhaled by a flower, made her beautiful with a beauty of a rustic and olympian order. To watch her reaching up to the clothes-line with both arms raised high above her head, caused you to fall a musing in a strain of pagan piety. Excellent Mrs. Hermann's baggy cotton gowns had some sort of rudimentary frills at neck and bottom, but this girl's print frocks hadn't even a wrinkle; nothing but a few straight folds in the skirt falling to her feet, and these, when she stood still, had a severe and statuesque quality. She was inclined naturally to be still whether sitting or standing. However, I don't mean to say she was statuesque. She was too generously alive; but she could have stood for an allegoric statue of the Earth. I

don't mean the worn-out earth of our possession, but a young Earth, a virginal
planet undisturbed by the vision of a future teeming with the monstrous forms
of life and death, clamorous with the cruel battles of hunger and thought.

The worthy Hermann himself was not very entertaining, though his English
was fairly comprehensible. Mrs. Hermann, who always let off one speech at
least at me in an hospitable, cordial tone (and in Platt-Deutsch I suppose) I could
not understand. As to their niece, however satisfactory to look upon (and she
inspired you somehow with a hopeful view as to the prospects of mankind) she
was a modest and silent presence, mostly engaged in sewing, only now and
then, as I observed, falling over that work into a state of maidenly meditation.
Her aunt sat opposite her, sewing also, with her feet propped on a wooden
footstool. On the other side of the deck Hermann and I would get a couple of
chairs out of the cabin and settle down to a smoking match, accompanied at
long intervals by the pacific exchange of a few words. I came nearly every
evening. Hermann I would find in his shirt sleeves. As soon as he returned
from the shore on board his ship he commenced operations by taking off his
coat; then he put on his head an embroidered round cap with a tassel, and
changed his boots for a pair of cloth slippers. Afterwards he smoked at the
cabin-door, looking at his children with an air of civic virtue, till they got caught
one after another and put to bed in various staterooms. Lastly, we would drink
some beer in the cabin, which was furnished with a wooden table on cross legs,
and with black straight-backed chairs—more like a farm kitchen than a ship's
cuddy. The sea and all nautical affairs seemed very far removed from the hos-
pitality of this exemplary family.

And I liked this because I had a rather worrying time on board my own
ship. I had been appointed ex-officio by the British Consul to take charge of her
after a man who had died suddenly, leaving for the guidance of his successor
some suspiciously unreceipted bills, a few dry-dock estimates hinting at bribery,
and a quantity of vouchers for three years' extravagant expenditure; all these
mixed up together in a dusty old violin-case lined with ruby velvet. I found
besides a large account-book, which, when opened, hopefully turned out to my
infinite consternation to be filled with verses—page after page of rhymed dog-
gerel of a jovial and improper character, written in the neatest minute hand I
ever did see. In the same fiddle-case a photograph of my predecessor, taken
lately in Saigon, represented in front of a garden view, and in company of a
female in strange draperies, an elderly, squat, rugged man of stern aspect in a
clumsy suit of black broadcloth, and with the hair brushed forward above the
temples in a manner reminding one of a boar's tusks. Of a fiddle, however, the
only trace on board was the case, its empty husk as it were; but of the two last
freights the ship had indubitably earned of late, there were not even the husks
left. It was impossible to say where all that money had gone to. It wasn't on
board. It had not been remitted home; for a letter from the owners, preserved
in a desk evidently by the merest accident, complained mildly enough that they
had not been favoured by a scratch of the pen for the last eighteen months.
There were next to no stores on board, not an inch of spare rope or a yard of
canvas. The ship had been run bare, and I foresaw no end of difficulties before
I could get her ready for sea.

As I was young then—not thirty yet—I took myself and my troubles very seriously. The old mate, who had acted as chief mourner at the captain's funeral, was not particularly pleased at my coming. But the fact is the fellow was not legally qualified for command, and the Consul was bound, if at all possible, to put a properly certificated man on board. As to the second mate, all I can say his name was Tottersen, or something like that. His practice was to wear on his head, in that tropical climate, a mangy fur cap. He was, without exception, the stupidest man I had ever seen on board ship. And he looked it too. He looked so confoundedly stupid that it was a matter of surprise for me when he answered to his name.

I drew ño great comfort from their company, to say the least of it; while the prospect of making a long sea passage with those two fellows was depressing. And my other thoughts in solitude could not be of a gay complexion. The crew was sickly, the cargo was coming very slow; I foresaw I would have lots of trouble with the charterers, and doubted whether they would advance me enough money for the ship's expenses. Their attitude towards me was unfriendly. Altogether I was not getting on. I would discover at odd times (generally about midnight) that I was totally inexperienced, greatly ignorant of business, and hopelessly unfit for any sort of command; and when the steward had to be taken to the hospital ill with choleraic symptoms I felt bereaved of the only decent person at the after end of the ship. He was fully expected to recover, but in the meantime had to be replaced by some sort of servant. And on the recommendation of a certain Schomberg, the proprietor of the smaller of the two hotels in the place, I engaged a Chinaman. Schomberg, a brawny, hairy Alsatian, and an awful gossip, assured me that it was all right. "First-class boy that. Came in the *suite* of his Excellency Tseng the Commissioner—you know. His Excellency Tseng lodged with me here for three weeks."

He mouthed the Chinese Excellency at me with great unction, though the specimen of the "*suite*" did not seem very promising. At the time, however, I did not know what an untrustworthy humbug Schomberg was. The "boy" might have been forty or a hundred and forty for all you could tell—one of those Chinamen of the death's-head type of face and completely inscrutable. Before the end of the third day he had revealed himself as a confirmed opium-smoker, a gambler, a most audacious thief, and a first-class sprinter. When he departed at the top of his speed with thirty-two golden sovereigns of my own hard-earned savings it was the last straw. I had reserved that money in case my difficulties came to the worst. Now it was gone I felt as poor and naked as a fakir. I clung to my ship, for all the bother she caused me, but what I could not bear were the long lonely evenings in her cuddy, where the atmosphere, made smelly by a leaky lamp, was agitated by the snoring of the mate. That fellow shut himself up in his stuffy cabin punctually at eight, and made gross and revolting noises like a water-logged trump. It was odious not to be able to worry oneself in comfort on board one's own ship. Everything in this world, I reflected, even the command of a nice little barque, may be made a delusion and a snare for the unwary spirit of pride in man.

From such reflections I was glad to make any escape on board that Bremen *Diana*. There apparently no whisper of the world's iniquities had ever penetrated. And yet she lived upon the wide sea: and the sea tragic and comic, the sea with its horrors and its peculiar scandals, the sea peopled by men and ruled by iron necessity is indubitably a part of the world. But that patriarchal old tub, like some saintly retreat, echoed nothing of it. She was world proof. Her venerable innocence apparently had put a restraint on the roaring lusts of the sea. And yet I have known the sea too long to believe in its respect for decency. An elemental force is ruthlessly frank. It may, of course, have been Hermann's skilful seamanship, but to me it looked as if the allied oceans had refrained from smashing these high bulwarks, unshipping the lumpy rudder, frightening the children, and generally opening this family's eyes out of sheer reticence. It looked like reticence. The ruthless disclosure was, in the end, left for a man to make; a man strong and elemental enough and driven to unveil some secrets of the sea by the power of a simple and elemental desire.

This, however, occurred much later, and meantime I took sanctuary in that serene old ship early every evening. The only person on board that seemed to be in trouble was little Lena, and in due course I perceived that the health of the rag-doll was more than delicate. This object led a sort of "in extremis" existence in a wooden box placed against the starboard mooring-bitts, tended and nursed with the greatest sympathy and care by all the children, who greatly enjoyed pulling long faces and moving with hushed footsteps. Only the baby— Nicholas—looked on with a cold, ruffianly leer, as if he had belonged to another tribe altogether. Lena perpetually sorrowed over the box, and all of them were in deadly earnest. It was wonderful the way these children would work up their compassion for that bedraggled thing I wouldn't have touched with a pair of tongs. I suppose they were exercising and developing their racial sentimentalism by the means of that dummy. I was only surprised that Mrs. Hermann let Lena cherish and hug that bundle of rags to that extent, it was so disreputably and completely unclean. But Mrs. Hermann would raise her fine womanly eyes from her needlework to look on with amused sympathy, and did not seem to see it, somehow, that this object of affection was a disgrace to the ship's purity. Purity, not cleanliness, is the word. It was pushed so far that I seemed to detect in this too a sentimental excess, as if dirt had been removed in very love. It is impossible to give you an idea of such a meticulous neatness. It was as if every morning that ship had been arduously explored with—with toothbrushes. Her very bowsprit three times a week had its toilette made with a cake of soap and a piece of soft flannel. Arrayed—I *must* say arrayed—arrayed artlessly in dazzling white paint as to wood and dark green as to ironwork the simple-minded distribution of these colours evoked the images of simple-minded peace, of arcadian felicity; and the childish comedy of disease and sorrow struck me sometimes as an abominably real blot upon that ideal state.

I enjoyed it greatly, and on my part I brought a little mild excitement into it. Our intimacy arose from the pursuit of that thief. It was in the evening, and Hermann, who, contrary to his habits, had stayed on shore late that day, was extricating himself backwards out of a little gharry on the river bank, opposite his ship, when the hunt passed. Realising the situation as though he had eyes in his shoulder-blades, he joined us with a leap and took the lead. The Chinaman fled silent like a rapid shadow on the dust of an extremely oriental road. I followed. A long way in the rear my mate whooped like a savage. A young moon threw a bashful light on a plain like a monstrous waste ground: the architectural mass of a Buddhist temple far away projected itself in dead black on the sky. We lost the thief of course; but in my disappointment I had to admire Hermann's presence of mind. The velocity that stodgy man developed in the interests of a complete stranger earned my warm gratitude—there was something truly cordial in his exertions.

He seemed as vexed as myself at our failure, and would hardly listen to my thanks. He said it was "nothings," and invited me on the spot to come on board his ship and drink a glass of beer with him. We poked sceptically for a while amongst the bushes, peered without conviction into a ditch or two. There was not a sound: patches of slime glimmered feebly amongst the reeds. Slowly we trudged back, drooping under the thin sickle of the moon, and I heard him mutter to himself, "Himmel! Zwei und dreissig Pfund!" He was impressed by the figure of my loss. For a long time we had ceased to hear the mate's whoops and yells.

Then he said to me, "Everybody has his troubles," and as we went on remarked that he would never have known anything of mine hadn't he by an extraordinary chance been detained on shore by Captain Falk. He didn't like to stay late ashore—he added with a sigh. The something doleful in his tone I put to his sympathy with my misfortune, of course.

On board the *Diana* Mrs. Hermann's fine eyes expressed much interest and commiseration. We had found the two women sewing face to face under the open skylight in the strong glare of the lamp. Hermann walked in first, starting in the very doorway to pull off his coat, and encouraging me with loud, hospitable ejaculations: "Come in! This way! Come in, captain!" At once, coat in hand, he began to tell his wife all about it. Mrs. Hermann put the palms of her plump hands together; I smiled and bowed with a heavy heart: the niece got up from her sewing to bring Hermann's slippers and his embroidered calotte, which he assumed pontifically, talking (about me) all the time. Billows of white stuff lay between the chairs on the cabin floor; I caught the words "Zwei und dreissig Pfund" repeated several times, and presently came the beer, which seemed delicious to my throat, parched with running and the emotions of the chase.

I didn't get away till well past midnight, long after the women had retired. Hermann had been trading in the East for three years or more, carrying freights of rice and timber mostly. His ship was well known in all the ports from Vladivostok to Singapore. She was his own property. The profits had been moderate, but the trade answered well enough while the children were small yet. In another year or so he hoped he would be able to sell the old *Diana* to a firm in Japan for a fair price. He intended to return home, to Bremen, by mailboat, second class, with Mrs. Hermann and the children. He told me all this stolidly, with slow puffs at his pipe. I was sorry when knocking the ashes out he began to rub his eyes. I would have sat with him till morning. What had I to hurry on board my own ship for? To face the broken rifled drawer in my state-room. Ugh! The very thought made me feel unwell.

I became their daily guest, as you know. I think that Mrs. Hermann from the first looked upon me as romantic person. I did not, of course, tear my hair *coram populo* over my loss, and she took it for lordly indifference. Afterwards, I daresay, I did tell them some of my adventures—such as they were—and they marvelled greatly at the extent of my experience. Hermann would translate what he thought the most striking passages. Getting upon his legs, and as if delivering a lecture on a phenomenon, he addressed himself, with gestures, to the two woman, who would let their sewing sink slowly to their laps. Meantime

I sat before a glass of Hermann's beer, trying to look modest. Mrs. Hermann would glance at me quickly, emit slight "Ach's!" The girl never made a sound. Never. But she too would sometimes raise her pale eyes to look at me in her unseeing gentle way. Her glance was by no means stupid; it beamed out soft and diffuse as the moon beams upon a landscape—quite differently from the scrutinising inspection of the stars. You were drowned in it, and imagined youself to appear blurred. And yet this same glance when turned upon Christian Falk must have been as efficient as the searchlight of a battle-ship.

Falk was the other assiduous visitor on board, but from his behaviour he might have been coming to see the quarter-deck capstan. He certainly used to stare at it a good deal when keeping us company outside the cabin door, with one muscular arm thrown over the back of the chair, and his big shapely legs, in very tight white trousers, extended far out and ending in a pair of black shoes as roomy as punts. On arrival he would shake Hermann's hand with a mutter, bow to the women, and take up his careless and misanthropic attitude by our side. He departed abruptly, with a jump, going through the performance of grunts, handshakes, bow, as if in a panic. Sometimes, with a sort of discreet and convulsive effort, he approached the women and exchanged a few low words with them, half a dozen at most. On these occasions Hermann's usual stare became positively glassy and Mrs. Hermann's kind countenance would colour up. The girl herself never turned a hair.

Falk was a Dane or perhaps a Norwegian, I can't tell now. At all events he was a Scandinavian of some sort, and a bloated monopolist to boot. It is possible he was unacquainted with the word, but he had a clear perception of the thing itself. His tariff of charges for towing ships in and out was the most brutally inconsiderate document of the sort I had ever seen. He was the commander and owner of the only tug-boat on the river, a very trim white craft of 150 tons or more, as elegantly neat as a yacht, with a round wheel-house rising like a glazed turret high above her sharp bows, and with one slender varnished pole mast forward. I daresay there are yet a few shipmasters afloat who remember Falk and his tug very well. He extracted his pound and a half of flesh from each of us merchant-skippers with an inflexible sort of indifference which made him detested and even feared. Schomberg used to remark: "I won't talk about the fellow. I don't think he has six drinks from year's end to year's end in my place. But my advice is, gentlemen, don't you have anything to do with him, if you can help it."

This advice, apart from unavoidable business relations, was easy to follow because Falk intruded upon no one. It seems absurd to compare a tug-boat skipper to a centaur: but he reminded me somehow of an engraving in a little book I had as a boy, which represented centaurs at a stream, and there was one, especially in the foreground, prancing bow and arrows in hand, with regular severe features and an immense curled wavy beard, flowing down his breast. Falk's face reminded me of that centaur. Besides, he was a composite creature. Not a man-horse, it is true, but a man-boat. He lived on board his tug, which was always dashing up and down the river from early morn till dewy eve. In the last rays of the setting sun, you could pick out far away down the reach his beard borne high up on the white structure, foaming up stream to anchor for the night. There was the white-clad man's body, and the rich brown patch of the hair, and nothing below the waist but the 'thwart-ship white lines of the bridge-screens, that led the eye to the sharp white lines of the bows cleaving the muddy water of the river.

Separated from his boat, to me at least he seemed incomplete. The tug herself without his head and torso on the bridge looked mutilated as it were. But he left her very seldom. All the time I remained in harbour I saw him only twice on shore. On the first occasion it was at my charterers, where he came in misanthropically to get paid for towing out a French barque the day before. The second time I could hardly believe my eyes, for I beheld him reclining under his beard in a cane-bottomed chair in the billiard-room of Schomberg's hotel.

It was very funny to see Schomberg ignoring him pointedly. The artificiality of it contrasted strongly with Falk's natural unconcern. The big Alsatian talked loudly with his other customers, going from one little table to the other, and passing Falk's place of repose with his eyes fixed straight ahead. Falk sat there with an untouched glass at his elbow. He must have known by sight and name every white man in the room, but he never addressed a word to anybody. He acknowledged my presence by a drop of his eyelids, and that was all. Sprawling there in the chair, he would, now and again, draw the palms of both his hands down his face, giving at the same time a slight, almost imperceptible, shudder.

It was a habit he had, and of course I was perfectly familiar with it, since you could not remain an hour in his company without being made to wonder at such a movement breaking some long period of stillness. It was a passionate and inexplicable gesture. He used to make it at all sorts of times; as likely as not after he had been listening to little Lena's chatter about the suffering doll, for instance. The Hermann children always besieged him about his legs closely, though, in a gentle way, he shrank from them a little. He seemed, however, to feel a great affection for the whole family. For Hermann himself especially. He sought his company. In this case, for instance, he must have been waiting for him, because as soon as he appeared Falk rose hastily, and they went out together. Then Schomberg expounded in my hearing to three or four people his theory that Falk was after Captain Hermann's niece, and asserted confidently that nothing would come of it. It was the same last year when Captain Hermann was loading here, he said.

Naturally, I did not believe Schomberg, but I own that for a time I observed closely what went on. All I discovered was some impatience on Hermann's part. At the sight of Falk, stepping over the gangway, the excellent man would begin to mumble and chew between his teeth something that sounded like German swear-words. However, as I've said, I'm not familiar with the language, and Hermann's soft, round-eyed countenance remained unchanged. Staring stolidly ahead he greeted him with, "Wie geht's," or in English, "How are you?" with a throaty enunciation. The girl would look up for an instant and move her lips slightly: Mrs. Hermann let her hands rest on her lap to talk volubly to him for a minute or so in her pleasant voice before she went on with her sewing again. Falk would throw himself into a chair, stretch his big legs, as like as not draw his hands down his face passionately. As to myself, he was not pointedly im-pertinent: it was rather as though he could not be bothered with such trifles as my existence; and the truth is that being a monopolist he was under no necessity to be amiable. He was sure to get his own extortionate terms out of me for towage whether he frowned or smiled. As a matter of fact, he did neither: but before many days elapsed he managed to astonish me not a little and to set Schomberg's tongue clacking more than ever.

It came about in this way. There was a shallow bar at the mouth of the river which ought to have been kept down, but the authorities of the State were piously busy gilding afresh the great Buddhist Pagoda just then, and I suppose had no money to spare for dredging operations. I don't know how it may be now, but at the time I speak of that sandbank was a great nuisance to the shipping. One of its consequences was that vessels of a certain draught of water, like Hermann's or mine, could not complete their loading in the river. After taking in as much as possible of their cargo, they had to go outside to fill up. The whole procedure was an unmitigated bore. When you thought you had as much on board as your ship could carry safely over the bar, you went and gave notice to your agents. They, in their turn, notified Falk that so-and-so was ready to go out. Then Falk (ostensibly when it fitted in with his other work, but, if the truth were known, simply when his arbitrary spirit moved him), after as-certaining carefully in the office that there was enough money to meet his bill, would come along unsympathetically, glaring at you with his yellow eyes from the bridge, and would drag you out dishevelled as to rigging, lumbered as to the decks, with unfeeling haste, as if to execution. And he would force you too to take the end of his own wire hawser, for the use of which there was of course an extra charge. To your shouted remonstrances against this extortion this tow-ering trunk with one hand on the engine-room telegraph only shook its bearded head above the splash, the racket and the clouds of smoke, in which the tug, backing and filling in the smother of churning paddle-wheels behaved like a ferocious and impatient creature. He had her manned by the cheekiest gang of lascars I ever did see, whom he allowed to bawl at you insolently, and, once fast, he plucked you out of your berth as if he did not care what he smashed. Eighteen miles down the river you had to go behind him, and then three more along the coast to where a group of uninhabited rocky islets enclosed a sheltered anchorage. There you would have to lie at single anchor with your naked spars showing to seaward over these barren fragments of land scattered upon a very intensely blue sea. There was nothing to look at besides but a bare coast, the muddy edge of the brown plain with the sinuosities of the river you had left, traced in dull green, and the Great Pagoda uprising lonely and massive with shining curves and pinnacles like the gorgeous and stony efflorescence of tropical rocks. You had nothing to do but to wait fretfully for the balance of your cargo, which was sent out of the river with the greatest irregularity. And it was open to you to console yourself with the thought that, after all, this stage of bother meant that your departure from these shores was indeed approaching at last.

We both had to go through that stage, Hermann and I, and there was a sort of tacit emulation between the ships as to which should be ready first. We kept on neck and neck almost to the finish, when I won the race by going personally to give notice in the forenoon; whereas Hermann, who was very slow in making up his mind to go ashore, did not get to the agents' office till late in the day. They told him there that my ship was first on turn for next morning, and I believe he told them he was in no hurry. It suited him better to go the day after.

That evening, on board the *Diana*, he sat with his plump knees well apart, staring and puffing at the curved mouthpiece of his pipe. Presently he spoke with some impatience to his niece about putting the children to bed. Mrs. Hermann, who was talking to Falk, stopped short and looked at her husband uneasily, but the girl got up at once and drove the children before her into the cabin. In a little while Mrs. Hermann had to leave us to quell what, from the sounds inside, must have been a dangerous mutiny. At this Hermann grumbled to himself. For half an hour longer Falk left alone with us fidgeted on his chair, sighed lightly, then at last, after drawing his hands down his face, got up, and as if renouncing the hope of making himself understood (he hadn't opened his mouth once) he said in English: "Well . . . Good night, Captain Hermann." He stopped for a moment before my chair and looked down fixedly; I may even say he glared: and he went so far as to make a deep noise in his throat. There was in all this something so marked that for the first time in our limited inter-course of nods and grunts he excited in me something like interest. But next moment he disappointed me—for he strode away hastily without a nod even.

His manner was usually odd it is true, and I certainly did not pay much attention to it; but that sort of obscure intention, which seemed to lurk in his nonchalance like a wary old carp in a pond, had never before come so near the surface. He had distinctly aroused my expectations. I would have been unable to say what it was I expected, but at all events I did not expect the absurd developments he sprung upon me no later than the break of the very next day.

I remember only that there was, on that evening, enough point in his behaviour to make me, after he had fled, wonder audibly what he might mean. To this Hermann, crossing his legs with a swing and settling himself viciously away from me in his chair, said: "That fellow don't know himself what he means."

There might have been some insight in such a remark. I said nothing, and, still averted, he added: "When I was here last year he was just the same." An eruption of tobacco smoke enveloped his head as if his temper had exploded like gunpowder.

I had half a mind to ask him point blank whether he, at least, didn't know why Falk, a notoriously unsociable man, had taken to visiting his ship with such assiduity. After all, I reflected suddenly, it was a most remarkable thing. I wonder now what Hermann would have said. As it turned out he didn't let me ask. Forgetting all about Falk apparently, he started a monologue on his plans for the future: the selling of the ship, the going home; and falling into a reflective and calculating mood he mumbled between regular jets of smoke about the expense. The necessity of disbursing passage-money for all his tribe seemed to disturb him in a manner that was the more striking because otherwise he gave no signs of a miserly disposition. And yet he fussed over the prospect of that voyage home in a mail-boat like a sedentary grocer who has made up his mind to see the world. He was racially thrifty I suppose, and for him there must have been a great novelty in finding himself obliged to pay for travelling—for sea travelling which was the normal state of life for the family—from the very cradle for most of them. I could see he grudged prospectively every single shilling which must be spent so absurdly. It was rather funny. He would become doleful over it, and then again, with a fretful sigh, he would suppose there was nothing for it now but to take three second-class tickets—and there were the four children to pay for besides. A lot of money that to spend at once. A big lot of money.

I sat with him listening (not for the first time) to these heart-searchings till

I grew thoroughly sleepy, and then I left him and turned in on board my ship. At daylight I was awakened by a yelping of shrill voices, accompanied by a great commotion in the water, and the short, bullying blasts of a steam-whistle. Falk with his tug had come for me.

I began to dress. It was remarkable that the answering noise on board my ship together with the patter of feet above my head ceased suddenly. But I heard more remote guttural cries which seemed to express surprise and annoyance. Then the voice of my mate reached me howling expostulations to somebody at a distance. Other voices joined, apparently indignant; a chorus of something that sounded like abuse replied. Now and then the steam-whistle screeched.

Altogether that unnecessary uproar was distracting, but down there in my cabin I took it calmly. In another moment, I thought, I should be going down that wretched river, and in another week at the most I should be totally quit of the odious place and all the odious people in it.

Greatly cheered by the idea, I seized the hair-brushes and looking at myself in the glass began to use them. Suddenly a hush fell upon the noise outside, and I heard (the ports of my cabin were thrown open)—I heard a deep calm voice, not on board my ship, however, hailing resolutely in English, but with a strong foreign twang, "Go ahead!"

There may be tides in the affairs of men which taken at the flood ... and so on. Personally I am still on the look out for that important turn. I am, however, afraid that most of us are fated to flounder for ever in the dead water of a pool whose shores are arid indeed. But I know that there are often in men's affairs unexpectedly—even irrationally—illuminating moments when an otherwise insignificant sound, perhaps only some perfectly commonplace gesture, suffices to reveal to us all the unreason, all the fatuous unreason, of our complacency. "Go ahead" are not particularly striking words even when pronounced with a foreign accent; yet they petrified me in the very act of smiling at myself in the glass. And then, refusing to believe my ears, but already boiling with indignation, I ran out of the cabin and up on deck.

It was incredibly true. It was perfectly true. I had no eyes for anything but the *Diana*. It was she that was being taken away. She was already out of her berth and shooting athwart the river. "The way this loonatic plucked that ship out is a caution," said the awed voice of my mate close to my ear. "Hey! Hallo! Falk! Hermann! What's this infernal trick?" I yelled in a fury.

Nobody heard me. Falk certainly could not hear me. His tug was turning at full speed away under the other bank. The wire hawser between her and the *Diana*, stretched as taut as a harpstring, vibrated alarmingly.

The high black craft careened over to the awful strain. A loud crack came out of her, followed by the tearing and splintering of wood. "There!" said the awed voice in my ear. "He's carried away their towing chock." And then, with enthusiasm, "Oh! Look! Look, sir! Look at them Dutchmen skipping out of the way on the forecastle. I hope to goodness he'll break a few of their shins before he's done with 'em."

I yelled my vain protests. The rays of the rising sun coursing level along the plain warmed my back, but I was hot enough with rage. I could not have believed that a simple towing operation could suggest so plainly the idea of abduction, of rape. Falk was simply running off with the *Diana*.

The white tug careered out into the middle of the river. The red floats of her paddle-wheels revolving with mad rapidity tore up the whole reach into foam. The *Diana* in mid-stream waltzed round with as much grace as an old barn, and flew after her ravisher. Through the ragged fog of smoke driving headlong upon the water I had a glimpse of Falk's square motionless shoulders under a white hat as big as a cart-wheel, of his red face, his yellow staring eyes, his great beard. Instead of keeping a look-out ahead, he was deliberately turning his back on the river to glare at his tow. The tall heavy craft, never so used before in her life, seemed to have lost her senses; she took a wild sheer against her helm, and for a moment came straight at us, menacing and clumsy, like a runaway mountain. She piled up a streaming, hissing, boiling wave halfway up her blunt stem, my crew let out one great howl,—and then we held our breaths. It was a near thing. But Falk had her! He had her in his clutch. I fancied I could hear the steel hawser ping as it surged across the *Diana's* forecastle, with the hands on board of her bolting away from it in all directions. It was a near thing. Hermann, with his hair rumpled, in a snuffy flannel shirt and a pair of mustard-coloured trousers, had rushed to help with the wheel. I saw his terrified round face; I saw his very teeth uncovered by a sort of ghastly fixed grin; and in a great leaping tumult of water between the two ships the *Diana* whisked past so close that I could have flung a hair-brush at his head, for, it seems, I had kept them in my hands all the time. Meanwhile Mrs. Hermann sat placidly on the skylight, with a woollen shawl on her shoulders. The excellent woman in response to my indignant gesticulations fluttered a handkerchief, nodding and smiling in the kindest way imaginable. The boys, only half-dressed, were jumping about the poop in great glee, displaying their gaudy braces; and Lena in a short scarlet petticoat, with peaked elbows and thin bare arms, nursed the rag-doll with devotion. The whole family passed before my sight as if dragged across a scene of unparalleled violence. The last I saw was Hermann's niece with the baby Hermann in her arms standing apart from the others. Magnificent in her close-fitting print frock, she displayed something so commanding in the manifest perfection of her figure that the sun seemed to be rising for her alone. The flood of light brought the opulence of her form and the vigour of her youth in a glorifying way. She went by perfectly motionless and as if lost in medication; only the hem of her skirt stirred in the draught; the sun rays broke on her sleek tawny hair; that bald-headed ruffian, Nicholas, was whacking her on the shoulder. I saw his tiny fat arm rise and fall in a workmanlike manner. And then the four cottage windows of the *Diana* came into view retreating swiftly down the river. The sashes were up, and one of the white calico curtains fluttered straight out like a streamer above the agitated water of the wake.

To be thus tricked out of one's turn was an unheard-of occurrence. In my agent's office, where I went to complain at once, they protested with apologies they couldn't understand how the mistake arose: but Schomberg, when I dropped in later to get some tiffin, though surprised to see me, was perfectly ready with an explanation. I found him seated at the end of a long narrow table, facing his wife—a scraggy little woman, with long ringlets and a blue tooth, who smiled abroad stupidly and looked frightened when you spoke to her. Between them a waggling punkah fanned twenty vacant cane-bottomed chairs and two rows of shiny plates. Three Chinamen in white jackets loafed with napkins in their hands around that desolation. Schomberg's pet *table-d'hôte* was not much of a success that day. He was feeding himself furiously and seemed to overflow with bitterness.

He began by ordering in a brutal voice the chops to be brought back for me, and turning in his chair: "Mistake they told you? Not a bit of it! Don't you believe it for a moment, captain! Falk isn't a man to make mistakes unless on purpose." His firm conviction was that Falk had been trying all along to curry favour on the cheap with Hermann. "On the cheap—mind you! It doesn't cost him a cent to put that insult upon you, and Captain Hermann gets in a day ahead of your ship. Time's money! Eh? You are very friendly with Captain Hermann I believe, but a man is bound to be pleased at any little advantage he may get. Captain Hermann is a good business man, and there's no such thing as a friend in business. Is there?" He leaned forward and began to cast stealthy glances as usual. "But Falk is, and always was, a miserable fellow. I would despise him."

I muttered, grumpily, that I had no particular respect for Falk.

"I would despise him," he insisted, with an appearance of anxiety which would have amused me if I had not been fathoms deep in discontent. To a young man fairly conscientious and as well-meaning as only the young man can be, the current ill-usage of life comes with a peculiar cruelty. Youth that is fresh enough to believe in guilt, in innocence, and in itself, will always doubt whether it have not perchance deserved its fate. Sombre of mind and without appetite, I struggled with the chop while Mrs. Schomberg sat with her everlasting stupid grin and Schomberg's talk gathered way like a slide of rubbish.

"Let me tell you. It's all about that girl. I don't know what Captain Hermann expects, but if he asked me I could tell him something about Falk. He's a miserable fellow. That man is a perfect slave. That's what I call him. A slave. Last year I started this *table d'hôte*, and sent cards out—you know. You think he had one meal in the house? Give the thing a trial? Not once. He has got hold now of a Madras cook—a blamed fraud that I hunted out of my cookhouse with a rattan. He was not fit to cook for white men. No, not for the white men's dogs either; but, see, any damned native that can boil a pot of rice is good enough for Mr. Falk. Rice and a little fish he buys for a few cents from the fishing-boats outside is what he lives on. You would hardly credit it—eh? A white man, too...."

He wiped his lips, using the napkin with indignation, and looking at me. It flashed through my mind in the midst of my depression that if all the meat in the town was like these *table-d'hôte* chops, Falk wasn't so far wrong. I was on the point of saying this, but Schomberg's stare was intimidating. "He's a vegetarian, perhaps," I murmured instead.

"He's a miser. A miserable miser," affirmed the hotel-keeper with great force. "The meat here is not so good as at home—of course. And dear too. But look at me. I only charge a dollar for the tiffin, and one dollar and fifty cents for the dinner. Show me anything cheaper. Why am I doing it? There's little profit in this game. Falk wouldn't look at it. I do it for the sake of a lot of young white fellows here that hadn't a place where they could get a decent meal and eat it decently in good company. There's first-rate company always at my table."

The convinced way he surveyed the empty chairs made me feel as if I had intruded upon a tiffin of ghostly Presences.

"A white man should eat like a white man, dash it all," he burst out impetuously. "Ought to eat meat, must eat meat. I manage to get meat for my patrons all the year round. Don't I? I am not catering for a dam' lot of coolies: Have another chop, captain.... No? You, boy—take away!"

He threw himself back and waited grimly for the curry. The half-closed jalousies darkened the room pervaded by the smell of fresh whitewash: a swarm of flies buzzed and settled in turns, and poor Mrs. Schomberg's smile seemed to express the quintessence of all the imbecility that had ever spoken, had ever breathed, had ever been fed on infamous buffalo meat within these bare walls. Schomberg did not open his lips till he was ready to thrust therein a spoonful of greasy rice. He rolled his eyes ridiculously before he swallowed the hot stuff, and only then broke out afresh.

"It is the most degrading thing. They take the dish up to the wheelhouse for him with a cover on it, and he shuts both the doors before he begins to eat. Fact! Must be ashamed of himself. Ask the engineer. He can't do without an engineer—don't you see—and as no respectable man can be expected to put up with such a table, he allows them fifteen dollars a month extra mess money. I assure you it is so! You just ask Mr. Ferdinand da Costa. That's the engineer he has now. You may have seen him about my place, a delicate dark young man, with very fine eyes and a little moustache. He arrived here a year ago from Calcutta. Between you and me, I guess the money-lenders there must have been after him. He rushes here for a meal every chance he can get, for just please tell me what satisfaction is that for a well-educated young fellow to feed all alone in his cabin—like a wild beast? That's what Falk expects his engineers to put up with for fifteen dollars extra. And the rows on board every time a little smell of cooking gets about the deck! You wouldn't believe! The other day da Costa got the cook to fry a steak for him—a turtle steak it was too, not beef at all—and the fat caught or something. Young da Costa himself was telling me of it here in this room. 'Mr. Schomberg'—says he—'if I had let a cylinder cover blow off through the skylight by my negligence Captain Falk couldn't have been more savage. He frightened the cook so that he won't put anything on the fire for me now.' Poor da Costa had tears in his eyes. Only try to put yourself in his place, captain: a sensitive, gentlemanly young fellow. Is he expected to eat his food raw? But that's your Falk all over. Ask any one you like. I suppose the fifteen dollars extra he has to give keep on rankling—in there."

And Schomberg tapped his manly breast. I sat half stunned by his irrelevant babble. Suddenly he gripped my forearm in an impressive and cautious manner, as if to lead me into a very cavern of confidence.

"It's nothing but enviousness," he said in a lowered tone, which had a stimulating effect upon my wearied hearing. "I don't suppose there is one person in this town that he isn't envious of. I tell you he's dangerous. Even I myself am not safe from him. I know for certain he tried to poison...."

"Oh, come now," I cried, revolted.

"But I know for certain. The people themselves came and told me of it. He went about saying everywhere I was a worse pest to this town than the cholera. He had been talking against me ever since I opened this hotel. And he poisoned Captian Hermann's mind too. Last time the *Diana* was loading here Captain Hermann used to come in every day for a drink or a cigar. This time he hasn't been here twice in a week. How do you account for that?"

He squeezed my arm till he extorted from me some sort of mumble.

"He makes ten times the money I do. I've another hotel to fight against, and there isd no other tug on the river. I am not in his way, am I? He wouldn't be fit to run an hotel if he tried. But that's just his nature. He can't bear to think I am making a living. I only hope it makes him properly wretched. He's like that in everything. He would like to keep a decent table well enough. But no—for the sake of a few cents. Can't do it. It's too much for him. That's what I call being a slave to it. But he's mean enough to kick up a row when his nose gets tickled a bit. See that? That just paints him. Miserly and envious. You can't account for it any other way. Can you? I have been studying him these three years."

He was anxious I should assent to his theory. And indeed on thinking it over it would have been plausible enough if there hadn't been always the essential falseness of irresponsibility in Schomberg's chatter. However, I was not disposed to investigate the psychology of Falk. I was engaged just then in eating despondently a piece of stale Dutch cheese, being too much crushed to care what I swallowed myself, let alone bothering my head about Falk's ideas of gastronomy. I could expect from their study no clue to his conduct in matters of business, which seemed to me totally unrestrained by morality or even by the commonest sort of decency. How insignificant and contemptible I must appear, for the fellow to dare treat me like this—I reflected suddenly, writhing in silent agony. And I consigned Falk and all his peculiarities to the devil with so much mental fervour as to forget Schomberg's existence, till he grabbed my arm urgently. "Well, you may think and think till every hair of your head falls off, captain; but you can't explain it in any other way."

For the sake of peace and quietness I admitted hurriedly that I couldn't; persuaded that now he would leave off. But the only result was to make his moist face shine with the pride of cunning. He removed his hand for a moment to scare a black mass of flies off the sugar-basin, and caught hold of my arm again.

"To be sure. And in the same way everybody is aware he would like to get married. Only he can't. Let me quote you an instance. Well, two years ago a Miss Vanlo, a very ladylike girl, came from home to keep house for her brother, Fred, who had an engineering shop for small repairs by the waterside. Suddenly Falk takes to going up to their bungalow after dinner and sitting for hours in the verandah saying nothing. The poor girl couldn't tell for the life of her what to do with such a man, so she would keep on playing the piano and singing to him evening after evening till she was ready to drop. And it wasn't as if she had been a strong young woman either. She was thirty, and the climate had been playing the deuce with her. Then—don't you know—Fred had to sit up with them for propriety, and during whole weeks on end never got a single chance to get to bed before midnight. That was not pleasant for a tired man—was it? And besides Fred had worries then because his shop didn't pay and he was dropping money fast. He just longed to get away from here and try his luck somewhere else, but for the sake of his sister he hung on and on till he ran himself into debt over his ears—I can tell you. I, myself, could show a handful of his chits for meals and drinks in my drawer. I could never find out tho' where he found all the money at last. Can't be but he must have got something out of that brother of his, a coal merchant in Port Said. Anyhow he paid everybody before he left, but the girl nearly broke her heart. Dissapoint-ment, of course, and at her age, don't you know.... Mrs. Schomberg here was very friendly with her, and she could tell you. Awful despair. Fainting fits. It was a scandal. A notorious scandal. To that extent that old Mr. Siegers—not your present charterer, but Mr. Siegers the father, the old gentleman who retired from business on a fortune and got buried at sea going home, *he* had to interview Falk in his private office. He was a man who could speak like a Dutch Uncle, and, besides, Messrs. Siegers had been helping Falk with a good bit of money from the start. In fact you may say they had made him as far as that goes. It so happened that just at the time he turned up here, their firm was chartering a lot of sailing-ships every year, and it suited their business that there should be good towing facilities on the river. See?... Well—there's always an ear at the keyhole—isn't there? In fact," he lowered his tone confidentially, "in this câse it was a good friend of mine; a man you can see here any evening; only they conversed rather low. Anyhow my friend's certain that Falk was trying to make all sorts of excuses, and old Mr. Siegers was coughing a lot. And yet Falk wanted all the time to be married too. Why! It's notorious the man has been longing for years to make a home for himself. Only he can't face the expense. When it comes to putting his hand in his pocket—it chokes him off. That's the truth and no other. I've always said so, and everybody agrees with me by this time. What do you think of that—eh?"

He appealed confidently to my indignation, but having a mind to annoy him I remarked, "that it seemed to me very pitiful—if true."

He bounced in his chair as if I had run a pin into him. I don't know what he might have said, only at that moment we heard through the half open door of the billiard-room the footsteps of two men entering from the verandah, a murmur of two voices; at the sharp tapping of a coin on a table Mrs. Schomberg half rose irresolutely. "Sit still," he hissed at her, and then, in an hospitable, jovial tone, contrasting amazingly with the angry glance that had made his wife sink in her chair, he cried very loud: "Tiffin still going on in here, gentlemen."

There was no answer, but the voices dropped suddenly. The head China-man went out. We heard the clink of ice in the glasses, pouring sounds, the shuffling of feet, the scraping of chairs. Schomberg, after wondering in a low mutter who the devil could be there at this time of the day, got up napkin in hand to peep through the doorway cautiously. He retreated rapidly on tip-toe, and whispering behind his hand informed me that it was Falk, Falk himself who was in there, and, what's more, he had Captain Hermann with him.

The return of the tug from the outer Roads was unexpected but possible, for Falk had taken away the *Diana* at half-past five, and it was now two o'clock. Schomberg wished me to observe that neither of these men would spend a dollar on a tiffin, which they must have wanted. But by the time I was ready to leave the dining-room Falk had gone. I heard the last of his big boots on the planks of the verandah. Hermann was sitting quite alone in the large, wooden room with the two lifeless billiard tables shrouded in striped covers, mopping his face diligently. He wore his best-go-ashore clothes, a stiff collar, black coat, large white waistcoat, grey trousers. A white cotton sunshade with a cane handle reposed between his legs, his side whiskers were neatly brushed, his chin had been freshly shaved; and he only distantly resembled the dishevelled and ter-rified man in a snuffy night shirt and ignoble old trousers I had seen in the morning hanging on to the wheel of the *Diana*.

He gave a start at my entrance, and addressed me at once in some confusion, but with genuine eagerness. He was anxious to make it clear he had nothing to do with what he called the "tam pizness" of the morning. It was most inconvenient. He had reckoned upon another day up in town to settle his bills and sign certain papers. There were also some few stores to come, and sundry pieces of "my ironwork," as he called it quaintly, landed for repairs, had been left behind. Now he would have to hire a native boat to take all this out to the ship. It would cost five or six dollars perhaps. He had had no warning from Falk. Nothing. . . . He hit the table with his dumpy fist. . . . Der verfluchte Kerl came in the morning like a "tam' ropper," making a great noise, and took him away. His mate was not prepared, his ship was moored fast—he protested it was shameful to come upon a man in that way. Shameful! Yet such was the power Falk had on the river that when I suggested in a chilling tone that he might have simply refused to have his ship moved, Hermann was quite startled at the idea. I never realised so well before that this is an age of steam. The exclusive possession of a marine boiler had given Falk the whip hand of us all. Hermann recovering, put it to me appealingly that I knew very well how unsafe it was to contradict that fellow. At this I only smiled distantly.

"Der Kerl!" he cried. He was sorry he had not refused. He was indeed. The damage! The damage! What for all that damage! Did I know how much damage he had done? It gave me a certain satisfaction to tell him that I had heard his old waggon of a ship crack fore and aft as she went by. "You passed close enough to me," I added significantly.

He threw both his hands up to heaven at the recollection. One of them grasped by the middle the white parasol, and he resembled curiously a caricature of a shopkeeping citizen in one of his own German comic papers. "Ach! That was dangerous," he cried. I was amused. But directly he added with an appearance of simplicity, "The side of your iron ship would have been crushed in like—like this matchbox."

"Would it?" I growled, much less amused now; but by the time I had decided that this remark was not meant for a dig at me he had worked himself into a high state of resentfulness against Falk. The inconvenience, the damage, the expense! Gottferdam! Devil take the fellow. Behind the bar Schomberg with a cigar in his teeth, pretended to be writing with a pencil on a large sheet of paper; and as Hermann's excitement increased it made me comfortingly aware of my own calmness and superiority. But it occurred to me while I listened to his revilings, that after all the good man had come up in the tug. There perhaps— since he must come to town—he had no option. But evidently he had had a drink with Falk, either accepted or offered. How was that ? So I checked him by saying loftily that I hoped he would make Falk pay for every penny of the damage.

"That's it! That's it! Go for him," called out Schomberg from the bar, flinging his pencil down and rubbing his hands.

We ignored his noise. But Hermann's excitement suddenly went off the boil as when you remove a sauce-pan from the fire. I urged on his consideration that he had done now with Falk and Falk's confounded tug. He, Hermann, would not, perhaps, turn up again in this part of the world for years to come, since he was going to sell the *Diana* at the end of this very trip ("Go home passenger in a mail boat," he murmured mechanically). He was therefore safe from Falk's malice. All he had to do was to race off to his consignees and stop payment of the towage bill before Falk had the time to get in and lift the money.

Nothing could have been less in the spirit of my advice than the thoughtful way in which he set about to make his parasol stay propped against the edge of the table.

While I watched his concentrated efforts with astonishment he threw at me one or two perplexed, half-shy glances. Then he sat down. "That's all very well," he said reflectively.

It cannot be doubted that the man had been thrown off his balance by being hauled out of the harbour against his wish. His stolidity had been profoundly stirred, else he would never have made up his mind to ask me unexpectedly whether I had not remarked that Falk had been casting eyes upon his niece. "No more than myself," I answered with literal truth. The girl was of the sort one necessarily casts eyes at in a sense. She made no noise, but she filled most satisfactorily a good bit of space.

"But you, captain, are not the same kind of man," observed Hermann.

I was not, I am happy to say, in a position to deny this. "What about the lady?" I could not help asking. At this he gazed for a time into my face, earnestly, and made as if to change the subject. I heard him beginning to mutter something unexpected, about his children growing old enough to require schooling. He would have to leave them ashore with their grandmother when he took up that new command he expected to get in Germany.

This constant harping on his domestic arrangements was funny. I suppose it must have been like the prospect of a complete alteration in his life. An epoch. He was going, too, to part with the *Diana*! He had served in her for years. He had inherited her. From an uncle, if I remember rightly. And the future loomed big before him, occupying his thought exclusively with all its aspects as on the eve of a venturesome enterprise. He sat there frowning and biting his lip, and suddenly he began to fume and fret.

I discovered to my momentary amusement that he seemed to imagine I could, should or ought, have caused Falk in some way to pronounce himself. Such a hope was incomprehensible, but funny. Then the contact with all this foolishness irritated me. I said crossly that I had seen no symptoms, but if there were any—since he, Hermann, was so sure—then it was stil worse. What pleasure Falk found in humbugging people in just that way I couldn't say. It was, however, my solemn duty to warn him. It had lately, I said, come to my knowledge that there was a man (not a very long time ago either) who had been taken in just like this.

All this passed in undertones, and at this point Schomberg, exasperated at our secrecy, went out of the room slamming the door with a crash that positively lifted us in our chairs. This, or else what I had said, huffed my Hermann. He supposed, with a contemptuous toss of his head towards the door which trembled yet, that I had got hold of some of that man's silly tales. It looked, indeed, as though his mind had been thoroughly poisoned against Schomberg. "His tales were—they were," he repeated, seeking for the word—"trash." They were trash, he reiterated and moreover I was young yet...

This horrid aspersion (I regret I am no longer exposed to that sort of insult) made me huffy too. I felt ready in my own mind to back up every assertion of Schomberg's and on any subject. In a moment, devil only knows why, Hermann and I were looking at each other most inimically. He caught up his hat without more ado and I gave myself the pleasure of calling after him:

"Take my advice and make Falk pay for breaking up your ship. You aren't likely to get anything else out of him."

When I got on board my ship later on, the old mate, who was very full of the events of the morning, remarked:

"I saw the tug coming back from the outer Roads just before two P.M." (He never by any chance used the words morning or afternoon. Always P.M. or A.M., log-book style.) "Smart work that. Man's always in a state of hurry. He's a regular chucker-out, ain't he, sir? There's a few pubs I know of in the East-end of London that would be all the better for one of his sort around the bar." He chuckled at his joke. "A regular chucker-out. Now he has fired out that Dutchman head over heels, I suppose our turn's coming to-morrow morning."

We were all on deck at break of day (even the sick—poor devils—had crawled out) ready to cast off in the twinkling of an eye. Nothing came. Falk did not come. At last, when I began to think that probably something had gone wrong in his engine-room, we perceived the tug going by, full pelt, down the river, as if we hadn't existed. For a moment I entertained the wild notion that he was going to turn round in the next reach. Afterwards I watched his smoke appear above the plain, now here, now there according to the windings of the river. It disappeared. Then without a word I went down to breakfast. I just simply went down to breakfast.

Not one of us uttered a sound till the mate, after imbibing—by means of suction out of a saucer—his second cup of tea, exclaimed: "Where the devil is the man gone to?"

"Courting!" I shouted, with such a fiendish laugh that the old chap didn't venture to open his lips any more.

I started to the office perfectly calm. Calm with excessive rage. Evidently they knew all about it already, and they treated me to a show of consternation. The manager, a soft-footed, immensely obese man, breathing short, got up to meet me, while all round the room the young clerks, bending over the papers on their desks, cast upward glances in my direction. The fat man, without waiting for my complaint, wheezing heavily and in a tone as if he himself were incredulous, conveyed to me the news that Falk—Captain Falk—had declined— had absolutely declined—to tow my ship—to have any thing to do with my ship—this day or any other day. Never!

I did my best to preserve a cool appearance, but, all the same, I must have shown how much taken aback I was. We were talking in the middle of the room. Suddenly behind my back some ass blew his nose with great force, and at the same time another quill-driver jumped up and went out on the landing hastily. It occurred to me I was cutting a foolish figure there. I demanded angrily to see the principal in his private room.

The skin of Mr. Siegers' head showed dead white between the iron grey streaks of hair lying plastered cross-wise from ear to ear over the top of his skull in the manner of a bandage. His narrow sunken face was of an uniform and permanent terra-cotta colour, like a piece of pottery. He was sickly, thin, and short, with wrists like a boy of ten. But from that debile body there issued a bullying voice, tremendously loud, harsh and resonant, as if produced by some powerful mechanical contrivance in the nature of a fog-horn. I do not know what he did with it in the private life of his home, but in the larger sphere of business it presented the advantage of overcoming arguments without the slightest mental effort, by the mere volume of sound. We had had several passages of arms. It took me all I knew to guard the interest of my owners—whom, *nota bene*, I had never seen—while Siegers (who had made their acquaintance some years before, during a business tour in Australia) pretended to the knowledge of their innermost minds, and, in the character of "our very good friends" threw them perpetually at my head.

He looked at me with a jaundiced eye (there was no love lost between us), and declared at once that it was strange, very strange. His pronunciation of English was so extravagant that I can't even attempt to reproduce it. For instance, he said "Fferie strantch." Combined with the bellowing intonation it made the language of one's childhood sound weirdly startling, and even if considered purely as a kind of unmeaning noise it filled you with astonishment at first. "They had," he continued, "been acquainted with Captain Falk for very many years, and never had any reason...."

"That's why I come to you, of course," I interrupted. "I've the right to know the meaning of this infernal nonsense." In the half-light of the room, which was greenish, because of the tree-tops screening the window, I saw him writhe his meagre shoulders. It came into my head, as disconnected ideas will come at all sorts of times into one's head, that this, most likely, was the very room where, if the tale were true, Falk had been lectured by Mr. Siegers, the father. Mr. Siegers' (the son's) overwhelming voice, in brassy blasts, as though he had been trying to articulate his words through a trombone, was expressing his great regret at conduct characterised by a very marked want of discretion... As I lived I was being lectured too! His deafening gibberish was difficult to follow, but it was *my* conduct—mine!—that... Damn! I wasn't going to stand this.

"What on earth are you driving at?" I asked in a passion. I put my hat on my head (he never offered a seat to anybody), and as he seemed for the moment struck dumb by my irreverence, I turned my back on him and marched out. His vocal arrangements blared after me a few threats of coming down on the ship for the demurrage of the lighters, and all the other expenses consequent upon the delays arising from my frivolity.

Once outside in the sunshine my head swam. It was no longer a question of mere delay. I perceived myself involved in hopeless and humiliating absurdities that were leading me to something very like a disaster. "Let us be calm," I muttered to myself, and ran into the shade of a leprous wall. From that short side-street I could see the broad main thoroughfare ruinous and gay, running away, away between stretches of decaying masonry, bamboo fences, ranges of arcades of brick and plaster, hovels of lath and mud, lofty temple gates of carved timber, huts of rotten mats—an immensely wide thoroughfare, loosely packed as far as the eye could reach with a barefooted and brown multitude paddling ankle deep in the dust. For a moment I felt myself about to go out of my mind with worry and desperation.

Some allowance must be made for the feeling of a young man new to responsibility. I thought of my crew. Half of them were ill, and I really began to think that some of them would end by dying on board if I couldn't get them out to sea soon. Obviously I should have to take my ship down the river, either working under canvas or dredging with the anchor down; operations which, in common with many modern sailors, I only knew theoretically. And I almost shrank from undertaking them shorthanded and without local knowledge of the river bed, which is so necessary for the confident handling of the ship. There were no pilots, no beacons, no buoys of any sort; but there was a very devil of a current for anybody to see, no end of shoal places, and at least two obviously awkward turns of the channel between me and the sea. But how dangerous these turns were I could not tell. I didn't even know what my ship was capable of! I had never handled her in my life. A misunderstanding between a man and his ship, in a difficult river with no room to make it up, is bound to end in trouble for the man. On the other hand, it must be owned I had not much reason to count upon a general run of good luck. And suppose I had the misfortune to pile her up high and dry on some beastly shoal? That would have been the final undoing of that voyage. It was plain that if Falk refused to tow me out he would also refuse to pull me off. This meant—what? A day lost at the very best; but more likely a whole fortnight of frizzling on some pestilential mudflat, of desperate work, of discharging cargo; more than likely it meant borrowing money at an exorbitant rate of interest—from the Siegers' gang too at that. They were a power in the port. And that elderly seaman of mine, Gambril, had looked pretty ghastly when I went forward to dose him with quinine that morning. *He* would certainly die—not to speak of two or three others that seemed nearly as bad, and of the rest of them just ready to catch any tropical disease going. Horror, ruin and everlasting remorse. And no help. None. I had fallen amongst a lot of unfriendly lunatics!

At any rate, if I must take my ship down myself it was my duty to procure if possible some local knowledge. But that was not easy. The only person I could think of for that service was a certain Johnson, formerly captain of a country ship, but now spliced to a country wife and gone utterly to the bad. I had only heard of him in the vaguest way, as living concealed in the thick of two hundred thousand natives, and only emerging into the light of day for the purpose of hunting up some brandy. I had a notion that if I could lay my hands on him I would sober him on board my ship and use him for a pilot. Better than nothing. Once a sailor always a sailor—and he had known the river for years. But in our Consulate (where I arrived dripping after a sharp walk) they could tell me nothing. The excellent young men on the staff, though willing to help me, belonged to a sphere of the white colony for which that sort of Johnson does not exist. Their suggestion was that I should hunt the man up myself with the help of the Consulate's constable—an ex-sergeant-major of a regiment of Hussars.

This man, whose usual duty apparently consisted in sitting behind a little table in an outer room of Consular offices, when ordered to assist me in my search for Johnson displayed lots of energy and a marvellous amount of local knowledge of a sort. But he did not conceal an immense and sceptical contempt for the whole business. We explored together on that afternoon an infinity of infamous grog shops, gambling dens, opium dens. We walked up narrow lanes where our gharry—a tiny box of a thing on wheels, attached to a jibbing Burmah pony—could by no means have passed. The constable seemed to be on terms of scornful intimacy with Maltese, with Eurasians, with Chinamen, with Klings, and with the sweepers attached to a temple, with whom he talked at the gate. We interviewed also through a grating in a mud wall closing a blind alley an immensely corpulent Italian, who, the ex-sergeant-major remarked to me perfunctorily, had "killed another man last year." Thereupon he addressed him as "Antonio" and "Old Buck," though that bloated carcase, apparently more than half filling the sort of cell wherein it sat, recalled rather a fat pig in a stye. Familiar and never unbending, the sergeant chucked—absolutely chucked— under the chin a horribly wrinkled and shrivelled old hag propped on a stick, who had volunteered some sort of information: and with the same stolid face he kept up an animated conversation with the groups of swathed brown women, who sat smoking cheroots on the doorsteps of a long range of clay hovels. We got out of the gharry and clambered into dwellings airy like packing crates, or descended into places sinister like cellars. We got in, we drove on, we got out again for the sole purpose, as it seemed, of looking behind a heap of rubble. The sun declined; my companion was curt and sardonic in his answers, but it appears we were just missing Johnson all along. At last our conveyance stopped once more with a jerk, and the driver jumping down opened the door.

A black mudhole blocked the lane. A mound of garbage crowned with the dead body of a dog arrested us not. An empty Australian beef tin bounded cheerily before the toe of my boot. Suddenly we clambered through a gap in a prickly fence. . . .

It was a very clean native compound: and the big native woman, with bare brown legs as thick as bedposts, pursuing on all fours a silver dollar that came rolling out from somewhere, was Mrs. Johnson herself. "Your man's at home," said the ex-sergeant, and stepped aside in complete and marked indifference to anything that might follow. Johnson—at home—stood with his back to a native house built on posts and with its walls made of mats. In his left hand he held a banana. Out of the right he dealt another dollar into space. The woman captured this one on the wing, and there and then plumped down on the ground to look at us with greater comfort.

"My man" was sallow of face, grizzled, unshaven, muddy on elbows and back; where the seams of his serge coat yawned you could see his white nakedness. The vestiges of a paper collar encircled his neck. He looked at us with a grave, swaying surprise. "Where do you come from?" he asked. My heart sank. How could I have been stupid enough to waste energy and time for this?

But having already gone so far I approached a little nearer and declared the purpose of my visit. He would have to come at once with me, sleep on board my ship, and to-morrow, with the first of the ebb, he would give me his assistance in getting my ship down to the sea, without steam. A six-hundred-ton barque, drawing nine feet aft. I proposed to give him eighteen dollars for his local knowledge; and all the time I was speaking he kept on considering attentively the various aspects of the banana, holding first one side up to his eye, then the other.

"You've forgotten to apologise," he said at last with extreme precision. "Not being a gentleman yourself, you don't know apparently when you intrude upon a gentleman. I am one. I wish you to understand that when I am in funds I don't work, and now . . ."

I would have pronounced him perfectly sober had he not paused in great concern to try and brush a hole off the knee of his trousers.

"I have money—and friends. Every gentleman has. Perhaps you would like to know my friend? His name is Falk. You could borrow some money. Try to remember. F-A-L-K. Falk." Abruptly his tone changed. "A noble heart," he said muzzily.

"Has Falk been giving you some money?" I asked, appalled by the detailed finish of the dark plot.

"Lent me, my good man, not given me," he corrected suavely. "Met me taking the air last evening, and being as usual anxious to oblige—Hadn't you better go to the devil out of my compound?"

And upon this, without other warning, he let fly with the banana, which missed my head and took the constable just under the left eye. He rushed at the miserable Johnson, stammering with fury. They fell. . . . But why dwell on the wretchedness, the breathlessness, the degradation, the senselessness, the weariness, the ridicule and humiliation and—and—the perspiration, of these moments? I dragged the ex-hussar off. He was like a wild beast. It seems he had been greatly annoyed at losing his free afternoon on my account. The garden of his bungalow required his personal attention, and at the slight blow of the banana the brute in him had broken loose. We left Johnson on his back still black in the face, but beginning to kick feebly. Meantime, the big woman had remained sitting on the ground, apparently paralysed with extreme terror.

For half an hour we jolted inside our rolling box, side by side, in profound silence. The ex-sergeant was busy staunching the blood of a long scratch on his cheek. "I hope you're satisfied," he said suddenly. "That's what comes of all that tomfool business. If you hadn't quarrelled with that tugboat skipper over some girl or other, all this wouldn't have happened."

"You heard *that* story?" I said.

"Of course I heard. And I shouldn't wonder if the Consul-General himself doesn't come to hear of it. How am I to go before him to-morrow with that thing on my cheek—I want to know. It's *you* who ought to have got this!"

After that, till the gharry stopped and he jumped out without leave-taking, he swore to himself steadily, horribly; muttering great, purposeful, trooper oaths, to which the worst a sailor can do is like the prattle of a child. For my part I had just the strength to crawl into Schomberg's coffee-room, where I wrote at a little table a note to the mate instructing him to get everything ready for dropping down the river next day. I couldn't face my ship. Well! she had a clever sort of skipper and no mistake—poor thing! What a horrid mess! I took my head between my hands. At times the obviousness of my innocence would reduce me to despair. What had I done? If I had done something to bring about the situation I should at least have learned not to do it again. But I felt guiltless to the point of imbecility. The room was empty yet; only Schomberg prowled round me goggle-eyed and with a sort of awed respectful curiosity. No doubt he had set the story going himself; but he was a good-hearted chap, and I am really persuaded he participated in all my troubles. He did what he could for me. He ranged aside the heavy matchstand, set a chair straight, pushed a spittoon slightly with his foot—as you show small attentions to a friend under a great sorrow—sighed, and at last, unable to hold his tongue:

"Well! I warned you, captain. That's what comes of running your head against Mr. Falk. Man'll stick at nothing."

I sat without stirring, and after surveying me with a sort of commiseration in his eyes, he burst out in a hoarse whisper: "But for a fine lump of a girl, she's a fine lump of a girl." He made a loud smacking noise with his thick lips. "The finest lump of a girl that I ever..." he was going on with great unction, but for some reason or other broke off. I fancied myself throwing something at his head. "I don't blame you, captain. Hang me if I do," he said with a patronising air.

"Thank you," I said resignedly. It was no use fighting against this false fate. I don't know even if I was sure myself where the truth of the matter began. The conviction that it would end disastrously had been driven into me by all the successive shocks my sense of security had received. I began to ascribe an extraordinary potency to agents in themselves powerless. It was as if Schomberg's baseless gossip had the power to bring about the thing itself or the abstract enmity of Falk could put my ship ashore.

I have already explained how fatal this last would have been. For my further action, my youth, my inexperience, my very real concern for the health of my crew must be my excuse. The action itself, when it came, was purely impulsive. It was set in movement quite undiplomatically and simply by Falk's appearance in the doorway of the coffee-room.

The room was full by then and buzzing with voices. I had been looked at with curiosity by every one, but how am I to describe the sensation produced by the appearance of Falk himself blocking the doorway? The tension of expectation could be measured by the profundity of the silence that fell upon the very click of the billiard balls. As to Schomberg, he looked extremely frightened; he hated mortally any sort of row (*fracas* he called it) in his establishment. *Fracas* was bad for business, he affirmed; but, in truth, this specimen of portly, middle-aged manhood was of a timid disposition. I don't know what, considering my presence in the place, they all hoped would come of it. A sort of stag fight, perhaps. Or they may have supposed Falk had come in only to annihilate me completely. As a matter of fact, Falk had come in because Hermann had asked him to inquire after the precious white cotton parasol which, in the worry and excitement of the previous day, he had forgotten at the table where we had held our little discussion.

It was this that gave me my opportunity. I don't think I would have gone to seek Falk out. No. I don't think so. There are limits. But there was an opportunity and I seized it—I have already tried to explain why. Now I will merely state that, in my opinion, to get his sickly crew into the sea air and secure a quick despatch for his ship a skipper would be justified in going to any length, short of absolute crime. He should put his pride in his pocket; he may accept confidences; he must explain his innocence as if it were a sin; he may take advantage of misconceptions, of desires and of weaknesses; he ought to conceal his horror and other emotions, and, if the fate of a human being, and that human being a magnificent young girl, is strangely involved—why, he should contemplate that fate (whatever it might seem to be) without turning a hair. And all these things I have done; the explaining, the listening, the pretending—even to the discretion—and nobody, not even Hermann's niece, I believe, need throw stones at me now. Schomberg at all events needn't, since from first to last, I am happy to say, there was not the slightest "*fracas.*"

Overcoming a nervous contraction of the windpipe, I had managed to exclaim "Captain Falk!" His start of surprise was perfectly genuine, but afterwards he neither smiled nor scowled. He simply waited. Then, when I had said, "I must have a talk with you," and had pointed to a chair at my table, he moved up to me, though he didn't sit down. Schomberg, however, with a long tumbler in his hand, was making towards us prudently, and I discovered then the only sign of weakness in Falk. He had for Schomberg a repulsion resembling that sort of physical fear some people experience at the sight of a toad. Perhaps to a man so essentially and silently concentrated upon himself (though he could talk well enough, as I was to find out presently) the other's irrepressible loquacity, embracing every human being within range of the tongue, might have appeared unnatural, disgusting, and monstrous. He suddenly gave signs of restiveness—positively like a horse about to rear, and, muttering hurriedly as if in great pain, "No. I can't stand that fellow," seemed ready to bolt. This weakness of his gave me the advantage at the very start. "Verandah," I suggested, as if rendering him a service, and walked him out by the arm. We stumbled over a few chairs; we had the feeling of open space before us, and felt the fresh breath of the river—fresh, but tainted. The Chinese theatres across the water made, in the sparsely twinkling masses of gloom an Eastern town presents at night, blazing centres of light, and of a distant and howling uproar. I felt him become suddenly tractable again like an animal, like a good-tempered horse when the object that scares him is removed. Yes. I felt in the darkness there how tractable he was, without my conviction of his inflexibility—tenacity, rather, perhaps—being in the least weakened. His very arm abandoning itself to my grasp was as hard as marble—like a limb of iron. But I heard a tumultuous scuffling of boot-soles within. The unspeakable idiots inside were crowding to the windows, climbing over each other's backs behind the blinds, billiard cues and all. Somebody broke a window-pane, and with the sound of falling glass, so suggestive of riot and devastation, Schomberg reeled out after us in a state of funk which had prevented his parting with his brandy and soda. He must have trembled like an aspen leaf. The piece of ice in the long tumbler he held in his hand tinkled with an effect of chattering teeth. "I beg you, gentlemen," he expostulated thickly. "Come! Really, now, I must insist..."

How proud I am of my presence of mind! "Hallo," I said instantly in a loud and naïve tone, "somebody's breaking your windows, Schomberg. Would you please tell one of your boys to bring out here a pack of cards and a couple of lights? And two long drinks. Will you?"

To receive an order soothed him at once. It was business. "Certainly," he said in an immensely relieved tone. The night was rainy, with wandering gusts of wind, and while we waited for the candles Falk said, as if to justify his panic, "I don't interfere in anybody's business. I don't give any occasion for talk. I am a respectable man. But this fellow is always making out something wrong, and can never rest till he gets somebody to believe him."

This was the first of my knowledge of Falk. This desire of respectability, of being like everybody else, was the only recognition he vouchsafed to the organisation of mankind. For the rest he might have been the member of a herd, not of a society. Self-preservation was his only concern. Not selfishness, but mere self-preservation. Selfishness presupposes consciousness, choice, the presence of other men; but his instinct acted as though he were the last of mankind nursing that law like the only spark of a sacred fire. I don't mean to say that living naked in a cavern would have satisfied him. Obviously he was the creature of the conditions to which he was born. No doubt self-preservation meant also the preservation of these conditions. But essentially it meant something much more simple, natural, and powerful. How shall I express it? It meant the preservation of the five senses of his body—let us say—taking it in its narrowest as well as in its widest meaning. I think you will admit before long the justice of this judgment. However, as we stood there together in the dark verandah I had judged nothing as yet—and I had no desire to judge—which is an idle practice anyhow. The light was long in coming.

"Of course," I said in a tone of mutual understanding, "it isn't exactly a game of cards I want with you."

I saw him draw his hands down his face—the vague stir of the passionate and meaningless gesture; but he waited in silent patience. It was only when the lights had been brought out that he opened his lips. I understood his mumble to mean that "he didn't know any game."

"Like this Schomberg and all the other fools will have to keep off," I said tearing open the pack. "Have you heard that we are universally supposed to be quarrelling about a girl? You know who—of course. I am really ashamed to ask, but is it possible that you do me the honour to think me dangerous?"

As I said these words I felt how absurd it was and also I felt flattered—for, really, what else could it be? His answer, spoken in his usual dispassionate undertone, made it clear that it was so, but not precisely as flattering as I supposed. He thought me dangerous with Hermann, more than with the girl herself; but, as to quarrelling, I saw at once how inappropriate the word was. We had no quarrel. Natural forces are not quarrelsome. You can quarrel with the wind that inconveniences and humiliates you by blowing off your hat in a street full of people. He had no quarrel with me. Neither would a boulder, falling on my head, have had. He fell upon me in accordance with the law by which he was moved—not of gravitation, like a detached stone, but of self-preservation. Of course this is giving it a rather wide interpretation. Strictly speaking, he had existed and could have existed without being married. Yet he told me that he had found it more and more difficult to live alone. Yes. He told me this in his low, careless voice, to such a pitch of confidence had we arrived at the end of half an hour.

It took me just about that time to convince him that I had never dreamed of marrying Hermann's niece. Could any necessity have been more extravagant? And the difficulty was the greater because he was so hard hit that he couldn't imagine anybody being able to remain in a state of indifference. Any man with eyes in his head, he seemed to think, could not help coveting so much bodily magnificence. This profound belief was conveyed by the manner he listened sitting sideways to the table and playing absently with a few cards I had dealt to him at random. And the more I saw into him the more I saw of him. The wind swayed the lights so that his sunburnt face, whiskered to the eyes, seemed to successively flicker crimson at me and to go out. I saw the extraordinary breadth of the high cheek-bones, the perpendicular style of the features, the massive forehead, steep like a cliff, denuded at the top, largely uncovered at the temples. The fact is I had never before seen him without his hat; but now, as if my fervour had made him hot, he had taken it off and laid it gently on the floor. Something peculiar in the shape and setting of his yellow eyes gave them the provoking silent intensity which characterised his glance. But the face was thin, furrowed, worn; I discovered that through the bush of his hair, as you may detect the gnarled shape of a tree trunk lost in a dense undergrowth. These overgrown cheeks were sunken. It was an anchorite's bony head fitted with a Capuchin's beard and adjusted to a herculean body. I don't mean athletic. Hercules, I take it, was not an athlete. He was a strong man, susceptible to female charms, and not afraid of dirt. And thus with Falk, who was a strong man. He was extremely strong, just as the girl (since I must think of them together) was magnificently attractive by the masterful power of flesh and blood, expressed in shape, in size, in attitude—that is by a straight appeal to the senses. His mind meantime, preoccupied with respectability, impervious to my protestations; and I went so far as to protest that I would just as soon think of marrying my mother's (dear old lady!) faithful female cook as Hermann's niece. Sooner, I protested, in my desperation, much sooner; but it did not appear that he saw anything outrageous in the proposition, and in his sceptical immobility he seemed to nurse the argument that at all events the cook was very, very far away. It must be said that, just before, I had gone wrong by appealing to the evidence of my manner whenever I called on board the *Diana*. I had never attempted to approach the girl, or to speak to her, or even to look at her in any marked way. Nothing could be clearer. But, as his own idea of—let us say—courting, seemed to consist precisely in sitting silently for hours in the vicinity of the beloved object, that line of argument inspired him with distrust. Staring down his extended legs he let out a grunt—as much as to say, "That's all very fine, but you can't throw dust in *my* eyes."

At last I was exasperated into saying, "Why don't you put the matter at rest by talking to Hermann?" and I added sneeringly: "You don't expect me perhaps to speak for you?"

To this he said, very loud for him, "Would you?"

And for the first time he lifted his head to look at me with wonder and incredulity. He lifted his head so sharply that there could be no mistake. I had touched a spring. I saw the whole extent of my opportunity, and could hardly believe in it.

"Why. Speak to . . . Well, of course," I proceeded very slowly, watching him with great attention, for, on my word, I feared a joke. "Not, perhaps, to the young lady herself. I can't speak German, you know. But . . ."

He interrupted me with the earnest assurance that Hermann had the highest opinion of me; and at once I felt the need for the greatest possible diplomacy at this juncture. So I demurred just enough to draw him on. Falk sat up, but except for a very noticeable enlargement of the pupils, till the irises of his eyes were reduced to two narrow yellow rings, his face, I should judge, was incapable of expressing excitement. "Oh, yes! Hermann did have the greatest . . ."

"Take up your cards. Here's Schomberg peeping at us through the blind!" I said.

We went through the motions of what might have been a game of écarté. Presently the intolerable scandalmonger withdrew, probably to inform the people in the billiard-room that we two were gambling on the verandah like mad.

We were not gambling, but it was a game; a game in which I felt I held the winning cards. The stake, roughly speaking, was the success of the voyage—

for me; and he, I apprehended, had nothing to lose. Our intimacy matured rapidly, and before many words had been exchanged I perceived that the excellent Hermann had been making use of me. That simple and astute Teuton had been, it seems, holding me up to Falk in the light of a rival. I was young enough to be shocked at so much duplicity. "Did he tell you that in so many words?" I asked with indignation.

Hermann had not. He had given hints only; and of course it had not taken very much to alarm Falk; but, instead of declaring himself, he had taken steps to remove the family from under my influence. He was perfectly straightforward about it—as straightforward as a tile falling on your head. There was no duplicity in that man; and when I congratulated him on the perfection of his arrangements—even to the bribing of the wretched Johnson against me—he had a genuine movement of protest. Never bribed. He knew the man wouldn't work as long as he had a few cents in his pocket to get drunk on, and, naturally (he said—"*naturally*") he let him have a dollar or two. He was himself a sailor, he said, and anticipated the view another sailor, like myself, was bound to take. On the other hand, he was sure that I should have to come to grief. He hadn't been knocking about for the last seven years up and down that river for nothing. It would have been no disgrace to me—but he asserted confidently I would have had my ship very awkwardly ashore at a spot two miles below the Great Pagoda. . . .

And with all that he had no ill-will. That was evident. This was a crisis in which his only object had been to gain time—I fancy. And presently he mentioned that he had written for some jewellery, real good jewellery—had written to Hong-Kong for it. It would arrive in a day or two.

"Well, then," I said cheerily, "everything is all right. All you've got to do is to present it to the lady together with your heart, and live happy ever after."

Upon the whole he seemed to accept that view as far as the girl was concerned, but his eyelids drooped. There was still something in the way. For one thing Hermann disliked him so much. As to me, on the contrary, it seemed as though he could not praise me enough. Mrs. Hermann too. He didn't know why they disliked him so. It made everything most difficult.

I listened impassive, feeling more and more diplomatic. His speech was not transparently clear. He was one of those men who seem to live, feel, suffer in a sort of mental twilight. But as to being fascinated by the girl and possessed by the desire of home life with her—it was as clear as daylight. So much being at stake, he was afraid of putting it to the hazard of the declaration. Besides, there was something else. And with Hermann being so set against him . . .

"I see," I said thoughtfully, while my heart beat fast with the excitement of my diplomacy. "I don't mind sounding Hermann. In fact, to show you how mistaken you were, I am ready to do all I can for you in that way."

A light sigh escaped him. He drew his hands down his face, and it emerged, bony, unchanged of expression, as if all the tissues had been ossified. All the passion was in those big brown hands. He was satisfied. Then there was that other matter. If there were anybody on earth it was I who could persuade Hermann to take a reasonable view! I had a knowledge of the world and lots of experience. Hermann admitted this himself. And then I was a sailor too. Falk thought that a sailor would be able to understand certain things best . . .

He talked as if the Hermanns had been living all their life in a rural hamlet, and I alone had been capable, with my practice in life, of a large and indulgent view of certain occurrences. That was what my diplomacy was leading me to. I began suddenly to dislike it.

"I say, Falk," I asked quite brusquely, "you haven't already a wife put away somewhere?"

The pain and disgust of his denial were very striking. Couldn't I understand that he was as respectable as any white man hereabouts; earning his living honestly. He was suffering from my suspicion, and the low undertone of his voice made his protestations sound very pathetic. For a moment he shamed me, but, my diplomacy notwithstanding, I seemed to develop a conscience, as if in very truth it were in my power to decide the success of this matrimonial enterprise. By pretending hard enough we come to believe anything—anything to our advantage. And I had been pretending very hard, because I meant yet to be towed safely down the river. But, through conscience or stupidity, I couldn't help alluding to the Vanlo affair. "You acted rather badly there. Didn't you?" was what I ventured actually to say—for the logic of our conduct is always at the mercy of obscure and unforeseen impulses.

His dilated pupils swerved from my face, glancing at the window with a sort of scared fury. We heard behind the blinds the continuous and sudden clicking of ivory, a jovial murmur of many voices, and Schomberg's deep manly laugh.

"That confounded old woman of a hotel-keeper then would never, never let it rest!" Falk exclaimed. "Well, yes! It had happened two years ago." When it came to the point he owned he couldn't make up his mind to trust Fred Valno—no sailor, a bit of a fool too. He could not trust him, but, to stop his row, he had lent him enough money to pay all his debts before he left. I was greatly surprised to hear this. Then Falk could not be such a miser after all. So much the better for the girl. For a time he sat silent; then he picked up a card, and while looking at it he said:

"You need not think of anything bad. It was an accident. I've been unfortunate once."

"Then in heaven's name say nothing about it."

As soon as these words were out of my mouth I fancied I had said something immoral. He shook his head negatively. It had to be told. He considered it proper that the relations of the lady should know. No doubt—I thought to myself—had Miss Valno not been thirty and damaged by the climate he would have found it possible to entrust Fred Valno with this confidence. And then the figure of Hermann's niece appeared before my mind's eye, with the wealth of her opulent form, her rich youth, her lavish strength. With that powerful and immaculate vitality, her girlish form must have shouted aloud of life to that man, whereas poor Miss Valno could only sing sentimental songs to the strumming of a piano.

"And that Hermann hates me, I know it!" he cried in his undertone, with a sudden recrudescence of anxiety. "I must tell them. It is proper that they should know. You would say so yourself."

He then murmured an utterly mysterious allusion to the necessity for peculiar domestic arrangements. Though my curiosity was excited I did not want to hear any of his confidences. I feared he might give me a piece of information that would make my assumed *rôle* of match-maker odious—however unreal it was. I was aware that he could have the girl for the asking; and keeping down a desire to laugh in his face, I expressed a confident belief in my ability to argue away Hermann's dislike for him. "I am sure I can make it all right," I said. He looked very pleased.

And when we rose not a word had been said about towage! Not a word! The game was won and the honour was safe. Oh! blessed white cotton umbrella! We shook hands and I was holding myself with difficulty from breaking into a step dance of joy when he came back, striding all the length of the verandah, and said doubtfully:

"I say, captain, I have your word? You—you—won't turn round?"

Heavens! The fright he gave me. Behind his tone of doubt there was something desperate and menacing. The infatuated ass. But I was equal to the situation.

"My dear Falk," I said, beginning to lie with a glibness and effrontery that amazed me even at the time—"confidence for confidence." (He had made no confidences.) "I will tell you that I am already engaged to an extremely charming girl at home, and so you understand . . ."

He caught my hand and wrung it in a crushing grip.

"Pardon me. I feel it every day more difficult to live alone . . ."

"On rice and fish," I interrupted smartly, giggling with the sheer nervousness of a danger escaped.

He dropped my hand as if it had become suddenly red hot. A moment of profound silence ensued, as though something extraordinary had happened.

"I promise you to obtain Hermann's consent," I faltered out at last, and it seemed to me that he could not help seeing through that humbugging promise. "If there's anything else to get over I shall endeavour to stand by you," I conceded further, feeling somehow defeated and overborne; "but you must do your best yourself."

"I have been unfortunate once," he muttered unemotionally, and turning his back on me he went away, thumping slowly the plank floor as if his feet had been shod with iron.

Next morning, however, he was lively enough as man-boat, a combination of splashing and shouting; of the insolent commotion below with the steady overbearing glare of the silent head-piece above. He turned us out most unnecessarily at an ungodly hour, but it was nearly eleven in the morning before he brought me up a cable's length from Hermann's ship. And he did it very badly too, in a hurry, and nearly contriving to miss altogether the patch of good holding ground, because, forsooth, he had caught sight of Hermann's niece on the poop. And so did I; and probably as soon as he had seen her himself. I saw the modest, sleek glory of the tawny head, and the full, grey shape of the girlish print frock she filled so perfectly, so satisfactorily, with the seduction of unfaltering curves—a very nymph of Diana the Huntress. And *Diana* the ship sat, high-walled and as solid as an institution, on the smooth level of the water, the most uninspiring and respectable craft upon the seas, useful and ugly, devoted to the support of domestic virtues like any grocer's shop on shore. At once Falk steamed away; for there was some work for him to do. He would return in the evening.

He ranged close by us, passing out dead slow, without a hail. The beat of the paddle-wheels reverberating amongst the stony islets, as if from the ruined walls of a vast arena, filled the anchorage confusedly with the clapping sounds of a mighty and leisurely applause. Abreast of Hermann's ship he stopped the engines; and a profound silence reigned over the rocks, the shore and the sea, for the time it took him to raise his hat aloft before the nymph of the grey print frock. I had snatched up my binoculars, and I can answer for it she didn't stir a limb, standing by the rail shapely and erect, with one of her hands grasping a rope at the height of her head, while the way of the tug carried slowly past her the lingering and profound homage of the man. There was for me an enormous significance in the scene, the sense of having witnessed a solemn declaration. The die was cast. After such a manifestation he couldn't back out. And I reflected that it was nothing whatever to me now. With a rush of black smoke belching suddenly out of the funnel, and a mad swirl of paddle-wheels provoking a burst of weird and precipitated clapping, the tug shot out of the desolate arena. The rocky islets lay on the sea like the heaps of a cyclopean ruin on a plain; the centipedes and scorpions lurked under the stones; there was not a single blade of grass in sight anywhere, not a single lizard sunning himself on a boulder by the shore. When I looked again at Hermann's ship the girl had disappeared. I could not detect the smallest dot of a bird on the immense sky, and the flatness of the land continued the flatness of the sea to the naked line of the horizon.

This is the setting now inseparably connected with my knowledge of Falk's misfortune. My diplomacy had brought me there, and now I had only to wait the time for taking up the *rôle* of an ambassador. My diplomacy was a success; my ship was safe; old Gambril would probably live; a feeble sound of a tapping hammer came intermittently from the *Diana*. During the afternoon I looked at times at the old homely ship, the faithful nurse of Hermann's progeny, or yawned towards the distant temple of Buddha, like a lonely hillock on the plain, where shaven priests cherish the thoughts of that Annihilation which is the worthy reward of us all. Unfortunate! He had been unfortunate once. Well, that was not so bad as life goes. And what the devil could be the nature of that misfortune? I remembered that I had known a man before who had declared himself to have fallen, years ago, a victim to misfortune; but this misfortune, whose effects appeared permanent (he looked desperately hard up) when considered dispassionately, seemed indistinguishable from a breach of trust. Could it be something of that nature? Apart, however, from the utter improbability that he would offer to talk of it even to his future uncle-in-law I had a strange feeling that Falk's physique unfitted him for that sort of delinquency. As the person of Hermann's niece exhaled the profound physical charm of feminine form, so her adorer's big frame embodied to my senses the hard, straight masculinity that would conceivably kill but would not condescend to cheat. The thing was obvious. I might just as well have suspected the girl of a curvature of the spine. And I perceived that the sun was about to set.

The smoke of Falk's tug hove in sight, far away at the mouth of the river. It was time for me to assume the character of an ambassador, and the negotiation would not be difficult except in the matter of keeping my countenance. It was all too extravagantly nonsensical, and I conceived that it would be best to compose for myself a grave demeanour. I practised this in my boat as I went along, but the bashfulness that came secretly upon me the moment I stepped on the deck of the *Diana* is inexplicable. As soon as we had exchanged greetings Hermann asked me eagerly if I knew whether Falk had found his white parasol.

"He's going to bring it to you himself directly," I said with great solemnity.

"Meantime I am charged with an important message for which he begs your favourable consideration. He is in love with your niece. . . ."

"*Ach So!*" he hissed with an animosity that made my assumed gravity change into the most genuine concern. What meant this tone? And I hurried on.

"He wishes, with your consent of course, to ask her to marry him at once—before you leave here, that is. He would speak to the Consul."

Hermann sat down and smoked violently. Five minutes passed in that furious meditation, and then, taking the long pipe out of his mouth, he burst into a hot diatribe against Falk—against his cupidity, his stupidity (a fellow that can hardly be got to say "yes" or "no" to the simplest question)—against his outrageous treatment of the shipping in port (because he saw they were at his mercy)—and against his manner of walking, which to his (Hermann's) mind showed a conceit positively unbearable. The damage to the old *Diana* was not forgotten, of course, and there was nothing of any nature said or done by Falk (even to the last offer of refreshment in the hotel) that did not seem to have been a cause of offence. "Had the cheek" to drag him (Hermann) into that coffee room; as though a drink from him could make up for forty-seven dollars and fifty cents of damage in the cost of wood alone—not counting two days' work for the carpenter. Of course he would not stand in the girl's way. He was going home to Germany. There were plenty of poor girls walking about in Germany.

"He's very much in love," was all I found to say.

"Yes," he cried. "And it is time too after making himself and me talked about ashore the last voyage I was here, and then now again; coming on board every evening unsettling the girl's mind, and saying nothing. What sort of conduct is that?"

The seven thousand dollars the fellow was always talking about did not, in his opinion, justify such behaviour. Moreover, nobody had seen them. He (Hermann) seriously doubted if there were seven thousand cents, and the tug, no doubt, was mortgaged up the top of the funnel to the firm of Siegers. But let that pass. He wouldn't stand in the girl's way. Her head was so turned that she had become no good to them of late. Quite unable even to put the children to bed without her aunt. It was bad for the children; they got unruly; and yesterday he actually had to give Gustav a thrashing.

For that, too, Falk was made responsible apparently. And looking at my Hermann's heavy, puffy, good-natured face, I knew he would not exert himself till greatly exasperated, and, therefore, would thrash very hard, and being fat would resent the necessity. How Falk had managed to turn the girl's head was more difficult to understand. I supposed Hermann would know. And then hadn't there been Miss Vanlo? It could not be his silvery tongue, or the subtle seduction of his manner; he had no more of what is called "manner" than an animal—which, however, on the other hand, is never, and can never be called vulgar. Therefore it must have been his bodily appearance, exhibiting a virility of nature as exaggerated as his beard, and resembling a sort of constant ruthlessness. It was seen in the very manner he lolled in the chair. He meant no offence, but his intercourse was characterised by that sort of frank disregard of susceptibilities a man of seven foot six, living in a world of dwarfs, would naturally assume, without in the least wishing to be unkind. But amongst men of his own stature, or nearly, this frank use of his advantages, in such matters as the awful towage bills for instance, caused much impotent gnashing of teeth.

When attentively considered it seemed appalling at times. He was a strange beast. But maybe women liked it. Seen in that light he was well worth taming, and I suppose every woman at the bottom of her heart considers herself as a tamer of strange beasts. But Hermann arose with precipitation to carry the news to his wife. I had barely the time, as he made for the cabin door, to grab him by the seat of his inexpressibles. I begged him to wait till Falk in person had spoken with him. There remained some small matter to talk over, as I understood.

He sat down again at once, full of suspicion.

"What matter?" he said surlily. "I have had enough of his nonsense. There's no matter at all, as he knows very well; the girl has nothing in the world. She came to us in one thin dress when my brother died, and I have a growing family."

"It can't be anything of that kind," I opined. "He's desperately enamoured of your niece. I don't know why he did not say so before. Upon my word, I believe it is because he was afraid to lose, perhaps, the felicity of sitting near her on your quarter deck."

I intimated my conviction that his love was so great as to be in a sense cowardly. The effects of a great passion are unaccountable. It has been known to make a man timid. But Hermann looked at me as if I had foolishly raved; and the twilight was dying out rapidly.

"You don't believe in passion, do you, Hermann?" I said cheerily. "The passion of fear will make a cornered rat courageous. Falk's in a corner. He will take her off your hands in one thin frock just as she came to you. And after ten years' service it isn't a bad bargain," I added.

Far from taking offence, he resumed his air of civic virtue. The sudden night came upon him while he stared placidly along the deck, bringing in contact with his thick lips, and taking away again after a jet of smoke, the curved mouthpiece fitted to the stem of his pipe. The night came upon him and buried in haste his whiskers, his globular eyes, his puffy pale face, his fat knees and the vast flat slippers on his fatherly feet. Only his short arms in respectable white shirt-sleeves remained very visible, propped up like the flippers of a seal reposing on the strand.

"Falk wouldn't settle anything about repairs. Told me to find out first how much wood I should require and he would see," he remarked; and after he had spat peacefully in the dusk we heard over the water the beat of the tug's floats. There is, on a calm night, nothing more suggestive of fierce and headlong haste than the rapid sound made by the paddle-wheels of a boat threshing her way through a quiet sea; and the approach of Falk towards his fate seemed to be urged by an impatient and passionate desire. The engines must have been driven to the very utmost of their revolutions. We heard them slow down at last, and, vaguely, the white hull of the tug appeared moving against the black islets, whilst a slow and rhythmical clapping as of thousands of hands rose on all sides. It ceased all at once, just before Falk brought her up. A single brusque splash was followed by the long drawn rumbling of iron links running through the hawse pipe. Then a solemn silence fell upon the Roadstead.

"He will soon be here," I murmured, and after that we waited for him without a word. Meantime, raising my eyes, I beheld the glitter of a lofty sky above the *Diana's* mastheads. The multitude of stars gathered into clusters, in rows, in lines, in masses, in groups, shone all together, unanimously—and the few isolated ones, blazing by themselves in the midst of dark patches, seemed to be of a superior kind and of an inextinguishable nature. But long striding footsteps were heard hastening along the deck; the high bulwarks of the *Diana* made a deeper darkness. We rose from our chairs quickly, and Falk, appearing before us, all in white, stood still.

Nobody spoke at first, as though we had been covered with confusion. His arrival was fiery, but his white bulk, of indefinite shape and without features, made him loom up like a man of snow.

"The captain here has been telling me..." Hermann began in a homely and amicable voice; and Falk had a low, nervous laugh. His cool, negligent undertone had no inflexions, but the strength of a powerful emotion made him ramble in his speech. He had always desired a home. It was difficult to live alone, though he was not answerable. He was domestic; there had been difficulties; but since he had seen Hermann's niece he found that it had become at last impossible to live by himself. "I mean—impossible," he repeated with no sort of emphasis and only with the slightest of pauses, but the word fell into my mind with the force of a new idea.

"I have not said anything to her yet," Hermann observed quietly. And Falk dismissed this by a "That's all right. Certainly. Very proper." There was a necessity for perfect frankness—in marrying, especially. Hermann seemed attentive, but he seized the first opportunity to ask us into the cabin. "And by-the-by, Falk," he said innocently, as we passed in, "the timber came to no less than forty-seven dollars and fifty cents."

Falk, uncovering his head, lingered in the passage. "Some other time," he said; and Hermann nudged me angrily—I don't know why. The girl alone in the cabin sat sewing at some distance from the table. Falk stopped short in the doorway. Without a word, without a sign, without the slightest inclination of his bony head, by the silent intensity of his look alone, he seemed to lay his herculean frame at her feet. Her hands sank slowly on her lap, and raising her clear eyes, she let her soft, beaming glance enfold him from head to foot like a slow and pale caress. He was very hot when he sat down; she, with bowed head, went on with her sewing; her neck was very white under the light of the lamp; but Falk, hiding his face in the palms of his hands, shuddered faintly. He drew them down, even to his beard, and his uncovered eyes astonished me by their tense and irrational expression—as though he had just swallowed a heavy gulp of alcohol. It passed away while he was binding us to secrecy. Not that he cared, but he did not like to be spoken about; and I looked at the girl's marvellous, at her wonderful, at her regal hair, plaited tight into that one astonishing and maidenly tress. Whenever she moved her well-shaped head it would stir stiffly to and fro on her back. The thin cotton sleeve fitted the irreproachable roundness of her arm like a skin; and her very dress, stretched on her bust, seemed to palpitate like a living tissue with the strength of vitality animating her body. How good her complexion was, the outline of her soft cheek and the small convoluted conch of her rosy ear! To pull her needle she kept the little finger apart from the others; it seemed a waste of power to see her sewing—eternally sewing—with that industrious and precise movement of her arm, going on eternally upon all the oceans, under all the skies, in innumerable harbours. And suddenly I heard Falk's voice declare that he could not marry a woman unless she knew of something in his life that had happened ten years ago. It was an accident. An unfortunate accident. It would affect the domestic arrangements of their home, but, once told, it need not be alluded to again for the rest of their lives. "I should want my wife to feel for me," he said. "It has made me unhappy." And how could he keep the knowledge of it to himself—he asked us—perhaps through years and years of companionship? What sort of companionship would that be? He had thought it over. A wife must know. Then why not at once? He counted on Hermann's kindness for presenting the affair in the best possible light. And Hermann's countenance, mystified before, became very sour. He stole an inquisitive glance at me. I shook my head blankly. Some people thought, Falk went on, that such an experience changed a man for the rest of his life. He couldn't say. It was hard, awful, and not to be forgotten, but he did not think himself a worse man than before. Only he talked in his sleep now, he believed.... At last I began to think he had accidentally killed some one; perhaps a friend—his own father maybe; when he went on to say that probably we were aware he never touched meat. Throughout he spoke English, of course on my account.

He swayed forward heavily.

The girl, with her hands raised before her pale eyes, was threading her needle. He glanced at her, and his mighty trunk overshadowed the table, bringing nearer to us the breadth of his shoulders, the thickness of his neck, and that incongruous, anchorite head, burnt in the desert, hollowed and lean as if by excesses of vigils and fasting. His beard flowed imposingly downwards, out of sight, between the two brown hands gripping the edge of the table, and his persistent glance made sombre by the wide dilations of the pupils, fascinated.

"Imagine to yourselves," he said in his ordinary voice, "that I have eaten man."

I could only ejaculate a faint "Ah!" of complete enlightenment. But Hermann, dazed by the excessive shock, actually murmured, "Himmel! What for?"

"It was my terrible misfortune to do so," said Falk in a measured undertone. The girl, unconscious, sewed on. Mrs. Hermann was absent in one of the state-rooms, sitting up with Lena, who was feverish; but Hermann suddenly put both his hands up with a jerk. The embroidered calotte fell, and, in the twinkling of an eye, he had rumpled his hair all ends up in a most extravagant manner. In this state he strove to speak; with every effort his eyes seemed to start further out of their sockets; his head looked like a mop. He choked, gasped, swallowed, and managed to shriek out the one word, "Beast!"

From that moment till Falk went out of the cabin the girl, with her hands folded on the work lying in her lap, never took her eyes off him. His own, in the blindness of his heart, darted all over the cabin, only seeking to avoid the sight of Hermann's raving. It was ridiculous, and was made almost terrible by the stillness of every other person present. It was contemptible, and was made appalling by the man's overmastering horror of his awful sincerity, coming to him suddenly, with the confession of such a fact. He walked with great strides; he gasped. He wanted to know from Falk how dared he to come and tell him this? Did he think himself a proper person to be sitting in this cabin where his wife and children lived? Tell his niece! Expected him to tell his niece! His own brother's daughter! Shameless! Did I ever hear tell of such impudence?—he appealed to me. "This man here ought to have gone and hidden himself out of sight instead of . . ."

"But it's a great misfortune for me. But it's a great misfortune for me," Falk would ejaculate from time to time.

However, Hermann kept on running frequently against the corners of the table. At last he lost a slipper, and crossing his arms on his breast, walked up with one stocking foot very close to Falk, in order to ask him whether he did think there was anywhere on earth a woman abandoned enough to mate with such a monster. "Did he? Did he? Did he?" I tried to restain him. He tore himself out of my hands; he found his slipper, and, endeavouring to put it on, stormed standing on one leg—and Falk, with a face unmoved and averted eyes, grasped all his mighty beard in one vast palm.

"Was it right then for me to die myself?" he asked thoughtfully. I laid my hand on his shoulder.

"Go away." I whispered imperiously, without any clear reason for this advice, except that I wished to put an end to Hermann's odious noise. "Go away."

He looked searchingly for a moment at Hermann before he made a move. I left the cabin too to see him out of the ship. But he hung about the quarter deck.

"It is my misfortune," he said in a steady voice.

"You were stupid to blurt it out in such a manner. After all, we don't hear such confidences every day."

"What does the man mean?" he mused in deep undertones. "Somebody had to die—but why me?"

He remained still for a time in the dark—silent; almost invisible. All at once he pinned my elbows to my sides. I felt utterly powerless in his grip, and his voice, whispering in my ear, vibrated.

"It's worse than hunger. Captain, do you know what that means? And I could kill then—or be killed. I wish the crowbar had smashed my skull ten years ago. And I've got to live now. Without her. Do you understand? Perhaps many years. But how? What can be done? If I had allowed myself to look at her once I would have carried her off before that man in my hands—like this."

I felt myself snatched off the deck, then suddenly dropped—and I staggered backwards, feeling bewildered and bruised. What a man! All was still; he was gone. I heard Hermann's voice declaiming in the cabin, and I went in.

I could not at first make out a single word, but Mrs. Hermann, who, attracted by the noise, had come in some time before, with an expression of surprise and mild disapproval depicted broadly on her face, was giving now all the signs of profound, helpless agitation. Her husband shot a string of guttural words at her, and instantly putting out one hand to the bulkhead as if to save herself from falling, she clutched the loose bosom of her dress with the other. He harangued the two women extraordinarily, with much of his shirt hanging out of his waistbelt, stamping his foot, turning from one to the other, sometimes throwing both his arms together, straight up above his rumpled hair, and keeping them in that position while he uttered a passage of loud denunciation; at others folding them tight across his breast—and then he hissed with indignation, elevating his shoulders and protruding his head. The girl was crying.

She had not changed her attitude. From her steady eyes that, following Falk in his retreat, had remained fixed wistfully on the cabin door, the tears fell rapid, thick, on her hands, on the work in her lap, warm and gentle like a shower in spring. She wept without grimacing, without noise—very touching, very quiet, with something more of pity than of pain in her face, as one weeps in compassion rather than in grief—and Hermann, before her, declaimed. I caught several times the word "Mensch," man; and also "Fressen," which last I looked up afterwards in my dictionary. It means "Devour." Hermann seemed to be requesting an answer of some sort from her; his whole body swayed. She remained mute and perfectly still; at last his agitation gained her; she put the palms of her hands together, her full lips parted, no sound came. His voice scolded shrilly, his arms went like a windmill—suddenly he shook a thick fist at her. She burst out into loud sobs. He seemed stupefied.

Mrs. Hermann rushed forward babbling rapidly. The two women fell on each other's necks, and, with an arm round her niece's waist, she led her away. Her own eyes were simply streaming, her face was flooded. She shook her head back at me negatively, I wonder why to this day. The girl's head dropped heavily on her shoulder. They disappeared together.

Then Hermann sat down and stared at the cabin floor.

"We don't know all the circumstances," I ventured to break the silence. He retorted tartly that he didn't want to know of any. According to his ideas no circumstances could excuse a crime—and certainly not such a crime. This was the opinion generally received. The duty of a human being was to starve. Falk therefore was a beast, an animal; base, low, vile, despicable, shameless, and deceitful. He had been deceiving him since last year. He was, however, inclined to think that Falk must have gone mad quite recently; for no sane person, without necessity, uselessly, for no earthly reason, and regardless of another's self-respect and peace of mind, would own to having devoured human flesh. "Why tell?" he cried. "Who was asking him?" It showed Falk's brutality because after all he had selfishly caused him (Hermann) much pain. He would have preferred not to know that such an unclean creature had been in the habit of caressing his children. He hoped I would say nothing of all this ashore, though. He wouldn't like it to get about that he had been intimate with an eater of men— a common cannibal. As to the scene he had made (which I judged quite unnecessary) he was not going to inconvenience and restrain himself for a fellow that went about courting and upsetting girls' heads, while he knew all the time that no decent housewifely girl could think of marrying him. At least he (Hermann) could not conceive how any girl could. "Fancy Lena! . . . No, it was impossible. The thoughts that would come into their heads every time they sat down to a meal. Horrible! Horrible!"

"You are too squeamish, Hermann," I said.

He seemed to think it was eminently proper to be squeamish if the word meant disgust at Falk's conduct; and turning up his eyes sentimentally he drew my attention to the horrible fate of the victims—the victims of that Falk. I said that I knew nothing about them. He seemed surprised. Could not anybody imagine without knowing? He—for instance—felt he would like to avenge them. But what if—said I—there had not been any? They might have died as it were, naturally—of starvation. He shuddered. But to be eaten—to death! To be devoured! He gave another deep shudder, and asked suddenly, "Do you think it is true?"

His indignation and his personality together would have been enough to spoil the reality of the most authentic thing. When I looked at him I doubted the story—but the remembrance of Falk's words, looks, gestures, invested it not only with an air of reality but with the absolute truth of primitive passion.

"It is true just as much as you are able to make it; and exactly in the way you like to make it. For my part, when I hear you clamouring about it, I don't believe it is true at all."

And I left him pondering. The men in my boat, lying at the foot of *Diana's* side-ladder, told me that the captain of the tug had gone away in his gig some time ago.

I let my fellows pull an easy stroke; because of the heavy dew the clear sparkle of the stars seemed to fall on me cold and wetting. There was a sense of lurking gruesome horror somewhere in my mind, and it was mingled with clear and grotesque images. Schomberg's gastronomic tittle-tattle was responsible for these; and I half hoped I should never see Falk again. But the first thing my anchor-watchman told me was that the captain of the tug was on board. He had sent his boat away and was now waiting for me in the cuddy.

He was lying full length on the stern settee, his face buried in the cushions. I had expected to see it discomposed, contorted, despairing. It was nothing of the kind; it was just as I had seen it twenty times, steady and glaring from the bridge of the tug. It was immovably set and hungry, dominated like the whole man by the singleness of one instinct.

He wanted to live. He had always wanted to live. So we all do—but in us the instinct serves a complex conception, and in him this instinct existed alone. There is in such simple development a gigantic force, and like the pathos of a child's naïve and uncontrolled desire. He wanted that girl, and the utmost that can be said for him was that he wanted that particular girl alone. I think I saw then the obscure beginning, the seed germinating in the soil of an unconscious need, the first shoot of that tree bearing now for a mature mankind the flower and the fruit, the infinite gradation in shades and in flavour of our discriminating love. He was a child. He was as frank as a child too. He was hungry for the girl, terribly hungry, as he had been terribly hungry for food.

Don't be shocked if I declare that in my belief it was the same need, the same pain, the same torture. We are in his case allowed to contemplate the foundation of all the emotions—that one joy which is to live, and the one sadness at the root of the innumerable torments. It was made plain by the way he talked. He had never suffered so. It was gnawing, it was fire; it was there, like this! And after pointing below his breastbone, he made a hard wringing motion with his hands. And I assure you that, seen as I saw it with my bodily eyes, it was anything but laughable. And again, as he was presently to tell me (alluding to an early incident of the disastrous voyage when some damaged meat had been flung overboard), he said that a time soon came when his heart ached (that was the expression he used), and he was ready to tear his hair out at the thought of all that rotten beef thrown away.

I had heard all this; I witnessed his physical struggles, seeing the working of the rack and hearing the true voice of pain. I witnessed it all patiently, because the moment I came into the cuddy he had called upon me to stand by him—and this, it seems, I had diplomatically promised.

His agitation was impressive and alarming in the little cabin, like the floundering of a great whale driven into a shallow cove in a coast. He stood up; he flung himself down headlong; he tried to tear the cushion with his teeth; and again hugging it fiercely to his face he let himself fall on the couch. The whole ship seemed to feel the shock of his despair; and I contemplated with wonder the lofty forehead, the noble touch of time on the uncovered temples, the unchanged hungry character of the face—so strangely ascetic and so incapable of portraying emotion.

What should he do? He had lived by being near her. He had sat—in the evening—I knew?—all his life! She sewed. Her head was bent—so. Her head—like this—and her arms. Ah! Had I seen? Like this.

He dropped on a stool, bowed his powerful neck whose nape was red, and with his hands stitched the air, ludicrous, sublimely imbecile and comprehensible.

And now he couldn't have her? No! That was too much. After thinking too that . . . What had he done? What was my advice? Take her by force? No? Mustn't he? Who was there then to kill him? For the first time I saw one of his features move; a fighting teeth-baring curl of the lip. . . . "Not Hermann, perhaps." He lost himself in thought as though he had fallen out of the world.

I may note that the idea of suicide apparently did not enter his head for a single moment. It occurred to me to ask:

"Where was it that this shipwreck of yours took place?"

"Down south," he said vaguely with a start.

"You are not down south now," I said. "Violence won't do. They would take her away from you in no time. And what was the name of the ship?"

"*Borgmester Dahl*," he said. "It was no shipwreck."

He seemed to be waking up by degrees from that trance, and waking up calmed.

"Not a shipwreck? What was it?"

"Break down," he answered, looking more like himself every moment. By this only I learned that it was a steamer. I had till then supposed they had been starving in boats or on a raft—or perhaps on a barren rock.

"She did not sink then?" I asked in surprise. He nodded. "We sighted the southern ice," he pronounced dreamily.

"And you alone survived?"

He sat down. "Yes. It was a terrible misfortune for me. Everything went wrong. All the men went wrong. I survived."

Remembering the things one reads of it was difficult to realise the true meaning of his answers. I ought to have seen at once—but I did not; so difficult is it for our minds, remembering so much, instructed so much, informed of so much, to get in touch with the real actuality at out elbow. And with my head full of preconceived notions as to how a case of "cannibalism and suffering at sea" should be managed I said—"You were then so lucky in the drawing of lots?"

"Drawing of lots?" he said. "What lots? Do you think I would have allowed my life to go for the drawing of lots?"

Not if he could help it, I perceived, no matter what other life went.

"It was a great misfortune. Terrible. Awful," he said. "Many heads went wrong, but the best men would live."

"The toughest, you mean," I said. He considered the word. Perhaps it was strange to him, though his English was so good.

"Yes," he asserted at last. "The best. It was everybody for himself at last and the ship open to all."

Thus from question to question I got the whole story. I fancy it was the only way I could that night have stood by him. Outwardly at least he was himself again; the first sign of it was the return of that incongruous trick he had of drawing both his hands down his face—and it had its meaning now, with that slight shudder of the frame and the passionate anguish of these hands uncovering a hungry immovable face, the wide pupils of the intent, silent, fascinating eyes.

It was an iron steamer of a most respectable origin. The burgomaster of Falk's native town had built her. She was the first steamer ever launched there. The burgomaster's daughter had christened her. Country people drove in carts from miles around to see her. He told me all this. He got the berth as, what we should call, a chief mate. He seemed to think it had been a feather in his cap; and, in his own corner of the world, this lover of life was of good parentage.

The burgomaster had advanced ideas in the ship-owning line. At that time not every one would have known enough to think of despatching a cargo steamer to the Pacific. But he loaded her with pitch-pine deals and sent her off to hunt for her luck. Wellington was to be the first port, I fancy. It doesn't matter, because in latitude 44° south and somewhere halfway between Good Hope and New Zealand the tail-shaft broke and the propeller dropped off.

They were steaming then with a fresh gale on the quarter and all their canvas set, to help the engines. But by itself the sail power was not enough to keep way on her. When the propeller went the ship broached-to at once, and the masts got whipped over-board.

The disadvantage of being dismasted consisted in this, that they had nothing to hoist flags on to make themselves visible at a distance. In the course of the first few days several ships failed to sight them; and the gale was drifting them out of the usual track. The voyage had been, from the first, neither very successful nor very harmonious. There had been quarrels on board. The captain was a clever, melancholic man, who had no unusual grip on his crew. The ship had been amply provisioned for the passage, but, somehow or other, several barrels of meat were found spoiled on opening, and had been thrown overboard soon after leaving home, as a sanitary measure. Afterwards the crew of the *Borgmester Dahl* thought of that rotten carrion with tears of regret, covetousness and despair.

She drove south. To begin with, there had been an appearance of organisation, but soon the bonds of discipline became relaxed. A sombre idleness succeeded. They looked with sullen eyes at the horizon. The gales increased: she lay in the trough, the seas made a clean breach over her. On one frightful night, when they expected their hulk to turn over with them every moment, a heavy sea broke on board, deluged the store-rooms and spoiled the best part of the remaining provisions. It seems the hatch had not been properly secured. This instance of neglect is characteristic of utter discouragement. Falk tried to inspire some energy into his captain, but failed. From that time he retired more into himself, always trying to do his utmost in the situation. It grew worse. Gale succeeded gale, with black mountains of water hurling themselves on the *Borgmester Dahl*. Some of the men never left their bunks; many became quarrelsome. The chief-engineer, an old man, refused to speak at all to anybody. Others shut themselves up in their berths to cry. On calm days the inert steamer rolled on a leaden sea under a murky sky, or showed, in sunshine, the squalor of sea waifs, the dried white salt, the rust, the jagged broken places. Then the gales came again. They kept body and soul together on short rations. Once, an English ship, scudding in a storm, tried to stand by them, heaving-to pluckily under their lee. The seas swept her decks; the men in oilskins clinging to her rigging looked at them, and they made desperate signs over their shattered bulwarks. Suddenly her main-topsail went, yard and all, in a terrific squall; she had to bear up under bare poles and disappeared.

Other ships had spoken them before, but at first they had refused to be taken off, expecting the assistance of some steamer. There were very few steamers in those latitudes then; and when they desired to leave this dead and drifting carcase, no ship came in sight. They had drifted south out of men's knowledge. They failed to attract the attention of a lonely whaler: and very soon the edge of the polar ice-cap rose from the sea and closed the southern horizon like a wall. One morning they were alarmed by finding themselves floating amongst detached pieces of ice. But the fear of sinking passed away like their vigour, like their hopes; the shocks of the floes knocking against the ship's side could not rouse them from their apathy: and the *Borgmester Dahl* drifted out again, unharmed, into open water. They hardly noticed the change.

The funnel had gone overboard in one of the heavy rolls; two of their three boats had disappeared, washed away in bad weather, and the davits swung to and fro, unsecured, with chafed rope's ends waggling to the roll. Nothing was done on board, and Falk told me how he had often listened to the water washing about the dark engine-room where the engines, stilled for ever, were decaying slowly into a mass of rust, as the stilled heart decays within the lifeless body. At first, after the loss of the motive power, the tiller had been thoroughly secured by lashings. But in course of time these had rotted, chafed, rusted, parting one by one: and the rudder, freed, banged heavily to and fro night and day, sending dull shocks through the whole frame of the vessel. This was dangerous. Nobody cared enough to lift a little finger. He told me that even now sometimes waking up at night, he fancied he could hear the dull vibrating thuds. The pintles carried away, and it dropped off at last.

The final catastrophe came with the sending off of their one remaining boat. It was Falk who had managed to preserve her intact, and how it was agreed that some of the hands should sail away into the track of the shipping to procure assistance. She was provisioned with all the food they could spare for the six who were to go. They waited for a fine day. It was long in coming. At last one morning they lowered her into the water.

Directly, in that demoralised crowd, trouble broke out. Two men who had no business there had jumped into the boat under the pretence of unhooking the tackles, while some sort of squabble arose on the deck amongst these weak, tottering spectres of a ship's company. The captain, who had been for days living secluded and unapproachable in the chart-room, came to the rail. He ordered the two men to come up on board and menaced them with his revolver. They pretended to obey, but suddenly cutting the boat's painter, gave a shove against the ship's side and made ready to hoist the sail.

"Shoot, sir! Shoot them down!" cried Falk—"and I will jump overboard to regain the boat." But the captain, after taking aim with an irresolute arm, turned suddenly away.

A howl of rage arose. Falk dashed into his cabin for his own pistol. When he returned it was too late. Two more men had leaped into the water, but the fellows in the boat beat them off with the oars, hoisted the boat's lug and sailed away. They were never heard of again.

Consternation and despair possessed the remaining ship's company, till the apathy of utter hopelessness re-asserted its sway. That day a fireman committed suicide, running up on deck with his throat cut from ear to ear, to the horror of all hands. He was thrown overboard. The captain had locked himself in the chart-room, and Falk, knocking vainly for admittance, heard him reciting over and over again the names of his wife and children, not as if calling upon them or commending them to God, but in a mechanical voice like an exercise of memory. Next day the doors of the chart-room were swinging open to the roll of the ship, and the captain had disappeared. He must during the night have jumped into the sea. Falk locked both the doors and kept the keys.

The organised life of the ship had come to an end. The solidarity of the men had gone. They became indifferent to each other. It was Falk who took in hand the distribution of such food as remained. They boiled their boots for soup to eke out the rations, which only made their hunger more intolerable. Sometimes whispers of hate were heard passing between the languid skeletons that drifted endlessly to and fro, north and south, east and west, upon that carcase of a ship.

And in this lies the grotesque horror of this sombre story. The last extremity of sailors, overtaking a small boat or a frail craft, seems easier to bear, because of the direct danger of the seas. The confined space, the close contact, the imminent menace of the waves, seem to draw men together, in spite of madness, suffering and despair. But there was a ship—safe, convenient, roomy: a ship with beds, bedding, knives, forks, comfortable cabins, glass and china, and a complete cook's galley, pervaded, ruled and possessed by the pitiless spectre of starvation. The lamp oil had been drunk, the wicks cut up for food, the candles eaten. At night she floated dark in all her recesses, and full of fears. One day Falk came upon a man gnawing a splinter of pine wood. Suddenly he threw the piece of wood away, tottered to the rail, and fell over. Falk, too late to prevent the act, saw him claw the ship's side desperately before he went down. Next day another man did the same thing, after uttering horrible imprecations. But this one somehow managed to get hold of the broken rudder chains and hung on there, silently. Falk set about trying to save him, and all the time the man, holding with both hands, looked at him anxiously with his sunken eyes. Then, just as Falk was ready to put his hand on him, the man let go his hold and sank like a stone. Falk reflected on these sights. His heart revolted against the horror of death, and he said to himself that he would struggle for every precious minute of his life.

One afternoon—as the survivors lay about on the after deck—the carpenter, a tall man with a black beard, spoke of the last sacrifice. There was nothing eatable left on board. Nobody said a word to this; but that company separated quickly, these listless feeble spectres slunk off one by one to hide in fear of each other. Falk and the carpenter remained on deck together. Falk liked the big carpenter. He had been the best man of the lot, helpful and ready as long as there was anything to do, the longest hopeful, and had preserved to the last some vigour and decision of mind.

They did not speak to each other. Henceforth no voices were to be heard conversing sadly on board that ship. After a time the carpenter tottered away forward; but later on, Falk going to drink at the fresh-water pump, had the inspiration to turn his head. The carpenter had stolen upon him from behind, and, summoning all his strength, was aiming with a crowbar a blow at the back of his skull.

Dodging just in time, Falk made his escape and ran into his cabin. While he was loading his revolver there, he heard the sound of heavy blows struck upon the bridge. The locks of the chart-room doors were slight, they flew open, and the carpenter, possessing himself of the captain's revolver, fired a shot of defiance.

Falk was about to go on deck and have it out at once, when he remarked that one of the ports of his cabin commanded the approaches to the fresh water-pump. Instead of going out he remained in and secured the door. "The best man shall survive," he said to himself—and the other, he reasoned, must at some time or other come here to drink. These starving men would drink often to cheat the pangs of their hunger. But the carpenter too must have noticed the position of the port. They were the two best men in the ship, and the game was with them. All the rest of the day Falk saw no one and heard no sound. At night he strained his eyes. It was dark—he heard a rustling noise once, but he was certain that no one could have come near the pump. It was to the left of his deck port, and he could not have failed to see a man, for the night was clear and starry. He saw nothing; towards morning another faint noise made him suspicious. Deliberately and quietly he unlocked his door. He had not slept, and had not given way to the horror of the situation. He wanted to live.

But during the night the carpenter, without at all trying to approach the pump, had managed to creep quietly along the starboard bulwark, and, unseen, had crouched down right under Falk's deck port. When daylight came he rose up suddenly, looked in, and putting his arm through the round brass framed opening, fired at Falk within a foot. He missed—and Falk, instead of attempting to seize the arm holding the weapon, opened his door unexpectedly, and with the muzzle of his long revolver nearly touching the other's side, shot him dead.

The best man had survived. Both of them had at the beginning just strength enough to stand on their feet, and both had displayed pitiless resolution, endurance, cunning and courage—all the qualities of classic heroism. At once Falk threw overboard the captain's revolver. He was a born monopolist. Then after the report of the two shots, followed by a profound silence, there crept out into the cold, cruel dawn of Antarctic regions, from various hiding-places, over the deck of that dismantled corpse of a ship floating on a grey sea ruled by iron necessity and with a heart of ice—there crept into view one by one, cautious, slow, eager, glaring, and unclean, a band of hungry and livid skeletons. Falk faced them, the possessor of the only fire-arm on board, and the second best man—the carpenter—was lying dead between him and them.

"He was eaten, of course," I said.

He bent his head slowly, shuddered a little, drawing his hands over his face, and said, "I had necer any quarrel with that man. But there were our lives between him and me."

Why continue the story of that ship, that story before which, with its fresh-water pump like a spring of death, its man with the weapon, the sea ruled by iron necessity, its spectral band swayed by terror and hope, its mute and un-hearing heaven?—the fable of the *Flying Dutchman* with its convention of crime and its sentimental retribution fades like a graceful wreath, like a wisp of white mist. What is there to say that every one of us cannot guess for himself? I believe Falk began by going through the ship, revolver in hand, to annex all the matches. Those starving wretches had plenty of matches! He had no mind to have the ship set on fire under his feet, either from hate or from despair. He lived in the open, camping on the bridge, commanding all the after deck and the only approach to the pump. He lived! Some of the others lived too—concealed, anxious, coming out one by one from their hiding-places at the seductive sound of a shot. And he was not selfish. They shared, but only three of them all were alive when a whaler, returning from her cruising-ground, nearly ran over the water-logged hull of the *Borgmester Dahl*, which, it seems, in the end had in some way sprung a leak in both her holds, but being loaded with deals could not sink.

"They all died," Falk said. "These three too, afterwards. But I would not die. All died, all! under this terrible misfortune. But was I too to throw away my life? Could I? Tell me, captain? I was alone there, quite alone, just like the others. Each man was alone. Was I to give up my revolver? Who to? Or was I to throw it into the sea? What would have been the good? Only the best man would survive. It was a great, terrible, and cruel misfortune."

He had survived! I saw him before me as though preserved for a witness to the mighty truth of an unerring and eternal principle. Great beads of per-spiration stood on his forehead. And suddenly it struck the table with a heavy blow, as he fell forward throwing his hands out.

"And this is worse," he cried. "This is a worse pain! This is more terrible."

He made my heart thump with the profound conviction of his cry. And after he had left me alone I called up before my mental eye the image of the girl weeping silently, abundantly, patiently, and as if irresistibly. I thought of her tawny hair. I thought how, if unplaited, it would have covered her all round as low as the hips, like the hair of a siren. And she had bewitched him. Fancy a man who would guard his own life with the inflexibility of a pitiless and immovable fate, being brought to lament that once a crowbar had missed his skull! The sirens sing and lure to death, but this one had been weeping silently as if for the pity of his life. She was the tender and voiceless siren of this appalling navigator. He evidently wanted to live his whole conception of life. Nothing else would do. And she too was a servant of that life that, in the midst of death, cries aloud to our senses. She was eminently fitted to interpret for him its feminine side. And in her own way, and with her own profusion of sensuous charms she also seemed to illustrate the eternal truth of an unerring principle. I don't know though what sort of principle Hermann illustrated when he turned up early on board my ship with a most perplexed air. It struck me, however, that he too would do his best to survive. He seemed greatly calmed on the subject of Falk, but still very full of it.

"What is it you said I was last night? You know," he asked after some preliminary talk. "Too—too—I don't know. A very funny word."

"Squeamish?" I suggested.

"Yes. What does it mean?"

"That you exaggerate things—to yourself. Without inquiry, and so on."

He seemed to turn it over in his mind. We went on talking. This Falk was the plague of his life. Upsetting everybody like this! Mrs. Hermann was unwell rather this morning. His niece was crying still. There was nobody to look after the children. He struck his umbrella on the deck. She would be like that for months. Fancy carrying all the way home, second class, a perfectly useless girl who is crying all the time. It was bad for Lena too, he observed; but on what grounds I could not guess. Perhaps of the bad example. That child was already sorrowing and crying enough over the rag doll. Nicholas was really the least sentimental person of the family.

"Why does she weep?" I asked.

"From pity," cried Hermann.

It was impossible to make out women. Mrs. Hermann was the only one he pretended to understand. She was very, very upset and doubtful.

"Doubtful about what?" I asked.

He averted his eyes and did not answer this. It was impossible to make them out. For instance, his niece was weeping for Falk. Now he (Hermann) would like to wring his neck—but then... He supposed he had too tender a heart. "Frankly," he asked at last, "what do you think of what we heard last night, captain?"

"In all these tales," I observed, "there is always a good deal of exaggeration."

And not letting him recover from his surprise I assured him that I knew all the details. He begged me not to repeat them. His heart was too tender. They made him feel unwell. Then, looking at his feet and speaking very slowly, he supposed that he need not see much of them after they were married. For, indeed, he could not bear the sight of Falk. On the other hand it was ridiculous to take home a girl with her head turned. A girl that weeps all the time and is of no help to her aunt.

"Now you will be able to do with one cabin only on your passage home," I said.

"Yes, I had thought of that," he said brightly, almost. "Yes! Himself, his wife, four children—one cabin might do. Whereas if his niece went..."

"And what does Mrs. Hermann say to it?" I inquired.

Mrs. Hermann did not know whether a man of that sort could make a girl happy—she had been greatly deceived in Captain Falk. She had been very upset last night.

Those good people did not seem to be able to retain an impression for a whole twelve hours. I assured him on my own personal knowledge that Falk possessed in himself all the qualities to make his niece's future prosperous. He said he was glad to hear this, and that he would tell his wife. Then the object of the visit came out. He wished me to help him to resume relations with Falk. His niece, he said, had expressed the hope I would do so in my kindness. He was evidently anxious that I should, for though he seemed to have forgotten nine-tenths of his indignation, yet he evidently feared to be sent to the right-about. "You told me he was very much in love," he concluded slyly, and leered in a sort of bucolic way.

As soon as he had left my ship I called Falk on board by signal—the tug still lying at the anchorage. He took the news with calm gravity, as though he had all along expected the stars to fight for him in their courses.

I saw them once more together, and only once—on the quarter-deck of the *Diana*. Hermann sat smoking with a shirt-sleeved elbow hooked over the back of his chair. Mrs. Hermann was sewing alone. As Falk stepped over the gang-way, Hermann's niece, with a slight swish of the skirt and a swift friendly nod to me, glided past my chair.

They met in sunshine abreast of the mainmast. He held her hands and looked down at them, and she looked up at him with her candid and unseeing glance. It seemed to me they had come together as if attracted, drawn and guided to each other by a mysterious influence. They were a complete couple. In her grey frock, palpitating with life, generous of form, olympian and simple, she was indeed the siren to fascinate that dark navigator, this ruthless lover of the five senses. From afar I seemed to feel the masculine strength with which he grasped those hands she had extended to him with a womanly swiftness. Lena, a little pale, nursing her beloved lump of dirty rags, ran towards her big friend; and then in the drowsy silence of the good old ship Mrs. Hermann's voice rang out so changed that it made me spin round in my chair to see what was the matter.

"Lena, come here!" she screamed. And this good-natured matron gave me a wavering glance, dark and full of fearsome distrust. The child ran back, sur-prised, to her knee. But the two, standing before each other in sunlight with clasped hands, had heard nothing, had seen nothing and no one. Three feet away from them in the shade a seaman sat on a spar, very busy splicing a strop, and dipping his fingers into a tar-pot, as if utterly unaware of their existence.

When I returned in command of another ship, some five years afterwards, Mr. and Mrs. Falk had left the place. I should not wonder if Schomberg's tongue had succeeded at last in scaring Falk away for good; and, indubitably, there was a tale still going about the town of a certain Falk, owner of a tug, who had won his wife at cards from the captain of an English ship.

TO-MORROW
TO-MORROW

What was known of Captain Hagberd in the little sea-port of Colebrook was not exactly in his favour. He did not belong to the place. He had come to settle there under circumstances not at all mysterious—he used to be very communicative about them at the time—but extremely morbid and unreasonable. He was possessed of some little money evidently, because he bought a plot of ground, and had a pair of ugly yellow brick cottages run up very cheaply. He occupied one of them himself and let the other to Josiah Carvil—blind Carvil, the retired boat-builder—a man of evil repute as a domestic tyrant.

These cottages had one wall in common, shared in a line of iron railing dividing their front gardens; a wooden fence separated their back gardens. Miss Bessie Carvil was allowed, as it were of right, to throw over it the tea-cloths, blue rags, or an apron that wanted drying.

"It rots the wood, Bessie my girl," the captain would remark mildly, from his side of the fence, each time he saw her exercising that privilege.

She was a tall girl; the fence was low, and she could spread her elbows on the top. Her hands would be red with the bit of washing she had done, but her forearms were white, and shapely, and she would look at her father's landlord in silence—in an informed silence which had an air of knowledge, expectation and desire.

"It rots the wood," repeated Captain Hagberd. "It is the only unthrifty, careless habit I know in you. Why don't you have a clothes line out in your back yard?"

Miss Carvil would say nothing to this—she only shook her head negatively. The tiny back yard on her side had a few stone-bordered little beds of black earth, in which the simple flowers she found time to cultivate appeared somehow extravagantly overgrown, as if belonging to an exotic clime; and Captain Hagberd's upright, hale person, clad in No. 1 sail-cloth from head to foot, would be emerging knee-deep out of rank grass and the tall weeds on his side of the fence. He appeared, with the colour and uncouth stiffness of the extraordinary material in which he chose to clothe himself—"for the time being," would be his mumbled remark to any observation on the subject—like a man roughened out of granite, standing in a wilderness not big enough for a decent billiard-room. A heavy figure of a man of stone, with a red handsome face, a blue wandering eye, and a great white beard flowing to his waist and never trimmed as far as Colebrook knew.

Seven years before, he had seriously answered, "Next month, I think," to the chaffing attempt to secure his custom made by that distinguished local wit, the Colebrook barber, who happened to be sitting insolently in the tap-room of the New Inn near the harbour, where the captain had entered to buy an ounce of tobacco. After paying for his purchase with three half-pence extracted from the corner of a handkerchief which he carried in the cuff of his sleeve, Captain Hagberd went out. As soon as the door was shut the barber laughed. "The old one and the young one will be strolling arm in arm to get shaved in my place presently. The tailor shall be set to work, and the barber, and the candlestick maker; high old times are coming for Colebrook, they are coming, to be sure. It used to be 'next week,' now it has come to 'next month,' and so on—soon it will be 'next spring,' for all I know."

Noticing a stranger listening to him with a vacant grin, he explained, stretching out his legs cynically, that this queer old Hagberd, a retired coasting-skipper, was waiting for the return of a son of his. The boy had been driven away from home, he shouldn't wonder; had run away to sea and had never been heard of since. Put to rest in Davy Jones's locker this many a day, as likely as not. That old man came flying to Colebrook three years ago all in black broadcloth (had lost his wife lately then), getting out of a third-class smoker as if the devil had been at his heels; and the only thing that brought him down was a letter—a hoax probably. Some joker had written to him about a seafaring man with some such name who was supposed to be hanging about some girl or other, either in Colebrook or in the neighbourhood. "Funny, ain't it?" The old chap had been advertising in the London papers for Harry Hagberd, and offering rewards for any sort of likely information. And the barber would go on to describe with sardonic gusto, how that stranger in mourning had been seen exploring the country, in carts, on foot, taking everybody into his confidence, visiting all the inns and alehouses for miles around, stopping people on the road with his questions, looking into the very ditches almost; first in the greatest excitement, then with a plodding sort of perseverance, growing slower and slower; and he could not even tell you plainly how his son looked. The sailor was supposed to be one of two that had left a timber ship, and to have been seen dangling after some girl; but the old man described a boy of fourteen or so—"a clever-looking, high-spirited boy." And when people only smiled at this he would rub his forehead in a confused sort of way before he slunk off, looking offended. He found nobody, of course; not a trace of anybody—never heard of anything worth belief, at any rate; but he had not been able somehow to tear himself away from Colebrook.

"It was the shock of this disappointment, perhaps, coming soon after the loss of his wife, that had driven him crazy on that point," the barber suggested, with an air of great psychological insight. After a time the old man abandoned the active search. His son had evidently gone away; but he settled himself to wait. His son had been once at least in Colebrook in preference to his native place. There must have been some reason for it, he seemed to think, some very powerful inducement, that would bring him back to Colebrook again.

"Ha, ha, ha! Why, of course, Colebrook. Where else? That's the only place in the United Kingdom for your long-lost sons. So he sold up his old home in Colchester, and down he comes here. Well, it's a craze, like any other. Wouldn't catch me going crazy over any of my youngsters clearing out. I've got eight of them at home." The barber was showing off his strength of mind in the midst of a laughter that shook the tap-room.

Strange, though, that sort of thing, he would confess, with the frankness of a superior intelligence, seemed to be catching. His establishment, for instance, was near the harbour, and whenever a sailorman came in for a hair-cut or a shave—if it was a strange face he couldn't help thinking directly, "Suppose he's the son of old Hagberd!" He laughed at himself for it. It was a strong craze. He could remember the time when the whole town was full of it. But he had his hopes of the old chap yet. He would cure him by a course of judicious chaffing. He was watching the progress of the treatment. Next week—next month—next year! When the old skipper had put off the date of that return till next year, he would be well on his way to not saying any more about it. In other matters he was quite rational, so this, too, was bound to come. Such was the barber's firm opinion.

Nobody had ever contradicted him; his own hair had gone grey since that time, and Captain Hagberd's beard had turned quite white, and had acquired a majestic flow over the No. 1 canvas suit, which he had made for himself secretly with tarred twine, and had assumed suddenly, coming out in it one fine morning, whereas the evening before he had been seen going home in his mourning of broadcloth. It caused a sensation in the High Street—shopkeepers coming to their doors, people in the houses snatching up their hats to run out— a stir at which he seemed strangely surprised at first, and then scared; but his only answer to the wondering questions was that startled and evasive, "For the present."

That sensation had been forgotten, long ago; and Captain Hagberd himself, if not forgotten had come to be disregarded—the penalty of dailiness—as the sun itself is disregarded unless it makes its power felt heavily. Captain Hagberd's movement showed no infirmity: he walked stiffly in his suit of canvas, a quaint and remarkable figure; only his eyes wandered more furtively perhaps than of yore. His manner abroad had lost its excitable watchfulness; it had become puzzled and diffident, as though he had suspected that there was somewhere about him something slightly compromising, some embarrassing oddity; and yet had remained unable to discover what on earth this something wrong could be.

He was unwilling now to talk with the townfolk. He had earned for himself the reputation of an awful skinflint, of a miser in the matter of living. He mumbled regretfully in the shops, bought inferior scraps of meat after long hesitations; and discouraged all allusions to his costume. It was as the barber had foretold. For all one could tell, he had recovered already from the disease of hope; and only Miss Bessie Carvil knew that he said nothing about his son's return because with him it was no longer "next week," "next month," or even "next year." It was "to-morrow."

In their intimacy of back yard and front garden he talked with her paternally, reasonably, and dogmatically, with a touch of arbitrariness. They met on the ground of unreserved confidence, which was authenticated by an affectionate wink now and then. Miss Carvil had come to look forward rather to these winks. At first they had discomposed her: the poor fellow was mad. Afterwards she had learned to laugh at them: there was no harm in him. Now she was aware of an unacknowledged, pleasurable, incredulous emotion, expressed by a faint blush. He winked not in the least vulgarly; his thin red face with a well-modelled curved nose, had a sort of distinction—the more so that when he talked to her he looked with a steadier and more intelligent glance. A handsome, hale, upright, capable man, with a white beard. You did not think of his age. His son, he affirmed, had resembled him amazingly from his earliest babyhood.

Harry would be one-and-thirty next July, he declared. Proper age to get married with a nice, sensible girl that could appreciate a good home. He was a very high-spirited boy. High-spirited husbands were the easiest to manage. These mean, soft chaps, that you would think butter wouldn't melt in their mouths, were the ones to make a woman thoroughly miserable. And there was nothing like home—a fireside—a good roof: no turning out of your warm bed in all sorts of weather. "Eh, my dear?"

Captain Hagberd had been one of those sailors that pursue their calling within sight of land. One of the many children of a bankrupt farmer, he had been apprenticed hurriedly to a coasting skipper, and had remained on the coast all his sea life. It must have been a hard one at first: he had never taken to it; his affection turned to the land, with its innumerable houses, with its quiet lives gathered round its firesides. Many sailors feel and profess a rational dislike for the sea, but his was a profound and emotional animosity—as if the love of the stabler element had been bred into him through many generations.

"People did not know what they let their boys in for when they let them go to sea," he expounded to Bessie. "As soon make convicts of them at once." He did not believe you ever got used to it. The weariness of such a life got worse as you got older. What sort of trade was it in which more than half your time you did not put your foot inside your house? Directly you got out to sea you had no means of knowing what went on at home. One might have thought him weary of distant voyages; and the longest he had ever made had lasted a fortnight, of which the most part had been spent at anchor, sheltering from the weather. As soon as his wife had inherited a house and enough to live on (from a bachelor uncle who had made some money in the coal business) he threw up his command of an East-coast collier with a feeling as though he had escaped from the galleys. After all these years he might have counted on the fingers of his two hands all the days he had been out of sight of England. He had never known what it was to be out of soundings. "I have never been further than eighty fathoms from the land," was one of his boasts.

Besse Carvil heard all these things. In front of their cottage grew an undersized ash; and on summer afternoons she would bring out a chair on the grass plot and sit down with her sewing. Captain Hagberd, in his canvas suit, leaned on a spade. He dug every day in his front plot. He turned it over and over several times every year, but was not going to plant anything "just at present."

To Bessie Carvil he would state more explicitly: "Not till our Harry comes home to-morrow." And she had heard this formula of hope so often that it only awakened the vaguest pity in her heart for that hopeful old man.

Everything was put off in that way, and everything was being prepared likewise for to-morrow. There was a boxful of packets of various flower-seeds to choose from, for the front garden. "He will doubtless let you have your say about that, my dear," Captain Hagberd intimated to her across the railing.

Miss Bessie's head remained bowed over her work. She had heard all this so many times. But now and then she would rise, lay down her sewing, and come slowly to the fence. There was a charm in these gentle ravings. He was determined that his son should not go away again for the want of a home all ready for him. He had been filling the other cottage with all sorts of furniture. She imagined it all new, fresh with varnish, piled up as in a warehouse. There would be tables wrapped up in sacking; rolls of carpets thick and vertical like fragments of columns, the gleam of white marble tops in the dimness of the drawn blinds. Captain Hagberd always described his purchases to her, carefully, as to a person having a legitimate interest in them. The overgrown yard of his cottage could be laid over with concrete... after to-morrow.

"We may just as well do away with the fence. You could have your drying-line out, quite clear of your flowers." He winked, and she would blush faintly.

This madness that had entered her life through the kind impulses of her heart had reasonable details. What if some day his son returned? But she could not even be quite sure that he ever had a son; and if he existed anywhere he had been too long away. When Captain Hagberd got excited in his talk she would steady him by a pretence of belief, laughing a little to salve her conscience.

Only once she had tried pityingly to throw some doubt on that hope doomed to disappointment, but the effect of her attempt had scared her very much. All at once over that man's face there came an expression of horror and incredulity, as though he had seen a crack open out in the firmament.

"You—you—you don't think he's drowned!"

For a moment he seemed to her ready to go out of his mind, for in his ordinary state she thought him more sane than people gave him credit for. On that occasion the violence of the emotion was followed by a most paternal and complacent recovery.

"Don't alarm yourself, my dear," he said a little cunningly: "the sea can't keep him. He does not belong to it. None of us Hagberds ever did belong to it. Look at me; I didn't get drowned. Moreover, he isn't a sailor at all; and if he is not a sailor he's bound to come back. There's nothing to prevent him coming back...."

His eyes began to wander.

"To-morrow."

She never tried again, for fear the man should go out of his mind on the spot. He depended on her. She seemed the only sensible person in the town; and he would congratulate himself frankly before her face on having secured such a level-headed wife for his son. The rest of the town, he confided to her once, in a fit of temper, was certainly queer. The way they looked at you—the way they talked to you! He had never got on with any one in the place. Didn't like the people. He would not have left his own country if it had not been clear that his son had taken a fancy to Colebrook.

She humoured him in silence, listening patiently by the fence; crocheting with downcast eyes. Blushes came with difficulty on her dead-white complexion, under the negligently twisted opulence of mahogany coloured hair. Her father was frankly carroty.

She had a full figure; a tired, unrefreshed face. When Captain Hagberd vaunted the necessity and propriety of a home and the delights of one's own fire-side, she smiled a little, with her lips only. Her home delights had been confined to the nursing of her father during the ten best years of her life.

A bestial roaring coming out of an upstairs window would interrupt their talk. She would begin at once to roll up her crochet-work or fold her sewing, without the slightest sign of haste. Meanwhile the howls and roars of her name would go on, making the fishermen strolling upon the sea-wall on the other side of the road turn their heads towards the cottages. She would go in slowly at the front door, and a moment afterwards there would fall a profound silence. Presently she would reappear, leading by the hand a man, gross and unwieldy like a hippopotamus, with a bad-tempered, surly face.

He was a widowed boat-builder, whom blindness had overtaken years before in the full flush of business. He behaved to his daughter as if she had been responsible for its incurable character. He had been heard to bellow at the top of his voice, as if to defy Heaven, that he did not care: he had made enough money to have ham and eggs for his breakfast every morning. He thanked God for it, in a fiendish tone as though he were cursing.

Captain Hagberd had been so unfavourably impressed by his tenant, that once he told Miss Bessie, "He is a very extravagant fellow, my dear."

She was knitting that day, finishing a pair of socks for her father, who expected her to keep up the supply dutifully. She hated knitting, and, as she was just at the heel part, she had to keep her eyes on her needles.

"Of course it isn't as if he had a son to provide for," Captain Hagberd went on a little vacantly. "Girls, of course, don't require so much—h'm—h'm. They don't run away from home, my dear."

"No," said Miss Bessie, quietly.

Captain Hagberd, amongst the mounds of turned-up earth, chuckled. With his maritime rig, his weather-beaten face, his beard of Father Neptune, he resembled a deposed sea-god who had exchanged the trident for the spade.

"And he must look upon you as already provided for, in a manner. That's the best of it with the girls. The husbands . . ." He winked. Miss Bessie, absorbed in her knitting, coloured faintly.

"Bessie! my hat!" old Carvil bellowed out suddenly. He had been sitting under the tree mute and motionless, like an idol of some remarkably monstrous superstition. He never opened his mouth but to howl for her, at her, sometimes about her; and then he did not moderate the terms of his abuse. Her system was never to answer him at all; and he kept up his shouting till he got attended to—till she shook him by the arm, or thrust the mouthpiece of his pipe between his teeth. He was one of the few blind people who smoke. When he felt the hat being put on his head he stopped his noise at once. Then he rose, and they passed together through the gate.

He weighed heavily on her arm. During their slow toilful walks she appeared to be dragging with her for a penance the burden of that infirm bulk. Usually they crossed the road at once (the cottages stood in the fields near the harbour, two hundred yards away from the end of the street), and for a long, long time they would remain in view, ascending imperceptibly the flight of wooden steps that led to the top of the sea-wall. It ran on from east to west, shutting out the Channel like a neglected railway embankment, on which no train had ever rolled within memory of man. Groups of sturdy fishermen would emerge upon the sky, walk along for a bit, and sink without haste. Their brown nets, like the cobwebs of gigantic spiders, lay on the shabby grass of the slope; and, looking up from the end of the street, the people of the town would recognise the two Carvils, by the creeping slowness of their gait. Captain Hagberd, pottering aimlessly about his cottages, would raise his head to see how they got on in their promenade.

He advertised still in the Sunday papers for Harry Hagberd. These sheets were read in foreign parts to the end of the world, he informed Bessie. At the same time he seemed to think that his son was in England—so near to Colebrook that he would of course turn up "tomorrow." Bessie, without committing herself to that opinion in so many words, argued that in that case the expense of advertising was unnecessary; Captain Hagberd had better spend that weekly half-crown on himself. She declared she did not know what he lived on. Her argumentation would puzzle him and cast him down for a time. "They all do it," he pointed out. There was a whole column devoted to appeals after missing relatives. He would bring the newspaper to show her. He and his wife had advertised for years; only she was an impatient woman. The news from Colebrook had arrived the very day after her funeral; if she had not been so impatient she might have been here now, with no more than one day more to wait. "You are not an impatient woman, my dear."

"I've no patience with you sometimes," she would say.

If he still advertised for his son he did not offer rewards for information any more; for, with the muddled lucidity of a mental derangement he had reasoned himself into a conviction as clear as day-light that he had already attained all that could be expected in that way. What more could he want? Colebrook was the place, and there was no need to ask for more. Miss Carvil praised him for his good sense, and he was soothed by the part she took in his hope, which had become his delusion; in that idea which blinded his mind to truth and probability, just as the other old man in the other cottage had been made blind, by another disease, to the light and beauty of the world.

But anything he could interpret as a doubt—any coldness of assent, or even a simple inattention to the development of his projects of a home with his returned son and his son's wife—would irritate him into flings and jerks and wicked side glances. He would dash his spade into the ground and walk to and fro before it. Miss Bessie called it his tantrums. She shook her finger at him. Then, when she came out again, after he had parted with her in anger, he would watch out of the corner of his eyes for the least sign of encouragement to approach the iron railings and resume his fatherly and patronising relations.

For all their intimacy, which had lasted some years now, they had never talked without a fence or a railing between them. He described to her all the splendours accumulated for the setting-up of their housekeeping, but had never invited her to an inspection. No human eye was to behold them till Harry had his first look. In fact, nobody had ever been inside his cottage; he did his own housework, and he guarded his son's privilege so jealously that the small objects of domestic use he bought sometimes in the town were smuggled rapidly across the front garden under his canvas coat. Then, coming out, he would remark apologetically, "It was only a small kettle, my dear."

And, if not too tired with her drudgery, or worried beyond endurance by her father, she would laugh at him with a blush, and say: "That's all right, Captain Hagberd; I am not impatient."

"Well, my dear, you haven't long to wait now," he would answer with a sudden bashfulness, and looking uneasily, as though he had suspected that there was something wrong somewhere.

Every Monday she paid him his rent over the railings. He clutched the shillings greedily. He grudged every penny he had to spend on his maintenance, and when he left her to make his purchases his bearing changed as soon as he got into the street. Away from the sanction of her pity, he felt himself exposed without defence. He brushed the walls with his shoulder. He mistrusted the queerness of the people; yet, by then, even the town children had left off calling after him, and the tradesmen served him without a word. The slightest allusion to his clothing had the power to puzzle and frighten especially, as if it were something utterly unwarranted and incomprehensible.

In the autumn, the driving rain drummed on his sailcloth suit saturated almost to the stiffness of sheet-iron, with its surface flowing with water. When the weather was too bad, he retreated under the tiny porch, and, standing close against the door, looked at his spade left planted in the middle of the yard. The ground was so much dug up all over, that as the season advanced it turned to a quagmire. When it froze hard, he was disconsolate. What would Harry say? And as he could not have so much of Bessie's company at that time of the year, the roars of old Carvil, that came muffled through the closed windows, calling her indoors, exasperated him greatly.

"Why don't that extravagant fellow get you a servant?" he asked impatiently one mild afternoon. She had thrown something over her head to run out for a while.

"I don't know," said the pale Bessie, wearily, staring away with her heavy-lidded, grey, and unexpectant glance. There were always smudgy shadows under her eyes, and she did not seem able to see any change or any end to her life.

"You wait till you get married, my dear," said her only friend, drawing closer to the fence. "Harry will get you one."

His hopeful craze seemed to mock her own want of hope with so bitter an aptness that in her nervous irritation she could have screamed at him outright. But she only said in self-mockery, and speaking to him as though he had been sane, "Why, Captain Hagberd, your son may not even want to look at me."

He flung his head back and laughed his throaty affected cackle of anger.

"What! That boy? Not want to look at the only sensible girl for miles around? What do you think I am here for, my dear—my dear—my dear?... What? You wait. You just wait. You'll see to-morrow. I'll soon—"

"Bessie! Bessie! Bessie!" howled old Carvil inside. "Bessie!—my pipe!" That fat blind man had given himself up to a very lust of laziness. He would not lift his hand to reach for the things she took care to leave at his very elbow. He would not move a limb; he would not rise from the chair, he would not put one foot before another, in that parlour (where he knew his way as well as if he had his sight) without calling her to his side and hanging all his atrocious weight on her shoulder. He would not eat one single mouthful of food without her close attendance. He had made himself helpless beyond his affliction, to enslave her better. She stood still for a moment, setting her teeth in the dusk, then turned and walked slowly indoors.

Captain Hagberd went back to his spade. The shouting in Carvil's cottage stopped, and after a while the window of the parlour downstairs was lit up. A man coming from the end of the street with a firm leisurely step passed on, but seemed to have caught sight of Captain Hagberd, because he turned back a pace or two. A cold white light lingered in the western sky. The man leaned over the gate in an interested manner.

"You must be Captain Hagberd," he said, with easy assurance.

The old man spun round, pulling out his spade, startled by the strange voice.

"Yes, I am," he answered nervously.

The other, smiling straight at him, uttered very slowly: "You've been advertising for your son, I believe?"

"My son Harry," mumbled Captain Hagberd, off his guard for once. "He's coming home to-morrow."

"The devil he is!" The stranger marvelled greatly, and then went on, with only a slight change of tone: "You've grown a beard like Father Christmas himself."

Captain Hagberd drew a little nearer, and leaned forward over his spade. "Go your way," he said, resentfully and timidly at the same time, because he was always afraid of being laughed at. Every mental state, even madness, has its equilibrium based upon self-esteem. Its disturbance causes unhappiness; and Captain Hagberd lived amongst a scheme of settled notions which it pained him to feel disturbed by people's grins. Yes, people's grins were awful. They hinted at something wrong: but what? He could not tell; and that stranger was obviously grinning—had come on purpose to grin. It was bad enough on the streets, but he had never before been outraged like this.

The stranger, unaware how near he was of having his head laid open with a spade, said seriously: "I am not trespassing where I stand, am I? I fancy there's something wrong about your news. Suppose you let me come in."

"*You* come in!" murmured old Hagberd, with inexpressible horror.

"I could give you some real information about your son—the very latest tip, if you care to hear."

"No," shouted Hagberd. He began to pace wildly to and fro, he shouldered his spade, he gesticulated with his other arm. "Here's a fellow—a grinning fellow, who says there's something wrong. I've got more information that you're aware of. I've all the information I want. I've had it for years—for years—for years—enough to last me till to-morrow. Let you come in, indeed! What would Harry say?"

Bessie Carvil's figure appeared in black silhouette on the parlour window; then, with the sound of an opening door, fitted out before the other cottage, all black, but with something white over her head. These two voices beginning to talk suddenly outside (she had heard them indoors) had given her such an emotion that she could not utter a sound.

Captain Hagberd seemed to be trying to find his way out of a cage. His feet squelched in the puddles left by his industry. He stumbled in the holes of the ruined grass-plot. He ran blindly against the fence.

"Here, steady a bit!" said the man at the gate, gravely, stretching his arm over and catching him by the sleeve. "Somebody's been trying to get at you. Hallo! what's this rig you've got on? Storm canvas, by George!" He had a big laugh. "Well, you *are* a character!"

Captain Hagberd jerked himself free, and began to back away shrinkingly. "For the present," he muttered, in a crestfallen tone.

"What's the matter with him?" The stranger addressed Bessie with the utmost familiarity, in a deliberate, explanatory tone. "I didn't want to startle the old man." He lowered his voice as though he had known her for years. "I dropped into a barber's on my way, to get a twopenny shave, and they told me there he was something of a character. The old man has been a character all his life."

Captain Hagberd, daunted by the allusion to his clothing, had retreated inside, taking his spade with him; and the two at the gate, startled by the unexpected slamming of the door, heard the bolts being shot, the snapping of the lock, and the echo of an affected gurgling laugh within.

"I didn't want to upset him," the man said, after a short silence.. "What's the meaning of all this? He isn't quite crazy."

"He has been worrying a long time about his lost son," said Bessie, in a low apologetic tone.

"Well, I am his son."

"Harry!" she cried—and was profoundly silent.

"Know my name? Friends with the old man, eh?"

"He's our landlord," Bessie faltered out, catching hold of the iron railing.

"Owns both them rabbit-hutches, does he?" commented young Hagberd scornfully: "just the thing he would be proud of. Can you tell me who's that chap coming to-morrow? You must know something of it. I tell you, it's a swindle on the old man—nothing else."

She did not answer, helpless before an insurmountable difficulty, appalled before the necessity, the impossibility and the dread of an explanation in which she and madness seemed involved together.

"Oh—I am so sorry," she murmured.

"What's the matter?" he said, with serenity. "You needn't be afraid of upsetting me. It's the other fellow that'll be upset when he least expects it. I don't care a hang; but there will be some fun when he shows his mug to-morrow. I don't care *that* for the old man's pieces, but right is right. You shall see me put a head on that coon—whoever he is!"

He had come nearer, and towered above her on the other side of the railings. He glanced at her hands. He fancied she was trembling, and it occurred to him that she had her part perhaps in that little game that was to be sprung on his old man to-morrow. He had come just in time to spoil their sport. He was entertained by the idea—scornful of the baffled plot. But all his life he had been full of indulgence for all sorts of women's tricks. She really was trembling very much; her wrap had slipped off her head. "Poor devil!" he thought. "Never mind about that chap. I daresay he'll change his mind before to-morrow. But what about me? I can't loaf about the gate till the morning."

She burst out: "It is *you* who come to-morrow."

He murmured. "Oh! It's me!" blankly, and they seemed to become breathless together. Apparently he was pondering over what he had heard; then, without irritation, but evidently perplexed, he said: "I don't understand. I hadn't written or anything. It's my chum who saw the paper and told me—this very morning . . . Eh? what?"

He bent his ear; she whispered rapidly, and he listened for a while, muttering the words "yes" and "I see" at times. Then, "But why won't to-day do?" he queried at last.

"You didn't understand me!" she exclaimed impatiently. The clear streak of light under the clouds died out in the west. Again he stooped slightly to hear better; and the deep night buried everything of the whispering woman and the attentive man, except the familiar contiguity of their faces, with its air of secrecy and caress.

He squared his shoulders; the broad-brimmed shadow of a hat sat cavalierly on his head. "Awkward this, eh?" he appealed to her. "To-morrow? Well, well! Never heard tell of anything like this. It's all to-morrow, then, without any sort of to-day, as far as I can see."

She remained still and mute.

"And you have been encouraging this funny notion," he said.

"I never contradicted him."

"Why didn't you?"

"What for should I?" she defended herself. "It would only have made him miserable. He would have gone out of his mind."

"His mind!" he muttered, and heard a short nervous laugh from her.

"Where was the harm? Was I to quarrel with the poor old man? It was easier to half believe it myself."

"Aye, aye," he meditated intelligently. "I suppose the old chap got around you somehow with his soft talk. You are good-hearted."

Her hands moved up in the dark nervously. "And it might have been true. It was true. It has come. Here it is. This is the to-morrow we have been waiting for."

She drew a breath, and he said good-humouredly: "Aye, with the door shut. I wouldn't care if . . . And you think he could be brought round to recognise me . . . Eh? What? . . . You could do it? In a week you say? H'm, I daresay you could—but do you think I could hold out a week in this dead-alive place? Not me! I want either hard work, or an all-fired racket, or more space than there is in the whole of England. I have been in this place, though, once before, and for more than a week. The old man was advertising for me then, and a chum I had with me had a notion of getting a couple of quid out of him by writing a lot of silly nonsense in a letter. That lark did not come off, though. We had to clear out—and none too soon. But this time I've a chum waiting for me in London, and besides . . ."

Bessie Carvil was breathing quickly.

"What if I tried a knock at the door?" he suggested.

"Try," she said.

Captain Hagberd's gate squeaked, and the shadow of his son moved on, then stopped, with another deep laugh in the throat, like the father's, only soft and gentle, thrilling to the woman's heart, awakening to her ears.

"He isn't frisky—is he? I would be afraid to lay hold of him. The chaps are always telling me I don't know my own strength."

"He's the most harmless creature that ever lived," she interrupted.

"You wouldn't say so if you had seen him chasing me upstairs with a hard leather strap," he said; "I haven't forgotten it in sixteen years."

She got warm from head to foot under another soft subdued laugh. At the rat-tat-tat of the knocker her heart flew into her mouth.

"Hey, dad! Let me in. I am Harry, I am. Straight! Come back home a day too soon."

One of the windows upstairs ran up.

"A grinning, information fellow," said the voice of old Hagberd, up in the darkness. "Don't you have anything to do with him. It will spoil everything."

She heard Harry Hagberd say, "Hallo, dad," then a clanging clatter. The window rumbled down, and he stood before her again.

"It's just like old times. Nearly walloped the life out of me to stop me going away, and now I come back he throws a confounded shovel at my head to keep me out. It grazed my shoulder."

She shuddered.

"I wouldn't care," he began, "only I spent my last shillings on the railway fare and my last twopence on a shave—out of respect for the old man."

"Are you really Harry Hagberd?" she asked swiftly. "Can you prove it?"

"Can I prove it? Can any one else prove it?" he said jovially. "Prove with what? What do I want to prove? There isn't a single corner in the world, barring England, perhaps, where you could not find some man, or more likely a woman, that would remember me for Harry Hagberd. I am more like Harry Hagberd than any man alive; and I can prove it to you in a minute, if you will let me step inside your gate."

"Come in," she said.

He entered then the front garden of the Carvils. His tall shadow strode with a swagger; she turned her back on the window and waited, watching the shape, of which the footfalls seemed the most material part. The light fell on a tilted hat; a powerful shoulder, that seemed to cleave the darkness; on a leg stepping out. He swung about and stood still, facing the illuminated parlour window at her back, turning his head from side to side, laughing softly to himself.

"Just fancy, for a minute, the old man's beard stuck on to my chin. Hey? Now say. I was the very spit of him from a boy."

"It's true," she murmured to herself.

"And that's about as far as it goes. He was always one of your domestic characters. Why, I remember how he used to go about looking very sick for three days before he had to leave home on one of his trips to South Shields for coal. He had a standing charter from the gas-works. You would think he was off on a whaling cruise—three years and a tail. Ha, ha! Not a bit of it. Ten days on the outside. The *Skimmer of the Seas* was a smart craft. Fine name, wasn't it? Mother's uncle owned her. . . ."

He interrupted himself, and in a lowered voice, "Did he ever tell you what mother died of?" he asked.

"Yes," said Miss Bessie, bitterly: "from impatience."

He made no sound for a while; then brusquely: "They were so afraid I would turn out badly that they fairly drove me away. Mother nagged at me for being idle, and the old man said he would cut my soul out of my body rather than let me go to sea. Well, it looked as if he would do it too—so I went. It looks to me sometimes as if I had been born to them by a mistake—in that other hutch of a house."

"Where ought you to have been born by rights?" Bessie Carvil interrupted him defiantly.

"In the open, upon a beach, on a windy night," he said, quick as lightning. Then he mused slowly. "They were characters, both of them, by George; and the old man keeps it up well—don't he? A damned shovel on the— Hark! who's that making that row? 'Bessie, Bessie,' It's in your house."

"It's for me," she said with indifference.

He stepped aside, out of the streak of light. "Your husband?" he inquired, with the tone of a man accustomed to unlawful trysts. "Fine voice for a ship's deck in a thundering squall."

"No; my father. I am not married."

"You seem a fine girl, Miss Bessie dear," he said at once.

She turned her face away.

"Oh, I say,—what's up? Who's murdering him?"

"He wants his tea." She faced him, still and tall, with averted head, with her hands hanging clasped before her.

"Hadn't you better go in?" he suggested, after watching for a while the nape of her neck, a patch of dazzling white skin and soft shadow above the sombre line of her shoulders. Her wrap had slipped down to her elbows. "You'll have all the town coming out presently. I'll wait here a bit."

Her wrap fell to the ground, and he stooped to pick it up; she had vanished. He threw it over his arm, and approaching the window squarely he saw a monstrous form of a fat man in an armchair, an unshaded lamp, the yawning of an enormous mouth in a big flat face encircled by a ragged halo of hair— Miss Bessie's head and bust. The shouting stopped; the blind ran down. He lost himself in thinking how awkward it was. Father mad; no getting into the house. No money to get back; a hungry chum in London who would begin to think he had been given the go-by. "Damn!" he muttered. He could break the door in, certainly; but they would perhaps bundle him into chokey for that without asking questions—no great matter, only he was confoundedly afraid of being locked up, even in mistake. He turned cold at the thought. He stamped his feet on the sodden grass.

"What are you?—a sailor?" said an agitated voice.

She had flitted out, a shadow herself, attracted by the reckless shadow waiting under the wall of her home.

"Anything. Enough of a sailor to be worth my salt before the mast. Came home that way this time."

"Where do you come from?" she asked.

"Right away from a jolly good spree," he said, "by the London train—see? Ough! I hate being shut up in a train. I don't mind a house so much."

"Ah," she said; "that's lucky."

"Because in a house you can at any time open the blamed door and walk away straight before you."

"And never come back?"

"Not for sixteen years at least,"he laughed. "To a rabbit hutch, and get a confounded old shovel..."

"A ship is not so very big," she taunted.

"No, but the sea is great."

She dropped her head, and as if her ears had been opened to the voices of the world, she heard beyond the rampart of sea wall the swell of yesterday's gale breaking on the beach with monotonous and solemn vibrations, as if all the earth had been a tolling bell.

"And then, why, a ship's a ship. You love her and leave her; and a voyage isn't a marriage." He quoted the sailor's saying lightly.

"It is not a marriage," she whispered.

"I never took a false name, and I've never yet told a lie to a woman. What

lie? Why, *the* lie—. Take me or leave me, I say: and if you take me, then it
is...." He hummed a snatch very low, leaning against the wall.

Oh, ho, ho, Rio!
And fare thee well,
My bonnie young girl,
We're bound to Rio Grande.

"Capstan song," he explained. Her teeth chattered.

"You are cold," he said. "Here's that affair of yours I picked up." She felt
his hands about her, wrapping her closely. "Hold the ends together in front,"
he commanded.

"What did you come here for?" she asked, repressing a shudder.

"Five quid," he answered promptly. "We let our spree go on a little too
long and got hard up."

"You've been drinking?" she asked.

"Blind three days; on purpose. I am not given that way—don't you think.
There's nothing and nobody that can get over me unless I like. I can be as steady
as a rock. My chum sees the paper this morning, and says he to me: 'Go on,
Harry: loving parent. That's five quid sure.' So we scraped all our pockets for
the fare. Devil of a lark!"

"You have a hard heart, I am afraid," she sighed.

"What for? For running away? Why! he wanted to make a lawyer's clerk
of me—just to please himself. Master in his own house; and my poor mother
egged him on—for my good, I suppose. Well, then—so long; and I went. No,
I tell you: the day I cleared out, I was all black and blue from his great fondness
for me. Ah! he was always a bit of a character. Look at that shovel, now. Off
his chump? Not much. That's just exactly like my dad. He wants me here just
to have somebody to order about. However, we two were hard up; and what's
five quid to him—once in sixteen hard years?"

"Oh, but I am sorry for you. Did you never want to come back home?"

"Be a lawyer's clerk and rot here—in some such place as this?" he cried in
contempt. "What! if the old man set me up in a home to-day, I would kick it
down about my ears—or else die there before the third day was out."

"And where else is it that you hope to die?"

"In the bush somewhere; in the sea; on a blamed mountain top for choice.
At home? Yes! the world's my home; but I expect I'll die in a hospital some day.
What of that? Any place is good enough, as long as I've lived; and I've been
everything you can think of almost but a tailor or a soldier. I've been a boundary
rider; I've sheared sheep; and humped my swag; and harpooned a whale. I've
rigged ships, and prospected for gold, and skinned dead bullocks,—and turned
my back on more money than the old man would have scraped in his whole
life. Ha, ha!"

He overwhelmed her. She pulled herself together and managed to utter,
"Time to rest now."

He straightened himself up, away from the wall, and in a severe voice said,
"Time to go."

But he did not move. He leaned back again, and hummed thoughtfully a
bar or two of an outlandish tune.

She felt as if she were about to cry. "That's another of your cruel songs,"
she said.

"Learned it in Mexico—in Sonora." He talked easily. "It is the song of the

Gambucinos. You don't know? The song of restless men. Nothing could hold them in one place—not even a woman. You used to meet one of them now and again, in the old days, on the edge of the gold country, away north there beyond the Rio Gila. I've seen it. A prospecting engineer in Mazatlan took me along with him to help look after the waggons. A sailor's a handy chap to have about you anyhow. It's all a desert: cracks in the earth that you can't see the bottom of; and mountains—sheer rocks standing up high like walls and church spires, only a hundred times bigger. The valleys are full of boulders and black stones. There's not a blade of grass to see; and the sun sets more red over that country than I have seen it anywhere—blood-red and angry. It *is* fine."

"You do not want to go back there again?" she stammered out.

He laughed a little. "No. That's the blamed gold country. It gave me the shivers sometimes to look at it—and we were a big lot of men together, mind; but these Gambucinos wandered alone. They knew that country before anybody had ever heard of it. They had a sort of gift for prospecting, and the fever of it was on them too; and they did not seem to want the gold very much. They would find some rich spot, and then turn their backs on it; pick up perhaps a little—enough for a spree—and then be off again, looking for more. They never stopped long where there were houses; they had no wife, no chick, no home, never a chum. You couldn't be friends with a Gambucino; they were too restless—here to-day, and gone, God knows where, to-morrow. They told no one of their finds, and there has never been a Gambucino well off. It was not for the gold they cared; it was the wandering about looking for it in the stony country that got into them and wouldn't let them rest: so that no woman yet born could hold a Gambucino for more than a week. That's what the song says. It's all about a pretty girl that tried hard to keep hold of a Gambucino lover, so that he should bring her lots of gold. No fear! Off he went, and she never saw him again."

"What became of her?" she breathed out.

"The song don't tell. Cried a bit, I daresay. They were the fellows: kiss and go. But it's the looking for a thing—a something. . . . Sometimes I think I am a sort of Gambucino myself."

"No woman can hold you, then," she began in a brazen voice, which quavered suddenly before the end.

"No longer than a week," he joked, playing upon her very heartstrings with the gay, tender note of his laugh; "and yet I am fond of them all. Anything for a woman of the right sort. The scrapes they got me into, and the scrapes they got me out of! I love them at first sight. I've fallen in love with you already, Miss—Bessie's your name—eh?"

She backed away a little, and with a trembling laugh: "You haven't seen my face yet."

He bent forward gallantly. "A little pale: it suits some. But you are a fine figure of a girl, Miss Bessie."

She was all in a flutter. Nobody had ever said so much to her before.

His tone changed. "I am getting middling hungry, though. Had no breakfast to-day. Couldn't you scare up some bread from that tea for me, or—"

She was gone already. He had been on the point of asking her to let him come inside. No matter. Anywhere would do. Devil of a fix! What would his chum think?

"I didn't ask you as a beggar," he said jestingly, taking a piece of bread-

and-butter from the plate she held before him. "I asked as a friend. My dad is rich, you know."

"He starves himself for your sake."

"And I have starved for his whim," he said, taking up another piece.

"All he has in the world is for you," she pleaded.

"Yes, if I come here to sit on it like a dam' toad in a hole. Thank you; and what about the shovel, eh? He always had a queer way of showing his love."

"I could bring him round in a week," she suggested timidly.

He was too hungry to answer her; and, holding the plate submissively to his hand, she began to whisper up to him in a quick, panting voice. He listened, amazed, eating slower and slower, till at last his jaws stopped altogether. "That's his game, is it?" he said, in a rising tone of scathing contempt. An ungovernable movement of his arm sent the plate flying out of her fingers. He shot out a violent curse.

She shrank from him, putting her hand against the wall.

"No!" he raged. "He expects! Expects *me* —for his rotten money!... Who wants his home? Mad—not he! Don't you think. He wants his own way. He wanted to turn me into a miserable lawyer's clerk, and now he wants to make of me a blamed tame rabbit in a cage. Of me! Of me!" His subdued angry laugh frightened her now.

"The whole world ain't a bit too big for me to spread my elbows in, I can tell you—what's your name—Bessie—let alone a dam' parlour in a hutch. Marry! He wants me to marry and settle! And as likely as not he has looked out the girl too—dash my soul! And do you know the Judy, may I ask?"

She shook all over with noiseless dry sobs; but he was fuming and fretting too much to notice her distress. He bit his thumb with rage at the mere idea. A window rattled up.

"A grinning, information fellow," pronounced old Hagberd dogmatically, in measured tones. And the sound of his voice seemed to Bessie to make the night itself mad—to pour insanity and disaster on the earth. "Now I know what's wrong with the people here, my dear. Why, of course! With this mad chap going about. Don't you have anything to do with him, Bessie. Bessie, I say!"

They stood as if dumb. The old man fidgeted and mumbled to himself at the window. Suddenly he cried piercingly: "Bessie—I see you. I'll tell Harry."

She made a movement as if to run away, but stopped and raised her hands to her temples. Young Hagberd, shadowy and big, stirred no more than a man of bronze. Over their heads the crazy night whimpered and scolded in an old man's voice.

"Send him away, my dear. He's only a vagabond. What you want is a good home of your own. That chap has no home—he's not like Harry. He can't be Harry. Harry is coming to-morrow. Do you hear? One day more," he babbled more excitedly; "never you fear—Harry shall marry you."

His voice rose very shrill and mad against the regular deep soughing of the swell coiling heavily about the outer face of the sea-wall.

"He will have to. I shall make him, or if not"—he swore a great oath—"I'll cut him off with a shilling to-morrow, and leave everything to you. I shall. To you. Let him starve."

The window rattled down.

Harry drew a deep breath, and took one step towards Bessie. "So it's you—the girl," he said, in a lowered voice. She had not moved, and she remained half turned away from him, pressing her head in the palms of her hands. "My word!" he continued, with an invisible half-smile on his lips. "I have a great mind to stop..."

Her elbows were trembling violently.

"For a week," he finished without a pause.

She clapped her hands to her face.

He came up quite close, and took hold of her wrists gently. She felt his breath on her ear.

"It's a scrape I am in—this, and it is you that must see me through." He was trying to uncover her face. She resisted. He let her go then, and stepping back a little, "Have you got any money?" he asked. "I must be off now."

She nodded quickly her shamefaced head, and he waited, looking away from her, while, trembling all over and bowing her neck, she tried to find the pocket of her dress.

"Here it is!" she whispered. "Oh, go away! go away for God's sake! If I had more—more—I would give it all to forget—to make you forget."

He extended his hand. "No fear! I haven't forgotten a single one of you in the world. Some gave me more than money—but I am a beggar now—and you women always had to get me out of my scrapes."

He swaggered up to the parlour window, and in the dim light filtering through the blind, looked at the coin lying in his palm. It was a half-sovereign. He slipped it into his pocket. She stood a little on one side, with her head drooping, as if wounded; with her arms hanging passive by her side, as if dead.

"You can't buy me in," he said, "and you can't buy yourself out."

He set his hat firmly with a little tap, and next moment she felt herself lifted up in the powerful embrace of his arms. Her feet lost the ground; her head hung back; he showered kisses on her face with a silent and over-mastering ardour, as if in haste to get at her very soul. He kissed her pale cheeks, her hard forehead, her heavy eyelids, her faded lips; and the measured blows and sighs of the rising tide accompanied the enfolding power of his arms, the over-whelming might of his caresses. It was as if the sea, breaking down the wall protecting all the homes of the town, had sent a wave over her head. It passed on; she staggered backwards, with her shoulders against the wall, exhausted, as if she had been stranded there after a storm and a shipwreck.

She opened her eyes after a while; and, listening to the firm, leisurely footsteps going away with their conquest, began to gather her skirts, staring all the time before her. Suddenly she darted through the open gate into the dark and deserted street.

"Stop!" she shouted. "Don't go!"

And listening with an attentive poise of the head, she could not tell whether it was the beat of the swell of his fateful tread that seemed to fall cruelly upon her heart. Presently every sound grew fainter, as though she were slowly turning into stone. A fear of this awful silence came to her—worse than the fear of death. She called upon her ebbing strength for the final appeal:

"Harry!"

Not even the dying echo of a footstep. Nothing. The thundering of the surf, the voice of the restless sea itself, seemed stopped. There was not a sound—

no whisper of life, as though she were alone, and lost in that stony country of which she had heard, where mad-men go looking for gold and spurn the find.

Captain Hagberd, inside his dark house, had kept on the alert. A window ran up; and in the silence of the stony country a voice spoke above her head, high up in the black air—the voice of madness, lies, and despair—the voice of inextinguishable hope. "Is he gone yet—that information fellow? Do you hear him about, my dear?"

She burst into tears. "No! no! no! I don't hear him any more," she sobbed.

He began to chuckle up there triumphantly. "You frightened him away. Good girl. Now we shall be all right. Don't you be impatient, my dear. One day more."

In the other house old Carvil, wallowing regally in his arm-chair, with a globe lamp burning by his side on the table, yelled for her in a fiendish voice: "Bessie! Bessie! You, Bessie!"

She heard him at last, and, as if overcome by fate, began to totter silently back towards her stuffy little inferno of a cottage. It had no lofty portal, no terrific inscription of forfeited hopes—she did not understand wherein she had sinned.

Captain Hagberd had gradually worked himself into a state of noisy happiness up there.

"Go in! Keep quiet!" she turned upon him tearfully, form the doorstep below.

He rebelled against her authority in his great joy at having got rid at last of that "something wrong." It was as if all the hopeful madness of the world had broken out to bring terror upon her heart, with the voice of that old man shouting of his trust in an everlasting to-morrow.

CHILDREN
of the
SEA

I

Mr. Baker, chief mate of the ship *Narcissus*, stepped in one stride out of his lighted cabin into the darkness of the quarter-deck. Above his head, on the break of the poop, the night-watchman rang a double stroke. It was nine o'clock. Mr. Baker, speaking up to the man above him, asked:—"Are all the hands aboard, Knowles?"

The man limped down the ladder, then said reflectively:—

"I think so, sir. All our old chaps are there, and a lot of new men has come. . . . . They must be all there."

"Tell the boatswain to send all hands aft," went on Mr. Baker; "and tell one of the youngsters to bring a good lamp here. I want to muster our crowd."

The main deck was dark aft, but halfway from forward, through the open doors of the forecastle, two streaks of brilliant light cut the shadow of the quiet night that lay upon the ship. A hum of voices was heard there, while port and starboard, in the illuminated doorways, silhouettes of moving men appeared for a moment, very black, without relief, like figures cut out of sheet tin. The ship was ready for sea. The carpenter had driven in the last wedge of the main-hatch battens, and, throwing down his maul, had wiped his face with great deliberation, just on the stroke of five. The decks had been swept, the windlass oiled and made ready to heave up the anchor; the big tow-rope lay in long bights along one side of the main deck, with one end carried up and hung over the bows, in readiness for the tug that would come paddling and hissing noisily, hot and smoky, in the limpid, cool quietness of the early morning. The captain was ashore, where he had been engaging some new hands to make up his full crew; and, the work of the day over, the ship's officers had kept out of the way, glad of a little breathing-time. Soon after dark the few liberty-men and the new hands began to arrive in shore-boats rowed by white-clad Asiatics, who clamoured fiercely for payment before coming alongside the gangway-ladder. The feverish and shrill babble of Eastern language struggled against the masterful tones of tipsy seamen, who argued against brazen claims and dishonest hopes by profane shouts. The resplendent and bestarred peace of the East was torn into squalid tatters by howls of rage and shrieks of lament raised over sums ranging from five annas to half a rupee; and every soul afloat in Bombay Harbour became aware that the new hands were joining the *Narcissus*.

Gradually the distracting noise had subsided. The boats came no longer in splashing clusters of three or four together, but dropped alongside singly, in a subdued buzz of expostulation cut short by a "Not a pice more! You go to the

339

devil!" from some man staggering up the accommodation-ladder—a dark figure, with a long bag poised on the shoulder. In the forecastle the newcomers, upright and swaying amongst corded boxes and bundles of bedding made friends with the old hands, who sat one above another in the two tiers of bunks, gazing at their future shipmates with glances critical but friendly. The two forecastle lamps were turned up high, and shed an intense hard glare; shore-going hard hats were pushed far on the backs of heads, or rolled about on the deck amongst the chain-cables; white collars, undone, stuck out on each side of red faces; big arms in white sleeves gesticulated; the growling voices hummed steady amongst bursts of laughter and hoarse calls. "Here, sonny, take that bunk!.... Don't you do it!.... What's your last ship?.... I know her..... Three years ago, in Puget Sound.... This here berth leaks, I tell you!.... Come on; give us a chance to swing that chest!.... Did you bring a bottle, any of you shore toffs?.... Give us a bit of 'baccy..... I know her; her skipper drank himself to death..... He was a dandy boy!.... Liked his lotion inside, he did!.... No!.... Hold your row, you chaps!.... I tell you, you came on board a hooker, where they get their money's worth out of poor Jack, by—!...."

A little fellow, called Craik and nicknamed Belfast, abused the ship violently, romancing on principle, just to give the new hands something to think over. Archie, sitting aslant on his sea-chest, kept his knees out of the way, and pushed the needle steadily through a white patch in a pair of blue trousers. Men in black jackets and stand-up collars, mixed with men bare-footed, bare-armed, with coloured shirts open on hairy chests, pushed against one another in the middle of the forecastle. The group swayed, reeled, turning upon itself with the motion of a scrimmage, in a haze of tobacco smoke. All were speaking together, swearing at every second word. A Russian Finn, wearing a yellow shirt with pink stripes, stared upwards, dreamy-eyed, from under a mop of tumbled hair. Two young giants with smooth, baby faces—two Scandinavians—helped each other to spread their bedding, silent, and smiling placidly at the tempest of good-humoured and meaningless curses. Old Singleton, the oldest able seaman in the ship, set apart on the deck right under the lamps, stripped to the waist, tattooed like a cannibal chief all over his powerful chest and enormous biceps. Between the blue and red patterns his white skin gleamed like satin; his bare back was propped against the heel of the bowsprit, and he held a book at arm's length before his big, sunburnt face. With his spectacles and a venerable white beard, he resembled a learned and savage patriarch, the incarnation of barbarian wisdom serene in the blasphemous turmoil of the world. He was intensely absorbed, and, as he turned the pages an expression of grave surprise would pass over his rugged features. He was reading "Pelham." The popularity of Bulwer Lytton in the forecastles of Southern-going ships is a wonderful and bizarre phenomenon. What ideas do his polished and so curiously insincere sentences awaken in the simple minds of the big children who people those dark and wandering places of the earth? What meaning their rough, inexperienced souls can find in the elegant verbiage of his pages? What excitement?—what forgetfulness?—what appeasement? Mystery! Is it the fascination of the incomprehensible?—is it the charm of the impossible? Or are those beings who exist beyond the pale of life stirred by his tales as by an enigmatical disclosure of a resplendent world that exists within the frontier of infamy and filth, within that border of dirt and hunger, of misery and dissipation, that comes down on all sides to the water's edge of the incorruptible ocean, and is the only thing they know of life, the only thing they see of surrounding land—those life-long prisoners of the sea? Mystery!

Singleton, who had sailed to the southward since the age of twelve, who in the last forty-five years had lived (as we had calculated from his papers) no more than forty months ashore—old Singleton, who boasted, with the mild composure of long years well spent, that generally from the day he was paid off from one ship till the day he shipped in another he seldom was in a condition to distinguish daylight—old Singleton sat unmoved in the clash of voices and cries, spelling through "Pelham" with slow labour, and lost in an absorption profound enough to resemble a trance. He breathed regularly. Every time he turned the book in his enormous and blackened hands the muscles of his big white arms rolled slightly under the smooth skin. Hidden by the white moustache, his lips, stained with tobacco-juice that trickled down the long beard, moved in inward whisper. His bleared eyes gazed fixedly from behind the glitter of black-rimmed glasses. Opposite to him, and on a level with his face, the ship's cat sat on the barrel of the windlass in the pose of a crouching chimera, blinking its green eyes at its old friend. It seemed to meditate a leap on to the old man's lap over the bent back of the ordinary seaman who sat at Singleton's feet. Young Charley was lean and long-necked. The ridge of his backbone made a chain of small hills under the old shirt. His face of a street-boy—a face precocious, sagacious, and ironic, with deep downward folds on each side of the thin, wide mouth—hung low over his bony knees. He was learning to make a lanyard knot with a bit of an old rope. Small drops of perspiration stood out on his bulging forehead; he sniffed strongly from time to time, glancing out of the corners of his restless eyes at the old seaman, who took no notice of the puzzled youngster muttering at his work.

The noise increased. Little Belfast seemed, in the heavy heat of the forecastle, to boil with facetious fury. His eyes danced; in the crimson of his face, comical as a mask, the mouth yawned black, with strange grimaces. Facing him, a half-undressed man held his sides, and, throwing his head back, laughed with wet eyelashes. Others stared with amazed eyes. Men sitting doubled up in the upper bunks smoked short pipes, swinging bare brown feet above the heads of those who, sprawling below on sea-chests, listened, smiling stupidly or scornfully. Over the white rims of berths stuck out heads with blinking eyes; but the bodies were lost in the gloom of those places, that resembled narrow niches for coffins in a whitewashed and lighted mortuary. Voices buzzed louder. Archie, with compressed lips, drew himself in, seemed to shrink into a smaller space, and sewed steadily, industrious and dumb. Belfast shrieked like an inspired Dervish:—". . . . So I seez to him, boys, seez I, 'Beggin' yer pardon, sorr,' seez I to that second mate of that steamer—'beggin' your-r-r pardon, sorr, the Board of Trade must 'ave been drunk when they granted you your certificate!' 'What do you say, you—!' seez he, comin' at me like a mad bull. . . . all in his white clothes; and I up with my tarpot and capsizes it all over his blamed lovely face and his lovely jacket. . . . . 'Take that!' seez I. 'I am a sailor, anyhow, you nosing, skipper-licking, useless, sooperfloos bridge-stanchion, you!' 'That's the kind of man I am!' shouts I. . . . . You should have seed him skip, boys! Drowned, blind with tar, he was! So. . . ."

"Don't 'ee believe him! He never upset no tar; I was there!" shouted somebody. The two Norwegians sat on a chest side by side, alike and placid, resembling a pair of love-birds on a perch, and with round eyes stared innocently; but the Russian Finn, in the racket of explosive shouts and rolling laughter, remained motionless, limp and dull, like a deaf man without a backbone. Near him Archie smiled at his needle. A broad-chested, slow-eyed newcomer spoke deliberately to Belfast during an exhausted lull in the noise:—"I wonder any of the mates here are alive yet with such a chap as you on board! I concloode they ain't that bad now, if you had the taming of them, sonny."

"Not bad! Not bad!" screamed Belfast. "If it wasn't for us sticking together. . . . . Not bad! They ain't never bad when they ain't got a chawnce, blast their black 'arts. . . . ." He foamed, whirling his arms, then suddenly grinned and, taking a tablet of black tobacco out of his pocket, bit a piece off with a funny show of ferocity. Another new hand—a man with shifty eyes and a yellow hatchet face, who had been listening open-mouthed in the shadow of the midship locker—observed in a squeaky voice:—"Well, it's a 'omeward trip, anyhow. Bad or good, I can do it hall on my 'ed—s'long as I get 'ome. And I can look after my rights! I will show 'em!" All the heads turned towards him. Only the ordinary seaman and the cat took no notice. He stood with arms akimbo, a little fellow with white eyelashes. He looked as if he had known all the degradations and all the furies. He looked as if he had been cuffed, kicked, rolled in the mud; he looked as if he had been scratched, spat upon, pelted with unmentionable filth. . . . and he smiled with a sense of security at the faces around. His ears were bending down under the weight of his battered hard hat. The torn tails of his black coat flapped in fringes about the calves of his legs. He unbuttoned the only two buttons that remained and every one saw he had no shirt under it. It was his deserved misfortune that those rags which nobody could possibly be supposed to own looked on him as if they had been stolen. His neck was long and thin; his eyelids were red; rare hairs hung about his jaws; his shoulders were peaked and drooped like the broken wings of a bird; all his left side was caked with mud which showed that he had lately slept in a wet ditch. He had saved his inefficient carcass from violent destruction by running away from an American ship where, in a moment of forgetful folly, he had dared to engage himself; and he had knocked about for a fortnight ashore in the native quarter, cadging for drinks, starving, sleeping on rubbish-heaps, wandering in sunshine: a startling visitor from a world of nightmares. He stood repulsive and smiling in the sudden silence. This clean white forecastle was his refuge; the place where he could be lazy; where he could wallow, and lie and eat—and curse the food he ate; where he could display his talents for shirking work, for cheating, for cadging; where he could find surely some one to wheedle and some one to bully—and where he would be paid for doing all this. They all knew him. Is there a spot on earth where such a man is unknown, an ominous survival testifying to the eternal fitness of lies and impudence? A taciturn long-armed shellback, with hooked fingers, who had been lying on his back smoking, turned in his bed to examine him dispassionately, then, over his head, sent a long jet of clear saliva towards the door. They all knew him! He was the man that cannot steer, that cannot splice, that dodges the work on dark nights; that, aloft, holds on frantically with both arms and legs, and swears at the wind, the sleet, the darkness; the man who curses the sea while others work. The man who is the last out and the first in when all hands are called. The man who can't do most things and won't do the rest. The pet of philanthropists and self-seeking land-lubbers. The sympathetic and deserving creature that knows all about his rights, but knows nothing of courage, of endurance, and of the unexpressed faith, of the unspoken loyalty that knits together a ship's company. The independent offspring of the ignoble freedom of the slums full of disdain and hate for the austere servitude of the sea.

Some one cried at him: "What's your name?"—"Donkin," he said, looking round with cheerful effrontery.—"What are you?" asked another voice.—"Why, a sailor like you, old man," he replied, in a tone that meant to be hearty but was impudent.—"Blamme if you don't look a blamed sight worse than a broken-down fireman," was the comment in a convinced mutter. Charley lifted his head and piped in a cheeky voice: "He is a man and a sailor"—then wiping his nose with the back of his hand bent down industriously over his bit of rope. A few laughed. Others stared doubtfully. The ragged newcomer was indignant.—"That's a fine way to welcome a chap into a fo'c'sle," he snarled. "Are you men or a lot of 'artless cannybals?"—"Don't take your shirt off for a word, shipmate," called out Belfast, jumping up in front, fiery, menacing, and friendly at the same time.—"Is that 'ere bloke blind?" asked the indomitable scarecrow, looking right and left with affected surprise. "Can't 'ee see I 'aven't got no shirt?"

He held both his arms out crosswise and shook the rags that hung over his bones with dramatic effect.

"'Cos why?" he continued very loud. "The bloody Yankees been tryin' to jump my guts hout 'cos I stood up for my rights like a good 'un. I ham a Henglishman, I ham. They set upon me an' I 'ad to run. That's why. A'n't yer never seed a man 'ard up? Yah! What kind of blamed ship is this? I'm dead broke. I 'aven't got nothink. No bag, no bed, no blanket, no shirt—not a bloomin' rag but what I stand in. But I 'ad the 'art to stand hup agin' them Yankees. 'As any of you 'art enough to spare a pair of old pants for a chum?"

He knew how to conquer the naïve instincts of that crowd. In a moment they gave him their compassion, jocularly, contemptuously, or surlily; and at first it took the shape of a blanket thrown at him as he stood there with the white skin of his limbs showing his human kinship through the black fantasy of his rags. Then a pair of old shoes fell at his muddy feet. With a cry:—"From under," a rolled-up pair of trousers, heavy with tar stains, struck him on the shoulder. The gust of their benevolence sent a wave of sentimental pity through their doubting hearts. They were touched by their own readiness to alleviate a shipmate's misery. Voices cried:—"We will fit you out, old man." Murmurs: "Never seed seech a hard case.....Poor beggar.....I've got an old sin-glet.....Will that be of any use to you?....Take it, matey....." Those friendly murmurs filled the forecastle. He pawed around with his naked foot, gathering the things in a heap and looked about for more. Unemotional Archie perfunc-torily contributed to the pile an old cloth cap with the peak torn off. Old Sin-gleton, lost in the serene regions of fiction, read on unheeding. Charley, pitiless with the wisdom of youth, squeaked:—"If you want brass buttons for your new unyforms I've got two for you." The filthy object of universal charity shook his fist at the youngster.—"I'll make you keep this 'ere fo'c'sle clean, young feller," he snarled viciously. "Never you fear. I will learn you to be civil to an able seaman, you hignorant hass." He glared harmfully, but saw Singleton shut his book, and his little beady eyes began to roam from berth to berth.—"Take that bunk by the door there—it's pretty fair," suggested Belfast. So advised, he gathered the gifts at his feet, pressed them in a bundle against his breast, then looked cautiously at the Russian Finn, who stood on one side with an unconscious gaze, contemplating, perhaps, one of those weird visions that haunt the men of his race.—"Get out of my road, Dutchy," said the victim of Yankee brutality. The Finn did not move—did not hear. "Get out, blast ye," shouted the other, shoving him aside with his elbow. "Get out, you blanked deaf and dumb fool. Get out." The man staggered, recovered himself, and gazed at the speaker in silence.—"Those damned furriners should be kept hunder," opined the amiable Donkin to the forecastle. "If you don't teach 'em their place they put on you like hanythink." He flung all his worldly possessions into the empty bedplace, gauged with another shrewd look the risks of the proceeding, then leaped up to the Finn, who stood pensive and dull.—"I'll teach you to swell around," he yelled. "I'll plug your eyes for you, you blooming square-head." Most of the men were now in their bunks and the two had the forecastle clear to themselves. The development of the destitute Donkin aroused interest. He danced all in tatters before the amazed Finn, squaring from a distance at the heavy, unmoved face. One or two men cried encouragingly: "Go it, Whitechapel!" settling themselves luxuriously in their beds to survey the fight. Others shouted: "Shut yer row!.... Go an' put yer 'ed in a bag!...." The hubbub was recommencing. Suddenly many heavy blows struck with a handspike on the deck above boomed like discharges of small cannon through the forecastle. Then the boatswain's voice rose outside the door with an authoritative note in its drawl:—"D'ye hear, below there? Lay aft! Lay aft to muster all hands!"

There was a moment of surprised stillness. Then the forecastle floor disappeared under men whose bare feet flopped on the planks as they sprang clear out of their berths. Caps were rooted for amongst tumbled blankets. Some, yawning, buttoned waistbands. Half-smoked pipes were knocked hurriedly against woodwork and stuffed under pillows. Voices growled:—"What's up?.... Is there no rest for us?" Donkin yelped:—"If that's the way of this ship, we'll 'ave to change hall that..... You leave me alone..... I will soon....." None of the crowd noticed him. They were lurching in twos and threes through the doors, after the manner of merchant Jacks who cannot go out of a door fairly, like mere landsmen. The votary of change followed them. Singleton, struggling into his jacket, came last, tall and fatherly, bearing high his head of a weather-beaten sage on the body of an old athlete. Only Charley remained alone in the white glare of the empty place, sitting between the two rows of iron links that stretched into the narrow gloom forward. He pulled hard at the strands in a hurried endeavour to finish his knot. Suddenly he started up, flung the rope at the cat, and skipped after the black tom that went off leaping sedately over chain compressors, with the tail carried stiff and upright, like a small flag pole.

Outside the glare of the steaming forecastle the serene purity of the night enveloped the seamen with its soothing breath, with its tepid breath flowing under the stars that hung countless above the mastheads in a thin cloud of luminous dust. On the town side the blackness of the water was streaked with trails of light which undulated gently on slight ripples, similar to filaments that float rooted to the shore. Rows of other lights stood away in straight lines as if drawn up on parade between towering buildings; but on the other side of the harbour sombre hills arched high their black spines, on which, here and there, the point of a star resembled a spark fallen from the sky. Far off, Byculla way, the electric lamps at the dock gates shone on the end of lofty standards with a glow blinding and frigid like captive ghosts of some evil moons. Scattered all over the dark polish of the roadstead, the ships at anchor floated in perfect stillness under the feeble gleam of their riding-lights, looming up, opaque and bulky, like strange and monumental structures abandoned by men to an everlasting repose.

Before the cabin door Mr. Baker was mustering the crew. As they stumbled and lurched along past the mainmast, they could see aft his round, broad face with a white paper before it, and beside his shoulder the sleepy head, with dropped eyelids, of the boy, who held, suspended at the end of his raised arm, the luminous globe of a lamp. Even before the shuffle of naked soles had ceased along the decks, the mate began to call over the names. He called distinctly in a serious tone befitting this roll-call to unquiet loneliness, to inglorious and obscure struggle, or to the more trying endurance of small privations and wearisome duties. As the chief mate read out a name, one of the men would answer: "Yes, sir!" or "Here!" and, detaching himself from the shadowy mob of heads visible above the blackness of starboard bulwarks, would step barefooted into the circle of light, and in two noiseless strides pass into the shadows on the port side of the quarter-deck. They answered in divers tones: in thick mutters, in clear, ringing voices; and some, as if the whole thing had been an outrage on their feelings, used an injured intonation: for discipline is not ceremonious in merchant ships, where the sense of hierarchy is weak, and where all fell themselves equal before the unconcerned immensity of the sea and the exacting appeal of the work.

Mr. Baker read on steadily:—"Hanssen—Campbell—Smith—Wamibo. Now, then, Wamibo. Why don't you answer? Always got to call your name twice." The Finn emitted at last an uncouth grunt, and, stepping out, passed through the patch of light, weird and gaudy, with the face of a man marching through a dream. The mate went on faster:—"Craik—Singleton—Donkin.....O Lord!" he involuntarily ejaculated as the incredibly dilapidated figure appeared in the light. It stopped; it uncovered pale gums and long, upper teeth in a malevolent grin.—"Is there anythink wrong with me, Mister Mate?" it asked, with a flavour of insolence in the forced simplicity of its tone. On both sides of the deck subdued titters were heard.—"That'll do. Go over," growled Mr. Baker, fixing the new hand with steady blue eyes. And Donkin vanished suddenly out of the light into the dark group of mustered men, to be slapped on the back and to hear flattering whispers. Round him men muttered to one another:—"He ain't afeard, he'll give sport to 'em, see if he don't.....Reg'lar Punch and Judy show.....Did ye see the mate start at him?....Well! Damme, if I ever!...."

The last man had gone over, and there was a moment of silence while the mate peered at his list.—"Sixteen, seventeen," he muttered. "I am one hand short, bo'sen," he said aloud. The big west-countryman at his elbow, swarthy and bearded like a gigantic Spaniard, said in a rumbling bass:—"There's no one left forward, sir. I had a look round. He ain't aboard, but he may turn up before daylight."—"Ay. He may or he may not," commented the mate; "can't make out that last name. It's all a smudge.....That will do, men. Go below."

The indistinct and motionless group stirred, broke up, began to move forward.

"Wait!" cried a deep, ringing voice.

All stood still. Mr. Baker, who had turned away yawning, spun round open-mouthed. At last, furious, he blurted out:—"What's this? Who said 'Wait'? What...."

But he saw a tall figure standing on the rail. It came down and pushed through the crowd, marching with a heavy tread towards the light on the quarter-deck. Then again the sonorous voice said with insistence:—"Wait!" The lamp-light lit up the man's body. He was tall. His head was away up in the shadows of lifeboats that stood on skids above the deck. The whites of his eyes and his teeth gleamed distinctly, but the face was indistinguishable. His hands were big and seemed gloved.

Mr. Baker advanced intrepidly. "Who are you? How dare you...." he began.

The boy, amazed like the rest, raised the light to the man's face. It was black. A surprised hum—a faint hum that sounded like the suppressed mutter of the word "Nigger"—ran along the deck and escaped out into the night. The nigger seemed not to hear. He balanced himself where he stood in a swagger that marked time. After a moment he said calmly:—"My name is Wait—James Wait."

"Oh!" said Mr. Baker. Then, after a few seconds of smouldering silence, his temper blazed out. "Ah! Your name is Wait. What of that? What do you want? What do you mean, coming shouting here?"

The nigger was calm, cool, towering, superb. The men had approached and stood behind him in a body. He overtopped the tallest by half a head. He said: "I belong to the ship." He enunciated distinctly, with soft precision. The deep, rolling tones of his voice filled the deck without effort. He was naturally scornful, unaffectedly condescending, as if from his height of six foot three he had surveyed all the vastness of human folly and had made up his mind not to be too hard on it. He went on:—"The captain shipped me this morning. I couldn't get aboard sooner. I saw you all aft as I came up the ladder, and could see directly you were mustering the crew. Naturally I called out my name. I thought you had it on your list, and would understand. You misapprehended." He stopped short. The folly around him was confounded. He was right as ever, and as ever ready to forgive. The disdainful tones had ceased, and, breathing heavily, he stood still, surrounded by all these white men. He held his head up in the glare of the lamp—a head vigorously modelled into deep shadows and shining lights—a head powerful and misshapen with a tormented and flattened face—a face pathetic and brutal: the tragic, the mysterious, the repulsive mask of a nigger's soul.

Mr. Baker, recovering his composure, looked at the paper close. "Oh, yes; that's so. All right, Wait. Take your gear forward," he said.

Suddenly the nigger's eyes rolled wildly, became all whites. He put his hand to his side and coughed twice, a cough metallic, hollow, and tremendously loud; it resounded like two explosions in a vault; the dome of the sky rang to it, and the iron plates of the ship's bulwarks seemed to vibrate in unison; then he marched off forward with the others. The officers lingering by the cabin door could hear him say: "Won't some of you chaps lend a hand with my dunnage? I've got a chest and a bag." The words, spoken sonorously, with an even intonation, were heard all over the ship, and the question was put in a manner that made refusal impossible. The short, quick shuffle of men carrying something heavy went away forward, but the tall figure of the nigger lingered by the main hatch in a knot of smaller shapes. Again he was heard asking: "Is your cook a coloured gentleman?" Then a disappointed and disapproving "Ah! h'm!" was his comment upon the information that the cook happened to be a mere white man. Yet, as they went all together towards the forecastle, he condescended to put his head through the galley door and boom out inside a magnificent "Good evening, doctor!" that made all the saucepans ring. In the dim light the cook dozed on the coal locker in front of the captain's supper. He jumped up as if he had been cut with a whip, and dashed wildly on deck to see the backs of several men going away laughing. Afterwards, when talking about that voyage, he used to say:—"The poor fellow had scared me. I thought I had seen the devil." The cook had been seven years in the ship with the same captain. He was a serious-minded man with a wife and three children, whose society he enjoyed on an average one month out of twelve. When on shore he took his family to church twice every Sunday. At sea he went to sleep every evening with his lamp turned up full, a pipe in his mouth, and an open Bible in his hand. Some one had always to go during the night to put out the light, take the book from his hand, and the pipe from between his teeth. "For"—Belfast used to say, irritated and complaining—"some night, you stupid cookie, you'll swallow your ould clay, and we will have no cook."—"Ah! sonny, I am ready for my maker's call.... wish you all were," the other would answer with a benign serenity that was altogether imbecile and touching. Belfast outside the galley door danced with vexation. "You holy fool! I don't want you to die," he howled, looking up with furious, quivering face and tender eyes. "What's the hurry? you blessed wooden-headed ould heretic, the divvle will have you soon enough. Think of Us.... of Us.... of Us!" And he would go away, stamping, spitting aside, disgusted and worried; while the other, stepping out, saucepan in hand, hot, begrimed, and placid, watched with a superior, cock-sure smile the back of his "queer little man" reeling in a rage. They were great friends.

Mr. Baker, lounging over the after-hatch, sniffed the humid night in the company of the second mate.—"Those West India niggers run fine and large— some of them.... Ough!.... Don't they? A fine, big man that, Mr. Creighton. Feel him on a rope. Hey? Ough! I will take him into my watch, I think." The second mate, a fair, gentlemanly young fellow, with a resolute face and a splen- did physique, observed quietly that it was just about what he expected. There could be felt in his tone some slight bitterness which Mr. Baker very kindly set himself to argue away. "Come, come, young man," he said, grunting between the words. "Come! Don't be too greedy. You had that big Finn in your watch all the voyage. I will do what's fair. You may have those two young Scandi- navians and I.... Ough!.... I get the nigger, and will take that.... Ough! that cheeky costermonger chap in a black frock-coat. I'll make him.... Ough!.... make him toe the mark, or my.... Ough!.... name isn't Baker. Ough! Ough! Ough!"

He grunted thrice—ferociously. He had that trick of grunting so between his words and at the end of sentences. It was a fine, effective grunt that went well with his menacing utterance, with his heavy, bull-necked frame, his jerky, rolling gait; with his big, seamed face, his steady eyes, and sardonic mouth. But its effect had been long ago discounted by the men. They liked him; Belfast— who was a favourite, and knew it—mimicked him, not quite behind his back. Charley—but with greater caution—imitated his walk. Some of his sayings became established, daily quotations in the forecastle. Popularity can go no farther! Besides, all hands were ready to admit that on a fitting occasion the mate could "jump down a fellow's throat in a reg'lar Western Ocean style."

Now he was giving his last orders. "Ough!.... You, Knowles! Call all hands at four. I want.... Ough!.... to heave short before the tug comes. Look out for the captain. I am going to lay down in my clothes..... Ough!.... Call me when you see the boat coming. Ough! Ough!.... The old man is sure to have something to say when he comes aboard," he remarked to Creighton. "Well, goodnight..... Ough! A long day before us tomorrow..... Ough!.... Better turn in now. Ough! Ough!"

Upon the dark deck a band of light flashed, then a door slammed, and Mr. Baker was gone into his neat cabin. Young Creighton stood leaning over the rail, and looked dreamily into the night of the East. And he saw in it a long country lane, a lane of waving leaves and dancing sunshine. He saw stirring boughs of old trees outspread, and framing in their arch the tender, the caressing blueness of an English sky. And through the arch a girl in a clear dress, smiling under a sunshade, seemed to be stepping out of the tender sky.

At the other end of the ship the forecastle, with only one lamp burning now, was going to sleep in a dim emptiness traversed by loud breathings, by sudden short sighs. The double row of berths yawned black, like graves tenanted by uneasy corpses. Here and there a curtain of gaudy chintz, half drawn, marked the resting-place of a sybarite. A leg hung over the edge very white and lifeless. An arm stuck straight out with a dark palm turned up, and thick fingers half closed. Two light snores, that did not synchronise, quarrelled in funny dialogue. Singleton stripped again—the old man suffered much from prickly heat—stood cooling his back in the doorway, with his arms crossed on his bare and adorned chest. His head touched the beam of the deck above. The nigger, half undressed, was busy casting adrift the lashing of his box, and spreading his bedding in an upper berth. He moved about in his socks, tall and noiseless, with a pair of braces beating about his heels. Amongst the shadows of stanchions and bowsprit, Donkin munched a piece of hard ship's bread, sitting on the deck with upturned feet and restless eyes; he held the biscuit up before his mouth in the whole fist, and snapped his jaws at it with a raging face. Crumbs fell between his outspread legs. Then he got up.

"Where's our water-cask?" he asked in a contained voice.

Singleton, without a word, pointed with a big hand that held a short smouldering pipe. Donkin bent over the cask, drank out of the tin, splashing the water, turned round and noticed the nigger looking at him over the shoulder with calm loftiness. He moved up sideways.

"There's a blooming supper for a man," he whispered bitterly. "My dorg at 'ome wouldn't 'ave it. It's fit enouf for you an' me. 'Ere's a big ship's fo'c'-sle!.... Not a blooming scrap of meat in the kids. I've looked in all the lockers....."

The nigger stared like a man addressed unexpectedly in a foreign language. Donkin changed his tone:—"Giv' us a bit of 'baccy, mate," he breathed out confidentially, "I 'aven't 'ad smoke or chew for the last month. I am rampin' mad for it. Come on, old man!"

"Don't be familiar," said the nigger. Donkin started and sat down on a chest near by, out of sheer surprise. "We haven't kept pigs together," continued James Wait in a deep undertone. "Here's your tobacco." Then, after a pause, he asked:—"What ship?"—"*Golden State*," muttered Donkin indistinctly, biting the tobacco. The nigger whistled low.—"Ran?" he said curtly. Donkin nodded: one of his cheeks bulged out.—"In course I ran," he mumbled. "They booted the life hout of one Dago chap on the passage 'ere, then started on me. I cleared hout 'ere."—"Left your dunnage behind?"—"Yes, dunnage and money," answered Donkin, raising his voice a little; "I got nothink. No clothes, no bed. A bandy-legged little Hirish chap 'ere 'as give me a blanket..... Think I'll go an' sleep in the fore topmast staysail to-night."

He went on deck trailing behind his back a corner of the blanket. Singleton, without a glance, moved slightly aside to let him pass. The nigger put away his shore togs and sat in clean working clothes on his box, one arm stretched over his knees. After staring at Singleton for some time he asked without emphasis:— "What kind of ship is this? Pretty fair? Eh?"

Singleton didn't stir. A long while after he said, with unmoved face:— "Ship!.... Ships are all right. It is the men in them!"

He went on smoking in the profound silence. The wisdom of half a century spent in listening to the thunder of the waves had spoken unconsciously through his old lips. The cat purred on the windlass. Then James Wait had a fit of roaring, rattling cough, that shook him, tossed him like a hurricane, and flung him panting with staring eyes headlong on his sea-chest. Several men woke up. One said sleepily out of his bunk: "'Struth! what a blamed row!"—"I have a cold on my chest," gasped Wait.—"Cold! you call it," grumbled the man; "should think 'twas something more..... "—"Oh! you think so," said the nigger upright and loftily scornful again. He climbed into his berth and began coughing persistently while he put his head out to glare all round the forecastle. There was no further protest. He fell back on the pillow, and could be heard there wheezing regularly like a man oppressed in his sleep.

Singleton stood at the door with his face to the light and his back to the darkness. And alone in the dim emptiness of the sleeping forecastle he appeared bigger, colossal, very old; old as Father Time himself, who should have come there into this place as quiet as a sepulchre to contemplate with patient eyes the short victory of sleep, the consoler. Yet he was only a child of time, a lonely relic of a devoured and forgotten generation. He stood, still strong, as ever unthinking; a ready man with a vast empty past and with no future, with his childlike impulses and his man's passions already dead within his tattooed breast. The men who could understand his silence were gone—those men who knew how to exist beyond the pale of life and within sight of eternity. They had been strong, as those are strong who know neither doubts nor hopes. They had been impatient and enduring, turbulent and devoted, unruly and faithful. Well-meaning people had tried to represent those men as whining over every mouthful of their food; as going about their work in fear of their lives. But in truth they had been men who knew toil, privation, violence, debauchery—but knew not fear, and had no desire of spite in their hearts. Men hard to manage, but easy to inspire; voiceless men—but men enough to scorn in their hearts the sentimental voices that bewailed the hardness of their fate. It was a fate unique and their own; the capacity to bear it appeared to them the privilege of the chosen! Their generation lived inarticulate and indispensable, without knowing the sweetness of affections or the refuge of a home—and died free from the dark menace of a narrow grave. They were the everlasting children of the mysterious sea. Their successors are the grown-up children of a discontented earth. They are less naughty, but less innocent; less profane, but perhaps also less believing; and if they had learned how to speak they have also learned how to whine. But the others were strong and mute; they were effaced, bowed and enduring, like stone caryatides that hold up in the night the lighted halls of a resplendent and glorious edifice. They are gone now—and it does not matter. The sea and the earth are unfaithful to their children: a truth, a faith, a generation of men goes—and is forgotten, and it does not matter! Except, perhaps, to the few of those who believed the truth, confessed the faith—or loved the men.

A breeze was coming. The ship that had been lying tide-rode swung to a heavier puff; and suddenly the slack of the chain cable between the windlass and the hawse-pipe clinked, slipped forward an inch, and rose gently off the deck with a startling suggestion as of unsuspected life that had been lurking stealthily in the iron. In the hawse-pipe the grinding links sent through the ship a sound like a low groan of a man sighing under a burden. The strain came on the windlass, the chain tautened like a string, vibrated—and the handle of the screwbrake moved in slight jerks. Singleton stepped forward.

Till then he had been standing meditative and unthinking, reposeful and hopeless, with a face grim and blank—a sixty-year-old child of the mysterious sea. The thoughts of all his lifetime could have been expressed in six words, but the stir of those things that were as much part of his existence as his beating heart called up a gleam of alert understanding upon the sternness of his aged face. The flame of the lamp swayed, and the old man, with knitted and bushy eyebrows, stood over the brake, watchful and motionless in the wild saraband of dancing shadows. Then the ship, obedient to the call of her anchor, forged ahead slightly and eased the strain. The cable relieved, hung down, and after swaying imperceptibly to and fro dropped with a loud tap on the hard wood planks. Singleton seized the high lever, and, by a violent throw forward of his body, wrung out another half-turn from the brake. He recovered himself, breathed largely, and remained for awhile glaring down at the powerful and compact engine that squatted on the deck at his feet, like some quiet monster—a creature amazing and tame.

"You . . . . hold!" he growled at it masterfully, in the incult tangle of his white beard.

II

Next morning, at daylight, the *Narcissus* went to sea.

A slight haze blurred the horizon. Outside the harbour the measureless expanse of smooth water lay sparkling like a floor of jewels, and as empty as the sky. The short black tug gave a pluck to windward, in the usual way, then let go the rope, and hovered for a moment on the quarter with her engines stopped; while the slim, long hull of the ship moved ahead slowly under lower topsails. The loose upper canvas blew out in the breeze with soft round contours, resembling small white clouds snared in the maze of ropes. Then the sheets were hauled home, the yards hoisted, and the ship became a high and lonely pyramid, gliding, all shining and white, through the sunlit mist. The tug turned short round and went away towards the land. Twenty-six pairs of eyes watched her low broad stern crawling languidly over the smooth swell between the two paddle-wheels that turned fast, beating the water with fierce hurry. She resembled an enormous and aquatic blackbeetle, surprised by the light, overwhelmed by the sunshine, trying to escape with ineffectual effort into the distant gloom of the land. She left a lingering smudge of smoke on the sky, and two vanishing trails of foam on the water. On the place where she had stopped a round black patch of soot remained, undulating on the swell—an unclean mark of the creature's rest.

The *Narcissus* left alone, heading south, seemed to stand resplendent and still upon the restless sea, under the moving sun. Flakes of foam swept past her sides; the water struck her with flashing blows; the land glided away, slowly fading; a few birds screamed on motionless wings over the swaying mastheads. But soon the land disappeared, the birds went away; and to the west the pointed sail of an Arab dhow running for Bombay, rose triangular and upright above the sharp edge of the horizon, lingered, and vanished like an illusion. Then the ship's wake, long and straight, stretched itself out through a day of immense solitude. The setting sun, burning on the level of the water, flamed crimson below the blackness of heavy rain clouds. The sunset squall, coming up from behind, dissolved itself into the short deluge of a hissing shower. It left the ship glistening from trucks to waterline, and with darkened sails. She ran easily before a fair monsoon, with her decks cleared for the night; and, moving along with her, was heard the sustained and monotonous swishing of the waves, mingled with the low whispers of men mustered aft for the setting of watches; the short plaint of some block aloft; or, now and then, a loud sigh of wind.

Mr. Baker, coming out of his cabin, called out the first name sharply before closing the door behind him. He was going to take charge of the deck. On the homeward trip, according to an old custom of the sea, the chief officer takes the first night-watch—from eight till midnight. So Mr. Baker, after he had heard the last "Yes, sir!" said moodily, "Relieve the wheel and look-out"; and climbed with heavy feet the poop ladder to windward. Soon after Mr. Creighton came down, whistling softly, and went into the cabin. On the doorstep the steward lounged, in slippers, meditative, and with his shirt-sleeves rolled up to the armpits. On the main deck the cook, locking up the galley doors, had an altercation with young Charley about a pair of socks. He could be heard saying impressively, in the darkness amidships: "You don't deserve a kindness. I've been drying them for you, and now you complain about the holes—and you swear, too! Right in front of me! If I hadn't been a Christian—which you ain't, you young ruffian—I would give you a clout on the head. . . . . Go away!" Men in couples or threes stood pensive or moved silently along the bulwarks in the waist. The first busy day of a homeward passage was sinking into the dull peace of resumed routine. Aft, on the high poop, Mr. Baker walked shuffling; grunted to himself in the pauses of his thoughts. Forward, the look-out man, erect between the flukes of the two anchors, hummed an endless tune, keeping his eyes fixed dutifully ahead in a vacant stare. A multitude of stars coming out into the clear night peopled the emptiness of the sky. They glittered, as if alive above the sea; they surrounded the running ship on all sides; more intense than the eyes of a staring crowd, and as inscrutable as the souls of men.

The passage had begun; and the ship, a fragment detached from the earth, went on lonely and swift like a small planet. Round her the abysses of sky and sea met in an unattainable frontier. A great circular solitude moved with her, ever changing and ever the same, always monotonous and always imposing. Now and then another wandering white speck, burdened with life, appeared far off—disappeared; intent on its own destiny. The sun looked upon her all day, and every morning rose with a burning, round stare of undying curiosity. She had her own future; she was alive with the lives of those beings who trod her decks; like that earth which had given her up to the sea, she had an intolerable load of regrets and hopes. On her lived timid truth and audacious lies; and, like the earth, she was unconscious, fair to see—and condemned by men to an ignoble fate. The august loneliness of her path lent dignity to the sordid inspiration of her pilgrimage. She drove foaming to the southward, as if guided by the courage of a high endeavour. The smiling greatness of the sea dwarfed the extent of time. The days raced after one another, brilliant and quick like the flashes of a lighthouse, and the nights, eventful and short, resembled fleeting dreams.

The men had shaken into their places, and the half-hourly voice of the bells ruled their life of unceasing care. Night and day the head and shoulders of a seaman could be seen aft by the wheel, outlined high against sunshine or starlight, very steady above the stir of revolving spokes. The faces changed, passing in rotation. Youthful faces, bearded faces, dark faces: faces serene, or faces moody, but all akin with the brotherhood of the sea; all with the same attentive expression of eyes, carefully watching the compass or the sails. Captain Allistoun, serious, and with an old red muffler round his throat, all day long pervaded the poop. At night, many times he rose out of the darkness of the companion, such as a phantom above a grave, and stood watchful and mute under the stars, his night-shirt fluttering like a flag—then, without a sound, sank down again. He was born on the shores of the Pentland Firth. In his youth he attained the rank of harpooner in Peterhead whalers. When he spoke of that time his restless grey eyes became still and cold, like the loom of ice. Afterwards he went into the East Indian trade for the sake of change. He had commanded the *Narcissus* since she was built. He loved his ship, and drove her unmercifully; for his secret ambition was to make her accomplish some day a brilliantly quick passage which would be mentioned in nautical papers. He pronounced his owner's name with a sardonic smile, spoke but seldom to his officers, and reproved errors in a gentle voice, with words that cut to the quick. His hair was iron-grey, his face hard and of the colour of pump-leather. He shaved every morning of his life— at six—but once (being caught in a fierce hurricane eighty miles southwest of Mauritius) he had missed three consecutive days. He feared naught but an unforgiving God, and wished to end his days in a little house, with a plot of ground attached—far in the country—out of sight of the sea.

He, the ruler of that minute world, seldom descended from the Olympian heights of his poop. Below him—at his feet, so to speak—common mortals led their busy and insignificant lives. Along the main deck Mr. Baker grunted in a manner bloodthirsty and innocuous; and kept all our noses to the grindstone, being—as he once remarked—paid for doing that very thing. The men working about the deck were healthy and contented— as most seamen are, when once well out to sea. The true peace of God begins at any spot a thousand miles from the nearest land; and when He sends there the messengers of His might it is not in terrible wrath against crime, presumption, and folly, but paternally, to chasten simple hearts—ignorant hearts that know nothing of life, and beat undisturbed by envy or greed.

In the evening the cleared decks had a reposeful aspect, resembling the autumn of the earth. The sun was sinking to rest, wrapped in a mantle of warm clouds. Forward, on the end of the spare spars, the boatswain and the carpenter sat together with crossed arms; two men friendly, powerful, and deep-chested. Beside them the short, dumpy sailmaker—who had been in the Navy—related, between the whiffs of his pipe, impossible stories about Admirals. Couples tramped backwards and forwards, keeping step and balance without effort, in a confined space. Pigs grunted in the big pigstye. Belfast, leaning thoughtfully on his elbow, above the bars, communed with them through the silence of his meditation. Fellows with shirts open wide on sunburnt breasts sat upon the mooring bits, and all up the steps of the forecastle ladders. By the foremast a few discussed in a circle the characteristics of a gentleman. One said:—"It's money as does it." Another maintained:—"No, it's the way they speak." Lame Knowles stumped up with an unwashed face (he had the distinction of being the dirty man of the forecastle), and, showing a few yellow fangs in a shrewd smile, explained craftily that he "had seen some of their pants." The backsides of them—he had observed—were thinner than paper from constant sitting down in offices, yet otherwise they looked first-rate and would last for years. It was all appearance. "It was," he said, "bloomin' easy to be a gentleman when you had a clean job for life." They disputed endlessly, obstinate and childish; they repeated in shouts and with inflamed faces their amazing arguments; while the soft breeze, eddying down the enormous cavity of the foresail, that stood out distended above their bare heads, stirred the tumbled hair with a touch passing light like an indulgent caress.

They were forgetting their toil, they were forgetting themselves. The cook approached to hear, and stood by, beaming with the inward consciousness of his faith, like a conceited saint unable to forget his glorious reward; Donkin, solitary and brooding over his wrongs on the forecastle-head, moved closer to catch the drift of the discussion below him; he turned his sallow face to the sea, and his thin nostrils moved, sniffing the breeze, as he lounged negligently by the rail. In the glow of sunset faces shone with interest, teeth flashed, eyes sparkled. The walking couples stood still suddenly, with broad grins; a man, bending over a washtub, sat up, entranced, with the soapsuds flecking his wet arms. Even the three petty officers listened leaning back, comfortably propped, and with superior smiles. Belfast left off scratching the ear of his favourite pig, and, open mouthed, tried with eager eyes to have his say. He lifted his arms, grimacing and baffled. From a distance Charley screamed at the ring:—"I know about gentlemen morn'n any of you. I've been hintymate with 'em.... I've blacked their boots." The cook, craning his neck to hear better, was scandalised. "Keep your mouth shut when your elders speak, you impudent young heathen— you." "All right, old Hallelujah, I'm done," answered Charley, soothingly. At some opinion of dirty Knowles, delivered with an air of supernatural cunning, a ripple of laughter ran along, rose like a wave, burst with a startling roar. They stamped with both feet; they turned their shouting faces to the sky; many, spluttering, slapped their thighs; while one or two, bent double, gasped, hugging themselves with both arms like men in pain. The carpenter and the boatswain, without changing their attitude, shook with laughter where they sat; the sailmaker, charged with an anecdote about a Commodore, looked sulky; the cook was wiping his eyes with a greasy rag; and lame Knowles, astonished at his own success, stood in their midst showing a slow smile.

Suddenly the face of Donkin leaning high-shouldered over the after-rail became grave. Something like a weak rattle was heard through the forecastle door. It became a murmur; it ended in a sighing groan. The washerman plunged both his arms into the tub abruptly; the cook became more crestfallen than an exposed backslider; the boatswain moved his shoulders uneasily; the carpenter got up with a spring and walked away—while the sailmaker seemed mentally to give his story up, and began to puff at his pipe with sombre determination. In the blackness of the doorway a pair of eyes glimmered white, and big, and staring. Then James Wait's head protruding, became visible, as if suspended between the two hands that grasped a doorpost on each side of the face. The tassel of his blue woollen nightcap, cocked forward, danced gaily over his left eyelid. He stepped out in a tottering stride. He looked powerful as ever, but showed a strange and affected unsteadiness in his gait; his face was perhaps a trifle thinner, and his eyes appeared rather startlingly prominent. He seemed to hasten the retreat of departing light by his very presence; the setting sun dipped sharply, as though fleeing before our nigger; a black mist emanated from him; a subtle and dismal influence; a something cold and gloomy that floated out and settled on all the faces like a mourning veil. The circle broke up. The joy of laughter died on stiffened lips. There was not a smile left among all the ship's company. Not a word was spoken. Many turned their backs, trying to look unconcerned; others, with averted heads, sent half-reluctant glances out of the corners of their eyes. They resembled criminals conscious of misdeeds more than honest men distracted by doubt; only two or three stared frankly, but stupidly, with lips slightly open. All expected James Wait to say something, and, at the same time, had the air of knowing beforehand what he would say. He leaned his back against the doorpost, and with heavy eyes swept over us a glance domineering and pained, like a sick tyrant overawing a crowd of abject but untrustworthy slaves.

No one went away. They waited in fascinated dread. He said ironically, with gasps between the works:—

"Thank you . . . . chaps. You . . . . are nice . . . . and . . . . quiet . . . . you are! Yelling so . . . . before . . . . the door . . . ."

He made a longer pause, during which he worked his ribs in an exaggerated labour of breathing. It was intolerable. Feet were shuffled. Belfast let out a groan; but Donkin above blinked his red eyelids with invisible eyelashes, and smiled bitterly over the nigger's head.

The nigger went on again with surprising ease. He gasped no more, and his voice rang, hollow and loud, as though he had been talking in an empty cavern. He was contemptuously angry.

"I tried to get a wink of sleep. You know I can't sleep o' nights. And you come jabbering near the door here like a blooming lot of old women. . . . . You think yourselves good shipmates. Do you? . . . . Much you care for a dying man!"

Belfast spun away from the pigstye. "Jimmy," he cried tremulously, "if you hadn't been sick I would—"

He stopped. The nigger waited awhile, then said in a gloomy tone:—"You would.....What? Go an' fight another such one as yourself. Leave me alone. It won't be for long. I'll soon die.....It's coming right enough!"

Men stood around very still, breathing lightly, and with exasperated eyes. It was just what they had expected, and hated to hear, that idea of a stalking death, thrust at them many times a day like a boast and like a menace by this obnoxious nigger. He seemed to take a pride in that death which, so far, had attended only upon the ease of his life; he was overbearing about it, as if no one else in the world had ever been intimate with such a companion; he paraded it unceasingly before us with an affectionate persistence that made its presence indubitable, and at the same time incredible. No man could be suspected of such monstrous friendship! Was he a reality—or was he a sham—this ever-expected visitor of Jimmy's? We hesitated between pity and mistrust, while, on the slightest provocation, he shook before our eyes the bones of his bothersome and infamous skeleton. He was for ever trotting him out. He would talk of that coming death as though it had been already there, as if it had been walking the deck outside, as if it would presently come in to sleep in the only empty bunk; as if it had sat by his side at every meal. It interfered daily with our occupations, with our leisure, with our amusements. We had no songs and no music in the evening, because Jimmy (we all lovingly called him Jimmy, to conceal our hate of his accomplice) had managed, with that prospective decease of his, to disturb even Archie's mental balance. Archie was the owner of the concertina; but after a couple of stinging lectures from Jimmy he refused to play any more. He said:— "Yon's an uncanny joker. I dinna ken what's wrang wi' him, but there's something verra wrang, verra wrang. It's nae manner of use asking me. I won't play." Our singers became mute because Jimmy was a dying man. For the same reason no chap—as Knowles remarked—could "drive in a nail to hang his few poor rags upon," without being made aware of the enormity he committed in disturbing Jimmy's interminable last moments. At night, instead of the cheerful yell, "One bell! Turn out! Do you hear there? Hey! hey! hey! Show leg!" the watches were called man by man, in whispers, so as not to interfere with Jimmy's, possibly, last slumber on earth. True, he was always awake, and managed, as we sneaked out on deck, to plant in our backs some cutting remark that, for the moment, made us feel as if we had been brutes, and afterwards made us suspect ourselves of being fools. We spoke in low tones within that fo'c'sle as though it had been a church. We ate our meals in silence and dread, for Jimmy was capricious with his food, and railed bitterly at the salt meat, at the biscuits, at the tea, as at articles unfit for human consumption—"let alone for a dying man!" He would say:—"Can't you find a better slice of meat for a sick man who's trying to get home to be cured—or buried? But there! If I had a chance, you fellows would do away with it. You would poison me. Look at what you have given me!" We served him in his bed with rage and humility, as though we had been the base courtiers of a hated prince; and he rewarded us by his unconciliating criticism. He had found the secret of keeping for ever on the run the fundamental imbecility of mankind; he had the secret of life, that confounded dying man, and he made himself master of every moment of our existence. We grew desperate, and remained submissive. Emotional little Belfast was for ever on the verge of assault or on the verge of tears. One evening he confided to Archie:—"For a ha'penny I would knock his ugly black head off— the skulking dodger!" And the straightforward Archie pretended to be shocked!

Such was the infernal spell which that casual St. Kitt's nigger had cast upon
our guileless manhood! But the same night Belfast stole from the galley the
officers' Sunday fruit pie, to tempt the fastidious appetite of Jimmy. He endan-
gered not only his long friendship with the cook but also—as it appeared—his
eternal welfare. The cook was overwhelmed with grief; he did not know the
culprit but he knew that wickedness flourished; he knew that Satan was abroad
amongst those men, whom he looked upon as in some way under his spiritual
care. Whenever he saw three or four of us standing together he would leave
his stove, to run out and preach. We fled from him; and only Charley (who
knew the thief) affronted the cook with a candid gaze which irritated the good
man. "It's you, I believe," he groaned, sorrowful, and with a patch of soot on
his chin. "It's you. You are a brand for the burning! No more of YOUR socks in
my galley." Soon, unofficially, the information was spread about that, should
there be another case of stealing, our marmalade (an extra allowance: half a
pound per man) would be stopped. Mr. Baker ceased to heap jocular abuse
upon his favourites, and grunted suspiciously at all. The captain's cold eyes,
high up on the poop, glittered mistrustful, as he surveyed us trooping in a small
mob from halyards to braces for the usual evening pull at all the ropes. Such
stealing in a merchant ship is difficult to check, and may be taken as a declaration
by men of their dislike for their officers. It is a bad symptom. It may end in God
knows what trouble. The Narcissus was still a peaceful ship, but mutual confidence was shaken. Donkin did not conceal his delight. We were dismayed.

Then illogical Belfast reproached our nigger with great fury. James Wait,
with his elbow on the pillow, choked, gasped out:—"Did I ask you to bone the
dratted thing? Blow your blamed pie. It has made me worse—you little Irish
lunatic, you!" Belfast, with scarlet face and trembling lips, made a dash at him.
Every man in the forecastle rose with a shout. There was a moment of wild
tumult. Some one shrieked piercingly:—"Easy, Belfast! Easy!...." We expected
Belfast to strangle Wait without more ado. Dust flew. We heard through it the
nigger's cough, metallic and explosive like a gong. Next moment we saw Belfast
hanging over him. He was saying plaintively:—"Don't! Don't, Jimmy! Don't be
like that. An angel couldn't put up with ye—sick as ye are." He looked round
at us from Jimmy's bedside, his comical mouth twitching, and through tearful
eyes; then he tried to put straight the disarranged blankets. The unceasing
whisper of the sea filled the forecastle. Was James Wait frightened, or touched,
or repentant? He lay on his back with a hand to his side, and as motionless as
if his expected visitor had come at last. Belfast fumbled about his feet, repeating
with emotion:—"Yes. We know. Ye are bad, but.... Just say what ye want
done, and.... We all know ye are bad—very bad....." No! Decidedly James
Wait was not touched or repentant. Truth to say, he seemed rather startled. He
sat up with incredible suddenness and ease. "Ah! You think I am bad, do you?"
he said gloomily, in his clearest baritone voice (to hear him speak sometimes
you would never think there was anything wrong with that man). "Do
you?.... Well, act according! Some of you haven't sense enough to put a blanket
shipshape over a sick man. There! Leave it alone! I can die anyhow!" Belfast
turned away limply with a gesture of discouragement. In the silence of the
forecastle, full of interested men, Donkin pronounced distinctly:—"Well, I'm
blowed!" and sniggered. Wait looked at him. He looked at him in a quite friendly
manner. Nobody could tell what would please our incomprehensible invalid:
but for us the scorn of that snigger was hard to bear.

Donkin's position in the forecastle was distinguished but unsafe. He stood on the bad eminence of a general dislike. He was left alone; and in his isolation he could do nothing but think of the gales of the Cape of Good Hope and envy us the possession of warm clothing and waterproofs. Our sea-boots, our oilskin coats, our well-filled sea-chests, were to him so many causes for bitter meditation: he had none of those things, and he felt instinctively that no man, when the need arose, would offer to share them with him. He was impudently cringing to us and systematically insolent to the officers. He anticipated the best results, for himself, from such a line of conduct—and was mistaken. Such natures forget that under extreme provocation men will be just—whether they want to be so or not. Donkin's insolence to long-suffering Mr. Baker became at last intolerable to us, and we rejoiced when the mate, one dark night, tamed him for good. It was done neatly, with great decency and decorum, and with little noise. We had been called—just before midnight—to trim the yards, and Donkin—as usual—made insulting remarks. We stood sleepily in a row with the forebrace in our hands waiting for the next order, and heard in the darkness a scuffly trampling of feet, an exclamation of surprise, sounds of cuffs and slaps, suppressed, hissing whispers:—"Ah! Will you!".... "Don't!.... Don't!".... "Then behave.".... "Oh! Oh!...." Afterwards there were soft thuds mixed with the rattle of iron things as if a man's body had been tumbling helplessly amongst the main-pump rods. Before we could realise the situation, Mr. Baker's voice was heard very near and a little impatient:—"Haul away, men! Lay back on that rope!" And we did lay back on the rope with great alacrity. As if nothing had happened, the chief mate went on trimming the yards with his usual and exasperating fastidiousness. We didn't at the time see anything of Donkin, and did not care. Had the chief officer thrown him overboard, no man would have said as much as "Hallo! he's gone!" But, in truth, no great harm was done—even if Donkin did lose one of his front teeth. We perceived this in the morning, and preserved a ceremonious silence: the etiquette of the forecastle commanded us to be blind and dumb in such a case, and we cherished the decencies of our life more than ordinary landsmen respect theirs. Charley, with unpardonable want of *savoir vivre*, yelled out:—"'Ave you been to your dentyst?.... Hurt ye, didn't it?" He got a box on the ear from one of his best friends. The boy was surprised, and remained plunged in grief for at least three hours. We were sorry for him, but youth requires even more discipline than age. Donkin grinned venomously. From that day he became pitiless; told Jimmy that he was a "black fraud"; hinted to us that we were an imbecile lot, daily taken in by a vulgar nigger. And Jimmy seemed to like the fellow!

Singleton lived untouched by human emotions. Taciturn and unsmiling, he breathed amongst us—in that alone resembling the rest of the crowd. We were trying to be decent chaps, and found it jolly difficult; we oscillated between the desire of virtue and the fear of ridicule; we wished to save ourselves from the pain of remorse, but did not want to be made the contemptible dupes of our sentiment. Jimmy's hateful accomplice seemed to have blown with his impure breath undreamt-of subtleties into our hearts. We were disturbed and cowardly. That we knew. Singleton seemed to know nothing, understand nothing. We had thought him till then as wise as he looked, but now we dared, at times, suspect him of being stupid—from old age. One day, however, at dinner, as we sat on our boxes round a tin dish that stood on the deck within the circle of our feet, Jimmy expressed his general disgust with men and things in words that were particularly disgusting. Singleton lifted his head. We became mute. The old man, addressing Jimmy, asked:—"Are you dying?" Thus interrogated, James Wait appeared horribly startled and confused. We all were startled. Mouths remained open; hearts thumped; eyes blinked; a dropped tin fork rattled in the dish; a man rose as if to go out, and stood still. In less than a minute Jimmy pulled himself together.—"Why? Can't you see I am?" he answered shakily. Singleton lifted a piece of soaked biscuit ("his teeth"—he declared—"had no edge on them now") to his lips.—"Well, get on with your dying," he said with venerable mildness; "don't raise a blamed fuss with us over that job. We can't help you." Jimmy fell back in his bunk, and for a long time lay very still wiping the perspiration off his chin. The dinner-tins were put away quickly. On deck we discussed the incident in whispers. Some showed a chuckling exultation. Many looked grave. Wamibo, after long periods of staring dreaminess, attempted abortive smiles; and one of the young Scandinavians, much tormented by doubt, ventured in the second dog-watch to approach Singleton (the old man did not encourage us much to speak to him) and ask sheepishly:—"You think he will die?" Singleton looked up.—"Why, of course he will die," he said deliberately. This seemed decisive. It was promptly imparted to every one by him who had consulted the oracle. Shy and eager, he would step up and with averted gaze recite his formula:—"Old Singleton says he will die." It was a relief! At last we knew that our compassion would not be misplaced, and we could again smile without misgivings—but we reckoned without Donkin. Donkin "didn't want to 'ave no truck with 'em dirty furriners." When Neillssen came to him with the news: "Singleton says he will die," he answered him by a spiteful "And so will you—you fat-headed Dutchman. Wish you Dutchmen were hall dead— 'stead comin' takin' our money hinto your starvin' country." We were appalled. We perceived that after all Singleton's answer meant nothing. We began to hate him for making fun of us. All our certitudes were going; we were on doubtful terms with our officers; the cook had given us up for lost; we had overheard the boatswain's opinion that "we were a crowd of softies." We suspected Jimmy, one another, and even our very selves. We did not know what to do. At every insignificant turn of our humble life we met Jimmy overbearing and blocking the way, arm-in-arm with his awful and veiled familiar. It was a weird servitude.

It began a week after leaving Bombay and came on us stealthily like any other great misfortune. Every one had remarked that Jimmy from the first was very slack at his work; but we thought it simply the outcome of his philosophy of life. Donkin said:—"You put no more weight on a rope than a bloody sparrer." He disdained him. Belfast, ready for a fight, exclaimed provokingly:—"You don't kill yourself, old man!"—"Would YOU?" he retorted with extreme scorn—and Belfast retired. One morning, as we were washing decks, Mr. Baker called to him:—"Bring your broom over here, Wait." He strolled languidly. "Move yourself! Ough!" grunted Mr. Baker; "what's the matter with your hind legs?" He stopped dead short. He gazed slowly with eyes that bulged out, with an expression audacious and sad.—"It isn't my legs," he said, "it's my lungs." Everybody listened.—"What's .... Ough! .... What's wrong with them?" inquired Mr. Baker. All the watch stood around on the wet deck, grinning, and with brooms or buckets in their hands. He said mournfully:—"Going—or gone. Can't you see I'm a dying man? I know it!" Mr. Baker was disgusted.—"Then why the devil did you ship aboard here?"—"I must live till I die—mustn't I?" he replied. The grins became audible.—"Go off the deck—get out of my sight," said Mr. Baker. He was nonplussed. It was an unique experience. James Wait, obedient, dropped his broom, and walked slowly forward. A burst of laughter followed him. It was too funny. All hands laughed. . . . . They laughed! . . . . Alas!

He became the tormentor of all our moments; he was worse than a nightmare. You couldn't see that there was anything wrong with him: a nigger does not show. He was not very fat—certainly—but then he was no leaner than other niggers we had known. He coughed often, but the most prejudiced person could perceive that, mostly, he coughed when it suited his purpose. He wouldn't, or couldn't, do his work—and he wouldn't lie-up. One day he would skip aloft with the best of them, and next time we would be obliged to risk our lives to get his limp body down. He was reported, he was examined; he was remonstrated with, threatened, cajoled, lectured. He was called into the cabin to interview the captain. There were wild rumours. It was said he had cheeked the old man; it was said he had frightened him. Charley maintained that the "skipper, weepin', 'as giv' 'im 'is blessin' an' a pot of jam." Knowles had it from the steward that the unspeakable Jimmy had been reeling against the cabin furniture; that he had groaned; that he had complained of general brutality and disbelief; and had ended by coughing all over the old man's meteorological journals which were then spread on the table. At any rate, Wait returned forward supported by the steward, who, in a pained and shocked voice, entreated us:—"Here! Catch hold of him, one of you. He is to lie-up." Jimmy drank a tin mugful of coffee, and, after bullying first one and then another, went to bed. He remained there most of the time, but when it suited him would come on deck and appear amongst us. He was scornful and brooding; he looked ahead upon the sea; and no one could tell what was the meaning of that black man sitting apart in a meditative attitude and as motionless as a carving.

He refused steadily all medicine; he threw sago and cornflour overboard till the steward got tired of bringing it to him. He asked for paregoric. They sent him a big bottle; enough to poison a wilderness of babies. He kept it between his mattress and the deal lining of the ship's side; and nobody ever saw him take a dose. Donkin abused him to his face, jeered at him while he gasped; and the same day Wait would lend him a warm jersey. Once Donkin reviled him for half an hour; reproached him with the extra work his malingering gave to the watch; and ended by calling him "a black-faced swine." Under the spell of our accursed perversity we were horror-struck. But Jimmy positively seemed to revel in that abuse. It made him look cheerful—and Donkin had a pair of old sea boots thrown at him. "Here, you East-end trash," boomed Wait, "you may have that."

At last Mr. Baker had to tell the captain that James Wait was disturbing the peace of the ship. "Knock discipline on the head—he will, Ough," grunted Mr. Baker. As a matter of fact, the starboard watch came as near as possible to refusing duty, when ordered one morning by the boatswain to wash out their forecastle. It appears Jimmy objected to a wet floor—and that morning we were in a compassionate mood. We thought the boatswain a brute, and, practically, told him so. Only Mr. Baker's delicate tact prevented an all-fired row: he refused to take us seriously. He came bustling forward, and called us many unpolite names, but in such a hearty and seamanlike manner that we began to feel ashamed of ourselves. In truth, we thought him much too good a sailor to annoy him willingly: and after all Jimmy might have been a fraud—probably was! The forecastle got a clean up that morning; but in the afternoon a sick-bay was fitted up in the deck-house. It was a nice little cabin opening on deck, and with two berths. Jimmy's belongings were transported there, and then—notwithstanding his protests—Jimmy himself. He said he couldn't walk. Four men carried him on a blanket. He complained that he would have to die there alone, like a dog. We grieved for him, and were delighted to have him removed from the forecastle. We attended him as before. The galley was next door, and the cook looked in many times a day. Wait became a little more cheerful. Knowles affirmed having heard him laugh to himself in peals one day. Others had seen him walking about on deck at night. His little place, with the door ajar on a long hook, was always full of tobacco smoke. We spoke through the crack cheerfully, sometimes abusively, as we passed by, intent on our work. He fascinated us. He would never let doubt die. He overshadowed the ship. Invulnerable in his promise of speedy corruption he trampled on our self-respect, he demonstrated to us daily our want of moral courage; he tainted our lives. Had we been a miserable gang of wretched immortals, unhallowed alike by hope and fear, he could not have lorded it over us with a more pitiless assertion of his sublime privilege.

III

Meantime the *Narcissus*, with square yards, ran out of the fair monsoon. She drifted slowly, swinging round and round the compass, through a few days of baffling light airs. Under the patter of short warm showers, grumbling men whirled the heavy yards from side to side; they caught hold of the soaked ropes with groans and sighs, while their officers, sulky and dripping with rain water, unceasingly ordered them about in wearied voices. During the short respites they looked with disgust into the smarting palms of their stiff hands, and asked one another bitterly:—"Who would be a sailor if he could be a farmer?" All the tempers were spoilt, and no man cared what he said. One black night, when the watch, panting in the heat and half-drowned with the rain, had been through four mortal hours hunted from brace to brace, Belfast declared that he would "chuck going to sea for ever and go in a steamer." This was excessive, no doubt. Captain Allistoun, with great self-control, would mutter sadly to Mr. Baker:— "It is not so bad—not so bad," when he had managed to shove, and dodge, and manœuvre his smart ship through sixty miles in twenty-four hours. From the doorstep of the little cabin, Jimmy, chin in hand, watched our distasteful labours with insolent and melancholy eyes. We spoke to him gently—and out of his sight exchanged sour smiles.

Then, again, with a fair wind and under a clear sky, the ship went on piling up the South Latitude. She passed outside Madagascar and Mauritius without a glimpse of the land. Extra lashings were put on the spare spars. Hatches were looked to. The steward in his leisure moments and with a worried air tried to fit washboards to the cabin doors. Stout canvas was bent with care. Anxious eyes looked to the westward, towards the cape of storms. The ship began to dip into a southwest swell, and the softly luminous sky of low latitudes took on a harder sheen from day to day above our heads: it arched high above the ship vibrating and pale, like an immense dome of steel, resonant with the deep voice of freshening gales. The sunshine gleamed cold on the white curls of black waves. Before the strong breath of westerly squalls the ship, with reduced sail, lay slowly over, obstinate and yielding. She drove to and fro in the unceasing endeavour to fight her way through the invisible violence of the winds: she pitched headlong into dark smooth hollows; she struggled upwards over the snowy ridges of great running seas; she rolled, restless, from side to side, like a thing in pain. Enduring and valiant, she answered to the call of men; and her slim spars waving for ever in abrupt semicircles, seemed to beckon in vain for help towards the stormy sky.

It was a bad winter off the Cape that year. The relieved helmsmen came off flapping their arms, or ran stamping hard and blowing into swollen, red fingers. The watch on deck dodged the sting of cold sprays or, crouching in sheltered corners, watched dismally the high and merciless seas boarding the ship time after time in unappeasable fury. Water tumbled in cataracts over the forecastle doors. You had to dash through a waterfall to get into your damp bed. The men turned in wet and turned out stiff to face the redeeming and ruthless exactions of their glorious and obscure fate. Far aft, and peering watchfully to windward, the officers could be seen through the mists of squalls. They stood by the weather-rail, holding on grimly, straight and glistening in their long coats; then, at times, in the disordered plunges of the hard-driven ship, they appeared high up, attentive, tossing violently above the grey line of a clouded horizon, and in motionless attitudes.

They watched the weather and the ship as men on shore watch the momentous chances of fortune. Captain Allistoun never left the deck, as though he had been part of the ship's fittings. Now and then the steward, shivering, but always in shirt sleeves, would struggle towards him with some hot coffee, half of which the gale blew out of the cup before it reached the master's lips. He drank what was left gravely in one long gulp, while heavy sprays pattered loudly on his oilskin coat, the seas swishing broke about his high boots; and he never took his eyes off the ship. He watched her every motion; he kept his gaze riveted upon her as a loving man who watches the unselfish toil of a delicate woman upon the slender thread of whose existence is hung the whole meaning and joy of the world. We all watched her. She was beautiful and had a weakness. We loved her no less for that. We admired her qualities aloud, we boasted of them to one another, as though they had been our own, and the consciousness of her only fault we kept buried in the silence of our profound affection. She was born in the thundering peal of hammers beating upon iron, in black eddies of smoke, under a grey sky, on the banks of the Clyde. The clamorous and sombre stream gives birth to things of beauty that float away into the sunshine of the world to be loved by men. The *Narcissus* was one of that perfect brood. Less perfect than many perhaps, but she was ours, and, consequently, incomparable. We were proud of her. In Bombay, ignorant landlubbers alluded to her as that "pretty grey ship." Pretty! A scurvy meed of commendation! We knew she was the most magnificent sea-boat ever launched. We tried to forget that, like many good sea-boats, she was at times rather crank. She was exacting. She wanted care in loading and handling, and no one knew exactly how much care would be enough. Such are the imperfections of mere men! The ship knew, and sometimes would correct the presumptuous human ignorance by the wholesome discipline of fear. We had heard ominous stories about past voyages. The cook (technically a seaman, but in reality no sailor)—the cook, when unstrung by some misfortune, such as the rolling over of a saucepan, would mutter gloomily while he wiped the floor:—"There! Look at what she has done! Some voy'ge she will drown all hands! You'll see if she won't." To which the steward, snatching in the galley a moment to draw breath in the hurry of his worried life, would remark philosophically:—"Those that see won't tell, anyhow. I don't want to see it." We derided those fears. Our hearts went out to the old man when he pressed her hard so as to make her hold her own, hold to every inch gained to windward; when he made her, under reefed sails, leap obliquely at enormous waves. The men, knitted together aft into a ready group by the first sharp order of an officer coming to take charge of the deck in bad weather:—"Keep handy the watch," stood admiring her valiance. Their eyes blinked in the wind; their dark faces were wet with drops of water more salt and bitter than human tears; beard and moustaches, soaked, hung straight and dripping like fine seaweed. They were fantastically misshapen; in high boots, in hats like helmets, and swaying clumsily, stiff and bulky in glistening oilskins, they resembled men strangely equipped for some fabulous adventure. Whenever she rose easily to a towering green sea, elbows dug ribs, faces brightened, lips murmured:—"Didn't she do it cleverly," and all the heads turning like one watched with sardonic grins the foiled wave go roaring to leeward, white with the foam of a monstrous rage. But when she had not been quick enough and, struck heavily, lay over trembling under the blow, we clutched at ropes, and looking up at the narrow bands of drenched and strained sails waving desperately aloft, we thought in our hearts:—"No wonder. Poor thing!"

The thirty-second day out of Bombay began inauspiciously. In the morning a sea smashed one of the galley doors. We dashed in through lots of steam and found the cook very wet and indignant with the ship:—"She's getting worse every day. She's trying to drown me in front of my own stove!" He was very angry. We pacified him, and the carpenter, though washed away twice from there, managed to repair the door. Through that accident our dinner was not ready till late, but it didn't matter in the end because Knowles, who went to fetch it, got knocked down by a sea and the dinner went over the side. Captain Allistoun, looking more hard and thin-lipped than ever, hung on to full topsails and foresail, and would not notice that the ship, asked to do too much, appeared to lose heart altogether for the first time since we knew her. She refused to rise, and bored her way sullenly through the seas. Twice running, as though she had been blind or weary of life, she put her nose deliberately into a big wave and swept the decks from end to end. As the boatswain observed with marked annoyance, while we were splashing about in a body to try and save a worthless wash-tub:—"Every blooming thing in the ship is going overboard this afternoon." Venerable Singleton broke his habitual silence and said with a glance aloft:—"The old man's in a temper with the weather, but it's no good bein' angry with the winds of heaven." Jimmy had shut his door, of course. We knew he was dry and comfortable within his little cabin, and in our absurd way were pleased one moment, exasperated the next, by that certitude. Donkin skulked shamelessly, uneasy and miserable. He grumbled:—"I'm perishin' with cold houtside in bloomin' wet rags, an' that 'ere black sojer sits dry on a blamed chest full of bloomin' clothes; blank his black soul!" We took no notice of him; we hardly gave a thought to Jimmy and his bosom friend. There was no leisure for idle probing of hearts. Sails blew adrift. Things broke loose. Cold and wet, we were washed about the deck while trying to repair damages. The ship tossed about, shaken furiously, like a toy in the hand of a lunatic. Just at sunset there was a rush to shorten sail before the menace of a sombre hail cloud. The hard gust of wind came brutal like the blow of a fist. The ship relieved of her canvas in time received it pluckily: she yielded reluctantly to the violent onset; then, coming up with a stately and irresistible motion, brought her spars to windward in the teeth of the screeching squall. Out of the abyssmal darkness of the black cloud overhead white hail streamed on her, rattled on the rigging, leaped in handfuls off the yards, rebounded on the deck—round and gleaming in the murky turmoil like a shower of pearls. It passed away. For a moment a livid sun shot horizontally the last rays of sinister light between the hills of steep, rolling waves. Then a wild night rushed in—stamped out in a great howl that dismal remnant of a stormy day.

There was no sleep on board that night. Most seamen remember in their life one or two such nights of a culminating gale. Nothing seems left of the whole universe but darkness, clamour, fury—and the ship. And like the last vestige of a shattered creation she drifts, bearing an anguished remnant of sinful mankind, through the distress, tumult, and pain of an avenging terror. No one slept in the forecastle. The tin oil-lamp suspended on a long string, smoking, described wide circles; wet clothing made dark heaps on the glistening floor; a thin layer of water rushed to and fro. In the bed-places men lay booted, resting on elbows and with open eyes. Hung-up suits of oilskin swung out and in, lively and disquieting like reckless ghosts of decapitated seamen dancing in a tempest. No one spoke and all listened. Outside the night moaned and sobbed to the accompaniment of a continuous loud tremor as of innumerable drums beating far off. Shrieks passed through the air. Tremendous dull blows made the ship tremble while she rolled under the weight of the seas toppling on her deck. At times she soared up swiftly as if to leave this earth for ever, then during interminable moments fell through a void with all the hearts on board of her standing still, till a frightful shock, expected and sudden, started them off again with a big thump. After every dislocating jerk of the ship, Wamibo, stretched full length, his face on the pillow, groaned slightly with the pain of his tormented universe. Now and then, for the fraction of an intolerable second, the ship, in the fiercer burst of a terrible uproar, remained on her side, vibrating and still, with a stillness more appalling than the wildest motion. Then upon all those prone bodies a stir would pass, a shiver of suspense. A man would protrude his anxious head and a pair of eyes glistened in the sway of light glaring wildly. Some moved their legs a little as if making ready to jump out. But several, motionless on their backs and with one hand gripping hard the edge of the bunk, smoked nervously with quick puffs, staring upwards; immobilised in a great craving for peace.

At midnight, orders were given to furl the fore and mizen topsails. With immense efforts men crawled aloft through a merciless buffeting, saved the canvas, and crawled down almost exhausted, to bear in panting silence the cruel battering of the seas. Perhaps for the first time in the history of the merchant service the watch, told to go below, did not leave the deck, as if compelled to remain there by the fascination of a venomous violence. At every heavy gust men, huddled together, whispered to one another:—"It can blow no harder"— and presently the gale would give them the lie with a piercing shriek, and drive their breath back into their throats. A fierce squall seemed to burst asunder the thick mass of sooty vapours; and above the wrack of torn clouds glimpses could be caught of the high moon rushing backwards with frightful speed over the sky, right into the wind's eye. Many hung their heads, muttering that it "turned their inwards out" to look at it. Soon the clouds closed up, and the world again became a raging, blind darkness that howled, flinging at the lonely ship salt sprays and sleet.

About half-past seven the pitchy obscurity round us turned a ghastly grey, and we knew that the sun had risen. This unnatural and threatening daylight, in which we could see one another's wild eyes and drawn faces, was only an added tax on our endurance. The horizon seemed to have come on all sides within arm's length of the ship. Into that narrowed circle furious seas leaped in, struck, and leaped out. A rain of salt, heavy drops flew aslant like mist. The main-topsail had to be goose-winged, and with stolid resignation every one prepared to go aloft once more; but the officers yelled, pushed back, and at last we understood that no more men would be allowed to go on the yard than were absolutely necessary for the work. As at any moment the masts were likely to be jumped out or blown overboard, we concluded that the captain didn't want to see all his crowd go over the side at once. That was reasonable. The watch then on duty, led by Mr. Creighton, began to struggle up the rigging. The wind flattened them against the ratlines; then, easing a little, would let them ascend a couple of steps; and again, with a sudden gust, pin all up the shrouds the whole crawling line in attitudes of crucifixion. The other watch plunged down on the main deck to haul up the sail. Men's heads bobbed up as the water flung them irresistibly from side to side. Mr. Baker grunted encouragingly in our midst, spluttering and blowing amongst the tangled ropes like an energetic porpoise. Favoured by an ominous and untrustworthy lull, the work was done without any one being lost either off the deck or from the yard. For the moment the gale seemed to take off, and the ship, as if grateful for our efforts, plucked up heart and made better weather of it.

At eight the men off duty, watching their chance, ran forward over the flooded deck to get some rest. The other half of the crew remained aft for their turn of "seeing her through her trouble," as they expressed it. The two mates urged the master to go below. Mr. Baker grunted in his ear:—"Ough! surely now . . . . Ough! . . . . confidence in us . . . . nothing more to do . . . . she must lay it out or go. Ough! Ough!" Tall young Mr. Creighton smiled down at him cheerfully:—". . . . She's right as a trivet! Take a spell, sir." He looked at them stonily with bloodshot, sleepless eyes. The rims of his eyelids were scarlet, and he moved his jaw unceasingly with a slow effort, as though he had been masticating a lump of india-rubber. He shook his head. He repeated:—"Never mind me. I must see it out—I must see it out," but he consented to sit down for a moment on the skylight, with his hard face turned unflinchingly to windward. The sea spat at it—and, stoical, it streamed with water as though he had been weeping. On the weather side of the poop the watch, hanging on to the mizen rigging and to one another, tried to exchange encouraging words. Singleton, at the wheel, yelled out:—"Look out for yourselves!" His voice reached them in a warning whisper. They were startled.

A big, foaming sea came out of the mist; it made for the ship, roaring wildly, and in its rush it looked as mischievous and discomposing as a madman with an axe. One or two, shouting, scrambled up the rigging; most, with a convulsive catch of the breath, held on where they stood. Singleton dug his knees under the wheel-box, and carefully eased the helm to the headlong pitch of the ship, but without taking his eyes off the coming wave. It towered close-to and high, like a wall of green glass topped with snow. The ship rose to it as though she had soared on wings, and for a moment rested poised upon the foaming crest, as if she had been a great sea-bird. Before we could draw breath a heavy gust struck her, another roller took her unfairly under the weather bow, she gave a toppling lurch, and filled her decks. Captain Allistoun leaped up, and fell; Archie rolled over him, screaming:—"She will rise!" She gave another lurch to leeward; the lower deadeyes dipped heavily; the men's feet flew from under them, and they hung kicking above the slanting poop. They could see the ship putting her side in the water, and shouted all together:—"She's going!" Forward the forecastle doors flew open, and the watch below were seen leaping out one after another, throwing their arms up; and, falling on hands and knees, scrambled aft on all fours along the high side of the deck, sloping more than the roof of a house. From leeward the seas rose, pursing them; they looked wretched in a hopeless struggle, like vermin fleeing before a flood; they fought up the weather ladder of the poop one after another, half naked and staring wildly; and as soon as they got up they shot to leeward in clusters, with closed eyes, till they brought up heavily with their ribs against the iron stanchions of the rail; then, groaning, they rolled in a confused mass. The immense volume of water thrown forward by the last scend of the ship had burst the lee door of the forecastle. They could see their chests, pillows, blankets, clothing, come out floating upon the sea. While they struggled back to windward they looked in dismay. The straw beds swam high, the blankets, spread out, undulated; while the chests, waterlogged and with a heavy list, pitched heavily, like dismasted hulks, before they sank; Archie's big coat passed with outspread arms, resembling a drowned seaman floating with his head under water. Men were slipping down while trying to dig their fingers into the planks; others, jammed in corners, rolled enormous eyes. They all yelled unceasingly:—"The masts! Cut! Cut! . . . ." A black squall howled low over the ship, that lay on her side with the weather yard-arms pointing to the clouds; while the tall masts, inclined nearly to the horizon, seemed to be of an unmeasurable length. The carpenter let go his hold, rolled against the skylight, and began to crawl to the cabin entrance, where a big axe was kept ready for just such an emergency. At that moment the topsail sheet parted, the end of the heavy chain racketed aloft, and sparks of red fire streamed down through the flying sprays. The sail flapped once with a jerk that seemed to tear our hearts out through our teeth, and instantly changed into a bunch of fluttering narrow ribbons that tied themselves into knots and became quiet along the yard. Captain Allistoun struggled, managed to stand up with his face near the deck, upon which men swung on the ends of ropes, like nest robbers upon a cliff. One of his feet was on somebody's chest; his face was purple; his lips moved. He yelled also; he yelled, bending down:—"No! No!" Mr. Baker, one leg over the binnacle-stand, roared out:—"Did you say no? Not cut?" He shook his head madly. "No! No!" Between his legs the crawling carpenter heard, collapsed at once, and lay full length in the angle of the skylight. Voices took up the shout—"No! No!" Then all became still. They waited for the ship to turn over altogether, and shake them out into the sea; and upon the terrific noise of wind and sea not a murmur of remonstrance came out from those men, who each would have given ever so many years of life to see "them damned sticks go overboard!" They all believed it their only chance; but a little hard-faced man shook his grey head and shouted "No!" without giving them as much as a glance. They were silent, and gasped. They gripped rails, they had wound ropes'-ends under their arms; they clutched ringbolts, they crawled in heaps where there was foothold; they held on with both arms, hooked themselves to anything to windward with elbows, with chins, almost with their teeth: and some, unable to crawl away from where they had been flung, felt the sea leap up, striking against their backs as they struggled upwards. Singleton had stuck to the wheel. His hair flew out in the wind; the gale seemed to take its life-long adversary by the beard and shake his old head. He wouldn't let go, and, with his knees forced between the spokes, flew up and down like a man on a bough. As Death appeared unready, they began to look about. Donkin, caught by one foot in a loop of some rope, hung, head down, below us, and yelled, with his face to the deck:—"Cut! Cut!" Two men lowered themselves cautiously to him; others hauled on the rope. They caught him up, shoved him into a safer place, held him. He shouted curses at the master, shook his fist at him with horrible blasphemies, called upon us in filthy words to "Cut! Don't mind that murdering fool! Cut, some of you!" One of his rescuers struck him a back-handed blow over the mouth; his head banged on the deck, and he became suddenly very quiet, with a white face, breathing hard, and with a few drops of blood trickling from his cut lip. On the lee side another man could be seen stretched out as if stunned; only the washboard prevented him from going over the side. It was the steward. We had to sling him up like a bale, for he was paralysed with fright. He had rushed up out of the pantry when he felt the ship go over, and had rolled down helplessly, clutching a china mug. It was not broken. With difficulty we tore it from him, and when he saw it in our hands he was amazed. "Where did you get that thing?" he kept on asking, in a trembling voice. His shirt was blown to shreds; the ripped sleeves flapped like wings. Two men made him fast, and, doubled over the rope that held him, he resembled a bundle of wet rags. Mr. Baker crawled along the line of men, asking:—"Are you all there?" and looking them over. Some blinked vacantly, others shook convulsively; Wamibo's head hung over his breast; and in painful attitudes, cut by lashings, exhausted with clutching, screwed up in corners, they breathed heavily. Their lips twitched, and at every sickening heave of the overturned ship they opened them wide as if to shout. The cook, embracing a wooden stanchion, unconsciously repeated a prayer. In every short interval of the fiendish noises around he could be heard there, without cap or slippers, imploring in that storm the Master of our lives not to lead him into temptation. Soon he also became silent. In all that crowd of cold and hungry men, waiting wearily for a violent death, not a voice was heard; they were mute, and in sombre thoughtfulness listened to the horrible imprecations of the gale.

Hours passed. They were sheltered by the heavy inclination of the ship from the wind that rushed in one long unbroken moan above their heads, but cold rain showers fell at times into the uneasy calm of their refuge. Under the torment of that new infliction a pair of shoulders would writhe a little. Teeth chattered. The sky was clearing, and bright sunshine gleamed over the ship. After every burst of battering seas, vivid and fleeting rainbows arched over the drifting hull in the flick of sprays. The gale was ending in a clear blow, which gleamed and cut like a knife. Between two bearded shellbacks Charley, fastened with somebody's long muffler to a deck ring-bolt, wept quietly, with rare tears wrung out by bewilderment, cold, hunger, and general misery. One of his neighbours punched him in the ribs, asking roughly:—"What's the matter with your cheek? In fine weather there's no holding you, youngster." Turning about with prudence he worked himself out of his coat and threw it over the boy. The other man closed up, muttering:—"'Twill make a bloomin' man of you, sonny." They flung their arms over and pressed against him. Charley drew his feet up and his eyelids dropped. Sighs were heard, as men, perceiving that they were not to be "drowned in a hurry," tried easier positions. Mr. Creighton, who had hurt his leg, lay amongst us with compressed lips. Some fellows belonging to his watch set about securing him better. Without a word or a glance he lifted his arms one after another to facilitate the operation, and not a muscle moved in his stern, young face. They asked him with solicitude:—"Easier now, sir?" He answered with a curt:—"That'll do." He was a hard young officer, but many of his watch used to say they liked him well enough because he had "such a gentlemanly way of damning us up and down the deck." Others, unable to discern such fine shades of refinement, respected him for his smartness. For the first time since the ship had gone on her beam ends Captain Allistoun gave a short glance down at his men. He was almost upright—one foot against the side of the skylight, one knee on the deck; and with the end of the vang round his waist swung back and forth with his gaze fixed ahead, watchful, like a man looking out for a sign. Before his eyes the ship, with half her deck below water, rose and fell on heavy seas that rushed from under her flashing in the cold sunshine. We began to think she was wonderfully buoyant—considering. Confident voices were heard shouting:—"She'll do, boys!" Belfast exclaimed with fervour:—"I would giv' a month's pay for a draw at a pipe!" One or two, passing dry tongues on their salt lips, muttered something about a "drink of water." The cook, as if inspired, scrambled up with his breast against the poop water-cask and looked in. There was a little at the bottom. He yelled, waving his arms, and two men began to crawl backwards and forwards with the mug. We had a good mouthful all round. The master shook his head impatiently, refusing. When it came to Charley one of his neighbours shouted:—"That bloomin' boy's asleep." He slept as though he had been dosed with narcotics. They let him be. Singleton held to the wheel with one hand while he drank, bending down to shelter his lips from the wind. Wamibo had to be poked and yelled at before he saw the mug held before his eyes. Knowles said sagaciously:—"It's better'n a tot o' rum." Mr. Baker grunted:—"Thank ye." Mr. Creighton drank and nodded. Donkin gulped greedily, glaring over the rim. Belfast made us laugh when with grimacing mouth he shouted:—"Pass it this way. We're all taytottlers here." The master, presented with the mug again by a crouching man, who screamed up at him:—"We all had a drink, captain," groped for it without ceasing to look ahead, and handed it back stiffly as though he could not spare half a glance away from the ship. Faces brightened. We shouted to the cook:—"Well done, doctor!" He sat to leeward, propped by the water-cask and yelled back abundantly, but the seas were breaking in thunder just then, and we only caught snatches that sounded like: "Providence" and "born again." He was at his old game of preaching. We made friendly but derisive gestures at him, and from below he lifted one arm, holding on with the other, moved his lips; he beamed up to us, straining his voice—earnest, and ducking his head before the sprays.

Suddenly some one cried:—"Where's Jimmy?" and we were appalled once more. On the end of the row the boatswain shouted hoarsely:—"Has any one seed him come out?" Voices exclaimed dismally:—"Drowned—is he?....No! In his cabin!....Good Lord!....Caught like a bloomin' rat in a trap.....Couldn't open his door....Aye! She went over too quick and the water jammed it....Poor beggar!....No help for 'im.....Let's go and see...." "Damn him, who could go?" screamed Donkin.—"Nobody expects you to," growled the man next to him; "you're only a thing."—"Is there half a chance to get at 'im?" inquired two or three men together. Belfast untied himself with blind impetuosity, and all at once shot down to leeward quicker than a flash of lightning. We shouted all together with dismay; but with his legs overboard he held and yelled for a rope. In our extremity nothing could be terrible; so we judged him funny kicking there, and with his scared face. Some one began to laugh, and, as if hysterically infected with screaming merriment, all those haggard men went off laughing, wild-eyed, like a lot of maniacs tied up on a wall. Mr. Baker swung off the binnacle-stand and tendered him one leg. He scrambled up rather scared, and consigning us with abominable words to the "divvle." "You are....Ough! You're a foul-mouthed beggar, Craik," grunted Mr. Baker. He answered, stuttering with indignation:—"Look at 'em, sorr. The bloomin' dirty images! laughing at a chum going overboard. Call themselves men, too." But from the break of the poop the boatswain called out:—"Come along," and Belfast crawled away in a hurry to join him. The five men, poised and gazing over the edge of the poop, looked for the best way to get forward. They seemed to hesitate. The others, twisting in their lashings, turning painfully, stared with open lips. Captain Allistoun saw nothing; he seemed with his eyes to hold the ship up in a superhuman concentration of effort. The wind screamed loud in sunshine; columns of spray rose straight up; and in the glitter of rainbows bursting over the trembling hull the men went over cautiously, disappearing from sight with deliberate movements.

They went swinging from belaying pin to cleat above the seas that beat the half-submerged deck. Their toes scraped the planks. Lumps of green cold water toppled over the bulwark and on their heads. They hung for a moment on strained arms, with the breath knocked out of them, and with closed eyes— then, letting go with one hand, balanced with lolling heads, trying to grab some rope or stanchion further forward. The long-armed and athletic boatswain swung quickly, gripping things with a fist hard as iron, and remembering suddenly snatches of the last letter from his "old woman." Little Belfast scrambled rageously, muttering "cursed nigger." Wamibo's tongue hung out with excitement; and Archie, intrepid and calm, watched his chance to move with intelligent coolness.

When above the side of the house, they let go one after another, and falling heavily, sprawled, pressing their palms to the smooth teak wood. Round them the backwash of waves seethed white and hissing. All the doors had become trap-doors, of course. The first was the galley door. The galley extended from side to side, and they could hear the sea splashing with hollow noises in there. The next door was that of the carpenter's shop. They lifted it, and looked down. The room seemed to have been devastated by an earthquake. Everything in it had tumbled on the bulkhead facing the door, and on the other side of that bulkhead there was Jimmy, dead or alive. The bench, a half-finished meat-safe, saws, chisels, wire rods, axes, crowbars, lay in a heap besprinkled with loose nails. A sharp adze stuck up with a shining edge that gleamed dangerously down there like a wicked smile. The men clung to one another peering. A sickening, sly lurch of the ship nearly sent them overboard in a body. Belfast howled "Here goes!" and leaped down. Archie followed cannily, catching at shelves that gave way with him, and eased himself in a great crash of ripped wood. There was hardly room for three men to move. And in the sunshiny blue square of the door, the boatswain's face, bearded and dark, Wamibo's face, wild and pale, hung over—watching.

Together they shouted: "Jimmy! Jim!" From above the boatswain contributed a deep growl: "You .... Wait!" In a pause, Belfast entreated: "Jimmy, darlin', are ye aloive?" The boatswain said: "Again! All together, boys!" All yelled excitedly. Wamibo made noises resembling loud barks. Belfast drummed on the side of the bulkhead with a piece of iron. All ceased suddenly. The sound of screaming and hammering went on thin and distinct—like a solo after a chorus. He was alive. He was screaming and knocking below us with the hurry of a man prematurely shut up in a coffin. We went to work. We attacked with desperation the abominable heap of things heavy, of things sharp, of things clumsy to handle. The boatswain crawled away to find somewhere a flying end of a rope; and Wamibo, held back by shouts:—"Don't jump! .... Don't come in here, muddle-head!"—remained glaring above us—all shining eyes, gleaming fangs, tumbled hair, resembling an amazed and half-witted fiend gloating over the extraordinary agitation of the damned. The boatswain adjured us to "bear a hand," and a rope descended. We made things fast to it and they went up spinning, never to be seen by man again. A rage to fling things overboard possessed us. We worked fiercely, cutting our hands, and speaking brutally to one another. Jimmy kept up a distracting row; he screamed piercingly, without drawing breath, like a tortured woman; he banged with hands and feet. The agony of his fear wrung our hearts so terribly that we longed to abandon him, to get out of that place deep as a well and swaying like a tree, to get out of his hearing, back on the poop where we could wait passively for death in incomparable repose. We shouted to him to "shut up, for God's sake." He redoubled his cries. He must have fancied we could not hear him. Probably he heard his own clamour but faintly. We could picture him crouching on the edge of the upper berth, letting out with both fists at the wood, in the dark, and with his mouth wide open for that unceasing cry. Those were loathsome moments. A cloud driving across the sun would darken the doorway menacingly. Every movement of the ship was pain. We scrambled about with no room to breathe, and felt frightfully sick. The boatswain yelled down at us:—"Bear a hand! Bear a hand! We two will be washed away from here directly if you ain't quick!" Three times a sea leaped over the high side and flung bucketfuls of water on our heads. Then Jimmy, startled by the shock, would stop his noise for a moment—waiting for the ship to sink, perhaps—and began again, distressingly loud, as if invigorated by the gust of fear. At the bottom the nails lay in a layer several inches thick. It was ghastly. Every nail in the world, not driven in firmly somewhere, seemed to have found its way into that carpenter's shop. There they were, of all kinds, the remnants of stores from seven voyages. Tin-tacks, copper tacks (sharp as needles), pump nails, with big heads, like tiny iron mushrooms; nails without any heads (horrible); French nails polished and slim. They lay in a solid mass more inabordable than a hedgehog. We hesitated, yearning for a shovel, while Jimmy below us yelled as though he had been flayed. Groaning, we dug our fingers in, and very much hurt, shook our hands, scattering nails and drops of blood. We passed up our hats full of assorted nails to the boatswain, who, as if performing a mysterious and appeasing rite, cast them wide upon a raging sea.

We got to the bulkhead at last. Those were stout planks. She was a ship, well finished in every detail—the *Narcissus* was. They were the stoutest planks ever put into a ship's bulkhead—we thought—and then we perceived that, in our hurry, we had sent all the tools overboard. Absurd little Belfast wanted to break it down with his own weight, and with both feet leaped straight up like a springbok, cursing the Clyde shipwrights for not scamping their work. Incidentally he reviled all North Britain, the rest of the earth, the sea—and all his companions. He swore, as he alighted heavily on his heels, that he would never, never any more associate with any fool that "hadn't savee enough to know his knee from his elbow." He managed by his thumping to scare the last remnant of wits out of Jimmy. We could hear the object of our exasperated solicitude darting to and fro under the planks. He had cracked his voice at last, and could only squeak miserably. His back or else his head rubbed the planks, now here, now there, in a puzzling manner. He squeaked as he dodged the invisible blows. It was more heartrending even than his yells. Suddenly Archie produced a crowbar. He had kept it back; also a small hatchet. We howled with satisfaction. He struck a mighty blow and small chips flew at our eyes. The boatswain above shouted:—"Look out! Look out there. Don't kill the man. Easy does it!" Wamibo, maddened with excitement, hung head down and insanely urged us:—"Hoo! Strook 'im! Hoo! Hoo!" We were afraid he would fall in and kill one of us and, hurriedly, we entreated the boatswain to "shove the blamed Finn overboard." Then, all together, we yelled down at the planks:—"Stand from under! Get forward," and listened. We only heard the deep hum and moan of the wind above us, the mingled roar and hiss of the seas. The ship, as if overcome with despair, wallowed lifelessly, and our heads swam with that unnatural motion. Belfast clamoured:—"For the love of God, Jimmy, where are ye? . . . . Knock! Jimmy darling! . . . . Knock! You bloody black beast! Knock!" He was as quiet as a dead man inside a grave; and, like men standing above a grave, we were on the verge of tears—but with vexation, the strain, the fatigue; with the great longing to be done with it, to get away, and lay down to rest somewhere where we could see our danger and breathe. Archie shouted:—"Gi'e me room!" We crouched behind him, guarding our heads, and he struck time after time in the joint of planks. They cracked. Suddenly the crowbar went halfway in through a splintered oblong hole. It must have missed Jimmy's head by less than an inch. Archie withdrew it quickly, and that infamous nigger rushed at the hole, put his lips to it, and whispered "Help" in an almost extinct voice; he pressed his head to it, trying madly to get out through that opening one inch wide and three inches long. In our disturbed state we were absolutely paralysed by his incredible action. It seemed impossible to drive him away. Even Archie at last lost his composure. "If ye don't clear oot I'll drive the crowbar thro' your head," he shouted in a determined voice. He meant what he said, and his earnestness seemed to make an impression on Jimmy. He disappeared suddenly, and we set to prising and tearing at the planks with the eagerness of men trying to get at a mortal enemy, and spurred by the desire to tear him limb from limb. The wood split, cracked, gave way. Belfast plunged in head and shoulders and groped viciously. "I've got 'im! Got 'im," he shouted. "Oh! There! . . . . He's gone; I've got 'im! . . . . Pull at my legs! . . . . Pull!" Wamibo hooted unceasingly. The boatswain shouted directions:—"Catch hold of his hair, Belfast; pull straight up, you two! . . . . Pull fair!" We pulled fair. We pulled Belfast out with a jerk, and dropped him with disgust. In a sitting posture, purple-faced, he sobbed despairingly:—"How can I hold on to 'is blooming short wool?" Suddenly Jimmy's head and shoulders appeared. He stuck half-way, and with rolling eyes foamed at our feet. We flew at him with brutal impatience, we tore the shirt off his back, we tugged at his ears, we panted over him; and all at once he came away in our hands as though somebody had let go his legs. With the same movement, without a pause, we swung him up. His breath whistled, he kicked our upturned faces, he grasped two pairs of arms above his head, and he squirmed up with such precipitation that he seemed positively to escape from our hands like a bladder full of gas. Streaming with perspiration, we swarmed up the rope, and, coming into the blast of cold wind, gasped like men plunged into icy water. With burning faces we shivered to the very marrow of our bones. Never before had the gale seemed to us more furious, the sea more mad, the sunshine more merciless and mocking, and the position of the ship more hopeless and appalling. Every movement of her was ominous of the end of her agony and of the beginning of ours. We staggered away from the door, and, alarmed by a sudden roll, fell down in a bunch. It appeared to us that the side of the house was more smooth than glass and more slippery than ice. There was nothing to hang on to but a long brass hook used sometimes to keep back an open door. Wamibo held on to it and we held on to Wamibo, clutching our Jimmy. He had completely collapsed now. He did not seem to have the strength to close his hand. We stuck to him blindly in our fear. We were not afraid of Wamibo letting go (we remembered that the brute was stronger than any three men in the ship), but we were afraid of the hook giving way, and we also believed that the ship had make up her mind to turn over at last. But she didn't. A sea swept over us. The boatswain spluttered:—"Up and away. There's a lull. Away aft with you, or we will all go to the devil here." We stood up surrounding Jimmy. We begged him to hold up, to hold on, at least. He glared with his bulging eyes, mute as a fish, and with all the stiffening knocked out of him. He wouldn't stand; he wouldn't even as much as clutch at our necks; he was only a cold black skin loosely stuffed with soft cotton wool; his arms and legs swung jointless and pliable; his head rolled about; the lower lip hung down, enormous and heavy. We pressed round him, bothered and dismayed; sheltering him we swung here and there in a body; and on the very brink of eternity we tottered all together with concealing and absurd gestures, like a lot of drunken men embarrassed with a stolen corpse.

Something had to be done. We had to get him aft. A rope was tied slack under his armpits, and, reaching up at the risk of our lives, we hung him on the foresheet cleet. He emitted no sound; he looked as ridiculously lamentable as a doll that had lost half its sawdust, and we started on our perilous journey over the main deck, dragging along with care that pitiful, that limp, that hateful burden. He was not very heavy, but had he weighed a ton he could not have been more awkward to handle. We literally passed him from hand to hand. Now and then we had to hang him up on a handy belaying-pin, to draw a breath and reform the line. Had the pin broken he would have irretrievably gone into the Southern Ocean, but he had to take his chance of that; and after a little while, becoming apparently aware of it, he groaned slightly, and with a great effort whispered a few words. We listened eagerly. He was reproaching us with our carelessness in letting him run such risks: "Now, after I got myself out from there," he breathed out weakly. "There" was his cabin. And he got himself out. We had nothing to do with it apparently!.... No matter..... We went on and let him take his chances, simply because we could not help it; for though at that time we hated him more than ever—more than anything under heaven—we did not want to lose him. We had so far saved him; and it had become a personal matter between us and the sea. We meant to stick to him. Had we (by an incredible hypothesis) undergone similar toil and trouble for an empty cask, that cask would have become as precious to us as Jimmy was. More precious, in fact, because we would have had no reason to hate the cask. And we hated James Wait. We could not get rid of the monstrous suspicion that this astounding black-man was shamming sick, had been malingering heartlessly in the face of our toil, of our scorn, of our patience—and now was malingering in the face of our devotion—in the face of death. Our vague and imperfect morality rose with disgust at his unmanly lie. But he stuck to it manfully—amazingly. No! It couldn't be. He was at all extremity. His cantankerous temper was only the result of the provoking invincibleness of that death he felt by his side. Any man may be angry with such a masterful chum. But, then, what kind of men were we—with our thoughts! Indignation and doubt grappled within us in a scuffle that trampled upon the finest of our feelings. And we hated him because of the suspicion; we detested him because of the doubt. We could not scorn him safely—neither could we pity him without risk to our dignity. So we hated him, and passed him carefully from hand to hand. We cried, "Got him?"—"Yes. All right. Let go." And he swung from one enemy to another, showing about as much life as an old bolster would do. His eyes made two narrow white slits in the black face. He breathed slowly, and the air escaped through his lips with a noise like the sound of bellows. We reached the poop ladder at last, and it being a comparatively safe place, we lay for a moment in an exhausted heap to rest a little. He began to mutter. We were always incurably anxious to hear what he had to say. This time he mumbled peevishly, "It took you some time to come. I began to think the whole smart lot of you had been washed overboard. What kept you back? Hey? Funk?" We said nothing. With sighs we started again to drag him up. The secret and ardent desire of our heart was the desire to beat him viciously with our fists about the head: and we handled him as tenderly as though he had been made of glass.....

The return on the poop was like the return of wanderers after many years amongst people marked by the desolation of time. Eyes were turned slowly in their sockets glancing at us. Faint murmurs were heard, "Have you got 'im after all?" The well-known faces looked strange and familiar; they seemed faded and grimy; they had a mingled expression of fatigue and eagerness. They seemed to have become much thinner during our absence, as if all these men had been starving for a long time in their abandoned attitudes. The captain, with a round turn of a rope on his wrist, and kneeling on one knee, swung with a face cold and stiff; but with living eyes he was still holding the ship up, heeding no one, as if lost in the unearthly effort of that endeavour. We fastened up James Wait in a safe place. Mr. Baker scrambled along to lend a hand. Mr. Creighton, on his back, and very pale, muttered, "Well done," and gave us, Jimmy and the sky, a scornful glance, then closed his eyes slowly. Here and there a man stirred a little, but most remained apathetic, in cramped positions, muttering between shivers. The sun was setting. A sun enormous, unclouded and red, declining low as if bending down to look into their faces. The wind whistled across long sunbeams that, resplendent and cold, struck full on the dilated pupils of staring eyes without making them wink. The wisps of hair and the tangled beards were grey with the salt of the sea. The faces were earthy, and the dark patches under the eyes extended to the ears, smudged into the hollows of sunken cheeks. The lips were livid and thin, and when they moved it was with difficulty, as though they had been glued to the teeth. Some grinned sadly in the sunlight, shaking with cold. Others were sad and still. Charley, subdued by the sudden disclosure of the insignificance of his youth, darted fearful glances. The two smooth-faced Norwegians resembled decrepid children, staring stupidly. To leeward, on the edge of the horizon, black seas leaped up towards the glowing sun. It sank slowly, round and blazing, and the crests of waves splashed on the edge of the luminous circle. One of the Norwegians appeared to catch sight of it, and, after giving a violent start, began to speak. His voice, startling the others, made them stir. They moved their heads stiffly, or turning with difficulty, looked at him with surprise, with fear, or in grave silence. He chattered at the setting sun, nodding his head, while the big seas began to roll across the crimson disc; and over miles of turbulent waters the shadows of high waves swept with a running darkness the faces of men. A crested roller broke with a loud hissing roar, and the sun, as if put out, disappeared. The chattering voice faltered, went out together with the light. There were sighs. In the sudden lull that follows the crash of a broken sea a man said wearily, "Here's that blooming Dutchman gone off his chump." A seaman, lashed by the middle, tapped the deck with his open hand with unceasing quick flaps. In the gathering greyness of twilight a bulky form was seen rising aft, and began marching on all fours with the movements of some big cautious beast. It was Mr. Baker passing along the line of men. He grunted encouragingly over every one, felt their fastenings. Some, with half-open eyes, puffed like men oppressed by heat; others mechanically and in dreamy voices answered him, "Aye! aye! sir!" He went from one to another grunting, "Ough!.... See her through it yet;" and unexpectedly, with loud angry outbursts, blew up Knowles for cutting off a long piece from the fall of the relieving tackle. "Ough!—Ashamed of yourself—Relieving tackle—Don't you know better!—Ough!—Able seaman! Ough!" The lame man was crushed. He muttered, "Get som'think for a lashing for myself, sir."—"Ough! Lashing—yourself. Are you a tinker or a sailor—What? Ough!—May want that tackle directly—Ough!—More use to the ship than your lame carcass. Ough!—Keep it!—Keep it, now you've done it." He crawled away slowly, muttering to himself about some men being "worse than children." It had been a comforting row.

Low exclamations were heard: "Hallo.... Hallo." .... Those who had been painfully dozing asked with convulsive starts, "What's up?.... What is it?" The answers came with unexpected cheerfullness: "The mate is going bald-headed for lame Jack about something or other." "No!" .... "What 'as he done?" Some one even chuckled. It was like a whiff of hope, like a reminder of safe days. Donkin, who had been stupefied with fear, revived suddenly and began to shout:—"'Ear 'im; that's the way they tawlk to hus. Vy donch 'ee 'it 'im—one ov yer? 'It 'im. 'It 'im! Comin' the mate hover hus. We are as good men as 'ee! We're hall goin' to 'ell now. We 'ave been starved in this rotten ship, an' now we're goin' to be drowned for them black-'earted bullies! 'It 'im!" He shrieked in the deepening gloom, he blubbered and sobbed, screaming:—"'It 'im! 'It 'im!" The rage and fear of his disregarded right to live tried the steadfastness of hearts more than the menacing shadows of the night that advanced through the unceasing clamour of the gale. From aft Mr. Baker was heard:—"Is one of you men going to stop him—must I come along?" "Shut up!".... "Keep quiet!" cried various voices, exasperated, trembling with cold.—"You'll get one across the mug from me directly," said an invisible seaman, in a weary tone, "I won't let the mate have the trouble." He ceased and lay still with the silence of despair. On the black sky the stars, coming out, gleamed over an inky sea that, speckled with foam, flashed back at them the evanescent and pale light of a dazzling whiteness born from the black turmoil of the waves. Remote in the eternal calm they glittered hard and cold above the uproar of the earth; they surrounded the vanquished and tormented ship on all sides: more pitiless than the eyes of a triumphant mob, and as unapproachable as the hearts of men.

The icy south wind howled exultingly under the sombre splendour of the sky. The cold shook the men with a resistless violence as though it had tried to shake them to pieces. Short moans were swept unheard off the stiff lips. Some complained in mutters of "not feeling themselves below the waist"; while those who had closed their eyes, imagined they had a block of ice on their chests. Others, alarmed at not feeling any pain in their fingers, beat the deck feebly with their hands—obstinate and exhausted. Wamibo stared vacant and dreamy. The Scandinavians kept on a meaningless mutter through chattering teeth. The spare Scotchmen, with determined efforts, kept their lower jaws still. The Westcountry men lay big and stolid in an invulnerable surliness. A man yawned and swore in turns. Another breathed with a rattle in his throat. Two elderly hardweather shellbacks, fast side by side, whispered dismally to one another about the landlady of a boarding-house in Sunderland, whon they both knew. They extolled her motherliness and her liberality; they tried to talk about the joint of beef and the big fire in the downstairs kitchen. The words dying faintly on their lips, ended in light sighs. A sudden voice cried into the cold night, "Oh Lord!" No one changed his position or took any notice of the cry. One or two passed, with a repeated and vague gesture, their hand over their faces, but most of them kept very still. In the benumbed immobility of their bodies they were excessively wearied by their thoughts, that rushed with the rapidity and vividness of dreams. Now and then, by an abrupt and startling exclamation, they answered the weird hail of some illusion; then, again, in silence contemplated the vision of known faces and familiar things. They recalled the aspect of forgotten shipmates and heard the voice of dead and gone skippers. They remembered the noise of gaslit streets, the steamy heat of tap-rooms, or the scorching sunshine of calm days at sea.

Mr. Baker left his insecure place, and crawled, with stoppages, along the poop. In the dark and on all fours her resembled some carnivorous animal prowling amongst corpses. At the break, propped to windward of a stanchion, he looked down on the main deck. It seemed to him that the ship had a tendency to stand up a little more. The wind had eased a little, he thought, but the sea ran as high as ever. The waves foamed viciously, and the lee side of the deck disappeared under a hissing whiteness as of boiling milk, while the rigging sang steadily with a deep vibrating note, and, at every upward swing of the ship, the wind rushed with a long-drawn clamour amongst the spars. Mr. Baker watched very still. A man near him began to make a blabbing noise with his lips, all at once and very loud, as though the cold had broken brutally through him. He went on:—"Ba—ba—ba—brrr—brr—ba—ba."—"Stop that!" cried Mr. Baker, groping in the dark. "Stop it!" He went on shaking the leg he found under his hand.—"What is it, sir?" called out Belfast, in the tone of a man awakened suddenly; "we are looking after that 'ere Jimmy."—"Are you? Ough! Don't make that row then. Who's that near you?"—"It's me—the boatswain, sir," growled the West-country man; "we are trying to keep life in that poor devil."—"Aye, aye!" said Mr. Baker, "Do it quietly, can't you."—"He wants us to hold him up above the rail," went on the boatswain, with irritation, "says he can't breathe here under our jackets."—"If we lift 'im, we drop 'im over-board," said another voice, "we can't feel our hands with the cold."—"I don't care. I am choking!' exclaimed James Wait in a clear tone.—"Oh, no, my son," said the boatswain, desperately, "you don't go till we all go on this fine night."— "You will see yet many a worse," said Mr. Baker, cheerfully.—"It's no child's play, sir!" answered the boatswain. "Some of us further aft, here, are in a pretty bad way."—"If the blamed sticks had been cut out of her she would be running along on her bottom now like any decent ship, an' giv' us all a chance," said some one, with a sigh.—"The old man wouldn't have it . . . . much he cares for us," whispered another.—"Care for you!" exclaimed Mr. Baker, angrily. "Why should he care for you? Are you a lot of women passengers to be taken care of? We are here to take care of the ship—and some of you ain't up to that. Ough! . . . . What have you done so very smart to be taken care of? Ough! . . . . Some of you can't stand a bit of a breeze without crying over it."—"Come, sorr. We ain't so bad," protested Belfast, in a voice shaken by shivers; "we ain't . . . . brr . . . ."— "Again," shouted the mate, grabbing at the shadowy form; "again! . . . . Why, you're in your shirt! What have you done?"—"I've put my oilskin and jacket over that half-dead nayggur—and he says he chokes," said Belfast, complain-ingly.—"You wouldn't call me nigger if I wasn't half dead, you Irish beggar!" boomed James Wait, vigorously.—"You . . . . brrr . . . . You wouldn't be white if you were ever so well . . . . I will fight you . . . . brrrr . . . . in fine weather . . . . brrr . . . . with one hand tied behind my back . . . . brrrrrr . . . ."—"I don't want your rags—I want air," gasped out the other faintly, as if suddenly exhausted.

The sprays swept over whistling and pattering. Men disturbed in their peaceful torpor by the pain of quarrelsome shouts, moaned, muttering curses. Mr. Baker crawled off a little way to leeward where a water-cask loomed up big, with something white against it. "Is it you, Podmore?" asked Mr. Baker. He had to repeat the question twice before the cook turned, coughing feebly.— "Yes, sir. I've been praying in my mind for a quick deliverance; for I am prepared for any call. . . . . I—"—"Look here, cook," interrupted Mr. Baker, "the men are perishing with cold."—"Cold!" said the cook mournfully; "they will be warm enough before long."—"What?" asked Mr. Baker, looking along the deck into the faint sheen of frothing water.—"They are a wicked lot," continued the cook solemnly, but in an unsteady voice, "about as wicked as any ship's company in this sinful world! Now, I"—he trembled so that he could hardly speak; his was an exposed place, and in a cotton shirt, a thin pair of trousers, and with his knees under his nose, he received, quaking, the flicks of stinging, salt drops; his voice sounded exhausted—"now, I—any time.... My eldest youngster, Mr. Baker.... a clever boy.... last Sunday on shore before this voyage he wouldn't go to church, sir. Says I, 'You go and clean yourself, or I'll know the reason why!' What does he do?.... Pond, Mr. Baker—fell into the pond in his best rig, sir!.... Accident?.... 'Nothing will save you, fine scholar though you are!' says I..... Accident!.... I whopped him, sir, till I couldn't lift my arm....." His voice faltered. "I whopped 'im!" he repeated, rattling his teeth; then, after a while, let out a mournful sound that was half a groan, half a snore. Mr. Baker shook him by the shoulders. "Hey! Cook! Hold up, Podmore! Tell me—is there any fresh water in the galley tank? The ship is lying along less, I think; I would try to get forward. A little water would do them good. Hallo! Look out! Look out!" The cook struggled.—"Not you, sir—not you!" He began to scramble to windward. "Galley!.... my business!" he shouted.—"Cook's going crazy now," said several voices. He yelled:—"Crazy, am I? I am more ready to die than any of you, officers incloosive—there! As long as she swims I will cook! I will get you coffee."—"Cook, ye are a gentleman!" cried Belfast. But the cook was already going over the weather ladder. He stopped for a moment to shout back on the poop:—"As long as she swims I will cook!" and disappeared as if he had gone overboard. The men who had heard sent after him a cheer that sounded like the wail of sick children. An hour or more afterwards some one said distinctly: "He's gone for good."—"Very likely," assented the boatswain; "even in fine weather he was as smart about the deck as a milch-cow on her first voyage. We ought to go and see." Nobody moved. As the hours dragged slowly through the darkness Mr. Baker crawled back and forth along the poop several times. Some men fancied they had heard him exchange murmurs with the master, but at that time the memories were incomparably more vivid than anything actual, and they were not certain whether the murmurs were heard now or many years ago. They did not try to find out. A mutter more or less did not matter. It was too cold for curiosity, and almost for hope. They could not spare a moment or a thought from the great mental occupation of wishing to live. And the desire of life kept them alive, apathetic and enduring, under the cruel persistence of wind and cold; while the bestarred black dome of the sky revolved slowly above the ship, that drifted, bearing their patience and their suffering, through the stormy solitude of the sea.

Huddled close to one another, they fancied themselves utterly alone. They heard sustained loud noises, and again bore the pain of existence through long hours of profound silence. In the night they saw sunshine, felt warmth, and suddenly, with a start, thought that the sun would never rise upon a freezing world. Some heard laughter, listened to songs; others, near the end of the poop, could hear loud human shrieks, and, opening their eyes, were surprised to hear them still, though very faint, and far away. The boatswain said:—"Why, it's the cook, hailing from forward, I think." He hardly believed his own words or recognised his own voice. It was a long time before the man next to him gave a sign of life. He punched hard his other neighbour and said:—"The cook's shouting!" Many did not understand, others did not care; the majority further aft did not believe. But the boatswain and another man had the pluck to crawl away forward to see. They seemed to have been gone for hours, and were very soon forgotten. Then suddenly men that had been plunged in a hopeless resignation became as if possessed with a desire to hurt. They belaboured one another with fists. In the darkness they struck persistently anything soft they could feel near, and, with a greater effort than for a shout, whispered excitedly:— "They've got some hot coffee. . . . . Boss'en got it. . . . . " "No! . . . . Where?". . . . "It's coming! Cook made it." James Wait moaned. Donkin scrambled viciously, caring not where he kicked, and anxious that the officers should have none of it. It came in a pot, and they drank in turns. It was hot, and while it blistered the greedy palates, it seemed incredible. The men sighed out parting with the mug:— "How 'as he done it?" Some cried weakly:—"Bully for you, doctor!"

He had done it somehow. Afterwards Archie declared that the thing was "meeraculous." For many days we wondered, and it was the one ever-interesting subject of conversation to the end of the voyage. We asked the cook, in fine weather, how he felt when he saw his stove "reared up on end." We inquired, in the north-east trade and on serene evenings, whether he had to stand on his head to put things right somewhat. We suggested he had used his bread-board for a raft, and from there comfortably had stoked his grate; and we did our best to conceal our admiration under the wit of fine irony. He affirmed not to know anything about it, rebuked our levity, declared himself, with solemn animation, to have been the object of a special mercy for the saving of our unholy lives. Fundamentally he was right, no doubt; but he need not have been so offensively positive about it—he need not have hinted so often that it would have gone hard with us had he not been there, meritorious and pure, to receive the inspiration and the strength for the work of grace. Had we been saved by his recklessness or his agility, we could have at length become reconciled to the fact; but to admit our obligation to anybody's virtue and holiness alone was as difficult for us as for any other handful of mankind. Like many benefactors of humanity, the cook took himself too seriously, and reaped the reward of irreverence. We were not ungrateful, however. He remained heroic. His saying— the saying of his life—became proverbial in the mouth of men as are the sayings of conquerors or sages. Later on, whenever one of us was puzzled by a task and advised to relinquish it, he would express his determination to persevere and to succeed by the words:—"As long as she swims I will cook!"

The hot drink helped us through the bleak hours that precede the dawn. The sky low by the horizon took on the delicate tints of pink and yellow like the inside of a rare shell. And higher, where it glowed with a pearly sheen, a small black cloud appeared, like a forgotten fragment of the night set in a border of dazzling gold. The beams of light skipped on the crests of waves. The eyes of men turned to the eastward. The sunlight flooded their weary faces. They were giving themselves up to fatigue as though they had done for ever with their work. On Singleton's black oilskin coat the dried salt glistened like hoar frost. He hung on by the wheel, with open and lifeless eyes. Captain Allistoun, unblinking, faced the rising sun. His lips stirred, opened for the first time in twenty-four hours, and with a fresh firm voice he cried, "Wear ship!"

The commanding sharp tones made all these torpid men start like a sudden flick of a whip. Then again, motionless where they lay, the force of habit made some of them repeat the order in hardly audible murmurs. Captain Allistoun glanced down at his crew, and several, with fumbling fingers and hopeless movements, tried to cast themselves adrift. He repeated impatiently, "Wear ship. Now then, Mr. Baker, get the men along. What's the matter with them?"— "Wear ship. Do you hear there?—Wear ship!" thundered out the boatswain suddenly. His voice seemed to break through a deadly spell. Men began to stir and crawl.—"I want the fore-top-mast staysail run up smartly," said the master, very loudly; "if you can't manage it standing up you must do it lying down— that's all. Bear a hand!"—"Come along! Let's give the old girl a chance," urged the boatswain.—"Aye! aye! Wear ship!" exclaimed quavering voices. The fore-castle men, with reluctant faces, prepared to go forward. Mr. Baker pushed ahead grunting on all fours to show the way, and they followed him over the break. The others lay still with a vile hope in their hearts of not being required to move till they got saved or drowned in peace.

After some time they could be seen forward appearing on the forecastle head, one by one in unsafe attitudes; hanging on to the rails; clambering over the anchors; embracing the cross-head of the windlass or hugging the fore-capstan. They were restless with strange exertions, waved their arms, knelt, lay flat down, staggered up, seemed to strive their hardest to go overboard. Suddenly a small white piece of canvas fluttered amongst them, grew larger, beating. Its narrow head rose in jerks—and at last it stood distended and triangular in the sunshine.—"They have done it!" cried the voices aft. Captain Allistoun let go the rope he had round his wrist and rolled to leeward headlong. He could be seen casting the lee main braces off the pins while the backwash of waves splashed over him.—"Square the main yard!" he shouted up to us—who stared at him in wonder. We hesitated to stir. "The main brace, men. Haul! haul anyhow! Lay on your backs and haul!" he screeched, half drowned down there. We did not believe we could move the main yard, but the strongest and the less discouraged tried to execute the order. Others assisted half-heartedly. Singleton's eyes blazed suddenly as he took a fresh grip of the spokes. Captain Allistoun fought his way up to windward.—"Haul men! Try to move it! Haul, and help the ship." His hard face worked suffused and furious. "Is she going off, Singleton?" he cried.—"Not a move yet, sir," croaked the old seaman in a horribly hoarse voice.—"Watch the helm, Singleton," spluttered the master. "Haul men! Have you no more strength than rats? Haul, and earn your salt." Mr. Creighton, on his back, with a swollen leg and a face as white as a piece of paper, blinked his eyes; his bluish lips twitched. In the wild scramble men grabbed at him, crawled over his hurt leg, knelt on his chest. He kept perfectly still, setting his teeth without a moan, without a sigh. The master's ardour, the cries of that silent man inspired us. We hauled and hung in bunches on the rope. We heard him say with violence to Donkin, who sprawled abjectly on his stomach,—"I will brain you with this belaying pin if you don't catch hold of the brace," and that victim of men's injustice, cowardly and cheeky, whimpered:— "Are you goin' ter murder hus now," while with sudden desperation he gripped the rope. Men sighed, shouted, hissed meaningless words, groaned. The yards moved, came slowly square against the wind, that hummed loudly on the yard-arms.—"Going off, sir," shouted Singleton, "she's just started."—"Catch a turn with that brace. Catch a turn!" clamoured the master. Mr. Creighton, nearly suffocated and unable to move, made a mighty effort, and with his left hand managed to nip the rope.—"All fast!" cried some one. He closed his eyes as if going off into a swoon, while huddled together about the brace we watched with scared looks what the ship would do now.

She went off slowly as though she had been weary and disheartened like the men she carried. She paid off very gradually, making us hold our breath till we choked, and as soon as she had brought the wind abaft the beam she started to move, and fluttered our hearts. It was awful to see her, nearly overturned, begin to gather way and drag her submerged side through the water. The dead-eyes of the rigging churned the breaking seas. The lower half of the deck was full of mad whirlpools and eddies; and the long line of the lee rail could be seen showing black now and then in the swirls of a field of foam as dazzling and white as a field of snow. The wind sang shrilly amongst the spars; and at every slight lurch we expected her to slip to the bottom sideways from under our backs. When dead before it she made the first distinct attempt to stand up, and we encouraged her with a feeble and discordant howl. A great sea came running up aft and hung for a moment over us with a curling top; then crashed down under the counter and spread out on both sides into a great sheet of bursting froth. Above its fierce hiss we heard Singleton's croak:—"She is steering!" He had both his feet now planted firmly on the grating, and the wheel spun fast as he eased the helm.—"Bring the wind on the port quarter and steady her!" called out the master, staggering to his feet, the first man up from amongst our prostrate heap. One or two screamed with excitement:—"She rises!" Far away forward, Mr. Baker and three others were seen erect and black on the clear sky, lifting their arms, and with open mouths as though they had been shouting all together. The ship trembled, trying to lift her side, lurched back, seemed to give up with a nerveless dip, and suddenly with an unexpected jerk swung violently to windward, as though she had torn herself out from a deadly grasp. The whole immense volume of water, lifted by her deck, was thrown bodily across to starboard. Loud cracks were heard. Iron ports breaking open thundered with ringing blows. The water topped over the starboard rail with the rush of a river falling over a dam. The sea on deck, and the seas on every side of her, mingled together in a deafening roar. She rolled violently. We got up and were helplessly run or flung about from side to side. Men, rolling over and over, yelled,—"The house will go!"—"She clears herself!" Lifted by a towering sea she ran along with it for a moment, spouting thick streams of water through every opening of her wounded sides. The lee braces having been carried away or washed off the pins, all the ponderous yards on the fore swung from side to side and with appalling rapidity at every roll. The men forward were seen crouching here and there with fearful glances upwards at the enormous spars that whirled about over their heads. The torn canvas and the ends of broken gear streamed in the wind like wisps of hair. Through the clear sunshine, over the flashing turmoil and uproar of the seas, the ship ran blindly, dishevelled and headlong, as if fleeing for her life; and on the poop we spun, we tottered about, distracted and noisy. We all spoke at once in a thin babble; we had the aspect of invalids and the gestures of maniacs. Eyes shone, large and haggard, in smiling, meagre faces that seemed to have been dusted over with powdered chalk. We stamped, clapped our hands, feeling ready to jump and do anything; but in reality hardly able to keep on our feet. Captain Allistoun, hard and slim, gesticulated madly from the poop at Mr. Baker: "Steady these fore-yards! Steady them the best you can!" On the main deck, men excited by his cries, splashed, dashing aimlessly here and there with the foam swirling up to their waists. Apart, far aft, and alone by the helm, old Singleton had deliberately tucked his white beard under the top button of his glistening coat. Swaying upon the din and tumult of the seas, with the whole battered length of the ship launched forward in a rolling rush before his steady old eyes, he stood rigidly still, forgotten by all, and with an attentive face. In front of his erect figure only the two arms moved crosswise with a swift and sudden readiness, to check or urge again the rapid stir of circling spokes. He steered with care.

IV

On men reprieved by its disdainful mercy, the immortal sea confers in its justice the full privilege of desired unrest. Through the perfect wisdom of its grace they are not permitted to meditate at ease upon the complicated and acrid savour of existence, lest they should remember and, perchance, regret the reward of a cup of inspiring bitterness, tasted so often, and so often withdrawn from before their stiffening but reluctant lips. They must without pause justify their life to the eternal pity that commands toil to be hard and unceasing, from sunrise to sunset, from sunset to sunrise: till the weary succession of nights and days tainted by the obstinate clamour of sages, demanding bliss and an empty heaven, is redeemed at last by the dumb fear and the dumb courage of men obscure, forgetful, and enduring.

The master and Mr. Baker coming face to face stared for a moment, with the intense and amazed looks of men meeting unexpectedly after years of trouble. Their voices were gone, and they whispered desperately at one another.— "Any one missing?" asked Captain Allistoun. —"No. All there."—"Anybody hurt?"—"Only the second mate."—"I will look after him directly. We're lucky."— "Very," articulated Mr. Baker, faintly. He gripped the rail and rolled bloodshot eyes. The little grey man made an effort to raise his voice above a dull mutter, and fixed his chief mate with a cold gaze, piercing like a dart.—"Get sail on the ship," he said, speaking authoritatively, and with an inflexible snap of his thin lips. "Get sail on her as soon as you can. This is a fair wind. At once, sir—Don't give the men time to feel themselves. They will get done up and stiff, and we will never.... We must get her along now".... He reeled to a long heavy roll; the rail dipped into the glancing hissing water. He caught a shroud, swung helplessly against the mate.... "now we have a fair wind at last.—Make—sail." His head rolled from shoulder to shoulder. His eyelids began to beat rapidly. "And the pumps—pumps, Mr. Baker." He peered as though the face within a foot of his eyes had been half a mile off. "Keep the men on the move to—to get her along," he mumbled in a drowsy tone, like a man going off into a doze. He pulled himself together suddenly. "Mustn't stand. Won't do," he said with a painful attempt at a smile. He let go his hold, and, propelled by the dip of the ship, ran aft unwillingly, with small steps, till he brought up against the binnacle stand. Hanging on there he looked up in an objectless manner at Singleton, who, unheeding him, watched anxiously the end of the jib-boom— "Steering gear works all right?" he asked. There was a noise in the old seaman's throat, as though the words had been rattling there together before they could come out.—"Steers . . . . like a little boat," he said, at last, with hoarse tenderness, without giving the master as much as half a glance—then, watchfully, spun the wheel down, steadied, flung it back again. Captain Allistoun tore himself away from the delight of leaning against the binnacle, and began to walk the poop, swaying and reeling to preserve his balance. . . . . .

The pump-rods, clanking, stamped in short jumps, while the fly-wheels turned smoothly, with great speed, at the foot of the mainmast, flinging back and forth with a regular impetuosity two limp clusters of men clinging to the handles. They abandoned themselves, swaying from the hip with twitching faces and stony eyes. The carpenter, sounding from time to time, exclaimed mechanically: "Shake her up! Keep her going!" Mr. Baker could not speak, but found his voice to shout; and under the goad of his objurgations, men looked to the lashings, dragged out new sails; and thinking themselves unable to move, carried heavy blocks aloft—overhauled the gear. They went up the rigging with faltering and desperate efforts. Their heads swam as they shifted their hold, stepped blindly on the yards like men in the dark; or trusted themselves to the first rope to hand with the negligence of exhausted strength. The narrow escapes from falls did not disturb the languid beat of their hearts; the roar of the seas seething far below them sounded continuous and faint like an indistinct noise from another world: the wind filled their eyes with tears, and with heavy gusts tried to push them off from where they swayed in insecure positions. With streaming faces and blowing hair they flew up and down between sky and water, bestriding the ends of yard-arms, crouching on foot-ropes, embracing lifts to have their hands free, or standing up against chain ties. Their thoughts floated vaguely between the desire of rest and the desire of life, while their stiffened fingers cast off head-earrings, fumbled for knives, or held with tenacious grip against the violent shocks of beating canvas. They glared savagely at one another, made frantic signs with one hand while they held their life in the other, looked down on the narrow strip of flooded deck, shouted along to leeward: "Light-to!". . . . "Haul out!". . . . "Make fast!" Their lips moved, their eyes stared, furious and eager with the desire to be understood, but the wind tossed their words unheard upon the disturbed sea. In an unendurable and unending strain they worked like men driven by a merciless dream to toil in an atmosphere of ice or flame. They burnt and shivered in turns. Their eyeballs smarted as if in the smoke of a conflagration; their heads were ready to burst with every shout. Hard fingers seemed to grip their throats. At every roll they thought: Now I must let go. It will shake us all off—and thrown about aloft they cried wildly: "Look out there—catch the end.". . . . "Reeve clear". . . . "Turn this block. . . . . " They nodded desperately; shook infuriated faces, "No! No! From down up." They seemed to hate one another with a deadly hate. The longing to be done with it all gnawed their breasts, and the wish to do things well was a burning pain. They cursed their fate, condemned their life, and wasted their breath in deadly implications upon one another. The sailmaker, with his bald head bared, worked feverishly, forgetting his intimacy with so many admirals. The boatswain, climbing up with marlinspikes and bunches of spunyarn rovings, or kneeling on the yard and ready to take a turn with the midship-stop, had acute and fleeting visions of his old woman and the youngsters in a moorland village. Mr. Baker, feeling very weak, tottered here and there, grunting and inflexible, like a man of iron. He waylaid those who, coming from aloft, stood gasping for breath. He ordered, encouraged, scolded. "Now then—to the main topsail now! Tally on to that gantline. Don't stand about there!"—"Is there no rest for us?" muttered voices. He spun round fiercely, with a sinking heart.—"No! No rest till the work is done. Work till you drop. That's what you're here for." A bowed seaman at his elbow gave a short laugh.—"Do or die," he croaked bitterly, then spat into his broad palms, swung up his long arms, and grasping the rope high above his head sent out a mournful, wailing cry for a pull all together. A sea boarded the quarter-deck and sent the whole lot sprawling to leeward. Caps, handspikes floated. Clenched hands, kicking legs, with here and there a spluttering face, stuck out of the white hiss of foaming water. Mr. Baker, knocked down with the rest, screamed—"Don't let go that rope! Hold on to it! Hold!" And sorely bruised by the brutal fling, they held on to it, as though it had been the fortune of their life. The ship ran, rolling heavily, and the topping crests glanced past port and starboard flashing their white heads. Pumps were freed. Braces were rove. The three topsails and foresail were set. She spurted faster over the water, outpacing the swift rush of waves. The menacing thunder of distanced seas rose behind her—filled the air with the tremendous vibrations of its voice. And devastated, battered, and wounded she drove foaming to the northward, as though inspired by the courage of a high endeavour....

The forecastle was a place of damp desolation. They looked at their dwelling with dismay. It was slimy, dripping; it hummed hollow with the wind, and was strewn with shapeless wreckage like a half-tide cavern in a rocky and exposed coast. Many had lost all they had in the world, but most of the starboard watch had preserved their chests; thin streams of water trickled out of them, however. The beds were soaked; the blankets spread out and saved by some nail squashed under foot. They dragged wet rags from evil-smelling corners, and, wringing the water out, recognised their property. Some smiled stiffly. Others looked round blank and mute. There were cries of joy over old waistcoats, and groans of sorrow over shapeless things found amongst the black splinters of smashed bed boards. One lamp was discovered jammed under the bowsprit. Charley whimpered a little. Knowles stumped here and there, sniffing, examining dark places for salvage. He poured dirty water out of a boot, and was concerned to find the owner. Those who, overwhelmed by their losses, sat on the forepeak hatch, remained elbows on knees, and, with a fist against each cheek, disdained to look up. He pushed it under their noses. "Here's a good boot. Yours?" They snarled, "No—get out." One snapped at him, "Take it to hell out of this." He seemed surprised. "Why? It's a good boot," but remembering suddenly that he had lost every stitch of his clothing, he dropped his find and began to swear. In the dim light cursing voices clashed. A man came in and, dropping his arms, stood still, repeating from the doorstep, "Here's a bloomin' old go! Here's a bloomin' old go!" A few rooted anxiously in flooded chests for tobacco. They breathed hard, clamoured with heads down. "Look at that, Jack!".... "Here! Sam! Here's my shore-going rig spoilt for ever." One blasphemed tearfully holding up a pair of dripping trousers. No one looked at him. The cat came out from somewhere. He had an ovation. They snatched him from hand to hand, caressed him in a murmur of pet names. They wondered where he had "weathered it out;" disputed about it. A squabbling argument began. Two men came in with a bucket of fresh water, and all crowded round it; but Tom, lean and mewing, came up with every hair astir and had the first drink. A couple of men went aft for oil and biscuits.

Then in the yellow light and in the intervals of mopping the deck they crunched hard bread, arranging to "worry through somehow." Men chummed as to beds. Turns were settled for wearing boots and having the use of oilskin coats. They called one another "old man" and "sonny" in cheery voices. Friendly slaps resounded. Jokes were shouted. One or two stretched on the wet deck, slept with heads pillowed on their bent arms, and several, sitting on the hatch, smoked. Their weary faces appeared through a thin blue haze, pacified and with sparkling eyes. The boatswain put his head through the door. "Relieve the wheel, one of you"—he shouted inside—"it's six. Blamme if that old Singleton hasn't been there more'n thirty hours. You are a fine lot." He slammed the door again. "Mate's watch on deck," said some one. "Hey, Donkin, it's your relief!" shouted three or four together. He had crawled into an empty bunk and on wet planks lay still. "Donkin, your wheel." He made no sound. "Donkin's dead," guffawed some one. "Sell 'is bloomin' clothes," shouted another. "Donkin, if ye don't go to the bloomin' wheel they will sell your clothes—d'ye hear?" jeered a third. He groaned from his dark hole. He complained about pains in all his bones, he whimpered pitifully. "He won't go," exclaimed a contemptuous voice, "your turn, Davies." The young seaman rose painfully squaring his shoulders. Donkin stuck his head out, and it appeared in the yellow light, fragile and ghastly. "I will giv' yer a pound of tobaccer," he whined in a conciliating voice, "so soon as I draw it from haft. I will—s'elp me . . . ." Davies swung his arm backhanded and the head vanished. "I'll go," he said, "but you will pay for it." He walked unsteady but resolute to the door. "So I will," yelped Donkin, popping out behind him. "So I will—s'elp me . . . . a pound . . . . three bob they chawrge." Davies flung the door open. "You will pay my price . . . . in fine weather," he shouted over his shoulder. One of the men unbuttoned his wet coat rapidly, threw it at his head. "Here, Taffy—take that, you thief!" "Thank you!" he cried from the darkness above the swish of rolling water. He could be heard splashing; a sea came on board with a thump. "He's got his bath already," remarked a grim shellback. "Aye, aye!" grunted others. Then, after a long silence, Wamibo made strange noises. "Hallo, what's up with you?" said some one grumpily. "He says he would have gone for Davy," explained Archie, who was the Finn's interpreter generally. "I believe him!" cried voices. . . . . . "Never mind, Dutchy. . . . You'll do, muddlehead . . . . Your turn will come soon enough . . . . You don't know when ye're well off." They ceased, and all together turned their faces to the door. Singleton stepped in, made two paces, and stood swaying slightly. The sea hissed, flowed roaring past the bows, and the forecastle trembled, full of a deep rumour; the lamp flared, swinging like a pendulum. He looked with a dreamy and puzzled stare, as though he could not distinguish the still men from their restless shadows. There were awestruck murmurs:— "Hallo, hallo". . . . "How does it look outside now, Singleton?" Those who sat on the hatch lifted their eyes in silence, and the next oldest seaman in the ship (those two understood one another, though they hardly exchanged three words in a day) gazed up at his friend attentively for a moment, then taking a short clay pipe out of his mouth, offered it without a word. Singleton put out his arm towards it, missed, staggered, and suddenly fell forward, crashing down, stiff and headlong like an uprooted tree. There was a swift rush. Men pushed, crying:—"He's done!".... "Turn him over!".... "Stand clear there!" Under a crowd of startled faces bending over him he lay on his back, staring upwards in a continuous and intolerable manner. In the breathless silence of a general consternation, he said in a grating murmur:—"I am all right," and clutched with his hands. They helped him up. He mumbled despondently:—"I am getting old.... old."—"Not you," cried Belfast, with ready tact. Supported on all sides, he hung his head.—"Are you better?" they asked. He glared at them from under his eyebrows with large black eyes, spreading over his chest the bushy whiteness of a beard long and thick.—"Old! old!" he repeated sternly. Helped along, he reached his bunk. There was in it a slimy soft heap of something that smelt, like does at dead low water a muddy foreshore. It was his soaked straw bed. With a convulsive effort he pitched himself on it, and in the darkness of the narrow place could be heard growling angrily, like an irritated and savage animal uneasy in its den:—"Bit of breeze.... small thing.... can't stand up.... old!" He slept at last. He breathed heavily, high-booted, sou'wester on head, and his oilskin clothes rustled, when with a deep sighing groan he turned over. Men conversed about him in quiet concerned whispers. "This will break 'im up".... "Strong as a horse".... "Aye. But he ain't what he used to be.".... In sad murmurs they gave him up. Yet at midnight he turned out to duty as if nothing had been the matter, and answered to his name with a mournful "Here!" He brooded alone more than ever, in an impenetrable silence and with a saddened face. For many years he had heard himself called "Old Singleton," and had serenely accepted the qualification, taking it as a tribute of respect due to a man who through half a century had measured his strength against the favours and the rages of the sea. He had never given a thought to his mortal self. He lived unscathed, as though he had been indestructible, surrendering to all the temptations, weathering many gales. He had panted in sunshine, shivered in the cold; suffered hunger, thirst, debauch; passed through many trials—known all the furies. Old! It seemed to him he was broken at last. And like a man bound treacherously while he sleeps, he woke up fettered by the long chain of disregarded years. He had to take up at once the burden of all his existence, and found it almost too heavy for his strength. Old! He moved his arms, shook his head, felt his limbs. Getting old.... and then? He looked upon the immortal sea with the awakened and groping perception of its heartless might; he saw it unchanged, black and foaming under the eternal scrutiny of the stars; he heard its impatient voice calling for him out of a pitiless vastness full of unrest, of turmoil, and of terror. He looked afar upon it, and he saw an immensity tormented and blind, moaning and furious, that claimed all the days of his tenacious life, and, when life was over, would claim the worn-out body of its slave.

This was the last of the breeze. It veered quickly, changed to a black southeaster, and blew itself out, giving the ship a famous shove to the northward into the joyous sunshine of the trade. Rapid and white she ran homewards in a straight path, under a blue sky and upon the plain of a blue sea. She carried Singleton's completed wisdom, Donkin's delicate susceptibilities, and the conceited folly of us all. The hours of ineffective turmoil were forgotten; the fear and anguish of these dark moments were never mentioned in the glowing peace of fine days. Yet from that time our life seemed to start afresh as though we had died and had been resuscitated. All the first part of the voyage, the Indian Ocean on the other side of the Cape, all that was lost in a haze, like an in- eradicable suspicion of some previous existence. It had ended—then there were blank hours: a livid blurr—and again we lived! Singleton was possessed of sinister truth; Mr. Creighton of a damaged leg; the cook of fame—and shame- fully abused the opportunities of his distinction. Donkin had an added grievance. He went about repeating with insistence:—"'E said 'e would brain me—did yer 'ear? They hare goin' to murder hus now for the least little thing." We began at last to think it was rather awful. And we were conceited! We boasted of our pluck, of our capacity for work, of our energy. We remembered honourable episodes: our devotion, our indomitable perseverance—and were proud of them as though they had been the outcome of our unaided impulses. We remembered our danger, out toil—and conveniently forgot our horrible scare. We decried our officers—who had done nothing—and listened to the fascinating Donkin. His care for our rights, his disinterested concern for our dignity, were not discouraged by the invariable contumely of our words, by the disdain of our looks. Our contempt for him was unbounded—and we could not but listen with interest to that consummate artist. He told us we were good men—a "blooming' condemned lot of good men." Who thanked us? Who took any notice of our wrongs? Didn't we lead a "dorg's loife for two poun' ten a month?" Did we think that miserable pay enough to compensate us for the risk to our lives and for the loss of our clothes? "We've lost hevery rag!" he cried. He made us forget that he, at any rate, had lost nothing of his own. The younger men listened, thinking—this 'ere Donkin's a long-headed chap, though no kind of man, anyhow. The Scandinavians were frightened at his audacities; Wamibo did not understand; and the older seamen thoughtfully nodded their heads making the thin gold earrings glitter in the fleshy lobes of hairy ears. Severe, sun-burnt faces were propped meditatively on tattooed forearms. Veined, brown fists held in their knotted grip the dirty white clay of smouldering pipes. They listened, impenetrable, broad-backed, with bent shoulders, and in grim silence. He talked with ardour, despised and irrefutable. His picturesque and filthy loquacity flowed like a troubled stream from a poisoned source. His beady little eyes danced, glancing right and left, ever on the watch for the approach of an officer. Sometimes Mr. Baker going forward to take a look at the head sheets would roll with his uncouth gait through the sudden stillness of the men; or Mr. Creighton limped along, smooth-faced, youthful, and more stern than ever, piercing our short silence with a keen glance of his clear eyes. Behind his back Donkin would begin again darting stealthy, sidelong looks.—"'Ere's one of 'em. Some of yer 'as made 'im fast that day. Much thanks yer got for hit. Ain't 'ee a-drivin yer wusse'n hever?.... Let 'im slip hoverboard.....Vy not? It would 'ave been less trouble. Vy not?" He advanced confidentially, backed away with great effect; he whispered, he screamed, waved his miserable arms no thicker than pipe-stems—stretched his lean neck—spluttered—squinted. In the pauses of his impassioned orations the wind sighed quietly aloft, the calm sea unheeded murmured in a warning whisper along the ship's side. We abominated the creature and could not deny the luminous truth of his contentions. It was all so obvious. We were indubitably good men; our deserts were great and our pay small. Through our exertions we had saved the ship and the skipper would get the credit of it. What had he done? we wanted to know. Donkin asked:—"What 'ee could do without hus?" and we could not answer. We were oppressed by the injustice of the world, surprised to perceive how long we had lived under its burden without realising our unfortunate state, annoyed by the uneasy suspicion of our undiscerning stupidity. Donkin assured us it was all our "good 'eartedness," but we would not be consoled by such shallow sophistry. We were men enough to courageously admit to ourselves our intellectual shortcomings; though from that time we refrained from kicking him, tweaking his nose, or from accidentally knocking him about, which last, after we had weathered the Cape, had been rather a popular amusement. Davies ceased to talk at him provokingly about black eyes and flattened noses. Charley, much subdued since the gale, did not jeer at him. Knowles deferentially and with a crafty air propounded questions such as:—"Could we all have the same grub as the mates? Could we all stop ashore till we got it? What would be the next thing to try for if we got that?" He answered readily with contemptuous certitude; he strutted with assurance in clothes that were much too big for him as though he had tried to disguise himself. These were Jimmy's clothes mostly—though he would accept anything from anybody; but nobody, except Jimmy, had anything to spare. His devotion to Jimmy was unbounded. He was for ever dodging in the little cabin, ministering to Jimmy's wants, humoring his whims, submitting to his exacting peevishness, often laughing with him. Nothing could keep him away from the pious work of visiting the sick, especially when there was some heavy hauling to be done on deck. Mr. Baker had on two occasions jerked him out from there by the scruff of the neck to our inexpressible scandal. Was a sick chap to be left without attendance? Were we to be ill-used for attending a shipmate?—"What?" growled Mr. Baker, turning menacingly at the mutter, and the whole half-circle like one man stepped back a pace. "Set the topmast stunsail. Away aloft, Donkin, overhaul the gear," ordered the mate inflexibly. "Fetch the sail along; bend the down-haul clear. Bear a hand." Then, the sail set, he would go slowly aft and stand looking at the compass for a long time, careworn, pensive, and breathing hard as if stifled by the taint of unaccountable ill-will that pervaded the ship. "What's up amongst them?" he thought. "Can't make out this hanging back and growling. A good crowd, too, as they go nowadays." On deck the men exchanged bitter words, suggested by a silly exasperation against something unjust and irremediable that would not be denied, and would whisper into their ears long after Donkin had ceased speaking. Our little world went on its curved and unswerving path carrying a discontented and aspiring population. They found comfort of a gloomy kind in an interminable and conscientious analysis of their unappreciated worth; and inspired by Donkin's hopeful doctrines they dreamed enthusiastically of the time when every lonely ship would travel over a serene sea, manned by a wealthy and well-fed crew of satisfied skippers.

It looked as if it would be a long passage. The south-east trades, light and unsteady, were left behind; and then, on the equator and under a low grey sky, the ship, in close heat, floated upon a smooth sea that resembled a sheet of ground glass. Thunder squalls hung on the horizon, circled round the ship, far off and growling angrily, like a troop of wild beasts afraid to charge home. The invisible sun, sweeping above the upright masts, made on the clouds a blurred stain of rayless light, and a similar patch of faded radiance kept pace with it from east to west over the unglittering level of the waters. At night, through the impenetrable darkness of earth and heaven, broad sheets of flame waved noiselessly; and for half a second the becalmed craft stood out with its masts and rigging, with every sail and every rope distinct and black in the centre of a fiery outburst, like a charred ship enclosed in a globe of fire. And, again, for long hours she remained lost in a vast universe of night and silence where gentle sighs wandering here and there like forlorn souls, made the still sails flutter as in sudden fear, and the ripple of a beshrouded ocean whisper its compassion afar—in a voice mournful, immense, and faint.....

When the lamp was put out, and through the door thrown wide open, Jimmy, turning on his pillow, could see vanishing beyond the straight line of top-gallant rail, the quick, repeated visions of a fabulous world made up of leaping fire and sleeping water. The lightning gleamed in his big sad eyes that seemed in a red flicker to burn themselves out in his black face, and then he would lay blinded and invisible in the midst of an intense darkness. He could hear on the quiet deck soft footfalls, the breathing of some man lounging on the doorstep; the low creak of swaying masts; or the calm voice of the watch-officer reverberating aloft, hard and loud, amongst the unstirring sails. He listened with avidity, taking a rest in the attentive perception of the slightest sound from the fatiguing wanderings of his sleeplessness. He was cheered by the rattling of blocks, reassured by the stir and murmur of the watch, soothed by the slow yawn of some sleepy and weary seaman settling himself deliberately for a snooze on the planks. Life seemed an indestructible thing. It went on in darkness, in sunshine, in sleep; tireless, it hovered affectionately round the imposture of his ready death. It was bright, like the twisted flare of lightning, and more full of surprises than the dark night. It made him safe, and the calm of its overpowering darkness was as precious as its restless and dangerous light.

But in the evening, in the dog-watches, and even far into the first night-watch, a knot of men could always be seen congregated before Jimmy's cabin. They leaned on each side of the door, peacefully interested and with crossed legs; they stood astride the doorstep discoursing, or sat in silent couples on his sea-chest; while against the bulwark along the spare top-mast, three or four in a row stared meditatively, with their simple faces lit up by the projected glare of Jimmy's lamp. The little place, repainted white, had, in the night, the brilliance of a silver shrine where a black idol, reclining stiffly under a blanket, blinked its weary eyes and received our homage. Donkin officiated. He had the air of a demonstrator showing a phenomenon, a manifestation bizarre, simple, and meritorious, that, to the beholders, should be a profound and an everlasting lesson. "Just look at 'im, 'ee knows what's what—never fear!" he exclaimed now and then, flourishing a hand hard and fleshless like the claw of a snipe. Jimmy, on his back, smiled with reserve and without moving a limb. He affected the languor of extreme weakness, so as to make it manifest to us that our delay in hauling him out from his horrible confinement, and then that night spent on the poop among our selfish neglect of his needs, had "done for him." He rather liked to talk about it, and of course we were always interested. He spoke spasmodically, in fast rushes with long pauses between, as a tipsy man walks....."Cook had just given me a pannikin of hot coffee.....Slapped it down there, on my chest—banged the door to.....I felt a heavy roll coming;

tried to save my coffee, burnt my fingers....and fell out of my bunk.....She
went over so quick.....Water came in through the ventilator.....I couldn't
move the door....dark as a grave....tried to scramble up into the upper
berth.....Rats....a rat bit my finger as I got up.....I could hear him swimming below me.....I thought you would never come.....I thought you were
all gone overboard....of course....Could hear nothing but the wind.....Then
you came....to look for the corpse, I suppose. A little more and...."

"Man! But ye made a rare lot of noise in here," observed Archie, thoughtfully.

"You chaps kicked up such a confounded row above.....Enough to scare
any one.....I didn't know what you were up to.....Bash in the blamed planks
....my head.....Just what a silly, scary gang of fools would do.....Not much
good to me anyhow.....Just as well....drown.....Pah."

He groaned, snapped his big white teeth, and gazed with scorn. Belfast
lifted a pair of dolorous eyes, with a broken-hearted smile, clenched his fists
stealthily; blue-eyed Archie caressed his red whiskers with a hesitating hand;
the boatswain at the door stared a moment, and brusquely went away with a
loud guffaw. Wamibo dreamed.....Donkin felt all over his sterile chin for the
few rare hairs, and said, triumphantly, with a sidelong glance at Jimmy:—"Look
at 'im! Wish I was 'arf has 'ealthy has 'e his—I do." He jerked a short thumb
over his shoulder towards the after end of the ship. "That's the blooming way
to do 'em!" he yelped, with forced heartiness. Jimmy said:—"Don't be a dam'
fool," in a pleasant voice. Knowles, rubbing his shoulder against the doorpost,
remarked shrewdly:—"We can't all go an' be took sick—it would be mutiny."—
"Mutiny—gawn!" jeered Donkin "there's no bloomin' law against bein' sick."—
"There's six weeks' hard for refoosing dooty," argued Knowles, "I mind I once
seed in Cardiff the crew of an overloaded ship—leastways she weren't overloaded, only a fatherly old gentleman with a white beard and an umbreller came
along the quay and talked to the hands. Said as how it was crool hard to be
drownded in winter just for the sake of a few pounds more for the owner—he
said. Nearly cried over them—he did; and he had a square mainsail coat, and
a gaff-topsail hat too—all proper. So they chaps they said they wouldn't go to
be drownded in winter—depending upon that 'ere Plimsoll man to see 'em
through the court. They thought to have a bloomin' lark and two or three days'
spree. And the beak giv' 'em six weeks—coss the ship warn't overloaded.
Anyways they made it out in court that she wasn't. There wasn't one overloaded
ship in Penarth Dock at all. 'Pears that old coon he was only on pay and allowance
from some kind people, under orders to look for overloaded ships, and he
couldn't see no further than the length of his umbreller. Some of us in the
boarding-house, where I live when I'm looking for a ship in Cardiff, stood by
to duck that old weeping spunger in the dock. We kept a good look out, too—
but he topped his boom directly he was outside the court.....Yes. They got
six weeks' hard....."

They listened, full of curiosity, nodding in the pauses their rough pensive
faces. Donkin opened his mouth once or twice, but restrained himself. Jimmy
lay still with open eyes and not at all interested. A seaman emitted the opinion
that after a verdict of atrocious partiality "the bloomin' beaks go an' drink at the
skipper's expense." Others assented. It was clear, of course. Donkin said:—
"Well, six weeks hain't much trouble. You sleep hall night in, reg'lar, in chokey.

Do it hon my 'ead." "You are used to it ainch'ee, Donkin?" asked somebody. Jimmy condescended to laugh. It cheered up every one wonderfully. Knowles, with surprising mental agility, shifted his ground. "If we all went sick what would become of the ship? eh?" He posed the problem and grinned all round.— "Let 'er go to 'ell," sneered Donkin. "Damn 'er. She ain't yourn."—"What? Just let her drift?" insisted Knowles in a tone of unbelief.—"Aye! Drift, an' be blowed," affirmed Donkin with fine recklessness. The other did not see it—meditated.— "The stores would run out," he muttered, "and . . . . never get anywhere . . . . and what about pay-day?" he added with greater assurance.—"Jack likes a good pay-day," exclaimed a listener on the doorstep. "Aye, because then the girls put one arm round his neck an' t'other in his pocket, an' call him ducky. Don't they, Jack?"—"Jack, you're a terror with the gals."—"He takes three of 'em in tow to once, like one of 'em Watkinses two-funnel tugs waddling away with three schooners behind."—"Jack, you're a lame scamp."—"Jack, tell us about that one with a blue eye and a black eye. Do."—"There's plenty of girls with one black eye along the Highway by . . . ."—"No, that's a speshul one—come Jack." Donkin looked severe and disgusted; Jimmy very bored; a grey-haired sea-dog shook his head slightly, smiling at the bowl of his pipe, discreetly amused. Knowles turned about bewildered; stammered first at one, them at another.—"No! . . . . I never! . . . . can't talk sensible sense midst you . . . . . Always on the kid." He retired bashfully—muttering and pleased. They laughed hooting in the crude light, around Jimmy's bed, where on a white pillow his hollowed black face moved to and fro restlessly. A puff of wind came, made the flame of the lamp leap, and outside, high up, the sails fluttered, while near by the block of the foresheet struck a ringing blow on the iron bulwark. A voice far off cried, "Helm up!" another, more faint, answered, "Hard-up, sir!" They became silent— waited expectantly. The grey-haired seaman knocked his pipe on the doorstep and stood up. The ship leaned over gently and the sea seemed to wake up, murmuring drowsily. "Here's a little wind comin'," said some one very low. Jimmy turned over slowly to face the breeze. The voice in the night cried loud and commanding:—"Haul the spanker out." The group before the door vanished out of the light. They could be heard tramping aft while they repeated with varied intonations:—"Spanker out!" . . . . "Out spanker, sir!" Donkin remained alone with Jimmy. There was a silence. Jimmy opened and shut his lips several times as if swallowing draughts of fresher air; Donkin moved the toes of his bare feet and looked at them thoughtfully.

"Ain't you going to give them a hand with the sail?" asked Jimmy.

"No. Hif six ov 'em hain't 'nough beef to set that blamed, rotten spanker, they hain't fit to live," answered Donkin in a bored, far-away voice, as though he had been talking from the bottom of a hole. Jimmy considered the conical, fowl-like profile with a queer kind of interest; he was leaning out of his bunk with the calculating, uncertain expression of a man who reflects how best to lay hold of some strange creature that looks as though it could sting or bite. But he said only:—"The mate will miss you—and there will be ructions."

Donkin got up to go. "I will do for 'im hon some dark night, see hif I don't," he said over his shoulder.

Jimmy went on quickly:—"You're like a poll-parrot, like a screechin' poll-parrot." Donkin stopped and cocked his head attentively on one side. His big ears stood out, transparent and veined, resembling the thin wings of a bat.

"Yuss?" he said, with his back towards Jimmy.

"Yes! Chatter out all you know—like . . . . like a dirty white cockatoo."

Donkin waited. He could hear the other's breathing, long and slow; the breathing of a man with a hundredweight or so on the breast-bone. Then he asked calmly:—"What do I know?"

"What? . . . . What I tell you . . . . not much. What do you want . . . . to talk about my health so . . . ."

"Hit's a blooming himposyshun. A bloomin', stinkin', first-class himposyshun—but hit don't tyke me hin. Not hit."

Jimmy kept still. Donkin put his hands in his pockets, and in one slouching stride came up to the bunk.

"I talk—what's the hodds. They hain't men here—sheep they hare. A driven lot of sheep. I 'old you hup . . . . Vy not? You're well hoff."

"I am . . . . I don't say anything about that . . . . ."

"Well. Let 'em see hit. Let 'em larn what a man can do. I ham a man, I know hall about yer . . . . ." Jimmy threw himself further away on the pillow; the other stretched out his skinny neck, jerked his bird face down at him as though pecking at the eyes. "I ham a man. I've seen the hinside of every chokey in the Colonies rather'n give hup my rights . . . . ."

"You are a jail-prop," said Jimmy weakly.

"I ham . . . . an' proud of it too. You! You 'aven't the bloomin' nerve—so you hinventyd this 'ere dodge . . . . ." He paused; then with marked afterthought accentuated slowly:—"Yer ain't sick—hare yer?"

"No," said Jimmy firmly. "Been out of sorts now and again this year," he mumbled with a sudden drop in his voice.

Donkin closed one eye, amicable and confidential. He whispered:—"Ye 'ave done hit afore—aven'tchee?" Jimmy smiled—then as if unable to hold back he let himself go:—"Last ship—yes. I was out of sorts on the passage. See? It was easy. They paid me off in Calcutta, and the skipper made no bones about it either . . . . . I got my money all right. Laid up fifty-eight days! The fools! O Lord! The fools! Paid right off." He laughed spasmodically. Donkin chummed giggling. Then Jimmy coughed violently. "I am as well as ever," he said, as soon as he could draw breath.

Donkin made a derisive gesture. "In course," he said profoundly, "hany one can see that."—"They don't," said Jimmy, gasping like a fish.—"They would swallow any yarn," affirmed Donkin.—"Don't you let on too much," admonished Jimmy in an exhausted voice.—"Your little gyme? Eh?" commented Donkin jovially. Then with sudden disgust: "Yer hall for yerself, s'long has ye're right . . . . ."

So charged with egoism James Wait pulled the blanket up to his chin and lay still for awhile. His heavy lips protruded in an everlasting black pout. "Why are you so hot on making trouble?" he asked without much interest.

"'Cos hit's a bloomin' shayme. We hare put hon . . . . bad food, bad pay . . . . I want hus to kick up a bloomin' row; a blamed 'owling row that would make 'em remember! Knocking people habout . . . . brain hus . . . . hindeed! Ain't we men?" His altruistic indignation blazed. Then he said calmly:—"I've been a-hairing ov yer clothes."—"All right," said Jimmy languidly, "bring them in."—"Giv' us the key of your chest, I'll put 'em away for yer," said Donkin with friendly eagerness.—"Bring 'em in, I will put them away myself," answered

James Wait with severity. Donkin looked down, muttering..... "What d'you say? What d'you say?" inquired Wait anxiously.—"Nothink. The night's dry? let 'em 'ang out till the morning," said Donkin, in a strangely trembling voice, as though restraining laughter or rage. Jimmy seemed satisfied.—"Give me a little water for the night in my mug—there," he said. Donkin took a stride over the door-step.—"Git it yerself," he replied in a surly tone. "You can do it, hunless you *hare* sick."—"Of course I can do it," said Wait, "only...."—"Well, then, do it," said Donkin viciously, "if yer can look hafter yer clothes, yer can look hafter yerself." He went on deck without a look back.

Jimmy reached out for the mug. Not a drop. He put it back gently with a faint sigh—and closed his eyes. He thought:—That lunatic Belfast will bring me some water if I ask. Fool. I am very thirsty.....It was very hot in the cabin, and it seemed to turn slowly round, detach itself from the ship, and swing out smoothly into a luminous, arid space where a black sun shone, spinning very fast. A place without any water! No water! A policeman with the face of Donkin drank a glass of beer by the side of an empty well, and flew away flapping vigorously. A ship whose mastheads protruded through the sky and could not be seen, was discharging grain, and the wind whirled the dry husks in spirals along the quay of a dock with no water in it. He whirled along with the husks— very tired and light. All his inside was gone. He felt lighter than the husks— and more dry. He expanded his hollow chest. The air streamed in carrying away in its rush a lot of strange things that resembled houses, trees, people, lamp-posts.....No more! There was no more air—and he had not finished drawing his long breath. But he was on gaol! They were locking him up. A door slammed. They turned the key twice, flung a bucket of water over him—Phoo! What for?

He opened his eyes, thinking the fall had been very heavy for an empty man—empty—empty. He was in his cabin. Ah! All right! His face was streaming with perspiration, his arms heavier than lead. He saw the cook standing in the doorway, a brass key in one hand and a bright tin hook-pot in the other.

"I have been locking up for the night," said the cook, beaming benevolently. "Eight-bells just gone. I brought you a pot of cold tea for your night's drinking, Jimmy. I sweetened it with some white cabin sugar, too. Well—it won't break the ship."

He came in, hung the pot on the edge of the bunk, asked perfunctorily, "How goes it?" and sat down on the box.—"H'm," grunted Wait inhospitably. The cook wiped his face with a dirty cotton rag, which, afterwards, he tied round his neck.—"That's how them firemen do in steamboats," he said serenely, and much pleased with himself. "My work is as heavy as theirs—I'm thinking— and longer hours. Did you ever see them down the stokehold? Like fiends they look—firing—firing—firing—down there."

He pointed his forefinger at the deck. Some gloomy thought darkened his shining face, fleeting, like the shadow of a travelling cloud over the light of a peaceful sea. The relieved watch tramped noisily forward, passing in a body across the sheen of the doorway. Some one cried, "Good night!" Belfast stopped for a moment and looked in at Jimmy, quivering and speechless as if with repressed emotion. He gave the cook a glance charged with dismal foreboding, and vanished. The cook cleared his throat. Jimmy stared upwards and kept as still as a man in hiding.

The night was clear, with a gentle breeze. The ship heeled over a little, slipping quietly over a sombre sea towards the inaccessible and festal splendour of a black horizon pierced by points of flickering fire. Above the mastheads the resplendent curve of the Milky Way spanned the sky like a triumphal arch of eternal light, thrown over the dark pathway of the earth. On the forecastle head a man whistled with loud precision a lively jig, while another could be heard faintly, shuffling and stamping in time. There came from forward a confused murmur of voices, laughter—snatches of song. The cook shook his head, glanced obliquely at Jimmy, and began to mutter. "Aye. Dance and sing. That's all they think of. I am surprised the Providence don't get tired . . . . . They forget the day that's sure to come . . . . but you . . . . ."

Jimmy drank a gulp of tea, hurriedly, as though he had stolen it, and shrank under his blanket, edging away towards the bulkhead. The cook got up, closed the door, then sat down again and said distinctly:—

"Whenever I poke my galley fire I think of you chaps—swearing, stealing, lying, and worse—as if there was no such thing as another world. . . . . Not bad fellows, either, in a way," he conceded slowly; then, after a pause of regretful musing, he went on in a resigned tone:—"Well, well. They will have a hot time of it. Hot! Did I say? The furnaces of one of them White Star boats ain't nothing to to."

He kept very quiet for a while. There was a great stir in his brain; an addled vision of bright outlines; an exciting row of rousing songs and groans of pain. He suffered, enjoyed, admired, approved. He was delighted, frightened, exalted—like on that evening (the only time in his life—twenty-seven years ago; he loved to recall the number of years) when as a young man he had—through keeping bad company—become intoxicated in an East-end music-hall. A tide of sudden feeling swept him clean out of his body. He soared. He contemplated the secret of the hereafter. It commended itself to him. It was excellent; he loved it, himself, all hands, and Jimmy. His heart overflowed with tenderness, with comprehension, with the desire to meddle, with anxiety for the soul of that black man, with the pride of possessed eternity, with the feeling of might. Snatch him up in his arms and pitch him right into the middle of salvation. . . . the black soul—blacker—body—rot—Devil. No! Talk—strength—Samson. . . . . There was a great din as of cymbals in his ears; he flashed through an ecstatic jumble of shining faces, lilies, prayer-books, unearthly joy, white shirts, gold harps, black coats, wings. He saw flowing garments, clean shaved faces, a sea of light—a lake of pitch. There were sweet scents, a smell of sulphur—red tongues of flame licking a white mist. An awesome voice thundered! . . . . It lasted three seconds.

"Jimmy!" he cried in an inspired tone. Then he hesitated. A spark of human pity glimmered yet through the infernal fog of his supreme conceit.

"What?" said James Wait, unwillingly. There was a silence. He turned his head just the least bit, and stole a cautious glance. The cook's lips moved inaudibly; his face was rapt, his eyes turned up. He seemed to be mentally imploring deck beams, the brass hook of the lamp, two cockroaches.

"Look here," said Wait, "I want to go to sleep. I think I could."

"This is no time for sleep!" exclaimed the cook, very loud. He had prayerfully divested himself of the last vestige of his humanity. He was a voice—a fleshless and sublime thing, as on that memorable night—the night when he went over the sea to make coffee for perishing sinners. "This is no time for sleeping," he repeated with exaltation. "I can't sleep."

"Don't care damn," said Wait, with factitious energy. "I can. Go an' turn in."

"Swear . . . . in the very jaws! . . . . In the very jaws! Don't you see the fire. . . . don't you feel it? Blind, chockful of sin! I can see it for you. I can't bear it. I hear the call to save you. Night and day. Jimmy let me save you!" The words of entreaty and menace broke out of him in a roaring torrent. The cockroaches ran away. Jimmy perspired, wriggling stealthily under his blanket. The cook yelled. . . . . "Your days are numbered! . . . ."—"Get out of this," boomed Wait, courageously.—"Pray with me! . . . ."—"I won't! . . . ." The little cabin was as hot as an oven. It contained an immensity of fear and pain; an atmosphere of shrieks and moans; prayers vociferated like blasphemies and whispered curses. Outside, the men called by Charley, who informed them in tones of delight that there was a row going on in Jimmy's place, pushed before the closed door, too startled to open it. All hands were there. The watch below had jumped out on deck in their shirts, as after a collision. Men running up, asked:—"What is it?" Others said:—"Listen!" The muffled screaming went on:—"On your knees! On your knees!"—"Shut up!"—"Never! You are delivered into my hands. . . . . Your life has been saved. . . . . . Purpose. . . . . . Mercy. . . . . Repent."—"You are a crazy fool! . . . ."—"Account of you. . . . you. . . . Never sleep in this world, if I . . . ."— "Leave off."—"No! . . . . stokehold. . . . only think! . . . ." Then an impassioned screeching babble where words pattered like hail.—"No!" shouted Jim.—"Yes. You are! . . . . No help. . . . . Everybody says so.'—"You lie!"—"I see you dying this minnyt . . . . before my eyes. . . . as good as dead now."—"Help!" shouted Jimmy, piercingly.—"Not in this valley. . . . . look upwards," howled the other.— "Go away! Murder! Help!" clamoured Jimmy. His voice broke. There were moanings, low mutters, a few sobs.

"What's the matter now?" said a seldom-heard voice.—"Fall back, men! Fall back, there!" repeated Mr. Creighton sternly, pushing through.—"Here's the old man," whispered some.—"The cook's in there, sir," exclaimed several, backing away. The door clattered open; a broad stream of light darted out on wondering faces; a warm whiff of vitiated air passed. The two mates towered head and shoulders above the spare, grey-headed man who stood revealed between them, in shabby clothes, stiff and angular, like a small carved figure, and with a thin, composed face. The cook got up from his knees. Jimmy sat high in the bunk, clasping his drawn-up legs. The tassel of the blue nightcap almost imperceptibly trembled over his knees. They gazed astonished at his long, curved back, while the white corner of one eye gleamed blindly at them. He was afraid to turn his head, he shrank within himself; and there was an aspect astounding and animal-like in the perfection of his expectant immobility. A thing of instinct—the unthinking stillness of a scared brute.

"What are you doing here?" asked Mr. Baker, sharply.—"My duty," said the cook, with ardour—"Your . . . . what?" began the mate. Captain Allistoun touched his arm lightly.—"I know his caper," he said, in a low voice. "Come out of that, Podmore," he ordered, aloud.

The cook wrung his hands, shook his fists above his head, and his arms dropped as if too heavy. For a moment he stood distracted and speechless.— "Never," he stammered, "I . . . . he . . . . I."—"What—do—you—say?" pronounced Captain Allistoun. "Come out at once—or . . . ."—"I am going," said the cook, with a hasty and sombre resignation. He strode over the doorstep firmly—hesitated—made a few steps. They looked at him in silence.—"I make you responsible!" he cried desperately, turning half round. "That man is dying. I make you...."—"You there yet?" called the master in a threatening tone.— "No, sir," he exclaimed hurriedly in a startled voice. The boatswain led him away by the arm; some one laughed; Jimmy lifted his head for a stealthy glance, and in one unexpected leap sprang out of his bunk; Mr. Baker made a clever catch and felt him very limp in his arms; the group at the door grunted with surprise.—"He lies," gasped Wait, "he talked about black devils—he is a devil— a white devil—I am all right." He stiffened himself, and Mr. Baker, experimentally, let him go. He staggered a pace or two; Captain Allistoun watched him with a quiet and penetrating gaze; Belfast ran to his support. He did not appear to be aware of any one near him; he stood silent for a moment, battling singlehanded with a legion of nameless terrors, amidst the eager looks of excited men who watched him far off, utterly alone in the impenetrable solitude of his fear. Heavy breathings stirred the darkness. The sea gurgled through the scuppers as the ship heeled over to a short puff of wind.

"Keep him away from me," said James Wait at last in his fine baritone voice, and leaning with all his weight on Belfast's neck. "I've been better this last week....I am well....I was going back to duty....to-morrow—now if you like—Captain." Belfast hitched his shoulders to keep him upright.

"No," said the master, looking at him fixedly.

Under Jimmy's armpit Belfast's red face moved uneasily. A row of eyes gleaming stared on the edge of light. They pushed one another with elbows, turned their heads, whispered. Wait let his chin fall on his breast and, with lowered eyelids, looked round in a suspicious manner.

"Why not?" cried a voice from the shadows, "the man's all right, sir."

"I am all right," said Wait with eagerness. "Been sick....better....turn-to now." He sighed.—"Howly Mother!" exclaimed Belfast with a heave of the shoulders, "stand up, Jimmy."—"Keep away from me then," said Wait, giving Belfast a petulant push, and reeling fetched against the door-post. His cheek-bones glistened as though they had been varnished. He snatched off his night-cap, wiped his perspiring face with it, flung it on the deck. "I am coming out," he said without stirring.

"No. You don't," said the master curtly. Bare feet shuffled, disapproving voices murmured all round; he went on as if he had not heard:—"You have been skulking nearly all the passage and now you want to come out. You think you are near enough to the pay-table now. Smell the shore, hey?"

"I've been sick....now—better," mumbled Wait glaring in the light.— "You have been shamming sick," retorted Captain Allistoun with severity; "Why...." he hesitated for less than half a second. "Why, anybody can see that. There's nothing the matter with you, but you choose to lie up to please yourself—and now you shall lie-up to please me. Mr. Baker, my orders are that this man is not to be allowed on deck to the end of the passage."

There were exclamations of surprise, triumph, indignation. The dark group of men swung across the light. "What for?" "Told you so...." "Bloomin' shame...."—"We've got to say something habout that," screeched Donkin from the rear.—"Never mind, Jim—we will see you righted," cried several together. An elderly seaman stepped to the front. "D'ye mean to say, sir," he asked ominously, "that a sick chap ain't allowed to get well in this 'ere hooker?" Behind him Donkin whispered excitedly amongst a staring crowd where no one spared him a glance, but Captain Allistoun shook a forefinger at the angry bronzed face of the speaker.—"You—you hold your tongue," he said warningly.—"This isn't the way," clamoured two or three younger men.—"Hare we bloomin' masheens?" inquired Donkin in a piercing tone, and dived under the elbows of the front rank.—"Soon show 'im we ain't boys . . . ."—"The man's a man if he is black."—"We ain't goin' to work this bloomin' ship shorthanded if Snowball's all right . . . ."—"He says he is."—"Well then, strike, boys, strike!"—"That's the bloomin' ticket." Captain Allistoun said sharply to the second mate: "Keep quiet, Mr. Creighton," and stood composed in the tumult, listening with profound attention to mixed growls and screeches, to every exclamation and every curse of the sudden outbreak. Somebody slammed the cabin door to with a kick; the darkness full of menacing mutters leaped with a short clatter over the streak of light, and the men became gesticulating shadows that growled, hissed, laughed excitedly. Mr. Baker whispered:—"Get away from them, sir." The big shape of Mr. Creighton hovered silently about the slight figure of the master.—"We have been hymposed upon all this voyage," said a gruff voice, "but this 'ere fancy takes the cake"—"That man is a shipmate."—"Are we bloomin' kids?"—"The port watch will refuse duty." Charley carried away by his feelings whistled shrilly, then yelped:—"Giv'us our Jimmy!" This seemed to cause a variation in the disturbance. There was a fresh burst of squabbling uproar. A lot of quarrels were set going at once.—"Yes"—"No."—"Never been sick."—"Go for them to once."—"Shut yer mouth, youngster—this is men's work."—"Is it?" muttered Captain Allistoun bitterly. Mr. Baker grunted: "Ough! They're gone silly. They've been simmering for the last month."—"I did notice," said the master.—"They have started a row amongst themselves now," said Mr. Creighton with disdain, "better get aft, sir. We will soothe them."—"Keep your temper, Creighton," said the master. And the three men began to move slowly towards the cabin door.

In the shadows of the fore rigging a dark mass stamped, eddied, advanced, retreated. There were words of reproach, encouragement, unbelief, execration. The elder seamen, bewildered and angry, growled their determination to go through with something or other; but the younger school of advanced thought exposed their and Jimmy's wrongs with confused shouts, arguing amongst themselves. They clustered round that moribund carcass, the fit emblem of their aspirations, and encouraging one another they swayed, they tramped on one spot, shouting that they would not be "put upon." Inside the cabin, Belfast, helping Jimmy into his bunk, twitched all over in his desire not to miss all the row, and with difficulty restrained the tears of his facile emotion. James Wait, flat on his back under the blanket, gasped complaints.—"We will back you up, never fear," assured Belfast, busy about his feet.—"I'll come out tomorrow morning—take my chance—you fellows must—" mumbled Wait, "I come out to-morrow—skipper or no skipper." He lifted one arm with great difficulty, passed the hand over his face; "Don't you let that cook . . . ." he breathed out.— "No, no," said Belfast, turning his back on the bunk, "I will put a head on him if he comes near you."—"I will smash his mug!" exclaimed faintly Wait, enraged and weak; "I don't want to kill a man, but . . . ." He panted fast like a dog after a run in sunshine. Some one just outside the door shouted, "He's as fit as any ov us!" Belfast put his hand on the door-handle.—"Here!" called James Wait hurriedly and in such a clear voice that the other spun round with a start. James Wait, stretched out black and deathlike in the dazzling light, turned his head on the pillow. His eyes stared at Belfast, appealing and impudent. "I am rather weak from lying-up so long," he said distinctly. Belfast nodded. "Getting quite well now," insisted Wait.—"Yes. I noticed you getting better this . . . . last month," said Belfast looking down. "Hallo! What's this!" he shouted and ran out.

He was flattened directly against the side of the house by two men who lurched against him. A lot of disputes seemed to be going on all round. He got clear and saw three indistinct figures standing alone in the fainter darkness under the arched foot of the mainsail, that rose above their heads like a convex wall of a high edifice. Donkin hissed:—"Go for them . . . . it's dark!" The crowd took a short run aft in a body—then there was a check. Donkin, agile and thin, flitted past with his right arm going like a windmill—and then stood still suddenly with his arm pointing rigidly above his head. The hurtling flight of some small heavy object was heard; it passed between the heads of the two mates, bounded heavily along the deck, struck the after hatch with a ponderous and deadened blow. The bulky shape of Mr. Baker grew distinct. "Come to your senses, men!" he cried, advancing at the arrested crowd. "Come back, Mr. Baker!" called the master's quiet voice. He obeyed unwillingly. There was a minute of silence, then a deafening hubbub arose. Above it Archie was heard energetically:—"If ye do oot ageen I wull tell!" There were shouts. "Don't!"—"Drop it!"—"We ain't that kind!" The black cluster of human forms reeled against the bulwark, back again towards the house. Shadowy figures could be seen tottering, falling, leaping up. Ringbolts rang under stumbling feet.—"Drop it!" "Let me!"—"No!"—"Curse you . . . . hah!" Then sounds as of some one's face being slapped; a piece of iron fell on the deck; a short scuffle, and some one's shadowy body scuttled rapidly across the main hatch before the shadow of a kick. A raging voice sobbed out a torrent of filthy language. . . . —"Throwing things—good God!" grunted Mr. Baker in dismay.—"That was meant for me," said the master quietly; "I felt the wind of that thing; what was it—an iron belaying-pin?"—"By Jove!" muttered Mr. Creighton. The confused voices of men talking amidships mingled with the wash of the sea, ascended between the silent and distended sails—seemed to flow away into the night, further than the horizon, higher than the sky. The stars burned steadily over the inclined mastheads. Trails of light lay on the water, broke before the advancing hull, and, after she had passed, trembled for a long time as if in awe of the murmuring sea.

Meantime the helmsman, anxious to know what the row was about, had let go the wheel, and, bent double, ran with long stealthy footsteps to the break of the poop. The *Narcissus*, left to herself, came up gently to the wind without any one being aware of it. She gave a slight roll, and the sleeping sails woke suddenly, coming all together with a mighty flap against the masts, then filled again one after another in a quick succession of loud reports that ran down the lofty spars, till the collapsed mainsail flew out last with a violent jerk. The ship trembled from trucks to keel; the sails kept on rattling like a discharge of musketry; the chain sheets and loose shackles jingled aloft in a thin peal; the gin blocks groaned. It was as if an invisible hand had given the ship an angry shake to recall the men that peopled her decks to the sense of reality, vigilance, and duty.—"Helm up!" cried the master sharply. "Run aft, Mr. Creighton, and see what that fool there is up to."—"Flatten in the head sheets. Stand by the weather fore-braces," growled Mr. Baker. Startled men ran swiftly repeating the orders. The watch below, abandoned all at once by the watch on deck, drifted towards the forecastle in twos and threes, arguing noisily as they went.—"We shall see to-morrow!" cried a loud voice, as if to cover with a menacing hint an inglorious retreat. And then only orders were heard, the falling of heavy coils of rope, the rattling of blocks. Singleton's white head flitted here and there in the night, high above the deck, like the ghost of a bird.—"Going off, sir!" shouted Mr. Creighton from aft.—"Full again."—"All right...."—"Ease off the head sheets. That will do the braces. Coil the ropes," grunted Mr. Baker, bustling about.

Gradually the tramping noises, the confused sound of voices, died out, and the officers, coming together on the poop, discussed the events. Mr. Baker was bewildered and grunted; Mr. Creighton was calmly furious; but Captain Allistoun was composed and thoughtful. He listened to Mr. Baker's growling argumentation, to Creighton's interjected and severe remarks, while looking down on the deck he weighed in his hand the iron belaying-pin—that a moment ago had just missed his head—as if it had been the only tangible fact of the whole transaction. He was one of those commanders who speak little, seem to hear nothing, look at no one—and know everything, hear every whisper, see every fleeting shadow of their ship's life. His two big officers towered above his lean, short figure; they talked over his head; they were dismayed, surprised, and angry, while between them the little quiet man seemed to have found his taciturn serenity in the profound depths of a larger experience. Lights were burning in the forecastle; now and then a loud gust of babbling chatter came from forward, swept over the decks, and became faint, as if the unconscious ship, gliding gently through the great peace of the sea, had left behind and for ever the foolish noise of turbulent mankind. But it was renewed again and again. Gesticulating arms, profiles of heads with open mouths appeared for a moment in the illuminated squares of doorways; black fists darted—withdrew..... "Yes. It was most damnable to have such an unprovoked row sprung on one," assented the master..... A tumult of yells rose in the light, abruptly ceased..... He didn't think there would be any further trouble just then..... A bell was struck aft, another, forward, answered in a deeper tone, and the clamour of ringing metal deeper spread round the ship in a circle of wide vibrations that ebbed away into the immeasurable night of an empty sea..... Didn't he know them! Didn't he! In past years. Better men, too. Real men to stand by one in a tight place. Worse than devils too sometimes—downright, horned devils. Pah! This—nothing. A miss as good as a mile..... The wheel was being relieved in the usual way.—"Full and by," said, very loud, the man going off.—"Full and by," repeated the other, catching hold of the spokes.—"This head wind is my trouble," exclaimed the master, stamping his foot in sudden anger; "head wind! all the rest is nothing." He was calm again in a moment. "Keep them on the move to-night, gentlemen; just to let them feel we've got hold all the time—quietly, you know. Mind you keep your hands off them, Creighton. To-morrow I will talk to them like a Dutch Uncle. A crazy crowd of tinkers! Yes, tinkers! I could count the real sailors amongst them on the fingers of one hand. Nothing will do but a row— if—you—please." He paused. "Did you think I had gone wrong there, Mr. Baker?" He tapped his forehead, laughed short. "When I saw him standing there, three parts dead and so scared—black amongst that gaping lot—no grit to face what's coming to us all—the notion came to me all at once, before I could think. Sorry for him—like you would be for a sick brute. If ever creature was in a mortal funk to die!....I thought I would let him go out in his own way. Kind of impulse. It never came into my head, those fools.....H'm! Stand to it now—of course." He stuck the belaying-pin in his pocket, seemed ashamed of himself, then sharply:—"If you see Podmore at his tricks again tell him I will have him put under the pump. Had to do it once before. The fellow breaks out like that now and then. Good cook tho'." He walked away quickly, came back to the companion. The two mates followed him through the starlight with amazed eyes. He went down three steps, and changing his tone, spoke with his head near the deck:—"I shan't turn in to-night, in case of anything; just call out if....Did you see the eyes of that sick nigger, Mr. Baker? I fancied he begged me for something. What? Past all help. One lone black beggar amongst the lot of us, and he seemed to look through me into the very hell. Fancy, this wretched Podmore! Well, let him die in peace. I am master here after all. Say what I like. Let him be. He might have been half a man once....Keep a good look-out." He disappeared down below, leaving his mates facing one another, and more impressed than if they had seen a stone image shed a miraculous tear of compassion over the incertitudes of life and death.....

In the blue mist spreading from twisted threads that stood upright in the bowls of pipes, the forecastle appeared as vast as a hall. Between the beams a heavy cloud stagnated; and the lamps surrounded by halos burned each at the core of a purple glow in two lifeless flames without rays. Wreaths drifted in denser wisps. Men sprawled about on the deck, sat in negligent poses, or, bending a knee, drooped with one shoulder against a bulkhead. Lips moved, eyes flashed, waving arms made sudden eddies in the smoke. The murmur of voices seemed to pile itself higher and higher as if unable to run out quick enough through the narrow doors. The watch below in their shirts, and striding on long white legs, resembled raving somnambulists; while now and then one of the watch on deck would rush in, looking strangely over-dressed, listen a moment, fling a rapid sentence into the noise and run out again; but a few remained near the door, fascinated, and with one ear turned to the deck.— "Stick together, boys," roared Davis. Belfast tried to make himself heard. Knowles grinned in a slow, dazed way. A short fellow with a thick clipped beard kept on yelling periodically:—"Who's afeard? Who's afeard?" Another one jumped up, excited, with blazing eyes, sent out a string of unattached curses and sat down quietly. Two men discussed familiarly, striking one another's breast in turn, to clinch arguments. Three others, with their heads in a bunch, spoke all together with a confidential air, and at the top of their voices. It was a stormy chaos of speech where intelligible fragments tossing, struck the ear. One could hear:—"In the last ship"—"Who cares? Try it on any one of us if—." "Knock under"—"Not a hand's turn"—"He says he is all right"—"I always thought"— "Never mind....." Donkin, crouching all in a heap against the bowsprit, hunched his shoulder-blades as high as his ears, and hanging a peaked nose, resembled a sick vulture with ruffled plumes. Belfast, straddling his legs, had a face red with yelling, and with arms thrown up, figured a Maltese cross. The two Scandinavians, in a corner, had the dumbfounded and distracted aspect of men gazing at a cataclysm. And, beyond the light, Singleton stood in the smoke, monumental, indistinct, with his head touching the beam; like a statue of heroic size in the gloom of a crypt.

He stepped forward, impassive and big. The noise subsided like a broken wave: but Belfast cried once more with uplifted arms:—"The man is dying I tell ye!" then sat down suddenly on the hatch and took his head between his hands. All looked at Singleton, gazing upwards from the deck, staring out of dark corners, or turning their heads with curious glances. They were expectant and appeased as if that old man, who looked at no one, had possessed the secret of their uneasy indignations and desires, a sharper vision, a clearer knowledge. And indeed standing there amongst them, he had the uninterested appearance of one who had seen multitudes of ships, had listened many times to voices such as theirs, had already seen all that could happen on the wide seas. They heard his voice rumble in his broad chest as though the words had been rolling towards them out of a rugged past. "What do you want to do?" he asked. No one answered. Only Knowles muttered—"Aye, aye," and somebody said low:— "It's a bloomin' shame." He waited, made a contemptuous gesture.—"I have seen rows aboard ship before some of you were born," he said slowly, "for something or nothing; but never for such a thing."—"The man is dying, I tell ye," repeated Belfast woefully, sitting at Singleton's feet.—"And a black fellow, too," went on the old seaman, "I have seen them die like flies." He stopped, thoughtful, as if trying to recollect gruesome things, details of horrors, heca- tombs of niggers. They looked at him fascinated. He was old enough to re- member slavers, bloody mutinies, pirates perhaps; who could tell through what violences and terrors he had lived! What would he say? He said:—"You can't help him; die he must." He made another pause. His moustache and beard stirred. He chewed words, mumbled behind tangled white hairs; incomprehen- sible and exciting, like an oracle behind a veil . . . . . —"Stop ashore—sick.— Instead—bringing all this head wind. Afraid. The sea will have her own.—Die in sight of land. Always so. They know it—long passage—more days, more dollars.—You keep quiet.—What do you want? Can't help him." He seemed to wake up from a dream. "You can't help yourselves," he said austerely, "Skipper's no fool. He has something in his mind. Look out—I say! I know 'em!" With eyes fixed in front he turned his head from right to left, from left to right, as if inspecting a long row of astute skippers.—"He said 'e would brain me!" cried Donkin in a heartrending tone. Singleton peered downwards with puzzled at- tention, as though he couldn't find him.—"Damn you!" he said vaguely, giving it up. He radiated unspeakable wisdom, hard unconcern, the chilling air of resignation. Round him all the listeners felt themselves somehow completely enlightened by their disappointment, and, mute, they lolled about with the careless ease of men who can discern perfectly the irremediable aspect of their existence. He, profound and unconscious, waved his arm once, and strode out on deck without another word.

Belfast was lost in a round-eyed meditation. One or two vaulted heavily into upper berths, and, once there, sighed; others dived head first inside lower bunks—swift, and turning round instantly upon themselves, like animals going into lairs. The grating of a knife scraping burnt clay was heard. Knowles grinned no more. Davies said, in a tone of ardent conviction:—"Then our skipper's looney." Archie muttered:—"My faith! we haven't heard the last of it yet!" Four bells were struck.—"Half our watch below is gone!" cried Knowles in alarm, then reflected. "Well, two hours' sleep is something towards a rest," he observed consolingly. Some already pretended to slumber; and Charley, sound asleep, suddenly said a few slurred words in an arbitrary, blank voice.—"This blamed boy has worrums!" commented Knowles from under a blanket, and in a learned manner. Belfast got up and approached Archie's berth.—"We pulled him out," he whispered sadly.—"What?" said the other, with sleepy discontent.—"And now we will have to chuck him overboard," went on Belfast, whose lower lip trembled.—"Chuck what?" asked Archie.—"Poor Jimmy," breathed out Belfast.—"He be blowed!" said Archie with untruthful brutality, and sat up in his bunk; "It's all through him. If it hadn't been for me, there would have been murder on board this ship!"—"'Tain't his fault, is it?" argued Belfast, in a murmur; "I've put him to bed . . . . an' he ain't no heavier than an empty beef-cask," he added, with tears in his eyes. Archie looked at him steadily, then turned his nose to the ship's side with determination. Belfast wandered about as though he had lost his way in the dim forecastle, and nearly fell over Donkin. He contemplated him from on high for awhile. "Ain't ye going to turn in?" he asked. Donkin looked up hopelessly.—"That black-'earted Scotch son of a thief kicked me!" he whispered from the floor, in a tone of utter desolation.—"And a good job, too!" said Belfast, still very depressed; "You were as near hanging as damn-it to-night, sonny. Don't you play any of your murthering games around my Jimmy! You haven't pulled him out. You just mind! 'Cos if I start to kick you"—he brightened up a bit—"if I start to kick you, it will be Yankee fashion— to break something!" He tapped lightly with his knuckles the top of the bowed head. "You moind, me bhoy!" he concluded, cheerily. Donkin let it pass.—"Will they split on me?" he asked, with pained anxiety.—"Who—split?" hissed Belfast, coming back a step. "I would split your nose this minyt if I hadn't Jimmy to look after! Who d'ye think we are?" Donkin rose and watched Belfast's back lurch through the doorway. On all sides invisible men slept, breathing calmly. He seemed to draw courage and fury from the peace around him. Venomous and thin-faced, he glared from the ample misfit of borrowed clothes as if looking for something he could smash. His heart leaped wildly in his narrow chest. They slept! He wanted to wring necks, gouge eyes, spit on faces. He shook a dirty pair of meagre fists at the smoking lights. "Ye're no men!" he cried, in a deadened tone. No one moved. "Yer 'aven't the pluck of a mouse!" His voice rose to a husky screech. Wamibo darted out a dishevelled head, and looked at him wildly. "Ye're sweepings ov ships! I 'ope you will hall rot before you die!" Wamibo blinked, uncomprehending but interested. Donkin sat down heavily; he blew with force through quivering nostrils, he ground and snapped his teeth, and, with the chin pressed hard against the breast, he seemed busy gnawing his way through it, as if to get at the heart within. . . . .

In the morning the ship, beginning another day of her wandering life, had an aspect of sumptuous freshness, like the spring-time of the earth. The washed decks glistened in a long clear stretch; the oblique sunlight struck the yellow brasses in dazzling splashes, darted over the polished rods in lines of gold, and the single drops of salt water forgotten here and there along the rail were as limpid as drops of dew, and sparkled more than scattered diamonds. The sails slept, hushed by a gentle breeze. The sun, rising lonely and splendid in the blue sky, saw a solitary ship gliding close-hauled on the blue sea.

The men pressed three deep abreast of the mainmast and opposite the cabin-door. They shuffled, pushed, had an irresolute mien and stolid faces. At every slight movement Knowles lurched heavily on his short leg. Donkin glided behind backs, restless and anxious, like a man looking for an ambush. Captain Allistoun came out suddenly. He walked to and fro before the front. He was grey, slight, alert, shabby in the sunshine, and as hard as adamant. He had his right hand in the side-pocket of his jacket, and also something heavy in there that made folds all down that side. One of the seamen cleared his throat ominously.—"I haven't till now found fault with you men," said the master, stopping short. He faced them with his worn, steely gaze, that by an universal illusion looked straight into every individual pair of the twenty pairs of eyes before his face. At his back Mr. Baker, gloomy and bull-necked, grunted low; Mr. Creighton, fresh as paint, had rosy cheeks and a ready, resolute bearing. "And I don't now," continued the master; "but I am here to drive this ship and keep every man-jack aboard of her up to the mark. If you knew your work as well as I do mine, there would be no trouble. You've been braying in the dark about 'See to-morrow morning!' Well, you see me now. What do you want?" He waited, stepping quickly to and fro, giving them searching glances. What did they want? They shifted from foot to foot, they balanced their bodies; some, pushing back their caps, scratched their heads. What did they want? Jimmy was forgotten; no one thought of him, alone forward in his cabin, fighting great shadows, clinging to brazen lies, chuckling painfully over his transparent deceptions. Ne, not Jimmy; he was more forgotten than if he had been dead. They wanted great things. And suddenly all the simple words they knew seemed to be lost for ever in the immensity of their vague and burning desire. They knew what they wanted, but they could not find anything worth saying. They stirred on one spot, swinging, at the end of muscular arms, big tarry hands with crooked fingers. A murmur died out.—"What is it—food?" asked the master, "you know the stores had been spoiled off the Cape."—"We know that, sir," said a bearded shell-back in the front rank.—"Work too hard—eh? Too much for your strength?" he asked again. There was an offended silence.—"We don't want to go short-handed, sir," began at last Davies in a wavering voice, "and this 'ere black—.... "—"Enough!" cried the master. He stood scanning them for a moment, then walking a few steps this way and that began to storm at them coldly, in gusts violent and cutting like the gales of those icy seas that had known his youth.— "Tell you what's the matter? Too big for your boots. Think yourselves damn good men. Know half your work. Do half your duty. Think it too much. If you did ten times as much it wouldn't be enough."—"We did our best by her, sir," cried some one with shaky exasperation.—"Your best," stormed on the master; "You hear a lot on shore, don't you? They don't tell you there your best isn't much to boast of. I tell you—your best is no better than bad. You can do no more? No, I know, and say nothing. But you stop your caper or I will stop it for you. I am ready for you! Stop it!" He shook a finger at the crowd. "As to that man," he raised his voice very much; "as to that man, if he puts his nose out on deck without my leave I will clap him in irons. There!" The cook heard him forward, ran out of the galley lifting his arms, horrified, unbelieving, amazed, and ran in again. There was a moment of profound silence during which a bow-legged seaman, stepping aside, expectorated decorously into the scupper. "There is another thing," said the master calmly. He made a quick stride and with a swing took an iron belaying-pin out of his pocket. "This!" His movement was so unexpected and sudden that the crowd stepped back. He gazed fixedly at their faces, and some at once put on a surprised air as though they had never seen a belaying-pin before. He held it up. "This is my affair. I don't ask you any questions, but you all know it; it has got to go where it came from." His eyes became angry. The crowd stirred uneasily. They looked away from the piece of iron, they appeared shy, they were embarrassed and shocked as though it had been something horrid, scandalous, or indelicate, that in common decency should not have been flourished like this in broad daylight. The master watched them attentively. "Donkin," he called out in a short, sharp tone.

Donkin dodged behind one, then behind another, but they looked over their shoulders and moved aside. The ranks kept on opening before him, closing behind, till at last he appeared alone before the master as though he had come up through the deck. Captain Allistoun moved close to him. They were much of a size, and at short range the master exchanged a deadly glance with the beady eyes. They wavered.—"You know this," asked the master.—"No, I don't," answered the other with cheeky trepidation.—"You are a cur. Take it," ordered the master. Donkin's arms seemed glued to his thighs; he stood, eyes front, as if drawn on parade. "Take it," repeated the master, and stepped closer; they breathed on one another. "Take it," said Captain Allistoun again, making a menacing gesture. Donkin tore away one arm from his side.—"Vy hare yer down hon me?" he mumbled with effort and as if his mouth had been full of dough.—"If you don't...." began the master. Donkin snatched at the pin as though his intention had been to run away with it, and remained stock still holding it like a candle. "Put it back where you took it from," said Captain Allistoun, looking at him fiercely. Donkin stepped back opening wide eyes. "Go, you blackguard, or I will make you," cried the master, driving him slowly backwards by a menacing advance. He dodged, and with the dangerous iron tried to guard his head from a threatening fist. Mr. Baker ceased grunting for a moment.—"Good! By Jove," murmured appreciatively Mr. Creighton in the tone of a connoisseur.—"Don't tech me," snarled Donkin, backing away.— "Then go. Go faster."—"Don't yer 'it me.....I will pull yer hup afore the magistryt.....I'll show yer hup." Captain Allistoun made a long stride, and Donkin, turning his back fairly, ran off a little, then stopped and over his shoulder showed yellow teeth.—"Further on, fore-rigging," urged the master, pointing with his arm.—"Hare yer goin' to stand by and see me bullied," screamed Donkin at the silent crowd that watched him. Captain Allistoun walked at him smartly. He started off again with a leap, dashed at the fore-rigging, rammed the pin into its hole violently. "I will be heven with yer yet," he screamed at the ship at large and vanished beyond the foremast. Captain Allistoun spun round and walked back aft with a composed face, as though he had already forgotten the scene. Men moved out of his way. He looked at no one.—"That will do, Mr. Baker. Send the watch below," he said quietly. "And you men try to walk straight for the future," he added in a calm voice. He looked pensively for a while at the backs of the impressed and retreating crowd. "Breakfast, steward," he called in a tone of relief through the cabin door.—"I didn't like to see you—Ough!—give that pin to that chap, sir," observed Mr. Baker; "he could have bust—Ough!—bust your head like an eggshell with it."—"O! he!" muttered the master absently. "Queer lot," he went on in a low voice. "I suppose it's all right now. Can never tell tho', nowadays, with such a.... Years ago; I was a young master then—one China voyage I had a mutiny; real mutiny, Baker. Different men tho'. I knew what they wanted: they wanted to broach cargo and get at the liquor. Very simple.....We knocked them about for two days, and

when they had enough—gentle as lambs. Good crew. And a smart trip I made."
He glanced aloft at the yards braced sharp up. "Head wind day after day," he
exclaimed bitterly. "Will we never get a decent slant this passage?"—"Ready,
sir," said the steward, appearing before them as if by magic and with a stained
napkin in his hand.—"Ah! All right. Come along, Mr. Baker—it's late—with
all this nonsense."

V

A heavy atmosphere of oppressive quietude pervaded the ship. In the afternoon
men went about washing clothes and hanging them out to dry in the unpros-
perous breeze with the meditative languor of disenchanted philosophers. Very
little was said. The problem of life seemed too voluminous for the narrow limits
of human speech, and by common consent it was abandoned to the great sea
that had from the beginning enfolded it in its immense grip; to the sea that
knew all, and would in time infallibly unveil to each the wisdom hidden in all
the errors, the certitude that lurks in doubts, the realm of safety and peace
beyond the frontiers of sorrow and fear. And in the confused current of impotent
thoughts that set unceasingly this way and that through bodies of men, Jimmy
bobbed up upon the surface, compelling attention, like a black buoy chained to
the bottom of a muddy stream. Falsehood triumphed. It triumphed through
doubt, through stupidity, through pity, through sentimentalism. We set ourselves to bolster it up, from compassion, from recklessness, from a sense of fun.
Jimmy's steadfastness to his untruthful attitude in the face of the inevitable truth
had the proportions of a colossal enigma—of a manifestation grand and incomprehensible that at times inspired a wondering awe; and there was also, to
many, something exquisitely droll in fooling him thus to the top of his bent.
The latent egoism of tenderness to suffering appeared in the developing anxiety
not to see him die. His obstinate non-recognition of the only certitude whose
approach we could watch from day to day was as disquieting as the failure of
some law of nature. He was so utterly wrong about himself that one could not
but suspect him of having access to some source of supernatural knowledge.
He was absurd to the point of inspiration. He was unique, and as fascinating
as only something inhuman could be; he seemed to shout his denials already
from beyond the awful border. He was becoming immaterial like an apparition;
his cheekbones rose, the forehead slanted more; the face was all hollows, patches
of shade; and the fleshless head resembled a disinterred black skull, fitted with
two restless globes of silver in the sockets of eyes. He was demoralising. Through
him we were becoming highly humanised, tender, complex, excessively deca-
dent: we understood the subtlety of his fear, sympathised with all his repulsions,
shrinkings, evasions, delusions—as though we had been over-civilised, and
rotten, and without any knowledge of the meaning of life. We had the air of
being initiated in some infamous mysteries; we had the profound grimaces of
conspirators, exchanged meaning glances, significant short words. We were
inexpressibly vile and very much pleased with ourselves. We lied to him with

gravity, with emotion, with unction, as if performing some moral trick with a
view to an eternal reward. We made a chorus of affirmation to his wildest
assertions, as though he had been a millionaire, a politician, or a reformer—
and we a crowd of ambitious lubbers. When we ventured to question his statements we did it after the manner of obsequious sycophants, to the end that his
glory should be augmented by the flattery of our dissent. He influenced the
moral tone of our world as though he had it in his power to distribute honours,
treasures, or pain; and he could give us nothing but his contempt. It was immense; it seemed to grow gradually larger, as his body day by day shrank a
little more, while we looked. It was the only thing about him—of him—that
gave the impression of durability and vigour. It lived within him with an un-
quenchable life. It spoke through the eternal pout of his black lips; it looked at
us through the profound impertinence of his large eyes, that stood far out of
his head like the eyes of crabs. We watched them intently. Nothing else of him
stirred. He seemed unwilling to move, as if distrustful of his own solidity. The
slightest gesture must have disclosed to him (it could not surely be otherwise)
his bodily weakness, and caused a pang of mental suffering. He was chary of
movements. He lay stretched out, chin on blanket, in a kind of sly, cautious
immobility. Only his eyes roamed over faces: his eyes disdainful, penetrating
and sad.

It was at that time that Belfast's devotion—and also his pugnacity—secured
universal respect. He spent every moment of his spare time in Jimmy's cabin.
He tended him, talked to him; was as gentle as a woman, as tenderly gay as an
old philanthropist, as sentimentally careful of his nigger as a model slave-owner.
But outside he was irritable, explosive as gunpowder, sombre, suspicious, and
never more brutal than when most sorrowful. With him it was a tear and a blow:
a tear for Jimmy, a blow for any one who did not seem to take a scrupulously
orthodox view of Jimmy's case. We talked about nothing else. The two Scandinavians, even, discussed the situation—but it was impossible to know in what
spirit, because they quarrelled in their own language. Belfast suspected one of
them of irreverence, and in this incertitude thought that there was no option
but to fight them both. They became very much terrified by his truculence, and
henceforth lived amongst us, dejected, like a pair of mutes. Wamibo never spoke
intelligibly, but he was as smileless as an animal—seemed to know much less
about it all than the cat—and consequently was safe. Moreover he had belonged
to the chosen band of Jimmy's rescuers, and was above suspicion. Archie was
silent generally, but often spent an hour or so talking to Jimmy quietly with an
air of proprietorship. At any time of the day and often through the night some
man could be seen sitting on Jimmy's box. In the evening, between six and
eight, the cabin was crowded, and there was an interested group at the door.
Every one stared at the nigger.

He basked in the warmth of our interest. His eyes gleamed ironically, and
in a weak voice he reproached us with our cowardice. He would say, "If you
fellows had stuck out for me I would be now on deck." We hung our heads.
"Yes, but if you think I am going to let them put me in irons just to show you
sport. . . . Well, no. . . . It ruins my health, this lying up, it does. You don't care."
We were as abashed as if it had been true. His superb impudence carried all
before it. We would not have dared to revolt. We didn't want to really. We
wanted to keep him alive till home—to the end of the voyage.

Singleton as usual held aloof, appearing to scorn the insignificant events of an ended life. Once only he came along, and unexpectedly stopped in the doorway. He peered at Jimmy in profound silence, as if desirous to add that black image to the crowd of Shades that peopled his old memory. We kept very quiet, and for a long time Singleton stood there as though he had come by appointment to call for some one, or to see some important event. James Wait lay perfectly still, and apparently not aware of the gaze scrutinising him with a steadiness full of expectation. There was a sense of tussle in the air. We felt the inward strain of men watching a wrestling bout. At last Jimmy with perceptible apprehension turned his head on the pillow.—"Good evening," he said in a conciliating tone.—"H'm," answered the old seaman, grumpily. For a moment longer he looked at Jimmy with severe fixity, then suddenly went away. It was a long time before any one spoke in the little cabin, though we all breathed more freely as men do after an escape from some dangerous situation. We all knew the old man's ideas about Jimmy, and nobody dared to combat them. They were unsettling, they caused pain; and, what was worse, they might have been true for all we knew. Only once did he condescend to explain them fully, but the impression was lasting. He said that Jimmy was the cause of head winds. Mortally sick men—he maintained—linger till the first sight of land, and then die; and Jimmy knew that the land would draw his life from him. It is so in every ship. Didn't we know it? He asked us with austere contempt: what did we know? What would we doubt next? Jimmy's desire encouraged by us and aided by Wamibo's (he was a Finn—wasn't he? Very well!) and Wimibo's spells delayed the ship in the open sea. Only lubberly fools couldn't see it. Whoever heard of such a run of calms and head winds? It wasn't natural. . . . We could not deny that it was strange. We felt uneasy. The common saying, "more days, more dollars," did not give the usual comfort because the stores were running short. Much had been spoiled off the Cape, and we were on half allowance of biscuit. Peas, sugar and tea had been finished long ago. Salt meat was giving out. We had plenty of coffee but very little water to make it with. We took up another hole in our belts and went on scraping, polishing, painting the ship from morning to night. And soon she looked as though she had come out of a band-box; but hunger lived on board of her. Not dead starvation, but steady, living hunger that stalked about the decks, slept in the forecastle; the tormentor of waking moments, the disturber of dreams. We looked to windward for signs of change. Every few hours of night and day we put her round with the hope that she would come up on that tack at last! She didn't. She seemed to have forgotten the way home; she rushed to and fro, heading north-west, heading east; she ran backwards and forwards, distracted, like a timid creature at the foot of a wall. Sometimes, as if tired to death, she would wallow languidly for a day in the smooth swell of an unruffled sea. All up the swinging masts the sails trashed furiously through the hot stillness of the calm. We were weary, hungry, thirsty; we commenced to believe Singleton, but with unshaken fidelity dissembled to Jimmy. We spoke to him with jocose allusiveness, like cheerful accomplices in a clever plot; but we looked to the westward over the rail with mournful eyes for a sign of hope, for a sign of fair wind; even if its first breath should bring death to our reluctant Jimmy. In vain! The universe conspired with James Wait. Light airs from the northward sprang up again; the sky remained clear; and round our weariness the glittering sea, touched by the breeze, basked voluptuously in the great sunshine, as though it had forgotten our life and trouble.

Donkin looked out for a fair wind along with the rest. No one knew the venom of his thoughts now. He was silent, and appeared thinner, as if consumed slowly by an inward rage at the injustice of men and of fate. He was ignored by all and spoke to no one, but his hate for every man looked out through his eyes. He talked with the cook only, having somehow persuaded the good man that he—Donkin—was a much calumniated and persecuted person. Together they bewailed the immorality of the ship's company. There could be no greater criminals than we, who by our lies conspired to send the soul of a poor ignorant black man to everlasting perdition. Podmore cooked what there was to cook, remorsefully, and felt all the time that by preparing the food of such sinners he imperilled his own salvation. As to the Captain—he had lived with him for seven years, he said, and would not have believed it possible that such a man.... "Well. Well.... There it is.... Can't get out of it. Judgment capsized all in a minute.... Struck in all his pride.... More like a sudden visitation than anything else." Donkin, perched sullenly on the coal-locker, swung his legs and concurred. He paid in the coin of spurious assent for the privilege to sit in the galley; he was disheartened and scandalised; he agreed with the cook; could find no words severe enough to criticise our conduct; and when in the heat of reprobation he swore at us, Podmore, who would have liked to swear also if it hadn't been for his principles, pretended not to hear. So Donkin, unrebuked, cursed enough for two, cadged for matches, borrowed tobacco, loafed for hours and very much at home before the stove. From there he could hear us on the other side of the bulkhead, talking to Jimmy. The cook knocked the pots about, slammed the oven door, muttered prophesies of damnation for all the ship's company; and Donkin, who did not admit of any hereafter, except for purposes of blasphemy, listened, concentrated and angry, gloating fiercely over a called-up image of infinite torment—like men gloat over the accursed images of cruelty and revenge, of greed, and of power.....

On clear evenings the silent ship, under the cold sheen of the dead moon, took on the false aspect of passionless repose resembling the winter of the earth. Under her a long band of gold barred the black disc of the sea. Footsteps echoed on her quiet decks. The moonlight clung to her like a frosted mist, and the white sails stood out in dazzling cones as of stainless snow. In the magnificence of the phantom rays the ship appeared pure like a vision of ideal beauty, illusive like a tender dream of serene peace. And nothing in her was real, nothing was distinct and solid but the heavy shadows that filled her decks with their unceasing and noiseless stir; the shadows blacker than the night and more restless than the thoughts of men.

Donkin prowled spiteful and alone amongst the shadows, thinking that Jimmy too long delayed to die. That evening, just before dark, land had been reported from aloft, and the master, while adjusting the tubes of the long glass, had observed with quiet bitterness to Mr. Baker that, after fighting our way inch by inch to the Western Islands, there was nothing to expect now but a spell of calm. The sky was clear and the barometer high. The light breeze dropped with the sun, and an enormous stillness, forerunner of a night without wind, descended upon the heated waters of the ocean. As long as daylight lasted, the hands collected on the forecastle-head watched on the eastern sky the island of

Flores, that rose above the level expanse of the sea with irregular and broken outlines like a sombre ruin upon a vast and deserted plain. It was the first land seen for nearly four months. Charley was excited, and in the midst of general indulgence took liberties with his betters. Men strangely elated without knowing why, talked in groups, and pointed with bared arms. For the first time that voyage Jimmy's sham existence seemed for a moment forgotten in the face of a solid reality. We had got so far anyhow. Belfast discoursed, quoting imaginary examples of short homeward passages from the Islands. "Them smart fruit schooners do it in five days," he affirmed. "What do you want?—only a good little breeze." Archie maintained that seven days was the shortest passage, and they disputed amicably with insulting words. Knowles declared he could already smell home from there, and with a heavy list on his short leg laughed fit to split his sides. A group of grizzled sea-dogs looked out for a time in silence and with grim absorbed faces. One said suddenly—"'Tain't far to London now."—"My first night ashore, blamme if I haven't steak and onions for supper . . . . and a pint of bitter," said another.—"A barrel ye mean," shouted some one.—"Ham an' eggs three times a day. That's the way I live!" cried an excited voice. There was a stir, appreciative murmurs; eyes began to shine; jaws champed; short nervous laughs were heard. Archie smiled with reserve all to himself. Singleton came up, gave a negligent glance, and went down again without saying a word, indifferent, like a man who had seen Flores an incalculable number of times. The night travelling from the East blotted out of the limpid sky the purple stain of the high land. "Dead calm," said somebody quietly. The murmur of lively talk suddenly wavered, died out; the clusters broke up; men began to drift away one by one, descending the ladders slowly and with serious faces as if sobered by that reminder of their dependence upon the invisible. And when the big yellow moon ascended gently above the sharp rim of the clear horizon it found the ship wrapped up in a breathless silence; a fearless ship that seemed to sleep profoundly, dreamlessly, on the bosom of the sleeping and terrible sea.

Donkin chafed at the peace—at the ship—at the sea that stretching away on all sides merged into the illimitable silence of all creation. He felt himself pulled up sharp by unrecognised grievances. He had been physically cowed, but his injured dignity remained indomitable, and nothing could heal his lacerated feelings. Here was land already—home very soon—a bad pay-day—no clothes—more hard work. How offensive all this was. Land. The land that draws away life from sick sailors. That nigger there had money—clothes—easy times; and would not die. Land draws life away. . . . He felt tempted to go and see whether it did. Perhaps already. . . . It would be a bit of luck. There was money in the beggar's chest. He stepped briskly out of the shadows into the moonlight, and, instantly, his craving, hungry face from sallow became livid. He opened the door of the cabin and had a shock. Sure enough, Jimmy was dead! He moved no more than a recumbent figure with clasped hands, carved on the lid of a stone coffin. Donkin glared with avidity. Then Jimmy, without stirring, blinked his eyelids, and Donkin had another shock. Those eyes were rather startling. He shut the door behind his back with gentle care, looking intently the while at James Wait as though he had come in there at a great risk to tell some secret of startling importance. Jimmy did not move but glanced languidly out of the corners of his eyes.—"Calm?" he asked.—"Yuss," said Donkin, very disappointed, and sat down on the box.

Jimmy breathed with composure. He was used to such visits at all times of night or day. Men succeeded one another. They spoke in clear voices, pronounced cheerful words, repeated old jokes, listened to him; and each, going out, seemed to leave behind a little of his own vitality, surrender some of his own strength, renew the assurance of life—the indestructible thing! He did not like to be alone in his cabin, because, when he was alone, it seemed to him as if he hadn't been there at all. There was nothing. No pain. Not now. Perfectly right—but he couldn't enjoy his healthful repose unless some one was by to see it. This man would do as well as anybody. Donkin watched him stealthily.— "Soon home now," observed Wait.—"Why d'yer whisper?" asked Donkin with interest, "can't yer speak hup?" Jimmy looked annoyed and said nothing for a while; then in a lifeless unringing voice:—"Why should I shout? You ain't deaf that I know."—"Oh! I can 'ear right 'enough," answered Donkin in a low tone, and looked down. He was thinking sadly of going out when Jimmy spoke again.—"Time we did get home . . . . to get something decent to eat . . . . I am always hungry." Donkin felt angry all of a sudden.—"What habout me," he hissed, "I am 'ungry too an' got ter work. You, 'ungry!"—"Your work won't kill you," commented Wait, feebly; "there's a couple of biscuits in the lower bunk there—you may have one. I can't eat them." Donkin dived in, groped in the corner, and when he came up again his mouth was full. He munched with ardour. Jimmy seemed to doze with open eyes. Donkin finished his hard bread and got up.—"You're not going?" asked Jimmy, staring at the ceiling.—"No," said Donkin impulsively, and instead of going out leaned his back against the closed door. He looked at James Wait, and saw him long, lean, dried up, as though all his flesh had shrivelled on his bones in the heat of a white furnace; the meagre fingers of one hand moved lightly upon the edge of the bunk playing an endless tune. To look at him was irritating and fatiguing; he could last like this for days; he was outrageous—belonging wholly neither to death nor life, and perfectly invulnerable in his apparent ignorance of both. Donkin felt tempted to enlighten him.—"What hare yer thinkin' of?" he asked surlily. James Wait had a grimacing smile that passed over the deathlike impassiveness of his bony face, incredible and frightful as would, in a dream, have been the sudden smile of a corpse.

"There is a girl," whispered Wait. . . . "Canton Street girl—She chucked a third engineer of a Rennie boat—for me. Cooks oysters just as I like. . . . She says—she would chuck—any toff—for a coloured gentleman. . . . That's me. I am kind to wimmen," he added a shade louder.

Donkin could hardly believe his ears. He was scandalised.—"Would she? Yer wouldn't be hany good to 'er," he said with unrestrained disgust. Wait was not there to hear him. He was swaggering up the East India Dock Road; saying kindly, "Come along for a treat," pushing glass swing-doors, posing with superb assurance in the gaslight above a mahogany counter.—"D'yer think yer will hever get ashore?" asked Donkin angrily. Wait came back with a start.—"Ten days," he said promptly, and returned at once to the regions of memory that know nothing of time. He felt untired, calm, and as if safely withdrawn within himself beyond the reach of every grave incertitude. There was something of the immutable quality of eternity in the slow moments of his complete restfulness. He was very quiet and easy amongst his vivid reminiscences which he mistook joyfully for images of an undoubted future. He cared for no one. Donkin felt this vaguely like a blind man may feel in his darkness the fatal antagonism of all the surrounding existences, that to him shall for ever remain irrealisable, unseen and enviable. He had a desire to assert his importance, to break, to crush; to be even with everybody for everything; to tear the veil, unmask, expose, leave no refuge—a perfidious desire of truthfulness! He laughed in a mocking splutter and said:

"Ten days. Strike me blind if I hever! . . . . You will be dead by this time to-morrow p'r'aps. Ten days!" He waited for a while. "D'ye 'ear me? Blamme if yer don't look dead halready."

Jimmy must have been collecting his strength for he said almost aloud— "You're a stinking, cadging liar. Every one knows you." And sitting up, against all probability, startled his visitor horribly. But very soon Donkin recovered himself. He blustered.

"What? What? Who's a liar? You hare—the crowd hare—the skipper— heverybody. I haint! Putting on hairs! Who's yer?" He nearly choked himself with indignation. "Who's yer to put on hairs," he repeated trembling. "'Ave one—'ave one, says 'ee—an' cawn't heat 'em 'isself. Now I'll 'ave both. By Gawd—I will! Yer nobody!"

He plunged into the lower bunk, rooted in there and brought to light another dusty biscuit. He held it up before Jimmy—then took a bite defiantly.

"What now?" he asked with feverish impudence. "Yer may take one—says yer. Why not giv' me both? No. I'm a mangy dorg. One fur a mangy dorg. I'll tyke both. Can yer stop me? Try. Come on. Try."

Jimmy was clasping his legs and hiding his face on the knees. His shirt clung to him. Every rib was visible. His emaciated back was shaken in repeated jerks by the panting catches of his breath.

"Yer won't? Yer can't! What did I say?" went on Donkin fiercely. He swallowed another dry mouthful with a hasty effort. The other's silent helplessness, his weakness, his shrinking attitude exasperated him. "Ye're done!" he cried. "Who's yer to be lied to; to be waited on 'and an' foot like a bloomin' hymperor. Yer nobody. Yer no one at all!" he spluttered with such a strength of unerring conviction that it shook him from head to foot in coming out, and left him vibrating like a released string.

Jimmy rallied again. He lifted his head and turned bravely at Donkin, who saw a strange face, an unknown face, a fantastic and grimacing mask of despair and fury. Its lips moved rapidly; and hollow, moaning, whistling sounds filled the cabin with a vague mutter full of menace, complaint and desolation, like the far-off murmur of a rising wind. Wait shook his head; rolled his eyes; he denied, cursed, menaced—and not a word had the strength to pass beyond the sorrowful pout of those black lips. It was incomprehensible and disturbing; a gibberish of emotions, a frantic dumb show of speech pleading for impossible things, threatening a shadowy vengeance. It sobered Donkin into a scrutinising watchfulness.

"Yer can't holler. See? What did I tell yer?" he said slowly after a moment of attentive examination. The other kept on headlong and unheard, nodding passionately, grinning with grotesque and appalling flashes of big white teeth. Donkin, as if fascinated by the dumb eloquence and anger of that black phantom, approached, stretching his neck out with distrustful curiosity; and it seemed to him suddenly that he was looking only at the shadow of a man crouching high in the bunk on the level with his eyes.—"What? What?" he said. He seemed to

catch the shape of some words in the continuous panting hiss. "Yer will tell
Belfast! Will yer? Hare yer a bloomin' kid?" He trembled with alarm and rage,
"Tell yer gran'mother! Yer afeard! Who's yer ter be afeard more'n hanyone?"
His passionate sense of his own importance ran away with a last remnant of
caution. "Tell an' be damned! Tell, if yer can!" he cried. "I've been treated
worser'n a dorg by your blooming back-lickers. They 'as set me on, honly to
turn aginst me. I ham the honly man 'ere. They clouted me, kicked me—an'
yer laffed—yer black, rotten hincumbrance, you! You will pay fur it. They giv'
yer their grub, their water—yer will pay fur hit to me, by Gawd! Who haxed
me ter 'ave a drink of water? They put their bloomin' rags on yer that night,
an' what did they giv' ter me—a clout on the bloomin' mouth—blast their . . . . S'elp
me! . . . . Yer will pay fur hit with yer money. Hi'm goin' ter 'ave it in a minyte;
has soon has ye're dead, yer bloomin' useless fraud. That's the man I ham. An'
ye're a thing—a bloody thing. Yah—you corpse!"

He flung at Jimmy's head the biscuit he had been all the time clutching
hard, but it only grazed, and striking with a loud crack the bulk-head beyond
burst like a hand-grenade into flying pieces. James Wait, as though wounded
mortally, fell back on the pillow. His lips ceased to move and the rolling eyes
became quiet and stared upwards with an intense and steady persistence. Donkin was surprised; he sat suddenly on the chest, and looked down, exhausted
and gloomy. After a moment he began to mutter to himself, "Die, you beggar—
die. Somebody'll come in. . . . I wish I was drunk. . . . Ten days. . . . Hoysters . . . ."
He looked up and spoke louder. "No. . . . No more for yer . . . . no more bloomin'
gals that cook hoysters. . . . Who's yer? Hit's my turn now. . . . I wish I was drunk;
I would soon giv' you a leg up haloft. That's where yer will go. Feet fust, through
a port. . . . Splash! Never see yer hany more. Hoverboard! Good 'nuff fur yer."

Jimmy's head moved slightly and he turned his eyes to Donkin's face; a
gaze unbelieving, desolated and appealing, of a child frightened by the menace
of being shut up alone in the dark. Donkin observed him from the chest with
hopeful eyes; then without rising he tried the lid. Locked. "I wish I was drunk,"
he muttered and getting up listened anxiously to the distant sound of footsteps
on the deck. They approached—ceased. Some one yawned interminably just
outside the door, and the foot-steps went away shuffling lazily. Donkin's fluttering heart eased its pace, and when he looked towards the bunk again Jimmy
was staring as before at the white beam.—"'Ow d'yer feel now?" he asked.—
"Bad," breathed out Jimmy.

Donkin sat down patient and purposeful. Every half-hour the bells spoke
to one another ringing along the whole length of the ship. Jimmy's respiration
was so rapid that it couldn't be counted, so faint that it couldn't be heard. His
eyes were terrified as though he had been looking at unspeakable horrors; and
by his face one could see that he was thinking of abominable things. Suddenly
with an incredibly strong and heart-breaking voice he sobbed out:

"Overboard! . . . . I! . . . . My God!"

Donkin writhed a little on the box. He looked unwillingly. Jimmy was mute.
His two long bony hands smoothed the blanket upwards, as though he had
wished to gather it all up under his chin. A tear, a big solitary tear, escaped
from the corner of his eye and, without touching the hollow cheek, fell on the
pillow. His throat rattled faintly.

And Donkin, watching the end of that hateful nigger, felt the anguishing grasp of a great sorrow on his heart at the thought that he himself, some day, would have to go through it all—just like this—perhaps! His eyes became moist. "Poor beggar," he murmured. The night seemed to go by in a flash; it seemed to him he could hear the irremediable rush of precious minutes. How long would this blooming affair last? Too long surely. No luck. He could not restrain himself. He got up and approached the bunk. Wait did not stir. Only his eyes appeared alive and his hands continued their smoothing movement with a horrible and tireless industry. Donkin bent over.

"Jimmy," he called low. There was no answer, but the rattle stopped. "D'yer see me?" he asked trembling. Jimmy's chest heaved. Donkin, looking away, bent his ear to Jimmy's lips, and heard a sound like the rustle of a single dry leaf driven along the smooth sand of a beach. It shaped itself.

"Light.... the lamp.... and.... go," breathed out Wait.

Donkin, instinctively, glanced over his shoulder at the blazing flame; then, still looking away, felt under the pillow for a key. He got it at once and for the next few minutes was shakily but swiftly busy about the box. When he got up, his face—for the first time in his life—had a pink flush—perhaps of triumph.

He slipped the key under the pillow again, avoiding to glance at Jimmy, who had not moved. He turned his back squarely from the bunk, and started to the door as though he were going to walk a mile. At his second stride he had his nose against it. He clutched the handle cautiously, but at that moment he received the irresistible impression of something happening behind his back. He spun round as though he had been tapped on the shoulder. He was just in time to see Jimmy's eyes blaze up and go out at once, like two lamps overturned together by a sweeping blow. Something resembling a scarlet thread hung down his chin out of the corner of his lips—and he had ceased to breathe.

Donkin closed the door behind him gently but firmly. Sleeping men, huddled under jackets, made on the lighted deck shapeless dark mounds that had the appearance of neglected graves. Nothing had been done all through the night and he hadn't been missed. He stood motionless and perfectly astounded to find the world outside as he had left it; there was the sea, the ship—sleeping men; and he wondered absurdly at it, as though he had expected to find the men dead, familiar things gone for ever: as though, like a wanderer returning after many years, he had expected to see bewildering changes. He shuddered a little in the penetrating freshness of the air, and hugged himself forlornly. The declining moon drooped sadly in the western board as if withered by the cold touch of a pale dawn. The ship slept. And the immortal sea stretched away, immense and hazy, like the image of life, with a glittering surface and lightless depths; promising, empty, inspiring—terrible. Donkin gave it a defiant glance and slunk off noiselessly as if judged and cast out by the august silence of its might.

Jimmy's death, after all, came as a tremendous surprise. We did not know till then how much faith we had put in his delusions. We had taken his chances of life so much at his own valuation that his death, like the death of an old belief, shook the foundations of our society. A common bond was gone; the strong, effective and respectable bond of a sentimental lie. All that day we mooned at our work, with suspicious looks and a disabused air. In our hearts we thought that in the matter of his departure Jimmy had acted in a perverse and unfriendly manner. He didn't back us up, as a shipmate should. In going he took away with himself the gloomy and solemn shadow in which our folly had posed, with humane satisfaction, as a tender arbiter of fate. And now we saw it was no such thing. It was just common foolishness; a silly and ineffectual meddling with issues of majestic import—that is, if Podmore was right. Perhaps he was? Doubt survived Jimmy; and, like a community of banded criminals disintegrated by a touch of grace, we were profoundly scandalised with each other. Men spoke unkindly to their best chums. Others refused to speak at all. Singleton only was not surprised. "Dead—is he? Of course," he said, pointing at the island right abeam: for the calm still held the ship spell-bound within sight of Flores. Dead—of course. *He* wasn't surprised. Here was the land, and there, on the forehatch and waiting for the sailmaker—there was that corpse. Cause and effect. And for the first time that voyage, the old seaman became quite cheery and garrulous, explaining and illustrating from the stores of experience how, in sickness, the sight of an island (even a very small one) is generally more fatal than the view of a continent. But he couldn't explain why.

Jimmy was to be buried at five, and it was a long day till then—a day of mental disquiet and even of physical disturbance. We took no interest in our work and, very properly, were rebuked for it. This, in our constant state of hungry irritation, was exasperating. Donkin worked with his brow bound in a dirty rag, and looked so ghastly that Mr. Baker was touched with compassion at the sight of this plucky suffering.—"Ough! You, Donkin! Put down your work and go lay-up this watch. You look ill."—"Hi ham, sir—in my ead," he said in a subdued voice, and vanished speedily. This annoyed many, and they thought the mate "bloomin' soft to-day." Captain Allistoun could be seen on the poop watching the sky cloud over from the south-west, and it soon got to be known about the decks that the barometer had begun to fall in the night, and that a breeze might be expected before long. This, by a subtle association of ideas, led to violent quarrelling as to the exact moment of Jimmy's death. Was it before or after "that 'ere glass started down"? It was impossible to know, and it caused much contemptuous growling at one another. All of a sudden there was a great tumult forward. Pacific Knowles and good-tempered Davies had come to blows over it. The watch below interfered with spirit, and for ten minutes there was a noisy scrimmage round the hatch, where, in the balancing shade of the sails, Jimmy's body, wrapped up in a white blanket, was watched over by the sorrowful Belfast, who, in his desolation, disdained the fray. When the noise had ceased, and the passions had calmed into surly silence, he stood up at the head of the swathed body, and lifting both arms on high, cried with pained indignation:—"You ought to be ashamed of yourselves! . . . ." We were.

Belfast took his bereavement very hard. He gave proofs of unextinguishable devotion. It was he, and no other man, who would help the sailmaker to prepare what was left of Jimmy for a solemn surrender to the insatiable sea. He arranged the weights carefully at the feet: two holystones, an old anchor-shackle without its pin, some broken links of a worn-out stream cable. He arranged them this way, then that. "Bless my soul! you aren't afraid he will chafe his heel?" said the sailmaker, who hated the job. He pushed the needle, puffing furiously, with his head in a cloud of tobacco smoke; he turned the flaps over, pulled at the stitches, stretched at the canvas.—"Lift his shoulders. . . . Pull to you a bit. . . . So— o—o. Steady." Belfast obeyed, pulled, lifted, overcome with sorrow, dropping tears on the tarred twine.—"Don't you drag the canvas too taut over his poor face, Sails," he entreated tearfully.—"What are you fashing yourself for? He will be comfortable enough," assured the sailmaker, cutting the thread after the last stitch, that came about the middle of Jimmy's forehead. He rolled up the remaining canvas, put away the needles. "What makes you take on so?" he asked. Belfast looked down at the long package of grey sailcloth.—"I pulled him out," he whispered, "and he did not want to go. If I had sat up with him last night he would have kept alive for me.... but something made me tired." The sailmaker took vigorous draws at his pipe and mumbled:—"When I.... West India Station.... In the *Blanche* frigate.... Yellow Jack.... sewed in twenty men a day.... Portsmouth—Devonport men—townies—knew their fathers, mothers—sisters—the whole boiling of 'em. Thought nothing of it. And these niggers like this one—you don't know where it comes from. Got nobody. No use to nobody. Who will miss him?"—"I do—I pulled him out," mourned Belfast dismally.

On two planks nailed together, and apparently resigned and still under the folds of the Union Jack with a white border, James Wait, carried aft by four men, was deposited slowly, with his feet pointing at an open port. A swell had set in from the westward, and following on the roll of the ship, the red ensign, at half-mast, darted out and collapsed again on the grey sky, like a tongue of flickering fire; Charley tolled the bell; and at every swing to starboard the whole vast semi-circle of steely waters visible on that side seemed to come up with a rush to the edge of the port, as if impatient to get at our Jimmy. Every one was there but Donkin, who was too ill to come; the Captain and Mr. Creighton stood bareheaded on the break of the poop; Mr. Baker, directed by the master, who had said to him gravely:—"You know more about the prayer book than I do," came out of the cabin door quickly and a little embarrassed. All the caps went off. He began to read in a low tone, and with his usual harmlessly menacing utterance, as though he had been for the last time reproving confidentially that dead seaman at his feet. The men listened in scattered groups; they leaned on the fife rail, gazing on the deck; they held their chins in their hands thoughtfully, or, with crossed arms and one knee slightly bent, hung their heads in an attitude of upright meditation. Wamibo dreamed. Mr. Baker read on, grunting reverently at the turn of every page. The words, missing the unsteady hearts of men, rolled out to wander without a home upon the heartless sea; and James Wait, silenced for ever, lay uncritical and passive under the hoarse murmur of despair and hopes.

Two men made ready and waited for those words that send so many of our brothers to their last plunge. Mr. Baker began the passage. "Stand by," muttered the boatswain. Mr. Baker read out: "To the deep," and paused. The men lifted the inboard end of the planks, the boatswain snatched off the Union Jack, and James Wait did not move.—"Higher," muttered the boatswain angrily. All the heads were raised; every man stirred uneasily, but James Wait gave no sign of going. In death and swathed up for all eternity, he yet seemed to hang on to the ship with the grip of an undying fear. "Higher! Lift!" whispered the boatswain fiercely.—"He won't go," stammered one of the men shakily, and both appeared ready to drop everything. Mr. Baker waited, burying his face in the book, and shuffling his feet nervously. All the men looked profoundly disturbed; from their midst a faint humming noise spread out—growing louder..... "Jimmy!" cried Belfast in a wailing tone, and there was a second of shuddering dismay.

"Jimmy, be a man!" he shrieked passionately. Every mouth was wide open, not an eyelid winked. He stared wildly, twitching all over; he bent his body forward like a man peering at an horror. "Go!" he shouted, and leaped off with his arm thrown out. "Go, Jimmy!—Jimmy, go! Go!" His fingers touched the head of the body, and the grey package started reluctantly to, all at once, whizz off the lifted planks with the suddenness of a flash of lightning. The crowd stepped forward like one man; a deep Ah—h—h! came out vibrating from the broad chests. The ship rolled as if relieved of an unfair burden; the sails flapped. Belfast, supported by Archie, gasped hysterically; and Charley, who anxious to see Jimmy's last dive, leaped headlong on the rail, was too late to see anything but the faint circle of a vanishing ripple.

Mr. Baker, perspiring abundantly, read out the last prayer in a deep rumour of excited men and fluttering sails. "Amen!" he said in an unsteady growl, and closed the book.

"Square the yards!" thundered a voice above his head. All hands gave a jump; one or two dropped their caps; Mr. Baker looked up surprised. The master, standing on the break of the poop, pointed to the westward. "Breeze coming," he said, "square the yards. Look alive, men!" Mr. Baker crammed the book hurriedly into his pocket.—"Forward, there—let go the foretack!" he hailed joyfully, bareheaded and brisk; "Square the foreyard, you port-watch!"—"Fair wind—fair wind," muttered the men going to the braces.—"What did I tell you?" mumbled old Singleton, flinging down coil after coil with hasty energy; "I knowed it—he's gone, and here it comes."

It came with the sound of a lofty and powerful sigh. The sails filled, the ship gathered way, and the waking sea began to murmur sleepily of home to the ears of men.

That night, while the ship rushed foaming to the Northward before a fresh-ening gale, the boatswain unbosomed himself to the petty officers' berth:—"The chap was nothing but trouble," he said, "from the moment he came aboard— d'ye remember—that night in Bombay? Been bullying all that softy crowd— cheeked the old man—we had to go fooling all over a half-drowned ship to save him. Dam' nigh a mutiny all for him—and now the mate abused me like a pickpocket for forgetting to dab a lump of grease on them planks. So I did, but you ought to have known better, too, than to leave a nail sticking up—hey, Chips?" "And you ought to have known better than to chuck all my tools overboard for 'im, like a skeary greenhorn," retorted the morose carpenter. "Well—he's gone after 'em now," he added in an unforgiving tone. "On the China Station, I remember once, the Admiral he says to me...." began the sailmaker.

A week afterwards the *Narcissus* entered the chops of the Channel.

Under white wings she skimmed low over the blue sea like a great tired bird speeding to its nest. The clouds raced with her mast-heads; they rose astern enormous and white, soared to the zenith, flew past, and falling down the wide curve of the sky seemed to dash headlong into the sea—the clouds swifter than the ship, more free, but without a home. The coast to welcome her stepped out of space into the sunshine. The lofty headlands trod masterfully into the sea; the wide bays smiled in the light; the shadows of homeless clouds ran along the sunny plains, leaped over valleys, without a check darted up the hills, rolled down the slopes; and the sunshine pursued them with patches of running brightness. On the brows of dark cliffs white lighthouses shone in pillars of light. The Channel glittered like a blue mantle shot with gold and starred by the silver of the capping seas. The *Narcissus* rushed past the headlands and the bays. Outward-bound vessels crossed her track, lying over, and with their masts stripped for a slogging fight with the hard sou'wester. And, inshore, a string of smoking steamboats waddled, hugging the coast, like migrating and amphibious monsters, distrustful of the restless waves.

At night the headlands retreated, the bays advanced into one unbroken line of gloom. The lights of the earth mingled with the lights of heaven; and above the tossing lanterns of a trawling fleet a great lighthouse shone steadily, such as an enormous riding light burning above a vessel of fabulous dimensions. Below its steady glow, the coast, stretching away straight and black, resembled the high side of an indestructible craft riding motionless upon the immortal and unresting sea. The dark land lay alone in the midst of waters, like a mighty ship bestarred with vigilant lights—a ship carrying the burden of millions of lives—a ship freighted with dross and with jewels, with gold and with steel. She towered up immense and strong, guarding priceless traditions and untold suffering, sheltering glorious memories and base forgetfulness, ignoble virtues and splendid transgressions. A great ship! For ages had the ocean battered in vain her enduring sides; she was there when the world was vaster and darker, when the sea was great and mysterious, and ready to surrender the prize of fame to audacious men. A ship mother of fleets and nations! The great flagship of the race; stronger than the storm! and anchored in the open sea.

The *Narcissus*, heeling over to off-shore gusts, rounded the South Foreland, passed through the Downs, and, in tow, entered the river. Shorn of the glory of her white wings, she wound obediently after the tug through the maze of invisible channels. As she passed them the red-painted light-vessels, swung at their moorings, seemed for an instant to sail with great speed in the rush of tide, and the next moment were left hopelessly behind. The big buoys on the tails of banks slipped past her sides very low, and, dropping in her wake, tugged at their chains like fierce watch-dogs. The reach narrowed; from both sides the land approached the ship. She went steadily up the river. On the riverside slopes the houses appeared in groups—seemed to stream down the declivities at a run to see her pass, and, checked by the mud of the foreshore, crowded on the banks. Further on, the tall factory chimneys appeared in insolent bands and watched her go by, like a straggling crowd of slim giants, swaggering and upright under the black plummets of smoke, cavalierly aslant. She swept round the bends; an impure breeze shrieked a welcome between her stripped spars; and the land, closing in, stepped between the ship and the sea.

A low cloud hung before her—a great opalescent and tremulous cloud, that seemed to rise from the steaming brows of millions of men. Long drifts of smoky vapours soiled it with livid trails; it throbbed to the beat of millions of hearts, and from it came an immense and lamentable murmur—the murmur of millions of lips praying, cursing, sighing, jeering—the undying murmur of folly, regret, and hope exhaled by the crowds of the anxious earth. The *Narcissus* entered the cloud; the shadows deepened; on all sides there was the clang of iron, the sound of mighty blows, shrieks, yells. Black barges drifted stealthily on the murky stream. A mad jumble of begrimed walls loomed up vaguely in the smoke, bewildering and mournful, like a vision of disaster. The tugs, panting furiously, backed and filled in the stream, to hold the ship steady at the dock-gates; from her bows two lines went through the air whistling, and struck at the land viciously, like a pair of snakes. A bridge broke in two before her, as if by enchantment; big hydraulic capstans began to turn all by themselves, as though animated by a mysterious and unholy spell. She moved through a narrow lane of water between two low walls of granite, and men with check-ropes in their hands kept pace with her, walking on the broad flagstones. A group waited impatiently on each side of the vanished bridge: rough heavy men in caps; sallow-faced men in high hats; two bareheaded women; ragged children, fascinated, and with wide eyes. A cart coming at a jerky trot pulled up sharply. One of the women screamed at the silent ship—"Hallo, Jack!" without looking at any one in particular, and all hands looked at her from the forecastle head.— "Stand clear! Stand clear of that rope!" cried the dockmen, bending over stone posts. The crowd murmured, stamped where they stood.—"Let go your quarter-checks! Let go!" sang out a ruddy-faced old man on the quay. The ropes splashed heavily falling in the water, and the *Narcissus* entered the dock.

The stony shores ran away right and left in straight lines, enclosing a sombre and rectangular pool. Brick walls rose high above the water—soulless walls, staring through hundreds of windows as troubled and dull as the eyes of over-fed brutes. At their base monstrous iron cranes crouched, with chains hanging from their long necks, balancing cruel-looking hooks over the decks of lifeless ships. A noise of wheels rolling over stones, the thump of heavy things falling, the racket of feverish winches, the grinding of strained chains, floated on the air. Between high buildings the dust of all the continents soared in short flights; and a penetrating smell of perfumes and dirt, of spices and hides, of things costly and of things filthy, pervaded the space, made for it an atmosphere precious and disgusting. The *Narcissus* came gently into her berth; the shadows of soulless walls fell upon her, the dust of all the continents leaped upon her deck, and a swarm of strange men, clambering up her sides, took possession of her in the name of the sordid earth. She had ceased to live.

A toff in a black coat and high hat scrambled with agility, came up to the second mate, shook hands, and said:—"Hallo, Herbert." It was his brother. A lady appeared suddenly. A real lady, in a black dress and with a parasol. She looked extremely elegant in the midst of us, and as strange as if she had fallen there from the sky. Mr. Baker touched his cap to her. It was the master's wife. And very soon the captain, dressed very smartly and in a white shirt, went with her over the side. We didn't recognise him at all till, turning on the quay, he called to Mr. Baker:—"Remember to wind up the chronometers to-morrow morning." An underhand lot of seedy-looking chaps with shifty eyes wandered in and out of the forecastle looking for a job—they said.—"More likely for something to steal," commented Knowles cheerfully. Poor beggars. Who cared? Weren't we home! But Mr. Baker went for one of them who had given him some cheek, and we were delighted. Everything was delightful.—"I've finished aft, sir," called out Mr. Creighton.—"No water in the well, sir," reported for the last time the carpenter, sounding-rod in hand. Mr. Baker glanced along the decks at the expectant groups of men, glanced aloft at the yards.—"Ough! That will do, men," he grunted. The groups broke up. The voyage was ended.

Rolled-up beds went flying over the rail; lashed chests went sliding down the gangway—mighty few of both at that. "The rest is having a cruise off the Cape," explained Knowles enigmatically to a dock-loafer with whom he had struck a sudden friendship. Men ran, calling to one another, hailing utter strangers to "lend a hand with the dunnage," then with sudden decorum approached the mate to shake hands before going ashore.—"Good-bye, sir," they repeated in various tones. Mr. Baker grasped hard palms, grunted in a friendly manner at every one, his eyes twinkled.—"Take care of your money, Knowles. Ough! Soon get a nice wife if you do." The lame man was delighted.—"Good-bye, sir," said Belfast with emotion, wringing the mate's hand, and looked up with swimming eyes. "I thought I would take 'im ashore with me," he went on plaintively. Mr. Baker did not understand, but said kindly:—"Take care of yourself, Craik," and the bereaved Belfast went over the rail mourning and alone.

Mr. Baker in the sudden peace of the ship moved about solitary and grunting, trying door handles, peering into dark places, never done—a model chief mate! No one waited for him ashore. Mother dead; father and two brothers, Yarmouth fishermen, drowned together on the Dogger Bank; sister married and unfriendly. Quite a lady. Married to the leading tailor of a little town, and its leading politician, who did not think his sailor brother-in-law quite respectable enough for him. Quite a lady, quite a lady, he thought, sitting down for a moment's rest on the quarter-hatch. Time enough to go ashore and get a bite, and sup, and a bed somewhere. He didn't like to part with a ship. No one to think about then. The darkness of a misty evening fell, cold and damp, upon the deserted deck; and Mr. Baker sat smoking, thinking of all the successive ships to whom through many long years he had given the best of a seaman's care. And never a command in sight. Not once!—"I haven't somehow the cut of a skipper about me," he meditated placidly, while the shipkeeper (who had taken possession of the galley), a wizened old man with bleared eyes, cursed him in whispers for "hanging about so."—"Now, Creighton," he pursued the unenvious train of thought, "quite a gentleman.... swell friends.... will get on. Fine young fellow....a little more experience." He got up and shook himself. "I'll be back first thing to-morrow morning for the hatches. Don't you let them touch anything before I come, shipkeeper," he called out. Then, at last, he also went ashore—a model chief mate!

The men scattered by the dissolving contact of the land came together once more in the shipping office.—"The *Narcissus* pays off," shouted outside a glazed door a brass-bound old fellow with a crown, and the capitals B. T. on his cap. A lot trooped in at once but many were late. The room was large, white-washed, and bare; a counter surmounted by a brass-wire grating fenced off a third of the dusty space, and behind the grating a pasty-faced clerk, with his hair parted in the middle, had the quick, glittering eyes and the vivacious, jerky movements of a caged bird. Poor Captain Allistoun also in there, and sitting before a little table with piles of gold and notes on it, appeared subdued by his captivity. Another Board of Trade bird was perching on a high stool near the door: an old bird that did not mind the chaff of elated sailors. The crew of the *Narcissus*, broken up into knots, pushed in the corners. They had new shore togs, smart jackets that looked as if they had been shaped with an axe, glossy trousers that seemed made of crumpled sheet-iron, collarless flannel shirts, shiny new boots. They tapped on shoulders, button-holed one another, asked:—"Where did you sleep last night?" whispered gaily, slapped their thighs, stamped, with bursts of subdued laughter. Most had clean radiant faces; only one or two were dishevelled and sad; the two young Norwegians looked tidy, meek, and altogether of a promising material for the kind ladies that patronise the Scandinavian Home. Wamibo, still in his working clothes, dreamed, upright and burly in the middle of the room, and, when Archie came in, woke up for a smile. But the wide-awake clerk called out a name, and the paying-off business began.

One by one they came up to the pay-table to get the wages of their glorious and obscure toil. They swept the money with care into broad palms, rammed it trustfully into trousers' pockets, or, turning their backs on the table, reckoned with difficulty in the hollow of their stiff hands.—"Money right? Sign the release. There—there," repeated the clerk, impatiently. "How stupid those sailors are!" he thought. Singleton came up, venerable—and uncertain as to daylight; brown drops of tobacco juice maculated his white beard; his hands, that never hesitated in the great light of the open sea, could hardly find the small pile of gold in the profound darkness of the shore. "Can't write?" said the clerk, shocked. "Make a mark, then." Singleton painfully sketched in a heavy cross, blotted the page. "What a disgusting old brute," muttered the clerk. Somebody opened the door for him, and the patriarchal seaman passed through unsteadily, without as much as a glance at any of us.

Archie had a pocket-book. He was chaffed. Belfast, who looked wild, as though he had already luffed up through a public-house or two, gave signs of emotion and wanted to speak to the Captain privately. The master was surprised. They spoke through the wires, and we could hear the Captain saying:—"I've given it up to the Board of Trade." "I should 've liked to get something of his," mumbled Belfast. "But you can't, my man. It's given up, locked and sealed, to the Marine Office," expostulated the master; and Belfast stood back, with drooping mouth and troubled eyes. In a pause of the business we heard the master and the clerk talking. We caught "James Wait—deceased—found no papers of any kind—no relations—no trace—the Office must hold his wages then." Donkin entered. He seemed out of breath, was grave, full of business. He went straight to the desk, talked with animation to the clerk, who thought him an intelligent man. They discussed the account, dropping h's against one another as if for a wager—very friendly. Captain Allistoun paid. "I give you a bad discharge," he said, quietly. Donkin raised his voice:—"I don't want your bloomin' discharge—keep it. I'm goin' ter 'ave a job hashore." He turned to us. "No more bloomin' sea fur me," he said, aloud. All looked at him. He had better clothes, had an easy air, appeared more at home than any of us; he stared with assurance, enjoying the effect of his declaration. "Yuss. I 'ave friends well hoff. That's more'n yer got. But I ham a man. Yer shipmates for all that. Who's comin fur a drink?"

No one moved. There was a silence; a silence of blank faces and stony looks. He waited a moment, smiled bitterly, and went to the door. There he faced round once more. "Yer won't? Yer bloomin' lot of yrpocrits. No? What 'ave I done to yer? Did I bully yer? Did I hurt yer? Did I?.... Yer won't drink? ....No!.... Then may yer die of thirst, hevery mother's son of yer! Not one of yer 'as the sperrit of a bug. Ye'rr the scum of the world. Work and starve!"

He went out, and slammed the door with such violence that the old Board of Trade bird nearly fell off his perch.

"He's mad," said Archie. "No! No! He's drunk," insisted Belfast, lurching about, and in a maudlin tone. Captain Allistoun sat smiling thoughtfully at the cleared pay-table.

Outside, on Tower Hill, they blinked, hesitated clumsily, as if blinded by the strange quality of the hazy light, as if discomposed by the view of so many men; and they who could hear one another in the howl of gales seemed deafened and distracted by the dull roar of the busy earth.—"To the Black Horse! To the Black Horse!" cried some. "Let us have a drink together before we part." They crossed the road, clinging to one another. Only Charley and Belfast wandered off alone. As I came up I saw a red-faced, blowsy woman, in a grey shawl, and with dusty, fluffy hair, fall on Charley's neck. It was his mother. She slobbered over him:—"O, my boy! My boy!"—"Leggo of me," said Charley, "Leggo, mother!" I was passing him at the time, and over the untidy head of the blubbering woman he gave me a humorous smile and a glance ironic, courageous, and profound, that seemed to put all my knowledge of life to shame. I nodded and passed on, but heard him say again, good-naturedly:—"If you leggo of me this minyt—ye shall 'ave a bob for a drink out of my pay." In the next few steps I came upon Belfast. He caught my arm with tremulous enthusiasm.—"I couldn't go wi' 'em," he stammered, indicating by a nod our noisy crowd, that drifted slowly along the other sidewalk. "When I think of Jimmy. . . . . Poor Jim! When I think of him I have no heart for drink. You were his chum, too . . . . but I pulled him out . . . . didn't I? Short wool he had. . . . . Yes. And I stole the blooming pie. . . . . He wouldn't go. . . . . He wouldn't go for nobody." He burst into tears. "I never touched him—never—!" he sobbed. "He went for me like . . . . like . . . . a lamb."

I disengaged myself gently. Belfast's crying fits generally ended in a fight with some one, and I wasn't anxious to stand the brunt of his inconsolable sorrow. Moreover, two bulky policemen stood near by, looking at us with a disapproving and incorruptible gaze.—"So long!" I said, and went off.

But at the corner I stopped to take my last look at the crew of the *Narcissus*. They were swaying irresolute and noisy on the broad flagstones before the Mint. They were bound for the Black Horse, where men, in fur caps with brutal faces and in shirt sleeves, dispense out of varnished barrels the illusions of strength, mirth, happiness; the illusion of splendour and poetry of life, to the paid-off crews of southern-going ships. From afar I saw them discoursing, with jovial eyes and clumsy gestures, while the sea of life thundered into their ears ceaseless and unheeded. And swaying about there on the white stones, surrounded by the hurry and clamour of men, they appeared to be creatures of another kind—lost, alone, forgetful, and doomed; they were like castaways, like reckless and joyous castaways, like mad castaways making merry in the storm and upon an insecure ledge of a treacherous rock. The roar of the town resembled the roar of topping breakers, merciless and strong, with a loud voice and cruel purpose; but overhead the clouds broke; a flood of sunshine streamed down the walls of grimy houses. The dark knot of seamen drifted in sunshine. To the left of them the trees in Tower Gardens sighed, the stones of the Tower gleaming, seemed to stir in the play of light, as if remembering suddenly all the great joys and sorrows of the past, the fighting prototypes of these men; press-gangs; mutinous cries; the wailing of women by the riverside, and the shouts of men welcoming victories. The sunshine of heaven fell like a gift of grace on the mud of the earth, on the remembering and mute stones, on greed, selfishness; on the anxious faces of forgetful men. And to the right of the dark group the stained front of the Mint, cleansed by the flood of light, stood out for a moment, dazzling and white, like a marble palace in a fairy tale. The crew of the *Narcissus* drifted out of sight.

I never saw them again. The sea took some, the steamers took others, the graveyards of the earth will account for the rest. Singleton has no doubt taken with him the long record of his faithful work into the peaceful depths of an hospitable sea. And Donkin, who never did a decent day's work in his life, no doubt earns his living by discoursing with filthy eloquence upon the right of labour to live. So be it! Let the earth and the sea each have its own.

A gone shipmate, like any other man, is gone for ever; and I never saw one of them again. But at times the spring-flood of memory sets with force up the dark River of the Nine Bends. Then on the waters of the forlorn stream drifts a ship—a shadowy ship manned by a crew of Shades. They pass and make a sign, in a shadowy hail. Haven't we, together and upon the immortal sea, wrung out a meaning from our sinful lives? Good-bye, brothers! You were a good crowd. As good a crowd as ever fisted with wild cries the beating canvas of a heavy foresail; or tossing aloft, invisible in the night, gave back yell for yell to a westerly gale.

YOUTH

This could have occurred nowhere but in England, where men and sea interpenetrate, so to speak—the sea entering into the life of most men, and the men knowing something or everything about the sea, in the way of amusement, of travel, or of bread-winning.

We were sitting round a mahogany table that reflected the bottle, the claret-glasses, and our faces as we leaned on our elbows. There was a director of companies, an accountant, a lawyer, Marlow, and myself. The director had been a *Conway* boy, the accountant had served four years at sea, the lawyer—a fine crusted Tory, High Churchman, the best of old fellows, the soul of honor—had been chief officer in the P. & O. service in the good old days when mail-boats were square-rigged at least on two masts, and used to come down the China Sea before a fair monsoon with stun'-sails set alow and aloft. We all began life in the merchant service. Between the five of us there was the strong bond of the sea, and also the fellowship of the craft, which no amount of enthusiasm for yachting, cruising, and so on can give, since one is only the amusement of life and the other is life itself.

Marlow (at least I think that is how he spelt his name) told the story, or rather the chronicle, of a voyage:

"Yes, I have seen a little of the Eastern seas; but what I remember best is my first voyage there. You fellows know there are those voyages that seem ordered for the illustration of life, that might stand for a symbol of existence. You fight, work, sweat, nearly kill yourself, sometimes do kill yourself, trying to accomplish something—and you can't. Not from any fault of yours. You simply can do nothing, neither great nor little—not a thing in the world—not even marry an old maid, or get a wretched 600-ton cargo of coal to its port of destination.

"It was altogether a memorable affair. It was my first voyage to the East, and my first voyage as second mate; it was also my skipper's first command. You'll admit it was time. He was sixty if a day; a little man, with a broad, not very straight back, with bowed shoulders and one leg more bandy than the other, he had that queer twisted-about appearance you see so often in men who work in the fields. He had a nut-cracker face—chin and nose trying to come together over a sunken mouth—and it was framed in iron-gray fluffy hair, that looked like a chin strap of cotton-wool sprinkled with coal-dust. And he had blue eyes in that old face of his, which were amazingly like a boy's, with that candid expression some quite common men preserve to the end of their days by a rare internal gift of simplicity of heart and rectitude of soul. What induced him to accept me was a wonder. I had come out of a crack Australian clipper, where I had been third officer, and he seemed to have a prejudice against crack clippers as aristocratic and high-toned. He said to me, 'You know, in this ship you will have to work.' I said I had to work in every ship I had ever been in. 'Ah, but this is different, and you gentlemen out of them big ships; . . . but there! I dare say you will do. Join to-morrow.'

"I joined to-morrow. It was twenty-two years ago; and I was just twenty. How time passes! It was one of the happiest days of my life. Fancy! Second mate for the first time—a really responsible officer! I wouldn't have thrown up my new billet for a fortune. The mate looked me over carefully. He was also an old chap, but of another stamp. He had a Roman nose, a snow-white, long beard, and his name was Mahon, but he insisted that it should be pronounced Mann. He was well connected; yet there was something wrong with his luck, and he had never got on.

"As to the captain, he had been for years in coasters, then in the Mediterranean, and last in the West Indian trade. He had never been round the Capes. He could just write a kind of sketchy hand, and didn't care for writing at all. Both were thorough good seamen of course, and between those two old chaps I felt like a small boy between two grandfathers.

"The ship also was old. Her name was the *Judea*. Queer name, isn't it? She belonged to a man Wilmer, Wilcox—some name like that; but he has been bankrupt and dead these twenty years or more, and his name don't matter. She had been laid up in Shadwell basin for ever so long. You can imagine her state. She was all rust, dust, grime—soot aloft, dirt on deck. To me it was like coming out of a palace into a ruined cottage. She was about 400 tons, had a primitive windlass, wooden latches to the doors, not a bit of brass about her, and a big square stern. There was on it, below her name in big letters, a lot of scroll work, with the gilt off, and some sort of a coat of arms, with the motto 'Do or Die' underneath. I remember it took my fancy immensely. There was a touch of romance in it, something that made me love the old thing—something that appealed to my youth!

"We left London in ballast—sand ballast—to load a cargo of coal in a northern port for Bankok. Bankok! I thrilled. I had been six years at sea, but had only seen Melbourne and Sydney, very good places, charming places in their way—but Bankok!

"We worked out of the Thames under canvas, with a North Sea pilot on board. His name was Jermyn, and he dodged all day long about the galley drying his handkerchief before the stove. Apparently he never slept. He was a dismal man, with a perpetual tear sparkling at the end of his nose, who either had been in trouble, or was in trouble, or expected to be in trouble—couldn't be happy unless something went wrong. He mistrusted my youth, my common-sense, and my seamanship, and made a point of showing it in a hundred little ways. I dare say he was right. It seems to me I knew very little then, and I know not much more now; but I cherish a hate for that Jermyn to this day.

"We were a week working up as far as Yarmouth Roads, and then we got into a gale—the famous October gale of twenty-two years ago. It was wind, lightning, sleet, snow, and a terrific sea. We were flying light, and you may imagine how bad it was when I tell you we had smashed bulwarks and a flooded deck. On the second night she shifted her ballast into the lee bow, and by that time we had been blown off somewhere on the Dogger Bank. There was nothing for it but go below with shovels and try to right her, and there we were in that vast hold, gloomy like a cavern, the tallow dips stuck and flickering on the beams, the gale howling above, the ship tossing about like mad on her side; there we all were, Jermyn, the captain, everyone, hardly able to keep our feet, engaged on that gravedigger's work, and trying to toss shovelfuls of wet sand up to the windward. At every tumble of the ship you could see vaguely in the dim light men falling down with a great flourish of shovels. One of the ship's boys (we had two), impressed by the weirdness of the scene, wept as if his heart would break. We could hear him blubbering somewhere in the shadows.

"On the third day the gale died out, and by-and-by a north-country tug picked us up. We took sixteen days in all to get from London to the Tyne! When we got into dock we had lost our turn for loading, and they hauled us off to a tier where we remained for a month. Mrs. Beard (the captain's name was Beard) came from Colchester to see the old man. She lived on board. The crew of runners had left, and there remained only the officers, one boy, and the steward, a mulatto who answered to the name of Abraham. Mrs. Beard was an old woman, with a face all wrinkled and ruddy like a winter apple, and the figure of a young girl. She caught sight of me once, sewing on a button, and insisted on having my shirts to repair. This was something different from the captains' wives I had known on board crack clippers. When I brought her the shirts, she said: 'And the socks? They want mending, I am sure, and John's—Captain Beard's—things are all in order now. I would be glad of something to do.' Bless the old woman. She overhauled my outfit for me, and meantime I read for the first time 'Sartor Resartus' and Burnaby's 'Ride to Khiva.' I didn't understand much of the first then; but I remember I preferred the soldier to the philosopher at the time; a preference which life has only confirmed. One was a man, and the other was either more—or less. However, they are both dead, and Mrs. Beard is dead, and youth, strength, genius, thoughts, achievements, simple hearts—all die. . . . No matter.

"They loaded us at last. We shipped a crew. Eight able seamen and two boys. We hauled off one evening to the buoys at the dock-gates, ready to go out, and with a fair prospect of beginning the voyage next day. Mrs. Beard was to start for home by a late train. When the ship was fast we went to tea. We sat rather silent through the meal—Mahon, the old couple, and I. I finished first, and slipped away for a smoke, my cabin being in a deck-house just against the poop. It was high water, blowing fresh with a drizzle; the double dock-gates were opened, and the steam colliers were going in and out in the darkness with their lights burning bright, a great plashing of propellers, rattling of winches, and a lot of hailing on the pier-heads. I watched the procession of head-lights gliding high and of green lights gliding low in the night, when suddenly a red gleam flashed at me, vanished, came into view again, and remained. The fore-end of a steamer loomed up close. I shouted down the cabin, 'Come up, quick!' and then heard a startled voice saying afar in the dark, 'Stop her, sir.' A bell jingled. Another voice cried warningly, 'We are going right into that bark, sir.' The answer to this was a gruff 'All right,' and the next thing was a heavy crash as the steamer struck a glancing blow with the bluff of her bow about our fore-rigging. There was a moment of confusion, yelling, and running about. Steam roared. Then somebody was heard saying, 'All clear, sir.' . . . 'Are you all right?' asked the gruff voice. I had jumped forward to see the damage, and hailed back, 'I think so.' 'Easy astern,' said the gruff voice. A bell jingled. 'What steamer is that?' screamed Mahon. By that time she was no more to us than a bulky shadow maneuvering a little way off. They shouted at us some name—a woman's name, Miranda or Melissa—or some such thing. 'This means another month in this beastly hole,' said Mahon to me, as we peered with lamps about the splintered bulwarks and broken braces. 'But where's the captain?'

"We had not heard or seen anything of him all that time. We went aft to look. A doleful voice arose hailing somewhere in the middle of the dock, '*Judea* ahoy!' . . . How the devil did he get there? . . . 'Hallo!' we shouted. 'I am adrift in our boat without oars,' he cried. A belated waterman offered his services, and Mahon struck a bargain with him for half-a-crown to tow our skipper alongside; but it was Mrs. Beard that came up the ladder first. They had been floating about the dock in that mizzly cold rain for nearly an hour. I was never so surprised in my life.

"It appears that when he heard my shout 'Come up,' he understood at once what was the matter, caught up his wife, ran on deck, and across, and down into our boat, which was fast to the ladder. Not bad for a sixty-year-old. Just imagine that old fellow saving heroically in his arms that old woman—the woman of his life. He set her down on a thwart, and was ready to climb back on board when the painter came adrift somehow, and away they went together. Of course in the confusion we did not hear him shouting. He looked abashed. She said cheerfully, 'I suppose it does not matter my losing the train now?' 'No, Jenny—you go below and get warm,' he growled. Then to us: 'A sailor has no business with a wife—I say. There I was, out of the ship. Well, no harm done this time. Let's go and look at what that fool of a steamer smashed.'

"It wasn't much, but it delayed us three weeks. At the end of that time, the captain being engaged with his agents, I carried Mrs. Beard's bag to the railway-station and put her all comfy into a third-class carriage. She lowered the window to say, 'You are a good young man. If you see John—Captain Beard—without his muffler at night, just remind him from me to keep his throat well wrapped up.' 'Certainly, Mrs. Beard,' I said. 'You are a good young man; I noticed how attentive you are to John—to Captain——' The train pulled out suddenly; I took my cap off to the old woman: I never saw her again. . . . Pass the bottle.

"We went to sea next day. When we made that start for Bankok we had been already three months out of London. We had expected to be a fortnight or so—at the outside.

"It was January, and the weather was beautiful—the beautiful sunny winter weather that has more charm than in the summer-time, because it is unexpected, and crisp, and you know it won't, it can't, last long. It's like a windfall, like a godsend, like an unexpected piece of luck.

"It lasted all down the North Sea, all down Channel; and it lasted till we were three hundred miles or so to the westward of the Lizards: then the wind went round to the sou'west and began to pipe up. In two days it blew a gale. The *Judea*, hove to, wallowed on the Atlantic like an old candlebox. It blew day after day; it blew with spite, without interval, without mercy, without rest. The world was nothing but an immensity of great foaming waves rushing at us, under a sky low enough to touch with the hand and dirty like a smoked ceiling. In the stormy space surrounding us there was as much flying spray as air. Day after day and night after night there was nothing round the ship but the howl of the wind, the tumult of the sea, the noise of water pouring over her deck. There was no rest for her and no rest for us. She tossed, she pitched, she stood on her head, she sat on her tail, she rolled, she groaned, and we had to hold on while on deck and cling to our bunks when below, in a constant effort of body, and worry of mind.

"One night Mahon spoke through the small window of my berth. It opened right into my very bed, and I was lying there sleepless, in my boots, feeling as though I had not slept for years, and could not if I tried. He said excitedly—

"'You got the sounding-rod in here, Marlow? I can't get the pumps to suck. By God! it's no child's play.'

"I gave him the sounding-rod and lay down again, trying to think of various things—but I thought only of the pumps. When I came on deck they were still at it, and my watch relieved at the pumps. By the light of the lantern brought on deck to examine the sounding-rod I caught a glimpse of their weary, serious faces. We pumped all the four hours. We pumped all night, all day, all week,—watch and watch. She was working herself loose, and leaked badly—not enough to drown us at once, but enough to kill us with the work at the pumps. And while we pumped the ship was going from us piecemeal: the bulwarks went, the stanchions were torn out, the ventilators smashed, the cabin-door burst in. There was not a dry spot in the ship. She was being gutted bit by bit. The long-boat changed, as if by magic, into matchwood where she stood in her gripes. I had lashed her myself, and was rather proud of my handiwork, which had withstood so long the malice of the sea. And we pumped. And there was no break in the weather. The sea was white like a sheet of foam, like a caldron of boiling milk; there was not a break in the clouds, no—not the size of a man's hand—no, not for so much as ten seconds. There was for us no sky, there were for us no stars, no sun, no universe—nothing but angry clouds and an infuriated sea. We pumped watch and watch, for dear life; and it seemed to last for months, for years, for all eternity, as though we had been dead and gone to a hell for sailors. We forgot the day of the week, the name of the month, what year it was, and whether we had ever been ashore. The sails blew away, she lay broadside on under a weather-cloth, the ocean poured over her, and we did not care. We turned those handles, and had the eyes of idiots. As soon as we had crawled on deck I used to take a round turn with a rope about the men, the pumps, and the mainmast, and we turned, we turned incessantly, with the water to our waists, to our necks, over our heads. It was all one. We had forgotten how it felt to be dry.

"And there was somewhere in me the thought: By Jove! this is the deuce of an adventure—something you read about; and it is my first voyage as second mate— and I am only twenty—and here I am lasting it out as well as any of these men, and keeping my chaps up to the mark. I was pleased. I would not have given up the experience for worlds. I had moments of exultation. Whenever the old dismantled craft pitched heavily with her counter high in the air, she seemed to me to throw up, like an appeal, like a defiance, like a cry to the clouds without mercy, the words written on her stern: 'Judea, London. Do or Die.'

"O youth! The strength of it, the faith of it, the imagination of it! To me she was not an old rattle-trap carting about the world a lot of coal for a freight—to me she was the endeavor, the test, the trial of life. I think of her with pleasure, with affection, with regret—as you would think of someone dead you have loved. I shall never forget her. . . . Pass the bottle.

"One night when tied to the mast, as I explained, we were pumping on, deafened with the wind, and without spirit enough in us to wish ourselves dead, a heavy sea crashed aboard and swept clean over us. As soon as I got my breath I shouted, as in duty bound, 'Keep on, boys!' when suddenly I felt something hard floating on deck strike the calf of my leg. I made a grab at it and missed. It was so dark we could not see each other's faces within a foot—you understand.

"After that thump the ship kept quiet for a while, and the thing, whatever it was, struck my leg again. This time I caught it—and it was a sauce-pan. At first, being stupid with fatigue and thinking of nothing but the pumps, I did not understand what I had in my hand. Suddenly it dawned upon me, and I shouted, 'Boys, the house on deck is gone. Leave this, and let's look for the cook.'

"There was a deck-house forward, which contained the galley, the cook's berth, and the quarters of the crew. As we had expected for days to see it swept away, the hands had been ordered to sleep in the cabin—the only safe place in the ship. The steward, Abraham, however, persisted in clinging to his berth, stupidly, like a mule—from sheer fright I believe, like an animal that won't leave a stable falling in an earthquake. So we went to look for him. It was chancing death, since once out of our lashings we were as exposed as if on a raft. But we went. The house was shattered as if a shell had exploded inside. Most of it had gone overboard—stove, men's quarters, and their property, all was gone; but two posts, holding a portion of the bulkhead to which Abraham's bunk was attached, remained as if by a miracle. We groped in the ruins and came upon this, and there he was, sitting in his bunk, surrounded by foam and wreckage, jabbering cheerfully to himself. He was out of his mind; completely and for ever mad, with this sudden shock coming upon the fag-end of his endurance. We snatched him up, lugged him aft, and pitched him head-first down the cabin companion. You understand there was no time to carry him down with infinite precautions and wait to see how he got on. Those below would pick him up at the bottom of the stairs all right. We were in a hurry to go back to the pumps. That business could not wait. A bad leak is an inhuman thing.

"One would think that the sole purpose of that fiendish gale had been to make a lunatic of that poor devil of a mulatto. It eased before morning, and next day the sky cleared, and as the sea went down the leak took up. When it came to bending a fresh set of sails the crew demanded to put back—and really there was nothing else to do. Boats gone, decks swept clean, cabin gutted, men without a stitch but what they stood in, stores spoiled, ship strained. We put her head for home, and—would you believe it? The wind came east right in our teeth. It blew fresh, it blew continuously. We had to beat up every inch of the way, but she did not leak so badly, the water keeping comparatively smooth. Two hours' pumping in every four is no joke—but it kept her afloat as far as Falmouth.

"The good people there live on casualties of the sea, and no doubt were glad to see us. A hungry crowd of shipwrights sharpened their chisels at the sight of that carcass of a ship. And, by Jove! they had pretty pickings off us before they were done. I fancy the owner was already in a tight place. There were delays. Then it was decided to take part of the cargo out and calk her topsides. This was done, the repairs finished, cargo reshipped; a new crew came on board, and we went out—for Bankok. At the end of a week we were back again. The crew said they weren't going to Bankok—a hundred and fifty days' passage—in a something hooker that wanted pumping eight hours out of the twenty-four; and the nautical papers inserted again the little paragraph: 'Judea. Bark. Tyne to Bankok; coals; put back to Falmouth leaky and with crew refusing duty.'

"There were more delays—more tinkering. The owner came down for a day, and said she was as right as a little fiddle. Poor old Captain Beard looked like the ghost of a Geordie skipper—through the worry and humiliation of it. Remember he was sixty, and it was his first command. Mahon said it was a foolish business, and would end badly. I loved the ship more than ever, and wanted awfully to get to Bankok. To Bankok! Magic name, blessed name. Mesopotamia wasn't a patch on it. Remember I was twenty, and it was my first second mate's billet, and the East was waiting for me.

"We want out and anchored in the outer roads with a fresh crew—the third. She leaked worse than ever. It was as if those confounded shipwrights had actually made a hole in her. This time we did not even go outside. The crew simply refused to man the windlass.

"They towed us back to the inner harbor, and we became a fixture, a feature, an institution of the place. People pointed us out to visitors as 'That 'ere bark that's going to Bankok—has been here six months—put back three times.' On holidays the small boys pulling about in boats would hail, '*Judea*, ahoy!' and if a head showed above the rail shouted, 'Where you bound to?—Bankok?' and jeered. We were only three on board. The poor old skipper mooned in the cabin. Mahon undertook the cooking, and unexpectedly developed all a Frenchman's genius for preparing nice little messes. I looked languidly after the rigging. We became citizens of Falmouth. Every shopkeeper knew us. At the barber's or tobacconist's they asked familiarly, 'Do you think you will ever get to Bankok?' Meantime the owner, the underwriters, and the charterers squabbled amongst themselves in London, and our pay went on. . . . Pass the bottle.

"It was horrid. Morally it was worse than pumping for life. It seemed as though we had been forgotten by the world, belonged to nobody, would get nowhere; it seemed that, as if bewitched, we would have to live for ever and ever in that inner harbor, a derision and a by-word to generations of long-shore loafers and dishonest boatmen. I obtained three months' pay and a five days' leave, and made a rush for London. It took me a day to get there and pretty well another to come back—but three month's pay went all the same. I don't know what I did with it. I went to a music-hall, I believe, lunched, dined, and supped in a swell place in Regent Street, and was back to time, with nothing but a complete set of Byron's works and a new railway rug to show for three months' work. The boatman who pulled me off to the ship said: 'Hallo! I thought you had left the old thing. *She* will never get to Bankok.' 'That's all *you* know about it,' I said scornfully—but I didn't like that prophecy at all.

"Suddenly a man, some kind of agent to somebody, appeared with full powers. He had grog blossoms all over his face, an indomitable energy, and was a jolly soul. We leaped into life again. A hulk came alongside, took our cargo, and then we went into dry dock to get our copper stripped. No wonder she leaked. The poor thing, strained beyond endurance by the gale, had, as if in disgust, spat out all the oakum of her lower seams. She was recalked, new coppered, and made as tight as a bottle. We went back to the hulk and reshipped our cargo.

"Then on a fine moonlight night, all the rats left the ship.

"We had been infested with them. They had destroyed our sails, consumed more stores than the crew, affably shared our beds and our dangers, and now, when the ship was made seaworthy, concluded to clear out. I called Mahon to enjoy the spectacle. Rat after rat appeared on our rail, took a last look over his shoulder, and leaped with a hollow thud into the empty hulk. We tried to count them, but soon lost the tale. Mahon said: 'Well, well! don't talk to me about the intelligence of rats. They ought to have left before, when we had that narrow squeak from foundering. There you have the proof how silly is the superstition about them. They leave a good ship for an old rotten hulk, where there is nothing to eat, too, the fools! . . . I don't believe they know what is safe or what is good for them, any more than you or I.'

"And after some more talk we agreed that the wisdom of rats had been grossly overrated, being in fact no greater than that of men.

"The story of the ship was known, by this, all up the Channel from Land's End to the Forelands, and we could get no crew on the south coast. They sent us one all complete from Liverpool, and we left once more—for Bankok.

"We had fair breezes, smooth water right into the tropics, and the old *Judea* lumbered along in the sunshine. When she went eight knots everything cracked aloft, and we tied our caps to our heads; but mostly she strolled on at the rate of three miles an hour. What could you expect? She was tired—that old ship. Her youth was where mine is—where yours is—you fellows who listen to this yarn; and what friend would throw your years and your weariness in your face? We didn't grumble at her. To us aft, at least, it seemed as though we had been born in her, reared in her, had lived in her for ages, had never known any other ship. I would just as soon have abused the old village church at home for not being a cathedral.

"And for me there was also my youth to make me patient. There was all the East before me, and all life, and the thought that I had been tried in that ship and had come out pretty well. And I thought of men of old who, centuries ago, went that road in ships that sailed no better, to the land of palms, and spices, and yellow sands, and of brown nations ruled by kings more cruel than Nero the Roman and more splendid that Solomon the Jew. The old bark lumbered on, heavy with her age and the burden of her cargo, while I lived the life of youth in ignorance and hope. She lumbered on through an interminable procession of days; and the fresh gilding flashed back at the setting sun, seemed to cry out over the darkening sea the words painted on her stern, '*Judea*, London. Do or Die.'

"Then we entered the Indian Ocean and steered northerly for Java Head. The winds were light. Weeks slipped by. She crawled on, do or die, and people at home began to think of posting us as overdue.

"One Saturday evening, I being off duty, the men asked me to give them an extra bucket of water or so—for washing clothes. As I did not wish to screw on the fresh-water pump so late, I went forward whistling, and with a key in my hand to unlock the forepeak scuttle, intending to serve the water out of a spare tank we kept there.

"The smell down below was as unexpected as it was frightful. One would have thought hundreds of paraffin-lamps had been flaring and smoking in that hole for days. I was glad to get out. The man with me coughed and said, "Funny smell, sir.' I answered negligently, 'It's good for the health, they say,' and walked aft.

"The first thing I did was to put my head down the square of the midship ventilator. As I lifted the lid a visible breath, something like a thin fog, a puff of faint haze, rose from the opening. The ascending air was hot, and had a heavy, sooty, paraffiny smell. I gave one sniff, and put down the lid gently. It was no use choking myself. The cargo was on fire.

"Next day she began to smoke in earnest. You see it was to be expected, for though the coal was of a safe kind, that cargo had been so handled, so broken up with handling, that it looked more like smithy coal than anything else. Then it had been wetted—more than once. It rained all the time we were taking it back from the hulk, and now with this long passage it got heated, and there was another case of spontaneous combustion.

"The captain called us into the cabin. He had a chart spread on the table, and looked unhappy. He said, 'The coast of West Australia is near, but I mean to proceed to our destination. It is the hurricane month too; but we will just keep her head for Bankok, and fight the fire. No more putting back anywhere, if we all get roasted. We will try to stifle this 'ere damned combustion by want of air.'

"We tried. We battened down everything, and still she smoked. The smoke kept coming out through imperceptible crevices; it forced itself through bulkheads and covers; it oozed here and there and everywhere in slender threads, in an invisible film, in an incomprehensible manner. It made its way into the cabin, into the forecastle; it poisoned the sheltered places on the deck, it could be sniffed as high as the mainyard. It was clear that if the smoke came out the air came in. This was disheartening. This combustion refused to be stifled.

"We resolved to try water, and took the hatches off. Enormous volumes of smoke, whitish, yellowish, thick, greasy, misty, choking, ascended as high as the trucks. All hands cleared out aft. Then the poisonous cloud blew away, and we went back to work in a smoke that was no thicker now than that of an ordinary factory chimney.

"We rigged the force pump, got the hose along, and by-and-by it burst. Well, it was as old as the ship—a prehistoric hose, and past repair. Then we pumped with the feeble head-pump, drew water with buckets, and in this way managed in time to pour lots of Indian Ocean into the main hatch. The bright stream flashed in sunshine, fell into a layer of white crawling smoke, and vanished on the black surface of coal. Steam ascended mingling with the smoke. We poured salt water as into a barrel without a bottom. It was our fate to pump in that ship, to pump out of her, to pump into her; and after keeping water out of her to save ourselves from being drowned, we frantically poured water into her to save ourselves from being burnt.

"And she crawled on, do or die, in the serene weather. The sky was a miracle of purity, a miracle of azure. The sea was polished, was blue, was pellucid, was sparkling like a precious stone, extending on all sides, all round to the horizon—as if the whole terrestrial globe had been one jewel, one colossal sapphire, a single gem fashioned into a planet. And on the luster of the great calm waters the *Judea* glided imperceptibly, enveloped in languid and unclean vapors, in a lazy cloud that drifted to leeward, light and slow: a pestiferous cloud defiling the splendor of sea and sky.

"All this time of course we saw no fire. The cargo smoldered at the bottom somewhere. Once Mahon, as we were working side by side, said to me with a queer smile: 'Now, if she only would spring a tidy leak—like that time when we first left the Channel—it would put a stopper on this fire. Wouldn't it?' I remarked irrelevantly, 'Do you remember the rats?'

"We fought the fire and sailed the ship too as carefully as though nothing had been the matter. The steward cooked and attended on us. Of the other twelve men, eight worked while four rested. Everyone took his turn, captain included. There was equality, and if not exactly fraternity, then a deal of good feeling. Sometimes a man, as he dashed a bucketful of water down the hatchway, would yell out, 'Hurrah for Bankok!' and the rest laughed. But generally we were taciturn and serious—and thirsty. Oh! how thirsty! And we had to be careful with the water. Strict allowance. The ship smoked, the sun blazed. . . . Pass the bottle.

"We tried everything. We even made an attempt to dig down to the fire. No good, of course. No man could remain more than a minute below. Mahon, who went first, fainted there, and the man who went to fetch him out did likewise. We lugged them out on deck. Then I leaped down to show how easily it could be done. They had learned wisdom by that time, and contented themselves by fishing for me with a chain-hook tied to a broom-handle, I believe. I did not offer to go and fetch up my shovel, which was left down below.

"Things began to look bad. We put the long-boat into the water. The second boat was ready to swing out. We had also another, a fourteen-foot thing, on davits aft, where it was quite safe.

"Then behold, the smoke suddenly decreased. We redoubled our efforts to flood the bottom of the ship. In two days there was no smoke at all. Everybody was on the broad grin. This was on a Friday. On Saturday no work, but sailing the ship of course was done. The men washed their clothes and their faces for the first time in a fortnight, and had a special dinner given them. They spoke of spontaneous combustion with contempt, and implied *they* were the boys to put out combustions. Somehow we all felt as though we each had inherited a large fortune. But a beastly smell of burning hung about the ship. Captain Beard had hollow eyes and sunken cheeks. I had never noticed so much before how twisted and bowed he was. He and Mahon prowled soberly about hatches and ventilators, sniffing. It struck me suddenly poor Mahon was a very, very old chap. As to me, I was as pleased and proud as though I had helped to win a great naval battle. O! Youth!

"The night was fine. In the morning a homeward-bound ship passed us hull down,—the first we had seen for months; but we were nearing the land at last, Java Head being about 190 miles off, and nearly due north.

"Next day it was my watch on deck from eight to twelve. At breakfast the captain observed, 'It's wonderful how that smell hangs about the cabin.' About ten, the mate being on the poop, I stepped down on the maindeck for a moment. The carpenter's bench stood abaft the mainmast: I leaned against it sucking at my pipe, and the carpenter, a young chap, came to talk to me. He remarked, 'I think we have done very well, haven't we?' and then I perceived with annoyance the fool was trying to tilt the bench. I said curtly, 'Don't, Chips,' and immediately became aware of a queer sensation, of an absurd delusion,—I seemed somehow to be in the air. I heard all round me like a pent-up breath released—as if a thousand giants simultaneously had said Phoo!—and felt a dull concussion which made my ribs ache suddenly. No doubt about it—I was in the air, and my body was describing a short parabola. But short as it was, I had the time to think several thoughts in, as far as I can remember, the following order: 'This can't be the carpenter—What is it?—Some accident—Submarine volcano?—Coals, gas!—By Jove! we are being blown up—Everybody's dead—I am falling into the afterhatch—I see fire in it.'

"The coal-dust suspended in the air of the hold had glowed dull-red at the moment of the explosion. In the twinkling of an eye, in an infinitesimal fraction of a second since the first tilt of the bench, I was sprawling full length on the cargo. I picked myself up and scrambled out. It was quick like a rebound. The deck was a wilderness of smashed timber, lying crosswise like trees in a wood after a hurricane; an immense curtain of soiled rags waved gently before me—it was the mainsail blown to strips. I thought, The masts will be toppling over directly; and to get out of the way bolted on all-fours towards the poop-ladder. The first person I saw was Mahon, with eyes like saucers, his mouth open, and the long white hair standing straight on end round his head like a silver halo. He was just about to go down when the sight of the main-deck stirring, heaving up, and changing into splinters before his eyes, petrified him on the top step. I stared at him in unbelief, and he stared at me with a queer kind of shocked curiosity. I did not know that I had no hair, no eyebrows, no eyelashes, that my young mustache was burnt off, that my face was black, one cheek laid open, my nose cut, and my chin bleeding. I had lost my cap, one of my slippers, and my shirt was torn to rags. Of all this I was not aware. I was amazed to see the ship still afloat, the poop-deck whole—and, most of all, to see anybody alive. Also the peace of the sky and the serenity of the sea were distinctly surprising. I suppose I expected to see them convulsed with horror. . . . Pass the bottle.

"There was a voice hailing the ship from somewhere—in the air, in the sky—I couldn't tell. Presently I saw the captain—and he was mad. He asked me eagerly, 'Where's the cabin-table?' and to hear such a question was a frightful shock. I had just been blown up, you understand, and vibrated with that experience,—I wasn't quite sure whether I was alive. Mahon began to stamp with both feet and yelled at him, 'Good God! don't you see the deck's blown out of her?' I found my voice, and stammered out as if conscious of some gross neglect of duty, 'I don't know where the cabin-table is.' It was like an absurd dream.

"Do you know what he wanted next? Well, he wanted to trim the yards. Very placidly, and as if lost in thought, he insisted on having the foreyard squared. 'I don't know if there's anybody alive,' said Mahon, almost tearfully, 'Surely,' he said, gently, 'there will be enough left to square the foreyard.'

"The old chap, it seems, was in his own berth, winding up the chronometers, when the shock sent him spinning. Immediately it occurred to him—as he said afterwards—that the ship had struck something, and he ran out into the cabin. There, he saw, the cabin-table had vanished somewhere. The deck being blown up, it had fallen down into the lazarette of course. Where we had our breakfast that morning he saw only a great hole in the floor. This appeared to him so awfully mysterious, and impressed him so immensely, that what he saw and heard after he got on deck were mere trifles in comparison. And, mark, he noticed directly the wheel deserted and his bark off her course—and his only thought was to get that miserable, stripped, undecked, smoldering shell of a ship back again with her head pointing at her port of destination. Bankok! That's what he was after. I tell you this quiet, bowed, bandy-legged, almost deformed little man was immense in the singleness of his idea and in his placid ignorance of our agitation. He motioned us forward with a commanding gesture, and went to take the wheel himself.

"Yes; that was the first thing we did—trim the yards of that wreck! No one was killed, or even disabled, but everyone was more or less hurt. You should have seen them! Some were in rags, with black faces, like coal-heavers, like sweeps, and had bullet heads that seemed closely cropped, but were in fact singed to the skin. Others, of the watch below, awakened by being shot out from their collapsing bunks, shivered incessantly, and kept on groaning even as we went about our work. But they all worked. That crew of Liverpool hard cases had in them the right stuff. It's my experience they always have. It is the sea that gives it—the vastness, the loneliness surrounding their dark stolid souls. Ah! Well! we stumbled, we crept, we fell, we barked our shins on the wreckage, we hauled. The masts stood, but we did not know how much they might be charred down below. It was nearly calm, but a long swell ran from the west and made her roll. They might go at any moment. We looked at them with apprehension. One could not foresee which way they would fall.

"Then we retreated aft and looked about us. The deck was a tangle of planks on edge, of planks on end, of splinters, of ruined woodwork. The masts rose from that chaos like big trees above a matted undergrowth. The interstices of that mass of wreckage were full of something whitish, sluggish, stirring—of something that was like a greasy fog. The smoke of the invisible fire was coming up again, was trailing, like a poisonous thick mist in some valley choked with dead wood. Already lazy wisps were beginning to curl upwards amongst the mass of splinters. Here and there a piece of timber, stuck upright, resembled a post. Half of a fife-rail had been shot through the foresail, and the sky made a patch of glorious blue in the ignobly soiled canvas. A portion of several boards holding together had fallen across the rail, and one end protruded overboard, like a gangway leading upon nothing, like a gangway leading over the deep sea, leading to death—as if inviting us to walk the plank at once and be done with our ridiculous troubles. And still the air, the sky—a ghost, something invisible was hailing the ship.

"Someone had the sense to look over, and there was the helmsman, who had impulsively jumped overboard, anxious to come back. He yelled and swam lustily like a merman, keeping up with the ship. We threw him a rope, and presently he stood amongst us streaming with water and very crest-fallen. The captain had surrendered the wheel, and apart, elbow on rail and chin in hand, gazed at the sea wistfully. We asked ourselves, What next? I thought, Now, this is something like. This is great. I wonder what will happen. O youth!

"Suddenly Mahon sighted a steamer far astern. Captain Beard said, 'We may do something with her yet.' We hoisted two flags, which said in the international language of the sea, 'On fire. Want immediate assistance.' The steamer grew bigger rapidly, and by-and-by spoke with two flags on her foremast, 'I am coming to your assistance.'

"In half an hour she was abreast, to windward, within hail, and rolling slightly, with her engines stopped. We lost our composure, and yelled all together with excitement, 'We've been blown up.' A man in a white helmet, on the bridge, cried, 'Yes! All right! all right!' and he nodded his head, and smiled, and made soothing motions with his hand as though at a lot of frightened children. One of the boats dropped in the water, and walked towards us upon the sea with her long oars. Four Calashes pulled a swinging stroke. This was my first sight of Malay seamen. I've known them since, but what struck me then was their unconcern: they came alongside, and even the bowman standing up and holding to our main-chains with the boat-hook did not deign to lift his head for a glance. I thought people who had been blown up deserved more attention.

"A little man, dry like a chip and agile like a monkey, clambered up. It was the mate of the steamer. He gave one look, and cried, 'O boys—you had better quit.'

"We were silent. He talked apart with the captain for a time,—seemed to argue with him. Then they went away together to the steamer.

"When our skipper came back we learned that the steamer was the *Sommerville*, Captain Nash, from West Australia to Singapore *viâ* Batavia with mails, and that the agreement was she should tow us to Anjer or Batavia, if possible, where we could extinguish the fire by scuttling, and then proceed on our voyage—to Bankok! The old man seemed excited. 'We will do it yet,' he said to Mahon, fiercely. He shook his fist at the sky. Nobody else said a word.

"At noon the steamer began to tow. She went ahead slim and high, and what was left of the *Judea* followed at the end of seventy fathom of tow-rope,—followed her swiftly like a cloud of smoke with mastheads protruding above. We went aloft to furl the sails. We coughed on the yards, and were careful about the bunts. Do you see the lot of us there, putting a neat furl on the sails of that ship doomed to arrive nowhere? There was not a man who didn't think that at any moment the masts would topple over. From aloft we could not see the ship for smoke, and they worked carefully, passing the gaskets with even turns. 'Harbor furl—aloft there!' cried Mahon from below.

"You understand this? I don't think one of those chaps expected to get down in the usual way. When we did I heard them saying to each other, 'Well, I thought we would come down overboard, in a lump—sticks and all—blame me if I didn't.' 'That's what I was thinking to myself,' would answer wearily another battered and bandaged scarecrow. And, mind, these were men without the drilled-in habit of obedience. To an onlooker they would be a lot of profane scallywags without a redeeming point. What made them do it—what made them obey me when I, thinking consciously how fine it was, made them drop the bunt of the foresail twice to try and do it better? What? They had no professional reputation—no examples, no praise. It wasn't a sense of duty; they all knew well enough how to shirk, and laze, and dodge—when they had a mind to it—and mostly they had. Was it the two pounds ten a month that sent them there? They didn't think their pay half good enough. No; it was something in them, something inborn and subtle and everlasting. I don't say positively that the crew of a French or German merchant-man wouldn't have done it, but I doubt whether it would have been done in the same way. There was a completeness in it, something solid like a principle, and masterful like an instinct—a disclosure of something secret—of that hidden something, that gift, of good or evil that makes racial difference, that shapes the fate of nations.

"It was that night at ten that, for the first time since we had been fighting it, we saw the fire. The speed of the towing had fanned the smoldering destruction. A blue gleam appeared forward, shining below the wreck of the deck. It wavered in patches, it seemed to stir and creep like the light of a glowworm. I saw it first, and told Mahon. 'Then the game's up,' he said. 'We had better stop this towing, or she will burst out suddenly fore and aft before we can clear out.' We set up a yell; rang bells to attract their attention; they towed on. At last Mahon and I had to crawl forward and cut the rope with an ax. There was no time to cast off the lashings. Red tongues could be seen licking the wilderness of splinters under our feet as we made our way back to the poop.

"Of course they very soon found out in the steamer that the rope was gone. She gave a loud blast of her whistle, her lights were seen sweeping in a wide circle, she came up ranging close alongside, and stopped. We were all in a tight group on the poop looking at her. Every man had saved a little bundle or a bag. Suddenly a conical flame with a twisted top shot up forward and threw upon the black sea a circle of light, with the two vessels side by side and heaving gently in its center. Captain Beard had been sitting on the gratings still and mute for hours, but now he rose slowly and advanced in front of us, to the mizzen-shrouds. Captain Nash hailed: 'Come along! Look sharp. I have mail-bags on board. I will take you and your boats to Singapore.'

"'Thank you! No!' said our skipper. 'We must see the last of the ship.'

"'I can't stand by any longer,' shouted the other. 'Mails—you know.'

"'Ay! ay! We are all right.'

"'Very well! I'll report you in Singapore. . . . Good-by!'

"He waved his hand. Our men dropped their bundles quietly. The steamer moved ahead, and passing out of the circle of light, vanished at once from our sight, dazzled by the fire which burned fiercely. And then I knew that I would see the East first as commander of a small boat. I thought it fine; and the fidelity to the old ship was fine. We should see the last of her. Oh the glamour of youth! Oh the fire of it, more dazzling than the flames of the burning ship, throwing a magic light on the wide earth, leaping audaciously to the sky, presently to be quenched by time, more cruel, more pitiless, more bitter than the sea—and like the flames of the burning ship surrounded by an impenetrable night.

.   .   .   .   .

"The old man warned us in his gentle and inflexible way that it was part of our duty to save for the underwriters as much as we could of the ship's gear. According we went to work aft, while she blazed forward to give us plenty of light. We lugged out a lot of rubbish. What didn't we save? An old barometer fixed with an absurd quantity of screws nearly cost me my life: a sudden rush of smoke came upon me, and I just got away in time. There were various stores, bolts of canvas, coils of rope; the poop looked like a marine bazaar, and the boats were lumbered to the gunwales. One would have thought the old man wanted to take as much as he could of his first command with him. He was very, very quiet, but off his balance evidently. Would you believe it? He wanted to take a length of old stream-cable and a kedge-anchor with him in the long-boat. We said, 'Ay, ay, sir,' deferentially, and on the quiet let the thing slip overboard. The heavy medicine-chest went that way, two bags of green coffee, tins of paint—fancy, paint!—a whole lot of things. Then I was ordered with two hands into the boats to make a stowage and get them ready against the time it would be proper for us to leave the ship.

"We put everything straight, stepped the long-boat's mast for our skipper, who was in charge of her, and I was not sorry to sit down for a moment. My face felt raw, every limb ached as if broken, I was aware of all my ribs, and would have sworn to a twist in the backbone. The boats, fast astern, lay in a deep shadow, and all around I could see the circle of the sea lighted by the fire. A gigantic flame arose forward straight and clear. It flared fierce, with noises like the whir of wings, with rumbles as of thunder. There were cracks, detonations, and from the cone of flame the sparks flew upwards, as man is born to trouble, to leaky ships, and to ships that burn.

"What bothered me was that the ship, lying broadside to the swell and to such wind as there was—a mere breath—the boats would not keep astern where they were safe, but persisted, in a pig-headed way boats have, in getting under the counter and then swinging alongside. They were knocking about dangerously and coming near the flame, while the ship rolled on them, and, of course, there was always the danger of the masts going over the side at any moment. I and my two boat-keepers kept them off as best we could with oars and boat-hooks; but to be constantly at it became exasperating, since there was no reason why we should not leave at once. We could not see those on board, nor could we imagine what caused the delay. The boat-keepers were swearing feebly, and I had not only my share of the work, but also had to keep at it two men who showed a constant inclination to lay themselves down and let things slide.

"At last I hailed 'On deck there,' and someone looked over. 'We're ready here,' I said. The head disappeared, and very soon popped up again. 'The captain says, All right, sir, and to keep the boats well clear of the ship.'

"Half an hour passed. Suddenly there was a frightful racket, rattle, clanking of chain, hiss of water, and millions of sparks flew up into the shivering column of smoke that stood leaning slightly above the ship. The catheads had burned away, and the two red-hot anchors had gone to the bottom, tearing out after them two hundred fathom of red-hot chain. The ship trembled, the mass of flame swayed as if ready to collapse, and the fore top-gallant-mast fell. It darted down like an arrow of fire, shot under, and instantly leaping up within an oar's-length of the boats, floated quietly, very black on the luminous sea. I hailed the deck again. After some time a man in an unexpectedly cheerful but also muffled tone, as though he had been trying to speak with his mouth shut, informed me, 'Coming directly, sir,' and vanished. For a long time I heard nothing but the whir and roar of the fire. There were also whistling sounds. The boats jumped, tugged at the painters, ran at each other playfully, knocked their sides together, or, do what we would, swung in a bunch against the ship's side. I couldn't stand it any longer, and swarming up a rope, clambered aboard over the stern.

"It was as bright as day. Coming up like this, the sheet of fire facing me, was a terrifying sight, and the heat seemed hardly bearable at first. On a settee cushion dragged out of the cabin, Captain Beard, with his legs drawn up and one arm under his head, slept with the light playing on him. Do you know what the rest were busy about? They were sitting on deck right aft, around an open case, eating bread and cheese and drinking bottled stout.

"On the background of flames twisting in fierce tongues above their heads they seemed at home like salamanders, and looked like a band of desperate pirates. The fire sparkled in the whites of their eyes, gleamed on patches of white skin seen through the torn shirts. Each had the marks as of a battle about him— bandaged heads, tied-up arms, a strip of dirty rag round a knee—and each man had a bottle between his legs and a chunk of cheese in his hand. Mahon got up. With his handsome and disreputable head, his hooked profile, his long white beard, and with an uncorked bottle in his hand, he resembled one of those reckless sea-robbers of old making merry amidst violence and disaster. 'The last meal on board,' he explained solemnly. 'We had nothing to eat all day, and it was no use leaving all this.' He flourished the bottle and indicated the sleeping skipper. 'He said he couldn't swallow anything, so I got him to lie down,' he went on; and as I stared, 'I don't know whether you are aware, young fellow, the man had no sleep to speak of for days—and there will be dam' little sleep in the boats.' 'There will be no boats by-and-by if you fool about much longer,' I said, indignantly. I walked up to the skipper and shook him by the shoulder. At last he opened his eyes, but did not move. 'Time to leave her, sir,' I said, quietly.

"He got up painfully, looked at the flames, at the sea sparkling round the ship, and black, black as ink farther away; he looked at the stars shining dim through a thin veil of smoke in a sky black, black as Erebus.

"'Youngest first,' he said.

"And the ordinary seaman, wiping his mouth with the back of his hand, got up, clambered over the taffrail, and vanished. Others followed. One, on the point of going over, stopped short to drain his bottle, and with a great swing of his arm flung it at the fire. 'Take this!' he cried.

"The skipper lingered disconsolately, and we left him to commune alone for awhile with his first command. Then I went up again and brought him away at last. It was time. The ironwork on the poop was hot to the touch.

"Then the painter of the long-boat was cut, and the three boats, tied together, drifted clear of the ship. It was just sixteen hours after the explosion when we abandoned her. Mahon had charge of the second boat, and I had the smallest— the 14-foot thing. The long-boat would have taken the lot of us; but the skipper said we must save as much property as we could—for the underwriters—and so I got my first command. I had two men with me, a bag of biscuits, a few tins of meat, and a breaker of water. I was ordered to keep close to the long-boat, that in case of bad weather we might be taken into her.

"And do you know what I thought? I thought I would part company as soon as I could. I wanted to have my first command all to myself. I wasn't going to sail in a squadron if there were a chance for independent cruising. I would make land by myself. I would beat the other boats. Youth! All youth! The silly, charming, beautiful youth.

"But we did not make a start at once. We must see the last of the ship. And so the boats drifted about that night, heaving and setting on the swell. The men dozed, waked, sighed, groaned. I looked at the burning ship.

"Between the darkness of earth and heaven she was burning fiercely upon a disc of purple sea shot by the blood-red play of gleams; upon a disc of water glittering and sinister. A high, clear flame, an immense and lonely flame, ascended from the ocean, and from its summit the black smoke poured continuously at the sky. She burned furiously, mournful and imposing like a funeral pile kindled in the night, surrounded by the sea, watched over by the stars. A magnificent death had come like a grace, like a gift, like a reward to that old ship at the end of her laborious days. The surrender of her weary ghost to the keeping of stars and sea was stirring like the sight of a glorious triumph. The masts fell just before daybreak, and for a moment there was a burst and turmoil of sparks that seemed to fill with flying fire the night patient and watchful, the vast night lying silent upon the sea. At daylight she was only a charred shell, floating still under a cloud of smoke and bearing a glowing mass of coal within.

"Then the oars were got out, and the boats forming in a line moved round her remains as if in procession—the long-boat leading. As we pulled across her stern a slim dart of fire shot out viciously at us, and suddenly she went down, head first, in a great hiss of steam. The unconsumed stern was the last to sink; but the paint had gone, had cracked, had peeled off, and there were no letters, there was no word, no stubborn device that was like her soul, to flash at the rising sun her creed and her name.

"We made our way north. A breeze sprang up, and about noon all the boats came together for the last time. I had no mast or sail in mine, but I made a mast out of a spare oar and hoisted a boat-awning for a sail, with a boat-hook for a yard. She was certainly over-masted, but I had the satisfaction of knowing that with the wind aft I could beat the other two. I had to wait for them. Then we all had a look at the captain's chart, and, after a sociable meal of hard bread and water, got our last instructions. These were simple: steer north, and keep together as much as possible. 'Be careful with that jury rig, Marlow,' said the captain; and Mahon, as I sailed proudly past his boat, wrinkled his curved nose and hailed, 'You will sail that ship of yours under water, if you don't look out, young fellow.' He was a malicious old man—and may the deep sea where he sleeps now rock him gently, rock him tenderly to the end of time!

"Before sunset a thick rain-squall passed over the two boats, which were far astern, and that was the last I saw of them for a time. Next day I sat steering my cockle-shell—my first command—with nothing but water and sky around me. I did sight in the afternoon the upper sails of a ship far away, but said nothing, and my men did not notice her. You see I was afraid she might be homeward bound, and I had no mind to turn back from the portals of the East. I was steering for Java—another blessed name—like Bankok, you know. I steered many days.

"I need not tell you what it is to be knocking about in an open boat. I remember nights and days of calm when we pulled, we pulled, and the boat seemed to stand still, as if bewitched within the circle of the sea horizon. I remember the heat, the deluge of rain-squalls that kept us baling for dear life (but filled our water-cask), and I remember sixteen hours on end with a mouth dry as a cinder and a steering-oar over the stern to keep my first command head on to a breaking sea. I did not know how good a man I was till then. I remember the drawn faces, the dejected figures of my two men, and I remember my youth and the feeling that will never come back any more—the feeling that I could last for ever, outlast the sea, the earth, and all men; the deceitful feeling that lures us on to joys, to perils, to love, to vain effort—to death; the triumphant conviction of strength, the heat of life in the handful of dust, the glow in the heart that with every year grows dim, grows cold, grows small, and expires—and expires, too soon—before life itself.

"And this is how I see the East. I have seen its secret places and have looked into its very soul; but now I see it always from a small boat, a high outline of mountains, blue and afar in the morning; like faint mist at noon; a jagged wall of purple at sunset. I have the feel of the oar in my hand, the vision of a scorching blue sea in my eyes. And I see a bay, a wide bay, smooth as glass and polished like ice, shimmering in the dark. A red light burns far off upon the gloom of the land, and the night is soft and warm. We drag at the oars with aching arms, and suddenly a puff of wind, a puff faint and tepid and laden with strange odors of blossoms, of aromatic wood, comes out of the still night—the first sigh of the East on my face. That I can never forget. It was impalpable and enslaving, like a charm, like a whispered promise of mysterious delight.

"We had been pulling this finishing spell for eleven hours. Two pulled, and he whose turn it was to rest sat at the tiller. We had made out the red light in that bay and steered for it, guessing it must mark some small coasting port. We passed two vessels, outlandish and high-sterned, sleeping at anchor, and, approaching the light, now very dim, ran the boat's nose against the end of a jutting wharf. We were blind with fatigue. My men dropped the oars and fell off the thwarts as if dead. I made fast to a pile. A current rippled softly. The scented obscurity of the shore was grouped into vast masses, a density of colossal clumps of vegetation, probably—mute and fantastic shapes. And at their foot the semicircle of a beach gleamed faintly, like an illusion. There was not a light, not a stir, not a sound. The mysterious East faced me, perfumed like a flower, silent like death, dark like a grave.

"And I sat weary beyond expression, exulting like a conqueror, sleepless and entranced as if before a profound, a fateful enigma.

"A splashing of oars, a measured dip reverberating on the level of water, intensified by the silence of the shore into loud claps, made me jump up. A boat, a European boat, was coming in. I invoked the name of the dead; I hailed: *Judea* ahoy! A thin shout answered.

"It was the captain. I had beaten the flagship by three hours, and I was glad to hear the old man's voice, tremulous and tired. 'Is it you, Marlow?' 'Mind the end of that jetty, sir,' I cried.

"He approached cautiously, and brought up with the deep-sea lead-line which we had saved—for the underwriters. I eased my painter and fell alongside. He sat, a broken figure at the stern, wet with dew, his hands clasped in his lap. His men were asleep already. 'I had a terrible time of it,' he murmured. 'Mahon is behind—not very far.' We conversed in whispers, in low whispers, as if afraid to wake up the land. Guns, thunder, earthquakes would not have awakened the men just then.

"Looking around as we talked, I saw away at sea a bright light traveling in the night. 'There's a steamer passing the bay,' I said. She was not passing, she was entering, and she even came close and anchored. 'I wish,' said the old man, 'you would find out whether she is English. Perhaps they could give us a passage somewhere.' He seemed nervously anxious. So by dint of punching and kicking I started one of my men into a state of somnambulism, and giving him an oar, took another and pulled towards the lights of the steamer.

"There was a murmur of voices in her, metallic hollow clangs of the engine-room, footsteps on the deck. Her ports shone, round like dilated eyes. Shapes moved about, and there was a shadowy man high up on the bridge. He heard my oars.

"And then, before I could open my lips, the East spoke to me, but it was in a Western voice. A torrent of words was poured into the enigmatical, the fateful silence; outlandish, angry words, mixed with words and even whole sentences of good English, less strange but even more surprising. The voice swore and cursed violently; it riddled the solemn peace of the bay by a volley of abuse. It began by calling me Pig, and from that went crescendo into unmentionable adjectives—in English. The man up there raged aloud in two languages, and with a sincerity in his fury that almost convinced me I had, in some way, sinned against the harmony of the universe. I could hardly see him, but began to think he would work himself into a fit.

"Suddenly he ceased, and I could hear him snorting and blowing like a porpoise. I said—

"'What steamer is this, pray?'

"'Eh? What's this? And who are you?'

"'Castaway crew of an English bark burnt at sea. We came here to-night. I am the second mate. The captain is in the long-boat, and wishes to know if you would give us a passage somewhere.'

"'Oh, my goodness! I say. . . . This is the *Celestial* from Singapore on her return trip. I'll arrange with your captain in the morning, . . . and, . . . I say, . . . did you hear me just now?'

"'I should think the whole bay heard you.'

"'I thought you were a shore-boat. Now, look here—this infernal lazy scoundrel of a caretaker has gone to sleep again—curse him. The light is out, and I nearly ran foul of the end of this damned jetty. This is the third time he plays me this trick. Now, I ask you, can anybody stand this kind of thing? It's enough to drive a man out of his mind. I'll report him. . . . I'll get the Assistant Resident to give him the sack, by . . . See—there's no light. It's out, isn't it? I take you to witness the light's out. There should be a light, you know. A red light on the—'

"'There was a light,' I said, mildly.

"'But it's out, man! What's the use of talking like this? You can see for yourself it's out—don't you? If you had to take a valuable steamer along this God-forsaken coast you would want a light too. I'll kick him from end to end of his miserable wharf. You'll see if I don't. I will—'

"'So I may tell my captain you'll take us?' I broke in.

"'Yes, I'll take you. Good night,' he said, brusquely.

"I pulled back, made fast again to the jetty, and then went to sleep at last. I had faced the silence of the East. I had heard some of its languages. But when I opened my eyes again the silence was as complete as though it had never been broken. I was lying in a flood of light, and the sky had never looked so far, so high, before. I opened my eyes and lay without moving.

"And then I saw the men of the East—they were looking at me. The whole length of the jetty was full of people. I saw brown, bronze, yellow faces, the black eyes, the glitter, the color of an Eastern crowd. And all these beings stared without a murmur, without a sigh, without a movement. They stared down at the boats, at the sleeping men who at night had come to them from the sea. Nothing moved. The fronds of palms stood still against the sky. Not a branch stirred along the shore, and the brown roofs of hidden houses peeped through the green foliage, through the big leaves that hung shining and still like leaves forged of heavy metal. This was the East of the ancient navigators, so old, so mysterious, resplendent and somber, living and unchanged, full of danger and promise. And these were the men. I sat up suddenly. A wave of movement passed through the crowd from end to end, passed along the heads, swayed the bodies, ran along the jetty like a ripple on the water, like a breath of wind on a field—and all was still again. I see it now—the wide sweep of the bay, the glittering sands, the wealth of green infinite and varied, the sea blue like the sea of a dream, the crowd of attentive faces, the blaze of vivid color—the water reflecting it all, the curve of the shore, the jetty, the high-sterned outlandish craft floating still, and the three boats with tired men from the West sleeping unconscious of the land and the people and of the violence of sunshine. They slept thrown across the thwarts, curled on bottom-boards, in the careless attitudes of death. The head of the old skipper, leaning back in the stern of the long-boat, had fallen on his breast, and he looked as though he would never wake. Farther out old Mahon's face was upturned to the sky, with the long white beard spread out on his breast, as though he been shot where he sat at the tiller; and a man, all in a heap in the bows of the boat, slept with both arms embracing the stem-head and with his cheek laid on the gunwale. The East looked at them without a sound.

"I have known its fascinations since: I have seen the mysterious shores, the still water, the lands of brown nations, where a stealthy Nemesis lies in wait, pursues, overtakes so many of the conquering race, who are proud of their wisdom, of their knowledge, of their strength. But for me all the East is contained in that vision of my youth. It is all in that moment when I opened my young eyes on it. I came upon it from a tussle with the sea—and I was young—and I saw it looking at me. And this is all that is left of it! Only a moment; a moment of strength, of romance, of glamour—of youth! . . . A flick of sunshine upon a strange shore, the time to remember, the time for a sigh, and—good-by!—Night—Good-by . . . !"

He drank.

"Ah! The good old time—the good old time. Youth and the sea. Glamour and the sea! The good, strong sea, the salt, bitter sea, that could whisper to you and roar at you and knock your breath out of you."

He drank again.

"By all that's wonderful, it is the sea, I believe, the sea itself—or is it youth alone? Who can tell? But you here—you all had something out of life: money, love—whatever one gets on shore—and, tell me, wasn't that the best time, that time when we were young at sea; young and had nothing, on the sea that gives nothing, except hard knocks—and sometimes a chance to feel your strength—that only—what you all regret?"

And we all nodded at him: the man of finance, the man of accounts, the man of law, we all nodded at him over the polished table that like a still sheet of brown water reflected our faces, lined, wrinkled; our faces marked by toil, by deceptions, by success, by love; our weary eyes looking still, looking always, looking anxiously for something out of life, that while it is expected is already gone—has passed unseen, in a sigh, in a flash—together with the youth, with the strength, with the romance of illusions.

HEART
of
DARKNESS

I

The *Nellie*, a cruising yawl, swung to her anchor without a flutter of the sails, and was at rest. The flood had made, the wind was nearly calm, and being bound down the river, the only thing for it was to come to and wait for the turn of the tide.

The sea-reach of the Thames stretched before us like the beginning of an interminable waterway. In the offing the sea and the sky were welded together without a joint, and in the luminous space the tanned sails of the barges drifting up with the tide seemed to stand still in red clusters of canvas sharply peaked, with gleams of varnished sprits. A haze rested on the low shores that ran out to sea in vanishing flatness. The air was dark above Gravesend, and farther back still seemed condensed into a mournful gloom, brooding motionless over the biggest, and the greatest, town on earth.

The Director of Companies was our captain and our host. We four affectionately watched his back as he stood in the bows looking to seaward. On the whole river there was nothing that looked half so nautical. He resembled a pilot, which to a seaman is trustworthiness personified. It was difficult to realize his work was not out there in the luminous estuary, but behind him, within the brooding gloom.

Between us there was, as I have already said somewhere, the bond of the sea. Besides holding our hearts together through long periods of separation, it had the effect of making us tolerant of each other's yarns—and even convictions. The Lawyer—the best of old fellows—had, because of his many years and many virtues, the only cushion on deck, and was lying on the only rug. The Accountant had brought out already a box of dominoes, and was toying architecturally with the bones. Marlow sat cross-legged right aft, leaning against the mizzen-mast. He had sunken cheeks, a yellow complexion, a straight back, an ascetic aspect, and, with his arms dropped, the palms of hands outwards, resembled an idol. The Director, satisfied the anchor had good hold, made his way aft and sat down amongst us. We exchanged a few words lazily. Afterwards there was silence on board the yacht. For some reason or other we did not begin that game of dominoes. We felt meditative, and fit for nothing but placid staring. The day was ending in a serenity of still and exquisite brilliance. The water shone pacifically; the sky, without a speck, was a benign immensity of unstained light; the very mist on the Essex marshes was like a gauzy and radiant fabric, hung from the wooded rises inland, and draping the low shores in diaphanous folds. Only the gloom to the west, brooding over the upper reaches, became more somber every minute, as if angered by the approach of the sun.

And at last, in its curved and imperceptible fall, the sun sank low, and from glowing white changed to a dull red without rays and without heat, as if about to go out suddenly, stricken to death by the touch of that gloom brooding over a crowd of men.

Forthwith a change came over the waters, and the serenity became less brilliant but more profound. The old river in its broad reach rested unruffled at the decline of day, after ages of good service done to the race that peopled its banks, spread out in the tranquil dignity of a waterway leading to the uttermost ends of the earth. We looked at the venerable stream not in the vivid flush of a short day that comes and departs for ever, but in the august light of abiding memories. And indeed nothing is easier for a man who has, as the phrase goes, "followed the sea" with reverence and affection, than to evoke the great spirit of the past upon the lower reaches of the Thames. The tidal current runs to and fro in its unceasing service, crowded with memories of men and ships it had borne to the rest of home or to the battles of the sea. It had known and served all the men of whom the nation is proud, from Sir Francis Drake to Sir John Franklin, knights all, titled and untitled—the great knights-errant of the sea. It had borne all the ships whose names are like jewels flashing in the night of time, from the *Golden Hind* returning with her round flanks full of treasure, to be visited by the Queen's Highness and thus pass out of the gigantic tale, to the *Erebus* and *Terror*, bound on other conquests—and that never returned. It had known the ships and the men. They had sailed from Deptford, from Greenwich, from Erith—the adventurers and the settlers; kings' ships and the ships of men on 'Change; captains, admirals, the dark "interlopers" of the Eastern trade, and the commissioned "generals" of East India fleets. Hunters for gold or pursuers of fame, they all had gone out on that stream, bearing the sword, and often the torch, messengers of the might within the land, bearers of a spark from the sacred fire. What greatness had not floated on the ebb of that river into the mystery of an unknown earth! . . . The dreams of men, the seed of commonwealths, the germs of empires.

The sun set; the dusk fell on the stream, and lights began to appear along the shore. The Chapman lighthouse, a three-legged thing erect on a mud-flat, shone strongly. Lights of ships moved in the fairway—a great stir of lights going up and going down. And farther west on the upper reaches the place of the monstrous town was still marked ominously on the sky, a brooding gloom in sunshine, a lurid glare under the stars.

"And this also," said Marlow suddenly, "has been one of the dark places of the earth."

He was the only man of us who still "followed the sea." The worst that could be said of him was that he did not represent his class. He was a seaman, but he was a wanderer too, while most seamen lead, if one may so express it, a sedentary life. Their minds are of the stay-at-home order, and their home is always with them—the ship; and so is their country—the sea. One ship is very much like another, and the sea is always the same. In the immutability of their surroundings the foreign shores, the foreign faces, the changing immensity of life, glide past, veiled not by a sense of mystery but by a slightly disdainful ignorance; for there is nothing mysterious to a seaman unless it be the sea itself, which is the mistress of his existence and as inscrutable as Destiny. For the rest, after his hours of work, a casual stoll or a casual spree on shore suffices to unfold for him the secret of a whole continent, and generally he finds the secret not worth knowing. The yarns of seamen have a direct simplicity, the whole meaning of which lies within the shell of a cracked nut. But Marlow was not typical (if his propensity to spin yarns be excepted), and to him the meaning of an episode was not inside like a kernel but outside, enveloping the tale which brought it out only as a glow brings out a haze, in the likeness of one of these misty halos that sometimes are made visible by the spectral illumination of moonshine.

His remark did not seem at all surprising. It was just like Marlow. It was accepted in silence. No one took the trouble to grunt even; and presently he said, very slow—

"I was thinking of very old times, when the Romans first came here, nineteen hundred years ago—the other day. . . . Light came out of this river since—you say Knights? Yes; but it is like a running blaze on a plain, like a flash of lightning in the clouds. We live in the flicker—may it last as long as the old earth keeps rolling! But darkness was here yesterday. Imagine the feelings of a commander of a fine—what d'ye call 'em?—trireme in the Mediterranean, ordered suddenly to the north; run overland across the Gauls in a hurry; put in charge of one of these craft the legionaries,—a wonderful lot of handy men they must have been too—used to build, apparently by the hundred, in a month or two, if we may believe what we read. Imagine him here—the very end of the world, a sea the color of lead, a sky the color of smoke, a kind of ship about as rigid as a concertina—and going up this river with stores, or orders, or what you like. Sandbanks, marshes, forests, savages,—precious little to eat fit for a civilized man, nothing but Thames water to drink. No Falernian wine here, no going ashore. Here and there a military camp lost in a wilderness, like a needle in a bundle of hay—cold, fog, tempests, disease, exile, and death,—death skulking in the air, in the water, in the bush. They must have been dying like flies here. Oh yes—he did it. Did it very well, too, no doubt, and without thinking much about it either, except afterwards to brag of what he had gone through in his time, perhaps. They were men enough to face the darkness. And perhaps he was cheered by keeping his eye on a chance of promotion to the fleet at Ravenna by-and-by, if he had good friends in Rome and survived the awful climate. Or think of a decent young citizen in a toga—perhaps too much dice, you know—coming out here in the train of some perfect, or tax-gatherer, or trader even, to mend his fortunes. Land in a swamp, march through the woods, and in some inland post feel the savagery, the utter savagery, had closed round him,—all that mysterious life of the wilderness that stirs in the forest, in the jungles, in the hearts of wild men. There's no initiation either into such mysteries. He has to live in the midst of the incomprehensible, which is also detestable. And it has a fascination, too, that goes to work upon him. The fascination of the abomination—you know. Imagine the growing regrets, the longing to escape, the powerless disgust, the surrender, the hate."

He paused.

"Mind," he began again, lifting one arm from the elbow, the palm of the hand outwards, so that, with his legs folded before him, he had the pose of a Buddha preaching in European clothes and without a lotus-flower—"Mind, none of us would feel exactly like this. What saves us is efficiency—the devotion to efficiency. But these chaps were not much account, really. They were no colonists; their administration was merely a squeeze, and nothing more, I suspect. They were conquerors, and for that you want only brute force—nothing to boast of, when you have it, since your strength is just an accident arising from the weakness of others.

They grabbed what they could get for the sake of what was to be got. It was just robbery with violence, aggravated murder on a great scale, and men going at it blind—as is very proper for those who tackle a darkness. The conquest of the earth, which mostly means the taking it away from those who have a different complexion or slightly flatter noses than ourselves, is not a pretty thing when you look into it too much. What redeems it is the idea only. An idea at the back of it; not a sentimental pretense but an idea; and an unselfish belief in the idea—something you can set up, and bow down before, and offer a sacrifice to. . . ."

He broke off. Flames glided in the river, small green flames, red flames, white flames, pursuing, overtaking, joining, crossing each other—then separating slowly or hastily. The traffic of the great city went on in the deepening night upon the sleepless river. We looked on, waiting patiently—there was nothing else to do till the end of the flood; but it was only after a long silence, when he said, in a hesitating voice, "I suppose you fellows remember I did once turn fresh-water sailor for a bit," that we knew we were fated, before the ebb began to run, to hear about one of Marlow's inconclusive experiences.

"I don't want to bother you much with what happened to me personally," he began, showing in this remark the weakness of many tellers of tales who seem so often unaware of what their audience would best like to hear; "yet to understand the effect of it on me you ought to know how I got out there, what I saw, how I went up that river to the place where I first met the poor chap. It was the farthest point of navigation and the culminating point of my experience. It seemed somehow to throw a kind of light on everything about me—and into my thoughts. It was somber enough too—and pitiful—not extraordinary in any way—not very clear either. No, not very clear. And yet it seemed to throw a kind of light.

"I had then, as you remember, just returned to London after a lot of Indian Ocean, Pacific, China Seas—a regular dose of the East—six years or so, and I was loafing about, hindering you fellows in your work and invading your homes, just as though I had got a heavenly mission to civilize you. It was very fine for a time, but after a bit I did get tired of resting. Then I began to look for a ship—I should think the hardest work on earth. But the ships wouldn't even look at me. And I got tired of that game too.

"Now when I was a little chap I had a passion for maps. I would look for hours at South America, or Africa, or Australia, and lose myself in all the glories of exploration. At that time there were many blank spaces on the earth, and when I saw one that looked particularly inviting on a map (but they all look that) I would put my finger on it and say, When I grow up I will go there. The North Pole was one of these places, I remember. Well, I haven't been there yet, and shall not try now. The glamour's off. Other places were scattered about the Equator, and in every sort of latitude all over the two hemispheres. I have been in some of them, and . . . well, we won't talk about that. But there was one yet—the biggest, the most blank, so to speak—that I had a hankering after.

"True, by this time it was not a blank space any more. It had got filled since my boyhood with rivers and lakes and names. It had ceased to be a blank space of delightful mystery—a white patch for a boy to dream gloriously over. It had become a place of darkness. But there was in it one river especially, a mighty big river, that you could see on the map, resembling an immense snake uncoiled, with its head in the sea, its body at rest curving afar over a vast country, and its tail lost in the depths of the land. And as I looked at the map of it in a shop-window, it fascinated me as a snake would a bird—a silly little bird. Then I remembered there was a big concern, a Company for trade on that river. Dash it all! I thought to myself, they can't trade without using some kind of craft on that lot of fresh water— steamboats! Why shouldn't I try to get charge of one. I went on along Fleet Street, but could not shake off the idea. The snake had charmed me.

"You understand it was a Continental concern, that Trading society; but I have a lot of relations living on the Continent, because it's cheap and not so nasty as it looks, they say.

"I am sorry to own I began to worry them. This was already a fresh departure for me. I was not used to get things that way, you know. I always went my own road and on my own legs where I had a mind to go. I wouldn't have believed it of myself; but, then—you see—I felt somehow I must get there by hook or by crook. So I worried them. The men said 'My dear fellow,' and did nothing. Then—would you believe it?—I tried the women. I, Charlie Marlow, set the women to work—to get a job. Heavens! Well, you see, the notion drove me. I had an aunt, a dear enthusiastic soul. She wrote: 'It will be delightful. I am ready to do anything, anything for you. It is a glorious idea. I know the wife of a very high personage in the Administration, and also a man who has lots of influence with,' &c., &c. She was determined to make no end of fuss to get me appointed skipper of a river steamboat, if such was my fancy.

"I got my appointment—of course; and I got it very quick. It appears the Company had received news that one of their captains had been killed in a scuffle with the natives. This was my chance, and it made me the more anxious to go. It was only months and months afterwards, when I made the attempt to recover what was left of the body, that I heard the original quarrel arose from a misunderstanding about some hens. Yes, two black hens. Fresleven—that was the fellow's name, a Dane—thought himself wronged somehow in the bargain, so he went ashore and started to hammer the chief of the village with a stick. Oh, it didn't surprise me in the least to hear this, and at the same time to be told that Fresleven was the gentlest, quietest creature that ever walked on two legs. No doubt he was; but he had been a couple of years already out there engaged in the noble cause, you know, and he probably felt the need at last of asserting his self-respect in some way. Therefore he whacked the old nigger mercilessly, while a big crowd of his people watched him, thunderstruck, till some man,—I was told the chief's son,— in desperation at hearing the old chap yell, made a tentative jab with a spear at the white man—and of course it went quite easy between the shoulder-blades. Then the whole population cleared into the forest, expecting all kinds of calamities to happen, while, on the other hand, the steamer Fresleven commanded left also in a bad panic, in charge of the engineer, I believe. Afterwards nobody seemed to trouble much about Fresleven's remains, till I got out and stepped into his shoes. I couldn't let it rest, though; but when an opportunity offered at last to meet my predecessor, the grass growing through his ribs was tall enough to hide his bones. They were all there. The supernatural being had not been touched after he fell. And the village was deserted, the huts gaped black, rotting, all askew within the fallen enclosures. A calamity had come to it, sure enough. The people had vanished. Mad terror had scattered them, men, women, and children, through the bush, and they had never returned. What became of the hens I don't know either. I should think the cause of progress got them, anyhow. However, through this glorious affair I got my appointment, before I had fairly begun to hope for it.

"I flew around like mad to get ready, and before forty-eight hours I was crossing the Channel to show myself to my employers, and sign the contract. In a very
few hours I arrived in a city that always makes me think of a white sepulcher. Prejudice no doubt. I had no difficulty in finding the Company's offices. It was the
biggest thing in the town, and everybody I met was full of it. They were going to
run an over-sea empire, and make no end of coin by trade.

"A narrow and deserted street in deep shadow, high houses, innumerable
windows with venetian blinds, a dead silence, grass sprouting between the
stones, imposing carriage archways right and left, immense double doors standing
ponderously ajar. I slipped through one of these cracks, went up a swept and un-
garnished staircase, as arid as a desert, and opened the first door I came to. Two
women, one fat and the other slim, sat on straw-bottomed chairs, knitting black
wool. The slim one got up and walked straight at me—still knitting with downcast
eyes—and only just as I began to think of getting out of her way, as you would for
a somnambulist, stood still, and looked up. Her dress was as plain as an umbrella-
cover, and she turned round without a word and preceded me into a waiting-
room. I gave my name, and looked about. Deal table in the middle, plain chairs all
round the walls, on one end a large shining map, marked with all the colors of a
rainbow. There was a vast amount of red—good to see at any time, because one
knows that some real work is done in there, a deuce of a lot of blue, a little green,
smears of orange, and, on the East Coast, a purple patch, to show where the jolly
pioneers of progress drink the jolly lager-beer. However, I wasn't going into any
of these. I was going into the yellow. Dead in the center. And the river was there—
fascinating—deadly—like a snake. Ough! A door opened, a white-haired secretarial head, but wearing a compassionate expression, appeared, and a skinny forefinger beckoned me into the sanctuary. Its light was dim, and a heavy writing-
desk squatted in the middle. From behind that structure came out an impression
of pale plumpness in a frock-coat. The great man himself. He was five feet six, I
should judge, and had his grip on the handle-end of ever so many millions. He
shook hands, I fancy, murmured vaguely, was satisfied with my French. *Bon voyage.*

"In about forty-five seconds I found myself again in the waiting-room with
the compassionate secretary, who, full of desolation and sympathy, made me sign
some document. I believe I undertook amongst other things not to disclose any
trade secrets. Well, I am not going to.

"I began to feel slightly uneasy. You know I am not used to such ceremonies,
and there was something ominous in the atmosphere. It was just as though I had
been let into some conspiracy—I don't know—something not quite right; and I
was glad to get out. In the outer room the two women knitted black wool feverishly. People were arriving, and the younger one was walking back and forth introducing them. The old one sat on her chair. Her flat cloth slippers were propped
up on a foot-warmer, and a cat reposed on her lap. She wore a starched white affair on her head, had a wart on one cheek, and silver-rimmed spectacles hung on
the tip of her nose. She glanced at me above the glasses. The swift and indifferent
placidity of that look troubled me. Two youths with foolish and cheery counte-
nances were being piloted over, and she threw at them the same quick glance of
unconcerned wisdom. She seemed to know all about them and about me too. An
eerie feeling came over me. She seemed uncanny and fateful. Often far away there
I thought of these two, guarding the door of Darkness, knitting black wool as for

a warm pall, one introducing, introducing continuously to the unknown, the other scrutinizing the cheery and foolish faces with unconcerned old eyes. *Ave!* Old knitter of black wool. *Morituri te salutant.* Not many of those she looked at ever saw her again—not half, by a long way.

"There was yet a visit to the doctor. 'A simple formality,' assured me the secretary, with an air of taking an immense part in all my sorrows. Accordingly a young chap wearing his hat over the left eyebrow, some clerk I suppose,—there must have been clerks in the business, though the house was as still as a house in a city of the dead,—came from somewhere up-stairs, and led me forth. He was shabby and careless, with ink-stains on the sleeves of his jacket, and his cravat was large and billowy, under a chin shaped like the toe of an old boot. It was a little too early for the doctor, so I proposed a drink, and thereupon he developed a vein of joviality. As we sat over our vermouths he glorified the Company's business, and by-and-by I expressed casually my surprise at him not going out there. He became very cool and collected all at once. 'I am not such a fool as I look, quoth Plato to his disciples,' he said sententiously, emptied his glass with great resolution, and we rose.

"The old doctor felt my pulse, evidently thinking of something else the while. 'Good, good for there,' he mumbled, and then with a certain eagerness asked me whether I would let him measure my head. Rather surprised, I said Yes, when he produced a thing like calipers and got the dimensions back and front and every way, taking notes carefully. He was an unshaven little man in a threadbare coat like a gaberdine, with his feet in slippers, and I thought him a harmless fool. 'I always ask leave, in the interests of science, to measure the crania of those going out there,' he said. 'And when they come back too?' I asked. 'Oh, I never see them,' he remarked; 'and, moreover, the changes take place inside, you know.' He smiled, as if at some quiet joke. 'So you are going out there. Famous. Interesting too.' He gave me a searching glance, and made another note. 'Ever any madness in your family?' he asked, in a matter-of-fact tone. I felt very annoyed. 'Is that question in the interests of science too?' 'It would be,' he said, without taking notice of my irritation, 'interesting for science to watch the mental changes of individuals, on the spot, but . . .' 'Are you an alienist?' I interrupted. 'Every doctor should be—a little,' answered that original, imperturbably. 'I have a little theory which you Messieurs who go out there must help me to prove. This is my share in the advantages my country shall reap from the possession of such a magnificent dependency. The mere wealth I leave to others. Pardon my questions, but you are the first Englishman coming under my observation. . . .' I hastened to assure him I was not in the least typical. 'If I were,' said I, 'I wouldn't be talking like this with you.' 'What you say is rather profound, and probably erroneous,' he said, with a laugh. 'Avoid irritation more than exposure to the sun. Adieu. How do you English say, eh? Good-by. Ah! Good-by. Adieu. In the tropics one must before everything keep calm.' . . . He lifted a warning forefinger. . . . '*Du calme, du calme. Adieu.*'

"One thing more remained to do—say good-by to my excellent aunt. I found her triumphant. I had a cup of tea—the last decent cup of tea for many days—and in a room that most soothingly looked just as you would expect a lady's drawing-room to look, we had a long quiet chat by the fireside. In the course of these confidences it became quite plain to me I had been represented to the wife of the high dignitary, and goodness knows to how many more people besides, as an exceptional and gifted creature—a piece of good furniture for the Company—a man you don't get hold of every day. Good heavens! and I was going to take charge of a two-penny-halfpenny river-steamboat with a penny whistle attached! It appeared, however, I was also one of the Workers, with a capital—you know. Something like an emissary of light, something like a lower sort of apostle. There had been a lot of such rot let loose in print and talk just about that time, and the excellent woman, living right in the rush of all that humbug, got carried off her feet. She talked about 'weaning those ignorant millions from their horrid ways,' till, upon my word, she made me quite uncomfortable. I ventured to hint that the Company was run for profit.

"'You forget, dear Charlie, that the laborer is worthy of his hire,' she said, brightly. It's queer how out of touch with truth women are. They live in a world of their own, and there had never been anything like it, and never can be. It is too beautiful altogether, and if they were to set it up it would go to pieces before the first sunset. Some confounded fact we men have been living contentedly with ever since the day of creation would start up and knock the whole thing over.

"After this I got embraced, told to wear flannel, be sure to write often, and so on—and I left. In the street—I don't know why—a queer feeling came to me that I was an imposter. Odd thing that I, who used to clear out for any part of the world at twenty-four hours' notice, with less thought than most men give to the crossing of a street, had a moment—I won't say of hesitation, but of startled pause, before this commonplace affair. The best way I can explain it to you is by saying that, for a second or two, I felt as though, instead of going to the center of a continent, I were about to set off for the center of the earth.

"I left in a French steamer, and she called in every blamed port they have out there, for, as far as I could see, the sole purpose of landing soldiers and custom-house officers. I watched the coast. Watching a coast as it slips by the ship is like thinking about an enigma. There it is before you—smiling, frowning, inviting, grand, mean, insipid, or savage, and always mute with an air of whispering, Come and find out. This one was almost featureless, as if still in the making, with an aspect of monotonous grimness. The edge of a colossal jungle, so dark-green as to be almost black, fringed with white surf, ran straight, like a ruled line, far, far away along a blue sea whose glitter was blurred by a creeping mist. The sun was fierce, the land seemed to glisten and drip with steam. Here and there grayish-whitish specks showed up, clustered inside the white surf, with a flag flying above them perhaps. Settlements some centuries old, and still no bigger than pin-heads on the untouched expanse of their background. We pounded along, stopped, landed soldiers; went on, landed custom-house clerks to levy toll in what looked like a God-forsaken wilderness, with a tin shed and a flag-pole lost in it; landed more soldiers—to take care of the custom-house clerks, presumably. Some, I heard, got drowned in the surf; but whether they did or not, nobody seemed particularly to care. They were just flung out there, and on we went. Every day the coast looked the same, as though we had not moved; but we passed various places—trading places—with names like Gran' Bassam Little Popo, names that seemed to belong to some sordid farce acted in front of a sinister backcloth. The idleness of a passenger, my isolation amongst all these men with whom I had no point of contact, the oily and languid sea, the uniform somberness of the coast, seemed to keep me away from the truth of things, within the toil of a mournful and senseless delusion. The voice of the surf heard now and then was a positive pleasure, like the speech of a brother. It was something natural, that had its reason, that had a meaning.

Now and then a boat from the shore gave one a momentary contact with reality. It was paddled by black fellows. You could see from afar the white of their eyeballs glistening. They shouted, sang; their bodies streamed with perspiration; they had faces like grotesque masks—these chaps; but they had bone, muscle, a wild vitality, an intense energy of movement, that was as natural and true as the surf along their coast. They wanted no excuse for being there. They were a great comfort to look at. For a time I would feel I belonged still to a world of straightforward facts; but the feeling would not last long. Something would turn up to scare it away. Once, I remember, we came upon a man-of-war anchored off the coast. There wasn't even a shed there, and she was shelling the bush. It appears the French had one of their wars going on thereabouts. Her ensign dropped limp like a rag; the muzzles of the long eight-inch guns stuck out all over the low hull; the greasy, slimy swell swung her up lazily and let her down, swaying her thin masts. In the empty immensity of earth, sky, and water, there she was, incomprehensible, firing into a continent. Pop, would go one of the eight-inch guns; a small flame would dart and vanish, a little white smoke would disappear, a tiny projectile would give a feeble screech—and nothing happened. Nothing could happen. There was a touch of insanity in the proceeding, a sense of lugubrious drollery in the sight; and it was not dissipated by somebody on board assuring me earnestly there was a camp of natives—he called them enemies!—hidden out of sight somewhere.

"We gave her her letters (I heard the men in that lonely ship were dying of fever at the rate of three a day) and went on. We called at some more places with farcical names, where the merry dance of death and trade goes on in a still and earthy atmosphere as of an overheated catacomb; all along the formless coast bordered by dangerous surf, as if Nature herself had tried to ward off intruders; in and out of rivers, streams of death in life, whose banks were rotting into mud, whose waters, thickened into slime, invaded the contorted mangroves, that seemed to writhe at us in the extremity of an impotent despair. Nowhere did we stop long enough to get a particularized impression, but the general sense of a vague and oppressive wonder grew upon me. It was like a weary pilgrimage amongst hints for nightmares.

"It was upward of thirty days before I saw the mouth of the big river. We anchored off the seat of the government. But my work would not begin till some two hundred miles farther on. So as soon as I could I made a start for a place thirty miles higher up.

"I had my passage on a little sea-going steamer. Her captain was a Swede, and knowing me for a seaman, invited me on the bridge. He was a young man, lean, fair, and morose, with lanky hair and a shuffling gait. As we left the miserable little wharf, he tossed his head contemptuously at the shore. 'Been living there?' he asked. I said, 'Yes.' 'Fine lot these government chaps—are they not?' he went on, speaking English with great precision and considerable bitterness. 'It is funny what some people will do for a few francs a month. I wonder what becomes of that kind when it goes up country?' I said to him I expected to see that soon. 'So-o-o!' he exclaimed. He shuffled athwart, keeping one eye ahead vigilantly. 'Don't be too sure,' he continued. 'The other day I took up a man who hanged himself on the road. He was a Swede, too.' 'Hanged himself! Why, in God's name?' I cried. He kept on looking out watchfully. 'Who knows? The sun too much for him, or the country perhaps.'

At last we opened a reach. A rocky cliff appeared, mounds of turned-up earth by the shore, houses on a hill, others, with iron roofs, amongst a waste of exca-vations, or hanging to the declivity. A continuous noise of the rapids above hov-ered over this scene of inhabited devastation. A lot of people, mostly black and naked, moved about like ants. A jetty projected into the river. A blinding sunlight drowned all this at times in a sudden recrudescence of glare. 'There's your Com-pany's station,' said the Swede, pointing to three wooden barrack-like structures on the rocky slope. 'I will send your things up. Four boxes did you say? So. Fare-well.'

"I came upon a boiler wallowing in the grass, then found a path leading up the hill. It turned aside for the bowlders, and also for an undersized railway-truck lying there on its back with its wheels in the air. One was off. The thing looked as dead as the carcass of some animal. I came upon more pieces of decaying machin-ery, a stack of rusty rails. To the left a clump of trees made a shady spot, where dark things seemed to stir feebly. I blinked, the path was steep. A horn tooted to the right, and I saw the black people run. A heavy and dull detonation shook the ground, a puff of smoke came out of the cliff, and that was all. No change ap-peared on the face of the rock. They were building a railway. The cliff was not in the way or anything; but this objectless blasting was all the work going on.

"A slight clinking behind me made me turn my head. Six black men advanced in a file, toiling up the path. They walked erect and slow, balancing small baskets full of earth on their heads, and the clink kept time with their footsteps. Black rags were wound round their loins, and the short ends behind wagged to and fro like tails. I could see every rib, the joints of their limbs were like knots in a rope; each had an iron collar on his neck, and all were connected together with a chain whose bights swung between them, rhythmically clinking. Another report from the cliff made me think suddenly of that ship of war I had seen firing into a continent. It was the same kind of ominous voice; but these men could by no stretch of imagi-nation be called enemies. They were called criminals, and the outraged law, like the bursting shells, had come to them, an insoluble mystery from over the sea. All their meager breasts panted together, the violently dilated nostrils quivered, the eyes stared stonily uphill. They passed me within six inches, without a glance, with that complete, deathlike indifference of unhappy savages. Behind this raw matter one of the reclaimed, the product of the new forces at work, strolled de-spondently, carrying a rifle by its middle. He had a uniform jacket with one button off, and seeing a white man on the path, hoisted his weapon to his shoulder with alacrity. This was simple prudence, white men being so much alike at a distance that he could not tell who I might be. He was speedily reassured, and with a large, white, rascally grin, and a glance at his charge, seemed to take me into partnership in his exalted trust. After all, I also was a part of the great cause of these high and just proceedings.

"Instead of going up, I turned and descended to the left. My idea was to let that chain-gang get out of sight before I climbed the hill. You know I am not par-ticularly tender; I've had to strike and to fend off. I've had to resist and to attack sometimes—that's only one way of resisting—without counting the exact cost, ac-cording to the demands of such sort of life as I had blundered into. I've seen the devil of violence, and the devil of greed, and the devil of hot desire; but, by all the stars! these were strong, lusty, red-eyed devils, that swayed and drove men—men, I tell you. But as I stood on this hillside, I foresaw that in the blinding sunshine of that land I would become acquainted with a flabby, pretending, weak-eyed devil of a rapacious and pitiless folly. How insidious he could be, too, I was only to find out several months later and a thousand miles farther. For a moment I stood appalled, as though by a warning. Finally I descended the hill, obliquely, towards the trees I had seen.

"I avoided a vast artificial hole somebody had been digging on the slope, the purpose of which I found it impossible to divine. It wasn't a quarry or a sandpit, anyhow: It was just a hole. It might have been connected with the philanthropic desire of giving the criminals something to do. I don't know. Then I nearly fell into a very narrow ravine, almost no more than a scar in the hillside. I discovered that a lot of imported drainage-pipes for the settlement had been tumbled in there. There wasn't one that was not broken. It was a wanton smash-up. At last I got under the trees. My purpose was to stroll into the shade for a moment; but no sooner within than it seemed to me I had stepped into a gloomy circle of some Inferno. The rapids were near, and an uninterrupted, uniform, headlong, rushing noise filled the mournful stillness of the grove, where not a breath stirred, not a leaf moved, with a mysterious sound—as though the tearing pace of the launched earth had suddenly become audible.

"Black shapes crouched, lay, sat between the trees, leaning against the trunks, clinging to the earth, half coming out, half effaced within the dim light, in all the attitudes of pain, abandonment, and despair. Another mine on the cliff went off, followed by a slight shudder of the soil under my feet. The work was going on. The work! And this was the place where some of the helpers had withdrawn to die.

"They were dying slowly—it was very clear. They were not enemies, they were not criminals, they were nothing earthly now,—nothing but black shadows of disease and starvation, lying confusedly in the greenish gloom. Brought from all the recesses of the coast in all the legality of time contracts, lost in uncongenial surroundings, fed on unfamiliar food, they sickened, became inefficient, and were then allowed to crawl away and rest. These moribund shapes were free as air—and nearly as thin. I began to distinguish the gleam of eyes under the trees. Then, glancing down, I saw a face near my hand. The black bones reclined at full length with one shoulder against the tree, and slowly the eyelids rose and the sunken eyes looked up at me, enormous and vacant, a kind of blind, white flicker in the depths of the orbs, which died out slowly. The man seemed young—almost a boy—but you know with them it's hard to tell. I found nothing else to do but to offer him one of my good Swede's ship's biscuits I had in my pocket. The fingers closed slowly on it and held—there was no other movement and no other glance. He had tied a bit of white worsted round his neck—Why? Where did he get it? Was it a badge—an ornament—a charm—a propitiatory act? Was there any idea at all connected with it? It looked startling round his black neck, this bit of white thread from beyond the seas.

"Near the same tree two more bundles of acute angles sat with their legs drawn up. One, with his chin propped on his knees, stared at nothing, in an intolerable and appalling manner: his brother phantom rested its forehead, as if overcome with a great weariness; and all about others were scattered in every pose of contorted collapse, as in some picture of a massacre or a pestilence. While I stood horror-struck, one of these creatures rose to his hands and knees, and went off on all-fours towards the river to drink. He lapped out of his hand, then sat up in the sunlight, crossing his shins in front of him, and after a time let his woolly head fall on his breastbone.

"I didn't want any more loitering in the shade, and I made haste towards the

station. When near the buildings I met a white man, in such an unexpected ele-
gance of get-up that in the first moment I took him for a sort of vision. I saw a high
starched collar, white cuffs, a light alpaca jacket, snowy trousers, a clear necktie,
and varnished boots. No hat. Hair parted, brushed, oiled, under a green-lined
parasol held in a big white hand. He was amazing, and had a penholder behind
his ear.

"I shook hands with this miracle, and I learned he was the Company's chief
accountant, and that all the bookkeeping was done at this station. He had come
out for a moment, he said, 'to get a breath of fresh air.' The expression sounded
wonderfully odd, with its suggestion of sedentary desk-life. I wouldn't have mentioned the fellow to you at all, only it was from his lips that I first heard the name
of the man who is so indissolubly connected with the memories of that time. Moreover, I respected the fellow. Yes; I respected his collars, his vast cuffs, his brushed
hair. His appearance was certainly that of a hairdresser's dummy; but in the great
demoralization of the land he kept up his appearance. That's backbone. His
starched collars and got-up shirt-fronts were achievements of character. He had
been out nearly three years; and, later on, I could not help asking him how he
managed to sport such linen. He had just the faintest blush, and said modestly,
'I've been teaching one of the native women about the station. It was difficult. She
had a distaste for the work.' This man had verily accomplished something. And he
was devoted to his books, which were in apple-pie order.

"Everything else in the station was in a muddle,—heads, things, buildings.
Strings of dusty niggers with splay feet arrived and departed; a stream of manu-
factured goods, rubbishy cottons, beads, and brass-wire set into the depths of
darkness, and in return came a precious trickle of ivory.

"I had to wait in the station for ten days—an eternity. I lived in a hut in the
yard, but to be out of the chaos I would sometimes get into the accountant's office.
It was built of horizontal planks, and so badly put together that, as he bent over
his high desk, he was barred from neck to heels with narrow strips of sunlight.
There was no need to open the big shutter to see. It was hot there too; big flies
buzzed fiendishly, and did not sting, but stabbed. I sat generally on the floor,
while, of faultless appearance (and even slightly scented), perching on a high
stool, he wrote, he wrote. Sometimes he stood up for exercise. When a truckle-
bed with a sick man (some invalided agent from up-country) was put in there, he
exhibited a gentle annoyance. 'The groans of this sick person,' he said, 'distract
my attention. And without that it is extremely difficult to guard against clerical
errors in this climate.'

"One day he remarked, without lifting his head, 'In the interior you will no
doubt meet Mr. Kurtz.' On my asking who Mr. Kurtz was, he said he was a first-
class agent; and seeing my disappointment at this information, he added slowly,
laying down his pen, 'He is a very remarkable person.' Further questions elicited
from him that Mr. Kurtz was at present in charge of a trading post, a very important one, in the true ivory-country, at 'the very bottom of there. Sends in as much
ivory as all the others put together. . . .' He began to write again. The sick man
was too ill to groan. The flies buzzed in a great peace.

"Suddenly there was a growing murmur of voices and a great tramping of
feet. A caravan had come in. A violent babble of uncouth sounds burst out on the
other side of the planks. All the carriers were speaking together, and in the midst
of the uproar the lamentable voice of the chief agent was heard 'giving it up' tear-

fully for the twentieth time that day. . . . He rose slowly. 'What a frightful row,' he said. He crossed the room gently to look at the sick man, and returning, said to me, 'He does not hear.' 'What! Dead?' I asked, startled. 'No, not yet,' he answered, with great composure. Then, alluding with a toss of the head to the tumult in the station-yard, 'When one has got to make correct entries, one comes to hate those savages—hate them to the death.' He remained thoughtful for a moment. 'When you see Mr. Kurtz,' he went on, 'tell him from me that everything here'—he glanced at the desk—'is very satisfactory. I don't like to write to him—with those messengers of ours you never know who may get hold of your letter—at that Central Station.' He stared at me for a moment with his mild, bulging eyes. 'Oh, he will go far, very far,' he began again. 'He will be a somebody in the Administration before long. They, above—the Council in Europe, you know—mean him to be.'

"He turned to his work. The noise outside had ceased, and presently in going out I stopped at the door. In the steady buzz of flies the homeward-bound agent was lying flushed and insensible; the other, bent over his books, was making correct entries of perfectly correct transactions; and fifty feet below the doorstep I could see the still tree-tops of the grove of death.

"Next day I felt that station at last, with a caravan of sixty men, for a two-hundred-mile tramp.

"No use telling you much about that. Paths, paths, everywhere; a stamped-in network of paths spreading over the empty land, through long grass, through burnt grass, through thickets, down and up chilly ravines, up and down stony hills ablaze with heat; and a solitude, a solitude, nobody, not a hut. The population had cleared out a long time ago. Well, if a lot of mysterious niggers armed with all kinds of fearful weapons suddenly took to traveling on the road between Deal and Gravesend, catching the yokels right and left to carry heavy loads for them, I fancy every farm and cottage thereabouts would get empty very soon. Only here the dwellings were gone too. Still I passed through several abandoned villages. There's something pathetically childish in the ruins of grass walls. Day after day, with the stamp and shuffle of sixty pair of bare feet behind me, each pair under a 60-lb. load. Camp, cook, sleep, strike camp, march. Now and then a carrier dead in harness, at rest in the long grass near the path, with an empty water-gourd and his long staff lying by his side. A great silence around and above. Perhaps on some quiet night the tremor of far-off drums, sinking, swelling, a tremor vast, faint; a sound weird, appealing, suggestive, and wild—and perhaps with as profound a meaning as the sound of bells in a Christian country. Once a white man in an unbuttoned uniform, camping on the path with an armed escort of lank Zanzibaris, very hospitable and festive—not to say drunk. Was looking after the upkeep of the road, he declared. Can't say I saw any road or any upkeep, unless the body of a middle-aged negro, with a bullet-hole in the forehead, upon which I absolutely stumbled three miles farther on, may be considered as a permanent improvement. I had a white companion too, not a bad chap, but rather too fleshy and with the exasperating habit of fainting on the hot hillsides, miles away from the last bit of shade and water. Annoying, you know, to hold your own coat like a parasol over a man's head while he is coming-to. I couldn't help asking him once what he meant by coming there at all. 'To make money, of course. What do you think?' he said, scornfully. Then he got fever, and had to be carried in a hammock slung under a pole. As he weighed sixteen stone I had no end of rows with the carriers. They jibbed, ran away, sneaked off with their loads in the night—quite a mutiny.

So, one evening, I made a speech in English with gestures, not one of which was lost to the sixty pairs of eyes before me, and the next morning I started the hammock off in front all right. An hour afterwards I came upon the whole concern wrecked in a bush—man, hammock, groans, blankets, horrors. The heavy pole had skinned his poor nose. He was very anxious for me to kill somebody, but there wasn't the shadow of a carrier near. I remembered the old doctor,—'It would be interesting for science to watch the mental changes of individuals, on the spot.' I felt I was becoming scientifically interesting. However, all that is to no purpose. On the fifteenth day I came in sight of the big river again, and hobbled into the Central Station. It was on a back water surrounded by scrub and forest, with a pretty border of smelly mud on one side, and on the three others inclosed by a crazy fence of rushes. A neglected gap was all the gate it had, and the first glance at the place was enough to let you see the flabby devil was running that show. White men with long staves in their hands appeared languidly from amongst the buildings, strolling up to take a look at me, and then retired out of sight somewhere. One of them, a stout, excitable chap with black mustaches, informed me with great volubility and many digressions, as soon as I told him who I was, that my steamer was at the bottom of the river. I was thunderstruck. What, how, why? Oh, it was 'all right.' The 'manager himself' was there. All quite correct. 'Everybody had behaved splendidly! splendidly!'—'you must,' he said in agitation, 'go and see the general manager at once. He is waiting!'

"I did not see the real significance of that wreck at once. I fancy I see it now, but I am not sure—not at all. Certainly the affair was too stupid—when I think of it—to be altogether natural. Still. . . . But at the moment it presented itself simply as a confounded nuisance. The steamer was sunk. They had started two days before in a sudden hurry up the river with the manager on board, in charge of some volunteer skipper, and before they had been out three hours they tore the bottom out of her on stones, and she sank near the south bank. I asked myself what I was to do there, now my boat was lost. As a matter of fact, I had plenty to do in fishing my command out of the river. I had to set about it the very next day. That, and the repairs when I brought the pieces to the station, took some months.

"My first interview with the manager was curious. He did not ask me to sit down after my twenty-mile walk that morning. He was commonplace in complexion, in feature, in manners, and in voice. He was of middle size and of ordinary build. His eyes, of the usual blue, were perhaps remarkably cold, and he certainly could make his glance fall on one as trenchant and heavy as an ax. But even at these times the rest of his person seemed to disclaim the intention. Otherwise there was only an indefinable, faint expression of his lips, something stealthy—a smile—not a smile—I remember it, but I can't explain. It was unconscious, this smile was, though just after he had said something it got intensified for an instant. It came at the end of his speeches like a seal applied on the words to make the meaning of the commonest phrase appear absolutely inscrutable. He was a common trader, from his youth up employed in these parts—nothing more. He was obeyed, yet he inspired neither love nor fear, nor even respect. He inspired uneasiness. That was it! Uneasiness. Not a definite mistrust—just uneasiness—nothing more. You have no idea how effective such a . . . a . . . faculty can be. He had no genius for organizing, for initiative, or for order even. That was evident in such things as the deplorable state of the station. He had no learning, and no intelligence. His position had come to him—why? Perhaps because he was never ill . . .

He had served three terms of three years out there . . . Because triumphant health in the general rout of constitutions is a kind of power in itself. When he went home on leave he rioted on a large scale—pompously. Jack ashore—with a difference— in externals only. This one could gather from his casual talk. He originated nothing, he could keep the routine going—that's all. But he was great. He was great by this little thing that it was impossible to tell what could control such a man. He never gave that secret away. Perhaps there was nothing within him. Such a suspicion made one pause—for out there there were no external checks. Once when various tropical diseases had laid low almost every 'agent' in the station, he was heard to say, 'Men who come out here should have no entrails.' He sealed the utterance with that smile of his, as though it had been a door opening into a darkness he had in his keeping. You fancied you had seen things—but the seal was on. When annoyed at meal-times by the constant quarrels of the white men about precedence, he ordered an immense round table to be made, for which a special house had to be built. This was the station's mess-room. Where he sat was the first place—the rest were nowhere. One felt this to be his unalterable conviction. He was neither civil nor uncivil. He was quiet. He allowed his 'boy'—an overfed young negro from the coast—to treat the white men, under his very eyes, with provoking insolence.

"He began to speak as soon as he saw me. I had been very long on the road. He could not wait. Had to start without me. The up-river stations had to be relieved. There had been so many delays already that he did not know who was dead and who was alive, and how they got on—and so on, and so on. He paid no attention to my explanations, and, playing with a stick of sealing-wax, repeated several times that the situation was 'very grave, very grave.' There were rumors that a very important station was in jeopardy, and its chief, Mr. Kurtz, was ill. Hoped it was not true. Mr. Kurtz was . . . I felt weary and irritable. Hang Kurtz, I thought. I interrupted him by saying I had heard of Mr. Kurtz on the coast. 'Ah! So they talk of him down there,' he murmured to himself. Then he began again, assuring me Mr. Kurtz was the best agent he had, an exceptional man, of the greatest importance to the Company; therefore I could understand his anxiety. He was, he said, 'very, very uneasy.' Certainly he fidgeted on his chair a good deal, exclaimed, 'Ah, Mr. Kurtz!' broke the stick of sealing-wax and seemed dumbfounded by the accident. Next thing he wanted to know 'how long it would take to' . . . I interrupted him again. Being hungry, you know, and kept on my feet too, I was getting savage. 'How could I tell,' I said. 'I hadn't even seen the wreck yet— some months, no doubt.' All this talk seemed to me so futile. 'Some months,' he said. 'Well, let us say three months before we can make a start. Yes. That ought to do the affair.' I flung out of his hut (he lived all alone in a clay hut with a sort of veranda) muttering to myself my opinion of him. He was a chattering idiot. Afterwards I took it back when it was borne in upon me startlingly with what extreme nicety he had estimated the time requisite for the 'affair.'

"I went to work the next day, turning, so to speak, my back on that station. In that way only it seemed to me I could keep my hold on the redeeming facts of life. Still, one must look about sometimes; and then I saw this station, these men strolling aimlessly about in the sunshine of the yard. I asked myself sometimes what it all meant. They wandered here and there with their absurd long staves in their hands, like a lot of faithless pilgrims bewitched inside a rotten fence. The word 'ivory' rang in the air, was whispered, was sighed. You would think they were praying to it. A taint of imbecile rapacity blew through it all, like a whiff from some corpse. By Jove! I've never seen anything so unreal in my life. And outside, the silent wilderness surrounding this cleared speck on the earth struck me as something great and invincible, like evil or truth, waiting patiently for the passing away of this fantastic invasion.

"Oh, these months! Well, never mind. Various things happened. One evening a grass shed full of calico, cotton prints, beads, and I don't know what else, burst into a blaze so suddenly that you would have thought the earth had opened to let an avenging fire consume all that trash. I was smoking my pipe quietly by my dismantled steamer, and saw them all cutting capers in the light, with their arms lifted high, when the stout man with mustaches came tearing down to the river, a tin pail in his hand, assured me that everybody was 'behaving splendidly, splendidly,' dipped about a quart of water and tore back again. I noticed there was a hole in the bottom of his pail.

"I strolled up. There was no hurry. You see the thing had gone off like a box of matches. It had been hopeless from the very first. The flame had leaped high, driven everybody back, lighted up everything—and collapsed. The shed was already a heap of embers glowing fiercely. A nigger was being beaten near by. They said he had caused the fire in some way; be that as it may, he was screeching most horribly. I saw him, later on, for several days, sitting in a bit of shade looking very sick and trying to recover himself: afterwards he arose and went out—and the wilderness without a sound took him into its bosom again. As I approached the glow from the dark I found myself at the back of two men, talking. I heard the name of Kurtz pronounced, then the words, 'take advantage of this unfortunate accident.' One of the men was the manager. I wished him a good evening. 'Did you ever see anything like it—eh? it is incredible,' he said, and walked off. The other man remained. He was a first-class agent, young, gentlemanly, a bit reserved, with a forked little beard and a hooked nose. He was stand-offish with the other agents, and they on their side said he was the manager's spy upon them. As to me, I had hardly ever spoken to him before. We got into talk, and by-and-by we strolled away from the hissing ruins. Then he asked me to his room, which was in the main building of the station. He struck a match, and I perceived that this young aristocrat had not only a silver-mounted dressing-case but also a whole candle all to himself. Just at that time the manager was the only man supposed to have any right to candles. Native mats covered the clay walls; a collection of spears, assegais, shields, knives was hung up in trophies. The business intrusted to this fellow was the making of bricks—so I had been informed; but there wasn't a fragment of a brick anywhere in the station, and he had been there more than a year—waiting. It seems he could not make bricks without something, I don't know what—straw maybe. Anyways, it could not be found there, and as it was not likely to be sent from Europe, it did not appear clear to me what he was waiting for. An act of special creation perhaps. However, they were all waiting—all the sixteen or twenty pilgrims of them—for something; and upon my word it did not seem an uncongenial occupation, from the way they took it, though the only thing that ever came to them was disease—as far as I could see. They beguiled the time by backbiting and intriguing against each other in a foolish kind of way. There was an air of plotting about that station, but nothing came of it, of course. It was as unreal as everything else—as the philanthropic pretense of the whole concern, as their talk, as their government, as their show of work. The only real feeling was a desire to get appointed to a trading-post where ivory was to he had, so that they could earn percentages. They intrigued and slandered and hated each other only on that ac- count,—but as to effectually lifting a little finger—oh, no. By heavens! there is something after all in the world allowing one man to steal a horse while another must not look at a halter. Steal a horse straight out. Very well. He has done it. Per- haps he can ride. But there is a way of looking at a halter that would provoke the most charitable of saints into a kick.

"I had no idea why he wanted to be sociable, but as we chatted in there it sud- denly occurred to me the fellow was trying to get at something—in fact, pumping me. He alluded constantly to Europe, to the people I was supposed to know there—putting leading questions as to my acquaintances in the sepulchral city, and so on. His little eyes glittered like mica discs—with curiosity,—though he tried to keep up a bit of superciliousness. At first I was astonished, but very soon I became awfully curious to see what he would find out from me. I couldn't pos- sibly imagine what I had in me to make it worth his while. It was very pretty to see how be baffled himself, for in truth my body was full of chills, and my head had nothing in it but that wretched steamboat business. It was evident he took me for a perfectly shameless prevaricator. At last he got angry, and, to conceal a move- ment of furious annoyance, he yawned. I rose. Then I noticed a small sketch in oils, on a panel, representing a woman, draped and blindfolded, carrying a lighted torch. The background was somber—almost black. The movement of the woman was stately, and the effect of the torchlight on the face was sinister.

"It arrested me, and he stood by civilly, holding a half-pint champagne bottle (medical comforts) with the candle stuck in it. To my question he said Mr. Kurtz had painted this—in this very station more than a year ago—while waiting for means to go to his trading-post. 'Tell me, pray,' said I, 'who is this Mr. Kurtz?'

"'The chief of the Inner Station,' he answered in a short tone, looking away. 'Much obliged,' I said, laughing. 'And you are the brickmaker of the Central Sta- tion. Everyone knows that.' He was silent for a while. 'He is a prodigy,' he said at last. 'He is an emissary of pity, and science, and progress, and devil knows what else. We want,' he began to declaim suddenly, 'for the guidance of the cause in- trusted to us by Europe, so to speak, higher intelligence, wide sympathies, a sin- gleness of purpose.' 'Who says that?' I asked. 'Lots of them,' he replied. 'Some even write that; and so *he* comes here, a special being, as you ought to know.' 'Why ought I to know?' I interrupted, really surprised. He paid no attention. 'Yes. To- day he is chief of the best station, next year he will be assistant-manager, two years more and . . . but I dare say you know what he will be in two years' time. You are of the new gang—the gang of virtue. The same people who sent him specially also recommended you. Oh, don't say no. I've my own eyes to trust.' Light dawned upon me. My dear aunt's influential acquaintances were producing an unexpected effect upon that young man. I nearly burst into a laugh. 'Do you read the Com- pany's confidential correspondence?' I asked. He hadn't a word to say. It was great fun. 'When Mr. Kurtz,' I continued severely, 'is General Manager, you won't have the opportunity.'

"He blew the candle out suddenly, and we went outside. The moon had risen. Black figures strolled about listlessly, pouring water on the glow, whence pro- ceeded a sound of hissing; steam ascended in the moonlight, the beaten nigger groaned somewhere. 'What a row the brute makes!' said the indefatigable man with the mustaches, appearing near us. 'Serve him right. Transgression—punishment—bang! Pitiless, pitiless. That's the only way. This will prevent all conflagrations for the future. I was just telling the manager . . .' He noticed my companion, and became crestfallen all at once. 'Not in bed yet,' he said, with a kind of servile heartiness; 'it's so natural. Ha! Danger-agitation.' He vanished. I went on to the river-side, and the other followed me. I heard a scathing murmur at my ear, 'Heap of muffs—go to.' The pilgrims could be seen in knots gesticulating, discussing. Several had still their staves in their hands. I verily believe they took these sticks to bed with them. Beyond the fence the forest stood up spectrally in the moonlight, and through the dim stir, through the faint sounds of that lamentable courtyard, the silence of the land went home to one's very heart,—its mystery, its greatness, the amazing reality of its concealed life. The hurt nigger moaned feebly somewhere near by, and then fetched a deep sigh that made me mend my pace away from there. I felt a hand introducing itself under my arm. 'My dear sir,' said the fellow, 'I don't want to be misunderstood, and especially by you, who will see Mr. Kurtz long before I can have that pleasure. I wouldn't like him to get a false idea of my disposition. . . .'

"I let him run on, this papier-maché Mephistopheles, and it seemed to me that if I tried I could poke my forefinger through him, and would find nothing inside but a little loose dirt, maybe. He, don't you see, had been planning to be assistant-manager by-and-by under the present man, and I could see that the coming of that Kurtz had upset them both not a little. He talked precipitately, and I did not try to stop him. I had my shoulders against the wreck of my steamer, hauled up on the slope like a carcass of some big river animal. The smell of mud, of primeval mud, by Jove! was in my nostrils, the high stillness of primeval forest was before my eyes; there were shiny patches on the black creek. The moon had spread over everything a thin layer of silver—over the rank grass, over the mud, upon the wall of matted vegetation standing higher than the wall of a temple, over the great river I could see through a somber gap glittering, glittering, as it flowed broadly by without a murmur. All this was great, expectant, mute, while the man jabbered about himself. I wondered whether the stillness on the face of the immensity looking at us two were meant as an appeal or as a menace. What were we who had strayed in here? Could we handle that dumb thing, or would it handle us? I felt how big, how confoundedly big, was that thing that couldn't talk, and perhaps was deaf as well. What was in there? I could see a little ivory coming out from there, and I had heard Mr. Kurtz was in there. I had heard enough about it too— God knows! Yet somehow it didn't bring any image with it—no more than if I had been told an angel or a fiend was in there. I believed it in the same way one of you might believe there are inhabitants in the planet Mars. I knew once a Scotch sailmaker who was certain, dead sure, there were people in Mars. If you asked him for some idea how they looked and behaved, he would get shy and mutter something about 'walking on all-fours.' If you as much as smiled, he would—though a man of sixty—offer to fight you. I would not have gone so far as to fight for Kurtz, but I went for him near enough to a lie. You know I hate, detest, and can't bear a lie, not because I am straighter than the rest of us, but simply because it appalls me. There is a taint of death, a flavor of mortality in lies,—which is exactly what I hate and detest in the world—what I want to forget. It makes me miserable and sick, like biting something rotten would do. Temperament, I suppose. Well, I went near enough to it by letting the young fool there believe anything he liked to imagine as to my influence in Europe. I became in an instant as much of a pretense as the rest of the bewitched pilgrims. This simply because I had a notion it somehow would be of help to that Kurtz whom at the time I did not see—you understand. He was just a word for me. I did not see the man in the name any more than you do. Do you see him? Do you see the story? Do you see anything? It seems to me I am trying to tell you a dream—making a vain attempt, because no relation of a dream can convey the dream-sensation, that commingling of absurdity, surprise, and bewilderment in a tremor of struggling revolt, that notion of being captured by the incredible which is of the very essence of dreams. . . ."

He was silent for a while.

". . . No, it is impossible; it is impossible to convey the life-sensation of any given epoch of one's existence,—that which makes its truth, its meaning—its subtle and penetrating essence. It is impossible. We live, as we dream—alone. . . ."

He paused again as if reflecting, then added—

"Of course in this you fellows see more than I could then. You see me, whom you know. . . ."

It had become so pitch dark that we listeners could hardly see one another. For a long time already he, sitting apart, had been no more to us than a voice. There was not a word from anybody. The others might have been asleep, but I was awake. I listened, I listened on the watch for the sentence, for the word, that would give me the clew to the faint uneasiness inspired by this narrative that seemed to shape itself without human lips in the heavy night-air of the river.

". . . Yes—I let him run on," Marlow began again, "and think what he pleased about the powers that were behind me. I did! And there was nothing behind me! There was nothing but that wretched, old, mangled steamboat I was leaning against, while he talked fluently about 'the necessity for every man to get on.' 'And when one comes out here, you conceive, it is not to gaze at the moon.' Mr. Kurtz was a 'universal genius,' but even a genius would find it easier to work with 'adequate tools—intelligent men.' He did not make bricks—why, there was a physical impossibility in the way—as I was well aware; and if he did secretarial work for the manager, it was because 'no sensible man rejects wantonly the confidence of his superiors.' Did I see it? I saw it. What more did I want? What I really wanted was rivets, by heaven! Rivets. To get on with the work—to stop the hole. Rivets I wanted. There were cases of them down at the coast—cases—piled up—burst—split! You kicked a loose rivet at every second step in that station yard on the hillside. Rivets had rolled into the grove of death. You could fill your pockets with rivets for the trouble of stooping down—and there wasn't one rivet to be found where it was wanted. We had plates that would do, but nothing to fasten them with. And every week the messenger, a lone negro, letter-bag on shoulder and staff in hand, left our station for the coast. And several times a week a coast caravan came in with trade goods,—ghastly glazed calico that made you shudder only to look at it, glass beads value about a penny a quart, confounded spotted cotton handkerchiefs. And no rivets. Three carriers could have brought all that was wanted to set that steamboat afloat.

"He was becoming confidential now, but I fancy my unresponsive attitude must have exasperated him at last, for he judged it necessary to inform me he feared neither God nor devil, let alone any mere man. I said I could see that very well, but what I wanted was a certain quantity of rivets—and rivets were what really Mr. Kurtz wanted, if he had only known it. Now letters went to the coast every week. . . . 'My dear sir,' he cried, 'I write from dictation.' I demanded rivets. There was a way—for an intelligent man. He changed his manner; became very cold, and suddenly began to talk about a hippopotamus; wondered whether sleeping on board the steamer (I stuck to my salvage night and day) I wasn't disturbed. There was an old hippo that had the bad habit of getting out on the bank and roaming at night over the station grounds. The pilgrims used to turn out in a body and empty every rifle they could lay hands on at him. Some even had sat up o' nights for him. All this energy was wasted, though. 'That animal has charmed life,' he said; 'but you can say this only of brutes in this country. No man—you apprehend me?—no man here bears a charmed life.' He stood there for a moment in the moonlight with his delicate hooked nose set a little askew, and his mica eyes glittering without a wink, then, with a curt Good night, he strode off. I could see he was disturbed and considerably puzzled, which made me feel more hopeful than I had been for days. It was a great comfort to turn from that chap to my influential friend, the battered, twisted, ruined, tin-pot steamboat. I clambered on board. She rang under my feet like an empty Huntley & Palmer biscuit-tin kicked along a gutter; she was nothing so solid in make, and rather less pretty in shape, but I had expended enough hard work on her to make me love her. No influential friend would have served me better. She had given me a chance to come out a bit— to find out what I could do. No, I don't like work. I had rather laze about and think of all the fine things that can be done. I don't like work—no man does—but I like what is in the work,—the chance to find yourself. Your own reality—for yourself, not for others—what no other man can ever know. They can only see the mere show, and never can tell what it really means.

"I was not surprised to see somebody sitting aft, on the deck, with his legs dangling over the mud. You see I rather chummed with the few mechanics there were in that station, whom the other pilgrims naturally despised—on account of their imperfect manners, I suppose. This was the foreman—a boiler-maker by trade—a good worker. He was a lank, bony, yellow-faced man, with big intense eyes. His aspect was worried, and his head was as bald as the palm of my hand; but his hair in falling seemed to have stuck to his chin, and had prospered in the new locality, for his beard hung down to his waist. He was a widower with six young children (he had left them in charge of a sister of his to come out there), and the passion of his life was pigeon-flying. He was an enthusiast and a connoisseur. He would rave about pigeons. After work hours he used sometimes to come over from his hut for a talk about his children and his pigeons; at work, when he had to crawl in the mud under the bottom of the steamboat, he would tip up that beard of his in a kind of white serviette he brought for the purpose. It had loops to go over his ears. In the evening he could be seen squatted on the bank rinsing that wrapper in the creek with great care, then spreading it solemnly on a bush to dry.

"I slapped him on the back and shouted 'We shall have rivets!' He scrambled to his feet exclaiming 'No! Rivets!' as though he couldn't believe his ears. Then in a low voice, 'You . . . eh?' I don't know why we behaved like lunatics. I put my finger to the side of my nose and nodded mysteriously. 'Good for you!' he cried, snapped his fingers above his head, lifting one foot. I tried a jig. We capered on the iron deck. A frightful clatter came out of that hulk, and the virgin forest on the other bank of the creek sent it back in a thundering roll upon the sleeping station. It must have made some of the pilgrims sit up in their hovels. A dark figure obscured the lighted doorway of the manager's hut, vanished, then, a second or so after, the doorway itself vanished too. We stopped, and the silence driven away by the stamping of our feet flowed back again from the recesses of the land. The great wall of vegetation, an exuberant and entangled mass of trunks, branches, leaves, boughs, festoons, motionless in the moonlight, was like a rioting invasion of soundless life, a rolling wave of plants, piled up, crested, ready to topple over the creek, to sweep every little man of us out of his little existence. And it moved not. A deadened burst of mighty splashes and snorts reached us from afar, as though an ichthyosaurus had been taking a bath of glitter in the great river. 'After all,' said the boiler-maker in a reasonable tone, 'why shouldn't we get the rivets?' Why not, indeed! I did not know of any reason why we shouldn't. 'They'll come in three weeks,' I said, confidently.

"But they didn't. Instead of rivets there came an invasion, an infliction, a visitation. It came in sections during the next three weeks, each section headed by a donkey carrying a white man in new clothes and tan shoes, bowing from the elevation right and left to the impressed pilgrims. A quarrelsome band of footsore sulky niggers trod on the heels of the donkeys; a lot of tents, camp-stools, tin boxes, white cases, brown bales would be shot down in the courtyard, and the air of mystery would deepen a little over the muddle of the station. Five such installments came, with their absurd air of disorderly flight with the loot of innumerable outfit shops and provision stores, that, one would think, they were lugging, after a raid, into the wilderness for equitable division. It was an inextricable mess of things decent in themselves but that human folly made look like the spoils of thieving.

"This devoted band called itself the Eldorado Exploring Expedition, and I believe they were sworn to secrecy. Their talk, however, was the talk of sordid buccaneers: it was reckless without hardihood, greedy without audacity, and cruel without courage; there was not an atom of foresight or of serious intention in the whole batch of them, and they did not seem aware these things are wanted for the work of the world. To tear treasure out of the bowels of the land was their desire, with no more moral purpose at the back of it than there is in burglars breaking into a safe. Who paid the expenses of the noble enterprise I don't know; but the uncle of our manager was leader of that lot.

"In exterior he resembled a butcher in a poor neighborhood, and his eyes had a look of sleepy cunning. He carried his fat paunch with ostentation on his short legs, and during the time his gang infested the station spoke to no one but his nephew. You could see these two roaming about all day long with their heads close together in an everlasting confab.

"I had given up worrying myself about the rivets. One's capacity for that kind of folly is more limited than you would suppose. I said Hang!—and let things slide. I had plenty of time for meditation, and now and then I would give some thought to Kurtz. I wasn't very interested in him. No. Still, I was curious to see whether this man, who had come out equipped with moral ideas of some sort, would climb to the top after all, and how he would set about his work when there."

II

"One evening as I was lying flat on the deck of my steamboat, I heard voices approaching—and there were the nephew and the uncle strolling along the bank. I laid my head on my arm again, and had nearly lost myself in a doze, when somebody said in my ear, as it were: 'I am as harmless as a little child, but I don't like to be dictated to. Am I the manager—or am I not? I was ordered to send him there. It's incredible.' . . . I became aware that the two were standing on the shore alongside the forepart of the steamboat, just below my head. I did not move; it did not occur to me to move: I was sleepy. 'It *is* unpleasant,' grunted the uncle. 'He has asked the Administration to be sent there,' said the other, 'with the idea of showing what he could do; and I was instructed accordingly. Look at the influence that man must have. Is it not frightful?' They both agreed it was frightful, then made several bizarre remarks: 'Make rain and fine weather—one man—the Council—by the nose'—bits of absurb sentences that got the better of my drowsiness, so that I had pretty near the whole of my wits about me when the uncle said, 'The climate may do away with this difficulty for you. Is he alone there?' 'Yes,' answered the manager; 'he sent his assistant down the river with a note to me in these terms: "Clear this poor devil out of the country, and don't bother sending more of that sort. I had rather be alone than have the kind of men you can dispose of with me." It was more than a year ago. Can you imagine such impudence!' 'Anything since then?' asked the other, hoarsely. 'Ivory,' jerked the nephew; 'lots of it—prime sort—lots—most annoying, from him.' 'And with that?' questioned the heavy rumble. 'Invoice,' was the reply fired out, so to speak. Then silence. They had been talking about Kurtz.

"I was broad awake by this time, but, lying perfectly at ease, remained still, having no inducement to change my position. 'How did that ivory come all this way?' growled the elder man, who seemed very vexed. The other explained that it had come with a fleet of canoes in charge of an English half-caste clerk Kurtz had with him; that Kurtz had apparently intended to return himself, the station being by that time bare of goods and stores, but after coming three hundred miles, had suddenly decided to go back, which he started to do alone in a small dug-out with four paddlers, leaving the half-caste to continue down the river with the ivory. The two fellows there seemed astounded at anybody attempting such a thing. They were at a loss for an adequate motive. As to me, I seemed to see Kurtz for the first time. It was a distinct glimpse: the dug-out, four paddling savages, and the lone white man turning his back suddenly on the headquarters, on relief, on thoughts of home—perhaps; setting his face towards the depths of the wilderness, towards his empty and desolate station. I did not know the motive. Perhaps he was just simply a fine fellow who stuck to his work for its own sake. His name, you understand, had not been pronounced once. He was 'that man.' The half-caste, who, as far as I could see, had conducted a difficult trip with great prudence and pluck, was invariably alluded to as 'that scoundrel.' The 'scoundrel' had reported that the 'man' had been very ill—had recovered imperfectly. . . . The two below me moved away then a few paces, and strolled back and forth at some little distance. I heard: 'Military post—doctor—two hundred miles—quite alone now—unavoidable delays—nine months—no news—strange rumors.' They approached again, just as the manager was saying, 'No one, as far as I know, unless a species of wandering trader—a pestilential fellow, snapping ivory from the natives.' Who was it they were talking about now? I gathered in snatches that this was some man supposed to be in Kurtz's district, and of whom the manager did not approve. 'We will not be free from unfair competition till one of these fellows is hanged for an example,' he said. 'Certainly,' grunted the other; 'get him hanged! Why not? Anything—anything can be done in this country. That's what I say; nobody here, you understand, *here*, can endanger your position. And why? You stand the climate—

you outlast them all. The danger is in Europe; but there before I left I took care to
——' They moved off and whispered, then their voices rose again. 'The extraordinary series of delays is not my fault. I did my possible.' The fat man sighed, 'Very
sad.' 'And the pestiferous absurdity of his talk,' continued the other; 'he bothered
me enough when he was here. "Each station should be like a beacon on the road
towards better things, a center for trade of course, but also for humanizing, improving, instructing." Conceive you—that ass! And he wants to be manager! No,
it's——' Here he got choked by excessive indignation, and I lifted my head the
least bit. I was surprised to see how near they were—right under me. I could have
spat upon their hats. They were looking on the ground, absorbed in thought. The
manager was switching his leg with a slender twig: his sagacious relative lifted his
head. 'You have been well since you came out this time?' he asked. The other gave
a start. 'Who? I? Oh! Like a charm—like a charm. But the rest—oh, my goodness!
All sick. They die so quick, too, that I haven't the time to send them out of the
country—it's incredible!' 'H'm. Just so,' grunted the uncle. 'Ah! my boy, trust to
this—I say, trust to this.' I saw him extend his short flipper of an arm for a gesture
that took in the forest, the creek, the mud, the river,—seemed to beckon with a
dishonoring flourish before the sunlit face of the land a treacherous appeal to the
lurking death, to the hidden evil, to the profound darkness of its heart. It was so
startling that I leaped to my feet and looked back at the edge of the forest, as
though I had expected an answer of some sort to that black display of confidence.
You know the foolish notions that come to one sometimes. The high stillness confronted these two figures with its ominous patience, waiting for the passing away
of a fantastic invasion.

"They swore aloud together—out of sheer fright, I believe—then pretending
not to know anything of my existence, turned back to the station. The sun was low;
and leaning forward side by side, they seemed to be tugging painfully uphill their
two ridiculous shadows of unequal length, that trailed behind them slowly over
the tall grass without bending a single blade.

"In a few days the Eldorado Expedition went into the patient wilderness, that
closed upon it as the sea closes over a diver. Long afterwards the news came that
all the donkeys were dead. I know nothing as to the fate of the less valuable animals. They, no doubt, like the rest of us, found what they deserved. I did not inquire. I was then rather excited at the prospect of meeting Kurtz very soon. When
I say very soon I mean it comparatively. It was just two months from the day we
left the creek when we came to the bank below Kurtz's station.

"Going up that river was like traveling back to the earliest beginnings of the
world, when vegetation rioted on the earth and the big trees were kings. An empty
stream, a great silence, an impenetrable forest. The air was warm, thick, heavy,
sluggish. There was no joy in the brilliance of sunshine. The long stretches of the
waterway ran on, deserted, into the gloom of overshadowed distances. On silvery
sandbanks hippos and alligators sunned themselves side by side. The broadening
waters flowed through a mob of wooded islands; you lost your way on that river
as you would in a desert, and butted all day long against shoals, trying to find the
channel, till you thought yourself bewitched and cut off for ever from everything
you had known once—somewhere—far away— in another existence perhaps.
There were moments when one's past came back to one, as it will sometimes when
you have not a moment to spare to yourself; but it came in the shape of an unrestful
and noisy dream, remembered with wonder amongst the overwhelming realities

of this strange world of plants, and water, and silence. And this stillness of life did not in the least resemble a peace. It was the stillness of an implacable force brooding over an inscrutable intention. It looked at you with a vengeful aspect. I got used to it afterwards; I did not see it any more; I had no time. I had to keep guessing at the channel; I had to discern, mostly by inspiration, the signs of hidden banks; I watched for sunken stones; I was learning to clap my teeth smartly before my heart flew out, when I shaved by a fluke some infernal sly old snag that would have ripped the life out of the tin-pot steamboat and drowned all the pilgrims; I had to keep a look-out for the signs of dead wood we could cut up in the night for next day's steaming. When you have to attend to things of that sort, to the mere incidents of the surface, the reality—the reality, I tell you—fades. The inner truth is hidden—luckily, luckily. But I felt it all the same; I felt often its mysterious stillness watching me at my monkey tricks, just as it watches you fellows performing on your respective tight-ropes for —what is it? half-a-crown a tumble——"

"Try to be civil, Marlow," growled a voice, and I knew there was at least one listener awake besides myself.

"I beg your pardon. I forgot the heartache which makes up the rest of the price. And indeed what does the price matter, if the trick be well done? You do your tricks very well. And I didn't do badly either, since I managed not to sink that steamboat on my first trip. It's a wonder to me yet. Imagine a blindfolded man set to drive a van over a bad road. I sweated and shivered over that business considerably, I can tell you. After all, for a seaman, to scrape the bottom of the thing that's supposed to float all the time under his care is the unpardonable sin. No one may know of it, but you never forget the thump—eh? A blow on the very heart. You remember it, you dream of it, you wake up at night and think of it—years after—and go hot and cold all over. I don't pretend to say that steamboat floated all the time. More than once she had to wade for a bit, with twenty cannibals splashing around and pushing. We had enlisted some of these chaps on the way for a crew. Fine fellows—cannibals—in their place. They were men one could work with, and I am grateful to them. And, after all, they did not eat each other before my face: they had brought along a provision of hippo-meat which went rotten, and made the mystery of the wilderness stink in my nostrils. Phoo! I can sniff it now. I had the manager on board and three or four pilgrims with their staves—all complete. Sometimes we came upon a station close by the bank, clinging to the skirts of the unknown, and the white men rushing out of a tumble-down hovel, with great gestures of joy and surprise and welcome, seemed very strange,—had the appearance of being held there captive by a spell. The word ivory would ring in the air for a while—and on we went again into the silence, along empty reaches, round the still bends, between the high walls of our winding way, reverberating in hollow claps the ponderous beat of the stern-wheel. Trees, trees, millions of trees, massive, immense, running up high; and at their foot, hugging the bank against the steam, crept the little begrimed steamboat, like a sluggish beetle crawling on the floor of a lofty portico. It made you feel very small, very lost, and yet it was not altogether depressing that feeling. After all, if you were small, the grimy beetle crawled on —which was just what you wanted it to do. Where the pilgrims imagined it crawled to I don't know. To some place where they expected to get something, I bet! For me it crawled toward Kurtz—exclusively; but when the steam-pipes started leaking we crawled very slow. The reaches opened before us and closed behind, as if the forest had stepped leisurely across the water to bar the way for our return. We penetrated deeper and deeper into the heart of darkness. It was very quiet there. At night sometimes the roll of drums behind the curtain of trees would run up the river and remain sustained faintly, as if hovering in the air high over our heads, till the first break of day. Whether it meant war, peace, or prayer we could not tell. The dawns were heralded by the descent of a chill still-ness; the woodcutters slept, their fires burned low; the snapping of a twig would make you start. We were wanderers on a prehistoric earth, on an earth that wore the aspect of an unknown planet. We could have fancied ourselves the first of men taking possession of an accursed inheritance, to be subdued at the cost of pro-found anguish and of excessive toil. But suddenly, as we struggled round a bend, there would be a glimpse of rush walls, of peaked grass-roofs, a burst of yells, a whirl of black limbs, a mass of hands clapping, of feet stamping, of bodies sway-ing, of eyes rolling, under the droop of heavy and motionless foliage. The steamer toiled along slowly on the edge of a black and incomprehensible frenzy. The pre-historic man was cursing us, praying to us, welcoming us—who could tell? We were cut off from the comprehension of our surroundings; we glided past like phantoms, wondering and secretly appalled, as sane men would be before an en-thusiastic outbreak in a madhouse. We could not understand, because we were too far and could not remember, because we were traveling in the night of first ages, of those ages that are gone, leaving hardly a sign—and no memories.

"The earth seemed unearthly. We are accustomed to look upon the shackled form of a conquered monster, but there—there you could look at a thing mon-strous and free. It was unearthly, and the men were—— No, they were not in-human. Well, you know, that was the worst of it—this suspicion of their not being inhuman. It would come slowly to one. They howled, and leaped, and spun, and made horrid faces; but what thrilled you was just the thought of their humanity—like yours—the thought of your remote kinship with this wild and passionate up-roar. Ugly. Yes, it was ugly enough; but if you were man enough you would admit to yourself that there was in you just the faintest trace of a response to the terrible frankness of that noise, a dim suspicion of there being a meaning in it which you—you so remote from the night of first ages—could comprehend. And why not? The mind of man is capable of anything—because everything is in it, all the past as well as all the future. What was there after all? Joy, fear, sorrow, devotion, valor, rage—who can tell?—but truth—truth stripped of its cloak of time. Let the fool gape and shudder—the man knows, and can look on without a wink. But he must at least be as much of a man as these on the shore. He must meet that truth with his own true stuff——with his own inborn strength. Principles? Principles won't do. Ac-quisitions, clothes, pretty rags—rags that would fly off at the first good shake. No; you want a deliberate belief. An appeal to me in this fiendish row—is there? Very well; I hear; I admit, but I have a voice too, and for good or evil mine is the speech that cannot be silenced. Of course, a fool, what with sheer fright and fine senti-ments, is always safe. Who's that grunting? You wonder I didn't go ashore for a howl and a dance? Well, no—I didn't. Fine sentiments, you say? Fine sentiments, be hanged! I had no time. I had to mess about with white-lead and strips of woolen blanket helping to put bandages on those leaky steam-pipes—I tell you. I had to watch the steering, and circumvent those snags, and get the tin-pot along by hook or by crook. There was surface-truth enough in these things to save a wiser man. And between whiles I had to look after the savage who was fireman. He was an improved specimen; he could fire up a vertical boiler. He was there below me, and, upon my word, to look at him was as edifying as seeing a dog in a parody of breeches and a feather hat, walking on his hind-legs. A few months of training had done for that really fine chap. He squinted at the steam-gauge and at the water-gauge with an evident effort of intrepidity—and he had filed teeth too, the poor devil, and the wool of his pate shaved into queer patterns, and three ornamental scars on each of his cheeks. He ought to have been clapping his hands and stamping his feet on the bank, instead of which he was hard at work, a thrall to strange witchcraft, full of improving knowledge. He was useful because he had been instructed; and what he knew was this—that should the water in that transparent thing disappear, the evil spirit inside the boiler would get angry through the greatness of his thirst, and take a terrible vengeance. So he sweated and fired up and watched the glass fearfully (with an impromptu charm, made of rags, tied to his arm, and a piece of polished bone, as big as a watch, stuck flatways through his lower lip), while the wooded banks slipped past us slowly, the short noise was left behind, the interminable miles of silence—and we crept on, towards Kurtz. But the snags were thick, the water was treacherous and shallow, the boiler seemed indeed to have a sulky devil in it, and thus neither that fireman nor I had any time to peer into our creepy thoughts.

"Some fifty miles below the Inner Station we came upon a hut of reeds, an inclined and melancholy pole, with the unrecognizable tatters of what had been a flag of some sort flying from it, and a neatly stacked woodpile. This was unexpected: We came to the bank, and on the stack of firewood found a flat piece of board with some faded pencil-writing on it. When deciphered it said: 'Wood for you. Hurry up. Approach cautiously.' There was a signature, but it was illegible—not Kurtz—a much longer word. Hurry up. Where? Up the river? 'Approach cautiously.' We had not done so. But the warning could not have been meant for the place where it could be only found after approach. Something was wrong above. But what—and how much? That was the question. We commented adversely upon the imbecility of that telegraphic style. The bush around said nothing, and would not let us look very far, either. A torn curtain of red twill hung in the doorway of the hut, and flapped sadly in our faces. The dwelling was dismantled; but we could see a white man had lived there not very long ago. There remained a rude table—a plank on two posts; a heap of rubbish reposed in a dark corner, and by the door I picked up a book. It had lost its covers, and the pages had been thumbed into a state of extremely dirty softness; but the back had been lovingly stitched afresh with white cotton thread, which looked clean yet. It was an extraordinary find. Its title was, 'An Inquiry into some Points of Seamanship,' by a man Tower, Towson—some such name—Master in his Majesty's Navy. The matter looked dreary reading enough, with illustrative diagrams and repulsive tables of figures, and the copy was sixty years old. I handled this amazing antiquity with the greatest possible tenderness, lest it should dissolve in my hands. Within, Towson or Towser was inquiring earnestly into the breaking strain of ships' chains and tackle, and other such matters. Not a very enthralling book; but at the first glance you could see there a singleness of intention, an honest concern for the right way of going to work, which made these humble pages, thought out so many years ago, luminous with another than a professional light. The simple old sailor, with his talk of chains and purchases, made me forget the jungle and the pilgrims in a delicious sensation of having come upon something unmistakably real. Such a book being there was wonderful enough; but still more astounding were the notes penciled in the margin, and plainly referring to the text. I couldn't believe my eyes! They were in cipher! Yes, it looked like cipher. Fancy a man lugging with him a book of that description into this nowhere and studying it—and making notes— in cipher at that! It was an extravagant mystery.

"I had been dimly aware for some time of a worrying noise, and when I lifted my eyes I saw the wood-pile was gone, and the manager, aided by all the pilgrims, was shouting at me from the river-side. I slipped the book into my pocket. I assure you to leave off reading was like tearing myself away from the shelter of an old and solid friendship.

"I started the lame engine ahead. 'It must be this miserable trader—this in- truder,' exclaimed the manager, looking back malevolently at the place we had left. 'He must be English,' I said. 'It will not save him from getting into trouble if he is not careful,' muttered the manager darkly. I observed with assumed innocence that no man was safe from trouble in this world.

"The current was more rapid now, the steamer seemed at her last gasp, the stern-wheel flopped languidly, and I caught myself listening on tiptoe for the next beat of the float, for in sober truth I expected the wretched thing to give up every moment. It was like watching the last flickers of a life. But still we crawled. Some- times I would pick out a tree a little way ahead to measure our progress towards Kurtz by, but I lost it invariably before we got abreast. To keep the eyes so long on one thing was too much for human patience. The manager displayed a beautiful resignation. I fretted and fumed and took to arguing with myself whether or no I would talk openly with Kurtz; but before I could come to any conclusion it oc- curred to me that my speech or my silence, indeed any action of mine, would be a mere futility. What did it matter what anyone knew or ignored? What did it mat- ter who was manager? One gets sometimes such a flash of insight. The essentials of this affair lay deep under the surface, beyond my reach, and beyond my power of meddling.

"Towards the evening of the second day we judged ourselves about eight miles from Kurtz's station. I wanted to push on; but the manager looked grave, and told me the navigation up there was so dangerous that it would be advisable, the sun being very low already, to wait where we were till next morning. Moreover, he pointed out that if the warning to approach cautiously were to be followed, we must approach in daylight—not at dusk, or in the dark. This was sensible enough. Eight miles meant nearly three hours' steaming for us, and I could also see sus- picious ripples at the upper end of the reach. Nevertheless, I was annoyed beyond expression at the delay, and most unreasonably too, since one night more could not matter much after so many months. As we had plenty of wood, and caution was the word, I brought up in the middle of the stream. The reach was narrow, straight, with high sides like a railway cutting. The dusk came gliding into it long before the sun had set. The current ran smooth and swift, but a dumb immobility sat on the banks. The living trees, lashed together by the creepers and every living bush of the undergrowth, might have been changed into stone, even to the slen- derest twig, to the lightest leaf. It was not sleep—it seemed unnatural, like a state of trance. Not the faintest sound of any kind could be heard. You looked on amazed, and began to suspect yourself of being deaf—then the night came sud- denly, and struck you blind as well. About three in the morning some large fish leaped, and the loud splash made me jump as though a gun had been fired. When the sun rose there was a white fog, very warm and clammy, and more blinding than the night. It did not shift or drive; it was just there, standing all round you like something solid. At eight or nine, perhaps, it lifted as a shutter lifts. We had a glimpse of the towering multitude of trees, of the immense matted jungle, with the blazing little ball of the sun hanging over it—all perfectly still—and then the white shutter came down again, smoothly, as if sliding in greased grooves. I ordered the chain, which we had begun to heave in, to be paid out again. Before it stopped running with a muffled rattle, a cry, a very loud cry, as of infinite desolation, soared slowly in the opaque air. It ceased. A complaining clamor, modulated in savage discords, filled our ears. The sheer unexpectedness of it made my hair stir under my cap. I don't know how it struck the others: to me it seemed as though the mist itself had screamed, so suddenly, and apparently from all sides at once, did this tumultuous and mournful uproar arise. It culminated in a hurried outbreak of almost intolerably excessive shrieking, which stopped short, leaving us stiffened in a variety of silly attitudes, and obstinately listening to the nearly as appalling and excessive silence. 'Good God! What is the meaning——?' stammered at my elbow one of the pilgrims,—a little fat man, with sandy hair and red whiskers, who wore side-spring boots, and pink pyjamas tucked into his socks. Two others remained open-mouthed a whole minute, then dashed into the little cabin, to rush out incontinently and stand darting scared glances, with Winchesters at 'ready' in their hands. What we could see was just the steamer we were on, her outlines blurred as though she had been on the point of dissolving, and a misty strip of water, perhaps two feet broad, around her—and that was all. The rest of the world was nowhere, as far as our eyes and ears were concerned. Just nowhere. Gone, disappeared; swept off without leaving a whisper or a shadow behind.

"I went forward, and ordered the chain to be hauled in short, so as to be ready to trip the anchor and move the steamboat at once if necessary. 'Will they attack?' whispered an awed voice. 'We will be all butchered in this fog,' murmured another. The faces twitched with the strain, the hands trembled slightly, the eyes forgot to wink. It was very curious to see the contrast of expressions of the white men and of the black fellows of our crew, who were as much strangers to that part of the river as we, though their homes were only eight hundred miles away. The whites, of course greatly discomposed, had besides a curious look of being painfully shocked by such an outrageous row. The others had an alert, naturally interested expression; but their faces were essentially quiet, even those of the one or two who grinned as they hauled at the chain. Several exchanged short, grunting phrases, which seemed to settle the matter to their satisfaction. Their headman, a young, broad-chested black, severely draped in dark-blue fringed cloths, with fierce nostrils and his hair all done up artfully in oily ringlets, stood near me. 'Aha!' I said, just for good fellowship's sake. 'Catch 'im,' he snapped, with a bloodshot widening of his eyes and a flash of sharp teeth—'catch 'im. Give 'im to us.' 'To you, eh?' I asked; 'what would you do with them?' 'Eat 'im!' he said curtly, and, leaning his elbow on the rail, looked out into the fog in a dignified and profoundly pensive attitude. I would no doubt have been properly horrified, had it not occurred to me that he and his chaps must be very hungry: that they must have been growing increasingly hungry for at least this month past. They had been engaged for six months (I don't think a single one of them had any clear idea of time, as we at the end of countless ages have. They still belonged to the beginnings of time—had no inherited experience to teach them as it were), and of course, as long as there was a piece of paper written over in accordance with some farcical law or other made down the river, it didn't enter anybody's head to trouble how they would live. Certainly they had brought with them some rotten hippo-meat, which couldn't have lasted very long, anyway, even if the pilgrims hadn't, in the midst of a shocking hullabaloo, thrown a considerable quantity of it overboard. It looked like a high-handed proceeding; but it was really a case of legitimate self-defense. You can't breathe dead hippo waking, sleeping, and eating, and at the same time keep your precarious grip on existence. Besides that, they had given them every week three pieces of brass wire, each about nine inches long; and the theory was they were to buy their provisions with that currency in river-side villages. You can see how *that* worked. There were either no villages, or the people were hostile, or the director, who like the rest of us fed out of tins, with an occasional old he-goat thrown in, didn't want to stop the steamer for some more or less recondite reason. So, unless they swallowed the wire itself, or made loops of it to snare the fishes with, I don't see what good their extravagant salary could be to them. I must say it was paid with a regularity worthy of a large and honorable trading company. For the rest, the only thing to eat—though it didn't look eatable in the least—I saw in their possession was a few lumps of some stuff like half-cooked dough, of a dirty lavender color, they kept wrapped in leaves, and now and then swallowed a piece of, but so small that it seemed done more for the looks of the thing than for any serious purpose of sustenance. Why in the name of all the gnawing devils of hunger they didn't go for us—they were thirty to five—and have a good tuck in for once, amazes me now when I think of it. They were big powerful men, with not much capacity to weigh the consequences, with courage, with strength, even yet, though their skins were no longer glossy and their muscles no longer hard. And I saw that something restraining, one of those human secrets that baffle probability, had come into play there. I looked at them with a swift quickening of interest—not because it occurred to me I might be eaten by them before very long, though I own to you that just then I perceived—in a new light, as it were—how unwholesome the pilgrims looked, and I hoped, yes, I positively hoped, that my aspect was not so—what shall I say?—so—unappetizing: a touch of fantastic vanity which fitted well with the dream-sensation that pervaded all my days at that time. Perhaps I had a little fever too. One can't live with one's finger everlastingly on one's pulse. I had often 'a little fever,' or a little touch of other things—the playful paw-strokes of the wilderness, the preliminary trifling before the more serious onslaught which came in due course. Yes; I looked at them as you would on any human being, with a curiosity of their impulses, motives, capacities, weaknesses, when brought to the test of an inexorable physical necessity. Restraint! What possible restraint? Was it superstition, disgust, patience, fear—or some kind of primitive honor? No fear can stand up to hunger, no patience can wear it out, disgust simply does not exist where hunger is; and as to superstition, beliefs, and what you may call principles, they are less than chaff in a breeze. Don't you know the devilry of lingering starvation, its exasperating torment, its black thoughts, its somber and brooding ferocity? Well, I do. It takes a man all his inborn strength to fight hunger properly. It's really easier to face bereavement, dishonor, and the perdition of one's soul—than this kind of prolonged hunger. Sad, but true. And these chaps too had no earthly reason for any kind of scruple. Restraint! I would just as soon have expected restraint from a hyena prowling amongst the corpses of a battle-field. But there was the fact facing me—the fact dazzling, to be seen, like the foam on the depths of the sea, like a ripple on an unfathomable enigma, a mystery greater—when I thought of it—than the curious, inexplicable note of desperate grief in this savage clamor that had swept by us on the river-bank, behind the blind whiteness of the fog.

"Two pilgrims were quarreling in hurried whispers as to which bank. 'Left.' 'No, no; how can you? Right, right, of course.' 'It is very serious,' said the manager's voice behind me; 'I would be desolated if anything should happen to Mr. Kurtz before we came up.' I looked at him, and had not the slightest doubt he was sincere. He was just the kind of man who would wish to preserve appearances. That was his restraint. But when he muttered something about going on at once, I did not even take the trouble to answer him. I knew, and he knew, that it was impossible. Were we to let go our hold of the bottom, we would be absolutely in the air—in space. We wouldn't be able to tell where we were going to—whether up or down stream, or across—till we fetched against one bank or the other,—and then we wouldn't know at first which it was. Of course I made no move. I had no mind for a smash-up. You couldn't imagine a more deadly place for a shipwreck. Whether drowned at once or not, we were sure to perish speedily in one way or another. 'I authorize you to take all the risks,' he said, after a short silence. 'I refuse to take any,' I said shortly; which was just the answer he expected, though its tone might have surprised him. 'Well, I must defer to your judgment. You are captain,' he said, with marked civility. I turned my shoulder to him in sign of my appreciation, and looked into the fog. How long would it last? It was the most hopeless look-out. The approach to this Kurtz grubbing for ivory in the wretched bush was beset by as many dangers as though he had been an enchanted princess sleeping in a fabulous castle. 'Will they attack, do you think?' asked the manager, in a confidential tone.

"I did not think they would attack, for several obvious reasons. The thick fog was one. If they left the bank in their canoes they would get lost in it, as we would be if we attempted to move. Still, I had also judged the jungle of both banks quite impenetrable—and yet eyes were in it, eyes that had seen us. The river-side bushes were certainly very thick; but the undergrowth behind was evidently penetrable. However, during the short lift I had seen no canoes anywhere in the reach—certainly not abreast of the steamer. But what made the idea of attack inconceivable to me was the nature of the noise—of the cries we had heard. They had not the fierce character boding of immediate hostile intention. Unexpected, wild, and violent as they had been, they had given me an irresistible impression of sorrow. The glimpse of the steamboat had for some reason filled those savages with unrestrained grief. The danger, if any, I expounded, was from our proximity to a great human passion let loose. Even extreme grief may ultimately vent itself in violence—but more generally takes the form of apathy. . . .

"You should have seen the pilgrims stare! They had no heart to grin, or even to revile me; but I believe they thought me gone mad—with fright, maybe. I delivered a regular lecture. My dear boys, it was no good bothering. Keep a look-out? Well, you may guess I watched the fog for the signs of lifting as a cat watches a mouse; but for anything else our eyes were of no more use to us than if we had been buried miles deep in a heap of cotton-wool. It felt like it too—choking, warm, stifling. Besides, all I said, though it sounded extravagant, was absolutely true to fact. What we afterwards alluded to as an attack was really an attempt at repulse. The action was very far from being aggressive—it was not even defensive, in the usual sense: it was undertaken under the stress of desperation, and in its essence was purely protective.

"It developed itself, I should say, two hours after the fog lifted, and its commencement was at a spot, roughly speaking, about a mile and a half below Kurtz's station. We had just floundered and flopped round a bend, when I saw an islet, a mere grassy hummock of bright green, in the middle of the stream. It was the only thing of the kind; but as we opened the reach more, I perceived it was the head of a long sandbank, or rather of a chain of shallow patches stretching down the middle of the river. They were discolored, just awash, and the whole lot was seen just under the water, exactly as a man's backbone is seen running down the middle of his back under the skin. Now, as far as I did see, I could go to the right or to the left of this. I didn't know either channel, of course. The banks looked pretty well alike, the depth appeared the same; but as I had been informed the station was on the west side, I naturally headed for the western passage.

"No sooner had we fairly entered it than I became aware it was much narrower than I had supposed. To the left of us there was the long uninterrupted shoal, and to the right a high, steep bank heavily overgrown with bushes. Above the bush the trees stood in serried ranks. The twigs overhung the current thickly, and from distance to distance a large limb of some tree projected rigidly over the stream. It was then well on in the afternoon, the face of the forest was gloomy, and a broad strip of shadow had already fallen on the water. In this shadow we steamed up—very slowly, as you may imagine. I sheered her well inshore—the water being deepest near the bank, as the sounding-pole informed me.

"One of my hungry and forbearing friends was sounding in the bows just below me. This steamboat was exactly like a decked scow. On the deck there were two little teak-wood houses, with doors and windows. The boiler was in the fore-end, and the machinery right astern. Over the whole there was a light roof, supported on stanchions. The funnel projected through that roof, and in front of the funnel a small cabin built of light planks served for a pilot-house. It contained a couch, two camp stools, a loaded Martini-Henry leaning in one corner, a tiny table, and the steering-wheel. It had a wide door in front and a broad shutter at each side. All these were always thrown open, of course. I spent my days perched up there on the extreme fore-end of that roof, before the door. At night I slept, or tried to, on the couch. An athletic black belonging to some coast tribe, and educated by my poor predecessor, was the helmsman. He sported a pair of brass earrings, wore a blue cloth wrapper from the waist to the ankles, and thought all the world of himself. He was the most unstable kind of fool I had ever seen. He steered with no end of a swagger while you were by; but if he lost sight of you, he became instantly the prey of an abject funk, and would let that cripple of a steamboat get the upper hand of him in a minute.

"I was looking down at the sounding-pole, and feeling much annoyed to see at each try, a little more of it stick out of that river, when I saw my poleman give up the business suddenly, and stretch himself flat on the deck, without even taking the trouble to haul his pole in. He kept hold on it though, and it trailed in the water. At the same time the fireman, whom I could also see below me, sat down abruptly before his furnace and ducked his head. I was amazed. Then I had to look at the river mighty quick, because there was a snag in the fairway. Sticks, little sticks, were flying about—thick: they were whizzing before my nose, dropping below me, striking behind me against my pilot-house. All this time the river, the shore, the woods, were very quiet—perfectly quiet. I could only hear the heavy splashing thump of the stern-wheel and the patter of these things. We cleared the snag clumsily. Arrows, by Jove! We were being shot at! I stepped in quickly to close the shutter on the land side. That fool-helsman, his hands on the spokes, was lifting his knees high, stamping his feet, champing his mouth, like a reined-in horse. Confound him! And we were staggering within ten feet of the bank. I had to lean right out to swing the heavy shutter, and I saw a face amongst the leaves on the level with my own, looked at me very fierce and steady; and then suddenly, as though a veil had been removed from my eyes, I made out, deep in the tangled gloom, naked breasts, arms, legs, glaring eyes,—the bush was swarming with human limbs in movement, glistening, of bronze color. The twigs shook, swayed, and rustled, the arrows flew out of them, and then the shutter came to. 'Steer her straight,' I said to the helmsman. He held his head rigid, face forward; but his eyes rolled, he kept on lifting and setting down his feet gently, his mouth foamed a little. 'Keep quiet!' I said in a fury. I might just as well have ordered a tree not to sway in the wind. I darted out. Below me there was a great scuffle of feet on the iron deck; confused exclamations; a voice screamed, 'Can you turn back?' I caught shape of a V-shaped ripple on the water ahead. What? Another snag! A fusillade burst out under my feet. The pilgrims had opened with their Winchesters, and were simply squirting lead into that bush. A deuce of a lot of smoke came up and drove slowly forward. I swore at it. Now I couldn't see the ripple or the snag either. I stood in the doorway, peering, and the arrows came in swarms. They might have been poisoned, but they looked as though they wouldn't kill a cat. The bush began to howl. Our wood-cutters raised a warlike whoop; the report of a rifle just at my back deafened me. I glanced over my shoulder, and the pilot-house was yet full of noise and smoke when I made a dash at the wheel. The fool-nigger had dropped everything, to throw the shutter open and let off that Martini-Henry. He stood before the wide opening, glaring, and I yelled at him to come back, while I straightened the sudden twist out of that steamboat. There was no room to turn even if I had wanted to, the snag was somewhere very near ahead in that confounded smoke, there was no time to lose, so I just crowded her into the bank—right into the bank, where I knew the water was deep.

"We tore slowly along the overhanging bushes in a whirl of broken twigs and flying leaves. The fusillade below stopped short, as I had foreseen it would when the squirts got empty. I threw my head back to a glinting whizz that traversed the pilot-house, in at one shutter-hole and out at the other. Looking past that mad helmsman, who was shaking the empty rifle and yelling at the shore, I saw vague forms of men running bent double, leaping, gliding, distinct, incomplete, evanescent. Something big appeared in the air before the shutter, the rifle went overboard, and the man stepped back swiftly, looked at me over his shoulder in an extraordinary, profound, familiar manner, and fell upon my feet. The side of his head hit the wheel twice, and the end of what appeared a long cane clattered round and knocked over a little camp-stool. It looked as though after wrenching that thing from somebody ashore he had lost his balance in the effort. The thin smoke had blown away, we were clear of the snag, and looking ahead I could see that in another hundred yards or so I would be free to sheer off, away from the bank; but my feet felt so very warm and wet that I had to look down. The man had rolled on his back and stared straight up at me; both his hands clutched that cane. It was the shaft of a spear that, either thrown or lunged through the opening, had caught him in the side just below the ribs; the blade had gone in out of sight, after making a frightful gash; my shoes were full; a pool of blood lay very still, gleaming dark-red under the wheel; his eyes shone with an amazing luster. The fusillade burst out again. He looked at me anxiously, gripping the spear like something precious, with an air of being afraid I would try to take it away from him. I had to make an effort to free my eyes from his gaze and attend to the steering. With one hand I felt above my head for the line of the steam-whistle, and jerked out screech after screech hurriedly. The tumult of angry and warlike yells was checked instantly, and then from the depths of the woods went out such a tremulous and prolonged wail of mournful fear and utter despair as may be imagined to follow the flight of the last hope from the earth. There was a great commotion in the bush; the shower of arrows stopped, a few dropping shots rang out sharply—then silence, in which the languid beat of the stern-wheel came plainly to my ears. I put the helm hard a-starboard at the moment when the pilgrim in pink pyjamas, very hot and agitated, appeared in the doorway. 'The manager sends me——' he began in an official tone, and stopped short. 'Good God!' he said, glaring at the wounded man.

"We two whites stood over him, and his lustrous and inquiring glance enveloped us both. I declare it looked as though he would presently put to us some question in an understandable language; but he died without uttering a sound, without moving a limb, without twitching a muscle. Only in the very last moment, as though in response to some sign we could not see, to some whisper we could not hear, he frowned heavily, and that frown gave to his black death-mask an inconceivably somber, brooding, and menacing expression. The luster of inquiring glance faded swiftly into vacant glassiness. 'Can you steer?' I asked the agent eagerly. He looked very dubious; but I made a grab at his arm, and he understood at once I meant him to steer whether or no. To tell you the truth, I was morbidly anxious to change my shoes and socks. 'He is dead,' murmured the fellow, immensely impressed. 'No doubt about it,' said I, tugging like mad at the shoe-laces. 'And, by the way, I suppose Mr. Kurtz is dead as well by this time.'

"For the moment that was the dominant thought. There was a sense of extreme disappointment, as though I had found out I had been striving after something altogether without a substance. I couldn't have been more disgusted if I had traveled all this way for the sole purpose of talking with Mr. Kurtz. Talking with. . . . I flung one shoe overboard, and became aware that that was exactly what I had been looking forward to—a talk with Mr. Kurtz. I made the strange discovery that I had never imagined him as doing, you know, but as discoursing. I didn't say to myself, 'Now I will never see him,' or 'Now I will never shake him by the hand,' but, 'Now I will never hear him.' The man presented himself as a voice. Not of course that I did not connect him with some sort of action. Hadn't I been told in all the tones of jealousy and admiration that he had collected, bartered, swindled, or stolen more ivory than all the other agents together. That was not the point. The point was in his being a gifted creature, and that of all his gifts the one that stood out pre-eminently, that carried with it a sense of real presence, was his ability to talk, his words—the gift of expression, the bewildering, the illuminating, the most exalted and the most contemptible, the pulsating stream of light, or the deceitful flow from the heart of an impenetrable darkness.

"The other shoe went flying unto the devil-god of that river. I thought, By Jove! it's all over. We are too late; he has vanished—the gift has vanished, by means of some spear, arrow or club. I will never hear that chap speak after all,—and my sorrow had a startling extravagance of emotion, even such as I had noticed in the howling sorrow of these savages in the bush. I couldn't have felt more of lonely desolation somehow, had I been robbed of a belief or had missed my destiny in life. . . . Why do you sigh in this beastly way, somebody? Absurd? Well, absurd. Good Lord! mustn't a man ever—— Here, give me some tobacco." . . .

There was a pause of profound stillness, then a match flared, and Marlow's lean face appeared, worn, hollow, with downward folds and dropped eyelids, with an aspect of concentrated attention; and as he took vigorous draws at his pipe, it seemed to retreat and advance out of the night in the regular flicker of the tiny flame. The match went out.

"Absurd!" he cried. "This is the worst of trying to tell. . . . Here you all are, each moored with two good addresses, like a hulk with two anchors, a butcher round one corner, a policeman round another, excellent appetites, and temperature normal—you hear—normal from year's end to year's end. And you say, Absurd! Absurd be—exploded! Absurd! My dear boys, what can you expect from a man who out of sheer nervousness had just flung overboard a pair of new shoes. Now I think of it, it is amazing I did not shed tears. I am, upon the whole, proud of my fortitude. I was cut to the quick at the idea of having lost the inestimable privilege of listening to the gifted Kurtz. Of course I was wrong. The privilege was waiting for me. Oh yes, I heard more than enough. And I was right, too. A voice. He was very little more than a voice. And I heard—him—it—this voice—other voices—all of them were so little more than voices—and the memory of that time itself lingers around me, impalpable, like a dying vibration of one immense jabber, silly, atrocious, sordid, savage, or simply mean, without any kind of sense. Voices, voices—even the girl herself—now——"

He was silent for a long time.

"I laid the ghost of his gifts at last with a lie," he began suddenly. "Girl! What? Did I mention a girl? Oh, she is out of it—completely. They—the women I mean—are out of it—should be out of it. We must help them to stay in that beautiful world of their own, lest ours gets worse. Oh, she had to be out of it. You should have heard the disinterred body of Mr. Kurtz saying, 'My Intended.' You would have perceived directly then how completely she was out of it. And the lofty frontal bone of Mr. Kurtz! They say the hair goes on growing sometimes, but this—ah—specimen, was impressively bald. The wilderness had patted him on the head, and, behold, it was like a ball—an ivory ball; it had caressed him, and—lo!—he had withered; it had taken him, loved him, embraced him, got into his veins, consumed his flesh, and sealed his soul to its own by the inconceivable ceremonies of some devilish initiation. He was its spoiled and pampered favorite. Ivory? I should think so. Heaps of it, stacks of it. The old mud shanty was bursting with it. You would think there was not a single tusk left either above or below the ground in the whole country. 'Mostly fossil,' the manager had remarked disparagingly. It was no more fossil than I am; but they call it fossil when it is dug up. It appears these niggers do bury the tusks sometimes—but evidently they couldn't bury this parcel deep enough to save the gifted Mr. Kurtz from his fate. We filled the steamboat with it, and had to pile a lot on the deck. Thus he could see and enjoy as long as he could see, because the appreciation of this favor had remained with him to the last. You should have heard him say, 'My ivory.' Oh yes, I heard him. 'My Intended, my ivory, my station, my river, my——' everything belonged to him. It made me hold my breath in expectation of hearing the wilderness burst into a prodigious peal of laughter that would shake the fixed stars in their places. Everything belonged to him—but that was a trifle. The thing was to know what he belonged to, how many powers of darkness claimed him for their own. That was the reflection that made you creepy all over. It was impossible—it was not good for one either—trying to imagine. He had taken a high seat amongst the devils of the land—I mean literally. You can't understand. How could you?—with solid pavement under your feet, surrounded by kind neighbors ready to cheer you or to fall on you, stepping delicately between the butcher and the policeman, in the holy terror of scandal and gallows and lunatic asylums—how can you imagine what particular region of the first ages a man's untrammeled feet may take him into by the way of solitude—utter solitude without a policeman—by the way of silence—utter silence, where no warning voice of a kind neighbor can be heard whispering of public opinion? These little things make all the great difference. When they are gone you must fall back upon your own innate strength, upon your own capacity for faithfulness. Of course you may be too much of a fool to go wrong—too dull even to know you are being assaulted by the powers of darkness. I take it, no fool ever made a bargain for his soul with the devil: the fool is too much of a fool, or the devil too much of a devil—I don't know which. Or you may be such a thunderingly exalted creature as to be altogether deaf and blind to anything but heavenly sights and sounds. Then the earth for you is only a standing place—and whether to be like this is your loss or your gain I won't pretend to say. But most of us are neither one nor the other. The earth for us is a place to live in, where we must put up with sights, with sounds, with smells too, by Jove!—breathe dead hippo, so to speak, and not be contaminated. And there, don't you see? your strength comes in, the faith in your ability for the digging of unostentatious holes to bury the stuff in—your power of devotion, not to yourself, but to an obscure, back-breaking business. And that's difficult enough. Mind, I am not trying to excuse or even explain—I am trying to account to myself for—for—Mr. Kurtz—for the shade of Mr. Kurtz. This initiated wraith from the back of Nowhere honored me with its amazing confidence before it vanished altogether. This was because it could speak English to me. The original Kurtz had been educated partly in England, and—as he was good enough to say himself—his sympathies were in the right place. His mother was half-English, his father was half-French. All Europe contributed to the making of Kurtz; and by-and-by I learned that, most appropriately, the International Society for the Suppression of Savage Customs had intrusted him with the making of a report, for its future guidance. And he had written it too. I've seen it. I've read it. It was eloquent, vibrating with eloquence, but too high-strung, I think. Seventeen pages of close writing he had found time for! But this must have been before his—let us say—nerves, went wrong, and caused him to preside at certain midnight dances ending with unspeakable rites, which—as far as I reluctantly gathered from what I heard at various times—were offered up to him—do you understand?—to Mr. Kurtz himself. But it was a beautiful piece of writing. The opening paragraph, however, in the light of later information, strikes me now as ominous. He began with the argument that we whites, from the point of development we had arrived at, 'must necessarily appear to them [savages] in the nature of supernatural beings—we approach them with the might as of a diety,' and so on, and so on. 'By the simple exercise of our will we can exert a power for good practically unbounded,' &c., &c. From that point he soared and took me with him. The peroration was magnificent, though difficult to remember, you know. It gave me the notion of an exotic Immensity ruled by an august Benevolence. It made me tingle with enthusiasm. This was the unbounded power of eloquence—of words—of burning noble words. There were no practical hints to interrupt the magic current of phrases, unless a kind of note at the foot of the last page, scrawled evidently much later, in an unsteady hand, may be regarded as the exposition of a method. It was very simple, and at the end of that moving appeal to every altruistic sentiment it blazed at you, luminous and terrifying, like a flash of lightning in a serene sky: 'Exterminate all the brutes!' The curious part was that he had apparently forgotten all about that valuable postscriptum, because, later on, when he in a sense came to himself, he repeatedly entreated me to take good care of 'my pamphlet' (he called it), as it was sure to have in the future a good influence upon his career. I had full information about all these things, and, besides, as it turned out, I was to have the care of his memory. I've done enough for it to give me the indisputable right to lay it, if I choose, for an everlasting rest in the dust-bin of progress, amongst all the sweepings and, figuratively speaking, all the dead cats of civilization. But then, you see, I can't choose. He won't be forgotten. Whatever he was, he was not common. He had the power to charm or frighten rudimentary souls into an aggravated witch-dance in his honor; he could also fill the small souls of the pilgrims with bitter misgivings: he had one devoted friend at least, and he had conquered one soul in the world that was neither rudimentary nor tainted with self-seeking. No; I can't forget him, though I am not prepared to affirm the fellow was exactly worth the life we lost in getting to him. I missed my late helmsman awfully,—I missed him even while his body was still lying in the pilot-house. Perhaps you will think it passing strange this regret for a savage who was no more account than a grain of sand in a black Sahara. Well, don't you see, he had done something, he had steered; for months I had him at my back—a help—an instrument. It was a kind of partnership. He steered for me—I had to look after him, I worried about his deficiencies, and thus a subtle bond had been created, of which I only became aware when it was suddenly broken. And the intimate profundity of that look he gave me when he received his hurt remains to this day in my memory—like a claim of distant kinship affirmed in a supreme moment.

"Poor fool! If he had only left that shutter alone. He had no restraint, no restraint—just like Kurtz—a tree swayed by the wind. As soon as I had put on a dry pair of slippers, I dragged him out, after first jerking the spear out of his side, which operation I confess I performed with my eyes shut tight. His heels leaped together over the little door-step; his shoulders were pressed to my breast; I hugged him from behind desperately. Oh! he was heavy, heavy; heavier than any man on earth, I should imagine. Then without more ado I tipped him overboard. The current snatched him as though he had been a wisp of grass, and I saw the body roll over twice before I lost sight of it for ever. All the pilgrims and the manager were then congregated on the awning-deck about the pilot-house, chattering at each other like a flock of excited magpies, and there was a scandalized murmur at my heartless promptitude. What they wanted to keep that body hanging about for I can't guess. Embalm it, maybe. But I had also heard another, and a very ominous, murmur on the deck below. My friends the wood-cutters were likewise scandalized, and with a better show of reason—though I admit that the reason itself was quite inadmissable. Oh, quite! I had made up my mind that if my late helmsman was to be eaten, the fishes alone should have him. He had been a very second-rate helmsman while alive, but now he was dead he might have become a first-class temptation, and possibly cause some startling trouble. Besides, I was anxious to take the wheel, the man in pink pyjamas showing himself a hopeless duffer at the business.

"This I did directly the simple funeral was over. We were going half-speed, keeping right in the middle of the stream, and I listened to the talk about me. They had given up Kurtz, they had given up the station; Kurtz was dead, and the station had been burnt—and so on—and so on. The red-haired pilgrim was beside himself with the thought that at least poor Kurtz had been properly revenged. 'Say! We must have made a glorious slaughter of them in the bush. Eh? What do you think? Say?' He positively danced, the bloodthirsty little gingery beggar. And he had nearly fainted when he saw the wounded man! I could not help saying, 'You made a glorious lot of smoke, anyhow.' I had seen, from the way the tops of the bushes rustled and flew, that almost all the shots had gone too high. You can't hit anything unless you take aim and fire from the shoulder; but these chaps fired from the hip with their eyes shut. The retreat, I maintained—and I was right—was caused by the screeching of the steam-whistle. Upon this they forgot Kurtz, and began to howl at me with indignant protests.

"The manager stood by the wheel murmuring confidentially about the necessity of getting well away down the river before dark at all events, when I saw in the distance a clearing on the river-side and the outlines of some sort of building. 'What's this?' I asked. He clapped his hands in wonder. 'The station!' he cried. I edged in at once, still going half-speed.

"Through my glasses I saw the slope of a hill interspersed with rare trees and perfectly free from undergrowth. A long decaying building on the summit was half buried in the high grass; the large holes in the peaked roof gaped black from afar; the jungle and the woods made a background. There was no inclosure or fence of any kind; but there had been one apparently, for near the house half-a-dozen slim posts remained in a row, roughly trimmed, and with their upper ends ornamented with round carved balls. The rails, or whatever there had been between, had disappeared. Of course the forest surrounded all that. The river-bank was clear and on the water-side I saw a white man under a hat like a cart-wheel beckoning persistently with his whole arm. Examining the edge of the forest above and below, I was almost certain I could see movements—human forms gliding here and there. I steamed past prudently, then stopped the engines and let her drift down. The man on the shore began to shout, urging us to land. 'We have been attacked,' screamed the manager. 'I know—I know. It's all right,' yelled back the other, as cheerful as you please. 'Come along. It's all right. I am glad.'

"His aspect reminded me of something I had seen—something funny I had seen somewhere. As I maneuvered to get alongside, I was asking myself, 'What does this fellow look like?' Suddenly I got it. He looked like a harlequin. His clothes had been made of some stuff that was brown holland probably, but it was covered with patches all over, with bright patches, blue, red, and yellow,—patches on the back, patches on front, patches on elbows, on knees; colored binding round his jacket, scarlet edging at the bottom of his trousers; and the sunshine made him look extremely gay and wonderfully neat withal, because you could see how beautifully all this patching had been done. A beardless, boyish face, very fair, no features to speak of, nose peeling, little blue eyes, smiles and frowns chasing each other over that open countenance like sunshine and shadow on a windswept plain. 'Look out, captain!' he cried; 'there's a snag lodged in here last night.' What!

Another snag? I confess I swore shamefully. I had nearly holed my cripple, to finish off that charming trip. The harlequin on the bank turned his little pug nose up to me. 'You English?' he asked, all smiles. 'Are you?' I shouted from the wheel. The smiles vanished, and he shook his head as if sorry for my disappointment. Then he brightened up. 'Never mind!' he cried encouragingly. 'Are we in time?' I asked. 'He is up there,' he replied, with a toss of the head up the hill, and becoming gloomy all of a sudden. His face was like the autumn sky, overcast one moment and bright the next.

"When the manager, escorted by the pilgrims, all of them armed to the teeth, had gone to the house, this chap came on board. 'I say, I don't like this. These natives are in the bush,' I said. He assured me earnestly it was all right. 'They are simple people,' he added; 'well, I am glad you came. It took me all my time to keep them off.' 'But you said it was all right,' I cried. 'Oh, they meant no harm,' he said; and as I stared he corrected himself, 'Not exactly.' Then vivaciously, 'My faith, your pilot-house wants a clean up!' In the next breath he advised me to keep enough steam on the boiler to blow the whistle in case of trouble. 'One good screech will do more for you than all your rifles. They are simple people,' he repeated. He rattled away at such a rate he quite overwhelmed me. He seemed to be trying to make up for lots of silence, and actually hinted, laughing, that such was the case. 'Don't you talk with Mr. Kurtz?' I said. 'You don't talk with that man—you listen to him,' he exclaimed with severe exaltation. 'But now——' He waved his arm, and in the twinkling of an eye was in the uttermost depths of despondency. In a moment he came up again with a jump, possessed himself of both my hands, shook them continuously, while he gabbed: 'Brother sailor . . . honor . . . pleasure . . . delight . . . introduce myself . . . Russian . . . son of an arch-priest . . . Government of Tambov . . . What? Tobacco! English tobacco; the excellent English tobacco! Now, that's brotherly. Smoke? Where's a sailor that does not smoke?'

"The pipe soothed him, and gradually I made out he had run away from school, had gone to sea in a Russian ship; ran away again; served some time in English ships; was now reconciled with the arch-priest. He made a point of that. 'But when one is young one must see things, gather experience, ideas; enlarge the mind.' 'Here!' I interrupted. 'You can never tell! Here I have met Mr. Kurtz,' he said, youthfully solemn and reproachful. I held my tongue after that. It appears he had persuaded a Dutch trading-house on the coast to fit him out with stores and goods, and had started for the interior with a light heart, and no more idea of what would happen to him than a baby. He had been wandering about that river for nearly two years alone, cut off from everybody and everything. 'I am not so young as I look. I am twenty-five,' he said. 'At first old Van Shuyten would tell me to go to the devil,' he narrated with keen enjoyment; 'but I stuck to him, and talked and talked, till at last he got afraid I would talk the hind-leg off his favorite dog, so he gave me some cheap things and a few guns, and told me he hoped he would never see my face again. Good old Dutchman, Van Shuyten. I've sent him one small lot of ivory a year ago, so that he can't call me a little thief when I get back. I hope he got it. And for the rest I don't care. I had some wood stacked for you. That was my old house. Did you see?'

'I gave him Towson's book. He made as though he would kiss me, but restrained himself. 'The only book I had left, and I thought I had lost it,' he said, looking at it ecstatically. 'So many accidents happen to a man going about alone, you know. Canoes get upset sometimes—and sometimes you've got to clear out so quick when the people get angry.' He thumbed the pages. 'You made notes in Russian?' I asked. He nodded. 'I tought they were written in cipher,' I said. He laughed, then became serious. 'I had lots of trouble to keep these people off,' he said. 'Did they want to kill you?' I asked. 'Oh no!' he cried, and checked himself. 'Why did they attack us?' I pursued. He hesitated, then said shamefacedly, 'They don't want him to go.' 'Don't they?' I said, curiously. He nodded a nod full of mystery and wisdom. 'I tell you,' he cried, 'this man has enlarged my mind.' He opened his arms wide, staring at me with his little blue eyes that were perfectly round."

III

"I looked at him, lost in astonishment. There he was before me, in motley, as though he had absconded from a troupe of mimes, enthusiastic, fabulous. His very existence was improbable, inexplicable, and altogether bewildering. He was an insoluble problem. It was inconceivable how he had existed, how he had succeeded in getting so far, how he had managed to remain—why he did not instantly disappear. 'I went a little farther,' he said, 'then still a little farther—till I had gone so far that I don't know how I'll ever get back. Never mind. Plenty time. I can manage. You take Kurtz away quick—quick—I tell you.' The glamour of youth enveloped his particolored rags, his destitution, his loneliness, the essential desolation of his futile wanderings. For months—for years—his life hadn't been worth a day's purchase; and there he was gallantly, thoughtlessly alive, to all appearance indestructible solely by the virtue of his few years and of his unreflecting audacity. I was seduced into something like admiration—like envy. Glamour urged him on, glamour kept him unscathed. He surely wanted nothing from the wilderness but space to breathe in and to push on through. His need was to exist, and to move onwards at the greatest possible risk, and with a maximum of privation. If the absolutely pure, uncalculating, unpractical spirit of adventure had ever ruled a human being, it ruled this be-patched youth. I almost envied him the possession of this modest and clear flame. It seemed to have consumed all thought of self so completely, that, even while he was talking to you, you forgot that it was he—the man before your eyes—who had gone through these things. I did not envy him his devotion to Kurtz, though. He had not meditated over it. It came to him, and he accepted it with a sort of eager fatalism. I must say that to me it appeared about the most dangerous thing in every way he had come upon so far.

"They had come together unavoidably, like two ships becalmed near each other, and lay rubbing sides at last. I suppose Kurtz wanted an audience, because on a certain occasion, when encamped in the forest, they had talked all night, or more probably Kurtz had talked. 'We talked of everything,' he said, quite transported at the recollection. 'I forgot there was such a thing as sleep. The night did not seem to last an hour. Everything! Everything! . . . Of love too.' 'Ah, he talked to you of love!' I said, much amused. 'It isn't what you think,' he cried, almost passionately. 'It was in general. He made me see things—things.'

"He threw his arms up. We were on deck at the time, and the headman of my wood-cutters, lounging near by, turned upon him his heavy and glittering eyes. I looked around, and I don't know why, but I assure you that never, never before, did this land, this river, this jungle, the very arch of this blazing sky, appear to me so hopeless and so dark, so impenetrable to human thought, so pitiless to human weakness. 'And, ever since, you have been with him, of course?' I said.

"On the contrary. It appears their intercourse had been very much broken by various causes. He had, as he informed me proudly, managed to nurse Kurtz through two illnesses (he alluded to it as you would to some risky feat), but as a rule Kurtz wandered alone, far in the depths of the forest. 'Very often coming to this station, I had to wait days and days before he would turn up,' he said. 'Ah, it was worth waiting for!—sometimes.' 'What was he doing? exploring or what?' I asked. 'Oh yes, of course;' he had discovered lots of villages, a lake too—he did not know exactly in what direction; it was dangerous to inquire too much—but mostly his expeditions had been for ivory. 'But he had no goods to trade with by that time,' I objected. 'There's a good lot of cartridges left even yet,' he answered, looking away. 'To speak plainly, he raided the country,' I said. He nodded. 'Not alone, surely!' He muttered something about the villages round that lake. 'Kurtz got the tribe to follow him, did he?' I suggested. He fidgeted a little. 'They adored him,' he said. The tone of these words was so extraordinary that I looked at him searchingly. It was curious to see his mingled eagerness and reluctance to speak of Kurtz. The man filled his life, occupied his thoughts, swayed his emotions. 'What can you expect?' he burst out; 'he came to them with thunder and lightning, you know—and they had never seen anything like it—and very terrible. He could be very terrible. You can't judge Mr. Kurtz as you would an ordinary man. No, no, no! Now—just to give you an idea—I don't mind telling you, he wanted to shoot me too one day—but I don't judge him.' 'Shoot you!' I cried. 'What for?' 'Well, I had a small lot of ivory the chief of that village near my house gave me. You see I used to shoot game for them. Well, he wanted it, and wouldn't hear reason. He declared he would shoot me unless I gave him the ivory and then cleared out of the country, because he could do so, and had a fancy for it, and there was nothing on earth to prevent him killing whom he jolly well pleased. And it was true too. I gave him the ivory. What did I care! But I didn't clear out. No, no. I couldn't leave him. I had to be careful, of course, till we got friendly again for a time. He had his second illness then. Afterwards I had to keep out of the way; but I didn't mind. He was living for the most part in those villages on the lake. When he came down to the river, sometimes he would take to me, and sometimes it was better for me to be careful. This man suffered too much. He hated all this, and somehow he couldn't get away. When I had a chance I begged him to try and leave while there was time; I offered to go back with him. And he would say yes, and then he would remain; go off on another ivory hunt; disappear for weeks; forget himself amongst these people—forget himself—you know.' 'Why! he's mad,' I said. He protested indignantly. Mr. Kurtz couldn't be mad. If I had heard him talk, only two days ago, I wouldn't dare hint at such a thing. . . . I had taken up my binoculars while we talked and was looking at the shore, sweeping the limit of the forest at each side and at the back of the house. The consciousness of there being people in that bush, so silent, so quiet—as silent and quiet as the ruined house on the hill—made me uneasy. There was no sign on the face of nature of this amazing tale that was not so much told as suggested to me in desolate exclamations, completed by shrugs, in interrupted phrases, in hints ending in deep sighs. The woods were unmoved, like a mask—heavy, like the closed door of a prison—they looked with their air of hidden knowledge, of patient expectation, of unapproachable silence. The Russian was explaining to me that it was only lately that Mr. Kurtz had come down to the river, bringing along with him all the fighting men of that lake tribe. He had been absent for several months—getting himself adored, I suppose—and had come down unexpectedly, with the intention to all appearance of making a raid either across the river or down stream. Evidently the appetite for more ivory had got the better of the—what shall I say?—less material aspirations. However he had got much worse suddenly. 'I heard he was lying helpless, and so I came up—took my chance,' said the Russian. 'Oh, he is bad, very bad.' I directed my glass to the house. There were no signs of life, but there was the ruined roof, the long mud wall peeping above the grass, with three little square window-holes, no two of the same size; all this brought within reach of my hand, as it were. And then I made a brusque movement, and one of the remaining posts of that vanished fence leaped up in the field of my glass. You remember I told you I had been struck at the distance by certain attempts at ornamentation, rather remarkable in the ruinous aspect of the place. Now I had suddenly a nearer view, and its first result was to make me throw my head back as if before a blow. Then I went carefully from post to post with my glass, and I saw my mistake. These round knobs were not ornamental but symbolic; they were expressive and puzzling, striking and disturbing—food for thought and also for the vultures if there had been any looking down from the sky; but at all events for such ants as were industrious enough to ascend the pole. They would have been even more impressive, those heads on the stakes, if their faces had not been turned to the house. Only one, the first I had made out, was facing my way. I was not so shocked as you may think. The start back I had given was really nothing but a movement of surprise. I had expected to see a knob of wood there, you know. I returned deliberately to the first I had seen—and there it was, black, dried, sunken, with closed eyelids,—a head that seemed to sleep at the top of that pole, and, with the shrunken dry lips showing a narrow white line of the teeth, was smiling too, smiling continuously at some endless and jocose dream of that eternal slumber.

"I am not disclosing any trade secrets. In fact the manager said afterwords that Mr. Kurtz's methods had ruined the district. I have no opinion on that point, but I want you clearly to understand that there was nothing exactly profitable in these heads being there. They only showed that Mr. Kurtz lacked restraint in the gratification of his various lusts, that there was something wanting in him—some small matter which, when the pressing need arose, could not be found under his magnificent eloquence. Whether he knew of this deficiency himself I can't say. I think the knowledge came to him at last—only at the very last. But the wilderness had found him out early, and had taken on him a terrible vengeance for the fantastic invasion. I think it had whispered to him things about himself which he did not know, things of which he had no conception till he took counsel with this great solitude—and the whisper had proved irresistibly fascinating. It echoed loudly within him because he was hollow at the core. . . . I put down the glass, and the head that had appeared near enough to be spoken to seemed at once to have leaped away from me into inaccessible distance.

"The admirer of Mr. Kurtz was a bit crestfallen. In a hurried, indistinct voice he began to assure me he had not dared to take these—say, symbols—down. He was not afraid of the natives; they would not stir till Mr. Kurtz gave the word. His ascendency was extraordinary. The camps of these people surrounded the place, and the chiefs came every day to see him. They would crawl. . . . 'I don't want to know anything of the ceremonies used when approaching Mr. Kurtz,' I shouted. Curious, this feeling that came over me that such details would be more intolerable than those heads drying on the stakes under Mr. Kurtz's windows. After all, that was only a savage sight, while I seemed at one bound to have been transported into some lightless region of subtle horrors, where pure, uncomplicated savagery was a positive relief, being something that had a right to exist—obviously—in the sunshine. The young man looked at me with surprise. I suppose it did not occur to him Mr. Kurtz was no idol of mine. He forgot I hadn't heard any of these splendid monologues on, what was it? on love, justice, conduct of life—or what not. If it had come to crawling before Mr. Kurtz, he crawled as much as the veriest savage of them all. I had no idea of the conditions, he said: these heads were the heads of rebels. I shocked him excessively by laughing. Rebels! What would be the next definition I was to hear? There had been enemies, criminals, workers—and these were rebels. Those rebellious heads looked very subdued to me on their sticks. 'You don't know how such a life tries a man like Kurtz,' cried Kurtz's last disciple. 'Well, and you?' I said. 'I! I! I am a simple man. I have no great thoughts. I want nothing from anybody. How can you compare me to . . .?' His feelings were too much for speech, and suddenly he broke down. 'I don't understand,' he groaned. 'I've been doing my best to keep him alive, and that's enough. I had no hand in all this. I have no abilities. There hasn't been a drop of medicine or a mouthful of invalid food for months here. He was shamefully abandoned. A man like this, with such ideas. Shamefully! Shamefully! I—I—haven't slept for the last ten nights. . . .'

"His voice lost itself in the calm of the evening. The long shadows of the forest had slipped down hill while we talked, had gone far beyond the ruined hovel, beyond the symbolic row of stakes. All this was in the gloom, while we down there were yet in the sunshine, and the stretch of the river abreast of the clearing glittered in a still and dazzling splendor, with a murky and over-shadowed bend above and below. Not a living soul was seen on the shore. The bushes did not rustle.

"Suddenly round the corner of the house a group of men appeared, as though they had come up from the ground. They waded waist-deep in the grass, in a compact body, bearing an improvised stretcher in their midst. Instantly, in the emptiness of the landscape, a cry arose flying straight to the very heart of the land; and, as if by enchantment, streams of human beings—of naked human beings—with spears in their hands, with bows, with shields, with wild glances and savage movements, were poured into the clearing by the dark-faced and pensive forest. The bushes shook, the grass swayed for a time, and then everything stood still in attentive immobility.

"'Now, if he does not say the right thing to them we are all done for,' said the Russian at my elbow. The knot of men with the stretcher had stopped too, halfway to the steamer, as if petrified. I saw the man on the stretcher sit up, lank and with an uplifted arm, above the shoulders of the bearers. 'Let us hope that the man who can talk so well of love in general will find some particular reason to spare us this time,' I said. I resented bitterly the absurd danger of our situation, as if to be at the mercy of that atrocious phantom had been a dishonoring necessity. I could not hear a sound, but through my glasses I saw the thin arm extended commandingly, the lower jaw moving, the eyes of that apparition shining darkly far in its bony head that nodded with grotesque jerks. Kurtz—Kurtz—that means short in German—don't it? Well, the name was as true as everything else in his life—and death. He looked at least seven feet long. His covering had fallen off, and his body emerged from it pitiful and appalling as from a winding-sheet. I could see the cage of his ribs all astir, the bones of his arm waving. It was as though an animated image of death carved out of old ivory had been shaking its hand with menaces at a motionless crowd of men made of dark and glittering bronze. I saw him open his mouth wide—it gave him a weirdly voracious aspect, as though he had wanted to swallow all the air, all the earth, all the men before him. A deep voice reached me faintly. He must have been shouting. He fell back suddenly. The stretcher shook as the bearers staggered forward again, and almost at the same time I noticed that the crowd of savages was vanishing without any perceptible movement of retreat, as if the forest that had ejected these beings so suddenly had drawn them in again as the breath is drawn in a long aspiration.

"Some of the pilgrims behind the stretcher carried his arms—two shot-guns, a heavy rifle, and a light revolver-carbine—the thunderbolts of that pitiful Jupiter. The manager bent over him murmuring as he walked beside his head. They laid him down in one of the little cabins—just a room for a bed-place and a camp-stool or two, you know. We had brought his belated correspondence, and a lot of torn envelopes and open letters littered his bed. His hand roamed feebly amongst these papers. I was struck by the fire of his eyes and the composed languor of his expression. It was not so much the exhaustion of disease. He did not seem in pain. This shadow looked satiated and calm, as though for the moment it had had its fill of all the emotions.

"He rustled one of the letters, and looking straight in my face said, 'I am glad.' Somebody had been writing to him about me. These special recommendations were turning up again. The volume of tone he emitted without effort, almost without the trouble of moving his lips, amazed me. A voice! a voice! It was grave, profound, vibrating, while the man did not seem capable of a whisper. However, he had enough strength in him—factitious no doubt—to very nearly make an end of us, as you shall hear directly.

"The manager appeared silently in the doorway; I stepped out at once and he drew the curtain after me. The Russian, eyed curiously by the pilgrims, was staring at the shore. I followed the direction of his glance.

"Dark human shapes could be made out in the distance, flitting indistinctly against the gloomy border of the forest, and near the river two bronze figures, leaning on tall spears, stood in the sunlight under fantastic headdresses of spotted skins, warlike and still in statuesque repose. And from right to left along the lighted shore moved a wild and gorgeous apparition of a woman.

"She walked with measured steps, draped in striped and fringed cloths, treading the earth proudly, with a slight jingle and flash of barbarous ornaments. She carried her head high; her hair was done in the shape of a helmet; she had brass leggings to the knee, brass wire gauntlets to the elbow, a crimson spot on her tawny cheek, innumerable necklaces of glass beads on her neck; bizarre things, charms, gifts of witch-men, that hung about her, glittered and trembled at every step. She must have had the value of several elephant tusks upon her. She was savage and superb, wild-eyed and magnificent; there was something ominous and stately in her deliberate progress. And in the hush that had fallen suddenly upon the whole sorrowful land, the immense wilderness, the colossal body of the fecund and mysterious life seemed to look at her, pensive, as though it had been looking at the image of its own tenebrous and passionate soul.

"She came abreast of the steamer, stood still, and faced us. Her long shadow fell to the water's edge. Her face had a tragic and fierce aspect of wild sorrow and of dumb pain mingled with the fear of some struggling, half-shaped resolve. She stood looking at us without a stir and like the wilderness itself, with an air of brooding over an inscrutable purpose. A whole minute passed, and then she made a step forward. There was a low jingle, a glint of yellow metal, a sway of fringed draperies, and she stopped as if her heart had failed her. The young fellow by my side growled. The pilgrims murmured at my back. She looked at us all as if her life had depended upon the unswerving steadiness of her glance. Suddenly she opened her bared arms and threw them up rigid above her head, as though in an uncontrollable desire to touch the sky, and at the same time the swift shadows darted out on the earth, swept around on the river, gathering the steamer into a shadowy embrace. A formidable silence hung over the scene.

"She turned away slowly, walked on, following the bank, and passed into the bushes to the left. Once only her eyes gleamed back at us in the dusk of the thickets before she disappeared.

"'If she had offered to come aboard I really think I would have tried to shoot her,' said the man of patches, nervously. 'I had been risking my life every day for the last fortnight to keep her out of the house. She got in one day and kicked up a row about those miserable rags I picked up in the storeroom to mend my clothes with. I wasn't decent. At least it must have been that, for she talked like a fury to Kurtz for an hour, pointing at me now and then. I don't understand the dialect of this tribe. Luckily for me, I fancy Kurtz felt too ill that day to care, or there would have been mischief. I don't understand. . . . No—it's too much for me. Ah, well, it's all over now.'

"At this moment I heard Kurtz's deep voice behind the curtain, 'Save me!— save the ivory, you mean. Don't tell me. Save *me*! Why, I've had to save you. You are interrupting my plans now. Sick! Sick! Not so sick as you would like to believe. Never mind. I'll carry my ideas out yet—I will return. I'll show you what can be done. You with your little peddling notions—you are interfering with me. I will return. I . . .'

"The manager came out. He did me the honor to take me under the arm and lead me aside. 'He is very low, very low,' he said. He considered it necessary to sigh, but neglected to be consistently sorrowful. 'We have done all we could for him—haven't we? But there is no disguising the fact, Mr. Kurtz has done more harm than good to the Company. He did not see the time was not ripe for vigorous action. Cautiously, cautiously—that's my principle. We must be cautious yet. The district is closed to us for a time. Deplorable! Upon the whole, the trade will suffer. I don't deny there is a remarkable quantity of ivory—mostly fossil. We must save it, at all events—but look how precarious the position is—and why? Because the method is unsound.' 'Do you,' said I, looking at the shore, 'call it "unsound method"?' 'Without doubt,' he exclaimed, hotly. 'Don't you?' . . . 'No method at all,' I murmured after a while. 'Exactly,' he exulted. 'I anticipated this. Shows a complete want of judgment. It is my duty to point it out in the proper quarter.' 'Oh,' said I, 'that fellow—what's his name?—the brickmaker, will make a readable report for you.' He appeared confounded for a moment. It seemed to me I had never breathed an atmosphere so vile, and I turned mentally to Kurtz for relief—positively for relief. 'Nevertheless I think Mr. Kurtz is a remarkable man,' I said with emphasis. He started, dropped on me a cold heavy glance, said very quietly, 'He *was*,' and turned his back on me. My hour of favor was over; I found myself lumped along with Kurtz as a partisan of methods for which the time was not ripe: I was unsound! Ah! but it was something to have at least a choice of nightmares.

"I had turned to the wilderness really, not to Mr. Kurtz, who, I was ready to admit, was as good as buried. And for a moment it seemed to me as if I also were buried in a vast grave full of unspeakable secrets. I felt an intolerable weight oppressing my breast, the smell of the damp earth, the unseen presence of victorious corruption, the darkness of an impenetrable night. . . . The Russian tapped me on the shoulder. I heard him mumbling and stammering something about 'brother seaman—couldn't conceal—knowledge of matters that would affect Mr. Kurtz's reputation.' I waited. For him evidently Mr. Kurtz was not in his grave; I suspect that for him Mr. Kurtz was one of the immortals. 'Well!' said I at last, 'speak out. As it happens, I am Mr. Kurtz's friend—in a way.'

"He stated with a good deal of formality that had we not been 'of the same profession,' he would have kept the matter to himself without regard to consequences. 'He suspected there was an active ill-will towards him on the part of these white men that—' 'You are right,' I said, remembering a certain conversation I had overheard. 'The manager thinks you ought to be hanged.' He showed a concern at this intelligence which amused me at first. 'I had better get out of the way quietly,' he said, earnestly. 'I can do no more for Kurtz now, and they would soon find some excuse. What's to stop them? There's a military post three hundred miles from here.' 'Well, upon my word,' said I, 'perhaps you had better go if you have any friends amongst the savages near by.' 'Plenty,' he said. 'They are simple people—and I want nothing, you know.' He stood biting his lip, then: 'I don't want any harm to happen to these whites here, but of course I was thinking of Mr. Kurtz's reputation—but you are a brother seaman and—' 'All right,' said I, after a time. 'Mr. Kurtz's reputation is safe with me.' I did not know how truly I spoke.

"He informed me, lowering his voice, that it was Kurtz who had ordered the attack to be made on the steamer. 'He hated sometimes the idea of being taken away—and then again. . . . But I don't understand these matters. I am a simple man. He thought it would scare you away—that you would give it up, thinking him dead. I could not stop him. Oh, I had an awful time of it this last month.' 'Very well,' I said. 'He is all right now.' 'Ye-e-es,' he muttered, not very convinced apparently. 'Thanks,' said I; 'I shall keep my eyes open.' 'But quiet—eh?' he urged, anxiously. 'It would be awful for his reputation if anybody here—' I promised a complete discretion with great gravity. 'I have a canoe and three black fellows waiting not very far. I am off. Could you give me a few Martini-Henry cartridges?' I could, and did, with proper secrecy. He helped himself, with a wink at me, to a handful of my tobacco. 'Between sailors—you know—good English tobacco.' At the door of the pilot-house he turned round—'I say, haven't you a pair of shoes you could spare?' He raised one leg. 'Look.' The soles were tied with knotted strings sandal-wise under his bare feet. I rooted out an old pair, at which he looked with admiration before tucking it under his left arm. One of his pockets (bright red) was bulging with cartridges, from the other (dark blue) peeped 'Towson's Inquiry,' &c., &c. He seemed to think himself excellently well equipped for a renewed encounter with the wilderness. 'Ah! I'll never, never meet such a man again. You ought to have heard him recite poetry—his own too it was, he told me. Poetry!' He rolled his eyes at the recollection of these delights. 'Oh, he enlarged my mind!' 'Good-by,' said I. He shook hands and vanished in the night. Sometimes I ask myself whether I had ever really seen him—whether it was possible to meet such a phenomenon! . . .

"When I woke up shortly after midnight his warning came to my mind with its hint of danger that seemed, in the starred darkness, real enough to make me get up for the purpose of having a look round. On the hill a big fire burned, illuminating fitfully a crooked corner of the station-house. One of the agents with a picket of a few of our blacks, armed for the purpose, was keeping guard over the ivory; but deep within the forest, red gleams that wavered, that seemed to sink and rise from the ground amongst confused columnar shapes of intense blackness, showed the exact position of the camp where Mr. Kurtz's adorers were keeping their uneasy vigil. The monotonous beating of a big drum filled the air with muffled shocks and a lingering vibration. A steady droning sound of many men chanting each to himself some weird incantation came out from the black, flat wall of the woods as the humming of bees comes out of a hive, and had a strange narcotic effect upon my half-awake senses. I believe I dozed off leaning over the rail, till an abrupt burst of yells, an overwhelming outbreak of a pent-up and mysterious frenzy, woke me up in a bewildered wonder. It was cut short all at once, and the low droning went on with an effect of audible and soothing silence. I glanced casually into the little cabin. A light was burning within, but Mr. Kurtz was not there.

"I think I would have raised an outcry if I had believed my eyes. But I didn't believe them at first—the thing seemed so impossible. The fact is I was completely unnerved by a sheer blank fright, pure abstract terror, unconnected with any distinct shape of physical danger. What made this emotion so overpowering was— how shall I define it?—the moral shock I received, as if something altogether monstrous, intolerable to thought and odious to the soul, had been thrust upon me unexpectedly. This lasted of course the merest fraction of a second, and then the usual sense of commonplace, deadly danger, the possibility of a sudden onslaught and massacre, or something of the kind, which I saw impending, was positively welcome and composing. It pacified me, in fact, so much, that I did not raise an alarm.

"There was an agent buttoned up inside an ulster and sleeping on a chair on deck within three feet of me. The yells had not awakened him; he snored very slightly; I left him to his slumbers and leaped ashore. I did not betray Mr. Kurtz— it was ordered I should never betray him—it was written I should be loyal to the nightmare of my choice. I was anxious to deal with this shadow by myself alone,— and to this day I don't know why I was so jealous of sharing with anyone the peculiar blackness of that experience.

"As soon as I got on the bank I saw a trail—a broad trail through the grass. I remember the exultation with which I said to myself, 'He can't walk—he is crawling on all-fours—I've got him.' The grass was wet with dew. I strode rapidly with clenched fists. I fancy I had some vague notion of falling upon him and giving him a drubbing. I don't know. I had some imbecile thoughts. The knitting old woman with the cat obtruded herself upon my memory as a most improper person to be sitting at the other end of such an affair. I saw a row of pilgrims squirting lead in the air out of Winchesters held to the hip. I thought I would never get back to the steamer, and imagined myself living alone and unarmed in the woods to an advanced age. Such silly things—you know. And I remember I confounded the beat of the drum with the beating of my heart, and was pleased at its calm regularity.

"I kept to the track though—then stopped to listen. The night was very clear: a dark blue space, sparkling with dew and starlight, in which black things stood very still. I thought I could see a kind of motion ahead of me. I was strangely cocksure of everything that night. I actually left the track and ran in a wide simi-circle (I verily believe chuckling to myself) so as to get in front of that stir, of that motion I had seen—if indeed I had seen anything. I was circumventing Kurtz as though it had been a boyish game.

"I came upon him, and, if he had not heard me coming, I would have fallen over him too, but he got up in time. He rose, unsteady, long, pale, indistinct, like a vapor exhaled by the earth, and swayed slightly, misty and silent before me; while at my back the fires loomed between the trees, and the murmur of many voices issued from the forest. I had cut him off cleverly; but when actually confronting him I seemed to come to my senses, I saw the danger in its right proportion. It was by no means over yet. Suppose he began to shout? Though he could hardly stand, there was still plenty of vigor in his voice. 'Go away—hide yourself,' he said, in that profound tone. It was very awful. I glanced back. We were within thirty yards from the nearest fire. A black figure stood up, strode on long black legs, waving long black arms, across the glow. It had horns—antelope horns, I think—on its head. Some sorcerer, some witch-man, no doubt: it looked fiend-like enough. 'Do you know what you are doing?' I whispered. 'Perfectly,' he answered, raising his voice for that single word: it sounded to me far off and yet loud, like a hail through a speaking-trumpet. If he makes a row we are lost, I thought to myself. This clearly was not a case for fisticuffs, even apart from the very natural aversion I had to beat the Shadow—this wandering and tormented thing. 'You will be lost,' I said—'utterly lost.' One gets sometimes such a flash of inspiration, you know. I did say the right thing, though indeed he could not have been more irretrievably lost than he was at this very moment, when the foundation of our intimacy were being laid—to endure—to endure—even to the end—even beyond.

"'I had immense plans,' he muttered irresolutely. 'Yes,' said I; 'but if you try to shout I'll smash your head with—' there was not a stick or a stone near. 'I will throttle you for good,' I corrected myself. 'I was on the threshold of great things,' he pleaded, in a voice of longing, with a wistfulness of tone that made my blood run cold. 'And now for this stupid scoundrel—' 'Your success in Europe is assured in any case,' I affirmed, steadily. I did not want to have the throttling of him, you understand—and indeed it would have been very little use for any practical purpose. I tried to break the spell—the heavy, mute spell of the wilderness—that seemed to draw him to its pitiless breast by the awakening of forgotten and brutal instincts, by the memory of gratified and monstrous passions. This alone, I was convinced, had driven him out to the edge of the forest, to the bush, towards the gleam of fires, the throb of drums, the drone of weird incantations; this alone had beguiled his unlawful soul beyond the bounds of permitted aspirations. And, don't you see, the terror of the position was not in being knocked on the head—though I had a very lively sense of that danger too—but in this, that I had to deal with a being to whom I could not appeal in the name of anything high or low. I had, even like the niggers, to invoke him—himself—his own exalted and incredible degradation. There was nothing either above or below him, and I knew it. He had kicked himself loose of the earth. Confound the man! he had kicked the very earth to pieces. He was alone, and I before him did not know whether I stood on the ground or floated in the air. I've been telling you what we said—repeating the phrases we pronounced,—but what's the good? They were common everyday words,—the familiar, vague sounds exchanged on every waking day of life. But what of that? They had behind them, to my mind, the terrific suggestiveness of words heard in dreams, of phrases spoken in nightmares. Soul! If anybody had ever struggled with a soul, I am the man. And I wasn't arguing with a lunatic either. Believe me or not, his intelligence was perfectly clear—concentrated, it is true, upon himself with horrible intensity, yet clear; and therein was my only chance—barring, of course, the killing him there and then, which wasn't so good, on account of unavoidable noise. But his soul was mad. Being alone in the wilderness, it had looked within itself, and, by heavens! I tell you, it had gone mad. I had—for my sins, I suppose—to go through the ordeal of looking into it myself. No eloquence could have been so withering to one's belief in mankind as his final burst of sincerity. He struggled with himself, too. I saw it,—I heard it. I saw the inconceivable mystery of a soul that knew no restraint, no faith, and no fear, yet struggling blindly with itself. I kept my head pretty well; but when I had him at last stretched on the couch, I wiped my forehead, while my legs shook under me as though I had carried half a ton on my back down that hill. And yet I had only supported him, his bony arm clasped round my neck—and he was not much heavier then a child.

"When next day we left at noon, the crowd, of whose presence behind the curtain of trees I had been acutely conscious all the time, flowed out of the woods again, filled the clearing, covered the slope with a mass of naked, breathing, quivering, bronze bodies. I steamed up a bit, then swung down-stream, and two thousand eyes followed the evolutions of the splashing, thumping, fierce river-demon beating the water with its terrible tail and breathing black smoke into the air. In front of the first rank, along the river, three men, plastered with bright red earth from head to foot, strutted to and fro restlessly. When we came abreast again, they faced the river, stamped their feet, nodded their horned heads, swayed their scarlet bodies; they shook towards the fierce river-demon a bunch of black feathers, a mangy skin with a pendent tail—something that looked like a dried gourd; they shouted periodically together strings of amazing words that resembled no sounds of human language; and the deep murmurs of the crowd, interrupted suddenly, were like the response of some satanic litany.

"We had carried Kurtz into the pilot-house: there was more air there. Lying on the couch, he stared through the open shutter. There was an eddy in the mass of human bodies, and the woman with helmeted head and tawny cheeks rushed out to the very brink of the stream. She put out her hands, shouted something, and all that wild mob took up the shout in a roaring chorus of articulated, rapid, breathless utterance.

"'Do you understand this?' I asked.

"He kept on looking out past me with fiery, longing eyes, with a mingled expression of wistfulness and hate. He made no answer, but I saw a smile, a smile of indefinable meaning, appear on his colorless lips that a moment after twitched convulsively. 'Do I not?' he said slowly, gasping, as if the words had been torn out of him by a supernatural power.

"I pulled the string of the whistle, and I did this because I saw the pilgrims on deck getting out their rifles with an air of anticipating a jolly lark. At the sudden screech there was a movement of abject terror through that wedged mass of bodies. 'Don't! don't! you frighten them away,' cried someone on deck disconsolately. I pulled the string time after time. They broke and ran, they leaped, they crouched, they swerved, they dodged the flying terror of the sound. The three red chaps had fallen flat, face down on the shore, as though they had been shot dead. Only the barbarous and superb woman did not so much as flinch, and stretched tragically her bare arms after us over the somber and glittering river.

"And then that imbecile crowd down on the deck started their little fun, and I could see nothing more for smoke.

"The brown current ran swiftly out of the heart of darkness, bearing us down towards the sea with twice the speed of our upward progress; and Kurtz's life was running swiftly too, ebbing, out of his heart into the sea of inexorable time. The manager was very placid, he had no vital anxieties now, he took us both in with a comprehensive and satisfied glance: the 'affair' had come off as well as could be wished. I saw the time approaching when I would be left alone of the party of 'unsound method.' The pilgrims looked upon me with disfavor. I was, so to speak, numbered with the dead. It is strange how I accepted this unforeseen partnership, this choice of nightmares forced upon me in the tenebrous land invaded by these mean and greedy phantoms.

"Kurtz discoursed. A voice! a voice! It rang deep to the very last. It survived his strength to hide in the magnificent folds of eloquence the barren darkness of his heart. Oh, he struggled! he struggled! The wastes of his weary brain were haunted by shadowy images now—images of wealth and fame revolving obsequiously round his unextinguishable gift of noble and lofty expression. My Intended, my station, my career, my ideas—these were the subjects for the occasional utterances of elevated sentiments. The shade of the original Kurtz frequented the bedside of the hollow sham, whose fate it was to be buried presently in the mold of primeval earth. But both the diabolic love and the unearthly hate of the mysteries it had penetrated fought for the possession of that soul satiated with primitive emotions, avid of lying fame, of sham distinction, of all the appearances of success and power.

"Sometimes he was contemptibly childish. He desired to have kings meet him at railway-stations on his return from some ghastly Nowhere, where he intended to accomplish great things. 'You show them you have in you something that is really profitable, and then there will be no limits to the recognition of your ability,' he would say. 'Of course you must take care of the motives—right motives—always.' The long reaches that were like one and the same reach, monotonous bends that were exactly alike, slipped past the steamer with their multitude of secular trees looking patiently after this grimy fragment of another world, the forerunner of change, of conquest, of trade, of massacres, of blessings. I looked ahead—piloting. 'Close the shutter,' said Kurtz suddenly one day; 'I can't bear to look at this.' I did so. There was a silence. 'Oh, but I will wring your heart yet!' he cried at the invisible wilderness.

"We broke down—as I had expected—and had to lie up for repairs at the head of an island. This delay was the first thing that shook Kurtz's confidence. One morning he gave me a packet of papers and a photograph,—the lot tied together with a shoe-string. 'Keep this for me,' he said. 'This noxious fool' (meaning the manager) 'is capable of prying into my boxes when I am not looking.' In the afternoon I saw him. He was lying on his back with closed eyes, and I withdrew quietly, but I heard him mutter, 'Live rightly, die, die . . .' I listened. There was nothing more. Was he rehearsing some speech in his sleep, or was it a fragment of a phrase from some newspaper article? He had been writing for the papers and meant to do so again, 'for the furthering of my ideas. It's a duty.'

"His was an impenetrable darkness. I looked at him as you peer down at a man who is lying at the bottom of a precipice where the sun never shines. But I had not much time to give him, because I was helping the engine-driver to take to pieces the leaky cylinders, to straighten a bent connecting-rod, and in other such matters. I lived in an infernal mess of rust, filings, nuts, bolts, spanners, hammers, ratchet-drills—things I abominate, because I don't get on with them. I tended the little forge we fortunately had aboard; I toiled wearily in a wretched scrap-heap—unless I had the shakes too bad to stand.

"One evening coming in with a candle I was startled to hear him say a little tremulously, 'I am lying here in the dark waiting for death.' The light was within a foot of his eyes. I forced myself to murmur, 'Oh, nonsense!' and stood over him as if transfixed.

"Anything approaching the change that came over his features I have never seen before, and hope never to see again. Oh, I wasn't touched. I was fascinated. It was as though a veil had been rent. I saw on that ivory face the expression of somber pride, of ruthless power, of craven terror—of an intense and hopeless despair. Did he live his life again in every detail of desire, temptation, and surrender during that supreme moment of complete knowledge? He cried in a whisper at some image, at some vision,—he cried out twice, a cry that was no more than a breath—

" 'The horror! The horror!'

"I blew the candle out and left the cabin. The pilgrims were dining in the mess-room, and I took my place opposite the manager, who lifted his eyes to give me a questioning glance, which I successfully ignored. He leaned back, serene, with that peculiar smile of his sealing the unexpressed depths of his meanness. A continuous shower of small flies streamed upon the lamp, upon the cloth, upon our hands and faces. Suddenly the manager's boy put his insolent black head in the doorway, and said in a tone of scathing contempt—

" 'Mistah Kurtz—he dead.'

"All the pilgrims rushed out to see. I remained, and went on with my dinner. I believe I was considered brutally callous. However, I did not eat much. There was a lamp in there—light, don't you know—and outside it was so beastly, beastly dark. I went no more near the remarkable man who had pronounced a judgment upon the adventures of his soul on this earth. The voice was gone. What else had been there? But I am of course aware that next day the pilgrims buried something in a muddy hole.

"And then they very nearly buried me.

"However, as you see, I did not go to join Kurtz there and then. I did not. I remained to dream the nightmare out to the end, and to show my loyalty to Kurtz once more. Destiny. My destiny! Droll thing life is—that mysterious arrangement of merciless logic for a futile purpose. The most you can hope from it is some knowledge of yourself—that comes too late—a crop of unextinguishable regrets. I have wrestled with death. It is the most unexciting contest you can imagine. It takes place in an impalpable grayness, with nothing underfoot, with nothing around, without spectators, without clamor, without glory, without the great desire of victory, without the great fear of defeat, in a sickly atmosphere of tepid skepticism, without much belief in your own right, and still less in that of your adversary. If such is the form of ultimate wisdom, then life is a greater riddle than some of us think it to be. I was within a hair's-breath of the last opportunity for pronouncement, and I found with humiliation that probably I would have nothing to say. This is the reason why I affirm that Kurtz was a remarkable man. He had something to say. He said it. Since I had peeped over the edge myself, I understand better the meaning of his stare, that could not see the flame of the candle, but was wide enough to embrace the whole universe, piercing enough to penetrate all the hearts that beat in the darkness. He had summed up—he had judged. 'The horror!' He was a remarkable man. After all, this was the expression of some sort of belief; it had candor, it had conviction, it had a vibrating note of revolt in its whisper, it had the appalling face of a glimpsed truth—the strange commingling of desire and hate. And it is not my own extremity I remember best—a vision of grayness without form filled with physical pain, and a careless contempt for the evanescence of all things—even of this pain itself. No! It is his extremity that I seem to have lived through. True, he had made that last stride, he had stepped over the edge, while I had been permitted to draw back my hesitating foot. And perhaps in this is the whole difference; perhaps all the wisdom, and all truth, and all sincerity, are just compressed into that inappreciable moment of time in which we step over the threshold of the invisible. Perhaps! I like to think my summing-up would not have been a word of careless contempt. Better his cry—much better. It was an affirmation, a moral victory paid for by innumerable defeats, by abominable terrors, by abominable satisfactions. But it was a victory! That is why I have remained loyal to Kurtz to the last, and even beyond, when a long time after I heard once more, not his own voice, but the echo of his magnificent eloquence thrown to me from a soul as translucently pure as a cliff of crystal.

"No, they did not bury me, though there is a period of time which I remember mistily, with a shuddering wonder, like a passage through some inconceivable world that had no hope in it and no desire. I found myself back in the sepulchral city resenting the sight of people hurrying through the streets to filch a little money from each other, to devour their infamous cookery, to gulp their unwholesome beer, to dream their insignificant and silly dreams. They trespassed upon my thoughts. They were intruders whose knowledge of life was to me an irritating pretense, because I felt so sure that could not possibly know the things I knew. Their bearing, which was simply the bearing of commonplace individuals going about their business in the assurance of perfect safety, was offensive to me like the outrageous flauntings of folly in the face of a danger it is unable to comprehend. I had no particular desire to enlighten them, but I had some difficulty in restraining myself from laughing in their faces, so full of stupid importance. I dare say I was not very well at that time. I tottered about the streets—there were various affairs to settle—grinning bitterly at perfectly respectable persons. I admit my behavior was inexcusable, but then my temperature was seldom normal in these days. My dear aunt's endeavors to 'nurse up my strength' seemed altogether beside the mark. It was not my strength that wanted nursing, it was my imagination that wanted soothing. I kept the bundle of papers given me by Kurtz, not knowing exactly what to do with it. His mother had died lately, watched over, as I was told, by his Intended. A clean-shaved man, with an official manner and wearing gold-rimmed spectacles, called on me one day and made inquiries, at first circuitous, afterwards suavely pressing, about what he was pleased to denominate certain 'documents.' I was not surprised, because I had had two rows with the manager on the subject out there. I had refused to give up the smallest scrap out of that package, and I took the same attitude with the spectacled man. He became darkly menacing at last, and with much heat argued that the Company had the right to every bit of information about its 'territories.' And, said he, 'Mr. Kurtz's knowl-edge of unexplored regions must have been necessarily extensive and peculiar—owing to his great abilities and to the deplorable circumstances in which he had been placed: therefore'—I assured him Mr. Kurtz's knowledge, however exten-sive, did not bear upon the problems of commerce or administration. He invoked then the name of science. 'It would be an incalculable loss if,' &c., &c. I offered him the report on the 'Suppression of Savage Customs,' with the postscriptum torn off. He took it up eagerly, but ended by sniffing at it with an air of contempt. 'This is not what we had a right to expect,' he remarked. 'Expect nothing else,' I said. 'There are only private letters.' He withdrew upon some threat of legal pro-ceedings, and I saw him no more; but another fellow, calling himself Kurtz's cou-sin, appeared two days later, and was anxious to hear all the details about his dear relative's last moments. Incidentally he gave me to understand that Kurtz had been essentially a great musician. 'There was the making of an immense success,' said the man, who was an organist, I believe, with lank gray hair flowing over a greasy coat-collar. I had no reason to doubt his statement; and to this day I am un-able to say what was Kurtz's profession, whether he ever had any—which was the greatest of his talents. I had taken him for a painter who wrote for the papers, or else for a journalist who could paint—but even the cousin (who took snuff during the interview) could not tell me what he had been—exactly. He was a universal genius—on that point I agreed with the old chap, who thereupon blew his nose noisily into a large cotton handkerchief and withdrew in senile agitation, bearing off some family letters and memoranda without importance. Ultimately a jour-nalist anxious to know something of the fate of his 'dear colleague' turned up. This visitor informed me Kurtz's proper sphere ought to have been politics 'on the pop-ular side.' He had furry straight eyebrows, bristly hair cropped short, an eye-glass on a broad ribbon, and, becoming expansive, confessed his opinion that Kurtz really couldn't write a bit—'but heavens! how that man could talk! He electrified large meetings. He had faith—don't you see?—he had the faith. He could get him-self to believe anything—anything. He would have been a splendid leader of an extreme party.' 'What party?' I asked. 'Any party,' answered the other. 'He was an—an—extremist.' Did I not think so? I assented. Did I know, he asked, with a sudden flash of curiosity, 'what it was that had induced him to go out there?' 'Yes,' said I, and forthwith handed him the famous Report for publication, if he thought fit. He glanced through it hurriedly, mumbling all the time, judged 'it would do,' and took himself off with this plunder.

"Thus I was left at last with a slim packet of letters and the girl's portrait. She struck me as beautiful—I mean she had a beautiful expression. I know that the sunlight can be made to lie too, yet one felt that no manipulation of light and pose could have conveyed the delicate shade of truthfulness upon those features. She seemed ready to listen without mental reservation, without suspicion, without a thought for herself. I concluded I would go and give her back her portrait and those letters myself. Curiosity? Yes; and also some other feeling perhaps. All that had been Kurtz's had passed out of my hands: his soul, his body, his station, his plans, his ivory, his career. There remained only his memory and his Intended—and I wanted to give that up too to the past, in a way,—to surrender personally all that remained of him with me to that oblivion which is the last word of our common fate. I don't defend myself. I had no clear perception of what it was I really wanted. Perhaps it was an impulse of unconscious loyalty, or the fulfillment of one of these ironic necessities that lurk in the facts of human existence. I don't know. I can't tell. But I went.

"I thought his memory was like the other memories of the dead that accumulate in every man's life,—a vague impress on the brain of shadows that had fallen on it in their swift and final passage; but before the high and ponderous door, between the tall houses of a street as still and decorous as a well-kept ally in a cemetery, I had a vision of him on the stretcher, opening his mouth voraciously, as if to devour all the earth with all its mankind. He lived then before me; he lived as much as he had ever lived—a shadow insatiable of splendid appearances, of frightful realities; a shadow darker than the shadow of the night, and draped nobly in the folds of a gorgeous eloquence. The vision seemed to enter the house with me—the stretcher, the phantom-bearers, the wild crowd of obedient worshipers, the gloom of the forests, the glitter of the reach between the murky bends, the beat of the drum, regular and muffled like the beating of a heart—the heart of a conquering darkness. It was a moment of triumph for the wilderness, an invading and vengeful rush which, it seemed to me, I would have to keep back alone for the salvation of another soul. And the memory of what I had heard him say afar there, with the horned shapes stirring at my back, in the glow of fires, within the patient woods, those broken phrases came back to me, were heard again in their ominous and terrifying simplicity. I remembered his abject pleading, his abject threats, the colossal scale of his vile desires, the meanness, the torment, the tempestuous anguish of his soul. And later on I seemed to see his collected languid manner, when he said one day, 'This lot of ivory now is really mine. The Company did not pay for it. I collected it myself at a very great personal risk. I am afraid they will try to claim it as theirs though. H'm. It is a difficult case. What do you think I ought to do—resist? Eh? I want no more than justice.' . . . He wanted no more than justice—no more than justice. I rang the bell before a mahogany door on the first floor, and while I waited he seemed to stare at me out of the glassy panel—stare with that wide and immense stare embracing, condemning, loathing all the universe. I seemed to hear the whispered cry, 'The horror! The horror!'

"The dusk was falling. I had to wait in a lofty drawing-room with three long windows from floor to ceiling that were like three luminous and bedraped columns. The bent gilt legs and backs of the furniture shone in indistinct curves. The tall marble fireplace had a cold and monumental whiteness. A grand piano stood massively in a corner, with dark gleams on the flat surfaces like a somber and polished sarcophagus. A high door opened—closed. I rose.

"She came forward, all in black, with a pale head, floating towards me in the dusk. She was in mourning. It was more than a year since his death, more than a year since the news came; she seemed as though she would remember and mourn for ever. She took both my hands in hers and murmured, 'I had heard you were coming.' I noticed she was not very young—I mean not girlish. She had a mature capacity for fidelity, for belief, for suffering. The room seemed to have grown

darker, as if all the sad light of the cloudy evening had taken refuge on her forehead. This fair hair, this pale visage, this pure brow, seemed surrounded by an
ashy halo from which the dark eyes looked out at me. Their glance was guileless,
profound, confident, and trustful. She carried her sorrowful head as though she
were proud of that sorrow, as though she would say, I—I alone know how to
mourn for him as he deserves. But while we were still shaking hands, such a look
of awful desolation came upon her face that I perceived she was one of those creatures that are not the playthings of Time. For her he had died only yesterday. And,
by Jove! the impression was so powerful that for me too he seemed to have died
only yesterday—nay, this very minute. I saw her and him in the same instant of
time—his death and her sorrow—I saw her sorrow in the very moment of his
death. Do you understand? I saw them together—I heard them together. She had
said, with a deep catch of the breath, 'I have survived;' while my strained ears
seemed to hear distinctly, mingled with her tone of despairing regret, the summing-up whisper of his eternal condemnation. I asked myself what I was doing
there, with a sensation of panic in my heart as though I had blundered into a place
of cruel and absurd mysteries not fit for a human being to behold. She motioned
me to a chair. We sat down. I laid the packet gently on the little table, and she put
her hand over it. . . . 'You knew him well,' she murmured, after a moment of
mourning silence.

" 'Intimacy grows quick out there,' I said. 'I knew him as well as it is possible
for one man to know another.'

" 'And you admired him,' she said. 'It was impossible to know him and not
admire him. Was it?'

" 'He was a remarkable man,' I said, unsteadily. Then before the appealing
fixity of her gaze, that seemed to watch for more words on my lips, I went on, 'It
was impossible not to——'

" 'Love him,' she finished eagerly, silencing me into an appalled dumbness.
'How true! how true! But when you think that no one knew him so well as I! I had
all his noble confidence. I knew him best.'

" 'You knew him best,' I repeated. And perhaps she did. But with every word
spoken the room was growing darker, and only her forehead, smooth and white,
remained illumined by the unextinguishable light of belief and love.

" 'You were his friend,' she went on. 'His friend,' she repeated, a little louder.
'You must have been, if he had given you this, and sent you to me. I feel I can speak
to you—and oh! I must speak. I want you—you who have heard his last words—
to know I have been worthy of him. . . . It is not pride. . . . Yes! I am proud to know
I understood him better than anyone on earth—he told me so himself. And since
his mother died I have had no one—no one—to—to——'

"I listened. The darkness deepened. I was not even sure whether he had
given me the right bundle. I rather suspect he wanted me to take care of another
batch of his papers which, after his death, I saw the manager examining under the
lamp. And the girl talked, easing her pain in the certitude of my sympathy; she
talked as thirsty men drink. I had heard that her engagement with Kurtz had been
disapproved by her people. He wasn't rich enough or something. And indeed I
don't know whether he had not been a pauper all his life. He had given me some
reason to infer that it was his impatience of comparative poverty that drove him
out there.

" '. . . Who was not his friend who had heard him speak once?' she was saying. 'He drew men towards him by what was best in them.' She looked at me with intensity. 'It is the gift of the great,' she went on, and the sound of her low voice seemed to have the accompaniment of all the other sounds, full of mystery, desolation, and sorrow, I had ever heard—the ripple of the river, the soughing of the trees swayed by the wind, the murmurs of wild crowds, the faint ring of incomprehensible words cried from afar, the whisper of a voice speaking from beyond the threshold of an eternal darkness. 'But you have heard him! You know!' she cried.

"'Yes, I know,' I said with something like despair in my heart, but bowing my head before the faith that was in her, before that great and saving illusion that shone with an unearthly glow in the darkness, in the triumphant darkness from which I could not have defended her—from which I could not even defend myself.

"'What a loss to me—to us!'—she corrected herself with beautiful generosity; then added in a murmur, 'To the world.' By the last gleams of twilight I could see the glitter of her eyes, full of tears—of tears that would not fall.

"'I have been very happy—very fortunate—very proud,' she went on. 'Too fortunate. Too happy for a little while. And now I am unhappy for—for life.'

"She stood up; her fair hair seemed to catch all the remaining light in a glimmer of gold. I rose too.

"'And of all this,' she went on, mournfully, 'of all his promise, and of all his greatness, of his generous mind, of his noble heart, nothing remains—nothing but a memory. You and I——'

"'We shall always remember him,' I said, hastily.

"'No!' she cried. 'It is impossible that all this should be lost—that such a life should be sacrificed to leave nothing—but sorrow. You know what vast plans he had. I knew of them too—I could not perhaps understand,—but others knew of them. Something must remain. His words, at least, have not died.'

"'His words will remain,' I said.

"'And his example,' she whispered to herself. 'Men looked up to him,—his goodness shone in every act. His example——'

"'True,' I said; 'his example too. Yes, his example. I forgot that.'

"'But I do not. I cannot—I cannot believe—not yet. I cannot believe that I shall never see him again, that nobody will see him again, never, never, never.'

"She put out her arms as if after a retreating figure, stretching them black and with clasped pale hands across the fading and narrow sheen of the window. Never see him! I saw him clearly enough then. I shall see this eloquent phantom as long as I live, and I shall see her too, a tragic and familiar Shade, resembling in this gesture another one, tragic also, and bedecked with powerless charms, stretching bare brown arms over the glitter of the infernal stream, the stream of darkness. She said suddenly very low, 'He died as he lived.'

"'His end,' said I, with dull anger stirring in me, 'was in every way worthy of his life.'

"'And I was not with him,' she murmured. My anger subsided before a feeling of infinite pity.

"'Everything that could be done——' I mumbled.

"'Ah, but I believed in him more than anyone on earth—more than his own mother, more than—himself. He needed me! Me! I would have treasured every sigh, every word, every sign, every glance.'

"I felt like a chill grip on my chest. 'Don't,' I said, in a muffled voice.

"'Forgive me. I—I—have mourned so long in silence—in silence. . . . You were with him—to the last? I think of his loneliness. Nobody near to understand him as I would have understood. Perhaps no one to hear. . . .'

"'To the every end,' I said, shakily. 'I heard his very last words. . . .' I stopped in a fright.

"'Repeat them,' she said in a heart-broken tone. 'I want—I want—something—something—to—to live with.'

"I was on the point of crying at her, 'Don't you hear them?' The dusk was repeating them in a persistent whisper all around us, in a whisper that seemed to swell menacingly like the first whisper of a rising wind. 'The horror! the horror!'

"'His last word—to live with,' she murmured. 'Don't you understand I loved him—I loved him—I loved him!'

"I pulled myself together and spoke slowly.

"'The last word he pronounced was—your name.'

"I heard a light sigh, and then my heart stood still, stopped dead short by an exulting and terrible cry, by the cry of inconceivable triumph and of unspeakable pain. 'I knew it—I was sure!' . . . She knew. She was sure. I heard her weeping; she had hidden her face in her hands. It seemed to me that the house would collapse before I could escape, that the heavens would fall upon my head. But nothing happened. The heavens do not fall for such a trifle. Would they have fallen, I wonder, if I had rendered Kurtz that justice which was his due? Hadn't he said he wanted only justice? But I couldn't. I could not tell her. It would have been too dark—too dark altogether. . . ."

Marlow ceased, and sat apart, indistinct and silent, in the pose of a meditating Buddha. Nobody moved for a time. "We have lost the first of the ebb," said the Director, suddenly. I raised my head. The offing was barred by a black bank of clouds, and the tranquil waterway leading to the uttermost ends of the earth flowed somber under an overcast sky—seemed to lead into the heart of an immense darkness.